EDGE
OF THE
WOODS

Also by Andrew Rowe

The War of Broken Mirrors Series

Forging Divinity

Stealing Sorcery

Defying Destiny

Arcane Ascension Series

Sufficiently Advanced Magic

On the Shoulders of Titans

The Torch that Ignites the Stars

The Silence of Unworthy Gods

Weapons and Wielders Series

Six Sacred Swords

Diamantine

Soulbrand

Other Books

How to Defeat a Demon King in Ten Easy Steps

Death Game Quality Assurance

Arcane Ascension Universe Books by Other Authors

Crystal Awakening by Kayleigh Nicol

EDGE OF THE WOODS

THE LOST EDGE ⁂ BOOK ONE

ANDREW ROWE

Podium

For my parents, who never questioned why I needed more swords.
Thanks for everything, Mom and Dad. I love you.

Cover design by Daniel Kamarudin

ISBN: 978-1-0394-7829-9

Published in 2025 by Podium Publishing
www.podiumaudio.com

CONTENTS

MAP OF DANIA

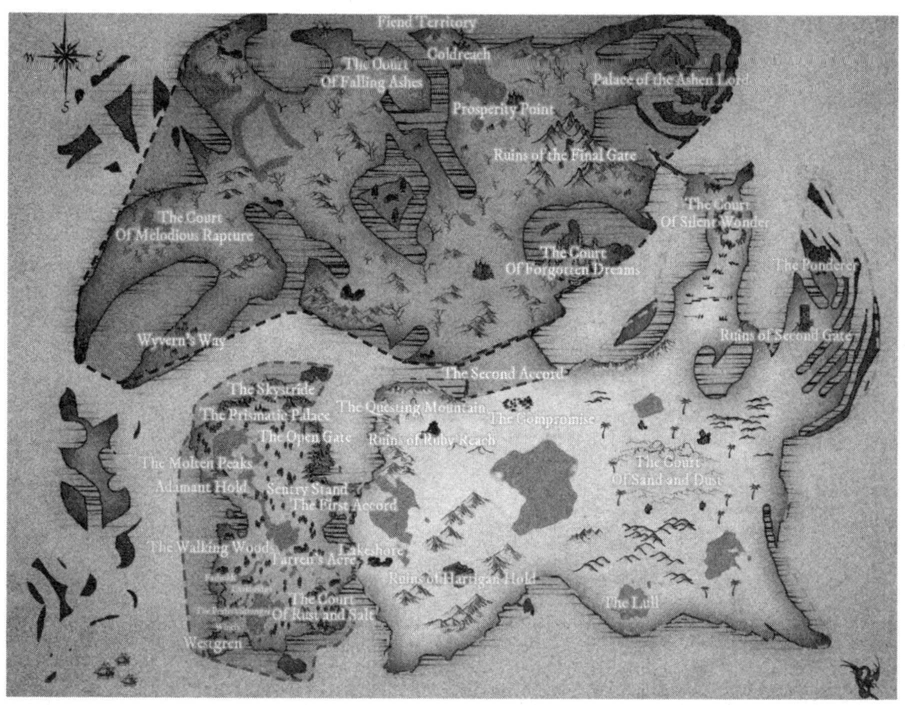

A general map of the continent of Dania, with lower detail on the areas outside our protagonist's homeland.

LOCAL MAP

A closer look at the local portion of the map. In the frame story (the Prologue and Interludes), our protagonists begin in the small town of Winch on the western coast and travel north from there.

In the main story, our protagonist begins in the Court of Rust and Salt on the southeastern side of the map.

MAP OF THE WOODS

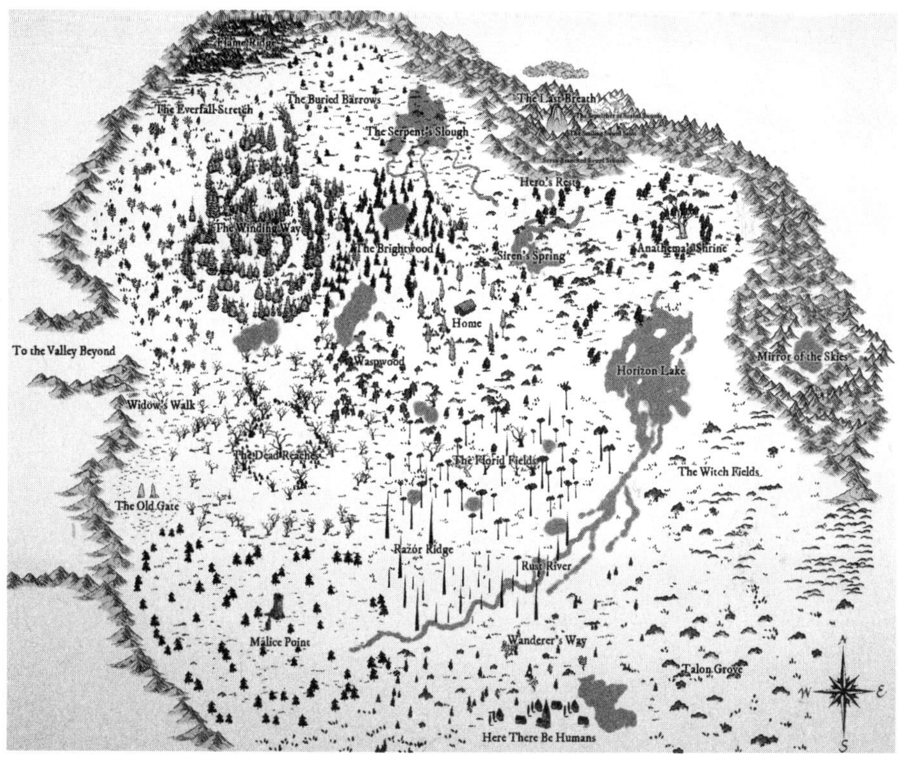

A rough map of the Court of Rust and Salt, though one may doubt at the authenticity, given that it was drawn from the stories of an unreliable narrator.

The main story begins in a glade north of the area marked "Home" on the map. From there, the protagonist travels to several other regions, the most notable being Anathema's shrine on the northeastern side.

STYLE NOTES

Some characters within this series communicate telepathically. To indicate this, rather than using quotes, I use different forms of punctuation based on the character initiating the telepathic communication.

I use different types of brackets to indicate telepathy for different characters. For example, <This would be one form of telepathic communication.> [This would what another form of telepathy looks like.]

This formatting difference is to make it immediately obvious which character is sending the telepathic message without repeatedly using dialogue tags or other indicators. The specific characters in question should be clear once the story actually reaches them.

I use the singular "they/them" for agender and non-binary characters as well as characters that have not had their gender determined by the narrator yet. For example, "I didn't know who wrote the note, but they had a peculiar style of writing."

Finally, I use spaces before and after em dashes (AP style). This is purely because I find this style easier to read.

EDGE
OF THE
WOODS

PROLOGUE

THE SCRIBE AND THE SWORDSMAN

There were days that Scribe would remember, even if time and fate conspired to leave them forgotten. This particular day was one of many first meetings with someone who could play an assortment of roles in his life, much to his potential delight or dismay.

The hapless Scribe first encountered the swordsman near a crossroads in the middle of nowhere. The street signs were hard to see in the dark and rain-swept evening, but Scribe raised a hand and squinted, focusing on the worn wood. The dim illumination of the ancient streetlight crystals was barely enough to discern the presence of letters on the wood and simply too feeble to parse them properly, at least for ordinary eyes.

Just a hint of sorcery, then. Let's see . . .

A familiar sensation and Scribe's vision cleared, no longer occluded by the incessant rainfall.

Fate Street . . . and Fortune Way.

Someone in civic engineering had a sense of humor.

With a groan, he released the simple spell. It had been a slight risk to use any sort of sorcery in a locale known for their loathing of anything they called "magical" — their hypocrisy and ignorance evident by the ubiquitous presence of enchanted lighting — though the chances that anyone would catch an instant of sight sorcery were minimal.

Scribe wiped his spectacles with a gloved hand, but that just spread the wetness on the lens, rather than clearing it. A moment later, he grimaced as the high winds carried something to smack him in the side of the face.

Just a leaf. There were dozens of them drifting in the breeze.

He was in the process of lifting his hand to the side of his face when he heard the screams.

"Help! Someone, help!"

With a sigh, Scribe lowered his head. He didn't precisely run to the stranger's aid. It was more like he trudged quickly, hearing and feeling the squelch of his wet boots and soaking socks with every step he took in the direction of the screams.

He sensed it before he rounded the corner and saw it: fire. He fought back the memories that came with that sensation but failed to still the trembling in his hands.

Wood creaked and cracked as flames consumed the upper floors of what must have been one of the largest houses in the comparatively humble city. It was nearly two blocks away, toward the very end of the street, but the blaze was easy to see in contrast to the darkness of the night. Scribe's eyes narrowed as he noted the way the fire and smoke seemed to writhe and churn on the building's rooftop, reacting to the rainfall almost as if alive.

Not an ordinary blaze, then. Arson, with a touch of thaumaturgy?

Already he saw people piling out of nearby homes, forming a small crowd, shouting, pointing, and presumably organizing. Buckets were being filled with water and what, at a distance, looked like sand.

Won't do a thing if that's what I think it is up there. If it's surviving this level of rainfall, it's too strong for buckets, too.

He heard another scream, this time coming from someone *inside* the building. This wasn't simply a matter of saving the structure, then. Someone couldn't escape.

He took a step closer, his hands trembling as images played across his mind. A closet door. The flames spreading. His sister . . .

I . . .

I . . . can't.

He shivered, his eyes shutting to hide his failures past and present. Then he turned to leave.

As he spun to abandon this place, something brushed past him in a blur. Purely on instinct, Scribe spun to follow whatever had just touched him.

As he shifted, Scribe beheld the stranger's wake. With ordinary senses, someone never would have noticed, but Scribe saw it clearly: where the stranger had moved, the leaves drifting in the wind had been sliced to pieces, as if struck a dozen times with a blade.

It was only then that he realized that the raindrops in the stranger's path had also been torn apart.

By the time he processed what was happening, the stranger was nearly at the building. At a distance, Scribe couldn't make out many details of the man's appearance — he was tall by Scribe's standards, and most likely skinny, but his form was near-entirely concealed by a dark green hooded cloak. Beyond that,

Scribe could tell from the man's stance that he held something beneath the cloak. By the way he stood and moved, Scribe judged it to likely be a poorly hidden sword, and thus mentally marked the figure as being a swordsman.

In a single motion that made Scribe gasp in uncharacteristic surprise, the hooded man leapt to the top of the building.

The flames rose to meet him, sweeping upward to tower above the building's chimney.

The stranger's stance shifted. His right hand went to something beneath his heavy green cloak, while his left hand came up in a gesture. His fingers moved into signs that the Scribe couldn't see at such a distance.

A somatic spell, or simply hand-signs for communication?

Whatever the intent, the flames simply rose higher, towering high above the building. Scribe felt his chest tighten as he saw the blaze coiled, and then like a python, it struck.

A trail of silver flashed across the sky.

The snakelike blaze froze in midmotion. Then, after a heartbeat, the top half of the blaze *slid* downward, parting like shorn paper.

Scribe's jaw might have slid open a little.

What . . . ? How . . . ?

The swordsman was moving again, then. Kneeling, then pressing his forehead against the rooftop's wood, as if in some sort of silent apology or prayer. The swordsman removed something from his cloak, but Scribe couldn't see what it was.

The rooftop blaze began to fade at once, but the interior of the building was still consumed with fire and filled with smoke.

The swordsman leapt from the roof to land near the building's door. With another swift movement of his arm, the door to the building split apart, and then the swordsman rushed inside.

Scribe felt himself walking closer in spite of himself. All around, villagers were doing the same. He saw some hurling buckets of water at still-exposed vestiges of flame, but most were doing as he was now. Watching. Waiting for the swordsman's return.

They were not waiting long.

The swordsman burst out the door carrying a child over each shoulder. He turned immediately to a man standing near the doorway who was wearing a panicked expression, then set the children down on the ground.

"Please." The panicked man looked back at the building, near-entirely consumed by smoke. "My baby is still in there."

The swordsman's eyes narrowed in determination. Then he nodded once and rushed straight into the smoke.

There was a *creak* as something in the top floor of the building began to give way. Someone screamed something like "Come back!," but if the swordsman heard it, he made no response.

Moments passed. There was a crack, louder this time.

Then the top of the building collapsed.

No!

Scribe raised a hand, power flooding through his veins. He couldn't fail here, not again, not when —

There was no sound, but he saw it — seven lines flashing across the building's front wall, just before it fell to pieces.

The swordsman stepped through the gap, cradling something gingerly in his arms. He let out a racking cough, the first sound Scribe had heard the swordsman produce, then thrust the bundle into the pleading man's arms.

"Thank you," the pleading man said, pulling back the blankets to reveal a perfectly healthy kitten. "Thank you, stranger."

The swordsman simply nodded once more and then turned to leave.

There were no other thanks for the stranger, only whispers.

"Fae . . ."

"Yokai . . ."

"Monster . . ."

The swordsman paused only for a moment, his shoulders slumping almost imperceptibly.

In a swift, seemingly unconscious motion, the swordsman pulled his cloak around himself tighter, then walked off into the night alone.

Their second encounter was, much like the first, not much of an encounter at all. More of an observation, really.

The rain and wind had given way to a clear sky and the kind of fresh air that only existed in small towns like this one — a tiny settlement called Winch with perhaps a couple hundred permanent residents — far from the bustle of the major cities.

Dislodging himself from his covers, Scribe went downstairs, paid for a breakfast that shockingly was not included in the public house's standard fees, and then made plans to leave the town.

Even *almost* using sorcery while surrounded by people had been a terrible risk. There was no formal inquisition presence here that he was aware of, thankfully, but a sufficient number of small-town folks could burn him just as easily if they'd noticed what he was doing.

I picked the worst possible time to come to Dania, didn't I?

There hadn't been an "inquisition" in his books. He'd only heard about it on the ship — it was a comparatively recent development, sparked by some sort of conflict between humanity and a faerie court that had sparked a general distrust for magic use over the last few years. Xenophobia and fear of the fae were nothing new, but some incident had escalated tensions, and he'd heard chatter that a war was looming. More immediately relevant to Scribe was that certain types of magic, particularly anything related to mental influence or illusion, were now considered signs of conspiring with faeries and witches.

This was, of course, patently absurd, and likely involved someone exploiting a conflict to increase their personal influence or stamp out political opponents . . . but that didn't make Scribe's job any easier.

He considered asking the owner of the public house about the swordsman, but he decided against it. Showing too much interest in what was apparently a pariah was only likely to draw more attention to himself, which was the exact opposite of what he needed.

As he departed the building, Scribe briefly checked the job board posted in the center of town, looking for anything quick and easy that he could do to earn a few coins before departing.

Extra hands needed at lumber mill.

New Explorer's Guild branch seeking members in Farholdt.

Child missing, last seen near forest.

There were two copies of each, except for the last: the poster of the missing child came with a drawing of the child's appearance and more information. One copy had been torn away.

The Explorer's Guild posting was interesting. He knew that the major branches of the guild would employ sorcerers openly. That would be useful, since in a place like this smaller town, he simply couldn't count on them to understand the difference between a dominion sorcerer and a "witch allied with the fae."

Ah, people hating something they don't understand. Not so different from home, in that respect. The guild might be a good option to look at, if I want to keep my head on my shoulders.

He shook his head, heading toward Caravan's Rest, which was exactly what it sounded like. His coin purse was a little bit anemic, but he still could afford a ride to Farholdt, where his particular services were more likely to be tolerated or even encouraged.

It was on his way there that he spotted the swordsman again, walking down the street in the opposite direction.

The swordsman walked with one hand held high to keep the hood of his cloak firmly in place. The other held the hand of a small, disheveled boy, who was looking up at the swordsman with obvious adoration in his eyes.

"Get you away from my son, monster!" shouted a voice from just outside one of the nearby shops.

The swordsman froze, then turned toward the source of the sound.

"Daddy!" The boy pulled away from the swordsman's hand and rushed toward the speaker — a huge man with a woodcutter's axe held in one hand.

The big man knelt as the boy approached. "Tobias, where have you been? Did that monster take you?"

The little boy shook his head fervently. "There was this big wolf, Daddy, and he came down like *whoosh* and then he—"

The father lifted a finger to hush his son, then turned toward the swordsman. "Don't think that you're getting a reward for this, *freak*."

The swordsman regarded the father silently for a moment, then bent down toward the child and made a hand-sign with his free hand. Then, seemingly self-consciously, the swordsman adjusted his cloak again as he turned to leave.

Someone threw a rock at the swordsman as he turned away, but they missed.

Scribe almost followed him. But they were, once again, going in opposite directions.

⁂

The next day, Scribe was riding in the back of one of several wagons in the caravan toward a larger city and the promise of greater opportunities.

Of course, there were people in the world who sought to profit through less *legitimate* means, and Scribe was reminded of that fact when the wagons abruptly stopped early the next morning.

At first, he wondered if something had simply happened to a wheel, or if one of the wagons had gotten stuck in the mud. It was only when he heard the shouting that he knew something was terribly wrong.

When he heard the first *thunk* of an arrow striking wood, he knew he had different types of risks to consider. Getting caught using sorcery by the wrong people would be bad, but getting riddled with arrows was arguably worse.

He was alone in the back of his wagon. That gave him options.

Let's be subtle about it.

He tapped the side of his head. An unnecessary gesture, but one that came from years of practice.

Hide.

And with that, he vanished from view. Not entirely — he'd opted for a camouflage effect rather than full invisibility, knowing that this situation might take time to resolve. Camouflage could potentially be seen through with keen eyes or close attention, but he could maintain it for close to an hour. Invisibility burned his essence much more rapidly: he could only safely maintain it for a matter of minutes. After that, the cost to his eyesight from using sight sorcery could cause permanent damage.

Cautiously, he swept aside the fabric at the back of the wagon, then crept out to get a better look at the situation.

The first arrow had, predictably, hit his particular wagon. A few inches higher and it might have pierced fabric, rather than wood, and hit either him or the supplies held inside.

A quick look at the arrow told him that something was off. The arrowhead was freshly polished steel and the pitch-black fletching pristine.

Too high quality for what I'd expect from random highwaymen. Former military, maybe? Maybe there's something more at work here, but I have more immediate concerns.

Fortunately, it seemed like the archers had decided to stop at one warning shot. Less fortunately, there were a *lot* of them.

Bandits. Of course, I had to run into bandits.

There were two hired guards for the caravan. They were, at present, in the process of hastily disarming themselves and surrendering.

Scribe couldn't have rolled his eyes any harder if he tried.

A quick look told him there were at least ten bandits: six in front of the wagon, blocking the road, and four with bows spread out on the sides of the wagons. With those sorts of numbers, two guards surrendering made a degree of sense. It was unlikely that the bandits would slaughter the travelers, anyway: banditry was, in Scribe's understanding, often the work of desperate people with few other options.

That didn't mean that he was going to take chances. He began to slink his way off toward the trees. He'd watch things from a safe distance, then rejoin the caravan if they were allowed to pass safely.

Attacking the bandits was, of course, completely out of the question. If the bandits did decide they were out for blood, he'd run. Plain and simple.

It wasn't until he'd gotten to a safe distance that he realized that someone was standing on top of one of the wagons, cloak pulled tightly against the cold morning air.

The swordsman.

When did he get here . . . ? Did he . . . teleport somehow? Hm.

He's certainly some kind of sorcerer, but there's a simpler explanation. They . . . probably just wouldn't let him inside the wagons. He's probably been riding on top of one this entire time.

Scribe felt a pang of uncharacteristic sympathy, but that wasn't his greatest concern at the moment.

The bandits had noticed the swordsman, too. And the swordsman had noticed *him*. He raised an eyebrow in Scribe's direction. There was no judgment there, only curiosity. The movement brought something else to Scribe's attention — the swordsman had something in his mouth.

A thin knife . . . ?

No, nothing of the sort. Just a thin strand of wheat.

Somehow, though, it *felt* like a knife.

That didn't matter. What mattered was that the swordsman had seen him.

Nonono, look away. He whipped his hand to the side, pointing toward the bandits. Another raised eyebrow from the swordsman, who switched his gaze, then looked right back at him.

At that point, it was too late.

One of the bandits followed the swordsman's gaze, squinted, and then . . .

"Hey! You! Get back here!"

Scribe was definitely not going to do that.

Bows were leveled in his direction. That was bad. Switching to full invisibility would make escaping into the woods possible, but it would diminish his eyesight faster, and he was still concerned that using obvious sorcery could draw attention. The kind of attention that could be more dangerous than the bandits themselves. And, even with that aside, playing his hand here would prevent him from rejoining the caravan if it was allowed to proceed.

Bolting into the woods was an option, but that would have required a degree of decisiveness that was, at the moment, beyond him. Instead, he simply raised his hands and froze.

One of the bandits, presumably the leader, turned toward the swordsman. "And you! Off the roof, now, and disarm! Don't try nothin' funny!"

The bandit leader looked a hint better equipped than the others, wearing a shirt of steel chain mail over the ubiquitous leather armor that the remaining bandits wore. That last part was another curious detail — the leather bits they wore were near-identical, but each seemed to fit the bandit properly.

Bandits with personally tailored armor? And that chain mail — it's pristine, like he's never worn it before. No rust, no gouges. Maybe he just maintains it very well, which could imply the "former soldiers" hypothesis, but . . .

His thought process was interrupted by movement.

The swordsman abandoned his curious expression, hopping down from the top of his wagon and leaping to a position in between the bandits and the scribe. He reached into his cloak.

"Easy, now," the bandit leader commanded. "Drop your sword, all slow-like."

Scribe couldn't see what was happening clearly, since the swordsman's back was facing him. He cautiously watched as the swordsman opened his cloak, reached to his belt, and tossed a long object out of reach.

Foolish. He should have kept it just at his . . .

Wait, what?

Scribe blinked at the object on the forest floor. It was about the right length for a sword, but with no visible handle, no metallic luster. At first, he thought it might simply be sheathed, but with a moment of concentration and a movement of his fingers, his vision focused to give him a closer look.

That . . .

That's just a stick.

Before Scribe could process this incongruity further, the bandit leader spoke again. "Cloak. Toss it. Don't want you havin' no hidden weapons."

The swordsman hesitated for the first time, then unclasped the cloak from his neck and tossed it aside.

Scribe blinked.

He'd been picturing some grizzled ranger beneath the cloak, or perhaps some fae thing with pointed ears. Maybe some combination of both.

The sight that greeted him was a lanky teenager dressed in forest greens. His black hair was long and wild, but that didn't make him look unnatural, just unkempt. His arm muscles were thick for his frame, but not beyond what Scribe might have expected from an ordinary blacksmith. From his vantage point, there was nothing to mark the swordsman as anything other than an ordinary youth, albeit one that needed a bath and good meal.

Before he could look more deeply — perhaps checking for sorcerous concealment effects, similar to his own — his priorities shifted.

"Good, good. You've made this faster." The bandit leader turned toward his archers. "Shoot the witch first."

Scribe cursed and stumbled back a step, and then the arrows were flying rapidly in his direction. Some were off course — these bandits either weren't aiming very carefully, or they weren't very good archers — but it didn't take more than one hit from an arrow to ruin his day. Or end his life, depending on where it hit. One arrow, he might have avoided, given the range they'd been fired from, but there were too many coming at him, too fast—

The swordsman moved even faster.

He vanished in a blur, reappearing in the path of the arrow fired in Scribe's direction. Then his arm moved with a *shink*, leaving a trail of silver in the air. The arrow split into two perfect halves, each of which fell harmlessly to the ground.

Deflecting an arrow was a classic mark of swordsmanship skill.

Slicing an arrow precisely in half was a sign of mastery.

Managing that when the arrow was fired at someone a hundred feet away . . . well, there was obviously more than mere swordsmanship going on at that point.

. . . And the swordsman wasn't carrying a sword.

In his right hand, the swordsman held his arrow-cleaving weapon: the humble strand of wheat that he'd been holding in his mouth.

Before Scribe's jaw could even finish dropping, the swordsman had rushed forward, closing the distance to the archers in an eyeblink. His hand blurred, and then he was moving again.

The archer stood uninjured. Their bowstrings, however, had been severed.

When Scribe's eyes next caught the swordsman, the wheat-wielding teen was standing in front of the leader of the bandits.

The swordsman leaned downward — he was only taller than the bandit leader by a couple of inches, but he somehow *felt* much taller — and raised his empty off hand. His fingers curled.

Then, as the bandit leader reached for his sword, the swordsman flicked him in the forehead.

Crack.

The bandit leader shot backward like he'd been fired out of a cannon, smashing into a tree and falling to the ground with a *thump*. He was still for a moment, then groaned, pushing himself to his knees.

The swordsman advanced with the general disposition and inevitability of a rockslide.

The bandit leader trembled, then reached for a knife on his belt.

Scribe barely saw the swordsman move, but suddenly his hand was empty. There was a *crack*, and then the bandit leader's hand froze in place.

A hurled straw of wheat had embedded itself into the tree between two of the bandit leader's fingers, arresting the path of his hand. He froze, abandoning any hope of claiming the weapon, then turned his head upward to find the swordsman looming over him.

"I . . ." the bandit leader stammered. "Please. Skyseeker, forgive me. Wasn't told one of you'd be here. I . . ."

Wasn't told? That's . . .

The swordsman's hand moved again, a blur of motion.

The bandit cringed and raised a hand to cover his face, far too late to defend himself. When the bandit leader finally opened his eyes and lowered his arm, the swordsman was still looming over him, but he had something in each of his hands.

In his left hand, the swordsman held a small pouch. In the right, a lock of the bandit leader's hair, cleanly cut through some means Scribe could not discern. As Scribe watched, the swordsman leaned down and offered the pouch to the bandit leader.

"Th-thank you for your mercy, Master Skyseeker. Is that . . ." The bandit looked at the pouch again, then took it. He hefted it in his hands, then opened it with widened eyes.

With his free hand, the swordsman made several hand-signs. Scribe couldn't follow it, but the bandit leader must have. When the swordsman lifted the bandit leader's severed hair and waved it meaningfully, Scribe understood the threat inherent in the gesture, but he wasn't quite certain of the context.

A gift in one hand, possible death in the other? Sounds like some people I know. But what's the exchange?

More hand-signs were made. Scribe tried to memorize them for later reference.

"Y-yes. I understand. I won't make the mistake again. Th-thank you, kind Skyseeker." The bandit lowered his head to the ground once, and then as the swordsman groaned in apparent discomfort, the bandit leader took to his feet and bolted into the woods with surprising speed.

The other bandits followed immediately thereafter. Or, as Scribe realized belatedly, some of them had already started to run.

Scribe paid them no further heed. He cautiously watched the swordsman, who was watching the bandits flee.

A Skyseeker? Scribe frowned. He'd heard of them, briefly. They were a specific category of essence sorcerers — people specialized in drawing in essence from outside sources like monsters and environments to gain new abilities. He'd heard conflicting things about what made someone a Skyseeker — it had to do with either literally looking for a mythological sky kingdom or possibly some kind of searching for inner power. Maybe both. It was something he'd been planning to study, but he'd thought of Skyseekers as monastic ascetics, not . . . wild teenagers in the woods.

I shouldn't exactly take the classifications given by bandits at face value. They may think of any kind of essence sorcerer as a Skyseeker, if they're not familiar with anything else.

The swordsman watched with intense focus as the bandits disappeared, then sighed and shook his head.

Then he turned to look straight toward Scribe. And, for the first time, Scribe saw it.

A six-petaled mark on the center of the swordsman's right cheek. It might have been mistaken for a tattoo if it hadn't been glowing green.

That must have been what the villagers had seen that first night, when he'd coughed after leaving the burning building. The sight that he'd been trying to hide with the hood of the cloak.

And the significance of it?

Scribe had absolutely no idea.

A dominion mark, perhaps? Or the local equivalent? It must be associated with the fae, causing the discrimination he's been experiencing. Perhaps it's an indication that he's actually of fae birth, but it might be another bit of inquisition propaganda.

And his eyes . . .

His eyes were strange, too. His irises were bright gray . . . or, perhaps more accurately, silver. They had a luster to them that made them look vaguely metallic. They had a hint of an unnatural glow, too, which lent a similar tone to his sclera.

Not rethri, then. He has sclera, it's just hard to see. Maybe some rethri blood? Or fae blood? Maybe the species are related.

His master had told him a bit about the local species, but she said a lot of things, and only a fraction of them were useful or true. He was expected to do his own research . . . and he'd only just arrived on the continent. He had a lot left to learn.

. . . Assuming he survived long enough.

The swordsman's silver gaze was fixed directly on him in a way that was unsettling. If the swordsman had seen through his camouflage, it was likely the man knew he was a sorcerer. If he had the same feelings on dominion sorcery that the locals did, then . . .

Scribe took a breath.

No. He helped me. That might have been impulsive, or perhaps opportunistic, but . . . I don't think he's going to murder me for trying to hide.

Time to take a chance.

He stepped forward cautiously, then went to the swordsman's fallen cloak. He lifted it from the ground, then extended a hand in the swordsman's direction.

By the time he'd stood up straight, the swordsman was already in front of him.

Fast. He's like a motion sorcerer, but . . . effortless. It's not like how Vee moved — he's not throwing himself around with bursts of motion. He's just running impossibly quickly, like he's under some kind of improved perpetual Haste spell, and without the usual side effects. Likely something to do with essence sorcery, since building up enough essence can improve physical traits.

The swordsman looked at the cloak, then took it from Scribe's outstretched hand. The swordsman frowned, wiping leaves and mud off the cloak with a strange look of sorrow, then tossed it back around his neck and fastened it in place. With the cloak fastened back on, he raised the hood, then nodded silently to Scribe.

"Thank you. For stopping the arrow." Glancing at the pieces of the broken projectile, Scribe wasn't sure the shot would have hit him in the first place, but he was still glad for the intervention.

The swordsman gave him a soft smile, raised his hands to make some kind of hand-signs, then turned away.

Scribe watched curiously as the swordsman moved to pick up his discarded stick, wipe it off with a sigh, then attach it to his belt using a tiny loop of rope that was attached to the stick's bottom.

Huh. Maybe that really is his weapon . . . ? Doesn't seem like he needs one, given how he handled those bandits.

If they were bandits at all.

On a hunch, Scribe swept up a couple pieces of the broken arrow, putting them in his pouch while the swordsman was cleaning his own weapon. He couldn't quite place the type of sorcery that had been used to cut through it. It looked metallic, but metal calling would have conjured a piece of metal. And . . . the arrowhead itself had been sliced in half. Whatever the swordsman had used had sliced clear through a piece of steel without any sign of resistance.

Some kind of hyperfocused light sorcery, maybe? Maybe a divine gift? Blade sorcery? That would be . . . unusual, given the location, but . . . I can't discount anything.

He's clearly capable of some kind of somatic sorcery method, similar to Assassin's Sorcery. It's possible the hand-signs he's using to communicate are the same language he uses for sorcery, but it's also possible he's casting spells through some other means entirely. He might not need any physical tells at all.

The swordsman turned back toward him after lifting the stick, nodded once with a sad expression, then turned toward the woods. Not the same direction the bandits had gone, but . . . away.

"Wait," Scribe called out, quickly stuffing a couple pieces of the arrow into one of his bags for future inspection. As he tucked away a piece of the shaft, he realized there was something etched into the side — a symbol — but the symbol had been marred when the arrow had been cleaved in two.

The swordsman turned toward him with a quizzical look.

"Where are you going?" Scribe asked, hastily tucking away the remains of the arrow and, for the moment, pushing aside that particular set of suspicions.

The swordsman shrugged, but otherwise didn't reply.

"You . . . you can understand me, right?"

The swordsman nodded.

"But . . . you're mute?"

The swordsman shook his head, sighing. He walked a little closer, making hand-signs, and opened his mouth. "Not . . . good . . . language?"

"Oh." Scribe blinked as understanding reached him. "This isn't your native language?"

The swordsman nodded hesitantly, like one might if they weren't quite sure they were answering correctly. That was all the confirmation he needed.

The signs . . . they're probably something more general that the locals understand, but that I don't. Okay. I can work with this.

"If that's not your native language, what is?"

The swordsman frowned. "Not understand. Sorry."

Scribe considered. *It's a long shot, but some of the local cultures sprung up from Mythralian explorers. Maybe . . .*

"Isendri?" he asked in Isendri.

"Cas? Melkain . . . ? Velthryn?"

The swordsman's eyes lit up in surprise, then narrowed. "Velthryn. I speak a bit."

Scribe's heart hammered faster. Velthryn was the most common language in his homeland and his own second language. His primary tongue was Liadran, but he hadn't mentioned that because it would have been too much of a tell for his own specific homeland, and depending on the swordsman's knowledge, that might have complicated things.

Was the swordsman another Mythralian traveler? That was . . . extremely unlikely, for a number of reasons, but it was possible Auntie had sent other agents. Or, maybe, one of her supposed siblings had put someone into play.

And those "bandits" . . . ugh.

Caution and care would be needed, given that he was clearly in the midst of something he didn't have enough information about, but a shared language was useful both for communication and investigation. "That should make things easier, then. I'm glad to be able to talk to you."

"Yes." The swordsman looked him up and down, seemingly renewing his assessment. "It *will* make things easier."

"I, uh . . ." Scribe coughed. "Are you Mythralian, then? Or just well-studied?"

The swordsman's eyes flicked to his, searching, and then he finally seemed to relax fractionally. "Originally, maybe. I've heard my parents were from there, but I was raised here."

"By another Mythralian?" Scribe asked.

"Perhaps. The man who raised me was a world traveler. He spoke little of his birth. And you?"

A difficult question, especially if this man knew how . . . challenging travel was from the homeland. "I'm from Mythralis. Just arrived a few weeks ago, actually. You're the first person I've met in this region who speaks Velthryn."

"It isn't common here," the swordsman said simply. "But it seems you have an understanding for the local tongue that eclipses mine. Unusual, if you've only been here for weeks."

This was a question he was more prepared for, at least. "Oh, I studied a number of languages back at home. It's a bit of a hobby of mine. I can't claim to be a master of any of the local languages, but I know bits of a few, and hope to learn more."

"A budding scholar, then." The swordsman nodded, seemingly more to himself than to Scribe. "Is that why you're here? To learn?"

"For the most part," Scribe said honestly. "I was also hoping to see some of the famous crystal shrines."

"Ah." The swordsman's stance subtly shifted, his guard lowering slightly as he seemed to accept that explanation. "I suppose a dominion sorcerer might find the idea of an additional type of magic with fewer side effects appealing."

"You know of the shrines, then?"

The swordsman gave him another measuring look. "I know of them, yes. But most were lost in a war long ago. There are organizations dedicated to digging them up — Shrineseekers. You'll find that sorcery as a whole is more acceptable to the north. This region is particularly . . . tense."

"Ah, yes. The locals seem to have been whipped into a fervor by this 'inquisition.' Do you happen to know anything about it?"

The swordsman winced. "More than I'd like, but less than I should."

Unusual phrasing, there. But I suppose it must be difficult to be a constant target because of his appearance. Perhaps I shouldn't press too hard about that subject.

As for the shrines . . . he's being evasive. He knows where at least one shrine is located, but he doesn't want to tell me. Not that I can blame him. I wouldn't give that kind of information to a stranger, either.

"Is that why you're heading north yourself? Hoping to get away from the sorcery-fearing locals?"

"Not exactly." The swordsman sighed. "Though I admit that finding a place where I can train openly would be pleasant."

The non-answer in that answer was even more obvious than before. It was clear that even if the swordsman had let his guard down slightly, he wasn't going to give everything away immediately. "Well, if we're both heading in the same direction . . . perhaps we can talk a bit while we travel." He glanced back to the wagons, which seemed to be getting back under way. "Are you planning to head back to those, or . . . ?"

The swordsman considered for a moment, then shook his head. "No. Too many people may have seen what I did. I'll be going now. Meeting you was a pleasant interlude."

Scribe looked at the wagon, frowned, then looked back to the swordsman.

Time to make a choice. Or, at least, to make what I've obviously been intended to think is a choice.

"You up for some company on the road?"

The swordsman shifted his stance again, his hand adjusting the empty scabbard on his side. Scribe tensed for a moment, bracing for a sudden assault, but no such thing came. Instead, the swordsman simply gave him a complicated look, then finally released his grip.

"It's a long walk. We'd better get moving."

Minutes later, Scribe had gathered his things from the wagon, collected the first arrow that struck it, and hastily retreated to follow the swordsman along a game path through the woods. It was a bit overgrown but far from the worst path he'd ever taken. The company, of course, would be worth going through far worse.

Someone who spoke Velthryn and practiced the local form of sorcery was an opportunity he couldn't possibly turn down, even if the man clearly didn't trust him. "Any idea where we're going?"

The swordsman nodded fractionally. "There was a poor-quality map in Winch, and I managed to get a look at a good one written in Velthryn a few towns back. This trail should lead down to a river, which we can follow all the way to a city."

"Thanks for letting me come with you."

"It's no trouble and no debt is owed."

Scribe blinked at the strange phrasing. Had . . . a debt been implied somehow? "That's . . . good to know."

The swordsman continued walking. "The wagons would be more comfortable for you, wouldn't they?"

Scribe shook his head. "Sure, maybe. But the locals aren't kind to sorcerers, and . . ."

"Ah, yes. You are concerned that the others noticed your abilities. Was that dominion sorcery that you used?"

Scribe hesitated, but only for a moment. "It was. Are you familiar with it?"

"Only a bit. Gramps told me the basic theory when I was young. Can't use it myself yet, but maybe someday."

I could potentially offer to teach him. It might be a good exchange for knowledge about local sorcery.

Was my arrival time and location planned specifically so that I'd run into this guy? Could she have planned that far ahead?

It wouldn't have been surprising. He'd been placed in stranger situations.

. . . *If so, what's the goal? Learning essence sorcery seems like an obvious enough starting place, I suppose.*

"What about you? You're an essence sorcerer, right?"

"Yes."

Not very talkative, is he?

"What convinced you to travel through a place that has so little tolerance for sorcerers, then? In my case, it's simply where my ship landed."

"I . . ." The swordsman sighed. "I was at home for too long. I wanted to get out, take a look at the world. See what's out there. And this place isn't far from where I grew up."

"What exactly do you want to see?"

The swordsman turned back toward him, offering a hint of a smile for the first time. *"Everything."*

Scribe couldn't help but smile in return. "Do you mind telling me about yourself a bit? We've got a long walk."

"I suppose I could tell you a bit. Not sure where to start, though."

Scribe shrugged, then reached up and adjusted the earring on his left ear. "The beginning, I suppose?"

The swordsman seemed to consider that. "No. That's boring. Let's skip ahead a bit."

"To where?"

The swordsman turned away, his silvery eyes shifting toward something long distant. "To the *adventure*."

CHAPTER I

STARTING SWORD

My world began with a single cut.

I lowered my stance, gripping my sword tightly, and pronounced my attack. “Eightfold Dragon Obliteration Strike!”

My sword came upward, tearing through the air. The dragon was defeated in an instant, freely spilling its precious lifeblood.

As the dragon fell, I took a breath. Victory had come with a single strike, but nevertheless, I couldn’t shake being nervous for what was to come.

She rushed to me with a smile, wearing an overlarge tiara and an ill-fitting dress. Her strawberry-blond hair was askew, no doubt from the horrifying conditions of her capture. “You’ve defeated the dragon, noble hero.”

“Only for you, princess.” I knelt in front of her. “My life is devoted to your service.”

Her expression shifted. “Serve me? . . . Yes, perhaps I might allow that. But there is something you should know.”

I turned my head upward toward her. Would she confess her love? Or perhaps tear my heart asunder by claiming she was already sworn to another knight, or a handsome prince?

“You see, brave hero . . .” She brought her hand up with a smirk. “The dragon was not my captor. He was merely fortunate enough to be my *previous* servant.”

My eyes widened. “But . . . then why . . .”

“A test of your abilities, dear knight.” Her eyes flashed, and she outstretched her right hand. A sword appeared in her grip. “And now I’ve seen through your ultimate technique.”

Her sword whipped downward. I raised my own to block, feeling a jolt of pain down my arm on impact. My hand trembled at the surprising force of the blow.

I scurried backward, barely managing to stumble to my feet before the next swing came. I parried again, but the force of the blow nearly snapped my sword and sent a tingling sensation through my hand and wrist.

She's too strong, I realized. I dodged the next attack rather than parrying it and attempted a counterstrike, but she was too fast. She stepped out of the way effortlessly, then batted my next swing aside with a bare hand.

"Why?" I stammered again, incoherently.

She paused, stretching out an open hand. A glowing ball appeared in her palm. "*Princess. Maiden.* Worst of all, *damsel.* Such despicable titles. Do you know what would have happened if I had stayed at home, and been a good princess? I'd be married off to some greedy duke twice my age. Perhaps a foreign prince if I'm lucky and *well-behaved.*" She shook her head. "No. I'll have no part in that. If this world wants to control me, I'll control *it* instead."

Her hand snapped shut around the sphere of light. The orb fractured, then spread in a gleaming pattern down her arm. The weave of lustrous light might have resembled scales to the unfamiliar, but with my trained eye, I recognized it as interwoven leaves.

My jaw tightened as I recognized the Golden Raiment technique. It would reinforce her body, further increasing her strength and durability, which already far exceeded my own.

Before, she'd nearly snapped my sword in half. With that technique active, I didn't think my blade could handle one more contact with hers.

Still, I couldn't give up. "That's Ashen Lord talk and you know it."

"Is it, now? Hm." She smirked. "Hadn't occurred to me. But, if that's what you want to call a woman with ambition, well . . ." She raised her sword. "You may kneel once again, before your new Ashen Lord."

She swung. I dodged.

Her blade impacted the ground, cutting a wide furrow into the dirt. I grimaced. If that had hit me . . .

I drew in a sharp breath and focused. I'd seen her fight before. I knew her moves. If I could just get in a single clean strike, maybe to her wrist . . .

She swung again, horizontally. This time the wind pressure from her swing, even without a technique, was enough to knock me back and off balance.

But when she lunged to follow up, she overextended herself.

There.

I swept upward, aiming for her wrist as planned. It was a well-executed attack, deliberate and fluid.

She batted my blade aside with casual ease.

And my well-worn sword cracked apart on the impact, just as I'd feared.

Left with only half a weapon, I stumbled backward again. I raised it in front of me, trying to think, search for any weakness. I knew the truth, of course.

She was too strong.

But I never let a little thing like certain defeat stop me.

"Do you yield, hero?" She leveled her weapon at me. "I can promise certain rewards, if you would swear your allegiance to me. I believe half the world would be the traditional offer?"

I glowered at her. "I wouldn't be much of a hero if I agreed to those terms, would I?"

"Weren't you ready to kneel and swear your fealty just moments ago?"

My hand tightened on the grip of my broken weapon. "That was, uh, different. I thought you were . . ."

"Vulnerable? *Compliant?*" She stepped forward, her sword pointed straight at my heart. "Yes, I can see now what you wanted. Easy victories, a vapid bride, and an adoring populace cheering your name. Perhaps they'd write stories about you." She tilted her head downward. "A pity. I hoped you'd be different from all the others. Ah, well. Dragons and heroes are both easily replaced."

I saw the moment she shifted the weight of her back foot, preparing to lunge.

With half a sword, my best option was probably to try to evade again, maneuver, and flee the scene. Her reinforcement technique would not last indefinitely, and I was a fast runner.

But if I was a hero, I couldn't think in those terms. I would face my enemies head-on, even if it meant certain death.

She lunged.

I didn't evade. I didn't block.

I lunged at the same time, knowing that she'd hit me. If I angled my attack just right, I could take her hit and still land a more serious injury in return.

What was victory without sacrifice?

Her eyes widened in surprise as she saw my move.

She was still faster than I was, but this time, it worked to my advantage. She interrupted her own attack, pulling her blade backward for an awkward parry.

I swept upward, meeting her sword with my broken one. In that moment, I envisioned with perfect clarity what I wanted to happen.

My weapon shimmered for an instant and passed cleanly through her blade.

A moment later, her sword fell into two neatly severed pieces. And a heartbeat after that, I saw a thin cut spreading across her cheek.

She stumbled backward, jaw dropping in shock.

I panicked a little. "Oh, ancestors. Ana! I'm *so sorry*!" I dropped my "sword." It was, of course, little more than a lovingly carved stick.

Ana dropped the other half of her wooden sword, raising a hand to her cheek and the wound spreading across her face. When she pulled her hands away, she looked almost comically shocked. "What—"

"I'm so sorry!" I glanced around, looking to see if anyone was watching. There were a couple other distant glowing lights that might have been local spirits. No elders nearby, fortunately, or I might be in trouble.

"You . . ." Ana turned, appraising me, then burst into laughter. "Oh, ancestors! Don't apologize!" She wiped her bloodstained hand on her dress, then rushed forward with her arms wide. "You finally woke up! I'm so *happy* for you!"

I widened my own arms to receive her hug, but I had to be cautious when I pulled her in. Not because of her strength, although that still was a risk if she squeezed me too tightly. No, because of her jagged wings that poked out of the back of her dress. She always forgot about how easily the bladelike wings could cut me. "Thanks, Ana. Are you okay? Maybe we should go to the spring and get you some healing water for that cut."

She snorted, pulling back. "Oh, it's fine. Don't be such a baby. It's just a scratch."

It *wasn't* just a scratch, but it didn't seem to bother her much. Injuries usually didn't. One of the advantages of her essence development level, I supposed. Or perhaps just a consequence of her particular faerie heritage.

Ana raised a hand, a glowing sphere appearing in her hand again, then concentrated. It reshaped itself, stretching out, and then shifted in color to white. In a moment, it had solidified into a bandage. She shoved it at me. "You can wrap me up, though, if you're so worried."

I accepted the bandage and lifted it up, pressing it against the wound to stop the bleeding.

"Ow! Not so hard! Ugh!"

"Sorry. Gramps taught me that you've gotta apply pressure to stop the blood from flowing." I held my hand against her face for a while. Ana tapped her foot impatiently. She'd never been good at staying still for more than, well, any time at all.

After a few minutes or so, I stopped pressing on the conjured cloth. I didn't have to wrap the bandage around her face; she'd managed to conjure one with adhesive on the edges, which was impressively complex for someone our age. Other faeries manifested essence powers at a young age, but Ana was advanced even by faerie standards.

"I'm going to get in *so* much trouble," I muttered.

"Bah, you'll be fine. I'll tell your grandfather it was my fault. Kind of was, I flipped the script on you a little."

I laughed. "Yeah, what *was* with that evil overlord monologue?"

"I wanted to surprise you! And you know I can't *stand* it when a princess just sits and waits to be rescued."

I snorted. "I *was* a little surprised you told me you were going to play a 'princess' today. I figured the hero-and-princess motif was just kind of a frame for you to make use of that guy."

I gestured at the now-deceased "dragon" on the ground, still leaking "lifeblood" from my "ultimate attack."

I'd never actually seen a piñata before. I'd heard of them, but they weren't a local custom. They were more of a human thing, as far as I understood, and specific to certain human cultures that were far away from our forest. Ana had arranged it as a surprise for me, since she knew I loved both hitting things with swords and eating candy.

It must have been difficult for her to arrange. She'd probably conjured the dragon piñata herself, but she couldn't make candy. Anything edible was beyond her abilities, at least for the moment — she hadn't developed her essence in that direction. And human candy wasn't easy to come by in the middle of our forest home. Humans were not allowed within our borders, and Ana couldn't leave — she was bound to this place even more closely than I was. The vast majority of faeries never left the woods, either because of their particular limitations — being bound to a specific tree, lake, or that sort of thing — or in the cases of faeries with less restrictive bindings, a general distaste for humanity.

That meant she'd probably bribed one of vanishingly few non-fae entities that traveled back and forth from the woods.

Oh, I should probably note that "fae" and "faerie" aren't quite the same thing. There's some argument, even among scholars, about what the distinction should be — but the way I was raised was to use "fae" as a broad category and "faerie" to refer to a specific subset of fae species. All faeries are fae, but not all fae are faeries — at least, the way I was taught. These are both human terms, rather than fae ones, anyway. They have their own languages and terms and tend to refer to individual species — or political courts — rather than the same type of human-made categories that we use. Unfortunately, those don't translate well, so . . . human terms it is, for this story, at least.

Anyway, there weren't a lot of non-fae in the woods that could have helped Ana out.

The Willowbark Witch, maybe, or Uncle Eiji. Potentially some of the witch's older children, if they were currently allowed to leave the woods. Regardless of the source, it would have cost Ana significantly; we always tried to do something impressive for each other for our name days.

My name day was technically the next day, but we had a tradition of celebrating across a three-day period rather than just on the day itself. I wasn't sure if that was actually a faerie tradition in general — they did like to do things in threes — or just a local one.

I held my hand against her face for a while longer. She bled through the first bandage, conjured another, and I replaced it. "We should probably get you cleaned up before something smells blood."

The fae were the masters of the wood, but they were hardly the only creatures that lived in our home. And for some particularly unfriendly beasts, the blood of a fae child was an enticing meal.

"Ugh. Fine. But candy first?" She gestured at the fallen dragon.

"Candy first," I agreed. "But, uh, maybe conjure us some towels? We have blood all over our hands."

Ana grinned. "I don't know, I think it looks kind of cool."

"It's actual blood, Ana. That's disgusting."

"*You're* disgusting." She stuck her tongue out at me.

⁂

We spent some time cleaning up with conjured towels. With a gesture, she made them vanish, blood and all.

"That's still really impressive," I noted.

"I appreciate it! I'm getting better at it. Couldn't make wet towels a few months ago, but now, it's pretty easy." She smiled, kneeling down and picking up the piñata.

". . . Where do your conjurations go when you dismiss the spell?"

She blinked. "What, the prospect of candy put you in a magic theory mood?"

"Just was wondering if you have a pile of bloodstained towels off in your shrine somewhere now."

Ana snorted. "Well, *that's* an image. To answer your question . . . no idea!" Ana shook the piñata with one hand, pouring candy into another. The dragon's head tore further as she shook it, nearly falling off. "You really mangled this guy, Mr. Hundred-Point Dragon-Killing Whatever."

"Eight-Point. Hundred-Point would have been really excessive for a dragon of that size. Not to mention a little over the top." I winked at her. She laughed.

"Everything you *do* is over the top."

I raised an eyebrow at her. "This coming from the new Ashen Lord Ana, First of Her Name."

"Point taken. But, uh, say that again. It sounded nice. Maybe make it clearer how much you worship me."

I rolled my eyes. "Ashen Lord Ana, First of Her Name, defeated by—"

She smacked me with the piñata, spraying more pieces of candy into the grass. "You did *not* defeat me!"

"I mean, I pretty much did. I broke your sword."

"I broke *your* sword first!"

"Well, I broke your sword better—"

She tried to tackle me, but I managed to step out of the way in time. She telegraphed her lunges too much.

She let out a growl, spinning around.

I raised my hands in surrender. "Okay, fine. We'll call it a draw for now. We can have a rematch after candy."

Her eyes narrowed . . . and then her face brightened right back up. "Deal."

We indulged ourselves in far, far too much candy that day.

That brought some sweetness to contrast the bitterness of what my name day meant.

In a few hours, I'd be thirteen years old.

I was still so far behind.

Fae children had the first sparks of essence when they were born, sometimes manifesting sorcerous abilities before they even opened their eyes.

My childhood playmates were, like Ana herself, almost exclusively fae. They were the primary populace of our home, after all.

. . . But I wasn't one of them.

Probably, at least. I wasn't quite sure *what* I was.

Gramps, my caretaker, looked like what I would have called an ancient and wizened human man . . . but humans weren't allowed in the forest. Not after the war. It was possible he was an exception, but he dodged every possible question on the subject with such evasiveness that I'd often joked that "dodging" was his favored essence type.

(That wasn't actually too far from the truth.)

As far as I could tell, I physically resembled a human more than anything else. That wasn't particularly telling — some fae looked almost identical to humans, like certain courtly fae subspecies — but I did have one unfortunate humanlike trait. I wasn't born with the ability to use essence, at least not in the same way that my fae companions did.

I did have something weird going on with my right hand — a strange mark that I'd identified as a kind of seal.

Seals, if you're not familiar, are forms of magic that are designed to suppress something else. You can think of a seal as a sort of magical barrier or container, but one specifically designed to keep something inside, unable to escape. The most famous seals are generally to prevent some sort of monster from escaping, like keeping the Buried trapped in the labyrinthine caverns beneath the world. Other seals, however, can be placed on individuals or items to limit their abilities. A seal on a cursed sword to prevent it from being drawn, for example, or to suppress the negative effects on drawing it.

In my case, I believed that my seal implied I had some kind of essence in my right hand that I'd been deliberately prevented from using. This was a little unusual, since most species that were born with large amounts of essence didn't tend to have it in their hands.

Most sapient creatures are born with locations in their body called Dianis Points. Dianis Points are the focal points of the essence structure of the body. They exist in every layer of the self — physical, essence, spirit, and so on — and serve as connection points between those layers. Dianis Points serve important regulatory functions even if they're not actively used, so even people from continents like Mythralis still benefit from them.

In order to actively use essence manifestations and techniques, or what you'd probably call spells, someone must first build a "complete" Dianis Point. This involves amassing enough essence of one type in a specific Dianis Point that it forms a crystalline structure, like a container. There are a few different culture-specific terms for these completed containers — fae often call them "wellsprings" and witches sometimes call them "vessels" — but I tend to stick with the boring scholarly term "completed Dianis Point."

For most species, their first completed Dianis Point was their Heart Point, Breathing Point, or Viewing Point. Those were located in the chest, throat, and forehead, respectively. There were Dianis Points in the hands — the Sword Point in the main hand and the Shield Point in the off hand — but I'd never heard of a human being born with a completed Dianis Point in one. And certainly not with a seal.

Of course, I wasn't necessarily human, but the seal was strange in any case.

The most likely explanation was that the seal didn't exist to seal off a standard essence type from a Dianis Point but rather something called a bloodline ability — a trait that people from specific powerful heritages were born with. These bloodline abilities could manifest at birth or much later in life, depending on the specific ability. I'd long imagined the possibility that

I was descended from the bloodline of one of the heroes that had defeated the Ashen Lord, the fiend that had nearly conquered the entire continent, but that was . . . unlikely, to say the least. There were numerous bloodlines out there and the vast majority of them were much more mundane. Moreover, being a member of a hero's bloodline would have been celebrated, not sealed away with the constant implication that I had some kind of forbidden power.

The more likely answer was that I was a part of some kind of *disgraced* bloodline, or simply a family that had taken to gathering essence of a type that was dangerous to incautious children.

Either way, bloodline abilities had a critical downside — the body had to acclimate to them, just like it had to acclimate to any other form of essence development. In my case, my body was stuck acclimating to a power type that it couldn't actually use because of the seal, slowing down my ability to accumulate essence without providing any useful benefit.

It was incredibly frustrating. Worse, I wasn't sure it was a bloodline ability at all. There were other possibilities — a spiritual bond to another creature, for example, or a property of a species I wasn't familiar with. The result was similar, leading to slow essence progress, but the distinction was meaningful to me. It was a mystery, and my inability to solve it had been a perpetual source of annoyance.

Maybe Gramps will tell me more about it, now that I've finally awakened my first Dianis Point . . . but I doubt it. Either way . . . at least I can finally start catching up to Ana and the others.

My first accessible Dianis Point is in my chest. My Heart Point. That's similar to how a human usually develops, so . . . that's one more point of evidence that I'm something related to humans, at least.

By human standards, developing a Heart Point at thirteen was just a razor-thin cut above average. Most humans would develop their first Dianis Point at fourteen to seventeen. Children who had resources shoved at them from a young age could complete their Heart Point in early childhood, but it was difficult to advance beyond that until the late teens. The body could process only a certain amount of essence at any given time. No matter how much power you tried to shove into it, a person's advancement speed was limited by their body's acclimation rate. There were tricks to working around that, and I'd always been very interested in studying those, but Gramps had kept me from trying too many of them. Now that I'd achieved Candle-level, though, I hoped to start experimenting more.

If I had human peers, I probably would have felt fine about being in an average range, but Ana had *four* completed Dianis Points already. She was midway through the second full level of essence development, the Torch-level, and I'd only just reached the first.

And Ana was hardly the only example. Nearly every creature I'd met in my lifetime up to that point was more powerful than I was in terms of essence development, since most fae were Candle-level at birth, and most non-fae in the forest were similarly powerful. That didn't mean I'd actually lose a fight to a newborn, mind you — I simply was behind them in terms of usable essence ability.

And with that, I'd always felt like . . . less. Intellectually, I knew that there wasn't anything wrong with me, and that there were other species and other places in the world where a lack of essence ability was perfectly normal — but it didn't feel like that when everyone else could throw blasts of fire or gusts of wind from early childhood.

Having essence I could actually wield . . . it finally made me feel a little more whole.

I'll go tell Gramps about this . . . and then it's time for some training. Lots of training. All of the training.

At that time, I could think of little that I wanted more than to grow strong enough to rival Ana. Thirteen-year-olds can be pretty single minded. They're almost as bad as adults.

You might think I was being childish for indulging in such fantasies, or playing hero-and-princess games at that age.

That's nonsense.

There's nothing stronger than a properly sharpened imagination.

I mean, other than maybe that one magic sword that can cut through concepts, like ambition and time. That's just . . . unfair.

Anyway, I consider a healthy imagination to be a useful asset, even now. And as important as it is for anyone, it was doubly so for Ana.

It was one of her essence types, after all.

As I bent down to pick up the (thankfully individually wrapped) pieces of candy that dropped out of the piñata, she conjured a wicker basket. Then, without pause, she ducked down and conjured a pair of chairs for us to sit in.

I'd seen her use her essence a hundred times before, but I always marveled at it. If an outsider had been watching us, they probably would have, too. Casually conjuring objects wasn't something ordinary children could manage, even among the fae.

But Ana had a special heart — the heart of a sword. A very special sword.

As a xiphiad, Ana was bound to a weapon, much like a dryad was bound to a tree. Her swordlike wings were the clearest visual hint of this, but if one looked closely, they could see a metallic sheen to her strawberry-blond hair and golden eyes.

Ordinarily, the main "tell" for a xiphiad was the sword itself . . . but that wasn't true with her. Ana's sword was sealed deep within a shrine in the center of the forest, awaiting a worthy champion that could claim it.

Obviously, I planned for that champion to be me . . . but there were complications.

Ana's full name was the same as the weapon she was bound to. Anathema, better known as the Bane of All Things, The Greatest Weakness, or sometimes the Dungeon Sword. While many swords had essence cores, much like monsters, Anathema was unique — it was powered by a dungeon core, a type of crystal that was capable of creating monsters, items, and terrain.

It was for this reason that Ana herself wielded such formidable powers. She was born with a connection to a dungeon core, and her essence abilities were naturally geared toward conjuration.

. . . And she was bound to use those abilities to stop anyone from claiming the weapon in her shrine.

If I wanted to free Ana, I had to both conquer the challenges of the shrine and defeat or outmaneuver Ana herself. At that point in my life, such a thing seemed nearly insurmountable . . . but at least I was finally making progress.

With a Dianis Point completed, I could begin to make more . . . or follow the "pure path" and simply focus on strengthening a single Dianis Point. My decision would determine the nature of my destiny mark, a visible mark that would appear on my body when I reached the Torch-level, the next level of essence development. Destiny marks granted specialized powers, similar to Kaldwynian attunement marks, and they served as a visible sign of an essence user's specialty. Choosing which destiny mark to work toward would be one of the most important decisions of my life. Plans spun in my mind as I devoured the candy.

So, with chocolate-stained hands, I turned back to Ana. "So, uh, weird question. How'd you figure out what your essence types were?"

"Oh!" She blinked at me. "I mean, my Heart Essence was clear from birth. I don't remember when someone first told me about it."

"What about the others, though? Imagination is a little more esoteric than dungeon essence."

"Yeah, sure. I thought it was dream essence at first, since I found that wellspring awakened when, well, I woke up one day. The queen is the one who told me what it was."

I pondered that, but there wasn't much I could do with the information. I was . . . not going to talk to the Queen of Rust and Salt any time soon. "And the third one?"

"Uh, lemme think. Oh! I think it was Uncle Eiji that told me about it." She tilted her head to the side curiously. "What, are you trying to figure yours out? Isn't it obvious?"

"Could be a lot of things. Cutting essence, breaking essence, weapon—"

"It's sword essence." She rolled her eyes. "It's *obviously* sword essence."

I felt my heart skip a beat, and not just because the Dianis Point that I'd completed was in my heart. "You're sure?"

"Uh, yeah. I'm a literal sword fae. I'd recognize it anywhere."

I frowned. "But you don't actually use sword essence."

"Not yet, sure, but I've been gathering some. Might make it my fifth well-spring, maybe my sixth."

She made it sound so easy. So casual. I shook my head. It wasn't worth getting discouraged over something like that. If anything, it would give us more in common to talk about. ". . . Sword essence. My plan . . . actually worked."

I felt a grin stretching across my face.

Ana snorted. "First time for everything."

I folded my arms. "Oh, come on! I haven't had *that* many failed plans."

"Like the time you tried to get the naiad twins to nearly drown you to 'awaken your power with a near-death experience'?"

"That's a well-documented phenomenon for essence wielders! It's not my fault the books don't talk about how inefficient it is at low levels."

"Or how you used to sleep with a wooden sword to try to get just a little bit of essence every night?"

"We still can't prove that didn't work."

Ana rolled her eyes.

"Or the time you nearly disrupted an ancient ritual by trying to pull one of the swords out of the Rust River?"

"They're all just standing there! How was I supposed to know they were a ritual formation?"

"Uh, you could have looked at the ley lines."

"I *can't see ley lines*."

Ana looked at me with sudden sadness in her eyes. "I . . . am so sorry, Lien. I should be more sensitive about your disabilities."

"It's not a disability!" I sighed. "Look, I admit I've had a few ideas that weren't exactly ideal—"

Ana snorted again.

"—but I have *sword essence* now. Finally."

It hadn't been easy.

Humans absorbed essence through exposure to large enough quantities of it. At later levels of essence development, a person had ways of manually compressing essence in their body to complete desired Dianis Points, but the Heart Point was trickier. There was very little manual control possible for essence before the first Dianis Point was established. The Heart Point was formed as soon as your body had absorbed enough essence of any one specific type — thus, in order to choose the Heart Point type you wanted, you needed to make sure you were absorbing more of that essence than anything else.

And it wasn't easy to find sword essence in a faerie forest. Not in pure form, at least.

So, for years and years, I'd done everything I could to skew the odds in my favor.

Ana had teased me about sleeping with a wooden sword, but she'd been wrong — I hadn't slept with one. I'd slept with as many as fifty-seven of them in and around my bedside, all crafted by hand.

I'd made frequent trips to the Rust River to visit the swords there, absorbing what essence I could from the nodes that appeared near the swords, as well as what little I could get out of the water and nearby plants.

I'd worked at the Ghost Forge, not as a formal apprentice but as an extra set of hands for Auntie Temper.

And, on the rare occasions when I had the opportunity, I'd traded, borrowed, and performed favors for raw sword essence in the form of essence vials and compressed nodes. Sadly, there weren't many opportunities to do this — it simply wasn't a common enough essence type for trade to be viable. Not in my homeland, anyway.

Even with all that effort, I hadn't known if I'd managed to succeed until that day. My efforts to nurture a sword essence Heart Point were a race against every other type of essence I was exposed to — and, given the type of faerie forest I was in, that was a staggering variety.

If I'd gone just a little slower, I might have ended up with one of the more common types in the forest flowing through my heart. Something like life, or water, or even air — such essence types were ubiquitous.

But I'd succeeded. And now . . . it was almost time for the next phase in my (somewhat dubious) plan. "So . . ." I grinned. "I can go to your shrine now, can't I?"

Ana's eyes widened. "Oh! You can! You can finally start visiting me now! I can't wait to brutalize you with my challenges!" She visibly brightened.

I grinned in return. "You can certainly try. In the meantime, though . . . a question for you. What was it like when you hit Torch?"

"Well, remember when I started glowing in the middle of our sparring match last winter?"

"Uh, yeah, hard to forget."

"I know." She batted her eyes at me. "I'm *unforgettable*."

"Ugh. Sure. I meant that it was hard to forget because you had your Destiny Dream right in the middle of our match and wouldn't stop talking about it afterward."

"Well, it was a good dream, okay?! Anyway, as for what it was like . . . I don't know how to describe it, exactly. The strength and speed were great, but . . . most of all, I felt more . . . whole, I guess? You'll understand when it happens. Everything felt more intuitive afterward. I was able to start using manifestations with my third wellspring immediately, and I'd picked up a new technique within a few months. Aren't I amazing?"

I grinned. "You *are* amazing. Your talent for manifestations is marvelous for our age. It's a shame about your swordsmanship."

She punched me in the arm. Not hard, of course, but she was *strong*. At Torch-level, her entire body had been reinforced considerably more than mine by her Dianis Points.

Still, the halfhearted punch didn't feel like it used to.

At Candle-level, I finally had power of my own. It was minimal by the standards of essence wielders, true — but even just reaching my first level of essence development was a tremendous advantage. In an instant, my strength, speed, and physical resilience had improved to somewhere around half again what they'd been before my Heart Point had formed. The specifics depended on the exact composition of my essence type. I'd have a bit of a skew toward striking power, as befitting a sword. It would also provide fewer advantages to things like magic resistance, as well as mental abilities and reflexes.

For the moment, though, I was more than happy with the new energy for me. I grinned and punched her back, just about as hard as she'd punched me. "Don't challenge me, I'm still good for another round."

"You're asking for it, buddy. I played easy because it's for your name day—"

"Oh, is that why you kept overextending yourself?"

She growled. "Your *face* overextended itself."

"That . . . doesn't even make any sense. But jumping back a topic . . ."

Ana grinned. "Right, running away. I see how it is."

"Where'd you learn your techniques?"

"Well, it depended on the specific technique type. I have different teachers for each. For sword essence . . . uh, that's going to be a problem, isn't it?"

"Yeah. Not a lot of sword teachers out here."

We paused, contemplating quietly for a time while we ate.

It took Ana twelve years to reach Torch from Candle . . . but it shouldn't take me that long. At our age, essence development should be faster than when she was first born . . . but . . . she's not going to slow down.

I'm going to need to figure out some tricks. But for now . . .

Taking a little break might be okay.

When the slain dragon was emptied, we rested together on the grass, chocolatey fingers intertwined.

". . . You think it'll always be like this for us?" Ana asked.

"I hope so."

We were quiet then.

Time passed. Day darkened until night.

And finally, as Ana fell asleep, she changed. Her body shrank down to its original size, barely larger than my hand. It had taken her years to learn the techniques necessary to shapeshift herself to my size, and even now, she couldn't maintain them in her sleep.

I knelt down and cautiously picked her up, then laid her atop my cloak as a makeshift bed. She mumbled something in her sleep about there "not being enough time," but I couldn't quite catch all of it.

I had to rest her facedown on the cloak to avoid her wings punching holes in it, but she settled in easily enough. "Sleep well, Ana."

Then finally, with a hint of regret at daylight's end, I carried her home.

CHAPTER II

SAGE STORIES

For me, home was down a long and winding path. A dangerous one, for the incautious — but one that was so familiar that I could have walked it blind.

With a bit of help, at least.

As I headed southward on the western side of a stream, I could hear faint sounds of chimes among the tall branches of the ancient trees. On occasion, if I risked a glance toward those branches, I'd catch the source of the tiny tines — glowing motes of light, and perhaps even a glimpse at a tiny mask.

Kodama, spirits of the wood. When I said that I could follow the path blindly, I meant that in a literal sense. As I drifted south and west, the whistling notes of the kodama would change. As their music shifted and softened, I would know when to turn.

I kept my eyes open, of course. Even if the music could serve as a guide, there was always the risk of tripping over something. Or just being eaten by one of the silent beasts that stalked the woods.

There were no beasts threatening to consume me that day, or at least none that dared show themselves before me. The walk was an easy one, my own whistle gradually blending in with the sounds of the forest spirits. I occasionally heard a giggle from the brush — the interest of a kodama in my own tune, perhaps, or a bit of mischief from one of the local faeries. Either was equally likely, really. Many of them knew it was my threefold name day celebration, and I'd already dodged a number of well-concealed (and affectionately intended) pranks in the earlier morning.

All told, it took about an hour before I'd moved beyond the stream and into the deep woods approaching the forest's heart. From there, the kodama were all around me, but more distant, their tune shifting toward a faint and eerie welcome.

One or two peeked out deliberately to wave at me. They were braver than most. Kodama were notoriously reclusive, even by the standards of spirits. Still, I was familiar to them, and known to be mostly harmless unless threatened. I paused briefly to reach into my bag and retrieve a handful of acorns to leave as a meager snack for my spirit friends. I had to do it slowly and carefully, both to avoid alarming the kodama and because I was still carrying a cloak-bundle with Ana in it tucked under one shoulder and a wooden sword in the other hand, making dexterous work a challenge.

(In spite of being tree spirits, kodama often consumed the products of trees readily. Don't think of it as cannibalism. Spirits are complicated.)

As my journey came to a close, my path slowed and my mind raced.

What am I going to focus on next?

There were so many options. The forest was rich with ambient essence, and now that I'd reached the stage where I could learn to perceive it, I could gather essence of many varieties to attempt to complete more Dianis Points. Or, of course, I could focus on making my existing one stronger.

When the cottage where I'd lived for as long as I could remember came into view, I hesitated.

And what am I going to tell Gramps?

My lips shifted fractionally southward as I pondered.

Maybe I should just . . .

The wind shifted.

I swung around, purely on instinct, my wooden blade cutting through the air with ease.

My weapon froze at the neck of an amused man. He raised one bushy gray eyebrow with deliberate slowness.

"Forgive me, Grandfather! I . . ." I withdrew the stick immediately, lowering it and bowing my head. "I was, uh, lost in thought."

"I can see that." He frowned, bending down. "None of that bowing, child. I may be old, but I am not so easily offended."

"Yes, Grandfather." I raised my head but kept the practice sword lowered. "Nevertheless, I apologize. I should not have attacked without warning."

"Not me, that's to be certain. You may have grown, but you have much growing yet to do before you can threaten someone at my stage." He smiled. "But you have grown, and that is what we should discuss. Come."

In a burst of smoke, he was gone. I was more than used to this — Gramps vanished from sight regularly. Typically, this seemed like some sort of deliberate teleportation technique, probably using air, vapor, or travel essence.

On occasion, though, he seemed to vanish *randomly*, even in the middle of a conversation. Perhaps that was just an indication that he was easily distracted by distant events beyond my sensory range, but I always wondered if perhaps Gramps had stumbled into a strange curse at some point or another.

Anyway, I knew his intent. I headed toward the door to our home, taking a moment to rest my freshly repaired wooden sword outside — with the point upward, of course. Putting a sword facedown was bad for maintenance, even if the sword wasn't a *proper* sword.

Then I reached for the old wooden door and pulled on the rusted iron ring. It was, critically, one of the very few pieces of iron in this region of the forest in general — the fae weren't generally tolerant of iron in their territory. An iron door ring was symbolic for protection. The rust on the iron, however, was symbolic of iron being conquered by the fae, making it tolerable.

It was just one of the many, many symbols in my childhood home.

I pulled on the ring to open the door. "Grandfather, I'm home!"

Announcing myself was entirely unnecessary, of course, since I'd just seen Gramps outside . . . but it was tradition.

And that might have been a different version of Gramps. Greeting each of them properly was important.

"Welcome home, child." Gramps was sitting at our lone table in the center of the cottage's main room, leaning back in his chair and lifting his teacup for a sip. He looked so casual that it felt a little bit staged, but I was used to that. "You can put Ana in your room for tonight."

I nodded, walking through the open space from the house's central living chamber into my own tiny bedchamber, where I set the cloak and Ana on my bed.

Ana had her own home — the shrine that housed the sword that carried her name — but she often ran out of energy and fell asleep if she was out past the falling of the sun. Thus, we'd sheltered her often.

She was a creature native to these woods, and thus under the protection of the forest itself . . . but it was always wise to sleep beneath a roof in fae lands, even if they were your own. Most of our faeries were gentle and pleasant folks, but they were not the only creatures of the wild woods. Not by any stretch of the imagination.

And the night was a danger to any that dared to travel alone — especially the faeries of the day.

As Ana rested in my bed, I returned to the main room.

Wordlessly, Gramps gestured at the second chair at the table. I took a seat across from him, flipped over my own cup, and poured myself some tea from the pot. It was still hot, of course. He'd either timed my return and brewed it recently or used some sort of technique to keep it fresh. Either was equally likely.

I took a sip of my own tea and waited for a moment. A brief silent interlude, while my mind continued to swim in anticipatory directions.

He lowered his cup, setting it on a dish. "Congratulations on reaching your Candle-level, child. That is a worthy accomplishment, and I am proud of you."

I could already sense the "but" coming and some sort of extended lesson. "Thank you, Grandfather." I lifted my cup for another sip. "Is this where you go into a lesson on how to change the essence composition of an already established Dianis Point?"

He seemed to consider that, then shook his head. "No, although that *is* an interesting subject. In spite of my . . . disagreement with your training choices, I'm aware that you would be reluctant to change your essence. I know how hard you've worked."

"Good." I set my cup down. "And on that point . . ." I let the terrible pun linger for a moment, but Gramps didn't even offer a groan, so I continued, "I'm a sword fighter now."

"Please, don't remind me." He reached up to rub his temples, looking suddenly exhausted. "And you're a sword essence wielder. That does not make you a sword fighter. You've never even used a real—"

He caught the trap a little too late. I didn't usually manage to pull one over on the old man, but he must have been flustered.

Either that, or he was playing some kind of ultra-long-term game where he made me think I'd tricked him, in order to trick me into following his own plan. Plausible, really, but at the time I chose to just cherish the victory.

"You know, you're right? I think it's about time I got a real sword to practice with. As a sword essence wielder, it would hurt my long-term growth if I don't start training with a metal sword early, wouldn't it?"

Gramps's eye twitched. "There are precious few metal swords in this forest."

"I could call in that favor that I'm owed . . ."

"Oh, certainly. If you wish to spend your entire life in service to the court, please, by all means, have them gift you with a blade." He snorted in derision.

"Well, I *could* use the favor to get permission to remove a magic sword from the river, rather than being given a fae one."

"Perhaps, but it would still be seen as a human weapon, then, and you would never be trusted. And you'd risk disrupting the ritual, even if I assisted you. No." Gramps raised a finger and wagged it at me. "No more tinkering with rituals!"

I brightened. "I came to the same conclusion, actually. I was thinking I'd leave tomorrow . . . for Ana's shrine."

"That's a bit ambitious, don't you think?" Gramps didn't truly look surprised, just . . . resigned. "You're technically eligible for the trials now, but . . ."

"I know, I know. Ana is a lot stronger than I am and she's had years to create traps, monsters, and all that stuff for me to face." I gave him a mischievous look. "But I beat her in a sword fight today."

"You did not." Gramps's tone was matter-of-fact.

"I . . . well, I sort of, marginally injured her. Accidentally. But in a way, that counts as winning!"

Gramps reached up to rub the top of his nose, as if he had a sudden headache for some inexplicable reason. "I won't bother to refute that. The shrine will be different, child. Do you remember the rule I taught you about attempting to challenge a vastly superior opponent?"

"Don't?"

"Precisely that. Now that you have completed your first Dianis Point, you should begin to develop techniques for utilizing your essence. Once you have learned several techniques and practiced them extensively, you will stand a more reasonable chance."

"Don't have to tell me twice." I grinned. "I can't wait to finally test out some of my technique ideas."

Coming up with hypothetical essence techniques was one of my hobbies. When I was little, I'd loved coming up with new technique ideas for characters I was reading about in books, or for the various heroes I loved in board games like Crowns.

When I'd gotten a little older, Gramps had convinced me to read an actual book on technique creation . . . and, to my surprise, I loved it. I'd spent years taking hypothetical technique concepts and trying to actually work on the mechanics of how to produce them.

I had stacks and stacks of what I called "technique scrolls" in my room, but they were all untested ideas. Now that I finally had the ability to manifest sword essence, I could finally start putting them to work.

. . . Except for one slight problem.

"Sure, sure. I absolutely plan to do that. Except . . . most sword essence techniques tend to require a *sword*."

There were a few technique concepts I'd come up with that didn't require a sword to work with, but in virtually every case, having a metal sword would make them easier to use — and ultimately, training without a metal sword wasn't going to be as useful for me in the long term as training with one.

"Your desire for such a tool is understandable. Were we in a better place for it, I would gladly provide one for you. But here . . ."

"I know. Not a lot of viable swords around here."

I'd run through the ideas for other sword options in my head a number of times. It's not that there weren't swords available at all, exactly — it's that they all had issues.

I already mentioned the problem with the swords in the Rust River. Tinkering with the ritual again was a bad idea.

The Ghost Forge was a potentially better option . . . if I was willing to serve the traditional seven years as an apprentice. I'd already helped out there from time to time, and benefited from the time spent there immensely, but I hadn't been truly eligible for apprenticeship until . . . well, just that day. Without a Dianis Point, I wasn't useful enough to call a true apprentice.

And while a Ghost Forge blade was a worthy goal, I wasn't willing to invest seven years into getting one. Certainly not before I'd obtained another sword to practice with during that time frame.

I'd considered trying to craft a sword out of a type of metal that the fae wouldn't have had a problem with. Silver was popular with the fae, but I didn't own nearly enough of it to make a sword. Copper was more plausible, but not the greatest material for sword making . . . and I didn't have a forge. And Auntie Temper wouldn't loan me the Ghost Forge to make an ordinary sword — that wasn't what it was for.

I'd considered making a forge, but unfortunately, that was one of my other brilliant plans that had to be abandoned after I learned that it might be considered, uh, an act of war against the fae people.

So . . . that was out.

There were other options, but they all posed similar problems. At least, as far as I knew.

"I don't suppose Uncle Eiji could get me one for my name day gift?"

"Bringing in a weapon from the human world would be a political statement. Perhaps with sufficient negotiation, it would be an attainable route — but you'd find working at the Ghost Forge faster."

"Right." I frowned, but I understood. The local faeries hadn't been on good terms with humanity since the whole, uh, attempted genocidal invasion thing. That hadn't gone well. "Is . . . he going to be here to celebrate tomorrow?"

"Unfortunately, no. Tasks keep him busy in other lands. He may be gone for some time."

Another disappointment, but hardly surprising. Uncle Eiji served as Gramps's eyes and ears in the outside world, seeking threats to the forest and . . . other, larger-scale threats. Ones I wasn't quite old enough to understand completely.

Of course, he wasn't just a scout or a spy — Uncle Eiji was powerful enough to swing wars in his chosen direction if he decided to step in. He just didn't.

Usually.

"Well, it seems I'm out of options, then, doesn't it?" I gave Gramps a look. "Unless you happen to know of any other suitable swords that I'm not aware of?"

"Perhaps a few." He gave me a soft smile. "But if you are so intent on challenging Ana's shrine . . . so be it. It is an insurmountable challenge, of course, and you will fail."

"Please. Conquering insurmountable challenges is my middle name."

"You don't have a middle name."

". . . I do now. It is my name day, after all."

"Not for another four hours. And being in the three-day window doesn't count." Gramps sounded surprisingly petulant about that.

I smiled at that. "Don't remind me tomorrow, then. Help me pack, instead."

"Hmph." Gramps set his tea down. "As if you'd be able to pack properly without my help."

Groaning aside, Gramps helped me without complaint. An hour later, I set my fully packed bags aside, and then finally, I went to my room.

I couldn't sleep, of course. I was too excited.

Instead, I pulled out my stack of half-made technique scrolls and got to work.

I laid out the first scroll in front of me, ran through the math in my head, and closed my eyes to picture the essence within my body.

I was so startled that I lost my concentration instantly.

As I'd approached Candle-level, I'd been able to loosely feel the essence forming within my chest, as well as the strange essence that was sealed within my right hand. If I really focused, I thought I could feel a bit of the flow within my star veins, but it was so faint that I couldn't tell if it was my imagination. It was right after I'd been sparring with Ana, or after I'd absorbed a node — sort of like how you could feel your heart pounding after a long run, even if you couldn't sense it more than a little most of the time.

Because my sense of my essence had been so weak prior to Candle, I couldn't do much of anything with it. I'd practiced basic exercises to try to adjust the flow of the essence right after a workout, and they were ostensibly working, but any progress I'd made had been so subtle that I'd barely been able to detect it. I'd tried to use that minimal control to nudge sword essence toward my heart whenever I absorbed enough of it, but I honestly couldn't even tell if that had been working. Prior to Candle-level, I couldn't even distinguish between the essence types within my body clearly — it was just "essence."

Now, with my eyes closed and my mind focused, essence shimmered star-bright in my imagination.

I could feel the flow within my body clearly, sensing several distinct streams of power that I couldn't have hoped to separate before. I could see the silver shining power at my Heart, the precious power that I'd hammered into my body through years of practice. And I could clearly feel a *tightness* around my right hand, and a sense of something within wrapped in so many layers of chains that the power within could barely be felt.

But barely wasn't "not at all." There was something in there, something that felt intimately familiar. Something I knew in that moment wasn't quite the same as the sword essence in my heart, but called to it regardless.

It has to be some kind of sword-related bloodline, or something at least similar. Maybe, if I free it, I could . . .

I pushed the thought from my mind. As much as I hated the feeling of the constriction on my hand, I'd been taught to demonstrate a great deal of caution when dealing with seals. There was something inherently unfair about being stuck with a power that I couldn't use, but I trusted Gramps, and every adult I'd spoken to on the subject had urged me to similar levels of caution.

I'd figure out my sealed power eventually, but for the moment, I could focus on mastering what *was* available.

I closed my eyes again, refocusing on the task at hand.

With a clearer image of the essence within my body, I was easily able to identify several types of essence flowing through my star veins, but I ignored that and focused on my Heart Point.

Now that I had a completed Dianis Point, it worked like a container that automatically refilled itself over time, and the essence within that container could be safely used without the risk of permanent harm. In truly desperate times, essence wielders could "burn" parts of the container itself for techniques, but they'd risk temporarily or permanently harming themselves in the process.

I wasn't going to risk anything like that any time soon, but my Heart Point had plenty of usable sword essence. I reached out for it, and with minimal effort, I was able to pull the less-solid usable essence out of the Heart Point and shift it freely within my internal essence structure. I took a moment just to marvel at how much easier it was than before I'd reached Candle.

This is wonderful. I . . . can finally make something of my own.

Let's get to work.

"Ultimate Blade Creation technique!"

I reached out my hand, concentrated on the essence I'd pulled out of my Heart Point, and pushed it outward, attempting to forge it into a massive greatsword.

Swirling silver essence emitted from my fingertips, forming a hilt, then a crossguard . . . then a rudimentary blade of swirling essence.

Instinctively, my hand closed around the grip . . . and my fingers went right through it.

As the hilt collapsed, I frowned . . . and the sword essence construct collapsed.

Bah. Just like I expected. It's not solid enough. But if I switch to deflection-core design . . .

I grinned.

Yeah. That might work. Let's find that scroll . . .

I practiced sword technique ideas well into the night.

Which is to say that I tried two dozen things that didn't work in the slightest . . .

And a single one that did.

It wasn't perfect, it wasn't easy, but that night, I had my first taste of my future path.

I went to sleep feeling contented for the first time in ages.

That night, I dreamed of adventure.

⁂

I woke burning with a quest in my heart. Or, possibly just regular heartburn. I might have eaten too many sweets the previous night . . . or, more likely, I'd overused my Dianis Point by practicing too many hypothetical sword techniques.

Either way, adventure was calling me.

I'll conquer that shrine, claim Ana's sword . . . and then, maybe, finally, Gramps will believe I'm ready to leave the forest. I'll get to see the world.

Ana was gone by the time I got out of bed. This wasn't unexpected. She was generally an earlier riser than I was, and given that she could both fly and teleport, she had an easy time getting around whenever she was awake enough to navigate safely.

After finishing my delicious tea and dealing with more eye-rolling concern from Gramps, I slipped my boots on at the doorway and headed back outside. I had plenty of preparation to do before leaving in the evening, but before that, I had chores to handle. I barely managed to convince Gramps to let me skip my morning history lessons, but I couldn't quite make myself skip the housework. Wasn't fair to leave the old man to do everything by himself, given that he was, as I've mentioned, ludicrously old.

(Not that he actually looked any older than when I'd been an infant, of course. I didn't know how he managed to keep his body ageless. He insisted it was "excellent tea," but it wasn't the tea. I drank the same tea, and I aged just fine. I suspected it was some kind of high-level stability essence ability, but I digress.)

The first chore was gathering wood. I set off toward the Dead Reaches, the part of the forest where the wood was, well, dead. I could have gathered dead branches from anywhere, of course, but it was easier to find it in the quantities I wanted in the region that had been killed in a single apocalyptic magical event.

It took me the better part of an hour to run there from the hut, which was good exercise . . . and easy. Shockingly easy. Advancing to Candle-level had increased my strength and speed even more than I'd realized the previous day. Perhaps sleeping had helped my body acclimate to the new level further, or maybe the change was just more pronounced at a run than a walk.

Either way, I felt *great*. I loved the feeling of the chill wind rushing through my hair, laughing as I waved to the gleaming spirits that hovered in the trees, and laughing as they whistled back to me in greeting.

I ignored the way that the air darkened as I approached: it was just a consequence of the tree canopy getting thicker and the presence of lingering death essence in the air. Hardly anything to worry about, really.

The only part about approaching the Dead Reaches that still creeped me out was the sound. Or, really, the absolute absence of it. There was no birdsong here, no shifting of small animals among the branches, not even the chittering of insects.

Nothing lived in the Dead Reaches.

That didn't mean that I was alone. Every so often, I'd catch a hint of movement at the corner of my vision. A stark blur of white, a fierce contrast to the pitch-black and withered wood of the forest itself.

More rarely, I'd feel the shifting of something within the ground, wriggling toward the surface to escape.

I ignored all that. The awakened dead present in the area weren't much of a threat to me — they weren't even Candle-level themselves, nor were they controlled by anything stronger. Those movements I sensed were just the undead running away from me.

"Don't worry, guys," I mumbled as I ran. "Not here to fight today."

As a smaller kid, I'd trained here often, fighting the awakened dead with my mighty blade, which was, at the time, even less of a sword and more of a stick. At first, the awakened dead had been happy to attempt to devour me, but over the course of a year or two, I'd put hundreds back in the ground. They'd learned their lesson.

It was good practice for me, too. They were too slow to be a major threat, and unlike more advanced undead like ghouls and wraiths, the ones I'd encountered were . . . basically just walking bodies. And I use the term "walking" loosely. More like . . . lurching, really. Stumbling? Something like that.

I didn't fight them out of any sort of animosity. It was the opposite, really. I felt bad for them, even if they weren't really conscious in the way that the living were.

I still hoped I'd eventually find a way to exorcise the whole place permanently, but that required a skill set that even Gramps didn't possess. (Hah! Possess.) He had a wide variety of skills and powers — far more than he'd been willing to reveal to me or teach — but whenever I asked about the Dead Reaches, he'd just told me sadly, "They'll move on when they're ready," and then added for clarity, "Punching them rarely helps."

Rarely meant sometimes, though, so I did a lot of punching anyway. And talking to them. And bringing them gifts.

On occasion, I'd find ghosts that were simply too aggressive to ignore. In those cases, I'd consult an elder, and we'd try to find the person's bones to burn. That was typically the easiest way to force a ghost to move on, merging back with the remainder of the person's spirit on the spirit plane to return to the cycle of reincarnation.

Anyway, I'd wandered in there a lot. Generally with an escort, to be fair, but I was old enough to find my way through it alone — especially now that I had a completed Dianis Point to work with. I made my way to the grove of the largest trees, knelt briefly to say a word of respect, and began to work.

The largest trees were nearest to the epicenter of the magical event that had killed the residents of this place. The same magic that had stolen the lives of everything in this portion of the grove had hardened the wood, much like the process of petrification. This was most pronounced with the great trees near the epicenter, rendering the black wood harder than ordinary iron.

I didn't possess any physical weapon or tool capable of cutting that blackened wood, but I didn't need one. Not anymore.

I moved to one of the withered trees in that grove, whispered another quick word of thanks, and extended my hand.

My mind reached out for the moment when I'd felt the surge of power during my battle with Ana. I recalled the feeling of the essence flowing smoothly from my heart to my hand, the tingling in my fingers, and the desperation with which I'd swung. Then, with knowledge honed from years of theory crafting and my exhausting practice the night before, I shaped that same essence differently, extending it and shifting the structure into three distinct aspects.

Sword Hand.

Then, with a moment of concentration, I cut.

My hand — or, rather, the bladelike aura around it — sliced cleanly through the withered wood.

I took a moment to marvel.

It had worked. It has actually *worked*!

I couldn't help myself. I burst into gleeful laughter, pumping my hand in victory.

Sword Hand had been the technique I'd managed to get to "work" the previous night, at least in terms of manifesting a blade of essence that remained stable for more than a few seconds . . . but by the time I'd managed to form it, I'd wasted so much essence on testing other ideas that I hadn't been able to try to cut anything with it.

Unlike my Ultimate Blade Creation technique, the Sword Hand technique didn't need to be gripped — it was just a field of essence that stretched out from my fingers. It had required several other modifications, too, but the important part was . . . it functioned.

The rudimentary technique was hardly perfect — it had cut a little *too* easily, enough so that I'd sliced into a second nearby tree after making my intended cut.

Oops. I'm . . . so sorry, Mr. Tree. I'll be more careful.

At least the trees were already dead, otherwise I would have felt *really* bad about it.

I'd have to adjust the cutting-aspected sword essence around the edges to allow for more resistance, at least for tasks like this one.

. . . But I couldn't feel too bad about the small mistake. It had *worked*. I had a functional technique!

I'd known it was supposed to be relatively easy once I had my Heart Point established, but I still couldn't help but feel jubilation at seeing my power manifest at my will.

There was something *right* about that power. Something that called to me when I felt the sword forming and cutting through an obstacle in my path. Something that felt like it had always been a part of me — something that had been long restrained, but never quite forgotten.

I tried to place that feeling, but without success. Instead, I focused on the immediate joy of the blade manifested from my hands . . . and the growing tingling sensation as my essence drained.

I didn't have much time. If each Dianis Point was like a container of fluid, my Heart Point was currently like a thin potion vial — easily drained in a single effort. It would grow larger both through specific training techniques and through absorbing more sword essence from outside sources to reinforce it, but for now, I didn't have much time to work with.

Another few quick motions and I'd separated a large section of the wood from tree, a block that I'd bring home to work on the repairs to our home. I'd have to alchemically treat the wood first, but after that it would retain its incredible hardness and serve as excellent building material to patch the gaps that the weather had wrought.

I picked up the lumber, slinging it over my shoulder . . . then paused.

I turned toward the single central tree of the grove. The heartwood had been the focus of the ritual that had killed this entire region, and out of a combination of respect and awe, I'd never really considered cutting into it. It simply didn't seem worth cutting into that massive thing for something as mundane as building materials.

But that evening, I had plans. My chances of succeeding in Ana's trial were better if I already had a sword.

I carried my lumber over to the great heartwood, set it down, and scanned for a branch of the right dimensions.

Perfect.

With that, I began to climb. And after that, I began to work.

When I returned home, I set the larger stack of lumber down on the ground, along with the single branch I'd taken from the heartwood.

I began to work on the regular wood first, preparing it for alchemical treatment. I retrieved my drawing rod, which was another type of stick, but one carved specifically for writing symbols in the dirt. Using the rod, I drew a circle around the branch, then marked the circle with salt from my pouch. Then I made two additional circles — one I filled with clear water, the next with a bit of liferoot. The end result was a threefold warding circle, a traditional form of defense against a wide variety of creatures.

Warding circles like this one didn't require any form of magic — the materials themselves were doing the work. Drawing circles had some significance in the context of ritual magic, but that wasn't what I was doing — the circles, in this case, were simply a physical means of keeping the materials for the ward properly separated. Using them was also important for practice if I ever decided I wanted to get into actual magical warding. That would have required infusing some of the materials and symbols with essence, similar to enchanting. I knew some of the theory behind it — it was the area of study for a close friend — but it wasn't something I was personally as interested in.

For the moment, the ritual circles were a simple precaution in case something went wrong with my alchemical treatment of the wood and it ended up releasing some sort of monster. That wasn't likely, but there was another lesser-known function. A nonmagical circle wouldn't stop essence from escaping, but the physical materials would react if significant amounts of opposing essence went over them, which would give me an early warning if something was going wrong.

Finally, I retrieved an implement from inside the house. Not a sword, but a silver knife. An instrument aligned with light essence used to counter corruption.

. . . It was a butter knife, but hey, it was silver. It'd work.

Then, with the knife, I carefully cut into the wood and poured a premixed solution.

Sorry, can't tell you the contents. That one is a trade secret.

Acrid black smoke rose from the wood. I wrinkled my nose in distaste, taking a few steps back immediately and keeping the knife in hand, just in case I needed to take further action. Fortunately, the smoke settled rapidly, and as it did, the wood I'd carved lightened just slightly in color, back to a healthier gray.

Good. Test case was a success.

I checked the integrity of the circles — it was fine, not even showing any discoloration — and then I repeated the process for the rest of the more-dead wood. There were no issues. That left only the branch from the heartwood tree.

When the knife cut into the heartwood, pitch-black essence exploded outward so quickly that I nearly dropped the silver blade. I probably should have pulled back immediately, but instead, I operated on instinct and cut *deeper*.

As I cut further into the wood, more essence flowed freely. I'd carved several gouges before I finally poured the solution into the wood, then, at last, retreated.

Three circles.

Salt blackened. Water stilled. Liferoot withered.

A final burst of blackness escaped from the wood, rushing straight toward me—

Sword Hand.

I cleaved the darkness in half. It twisted on contact with my essence blade, writhing and hissing — and then finally vanished into nothingness.

Breathing heavily, I watched the branch cautiously, but no further power escaped . . . and the branch had *changed.* Unlike the wood pile, the material remained black, but now it shined with a brilliant metallic luster. I grinned, and then with trepidation, I reached out and touched the wood.

It felt *warm.*

I turned the branch over in my hands, perplexed at the way the transformation had manifested. Then, with only a moment of pause, I returned to work.

The wood had been scoured. Now it needed to be carved.

⁂

I turned the newly carved sword over in my hands, admiring my own craftwork. I'd never been good at detail, but I'd taken the time to painstakingly carve a series of Nyn letters for "sharp" and "resilient" into the wood, thinking forward for a day when I might learn how to imbue them with essence someday if my talents leaned in that direction.

I'd carefully carved another section of the branch, hollowed a section of it, and then attached it with adhesive to form a crossguard. After adhering it on, I'd also wrapped that section with a thin line of rope to help it stay in place until the adhesive set properly.

After that, I'd wrapped the guard, using a bit of the hide from a recently hunted stag as a grip. The faeries taught never to waste, and there was no greater way to honor a beast that I had defeated in battle than to wear or wield it. In that way, the beast would live on as a part of me, and continue to hunt alongside me.

Upon completing the woodcarving project, I lashed the newly carved sword to my belt, then began the next of my tasks.

First, I picked up the larger segment of wood, and then I walked to the side of the hut. I measured the distance, then leapt to the roof, landing just at the edge. The old wood trembled just slightly on impact, but it was well-mortared and secure.

From there, the next stage was finding the areas where the wood had weakened, removing the old pieces, and carving new ones into shape to replace them. This was a simple process: once again, a rudimentary Sword Hand technique served as the only tool I needed to make each cut.

With the new pieces in place, I set the remaining new wood next to the house, then went to find the mortar and pestle in the supply shack next to the house. Fortunately, the closet also contained the necessary herbs to make the mortar for the roof, and they remained fresh enough to use.

I sat down, beginning the familiar process of mixing herbs in the bowl and mashing them into paste, then adding the appropriate liquids from the carefully sealed bottles on the shelf nearby.

Should I make some poultices while I'm here? Hm, nah. I can do it before I leave tonight if I feel like it.

I did, however, grab three potions that I'd finished brewing earlier in the week and fasten them to my belt. I'd likely need those later in the day and didn't want to forget them.

With mixing my compound finished, I leapt back to the roof and carefully painted the mortar to the new pieces. Regrettably, I couldn't accelerate the drying process with the type of essence at my disposal. Death essence would have worked for that, or possibly time essence, but I didn't use those. Theoretically, I could have tried to salvage death essence from the plants in the Dead Reaches to make some kind of alchemical drying elixir, but that would have been a whole other task. After that, I returned my supplies to the cabinet and got to my next chore.

I headed inside the hut. Gramps was sitting at the table reading, although for the moment he'd set aside his seemingly endless supply of tea. "I'm going hunting," I told him, slipping my bow and quiver off the hook on the nearby wall.

"Don't get overzealous. And if you're going anywhere beyond the Brightwood, bring an elder."

I groaned. "I can handle anything in Serpent's Slough or the Winding Way by myself."

"And carry it back?"

I gave him a resigned sound in reply. "*Fine.* I'll think about it."

I slung my bow over my shoulder and attached the quiver to my belt. I'd always found a side draw more comfortable than a back draw for arrows.

I glanced at my gloves and armguard, debating wearing them, but decided against it. The bowstring slapping against my bare arm was annoying, but it couldn't hurt me, and I didn't want to get my gloves or armguard dirty. Getting them dirty would mean I'd have to wash them, which was a pain and a half.

And it wasn't like I was planning to use the bow, anyway. I'd taken it because I needed Gramps to feel comfortable knowing I was armed properly for doing something dangerous . . . but I hadn't fired an arrow during a hunt in years. I'd practiced archery with targets, sure, but ranged attacks had never felt like my style.

I was much more comfortable with a blade in my hand . . . or, at least, the rough wooden approximation of one. And now that I had sword essence to go with it? Well, the bow was little more than a prop, unless I ran into something truly unusual. It would have been helpful for hunting birds, but I'd learned long ago to avoid shooting at anything in flight — half the time it was a faerie in disguise.

I set off toward the Brightwood at a comfortable run, conserving my essence rather than trying to use it to boost my speed. Sword essence was loosely in the "enhancement" family, meaning I could theoretically use it to boost my physical attributes, but it wouldn't be very efficient until I learned a technique specifically designed for that purpose. Moreover, I'd drained my Heart Point twice already, and while it would refill again, using my entire essence pool more than a few times in a day was generally a bad idea. That would potentially put strain on the Dianis Point and form cracks if I did it regularly, so I hoped to avoid overdoing it, at least until I figured out more about my tolerance levels.

Besides, I *liked* running. Especially in beautiful parts of the woods like that one.

A smile crossed my face as I approached the Brightwood. Unlike some of the segments of the forest, the name was accurate: the entire region was lit by tiny floating balls of light, glowing orbs fixed to the trees, and bioluminescent flowers and vines. Even in the deepest of night, the Brightwood shone. Not like daylight: more like a field of brilliant stars.

Of course, those hovering spheres weren't actually celestial in nature. They were an entirely different form of wonder. One of the glimmering orbs floated toward me as I approached the forest edge. Without years of familiarity with the place, I might have mistaken the globes for simple manifestations of light mana. But I'd been there a thousand times, and I knew how to narrow my eyes and focus just right to see the figure within the glow.

A tiny person floated within the sphere, flapping his butterfly wings to remain aloft and enthusiastically waving his arms as I approached. "Lo, Edge! What brings?"

The speaker looked very much like a small boy, but with an emphasis on small: he was only about five inches tall. Aside from that, his appearance was roughly that of a ten-year-old human boy with butterfly wings, an outfit wrought from green and gold leaves, and a tiny twig sword on his belt. He wore what appeared to be a human-sized gold ring as a circlet on his head. Occasionally, I wondered how that ring had found its way into the forest, but it wasn't really much of a concern.

In spite of his diminutive size, I could hear him speaking without difficulty. This was likely a property of his Breathing Point, but I wasn't actually sure. Like most people outside my family, this particular faerie usually called me Edge, which was a part of a title I'd earned when I was younger. It was a translation of my personal name, and it had more personal significance to him than it did to most.

I returned his wave, feeling a warm smile cross my lips. "Seeking safe passage through your home, Lindt. I've brought my traditional offering." I reached into my belt pouch, fishing out a tiny hollowed-out acorn filled with honey. I carried about a half dozen of them most of the time: honey was easy enough to find in the Waspwood, which I visited often, but the faeries of the Brightwood disdained the place.

(There *were* Waspwood faeries, but they didn't tend to trade goods with the Brightwood faeries. That's a whole other topic, though, and I'm digressing again.)

I reverently extended a hand toward Lindt, offering the gift. He floated over with excited eyes, then wrapped both of his tiny arms around the acorn in a hug, like he'd just found a long-lost friend. "Tribute, wonderful tribute . . ."

"You accept it, then?" I asked.

"Ahem." He blinked, briefly pulling out of his stupor. "I, Lindt, hereby accept your gift on behalf of the Brightwood Elders. In exchange, your request for safe passage through our lands is granted."

"Excellent. You may now take my gift." I was careful not to say "thank you" — thanking a faerie often implied a debt, and there was no debt when an exchange had already been made.

This was largely a needless formality; the faeries of this particular forest knew me well, and I would have been permitted to travel their lands without any exchange being necessary. I bore the petals of a fae kiss on my right cheek (long story): that symbol was sufficient to mark me as a friend of the Brightwood and any of their allied courts.

I brought the gifts because I liked to, and because it was fun. And I paid it in "exchange for safe passage" because that meant the faeries didn't have to feel any obligation to owe me anything in return for my gifts. Both sides were well aware of this, and it suited everyone perfectly well.

I slowed my running pace a bit as I entered the Brightwood proper, feeling a shift in the essence composition in the air as I crossed the threshold into the faeries' territory. Lindt followed alongside me, serving as an "escort," which gave us a chance to chat along the way.

"I see you take the northward path," Lindt remarked as I ran. "Such a path could lead past Eliree's guest tree, if you wished it." His phrasing was careful: he did not wish to form an obligation, or imply that one already existed.

"I choose another path today," I responded, trying not to get too exasperated. The faeries loved it when I visited Eliree: they thought ours was one of the great stories of love that would be told for centuries. In truth, Eliree and I were adolescents who had found a similarity in our spirits, but with very different goals. We shared some interests, but for the most part, we were in a sort of casual courtship out of a lack of any other viable options.

While I still enjoyed spending time with Eliree, I couldn't afford the visit. We tended to get caught up talking for hours. A visit to her never lasted as short a time as I planned.

Lindt and I bantered as we traveled, and I gave passing greetings to many of the other faeries as we passed through. I gave no further gifts for the moment, though I planned to offer another to whoever guarded the north side of the region when I returned home.

"It would be a simple thing to visit the elders and acquire assistance with your coming hunt," Lindt offered. "Especially for one bearing so much tribute . . ."

I grinned. "A simple thing, but unneeded for now."

"So you say." Lindt nodded.

We reached the northern border not long after that and parted ways. I briefly considered asking Lindt to give Eliree a message, but I decided against it. It was best to avoid drawing her attention: she would not have approved of some of my plans.

Most of my plans.

All of my plans?

Anyway, I exited the Brightwood on the northern side, on the border of the Serpent's Slough and the Buried Barrows. I chose to enter the latter of the two. They were about equally dangerous, provided I stayed out of the *actual* barrows, and the terrain in the Buried Barrows was far more comfortable. It was merely uneven ground with occasional pitfalls leading into deadly monster-filled lairs, as opposed to the Serpent's Slough, which was a swamp.

Nobody sane enjoyed going to swamps.

As I entered the Buried Barrows, I sighed, removed a bottle from a pouch on my left hip, and removed the cork. With a grimace, I drank the potion, bracing myself for the sensations that slammed into me in the aftermath.

Swamps were, after all, even worse when you had an enhanced sense of smell. Even just being *near* the Serpent's Slough was awful with my senses augmented. I was glad I was going another direction.

Ugh. I really need to get a Viewing Point established so I don't have to keep dealing with this.

I fastened a scarf over my lower face. I'd doused the scarf with peppermint oil to try to overwhelm the stench of the region — enhanced smell wasn't the reason I needed the potion, so blocking off the unfortunate side effect wasn't going to get me into any trouble. Unfortunately, the peppermint scarf wasn't quite good enough to stanch the smell entirely, but at least it helped.

I grunted, then stepped forward, more keenly *feeling* my first step, then the next and the next.

The potion I'd consumed was a Threatseer Tonic. The creative name was, much like many of my grandfather's more esoteric recipes, completely useless at describing the actual function. It barely interacted with my eyesight at all, save for making certain specific essence types glow a little. The principal enhancements were twofold: a significant increase to my sense of smell, and, more importantly for the moment, an enhanced sense of "pressure."

The latter might require some explanation. Basically, it made it easier to sense the hardness of what you were touching. This was, according to Gramps, a combination of enhancements to the senses of touch and hearing, as well as a less obvious internal sense for how you're applying your own strength and weight. I could tell that my hearing was a little better when I drank the potion, but the other stuff was too subtle for me to detect on an individual basis, at least at my skill level. Apparently, "pressure sense" was something that many higher-level Skyseekers had to work on developing for virtually everything they did; otherwise their absurdly enhanced strength would break everything they were using.

I wasn't using it for that purpose. I was probably a little too strong for my level of control, even back then, but it was more immediately important for specific environmental threats.

I took a breath and more measured steps forward, trying to ignore the glowing in the periphery of my vision. In spite of — and also because of — the presence of the awakened dead, there were numerous sources of essence in the area. After I'd taken a few more moments to acclimate to the potion, I closed my eyes to improve my focus.

Then I began my run.

That was a calculated risk. Swift movements would increase the odds of attracting the attention of a predator, but running synergized with the purpose of the potion: avoiding falling when I inevitably hit an unstable portion of the barrow ground.

I reached the first one almost immediately, feeling the difference in how my boot sank just a fraction too far into the ground and the subtlest hints of the tremor that began in the instant of contact. As my second foot landed, I immediately pushed myself into a jump, leaping clear of the newly formed barrow-pit that had just emerged beneath where I'd been standing.

I didn't pause for an instant. Standing still was death.

. . . Or, at least the inconvenience of having to climb out of a pit, if it was one of the empty ones. If I hit one that was carrying something larger and hungrier than the creatures on the surface, well . . . this would be a very short trip.

My running steps carried me deeper and deeper into the barrows, hitting more and more pits. Each and every jump sent a thrill through me, the exhilaration of a narrowly avoided danger flooding my mind and body with delight. I might have let out a joyful laugh, muffled only slightly by my scarf.

In retrospect, that was probably what first attracted the monster's attention.

While the truly dangerous creatures were hidden in those pits that went deep into the depths of the earth, there were plenty of still horrendously lethal creatures prowling the forest above.

And those were *exactly* what I was looking for.

After a near-miss where even my enhanced senses proved insufficient to process a minute depression in the ground that I barely managed to tumble away from, my last-minute dodge took me off my usual path.

Faerie rules handed down by humans aren't reliable — many of them are absolute nonsense.

But there's one rule that has managed to remain known in human society that is true enough:

Never, ever leave the clear path in a dangerous place.

Naturally, once I realized I'd jumped off the path, I kept running . . . farther and farther away from it.

I *loved* exploring.

I had time constraints that day, so I didn't plan to go *too* far out of my way, but as it happened, I strayed a little farther off course than I'd intended. It hadn't been more than a few minutes when I realized that something was wrong.

Empty.

I shifted my glance from side to side, noting the odd absence of any noticeable monsters in the region.

Huh. That's . . . not a good sign.

Monsters were born naturally in areas like this one, from both mundane reproduction and the machinations of spawning entities like dungeon cores. An area that was visibly "empty" usually meant . . .

Crack.

I spun just in time to see the charge of a beast about three times my size. In spite of the creature's ludicrous mass, it had been almost perfectly silent — and camouflaged — until my potion-augmented hearing picked out the snapping of a branch.

Oh, nope.

I sprang out of the charging beast's way . . . at least mostly.

In spite of managing to jump before it ran me over, I was still slammed into a tree by a colossal wave of force that followed behind the creature's charge. The aura was much wider than the creature itself and near-invisible, but fortunately, it didn't hit *quite* as hard as the creature itself.

I blinked away the disorientation from the impact, then quickly dislodged myself from the shattered tree, whispered an apology to the wood, and brushed myself off.

The next crack was my neck. No, that's unclear, I don't mean something snapped my spine — that would have been a pretty bad end to my name day celebrations. I mean, I cracked my neck because I was about to break that monster to pieces.

I laughed again.

"I welcome your challenge, great one."

The next time the near-invisible creature charged, which wasn't a long wait, I jumped. The tidal wave of force that followed behind the creature couldn't hit me if I was on top of it.

I landed less than gracefully atop the charging beast, immediately ducking and swinging a fist into the creature's back.

Thump.

Big guy barely noticed my punch.

Then I was tumbling off as it shook itself. I hit the ground a moment later, grabbing onto the monster's leg.

At that close of range, I finally got a good look at it.

The beast looked like a wild boar, except it was several times larger than it should have been and had a coat that was pitch-black and slick with something that resembled oil.

Shadow hide. Just my luck. No wonder I didn't hear it until it was nearly on top of me.

I rolled, flipped myself back to my feet, and raised my fists.

Shock wave follows behind it, but not above or below. I could leap again and hit it from behind, if I had a decent attack technique to use.

Weak to the light element. Which, of course, I don't have.

Also weak to fire, but less so. I could fashion a torch, but . . . there's no time.

The shadow-hide boar snorted and stomped a foot, and silently I thanked the universe for making so many monsters telegraph their attacks. When the boar charged at me again, tusks primed to pierce straight through my torso, I dropped to the ground.

As the boar rushed over me, I stuck my hand upward.

Sword Hand.

A blade of flickering energy manifested around my outstretched hand and . . .

Well, it did what I was hoping for. Mostly.

The problem with slicing through monsters covered in black gunk is that you have an unfortunate tendency to get, well, drenched in black gunk.

Ick.

The boar crashed into a tree as it continued to rush beyond me, bleeding furiously.

I stood up, sighed, and turned back toward it.

The boar's tusks had gotten caught in the tree.

I stepped in close. "You fought well, and you will be remembered."

My hand swept down.

Gramps had been right.

Carrying a titanic boar all the way home was, in fact, a terrible idea. I ended up having to hastily construct a sled, and even then, hauling it onto the sled and then dragging it the rest of the way home was a huge pain.

. . . But it was worth it to see his stunned expression when I slammed the beast down on the ground outside the door.

"Alone?" Gramps asked.

I grinned. "Yup."

"Hm." He furrowed his brow, trying to look inscrutable. Then, after a moment, he simply sighed, shook his head, and said, "Well, then you can carry it a bit farther. Come on. Go strip it by the river."

I groaned.

It was a long walk, but he was right.

Monstrous beasts, as a general rule, had a stronger scent than ones with smaller amounts of essence. Shadow-hide boars were no exception, and thus, stripping the boar at home would have led to particularly terrible odor that would have lasted for a considerable time.

Carrying the boar farther was . . . well, a bore. But I got through the process, then methodically began to carve it, separating hide, meat, organs, and bone.

The meat, once purified and cooked, would provide days of excellent, strength-building meals. Monster meat contained a small portion of the creature's essence, and thus it was extremely valuable for anyone working to refine their body.

The bones would be useful as well, either for building tools or as components in certain alchemical concoctions.

The hide had considerable value, maintaining its sensory-blocking properties, as well as a high degree of durability. It was kind of icky, though, so I didn't want to wear it. Maybe it would be worth something on the market once I left for human civilization. More likely, Uncle Eiji could take it with him on his next trip and sell it to purchase some of the goods we needed for the household as a whole.

The real prize was the monster's core: a simple green sphere that contained much of the creature's accumulated essence. Different monsters had different types of cores, each of which contained properties linked to the type of monster. These cores could be used as sources of essence for rituals or essence-bonded items, but there was another use that was more immediately useful:

They were edible, too.

Most intelligent creatures tended to dislike the idea of consuming anything that resembled a soul. Fortunately, this wasn't actually the monster's spirit: that would have departed to the spirit world at or near the moment of the creature's demise. Rather, the core was a simple container of raw essence that the creature had been able to draw from in life. It was, in effect, the same thing as a completed Dianis Point for a person — but fully corporeal, unlike the ones in a human or similar creature.

Some cores were more spongy or gelatin-like. Others had a hard shell and a gooey interior, like an egg. This one, however, was rock-solid, like a spherical gem. Eating a crystalline structure in its raw state wasn't something most humans could do, unless they had crystal or bone essence, which I didn't.

So instead of trying to gnaw on it, before we had our meal, Gramps and I would prepare the core. We'd crush it into powder, then mix it with a handful of herbs and water in order to make a type of simple essence elixir.

Or, as Gramps called it, "tea."

That essence, much like the meat, could be processed by the body in a couple different ways.

Essence in the body falls into two main categories, at least in the specific categorical system that local scholars use — primary essence and secondary essence.

Primary essence is used for the completion of Dianis Points, like the Heart Point that I'd already formed in my chest. Essentially (heh), primary essence is what defines an essence wielder's abilities.

The essence generated by Dianis Points is also considered primary essence, but it's different in composition. The essence that forms a Dianis Point is more "solid," like a container, whereas the essence generated by the Dianis Point remains in a more diffuse state. This allows the essence generated by the Dianis Point to be distinguished from the container itself and pulled out of it for direct use. Academics generally distinguish between these types, calling them "compressed" primary essence and "usable" primary essence.

Primary essence is generally considered the most important thing for prospective Skyseekers — and most other essence sorcerers — to pay attention to. Compressed primary essence is the main resource used to advance in essence sorcery levels — meaning from Candle to Torch, or Torch to Hearth, or that sort of thing. Higher levels get a bit more complex. Usable essence is the most important for everyday things — it's a pool of energy that is used to power spells, techniques, and other forms of sorcery.

Secondary essence is the essence that fuels your body's basic functions. Everyone is born with some of this in several varieties. Building up more of this doesn't make you an essence wielder or improve your techniques, but it makes you better at things related to that essence type. For example, building up more secondary sight essence helps your eyesight. I'd heard that rich nobles used to eat normal carrots based on a rumor that they contained sight essence, but that's not actually the case — not with ordinary carrots, anyway. You need specialized sight-essence-bearing carrots for that.

Building up any of the more physically oriented essence types can improve physical abilities. Earth secondary essence, for example, increases physical strength and durability. Motion secondary essence increases speed. Stability secondary essence increases all of those, but to a lesser degree than the more specialized types.

Essence types like knowledge and deception improve cognitive abilities. Knowledge essence increases your mental processing speed and memory, while deception essence improves general sensory abilities.

Elemental essence types provide resistance to those elements and also have some useful secondary functions. Aside from obvious benefits like earth increasing durability and strength, there are more esoteric benefits, like water essence massively improving resistance to poison and disease.

The most important part of this to remember is that anyone can build up secondary essence of any type and benefit from it — but it's not usable for techniques or for increasing your overall essence wielder level, so generally, it's considered a much lower priority than building primary essence. This is also a slow process. Most foods only retain marginal trace amounts of essence from the original creature, and it takes eating a lot of it to have a major impact.

If you want to use essence from food to complete a Dianis Point, you need to build a foundation first. A foundation is a Dianis Point that isn't finished but has enough compressed essence that it serves as a sort of magnet that attracts more essence of that type. People at Candle-level and above can make a foundation manually by compressing the desired essence type in whichever Dianis Point they want. Prior to that, your best way to form a foundation is to consume a bunch of a specific essence type all at once and hope it sticks. Food usually isn't enough for that — you generally want to consume entire nodes or vials of the right types to get the process started. I'd done that, as well as other things to help skew my odds, like my "sleep with fifty-plus swords in my room" strategy.

The boar's essence core wouldn't make for quite as tasty a tea as we'd had earlier in the day: that tea had been made from the essence of a spiritual wasp from the Waspwood, and their cores tasted like honey. This one would probably taste a bit like bacon, which was pretty strange in a tea, but hey, bacon was bacon.

I washed salvageable parts of the boar in the river, wrapped them in the cleaned hide, and then carried them back to the house. We quickly prepared the core, cooked some of the meat, then salted the rest of it and set it up to dry.

After that, we finally had lunch.

"You have grown stronger," Gramps admitted.

"I'm sensing a 'but don't get arrogant' coming." I smirked.

"No." He shook his head. "That is not what I wish to convey right now. It is a much more important lesson."

"Oh?" I raised an eyebrow.

"Yes." He nodded sagely. "Listen closely. When one hunts a tremendous beast like this, harvests the necessary parts, and prepares them for use . . ."

I prepared myself for some sort of moral lesson.

"Take a bath. Please, for the love of the dead gods. Take a bath, child. You stink like an army of the dead."

". . . Fair."

After bathing in the stream and a bit of play with the local naiads, I went back home. I'd wasted more time than I'd wanted to, but I still refused to rush off without making the proper preparations. I was confident in my abilities, but I had no illusions about my chances of defeating Ana's tests without using every tool at my disposal.

. . . And, beyond that, my tricks wouldn't do me any good if I died before making it to the shrine.

I threw on my heavy cloak — the night would be cold, especially now that I was soaking wet — and the backpack full of basic travel supplies that

I'd packed with Gramps earlier in the day. Food, water, rope, flint, lots of oilweed, my flute, a mirror, my brush and quill set, ink, blank parchment, a bronze whittling knife and whetstone, that sort of thing.

I didn't bring my bow. I didn't need the extra weight. My newly forged wooden blade would be the only weapon I needed.

Next, I fastened my travel pouches onto my belt and double-checked their contents.

The left set, color-coded green, was my offering pouches. Each had simple gifts that could be used in exchange for services, or simply to avoid an unwanted confrontation.

Acorns with honey. Milk. Blood. Three essence vials: water, life, and earth essences. Coins. Dried meat. Feathers. Ink. Packets of tea leaves.

The right set, color-coded red, was my warding pouches. They carried components that could be used to scare off specific types of creatures to prevent a fight, or as potent tools if a fight did occur.

Iron powder for fae and certain types of fiends. Salt for ghosts. Essence of sunlight for wraiths and specters. Charcoal for phantasms. Silver spikes for lycanthropes. Wolfsbane for wolves. Garlic. Dawnflowers. Redbane. Stagnant water for naiads. First drops of rain from a sunny day for . . . more obscure stuff. Razorgrass for trapping.

All the basics, really. I also kept an empty pouch, in case I needed to pick things up.

I didn't think I'd need my warding pouches to quite the same degree now that I had the ability to form a blade from sword essence — that would scare off a lot of lower-level monsters on its own — but the pouches were useful for when I was sleeping in dangerous territory. I'd learned long ago to set up rings of specific materials to keep my sleeping place secure. Beyond that, they'd be helpful for keeping creatures at bay that were too powerful for me to fight directly . . . and there were still an awful lot of those. At Candle-level, I was still one of the weakest entities in the forest in terms of raw essence ability. My raw physical abilities were better developed than the average person my age, thanks to the properties of sword essence and a lifetime of delicious tea and monster meat to fuel other types of secondary essence, but that wouldn't be enough to close the gap against anything that was truly strong — and there were many, many creatures in my home forest that qualified.

I didn't have any particular deterrents for a couple of the deadliest categories of creatures: dragons and humans. Dragons didn't tend to have any universal weaknesses. Some specific flowers and other fauna were toxic to them, but I didn't have any on hand.

Humans weren't easily warded off by much of anything, either. It wasn't that they didn't have weaknesses: they simply had so many that they tended to be unaware of them and ignore them entirely. That, and live snakes were a pain to carry around. Fortunately, humans were almost unheard of in these parts, and dragons . . .

Well, if I ran into a dragon, throwing a plant at them wasn't going to save me.

I brewed a couple quick potions for emergencies: a stamina restoration potion and a poison suppression potion. I packed those in my backpack.

By the time that was done, the sun had fallen.

I bid my grandfather goodbye. I was prepared.

It was time to earn myself a sword.

INTERLUDE I

SCRIBE'S SORCERY

As Scribe followed the strange youth through the brush, he processed each bit of the story carefully. He had little interest in the minutiae of the Skyseeker's childhood, but the bits and pieces about the functionality of the essence system were absolute treasure. He'd gleaned some of the same information from his own scattered studies since he'd arrived on the continent — and heard a few tiny bits prior to that — but an actual essence wielder was a font of information beyond anything he'd managed to find thus far.

Need to be careful about how overt I am with my questions, but . . . there's potential here.

Scribe bit his lip, thinking, then interjected as soon as the youth paused for breath. With a practiced motion, he reached up and shifted his earring. "This is a fascinating story, thank you for sharing. If you don't mind, can I ask a few small questions before you continue?"

"Of course." The youth nodded. "I'm pleased that you're enjoying it."

"Enjoying" wasn't exactly the word he would have used, but there was no need to issue a correction. In some senses, he did enjoy learning things that were useful. He might have found more joy in it if not for the looming sense of doom related to his current assignment, as well as the potential risks if this youth discovered more about his goals.

"A practical one, first. Do you know where we're going? You said you'd seen a map, but . . ."

"Oh!" The swordsman blinked, then raised a hand to scratch the back of his head, looking abashed. "I probably should have been clearer about that earlier. Yes, of course I know where we're going. I mean, mostly."

"Mostly?"

The swordsman laughed. "Well, I haven't precisely been out in this region before, but like I mentioned, the map I saw a few towns back was reasonably good quality. There were some landmarks, and I think the scale was about right."

Scribe's eyes narrowed. "Did you happen to make a copy of said map?"

"Oh, no. Didn't think to, sorry. I'm not bad with directions, though. Usually."

That . . . was not reassuring. Especially given what he'd heard about the wilderness on Dania, both from Edge himself and otherwise. "Maybe it would be best to stay on the path? You mentioned that was the common wisdom in these lands, correct? And the roads have wards against the local threats, do they not?"

Edge shrugged a shoulder. "I suppose, but they're not very good. Spread too far apart to cover every area, and they get worn down over time. Doubt they'd repel many of the more dangerous threats, in any case. That's why you get people traveling in larger groups. You know, caravans . . ."

"Groups of bandits . . ." Scribe offered.

Edge laughed. "Right. 'Bandits.' Oh, you aren't expecting to stumble into more of those 'bandits,' are you?"

The swordsman's emphasis on the word made it clear that he had suspicions of his own, but it was tough to know exactly how much the swordsman had guessed, and it didn't seem like the time to pry. He needed more information of his own first. So, instead, he replied casually, "Well, I *wasn't* expecting it. Not until you asked. Now, I feel like it's almost unavoidable."

"Hah!" Edge chuckled, then gestured to the woods around him. "I know how that can feel. Realistically, though, there's no need to worry. Won't find too many hideouts in these woods — for bandits or otherwise. Too far off the trail at this point, it's not a good place to hide. Nothing but ruins and monsters out here, it's way too dangerous for ordinary folk to wander."

"That's . . . not exactly as comforting as you might think it is."

The swordsman paused in his tracks, turning and raising an eyebrow. "If you're really that concerned, we can turn toward the road. It's not that far, probably a mile or so."

"How do you know? We've been walking for quite a while."

"Well, assuming that map was accurate, I have a pretty good idea of the curve. We've been walking about two and a half hours from where the bandits stopped us. Your stride is about two and a half feet, with about a stride every three quarters of a second. Given that we're slowing down a little here and there, we're probably going about two miles an hour."

"Meaning we've only gone about five miles, and based on the angle, you think we're not far from the road." Scribe nodded in understanding, but furrowed his brow.

. . . When did he calculate the length of our steps and how quickly we were stepping?

Edge had been narrating almost constantly, with only a few brief pauses. It wasn't exactly a difficult calculation — Scribe could have done the math just as easily — but he hadn't really considered it the type of thing to think about.

Might just be an element of having to survive in a strange forest for much of his life, Scribe considered; *if wandering too far from a path is death where he comes from, having a good idea of exactly how far you've traveled is probably second nature to him.*

He wasn't entirely satisfied by that answer, but asking directly seemed awkward, so he approached it from a different angle. "If you know where we are, roughly, then what was your plan? I know you mentioned a river, but I haven't seen one."

"Ah. My apologies, I likely should have been clearer from the start, but I don't often have people to tell stories to. Or, you know, talk to in general." The swordsman turned and pointed into the distance. "Up that way about ten more miles and we'll hit the Lark River, I think. From there, we just follow the river, like I said. Eventually, we'll hit a rather famous riverside public house, where we can stay for a night or so and resupply. After that, we can either go back into wilderness, or follow the road from the public house for another several days. We should hit a major city after about a week of travel."

A riverside public house? What are the odds . . . ?

He frowned, thinking of the arrow, and the symbol he'd seen. He'd still have to look at it more closely, but . . .

"Something the matter?" Edge asked.

Scribe shook his head. "No, just thinking. The city you mentioned. Is it the same city the caravan was traveling to? Farholdt, I believe?"

The swordsman shook his head. "Nope. The road to Farholdt curves farther north, rather than east like the river. But I didn't have pressing business there — did you?"

"Not at all, but I do need to find a major city of some kind. Was hoping to register as an explorer and get a license."

"Ah. A good plan. I doubt that would help with the torches and pitchforks this far to the south . . . the inquisition's influence is too strong. Once you get into the major cities, though, a license would be a significant boon. I'd considered doing something similar myself — if I spoke the language."

Scribe could obviously sense the implication in that. "If we get to a city together that has a guild offering licensing, I'd be willing to translate, but I don't think I have enough coin to pay for two licenses."

"I can figure out a way to get the money."

The swordsman sounded unconcerned, so Scribe didn't press on that subject, but he did have other questions. "Why not just go back to the road and walk to Farholdt that way? We're probably well ahead of the caravan at this point. They must have taken a while to recover after the chaos."

"Sure. But I don't want to run into road patrols if we're not with a caravan — we will, ironically, look like bandits."

Scribe chuckled softly. ". . . Not very good ones, I'd imagine, given our lack of numbers."

"Sure. But our situations are complex, and I can't talk through them. I imagine you wouldn't want to, either. Beyond that, if we proceed on that path, we'd likely end up stopping overnight in the same places as the caravan — and thus, have more opportunities to be seen by those people again."

"True. But couldn't we just go off-road to camp at night?"

The swordsman shrugged at that. "We could, but assuming Farholdt is our eventual stopping point, we'd potentially be recognized by caravan members there. Beyond that, I had planned to eventually visit Larkbridge — that's the city along the river — at some point. I've heard they have a particular shop that sells essence collection vials, and I need to restock my supply. Beyond that, there should be an explorer's guild hall, I believe. So it's a superior option all around. Do you disagree?"

"Not really, you raise good points. But I might rather deal with a bit of suspicion than monsters."

"Oh, don't be too concerned. I can handle most things out here. Probably."

"It's that *probably* that worries me."

Edge gave him a charming grin. "Well, if I can't, you can always go invisible or run. You can run a mile, can't you?"

". . . Probably."

Edge grinned wider at the mirrored phrase. Scribe groaned.

"Fine. We'll try it your way, at least for now. But if things get too dangerous . . ."

"You'll abandon me in a heartbeat. Got it." The swordsman clapped. "So, shall we keep moving?"

They continued walking for a time, while Edge paused his storytelling to take a few drinks of water and eat some sort of dried snack.

Scribe resolved to use some reconnaissance magic at some point after they stopped to establish if Edge really had any idea of where they were going, but they hadn't paused long enough for him to separate himself and try anything just yet. It would likely need to wait until nightfall.

In the meantime, however, he had questions. "This has been very useful, thank you. I do have something to ask before you resume your story, however."

The swordsman adjusted his hood and gave Scribe a curious expression. "Sure, I don't mind."

"When you defeated that bandit leader, you not only let him live, but you gave him something. Why?"

"Ah, that." The swordsman looked momentarily pensive, then shook his head. "Most bandits don't pick that career out of joy — they do it out of desperation."

"So, you thought to remove that element, and hoped he'd stop? If you'll forgive me, that sounds a bit naïve."

"Oh, if I'd just handed him a sack of coins, I'd absolutely agree. I did a bit more than that." The stranger's look grew momentarily mischievous. "I've learned that my appearance frightens people, however, and as much as I loathe that, it's a usable tool."

"A threat, then, on top of the coins? That seems unenforceable."

"Oh, a simple 'I'll come back if you ever rob someone again' would be. But where an overt warning might fail, a subtler one might succeed. I couldn't speak his language, but in some cases, that serves me further. I signed 'Faerie gold, give to your people.' 'Accept this and you must never steal again.' Incredibly vague, but given my demonstrated powers, taking some of his hair, and the local association with fae and horrific curses and baby stealing, he probably assumed that taking the money would bind him into some kind of magical pact."

". . . Did it?"

"Of course not. I wasn't going to waste a soul-binding on some random bandit, and I have no talent for curses. But I'll use any weapon at my disposal — and someone else's imagination can be just as sharp as my own."

Scribe gave the swordsman a skeptical look. While the intention behind the trickery was pure enough, it still struck him as being overly optimistic to assume that such a tactic would actually deter the bandits for any length of time.

"Do you really think that the mere threat of a nonexistent curse will stop them?"

"Not that on its own, no." The swordsman shook his head. "The way I see it, I gave them three layers of deterrents. One, the risk of being physically killed by a Skyseeker if they try banditry, either myself or another. Two, by offering them coin, I've reduced their desperation. I didn't have much, but it should be enough to help them eat for a while, and hopefully find other work.

And three, the nonexistent curse. The bandits likely fled the area as a group. When they regroup, they'll share stories and feed upon their shared fears. My hope is that these things will be enough to dissuade them from further crimes."

"I . . . see."

It wasn't that Scribe couldn't see the logic behind the swordsman's approach.

But to sacrifice his own meager coins for the mere *chance* that bandits might change their ways?

The swordsman was gambling a great deal on hope. Scribe wouldn't have put money on that bet. It didn't strike him as naïve, exactly, not in in the way that it would have if the swordsman had simply handed them coins and hoped for the best.

No, it simply struck him as *uncertain.* And Scribe loathed that kind of uncertainty. Simply eliminating the bandit threat would have been cleaner. And potentially profitable, rather than operating at a loss. The caravan might have rewarded such bravery and the bandits themselves might not have been entirely penniless.

But that isn't what he cares about, is it?

Looking at the swordsman, the Scribe saw uncertainty, too . . . but that uncertainty was twinged with a degree of pride and hope.

And in that, the Scribe saw something he'd lost in a blistering inferno so many years before.

There was a moment of silence as Scribe processed that difference between them and wondered what it might have been like if he'd still been able to act on hopes of his own.

"Shall I continue my tale?" the swordsman asked.

Scribe blinked away his introspection. "Oh, yes. Of course. Thank you for humoring my questions." Absently, he reached up to twist his earring.

"It's my pleasure. So, where was I? Ah, yes. I'd just left home . . . and a long journey waited for me."

CHAPTER III

SHARPENED SENSES

Traveling at night had risks, even for me. The easiest path would have been to travel through the Brightwood. The night fae that lived there were just as accommodating as those of the day, if one knew their traditions — and I knew them well.

Friendly voices and faces weren't what I was looking for that night, nor did I wish to be delayed by their playful games and tricks.

And beyond that? I rarely took the easy path. Living on the razor-thin edge between life and death was far more satisfying.

I took the rough game path south from home, brushing branches aside and pushing toward the first locale I'd need to cross: the Florid Fields.

Much like the Brightwood, the Florid Fields were visible at night, but the look was quite distinct. The brilliant flowers and bioluminescent moss glowed with crimson light.

Oftentimes, nature's color scheme could be misleading to the uninitiated: humans with a fondness for gold might find a yellow flower attractive, only to find that yellow was nature's way of saying "I'm a deadly poison, do not touch."

In this particular case, however, the crimson flowers were exactly what one might assume: the scarlet tone came from their propensity to drink the blood of anything that wandered close.

Humans had an uncreative name for these flowers: blood roses.

The local fae had a different name: *Vasendra cortair.* Which, uh, also meant blood roses.

Sometimes the fae weren't very creative, either.

As I wandered through the gleaming flowers, I pulled the first vial out of one of my warding pouches. The moment a vine began to reach upward to wrap around my leg, I sighed, unstoppered the vial, and shook a tiny bit of garlic powder out on the vine. It withdrew immediately.

I almost felt disappointed. Such simple solutions were boring, but I didn't have the time to tangle with deadly plants.

I pushed forward, reaching a patch of glowing vines. These weren't vampiric, nor were they all one variety. Mentally, I categorized them:

Vorinlief. Do not eat, paralytic poison.

Galilief. Do not eat, tastes terrible.

Falilief. Do not eat, causes stomach cramps.

I shook my head, pulled out my pouch of charcoal, and sprinkled some on my legs — that was going to be a pain to clean later, but it'd help if I made mistakes — then got to work.

Sword Hand.

I cut a few vorinlief tips and dismissed my Sword Hand. Then, carefully, I used a brush to sweep the severed vine ends into my charcoal pouch. Charcoal had a preserving effect on vorinlief — in theory, the paralytic properties of it would be maintained for years if it was kept properly contained.

Once that was done, I wiped the brush in the dirt, which would be sufficient to diffuse any lingering poison on it to a negligible amount. I'd wash the brush properly later. For the moment, I stowed it in an empty bag.

I didn't like using poison in a fight, but vorinlief was a good deterrent against some kinds of dire animals. It was also useful as an anesthetic — skin contact with vorinlief caused numbness, which could be useful. It only worked as a paralytic when ingested or if it got into an injury.

With that acquired, I started walking toward the razorgrass. I stopped at the edge of the field, then began tapping my foot and humming to myself.

Doot doot doot, goin' through the grass.

There was an audible *shink* as the razorgrass nearest to me pulled down into the ground, responding to my rhythm. I stepped forward onto the seemingly bare ground and kept tapping.

Doot doot doot, gotta move real fast.

The path through the grass gradually cleared. As long as I kept time with the music in my head, I wouldn't have to worry about.

Doot doot doot, nothing scary here,
Doot doot doot, nothing I should fear,
Doot doot doot, just gotta keep the beat,
Doot doot doot, have to move my feet,
Doot doot doot, sing a happy tune,
Doot doot doot, dance beneath the moon,
Doot doot doot, almost to the tree,
Doot doot doot, someone's behind me—

I whirled, a blade of concentrated essence manifesting around my right hand and arcing unerringly toward the neck of my pursuer.

"Hi, Lien!" Ana grinned brightly, completely ignoring the sword of phantasmal power at her throat. This was only natural: she had no reason to feel threatened. Not only did she know that I would never deliberately harm her — well, outside of a sparring match — she was under the impression that she'd probably reconstitute herself if someone managed to destroy her body. Being tied to a dungeon core had some significant advantages. I wasn't actually sure the core would be able to revive her if she died, but she *felt* like it would, and her behavior reflected that.

I certainly had no intention of testing it.

Another advantage from her dungeon core was how she'd snuck up on me — she'd likely teleported somewhere nearby, then flown after me. While she was in the forest, she could draw from the ley lines as a means to teleport herself virtually anywhere. There were limitations, but I won't get into all that right now.

I pulled my arm back immediately when I realized who I was dealing with. I was torn between groaning and grinning at her sudden appearance. I opted for the latter, but only briefly before breaking into a run.

"Bye, Lien!" Ana waved a tiny hand as I shot forward.

I was no threat to her, nor she to me, unless something had drastically changed. I did, however, have to deal with the very real threat of the grass beneath me that was already beginning to shift in the absence of my rhythm.

I abandoned finesse for speed, dismissing my Sword Hand and spinning back to rush toward the relative safety of the Heart's Burden, a large tree on the border of the razorgrass. I heard a *shink* right behind me and leapt the last dozen feet, grabbing hold of a low-hanging branch and pulling myself upward just before the grass burst beneath where I'd been standing a moment earlier.

The branch creaked.

Oh, no.

I dropped . . . but not far enough to reach the grass. It took me only a moment to realize that I was floating, and that I probably wouldn't be for long. I grabbed onto the tree again, finding a more stable branch, and pulled myself up.

Then I turned to find myself nearly face to face with Ana.

Or, really, face to entire body. Ana was presently in her natural form, meaning she was only about the length of my hand.

She was striking in her current outfit, which she'd undoubtedly prepared just for the occasion. She wore plain brown traveling pants, a stylish white swashbuckler shirt, and a tiny rapier on her left hip. The rapier was thinner than the many other blades that protruded from her back to form her wings. She was also wearing a jaunty hat, which she did not seem to realize was on fire.

I suppose I should also mention that her hair was, at that moment, like molten gold. Not in the "golden blond" sense. Like, literal gold, and also hot to the point that it was in a near-liquid state. That heat helped to give it a little bit of a reddish tone. It often got that way when she was overly excited. Fortunately, she could turn down the heat to a more reasonable temperature if she paid attention, otherwise she probably would have burned me very badly on a number of occasions. It also cooled off whenever she went to sleep.

The fire wouldn't harm her, but I mourned that poor hat. I hoped it hadn't been a gift. Ana could (and often did) make her own clothing with magic alone, and it would be less tragic if she could just poof herself a replacement.

And if it was a gift . . . well, she didn't have any shortage of suitors to offer her new ones.

Sword faeries were rare, after all. Even in a fae-guarded forest, Ana was one of only half a dozen I was aware of, and she had something of celebrity status for the particular weapon she was bound to.

I knew better than to comment on Ana's burning hat. Instead, I focused on the present.

I let out a sigh of relief. "I appreciate the save there. Razorgrass doesn't sting quite as bad as it used to, but I'd hate to ruin these boots."

"No problem!" Ana beamed. "No debt is owed. It's my duty to protect all the creatures of the forest. You're included in that, you know."

I laughed. "It's funny you say that, given how much of the time you're trying to kill me."

Ana gave me a pouty face. "I'm not *trying* to kill you. You're just, you know, hilariously weak."

I rolled my eyes. "I'm not hilariously weak, Ana. I'm probably quite strong by the standards of . . . whatever species I am. *Most* people would die if you drop boulders on top of them."

"Please! You were *fine*. I haven't killed you even once yet!"

"It only takes once for me, Ana."

She shrugged. "Not my fault you've only got one life. And hey, we haven't proven that. You might be immortal. We could check right now?"

I shook my head. "I'm going to pass on that one."

"But then how will we know?" She wrinkled her nose in distaste. "Ugh. Fine. Anyway, what are you doing out here so late? Shouldn't you be sleeping, or thinking romantic things about Eliree?"

I furrowed my brow. The branch beneath me creaked precariously, so I climbed a bit higher, finding stronger support. "I could ask you the same thing."

"I'm not a teenaged boy, Lien. You're aware of that. And Eliree is cute, but not my type. Nowhere near swordy enough."

"I meant the other part."

"There was another part? . . . Oh. It's *my* forest, of course I'm here!"

I shook my head. "I don't usually see you this far from your shrine at night. You weren't following me, were you?"

"Pfft. Why would I do a silly thing like what I was definitely just doing?"

I gave her a suspicious look. "Why were you following me, Ana?"

"I dunno. I was bored. It's your name day. You weren't at your house *or* my house. And you're going a weird direction."

Her "house" she referred to was the shrine at the center of the forest — as opposed to my own little hut. I hadn't been inside there yet, but the area outside was almost as much of a home to me as my own hut. I visited her often, but she was right — I was taking a strange route. "I'm on my way to your place . . . but I'm preparing for the visit."

I patted the wooden sword on my hip for emphasis.

"Ooh!" Her eyes widened in excitement. "A sword! You got a new sword!"

"I *made* a new sword." I laughed.

"Oooh! And it's even rune-etched! What's it do?" she asked eagerly.

"It, uh . . . I hit things with it?"

She sighed. "That's . . . kind of boring, you know."

"I'm not exactly an enchanter." Belatedly, I added, "Not yet, at least."

"How's it going to help you, then?"

"Mostly with blocking. My Sword Hand has fantastic cutting power, but since it isn't solid, I can't use it to defend myself very effectively. Having a physical weapon to block with will help with things like deflecting projectiles, prodding traps from a distance, and that sort of thing."

"I guess that makes sense. Still kind of boring, though."

"Well, I'll have a magic sword soon enough." I winked at her.

"You . . . you mean. You're *attempting my trial*?" Her eyes went comically wide.

"You bet."

"Tonight?!"

"Tomorrow morning, more likely. But yes, that's the plan. I'm finally eligible, so . . ."

"Lien . . . not to be rude, but you know that you're like, absolutely not even close to ready for that, right?" She gave me a pointed look.

I grinned at her. "There's always hope. You just have to make it."

Ana blinked. "Are you generating hope essence now?"

". . . Not what I meant."

"Oh." She frowned. "Okay."

Ana and I knew each other very well — we'd been playing together since we were kids, after all. By "playing together" I mean that she made conjured monsters and traps that threatened my life on a weekly basis, but hey, friendship can come from stranger places.

In spite of knowing each other as well as we did, though, we often had some disconnects in communication. This was pretty unsurprising, given that I was whatever I was, and she was the faerie responsible for the murder death traps surrounding her namesake weapon — Anathema.

Most sword faeries would conduct simple tests of worthiness to determine what sort of person was worthy to wield their sword. Many times, these tests were what you'd expect: go slay a princess, save a dragon that was cruelly imprisoned in a tall tower, that sort of thing.

Ana, however, had a somewhat significant advantage.

Her sword was a challenge all to itself.

Anathema was, as far as I knew, a unique weapon. Many weapons had powerful crystals or enchantments that supplied them with essence, giving them special functions . . .

But Anathema? That was a whole different story.

Not a lot of swords had the ability to construct entire buildings, shift terrain, and conjure monsters from nothing.

I didn't know *how* a sword had been built with a dungeon core inside it. I wasn't even sure the core was an original part of the weapon: it had multiple other crystals inside it, as well as multiple empty "slots" that implied other crystals had once been housed by the weapon.

But regardless of how it had gotten that way and why, Anathema's unusual core gave it powers that no other weapon I was aware of could match:

Anathema was a sword that could be used to build dungeons. And with that, everything that came along with a traditional dungeon. Anathema could make deadly traps, terrifying monsters, and even other items. There were limits, of course — not all dungeon cores had equal strength, and not all dungeon cores had access to every type of essence. She could not, for example, make metal swords, even though she'd tried on more than one occasion. For that, she'd need actual metal essence to work with. But even with limitations, Anathema was powerful and unusual.

And with an unusual sword came an unusual faerie. And with that unusual faerie came creative and deadly challenges.

There was a reason that no one had ever managed to complete Anathema's tests — and a large part of that reason was Ana herself. Ana, the faerie bound to the sword, had developed dungeon essence, allowing her to manifest similar abilities even outside the shrine, albeit on a much smaller scale. That gave her incredible flexibility, making her well-known and respected even among older and more powerful faeries.

She was a worthy opponent. Defeating her would not be easy.

I'd prepared myself as much as I could for the day when I could fight my way through her challenges and seek her blessing to claim the sword. Each week, I'd try my hand against weaker versions of the same types of challenges she was creating for her challengers. She'd make them for me outside the shrine, and I'd "test" the ideas, typically by getting beaten into the ground by newly made ghouls and golems and falling into hundreds of her traps.

We were great friends.

. . . But we didn't think precisely the same way.

Even with her chosen humanoid visage, Ana still didn't see the world quite in the same terms that humans did. She'd learned a great deal from our interactions, but I wasn't exactly a conventional human, either, so I might not have been the best example. I wasn't sure if I was even more similar to a human than she was, in truth, but I read more human books and thought I had more similarities to their behaviors and thought processes.

Her other visitors — the other fae or wandering monsters — weren't much more help to her in understanding human thoughts and behavior.

So, because of those disconnects, we tried to take the time to explain things to each other when possible. Ordinarily, I might have taken some time to just chat with her, but night was in limited supply and I needed to get moving. "I need to get going. Can you come with me?"

"Sure! Want help getting down?"

I nodded.

Ordinarily, accepting help from any sort of fae was dangerous. They'd expect some kind of favor in return.

There were two reasons why this case was an exception, and I didn't have to worry.

One, Ana had explicitly stated that the forest was under her protection, and that such protection extended to me. That by itself meant that I could indulge myself in asking for her assistance with things without the expectation of anything in return.

This was theoretically similar to guest rights in some human cultures, but with some additional nuances, including the magically binding nature of faerie promises.

If I'd been unscrupulous, an open-ended statement like Ana's could have been potentially abusable. It was a sign of *significant* trust that she'd said something like that, since technically she was now obligated to help me even if I, say, decided to go fight a dragon or something.

(Unless the dragon was a resident of the forest and also under her protection, which would get messier, and . . . I digress.)

The second reason was that I, as previously mentioned, carried the mark of a faerie's kiss. That also offered me a degree of protection in any fae realm, so long as I didn't betray the trust in which that kiss had been given.

If the mark of that kiss ever turned black . . . well, I'd have a lot more than Ana to worry about.

Anyway, summing up: I accepted Ana's help. She levitated me down to a safe spot outside the razorgrass. I whispered a quick apology to the tree for hurting its arm, and then I took back off toward the next part of the forest while Ana floated next to me.

"So, your sword. You are going to make it into a real magic sword eventually, right?"

"Sure, that's the plan."

She bounced in midair, clapping gleefully. "What sort of magic sword? And are you going to keep it in that shape? Is it going to be a longsword, or a shortsword, or a broadsword, or a rapier, or a scimitar, or—"

"I'm not sure."

She frowned at that. "You're not sure? But, but, that's so important!"

I didn't disagree with her, but I couldn't put what I wanted into words.

There was a sword I'd seen since I was a child in my dreams — a single weapon that felt like it was meant to be mine. But . . . when I looked at it too closely, or reached for it—

I always failed. Something always stopped me. A shadow would pass in front of my vision, or I'd fall off a cliffside, or the sword itself would vanish, or . . .

I shook my head, dismissing that line of thought. I'd solve that mystery later. I took a moment to stretch and breathe. "I've got time to sort out what style suits me best. For now . . . I'll probably make it something short that I can use in my off hand after I've got *your* sword to use in my main hand."

"Hmmm." She wrinkled her nose. It was kind of cute. "You're awfully confident. You aren't planning to *cheat* at my tests, are you?"

I gasped in faux shock, holding a hand over my chest. "That doesn't sound like something I would do, does it?" I didn't sound convincing, even to myself.

She put her hands on her hips. "You very definitely would. You have, in fact, cheated in our games before. Repeatedly."

I coughed. "Is it really cheating when you're ten times more powerful than I am and I'm just evening the odds?"

"Uh, yeah. I'm supposed to be better than you. Evening the odds is obviously cheating."

I snorted. "If you say so. Fine, fine . . . I won't do so more than usual?"

She snorted. "*More* convincing, at least, but I'm still doubtful."

"Sorry, sorry." I wasn't sorry. She knew that. I had my own particular way of "solving" problems, and by "solving," I mean generally ignoring the intent of the puzzle and finding a way to handle it that I found more personally entertaining.

Fortunately, that was probably the most fae-like characteristic I had, and my "puzzle-breaking" antics were both well-known and well-loved among the locals.

"You *should* be sorry," she said quietly, barely a whisper.

"What was that?" I asked.

"Nothing you should have heard." Again, a whisper.

I turned back around to face her, then kept walking, but backward. This particular patch of forest was familiar enough that I didn't need to see where I was going. I'd be hitting Razor Ridge soon, which was one of my favorite places in the whole forest. "You sound upset. Is something wrong?"

She wrinkled her nose. "It's, uh, fine," she lied.

That was dangerous.

Faeries, as a general rule, did not lie. They could skirt the truth, dance around it . . .

But lying outright?

That was some dangerous business, there.

"It doesn't sound fine." I was careful not to accuse her of lying, given the consequences of that kind of discussion. Instead, I raised an eyebrow, deftly stepping over a deathrock as it started ticking. I walked a little faster to make sure I cleared the area before it exploded. "Something happen? You didn't see a human in the forest, did you?"

"Pfft. Obviously not. It's just . . . ugh." She threw up her hands. "Never mind, I'm just . . . overthinking things."

I gave her a concerned look. "You can talk to me, you know."

"I know. I just don't think I should—" She paused. We both covered our ears while the deathrock detonated, then kept walking. Or, well, floating in her case. "I don't think it's fair for me to impose this on you."

"Sounds serious. Come on, talk."

Ana frowned, her perpetual luster seeming to dim for a moment. "I'll think about it."

We walked (and floated) on in silence for a little while after that.

Eventually, the lush vegetation of the Florid Fields gave way to one of my personal favorite locales: Razor Ridge.

In spite of the name, Razor Ridge didn't have quite as much razorgrass as the Florid Fields. Instead, it was filled with a larger cousin with a similar style: bladebrambles. Bladebrambles were huge shafts of sharpened wood that protruded from the ground throughout the region, anywhere from waist height to taller than a building. While somewhat foreboding-looking, they were essentially harmless unless you decided you wanted to reach out and touch one . . . at which point, you'd probably want to say goodbye to your fingers.

Unlike razorgrass, bladebrambles didn't do anything to actively "attack" — they simply produced a thin but vicious aura of sharpness essence. Anyone without the proper preparations would have their flesh torn apart by the equivalent of thousands of tiny blades the moment they tried to touch one.

Why did I love these cheerful little stabby things so much?

Bladebrambles were a source of bladeberries.

No, not at the top: bladebrambles weren't trees, exactly. Rather, bladeberries grew on bushes that grew in areas with bladebrambles.

Like bladebrambles, bladeberries produced a cutting aura . . . but in such small amounts that even an ordinary human could eat one or two without too much risk. And, like most essence-bearing food, consuming it would help you build up that type of essence in your body over time.

In this particular case, bladeberries contained three main types of essence: life, metal, and sharpness. All three of them were parts of my possible longer-term plans, although the metal essence in these particular berries was copper-aspected, because of the type of metal that had given birth to them, and I didn't plan to utilize that. Technically, that made them "copper-aspected bladeberries" — with a coppery tone to their crunchy exterior that looked like a cut gemstone — but I rarely ran into the other types, so I just called them bladeberries.

Anyway, I didn't really need the life or copper-aspected metal essence, but sharpness essence was an absolute must.

Sharpness essence was a cousin of the far more commonly utilized sword essence. It was a popular essence for binding into weapons, but people rarely chose to incorporate it into their own essence framework. Not because it was too dangerous for most people to utilize safely (even though it was), but rather because it was generally considered too niche and impractical to gather in the first place.

This particular sharpness essence was sword-aspected sharpness essence, meaning it was only one step removed from sword essence. That made it one of the few things even similar to sword essence that was easily available in my homeland.

Gramps had told me not to bother with it, which is probably why I'd spent the better part of the last two years coming to this grove weekly and gathering every bit of sharpness essence that I could.

I picked several berries from the nearest bush, popped one in my mouth, and bagged some others for later. They'd replenish themselves over time as long as I didn't pick any particular bush completely clean.

Then, I went hunting for the real prize: sword-aspected sharpness motes. As with any area saturated with a great deal of essence of a particular type, there was a high probability that eventually, essence would coalesce into motes — or even cores — in this region. I went through regularly, checking the common locations where they appeared.

And, sure enough, I found one without much difficulty. It was a glimmering spiky orb that hovered in the air between three of the larger bladebrambles.

"Oooh." Ana gazed at it. "Want me to get it down for you?"

"Nah." I shook my head. "I've got it."

Ordinarily, one would gather dangerous things like sharpness essence with the utmost care. I, being familiar with what I was dealing with, threw a rock at it. The first rock missed — rock throwing wasn't my specialty — but the second knocked it right out of the air. The sphere fell to the ground. The remains of the rock, now split in twain, fell along with it.

I had a habit of breaking rocks like that.

Ana clapped appreciatively at my performance. I walked over, half-consciously stepping over a silversnake that was slithering in the soil, then picked up the orb with my right hand and concentrated. The spiky sphere flickered, then vanished in a puff of silvery sparks.

As the sharpness essence flowed into my body, I closed my eyes and concentrated, sensing silvery power flowing into me.

I could have easily begun to compress the essence in a specific Dianis Point to work toward completing it, but I wasn't sure if I was ready to make the decision on which additional Dianis Points I wanted to form. Instead, I concentrated on the sharpness essence and shifted it toward my Heart Point.

As the sharpness essence approached the center of my chest, I began a new process that I'd studied extensively. I extracted a bit of sword essence that my Heart Point had generated, then mixed it together with the sharpness essence. This was very simple, given that they were related essence types. After merging them, I ran the merged essence through my star veins, continuing the mixing process. After several repetitions of this process, I'd refined the essence into a type of sword-aspected essence, which I moved back toward my Heart Point. Then I simply compressed that essence against the Heart Point itself, working toward strengthening my heart.

The Heart Point would do the rest of the work, gradually converting the essence mixture into sword essence that matched the rest of the essence it used. By doing this, I was able to use sharpness essence to strengthen my Heart Point.

Converting similar essence types was an extremely common practice for reinforcing an existing Dianis Point. Given the sheer variety of types of essence in the world, converting similar essences was much more reliable than simply looking for exactly the same essence type and using that exclusively.

I was at the stage where developing more Dianis Points rather than just converting essence would potentially be wise, but I'd worry about that later. For the moment, more power for my Heart Point was more immediately relevant.

I opened my eyes to find Ana floating in front of me. She'd shifted her outfit — which was, it seemed, now simply composed of her own essence — while I wasn't looking, and now she wore a crimson suit of armor matching the tones of the bladebrambles.

"Working on making yourself even edgier?" She gave me a knowing grin.

I rolled my eyes. "Ugh, don't you start. The name puns are bad enough when *I* make them."

"I think they're endearing, personally. And they suit you more and more with each weird fruit you creepily absorb."

"I'm not sure these are technically fruit. But either way, I'm sure I'll earn a better nickname after I get out of this place."

". . . You're really planning to leave home after you go to the shrine?"

I blinked. "Obviously? That's . . . sort of the main reason I need a sword. I'll need one to protect myself when I get to the outside world . . . and Gramps seems to think that conquering your shrine is something I need to do for other reasons, too."

"I just thought . . . never mind." She gave me another bright look, but this one was obviously fake.

I winced, knowing I'd made a mistake.

Had something changed? Was she worried about leaving her dungeon behind? Or was there something subtler going on, something I'd somehow missed entirely?

I wasn't willing to simply let that go. Secrets between friends were fine, but this one was hurting her. Somehow, *I* was hurting her. That wasn't acceptable. "Ana, what is it that you're not telling me? Is there some reason you don't want to leave the forest?"

"Oh, it's, uh. Sorry. I . . ." She turned away. "It's late. I have very important sword things."

"Ana, wai—"

And then she was gone, vanishing in a burst of sparks. I sighed.

That's a problem, but . . . I can't stop myself because she's being vague and mysterious. I can ask her about it if I see her before I go in the shrine.

I spent a while searching the area for other sources of sharpness essence, finding a couple smaller motes in their usual locations, then headed farther to the south.

Soon I reached one of the most iconic parts of the woods. The reason why our forest grew razorgrass and bladebrambles.

The Rust River.

That wasn't actually the local name for it. Instead, the locals called it *Ithrenkael*, a fae word that translated to "The Death of Iron." A much more foreboding name, but in spite of the accuracy involved, I found myself using the human name for the region more frequently.

The reason for the human name was obvious to anyone who came by: the waters of the river were stained crimson, even hundreds of years after the event that had caused it. No, not because of blood. Thousands had died on that river, but their blood wouldn't have stained it to that degree.

It was their swords, thousands and thousands of swords, littering the water. Centuries after the bodies themselves had worn away, the swords remained in the water, many — but not all — covered in rust.

The ancient swords weren't precisely the source of the color, either. Even a bunch of rusty swords wouldn't perpetually taint the water enough to completely change the water's color. This was, instead, a consequence of a faerie warning. Fae magic preserved the rusted weapons and gave the water the crimson hue as a lesson to the humans who had attempted to invade their kingdom: this is the fate of those who would dare to desecrate the forest.

Humanity got the message.

Thus, the Rust River served as a clear border between fae and human territory. The forest continued beyond it, and the fae still inhabited the region beyond, but humans knew not to cross the river or get anywhere close to it.

A consequence of that faerie magic was that the preserved swords continued to generate sword essence, as well as other types of related essences. That, in turn, had gradually influenced the flora and the fauna of the forest. Animals that drank from the Rust River would develop properties related to sword essence, sharpness essence, and even rust essence.

I'd occasionally drink some of the water when I was first starting to build the essence in my body, but at this point, it wasn't an efficient form of essence development.

Instead, I waded through the water of the river, seeking out the few swords that remained in the river that *hadn't* rusted. These were weapons that had been enchanted with human magic at the time they had been plunged into the water. Some had probably been the swords of famous knights and royals.

Now they served as little more than a deadly warning . . . and, of course, a few better-than-average sources of sword essence.

I'd learned my lesson about trying to take the swords out of the ritual formation, but taking the nodes that appeared nearby was a whole different story. The fae didn't have the slightest problem with it. They hated the idea of wasting resources. Honestly, I think they were happy I'd thought of the idea.

I regularly came by to find these nodes and absorb them — it was my single most reliable source of sword essence. Beyond that, I'd begun trying to siphon off essence from the swords directly, hoping to supplement my sword essence supply further. I'd been given permission for that as well, but it had proven too challenging.

At least until that day.

As I put my hands on one of the swords, I closed my eyes and envisioned my core self — and cautiously extended my senses into the sword in my grip.

A burst of colors flooded my vision — and bled into my other senses. I saw metal plunged into water, worn away by time. My ears rang with the sounds of swords clashing against each other and blades broken by fang and claw. I tasted iron on my mouth, smelled it. I felt broken blades pressed against my neck.

I pulled back instantly, overwhelmed.

My heart pounded in my chest.

That . . . wasn't just one sword I was sensing. It was something related to the ritual and the river itself.

The sensation I'd felt when I'd opened up my essence sense was impossibly strong, terrifyingly intense.

So, naturally, I did it again immediately.

I staggered again, but managed to maintain my grip for another moment this time. I felt myself falling to my knees in the water, but tightened my grip rather than loosening it, and focused on a portion of the sense — the sight, sound, and touch of blades.

Then I *pulled.*

I felt resistance, the image of a sword stuck in between the stones of a river, but I responded with the image of my own legs braced against the stones as I put both hands on the grip and wrenched upward—

I sensed something else, then. Something almost like a feeling, an acknowledgment, one that came from outside myself.

And with it, the image of the sword came free — and essence flowed into my body.

I fell backward into the water, my hands coming free from the grip of the actual weapon I'd held. It was, of course, still stuck in the water. The image of pulling a sword out had only been a mental exercise, one designed to wrench loose the essence held within the ritual's grasp.

I . . . hadn't expected it to work.

I felt sword essence flowing freely through my star veins and grinned to myself. It wasn't a truly overwhelming amount, but I'd pulled free more power than I typically managed from a good day of hunting for sword essence nodes.

It wouldn't give me any more immediate power, but as my body processed that essence, my Dianis Point would grow stronger, and the portion that became secondary essence would increase my physical abilities as well.

Well, I considered, *I'm definitely trying that again sometime.*

I'd have to be cautious, of course. Repeating that process regularly was a risk — I didn't want to disrupt the ritual that kept the swords stable. And beyond that . . . I'd felt something beyond just essence when I'd reached into that sword.

The river . . . does it have a spirit?

It wouldn't have been surprising — virtually everything in the lands where I'd been raised had a spirit of some kind, but I hadn't actually heard of a spirit for the Rust River. I knew other river spirits — the naiads Current and Flow, for example, in the river farther to the north near the healing spring — but I'd never seen naiads in this river, nor heard of them.

Maybe it's an incorporeal spirit?

I was curious, but it was beyond my immediate ability to explore. Instead, I shifted back to the sword I'd gripped, put my hands on it, and whispered.

"Spirit of the sword, spirit of the river, spirit of the ritual, I offer you this humble offering in return for your generous gift."

I reached into one of my gift pouches and retrieved three tiny silver coins, casting them into the waters. I hoped that the spirit — or spirits — would find the offering pleasing. Knowing what to offer a spirit I couldn't communicate with was difficult, but it was better to make sure I *offered* something, rather than accruing a debt to an unknown entity.

It was a subtle thing, but I thought I heard a melodious sound as each coin struck the water. I hoped that signaled acceptance, but I didn't know.

With that completed, I stood and headed downriver. This path took me even farther from the shrine — it was almost entirely in the wrong direction

— but I had one more important place to visit. After that, I'd make my way back up the river toward the shrine and find a place to sleep nearby before the attempt.

To the southwest of the river was one of the most ominous places in the forest: Malice Point. An ancient, crumbling tower, the location radiated essence of a dozen varieties. Flame. Ruin. Decay. Fear.

Given the aura of the place, it didn't get a lot of visitors. As I walked closer, the essence thickened until the ominous aura felt almost like a mist hovering in the air. Or, perhaps "smoke" would be a better word, given that flame essence was involved.

I pressed on farther, pushing through the smoky haze. The aura hardened until pressing on felt almost like walking through mud.

It took minutes, but finally I struggled through the thickest region of aura and came to a place where I could breathe more easily on the inside.

I stood at the base of the crumbled tower and looked up.

The eye that met my gaze was taller than my entire body.

And when the creature spoke, the air itself cracked at the sound of his voice.

CHAPTER IV

SCORCHING SMOKE

The air-splitting roar nearly deafened me, the gale force of the breath that accompanied it driving me back a step. My ears rang in the aftermath, but fortunately, not too much to hear the words that followed.

"Who dares intrude on my domain?"

Every word reverberated in my body and spirit simultaneously, and I felt potent fear and thunder essence threaten to overwhelm me. I gritted my teeth and focused, then offered a traditional reply.

"Forgive my insolence for intruding upon your lair. This humble one has brought gifts to—"

"What? Speak up, I cannot hear you over your insignificance!"

I sighed, then raised my voice. "I have brought gifts in hopes you will grant me forgiveness and safe passage through your domain."

The gigantic eye blinked, then pulled back, giving me a better view of the titanic head that held it.

Every coppery scale on that head was larger than my entire body. The teeth in his mouth were large enough to rival some of the tallest trees of the wood. The horns on the sides of his head were each larger than an elephant.

Verthrimax was so large that I'd never been able to see his entire draconic form at once, not even from a great distance: but I didn't need to.

It was obvious, even just looking at his face, that I was greeting a dragon.

Smoke poured from his nostrils as his eyes narrowed at me. Then, after a moment of silence, he spoke again with words of thunder. ". . . Edge? Is that your voice I hear?"

His narrowed eyes continued to focus on me, but without seeing.

Verthrimax was ancient and powerful beyond anyone I knew. He was, however, almost completely blind.

"Yes, it's me, great one. Please forgive me for coming without warning."

There was a louder snort, and then the dragon looked upward and let out a booming laugh with such volume that the ground beneath me shook and cracks formed in the earth. In the distance, animals were probably fleeing the area in fear, which I felt slightly guilty about.

"Edge! It's been too long." He cleared his throat, which sounded something like a part of the forest going through a very large wood chipper. "Ahem. That is, Child of the Forest, I will permit you this once to intrude on my domain."

I grinned. Verthrimax didn't get visitors very often, because of the whole "being a terrifying dragon that could eat a small town in a gulp" thing, so I tried to come by whenever I could to greet him. Doing so with proper formalities was important, too, even if he didn't always remember to use them in return.

Treating him with respect helped him remember.

I headed to the front door of the colossal tower. It had been ripped off the hinges again, probably through some sort of small accident. I'd have to fix it later, during daylight.

I headed in, following the brittle spiral staircase toward the top of the tower, where the dragon perched atop what remained of the roof.

Once, the tower had housed thousands of people: now it served as home for only the resident I visited atop it. Ancient wards on the building kept it from collapsing under his weight, but only just barely. Gramps came by from time to time to renew those wards, while Ana and I did what we could to periodically fix the structural damage.

When I reached the top, I took off my backpack and opened it. "A few humble gifts for you. First, something to drink. It's not a lot, though, so if you'll forgive my impertinence, you may wish to take your smaller form to drink it."

I pulled out a flask of water I'd gathered from a healing pool. I had laboriously gathered two full flasks over the last couple months to prepare for my shrine challenge, but I wasn't the only one that deserved to benefit from the waters.

I heard a snort of derision. "You have grown audacious, child, but I will not refuse a gift in the manner in which it is offered."

The titanic beast shimmered for an instant, then re-formed into the body of an ancient, brown-skinned man. He was massive and muscular in spite of his advanced age. His copper hair and beard made it obvious that he wasn't human, or at the least had a very special form of hair dye. It looked like actual copper, complete with metallic luster, although my understanding was that it wasn't exactly made of metal.

I opened the top of the flask and handed it to him. He sniffed at it, then replied in a voice that remained powerful, but not earth-shattering. "Healing essence. You waste your gift, I fear. *Again.*"

I shook my head. We'd had this argument before. "Maybe if you drink enough of it . . ."

"My sight will not return, Edge. The wound was struck too long ago." He sighed, then took a drink regardless, closing his eyes.

We were quiet for a moment while he savored the liquid.

". . . It is good, though. The eyes may not heal, but it does well to soothe the aches of old bones."

I was glad he'd accepted the gift at all. Some days, he might have been offended or saddened by the gesture. He always held a twinge of melancholy, but he seemed to be in one of his better moods.

I wasn't going to ruin that by arguing with him about his eyes. Grandfather had assured me that fixing old wounds like the dragon's was possible, but the quantity of healing essence it would require was staggering. If he'd consumed the whole healing pool at once, it might have been enough . . . but it seemed a better strategy to keep feeding him a bit at a time over years, allowing his body to naturally accumulate more life essence. The life essence in the pool gradually regenerated as long as there was some of it left within, and thus, taking from it sparingly allowed for a net increase in healing available over time. And while essence for creatures like dragons didn't work identically to that of humans, they still could improve their essence by consuming the right types.

I didn't know if he was using that essence to complete another Dianis Point or if it was simply being used as secondary essence to gradually improve his recovery process. Either would help, but he was too stubborn to tell me if he was going to build a Dianis Point or not. That type of thing was "private," at least by the standards of ancient dragons.

It would take years, many years, if it worked at all . . . but I'd already been doing it for quite a while. So had Ana.

I had to hope someone would keep doing it after I left. Maybe Grandfather could help. Or perhaps Auntie Temper would finally manage to make a pair of glasses that worked for him. She'd tried several times, but conventional corrective lenses didn't work for him, even when he wore a humanoid form.

We stood in quiet for a time while he sipped. For a creature with a life span like his, a few minutes of silence wasn't even a heartbeat. Then finally, he said, "I have been remiss. You offered a gift. You are my guest now and may be seated."

I thanked him and took a seat. "I did bring another gift, if you would allow me to present it."

"Oh?" He sounded surprised. More than one gift in one visit was unusual. "Do you require some aid, that you bring me additional tribute?"

"No." I shook my head. Then, after a beat, I added, "I'm . . . leaving soon. Assuming everything goes according to plan."

"Leaving? Hold a moment." The older man frowned, then found his way to a large chunk of debris and sat down on it. "Thank you, these old bones aren't fond of standing. Now, where are you going?"

"Human territory."

He almost shot back to his feet. "Humans!" Fire flashed in his mouth as he spat the word. "Why would you do such a thing?"

"To explore. I love my home, my family, my friends . . . but I've read so many stories about all the things out there. Hundreds of Destiny Shrines with their unique trials, the lost labyrinths of the old fae courts, the ruins of forgotten civilizations, the Tower of Trials where only the Hero's Party reached the top . . . even whole other worlds, like the ruins of Rendalir . . ."

"Ah, Child of the Wood . . . There are stories, yes, and some fragments of truth among them. But if you seek them out, I fear you will not like what you find."

"Perhaps." I'd heard the same thing from Gramps on numerous occasions. "But learning the truth is another sort of adventure. And I . . . there are parts of me that I can't learn about here, either. Not entirely. And to that end . . . I've finally completed my first Dianis Point."

"What? Truly? This is a cause for celebration! I . . . I believe I have some sweets somewhere . . ."

I smiled. He definitely didn't. "Oh, don't worry. I've had plenty to eat today already."

"Hm. If you insist. But why would that require you to explore?"

"It's sword essence, great one. And to hone it properly, I must find swords and train with them."

"Bah." He folded his arms. "Why do you seek such crude tools? Your essence should be weapon enough. Simply develop techniques and learn to wield your own power as a blade."

He wasn't alone in espousing that sort of viewpoint — most creatures that fought with natural weapons like claws and flaming breath had great disdain for human weaponry. "I am young yet, and nowhere near your might, great one. While I have already formed my first technique, and I will practice wielding my essence, of course . . . I require proper teachings and better techniques to sharpen my skills properly. I know of few in these parts who train with a sword at all."

"Hmph. And for good reason. Human tools. Human lands. Neither will avail you, Child of the Forest. You should not leave. A more foolish decision I have never heard." He snorted. Again, flames and smoke from his nostrils. I had to dodge to the side to avoid being lit on fire.

"Nevertheless, it was my choice, and I must make the decisions that—"

"Yes, yes." He cut me off. Then, after a moment of hesitation, he said, "You don't have to leave to find a sword. You could . . . take one from here." Hastily, he added, "As an exchange for your gifts."

I nearly gasped aloud.

Dragons did *not*, as a general rule, offer objects from their hoard except under the most extreme circumstances. It went against their every instinct. Their hoard was symbolic of their life's accomplishments and prestige: diminishing a hoard was diminishing a dragon.

This was not an insignificant gesture.

And so I had every reason to be surprised, and my refusal did not seem particularly out of place. "I am deeply honored by your offer." I stood, bowed at the waist, then took a seat again. "But I cannot accept such a generous gift. I have not done enough to earn such favor, and . . . I must confess that, if I am to earn a sword, I wish to earn it in battle, or as a gift from my sword teacher, much as the old ways dictate."

The dragon's shoulders slumped. "Very well. I . . . understand."

Using the "old ways" as an excuse had proven effective, just as I had hoped. It was a bit of a gamble, but I didn't think I'd upset him, which was important.

There was a different reason I'd refused to take something from his hoard, though.

There wasn't much of a hoard left to begin with. And it certainly didn't have any legendary swords.

Verthrimax had been blinded in the great battle that had caused the creation of the Rust River, centuries before. He had been at the height of his power and prestige during that battle, striking down hundreds, maybe thousands, of the invaders to protect the forest.

But he had lost more than just his vision that day. His injuries had been severe, and in the aftermath, he had slept for a long, long time.

And humans, while fearful, were often cunning and cruel.

In the early days of his slumber, his hoard had been plundered.

And even after he woke, some wretched few had learned of his blindness, found their way into his lair, and stolen from the little that remained.

It was, perhaps, some comfort that his blindness had not allowed him to know the scope of what he had lost.

Ana and I had learned of this story when we were young and, through a series of misadventures, conspired to refill his once-great hoard with tiny baubles and worthless trinkets. Now, when Verthrimax slept upon his hoard, the pile was nearly as large as it had been in his glory days . . .

. . . But it contained virtually nothing of worth. Just abandoned pots and pans, copper coins, broken blades, and lost arrowheads.

For the blind dragon, that hardly seemed to matter.

Somehow, his hoard had returned. In the years since, he seemed to have almost forgotten that it had ever been stolen at all.

And slowly but surely, his confidence had been growing back along with it.

A part of me feared what might happen if his eyesight returned and he realized that his renewed hoard was a pile of trinkets gathered by precocious children.

. . . But another part of me just wanted him to be comfortable and happy. And if Verthrimax the Iron Breaker could regain his sight, well . . . making a new hoard of much vaster scope was not by any means out of the question.

Finally, with a hint of melancholy, the dragon spoke again. "When do you leave, child?"

"I will leave here in a few hours. As for leaving the forest . . . that could be days, if I succeed at my first attempt, or it could be a year or two before I succeed. Though I may not be leaving immediately, I felt you should know I intend to begin my attempts now."

"Only a year or two more. Even a dozen would be such a short time. You are certain you must do this?"

"Yes. It's my path. I . . . need to explore the world. To learn. To grow."

"And how long will you be gone, once you leave?"

"I don't know." I shook my head. "But I do hope to visit soon. I have a feeling Ana will get bored and want to come home from time to time."

"Hah! Indeed. Even *I* would not challenge that one when she has not been entertained in too long."

I smiled at that. "And that leads me to my gift." I pulled it out of my bag.

He sniffed at the air. "Is . . . that leather that I smell? And . . . ah, parchment. A book! You've brought me a book. But, ah, this one does not have touch-lines, so I . . ."

Before he could turn his thoughts in a sad direction, I hastily intervened. "It's a magic book, won in a faerie trial. When opened, if you will it, the book will read itself aloud."

The dragon gasped. "A book that reads itself. How wonderous! I have not held one of these in . . . quite some time. This . . . this is a grand gift, Edge. I am in your . . ."

I couldn't let him finish that. "No, you've taught me a great deal. You owe me nothing. But if you insist on repaying me, perhaps allow me the indulgence of reading you some of the early pages myself?"

The dragon settled down with a broad smile. "Nothing would make me happier, child."

I grinned and opened the book. "Once upon a time, there was a great and mighty dragon . . ."

My words carried us both until late in the night, until finally, I carried the sleeping dragon himself to his hoard, deep below the tower.

He slept with a smile upon trinkets that were, to him, more valuable than a world of gold.

***

The morning light had nearly arrived before I departed the tower. I was exhausted, but refreshed by my encounter. Visiting the old dragon always left a smile on my face and gave me fresh determination to face the world.

Someday, perhaps, I'd etch myself into legend the way that he had.

I fought my fatigue and pushed out of the dragon's territory back toward the Rust River.

Once I reached the river, I simply stayed on the southern side of it this time, following the path toward the northeast. It would lead all the way to Horizon Lake, which was just south of the shrine.

My original plan was to get all the way to the northern bank of the lake, then make camp there to head straight into the shrine in the afternoon when I woke up.

As the sun began to creep up the horizon, I knew I'd have to adjust. I'd spent longer than planned with my visit to Verthrimax. I couldn't possibly regret that, but exhaustion was setting in. I knew from experience that if I pushed myself too hard, I'd end up suffering for it the next day, and I couldn't afford that.

So, I evaluated my options.

If I called out to Ana, she'd probably hear me. She could make an instant shelter for me just about anywhere. Her powers were strongest at the shrine itself, but she was connected to the entire forest. Creating a little hut for me to sleep in would be effortless for her.

. . . But she'd been acting strange, and I wasn't sure that asking her for a favor was a good idea. Especially on my threefold name day. That had significance to us both.

So, Ana was an option, but a poor one.

Heading home was an option. It wasn't actually a terrible one, either. Cutting across the river and retracing my steps would have been quick and simple. If I did that, I could simply head east whenever I woke up, taking a more direct route to the shrine.

But Gramps would take that as an opportunity to tease me, so it wasn't acceptable.

Making my own shelter was viable. I'd done it plenty of times. As long as I used dead wood and rocks, the fae wouldn't mind. I had my warding pouches. I could protect myself from most threats with those, especially now that I could fight a bit more directly with my essence. My quality of sleep would be questionable, though.

Instead of all of those, I decided on another slight detour. Just before the Rust River met Horizon Lake, I turned east into one of the few areas of the forest that wasn't strictly fae territory:

The Witch Fields.

No, the fields weren't made of witches. That would be a little extreme, even by the standards of my homeland. Instead, it was a flat plain that held a single distinctive feature: a small, innocuous-seeming hut toward the center.

The Witch's Hut.

The sun was shining brightly by the time I trudged through the grassy fields to reach the door to the witch's home. Without hesitation, I knocked three times, then pulled a small trinket out of my bag — a packet of tea. The traditional kind, not the "made from dead monster cores" kind.

The door swung open, seemingly of its own accord. Inside, I could see no one — just darkness.

Without hesitation, I stepped inside, closing the door behind me.

Instantly, the magical darkness cleared.

I found myself standing inside a space that was much larger than the hut appeared to be from the outside. The entry room to the Witch's Hut still looked, well, hutlike. Wooden walls and floors with a layer of dust that never seemed to vanish, regardless of how much it was cleaned. Spiderwebs in the corners that were, as far as I could tell, largely decorative. There were plenty of spiders in the hut, but they didn't need webs to hunt.

A set of seven brooms — one large, six smaller — rested near the entrance door. The entrance room had four doors: one behind me, two on the sides, and one straight ahead. I didn't go toward any of them.

With practiced ease, I sidestepped the leap of the monster that attempted to ambush me from the left side.

I heard the creature land, but I still couldn't see her, save for the telltale blur that indicated the presence of an invisible creature.

I ducked down, then reached out with my hand. "Good try, Hemlock. You almost had me."

I heard a sniff, and then I felt something scratch one of my fingers in apparent resignation. That was good, because Hemlock could be a real problem if she was in a bad mood.

"Where's Mommy?" I asked. I wasn't expecting a verbal reply. I wasn't sure if Hemlock could reply verbally, or even telepathically — she was old enough and powerful, but she was the quiet type.

I wasn't even sure what Hemlock was. She was perpetually invisible, and while most people would have assumed a mischievous witch's familiar would be a cat, I personally suspected that Hemlock was some kind of deadly venomous chicken.

That would have suited the witch's personality better than a cat.

Since I wasn't expecting a direct reply, I was more than a little surprised when I got one.

"She's still asleep."

The sound came from behind me. I swung around, startled, and barely resisted my instinct to strike. That was fortunate, because the boy in the floppy hat behind me had rings under his eyes and didn't look like he was ready to be awake, let alone fight.

He was about my age, but a whole head shorter, with dark eyes and darker skin. The rough robes and floppy hat he wore, the staff he carried, and the belt of trinkets all gave him something of a traditional wizard aesthetic. All he was missing was a fake beard.

In spite of that, he wasn't a wizard — well, at least, not of the traditional variety.

Darryl was a witch, like his mother before him. And like everyone else in the household, *possibly* excluding the familiars. I honestly wasn't clear on if they were somehow witches, too.

Darryl plucked the tea bag out of my hand without the slightest hesitation. "Thanks."

Then, without a moment of hesitation, he tossed it in his mouth.

I tried not to stare at him. ". . . You're welcome."

"Mmf." He kept the tea bag in his mouth but spoke again anyway. "Think I got you this time."

I grunted in grudging acknowledgment. "You did. Was Hemlock's little ambush a trick so you could sneak up on me?"

He nodded. "Mmf."

"Were you scrying on the road with a crystal ball or something?"

He shook his head. "No. New security wards around the whole house. Something of a personal project."

When Darryl discussed wards, he meant the magical variety — they were his primary area of expertise. He used several types of essence to create potent localized effects, which could repel monsters, create barriers, or even create certain beneficial effects in specific areas.

I nodded in appreciation. "Not bad. I don't suppose you have any personal talismans for sale that might be useful in the shrine?"

He rolled his eyes. "Don't joke. Ana would kill me if I helped you."

". . . Fair."

Without saying anything else, Darryl turned and waved a hand. I followed him as he walked toward the left door, opened it, and took me down an implausibly long hall.

"Your mom is usually up earlier," I noted.

"Moon ritual last night. We were all up late."

"Oh. Red Moon. I keep forgetting." I nodded in understanding.

"Mm" was his only reply, which was probably a good thing, since talking with my tea bag in his mouth had to be a challenge. I didn't question the behavior, though. I'd seen far stranger things, and I supposed it would probably help him wake up.

"You took the gift, so I take it you're giving me safe passage and guest rights?"

He nodded and kept walking.

"Verbally, please."

He groaned. "By my name, I, Darryl, grant you safe passage through our lands and guest rights in our home. Now, you need crash space, I take it?"

"Yeah, thanks. Hitting the shrine tomorrow. Or, uh, today, since it's morning now, and I've been up all night."

"Your threefold name day. A bit of a gamble, going during that. Might be good luck, or . . ." He nodded, then stopped at a door. He drew a shape on it with a finger, then pushed it open. "Get some sleep. We'll eat and give you gifts before you leave."

I smiled. "That's not necessary."

"You're wrong." He shook his head. "I'm not much for tradition, either, Edge. But not all traditions are bad. Now, in. You've got a long day ahead of you."

I nodded, then opened my arms.

Darryl stepped in and hugged me. "Good night, Edge. And I'll hope that it's good luck that you gain from this chosen path."

"Thanks." I smiled. "But I won't need it."

I woke an indeterminable period of time later to the sound of incessant knocking.

"Wake up! Wake up! Wake up!" A tiny voice outside the door insisted with all of the fervor of a five-year-old that had been assigned an important, nay, *crucial* task.

I sighed, rubbing my face and instinctively stretching. "I'm up, Poppy."

"Okay, but you can't stay in bed! Mom says it's time to eat!"

I shoved myself out of the warmth and comfort of the covers with great reluctance. One simply did not stay in bed when the Willowbark Witch insisted otherwise. I gathered my things and proceeded to the door, pushing it open.

Poppy gasped in surprise at seeing me, as if I'd pulled some kind of magic trick. I didn't understand at first: I was hardly a stranger to the tiny black-eyed girl. "You have a sword!"

I laughed. "I sure do. Well, a stick on the way to being a real sword, at any rate." I knelt down and mussed her hair.

"You can't call it that. You carved it, it needs a name!" Her eyes widened as she remembered something. "And it's the perfect day!"

That was surprisingly insightful on her part. Naming an item that I'd recently crafted on my own name day was, in a way, thematically appropriate.

I stood up suddenly as I felt something to my right, then turned and opened my hand as Darryl shoved a cup of something hot into it. "Thanks," I responded instinctively. Fortunately, he'd already offered me guest rights, and the witches weren't exactly traditional fae, so thanking him for a beverage wasn't a mistake that would cost me returned favors in the future.

I lifted the stone cup and sniffed at the contents, then closed my eyes in delight at the scent of herbs and cinnamon. He'd made me tea of the traditional variety, and he'd remembered my love for cinnamon, too.

"Just a small thing. Come on. Mom is going to sacrifice us in some kind of ritual if we don't get food while it's hot."

That was probably an exaggeration, but given how Poppy gasped and tugged at my pants, I decided it was wiser not to find out.

Darryl expertly led me down the house's corridors — ones that I knew well enough, but that changed frequently, meaning that even my relative familiarity with the home wouldn't be a reliable means to get around on my own.

I didn't think the witch's house was *technically* a dungeon, but I wouldn't have been surprised if it was. When I'd been a foolish enough child to ask how it worked, she'd been extremely cagey about it. Now that I was older, I knew there were a few distinct possibilities. Dimensional essence, something like a non-dungeon magical core, illusions and memory alterations, that sort of thing.

Anyway, Darryl gave me no new hints toward the house's nature as he led me to the dining room, where we found the table already set.

The dining room had seemed colossal when I was a child, but now, I could see it was *just right* for a family of their size that occasionally welcomed a guest. The whole room appeared to be crafted from a single piece of wood, like we were inside a living tree (which was technically possible).

The remains of several dangerous beasts were mounted on and near the walls, but not as hunting trophies: the plaque beneath each was a memorial to the creature's service to the Willowbark Witch. In other words, they were her pets and friends, stuffed as memorials to their long years of service.

A scaled worm was mounted around nearly half the room, large enough to swallow whole any of the humanlike people in the chamber whole.

A deer with golden fur and antlers stood proudly in the right corner, neck raised high.

A tiny rabbit hung mounted on the right wall, the only sign that it wasn't a mundane creature the single sharp horn that protruded from the creature's forehead.

And so on and so on.

When I was a kid, the stuffed creatures had absolutely creeped the resh out of me.

Now that I was a near-adult, they *still* absolutely creeped the resh out of me. Every once in a while, I thought I saw the deer's long-dead eyes focusing on me.

It was probably a trick of the light or a trick of my mind. Or, equally likely, a prank from the witch herself or one of the kids.

. . . But sometimes, even knowing that, it was hard to ignore the distinct feeling that I was being watched, and that the monsters there might rise at any time and try to eat me.

The funny thing was I wouldn't have even been afraid of the monsters if they *were* alive. I'd fought much, much scarier beasts. But somehow, the feeling that they might be more alive than they seemed set all of my senses on edge, and not in a fun, punlike way. I had to restrain my instinct to attack every time I saw them, especially when I thought I sensed a hint of movement.

The accoutrements of the room didn't end there. The rocking chair in the corner liked to rock on its own, especially when I wasn't looking. The paintings of fantastical characters were my favorite part of the chamber, but it was somewhat unnerving to note that the characters in them would move from painting to painting, seemingly visiting each other whenever I was absent.

The tall grandfather clock was the only part of the room that seemed normal, which somehow was the most suspicious thing of all. I'd always watched it for any indication that it was going to move faster or slower than normal, or perhaps backward, signaling an incident of time travel.

But no, the clock was always precise. It reminded me of that when it loudly gonged exactly six times the moment I stepped into the room.

Six seated figures stood simultaneously with the chime, turning toward the part of the room where I'd entered.

Five were the remaining children of the witch.

Belladonna, the oldest of the children at twenty-something. She was considered a "full" witch in her own right, although I wasn't entirely sure what that meant. My impression was that it probably meant she had a destiny mark with the Witch destiny — or perhaps a more specialized version thereof — but I'd never been able to get a straight answer when I'd asked about that subject as a child. I'd always been obnoxiously curious, but I couldn't blame the witches for being secretive.

If she had exactly the same destiny mark as her mother, that implied a strong possibility that the family knew where a Destiny Shrine was located. And entire wars had been waged over the locations of a single still-functional Destiny Shrine.

It was possible she'd simply gotten the same destiny mark as her mother (or a similar one) through her Destiny Dream, which would have simply required having the base essence types to meet the requirements of that destiny and the good luck or lucidity to take the right path during her dream. It was possible she'd picked her essence types carefully to end up with that specific destiny, much in the same way I'd already been planning to . . . but I didn't think that was likely. I knew a bit about her essence types, and they were different enough from her mother's that it didn't feel right.

Being older, I was still extremely curious, but I'd learned enough to stop asking the potential murder-inviting questions about it.

As the oldest child, Belladonna was obviously the first one I'd gotten a crush on when I'd been old enough to do that sort of thing. She had chestnut hair and dark brown skin that I'd always found quite fetching. She had tolerated my crush as a small child, then kindly let me know that she was both *far* too old for me and that she preferred girls when I got more obnoxious about my brief infatuation. I was very briefly heartbroken, then mended rapidly in the way of the young.

More notably, Belladonna was far more powerful and wise than the average person of her years, already serving as a mentor to young Skyseekers during the summer season when she visited the outside world. In spite of her name, she wasn't a poison specialist, but she liked people to think that she was.

Cascade was the next oldest and, aside from Darryl, the only other one of the children who was my elder. I wasn't quite clear on her age, but probably nineteenish. Her complexion was pitch-black, with her hair the teal color of the water from which she drew her power. She was the great traveler of the children, having bonded to the ocean as a child under circumstances that remained secret to me. I envied her more than words could say.

Flare was next, with the quintessential crimson hair and eyes that marked her as bound to the essence of fire. Those blazing eyes focused on me with absolute intensity, effortlessly drawing me into meeting them. Tiny sparks played around her irises, drawing my attention to the ever-growing number of freckles on her face. At only a few months my junior, she was getting more dangerous and more attractive by the year. Those qualities, were, of course, nearly synonymous in my own mind.

Next was Root, the first of the children who was considerably younger than I was. Dark-skinned and green-haired, she was easily distracted and effortlessly talented. She'd chosen her name when she'd hoped to focus on plant magic, but in recent years she'd focused more on earth and crystal. She had not yet decided to change her name.

The youngest was Blink, a perfectly appropriate name for a child who could be there one moment and gone in the next. At three years of age, she shouldn't have been old enough to be actively using magic, and yet, somehow, she had a propensity for vanishing without a trace. She was pale as a sheet, with matching paper-white hair and eyes. I was too polite to say it, but I thought there was at least a one-in-four chance she was a ghost.

And finally, there was the witch herself. Today, she was wearing her most traditional face: that of an older woman with thinning hair, a crooked nose, a pointed hat, and long, rough-spun robes. She was probably feeling sentimental, given the occasion.

I'd seen her look even older, with skin like dry and wrinkled parchment. I'd seen her look younger than Belladonna, like a teenager with dark hair and pristine skin. I'd seen her most often as an unremarkable adult, perhaps forty years old, with the brown and gray of her hair still actively at war, neither side prevailing.

If she had a true face, I'd never seen it. But the closest, perhaps, was when I'd seen her with no face at all.

On the rare occasions when she was busy or startled, at times, I'd seen her wearing long black robes and a scarf around the lower half of her face. Between the scarf and hat, I couldn't see much of her features . . . but what I could see looked like a black void where her head should be.

I had no idea what I had seen on those days, save for the absence of a person. Perhaps that was the true witch, or perhaps it was just another veil.

I turned my gaze away from her knowing smile to the other figures at the table, the ones that hadn't stood up. The familiars. I won't name them all now, since I don't have permission. But there were seven of them, too. They didn't bother to greet me: at the moment, I wasn't worthy of their notice.

"Come, children." The witch greeted us in a tone that at once sounded affectionate and stern. She was including me in "children," which was a good sign: one that granted an additional layer of safety but also one of responsibility. I would need to play my role properly.

Darryl and Poppy led the way to the table. There was an empty seat for each of us, of course. I took my seat next to Darryl, as appropriate. If I had been treated as just a guest, I would have been seated next to the witch, but I had been given a chair based on the order of our age, placing me as part of the family.

I smiled at that, sitting down simultaneously with Darryl, then giving a nod of greeting to the bright orange cat seated to my right. As I mentioned, children were seated in order of age, and Flare's familiar was just slightly her senior.

"Mew." Miss Mewthos greeted me in traditional fashion. As with many of the familiars, Miss Mewthos probably wasn't an ordinary animal, but I wasn't aware of the specifics. A cait sith — which basically just means "faerie cat" — was the most likely, but she could have been something more esoteric like a chess cat or a shade slinker. As an appropriate reply, I immediately fetched her an offering, pouring her a saucer of milk. "Mrr." The cat accepted my gift but did not immediately partake. She knew to wait for the witch's permission before eating.

The witch waited for us to settle, remaining standing as she spoke.

"A child joins us today for an old tradition. We are honored that you have come here on your name day." The witch nodded to me.

I knew the formula. "I thank you and gratefully accept your offered hospitality."

"Good. Then all is well." The witch sat down. "But before we eat, a few brief formalities."

I heard some of the kids groan. Root rolled her eyes and made a gesture of running a finger across her throat, triggering a gasp and a giggle from Blink. The witch ignored her kids, looking straight at me. "The name day is an old tradition — older even than me, if you can believe it."

I can't, Cascade silently mouthed.

The witch ignored her. "Though in many cultures it has degenerated into a ceremony of toys and cakes, we remember the true purpose of the day: the choosing. Do you recall the words?"

I nodded in response. "I do."

"Good." The witch nodded. "Then, tell us. This year, what is your name, child?"

I closed my eyes and took a breath, remembering. "I am Lien, Child of the Unknown and bearing the title Edge of the Woods. I was once offered another title that I have not yet claimed, for I have been deemed unready. By my will, by my word, and by my wish, I mark myself so."

I thought I felt something when I spoke those last words, a brief chill that ran down my spine. Goose bumps ran across my arms.

Was it old magic at work, or just my mind? I could never tell.

"Good. It is sealed, then." The witch clapped. "Lien for another year, it is. And you continue to honor Eiji with your chosen title."

I nodded. My commonly used nickname, Edge, had layers of meaning. It was a translation of "Lien" into Velthryn, but it was also a reference to Uncle Eiji, one of the ancient guardians of the forest. Uncle Eiji wasn't my bloodline uncle, but that didn't matter much — he was family. Taking on a name similar to his was a way of marking myself as a part of the tradition of the forest's guardians, much like a human might be given a birth name based on a grandparent.

The latter part of the title — "of the woods," that is — was a granted title. I'd earned it, along with the mark on my cheek, for protecting someone who needed it.

Nothing in my life had made me prouder.

The witch gave me a toothy grin. "Now, with that finished, there's one more question we have at this table. Not an old tradition, but a recent one that is just as important."

Blink made a gleeful gasp. "I know this one!" She turned toward me. "Are you a boy or a girl? Or, uh, neither? Or both?"

I turned and gave her a warm smile. "I'm a boy. Thank you for asking."

It was a good question to ask. An important one. Something that eased the process for any children that might discover throughout the year that they might be something that they hadn't realized or been able to articulate earlier in their lives. They could share with the family at any time, but by making it a name-day question, they'd provided an easy window to discuss it without the burden of choosing a time.

I still remember working with Cascade to sew Darryl his first binder when he'd told us about what he'd realized. I'd been honored that he'd chosen to include me when he'd told the family. He'd been a little embarrassed at first, but we'd been through a lot together, and the whole family had learned and grown from the experience.

"You're welcome!" Blink turned to the witch. "Can we eat now? I'm hungry."

The witch nodded to her. "A third thing, and then we will be done. What will you do this year, Lien?"

I considered it. Not a new question, but one that I had a harder time answering than the others.

With a pause, I bit my lip absently, then spoke. "Grow."

⁂

After I made my third name day declaration, the witch quickly gave us permission to eat. I dug into my meal, the most substantial thing I'd eaten since leaving home the day before, then gratefully and hastily bid the witch's family goodbye.

Staying longer would have been easy. Too easy. But I had work to do. I couldn't abandon that, as tempting as the prospect may have been.

With daylight shining, I walked a familiar path back to the river, then to the north.

My mind wandered as my footsteps carried me invariably forward.

My questions of the day had been easy ones, but I still wondered . . .

Why did it feel like part of my name was missing?

⁂

The shrine was located in a distant part of the forest, but I knew the weaving paths of the wood well enough to walk them blind. There was no danger in the grove surrounding the shrine — Ana's potent power kept the area free from any but the most benign of beasts.

No, the danger sat just outside the shrine's entrance, resplendent in her robe of leaves and crown of flowers. The outfit was a near-match for her natural qualities: her skin was covered in patches of leaves and bark, and her hair matched the dark brown of the surrounding trees. The shadows from the massive tree seemed to wrap around her like a cloak, which wasn't surprising, given that shade was her primary essence type. She could have been nearly invisible if she didn't want to be seen, but she wasn't hiding. She wanted me to see her, then. To see her disapproval.

Eliree. Half dryad, half human . . . all first love.

"You didn't think to tell me you were in my part of the woods yesterday?" Her voice was rich as maple syrup. I mean that in as literal a sense as possible, given that she was, in fact, part tree-spirit.

Mentally, I noted the need to flick a faerie the next time I saw him. "I've been busy."

"Busy avoiding me, you mean." She gave an adorable little pout. "Have I disappointed you so?"

"It's not that." I shook my head. "I'm just . . . getting antsy. I've lived here my whole life, and I'm not . . ."

"Not affixed to the ground. Yes, I know." She closed her eyes. "I won't wish you luck."

I frowned at her. "No?"

She looked away. "Because if you're lucky, if you succeed . . . then you'll leave."

"You could come with me, you know. You're not a full dryad. You don't need to stay near your tree. We could find you another one, like your guest tree in the Brightwood . . ."

"No." Eliree didn't turn to look at me. "I . . . it doesn't feel right. I'm sorry. I shouldn't have come here."

She stood up suddenly, focusing her almond (not literally, she was a different type of tree) eyes on my own. "I wish you happiness." Then, after a pause, she added, "With me or without. Happy name day, whatever your true name may be."

"Eliree . . ." I reached out for her, but she walked past me without looking back.

"I won't be waiting here to heal you. Not from this. Don't get killed in there."

I smiled sadly at her retreating form. "Wouldn't dream of it."

I was lying, then.

I dreamed of dying all the time.

The entrance to the shrine was all too familiar.

Three stone tablets stood near the door at the center of the titanic tree, each of which contained writing. Some ancient, some very new.

I glanced at each of them in turn, in spite of knowing the contents nearly by heart.

It'd be important to see if Ana had changed anything at the last minute, after all.

The first was the simplest. It was a marker that always struck me as having a somber tone that I couldn't quite understand at that age.

Here lies Anathema—
Blade of the lost,
Scourge of the wicked,
Bane of all things.

The next tablet was equally ancient, holding the text that served as a warning and hint to all those that would hope to traverse the shrine's depths. I found myself whispering the words aloud as I read them for the thousandth time.

Ware thee of challenges three,
Of steel, and stone, and destiny—
With blade of dark a hero lies,
And with her soul an ember dies.
To claim the blade that once she earned,
Thou must choose the path all spurned,
To seek within and cast aside,
The rage that burns hearts deep inside.
If anger guides thee, turn aside,
Your deepest dreams you cannot hide—
For only one with gentle hand,
Can wield the sword that ends our land.

I'd spent many years speculating on the specific meaning of that poem. It was obvious enough that Anathema had supposedly been wielded by some ancient hero, but research had given me nothing about her. I daydreamed about the possibility that this hero was the capital-*H* Hero — that is, the woman who once had the fabled Hero destiny mark — who had confronted and defeated the Ashen Lord. That, of course, seemed incredibly unlikely. There were hundreds of stories about her, and many of them included specific weapons or items she was supposed to have wielded at one point or another, but Anathema was known to be a *cursed* sword. The Hero had wielded a *sacred* sword — everyone agreed on that. And while a sacred sword hypothetically could have been cursed somehow, the odds that this was the hero's personal weapon that somehow had gotten cursed seemed very low. If nothing else, such an important weapon probably would have been collected by her companions if she'd died after the battle, as some stories indicated . . . and I doubted they would have hid it in some weird shrine.

Other parts of the poem were both easier and harder to parse. There would be three types of challenges, although each challenge could be represented by more than one thing. Steel seemed the most straightforward, likely involving combat of some kind. It was noteworthy that steel was also an alloy of iron, which meant that it was something that had deleterious effects against fae. That could have meant that the steel test also would involve the weaknesses of whoever was being tested, but it was possible I was reading too much into it.

Stone was a little tougher. It could have meant challenges based around physical resilience, strength, or that sort of thing. It also might have meant challenges of patience, or perhaps crafting skill. It was also possible it would be puzzles, since moving things like boulders and statues were very common historical shrine challenges. Given the number of possible interpretations, I'd trained very broadly to try to be prepared for whatever they might have been.

Destiny challenges were so open-ended that they could have meant anything. That didn't mean I couldn't speculate, but I considered everything from "confront a version of your possible future self" to "be born with the right family." Some possibilities I could plan for, others were purely luck . . . unless, of course, I found a way to nudge destiny in the right direction.

I suspected the most likely scenario was that the destiny challenges would have something to do with the part at the end of the poem, indicating that one had to . . . not be angry? That seemed straightforward enough — it might have meant that there would be tests that deliberately tried to annoy or provoke the person doing the trial, or perhaps that there would be some kind of intangible test of spiritual worthiness. I'd grown up with lessons on meditation to control my emotions, and I liked to think I was pretty good at it, but I suspected whatever I was going to be dealing with would be a little trickier than "don't get mad when you get punched by the monster."

If Ana tested my soul, I hoped she'd like what she found.

With that in mind, I looked at the third tablet.

Hi! I'm Ana. This shrine is my home, but don't feel the need to take your shoes off at the entrance.

There are some rules, though! Three, to be specific.

Only those with a completed wellspring with sword essence can enter the shrine. Sorry, non-swordy folks! You can't hope to wield all this without it.

No one may enter if they are above Hearth-level. No exceptions!!!

There will be risks, dangers, etc. in the shrine. You consent to the risks of taking these tests, up to and including risk of death, when you enter the door. In addition, you consent to have your memories of the shrine's trials suppressed if you fail. This is to preserve the integrity of the trials for future trial-takers!

Addendum: Edge, just because it only says "no exceptions" on the second rule doesn't mean there are exceptions to the other two, so quit trying to sneak in before you have sword essence!

I had, in fact, tried to sneak into the shrine a few times as a kid before I had essence. But come on, you can't blame me for exploring such an obvious loophole!

Fortunately, Ana hadn't blamed me, either. Or killed me. She easily could have, at that point. I was lucky she liked me.

Anyway, I finished studying the tablets, then turned back to the main entrance and took a deep breath.

A single door of blue metal was held firmly in place by the roots of the titanic tree. When I touched the handle, strange glyphs glowed white on the door's surface, and then the handle unlocked to allow me to pull it open.

I took another breath. It was really happening. It was the first time I'd been able to open the door on my own, my sword essence proving worthy to activate the runes.

I can do this.

When the door finished opening, I saw a pure white void ahead of me. Then I stepped into the void, and the world around me changed.

I've got this. I've trained my whole life for this. I won't fail was my last thought as I stepped in the door.

My next thoughts were less coherent.

Pain came first, then disorientation as my eyes flickered open.

I was on the ground outside the shrine, facing upward. My right arm was wrapped in soft white bandages, but they'd bled through. My tunic was torn apart. The wounds there were shallower but unbandaged.

A half-empty healing flask lay just out of my reach. My belt pouch was torn to shreds, the other contents missing.

My fingers were wrapped around the grip of what little remained of a broken stick that I'd honed with hope for victory. Beyond the portion in my hand, the once beautiful piece of blackened wood was little more than splinters.

Did I give you a name while I was in there? I can't remember.

My eyes shut. My hand tightened further around the bit of stag hide that I'd wrapped lovingly around the grip.

I'm sorry.

I couldn't remember my encounters inside the shrine — that was part of the test, as the third rule had indicated. I knew what it had to mean, though.

I had failed.

I hadn't earned Ana's sword.

And I couldn't leave home.

Happy name day, I whispered to myself without rising from the stone.

Then I closed my eyes and I cried.

INTERLUDE II

SHARDS OF SELF

The swordsman was silent for a time, his steps falling quietly on the forest floor. For a time, Scribe was uncertain as to what to say. Was he expected to offer some sort of comfort to the young man for whatever frustration he still felt from a childhood failure?

Scribe absently reached up and fiddled with his earring. After that, he simply kept walking in silent contemplation.

Fortunately, the swordsman eventually just turned around, continuing to walk backward. His expression wasn't as dour as Scribe might have expected, merely contemplative. "I made a lot of mistakes back then. In retrospect, it's so easy to see them now. At times, I wonder if I'll look back at these years and find this version of myself to be equally naïve."

"Eh." Scribe shrugged as he kept walking, wondering if the swordsman would blunder into a tree or trip over a root if he insisted on continuing to walk backward. "I wouldn't overthink it. People make mistakes regardless of age and experience."

"While that's true, I'd like to hope that my future failures won't be quite as embarrassing as those of the past." Edge chuckled, hopping backward over an outstretched root. That, while made without any overt showmanship, seemed like it might have been a calculated bit of subtle performance — perhaps to demonstrate that Edge could detect things behind him to some limited degree. Or, of course, maybe Scribe was the one overthinking things.

As usual.

But he was thinking about one thing in particular quite a bit — something that had stuck with him. "Not to be rude, but . . . from everything you explained beforehand, it sounds like your foray into the shrine was, well . . ."

"Foolhardy?" Edge's lips curled up. "Doomed from the start?"

"I was looking for a softer way to put it, but yes." Scribe shook his head. "It sounded as if Anathema herself would be too much for you in most direct confrontations. She was still a level higher in essence-wielding ability, yes?"

"She was. More than a full level, really — I'd just reached the first step of the first stage. She was midway through the second."

Scribe frowned. "I see. So . . . assuming she had an advantage in essence level . . . why would you expect to be able to beat her? And . . . weren't there supposed to be other challenges, too? Traps, puzzles, monsters? I can't even imagine how many monsters she might have available if she'd been able to conjure them repeatedly over the course of years. Do . . . her conjured monsters last indefinitely? Are they intelligent?"

"Getting into a lot of different issues there, so let's back up a bit." Edge was, of course, still walking backward as he said that. "You're right. I had no chance against Ana alone in a fair encounter. Certainly not after dealing with a mountain of puzzles, traps, and monsters. And yes, she could create permanent ones — and she could make them stronger by investing more essence over time."

"Meaning she might have had monsters inside her shrine that were stronger than her, possibly by orders of magnitude."

"I wouldn't go as far as that last part — there were practical limits. Maybe a level or two, but if that."

"Even so, she was capable of creating a defensive structure with monsters that were not only stronger than you, but even stronger than *her*. So . . . how did you expect to be able to make it through her shrine?"

Edge scratched the back of his head, looking briefly abashed. "When you put it like that, it really does sound childish for me to expect any chance of victory — but there's a layer to that you're not considering."

"Oh?" Scribe was genuinely curious. "Your equipment, or that sealed power, perhaps?"

"Oh, no. Nothing quite so direct." The swordsman laughed, shaking his head, then lowering it sadly. "I thought she'd let me win."

He was quiet for a moment, stopping his movement.

It was only then, with that admission, that Edge took a step backward and promptly tripped over a rock.

He stumbled, an expression of comical surprise crossing his features as he fell to the ground—

Then caught himself, laughing gleefully, and pushed himself right back to his feet.

"Well." He smiled as he pushed himself back up. "I suppose I still haven't learned to watch where I'm walking, though. Always another lesson, isn't there?"

"Always another lesson," Scribe agreed, but he didn't think they were necessarily learning the same things. "Why did you think she'd let you win?"

Edge seemed to consider that for a moment, then turned back toward walking straight ahead and gestured for Scribe to follow. "I was weak, at least by the standards of the people around me. I knew that. Everyone knew that. And while I always insisted that I didn't like it when Ana, or anyone else, went easy on me in things like games and sparring practice . . . it was a necessity. An ordinary teenager isn't going to use their full strength when practicing with a five-year-old, you know?"

"Was the difference in strength between you really that glaring?"

"That depends on what you mean by strength. In terms of primary essence-wielding ability, absolutely. If you mean literal physical strength, my essence was skewed that way, so I could match her there. Unless, of course, she was using a technique like the Golden Raiment."

Scribe nodded. "I've heard of body-enhancement techniques like that back at home. Body of Stone, that sort of thing."

"Right. Similar principle. I didn't have anything like that, either for training or for direct combat use. The benefit would have scaled with how much essence she used, so she'd need to use more power to keep the technique useful as she grew older."

"That's good to know, but I think we're getting distracted from the original question. Why did you think she'd let you win?"

"Oh, right. Sorry, I don't talk to people often, and the minutiae of essence techniques is something of a personal interest of mine." Edge made a wistful sigh. "Up until that point in my life, I'd been taught to expect people to go easy on me, since I was comparatively weak. My friends and family didn't want to make me feel inferior or anything — they just loved me and felt bad crushing me at every possible task. Ana didn't always let me win at things, but she calibrated her abilities to be more similar to my own, especially for games. And . . . I was still treating the shrine as something more like that. Ana and I played together all the time, with hundreds of myriad scenarios. The shrine . . ."

He paused, seeming to search for words.

"I knew, intellectually, the shrine was more important. It was more important to me, too — vastly so. To me, it was the way to prove that I was finally worth something. That I wasn't just a child to take pity on. If I earned the sword, I wouldn't be a weakling — I'd be special. The only one who had passed those tests. And with a metal sword that the forest approved of, I could begin learning proper sword techniques, which I could use to make my way in the world when I left home."

He let out a bitter laugh.

"Nothing was more important to me than earning that sword. I'd built it up in my mind as a key to my feelings of self-worth — and my freedom. Ana knew that I wanted to see the human lands outside the forest, and that I saw earning the sword as a critical part of proving I was ready to leave home to do that. When I failed — when she let me fail — it hurt. I didn't understand what had gone wrong. I'd thought she would have wanted me to have the sword. We'd daydreamed many times about wanting to explore the world together, as partners. For a child that had grown up with a dangerous degree of conflating stories with reality, it felt like Ana had gone off script. Like she was punishing me somehow, for something I couldn't understand."

Scribe nodded along. "But that wasn't it at all, was it?"

"No, of course not." Edge kept walking but slowed his steps a little to glance backward toward Scribe. "Truth is, I was so fixated on what earning the sword meant to me — to how I could use it — that I'd failed to properly consider what it meant to *her*. It was literally an extension of herself. If she gave it to anyone who didn't earn the sword properly, what would that mean for the sword's future, or for her own? And I think Ana was a little more mature than I was in another way, too. I think she already knew, even at that age, that if I realized she'd given the sword to me out of pity, it would hurt me more when I was old enough to process it properly. And beyond that . . . well, succeeding at the trials of the sword would have had consequences she understood, but I couldn't have possibly known at that age. So, as much as she wanted me to succeed, she didn't go easy on me, at least not to such a degree that she offered me a free victory. And when I was woefully unprepared to handle trials that she'd spent years creating, I failed."

His lips tightened for a moment. "It must have been hard for her to watch. She'd tried to warn me. So had Gramps. It's not that I hadn't heard them, but I hadn't really understood what they were trying to say. Not then."

"But you learned, didn't you?"

He shrugged a shoulder, then turned back to walking straight. ". . . I learned that she wasn't going to just hand me the victory. That was obvious enough. It was a long time before I truly understood why. I needed to learn a number of other things first."

Scribe reached up and rubbed at the earring on his left ear. "Did you learn any other interesting lessons?"

"I did." Edge paused in his step, taking a drink of water from his flask. "As with many chapters of my life, failure was only the beginning."

CHAPTER V

SURRENDER

I wiped tears from my eyes with dirt-stained sleeves. That only made my eyes burn more, so I groaned and reached for my waterskin, which still had a bit of ordinary water left. Just trying to lift something sent a flare of agony through my wrist, but I muscled through it, trembling as I lifted the flask to wash my eyes. With the little remaining fluid, I washed my hands as well, revealing minor lacerations on my knuckles that I'd barely noticed before.

Well, I thought, *at least I managed to punch something.*

I shook my flask to get the last few drops of water in my mouth, grimaced, then packed it away.

I took stock of my remaining supplies — they weren't great. I'd lost one entire warding pouch, save for the loop that had previously attached it to my belt and a tiny scrap of fabric.

Torn by claws, likely.

My other pouches were intact, but somewhat depleted.

Salt is all gone.

Silver spikes are missing, as are the Dawnflowers and sun-rain drops.

Still have all my iron sand, charcoal, vorinlief, wolfsbane, and essence vials.

I winced, shifting into a sitting position to contemplate.

Based on that . . . I probably hadn't encountered many fae, or if I had, I hadn't had a chance to offer them gifts or repel them.

And with what's missing . . . silver, Dawn . . . vampires? No, that's absurd, she can't have vampires in there.

Can she?

I shook my head. The missing supplies painted a picture, but it wasn't enough to be certain about anything. It was easily possible that the lost pouch had been incidental, or that I'd used the supplies for barter, or that

Ana had taken them after I'd been defeated as some kind of misdirection, or . . .

I tightened my fists in frustration.

This is pointless. I can't learn a thing if I lose my memories after the challenge. It's not fair.

I slammed a fist into a nearby stone hard enough to leave a crack, then regretted it immediately as my bruised knuckles flared with renewed pain.

I growled, sucked in a deep breath, then shoved myself to my feet.

Fine. If it isn't going to be fair, if she's not going to let me learn, then I'm just going to have to punch through the reshing shrine with force alone.

I cracked my neck and stared at the still-open doors. I flexed half-numb fingers in the air.

This time, I drew in a breath, *no holding back.*

I stepped into the shrine with my head held high.

. . . And woke, once again, crumbled like a discarded piece of parchment on the ground.

Recovery was slower after my second attempt. I had no water left to wash my wounds . . . which were, unfortunately, more serious. My left arm throbbed with the kind of agony that told me something had probably bruised the bone. My right arm carried a long cut that had been wrapped with cloth from my left leg, which was unfortunate, since that was also lacerated.

I trembled with pain and anger, then flexed my right hand, tightened my jaw, and projected a blade of essence from my hand.

Well, I sucked in a breath, *at least that isn't broken.*

I dismissed the essence blade, slowly rose to my feet, and stared at the door.

And that means . . . I can still fight.

I stepped back through the door.

. . . And woke, for the third time, with a body caked with mud and blood.

Once more.

I pushed myself to my feet, swayed, and would have fallen if I hadn't been caught by a tiny hand.

"Easy, there." Ana barely managed to keep me from falling in her diminutive state. She hovered behind me, beating her wings for extra strength to help stabilize me. Eventually, I found my footing and turned to see her. I felt my hands tightening before I even saw her, the desire to lash out —

But that faded the moment I saw the worry on her face.

For a moment, I just stared at her, tightening my jaw and willing my eyes to stay dry. Anger was a better response, I told myself. Crying was for children and I . . . I couldn't let Ana see me that way.

I couldn't let the day end in failure, either. "I . . . could you make me some bandages? And some water?" I turned my eyes toward the sky. It was getting dark. "I don't think I'll have time to go home for them and get back before my next attempt."

"Your next . . . Lien." Her blazing eyes shut. "You . . . you have to stop, Lien. You're done for the day."

"I think I can make that choice on my own. I just . . . need a few more supplies, and I'll—"

"No." Ana folded her arms as her eyes fluttered back open. "It's not just your decision. As it happens, there's a rule." She pointed behind me.

I turned around, frowning, and swayed on my feet, nearly losing my balance from that simple motion. As my swimming vision slowly cleared, I focused on one of the tablets outside the shrine — one that held the many rules for entering the shrine.

. . . And saw new lettering in gold at the bottom of the tablet.

Thrice may thou enter with the passing of each year.

My jaw tightened again as I turned back to her. "You . . . you made a new rule? That's . . . that's not . . ."

Ana drew in a sharp breath. Her eyes narrowed. "Be careful, Lien. Watch your words. You didn't actually mean to imply that my trial is *unfair*, did you?"

My tongue felt dry in my mouth. I almost spat something vitriolic back at her, something angry, something foolish—

But seeing the expression on her face, not just of warning, but the lines of pain around her eyes . . . my mouth opened, then closed again. I closed my eyes, drew in a breath, focused . . . and found myself again.

Saying to Ana that her challenges were unfair would have been a terrible slight, akin to calling her a liar — which, if repeated enough and with any degree of accuracy to the claim, could cause harm to her very spirit. It was more than just an insult. It was a rejection of her being . . . and that, fortunately, was a line that even my anger and frustration did not allow me to cross.

"I . . . forgive me. Your rules are clear and fair. I was simply surprised, and I'm . . . not in the best of shape."

"That's an understatement, mister. Can . . . we just head back to your place for the night? Put this behind us, for now?"

I stared at her, saw the pleading in her gaze. My lip trembled.

"I . . ." I glanced back at the shrine door, now closed to me. A sign of my absolute inadequacy. "I don't . . ."

"Come on, Lien. It's . . . still your name day. I could make *cake*!"

I laughed in spite of myself.

I'd always hated cake.

"Well . . ." I took one last look at the door, then back to Ana. "How could I refuse a sweet offer like that?"

Ana shifted to her human size with what seemed like surprising difficulty, then slipped an arm around my back. She didn't say anything, but she clearly knew I couldn't walk on my own.

Together, with pain surging through my injured leg with every step, we walked to our other home.

CHAPTER VI

SIMPLE SUCCOR

When Ana and I finally made it back to my home, it was nearly pitch-black. I'd say I was lucky that we weren't eaten by something while traveling so late when I was injured, but in reality, it probably had more to do with Ana's presence than luck. Most of the creatures of the forest had close ties with her, and those that weren't intelligent enough to communicate still generally had an inherent understanding of the threat that she posed.

That didn't make travel risk-free by any means, but it was certainly better than if I'd made the attempt on my own. Ana half carried me as long as she could, but she wasn't able to retain her human-sized form long enough to make the entire journey. Eventually, I had to find a piece of dead wood to use as a walking stick, which only brought back sharp memories of the one I'd carved.

I'm sorry that I failed you. I'm sorry that I can't remember your end. I'll try to grow strong enough to be worthy of your forgiveness.

I was still in a dour mood when we reached the hut. The lanterns were still lit in spite of the late hour, presumably to make the place feel warm and inviting for my return.

"Gramps?" I whispered as I opened the door. There wasn't any reply, but I saw a note on the table.

Went to bed. There's dinner for Ana and yourself in the stasis box. Happy name day, child.

I didn't let myself cry again.

Instead, I set Ana down on one of the chairs — she'd fallen asleep on my shoulder — closed the door, then opened the stasis box.

Beef stew. Gramps hates it, but it's one of my favorites. He must have cooked it for me and waited.

I poured some of the still-hot stew into a bowl — the stasis box having preserved it, as the name indicated — and sat down, ignoring the aching in my arm as I ate in silence. Ana didn't wake up, and though I debated waking her to eat, instead I just picked her up gingerly after I finished cleaning my bowl and tucked her into her own little bed.

I bathed as best I could with a few buckets of water from the well outside, then dressed my wounds and changed my clothes. A real bath in the healing spring would have been better, but it was too late at night to go out there on my own.

I shivered as I headed back into the house and pulled up my covers.

After that, I fought my way toward sleep. It was a losing battle.

My mind simply wouldn't shut down.

What had I done wrong? How had I failed? Why was I so infuriatingly *weak*?

Could . . . could I have won if I'd broken that strange seal on my right hand? What was it, and why wouldn't Gramps tell me about it?

My mind flashed through anger, disappointment, and frustration in sequence, over and over again. I searched for answers, thinking about every clue I could from the patterns of the wounds on my body to the way that my clothes and pouches had been torn.

I found no answers that night and precious little sleep.

When the dawn finally came, I pulled an extra shirt over my eyes and finally, as my anger guttered out in the wake of absolute exhaustion, found my way to sleep.

I woke up. That was, in retrospect, probably a mistake.

I felt *awful*. It turns out that getting absolutely beaten to a pulp and then going to sleep doesn't magically fix all of your injuries. I mean, unless you're some kind of magical construct or something, I suppose, in which case it might? It depends on the specific variety of creature.

Anyway, I didn't heal overnight, and I'd rolled over onto my more wounded arm at some point during the night. That was bad.

With a groan and what might have been generously described as a flail, I dislodged my eye-shirt and covers, then rolled gracelessly out of bed.

Ana fluttered enthusiastically in front of me, positively gleaming with an inappropriate level of energy for the morn . . . evening. It was definitely evening.

"Mrr," I greeted her, master of articulation that I was. I tried to raise an arm to wave, but that didn't work, since my arm was still about three-quarters of the way to useless.

"Good morning, Lien! Come on, Gramps and I were waiting for you before we had dinner!"

"Mmm," I replied, still setting records for mastery of poetic language. "Minute. Clothes."

"Oh! Sure, take your time."

I changed from my nightclothes into a fresh traveling outfit, which was probably pointless, because I was barely able to travel the distance necessary to reach the kitchen table. The laceration on my leg throbbed worryingly in a way that hinted that maybe it was a bad idea to walk a dozen miles while I was injured.

Oops.

Well, I've made worse choices.

Anyway, I sat down at the table. Gramps thrust a large mug of steaming tea at me, which I gratefully accepted. I took several deep breaths of it, just savoring the smell — had he put cinnamon in there? — and warming my hands on the cup before beginning to cautiously sip at it.

Ana, in her six-inch-sized state, leaned up against her own mug like a lizard warming itself on a sunbaked rock. She was small enough that she could have used her teacup as a bathtub, and at the moment, my aching bones envied that. (At least in theory. In reality, the cinnamon and injuries probably didn't mix well. I hadn't actually tried, but it seemed like a bad idea.)

"So," Gramps began slowly, "what have you learned?"

I sighed, closing my eyes for a moment and warming my hands on the tea again. There was food on the table, too, but I didn't think my stomach was quite ready for it.

My mind was equally unready for this conversation.

"I wasn't ready," I said after a time. It was a difficult statement to make. I didn't like demonstrating weakness, especially to Ana and Gramps. I . . . wanted them to think I was capable. Both because of pride and because I knew that Gramps wouldn't let me leave home for the outside world until he felt I was "ready."

"Good." Gramps nodded. "That is valuable to know. What else?"

"I need a better sword. A real one. The weapon I carved . . ." I shook my head. "I'm not going to be able to face Ana's challenges with something like that."

Ana nodded enthusiastically, but Gramps seemed less pleased.

"How do you know a weapon was the problem?" Gramps asked. "There may not have even been any monsters — you could have faced puzzles and traps alone."

"I don't know for certain . . . but the way one of my pouches was torn off my belt seemed consistent with claws. And beyond that? Even if I'm only dealing with traps — which I doubt — a metal blade would help me focus my essence. I could deflect arrows, cut down swinging pendulums . . ."

"Perhaps. But the problem of supply remains. How will you find such a blade? Will you spend your seven years in service to the Ghost Forge?"

I frowned at that. "I . . . I'd rather not wait that long. Maybe Uncle Eiji could find me something if I ask next time he visits. If the court would be hesitant to allow anything with iron, maybe a weapon with a different metallic base, like silver."

"Silver is a good metal. The queen might permit it," Ana mused, "but a sword forged by human hands would still be a potential problem."

"Tengu-forged, then? They're known for their sword arts, and some still have good relations with the court."

"It is unlikely your uncle could find the time for a journey into their territory. And tengu-forged blades are hardly common outside the mountains," Gramps posed.

"I . . . I'll have to think on it. I'm sure there are options." I hesitated for a moment out of sheer stubbornness, then gathered my resolve. "What would you recommend?"

"I would recommend focusing less on earning a blade and thinking more in terms of building your essence. Your chances of completing the shrine will be vastly greater if you reach Torch-level and earn a destiny mark."

I nodded slowly, sipping at my tea. "I can work on that, and I appreciate your advice . . . but I'm not going to entirely abandon searching for a sword to use. Even aside from using a sword to help me through the shrine, there's no way for me to properly practice developing sword techniques without one. Sure, I could try to adapt techniques for wooden swords, but then I'd have to unlearn the habits I form from that when I eventually get a metal one. Do you know of any other swords nearby I'm not already aware of?"

He seemed to consider that. "None that would be good options for you, I'm afraid. I am sorry, child."

"Actually . . ." Ana flashed a grin my way. "*I* might."

Gramps turned to her with a mixture of surprise and . . . alarm, maybe? Both were unusual. Gramps had essence abilities geared toward detection — he wasn't omniscient, but he had a tendency to just . . . know things.

I promptly ignored my suspicions in favor of excitement. "What kind of sword? Where?"

"Well, I don't know, exactly, but . . . check your bags from yesterday."

I blinked. Gramps's look of alarm deepened into grave concern.

I stood up with great effort, then went and found my remaining bags from the day before. Ana helpfully pointed me to my main backpack. I opened it, images of finding a half-broken sword in my mind . . . but I found something else. Something much more mysterious and potentially more valuable.

A scrap of cloth. A large one, well-worn but carefully folded.

I gingerly lifted the torn and smudged piece of fabric out of my bag, then rested it on the table and gently unfolded it to get a better look.

My eyes widened at the sight.

A map.

It was a *map*.

And not just a map . . . it contained an area I recognized in an instant. Hero's Rest, the spring of healing water where I'd often gradually gathered enough essence to make healing elixirs.

That was at the bottom of the map, however, and not the focus. It showed a long, curvy trail leading north — outside of fae territory into the mountains above. And as it climbed, my heart soared along with it.

I knew that trail, too. I'd never walked it, but I knew where it led: The Last Breath. A high point in the mountains, named for being the site of the final battle for an ancient hero.

. . . Or possibly for the difficulty people had with breathing there, due to the high altitude. Maybe both.

It was near that height that I saw the symbol that made my heart sing — a sword.

"Is . . . this a treasure map?" I asked, half to Ana and half to myself.

While I wasn't allowed to travel into human territory, the mountains on the map weren't faerie territory *or* human territory, at least in the modern era. They were, as far as I knew, largely uninhabited. I'd been forbidden from wandering there when I was younger, since I couldn't use essence to defend myself, but now that I was at Candle-level . . .

I looked to Ana with hope in my eyes.

"I don't know! Isn't it wonderful?"

She didn't know? That was . . . odd, considering where I'd supposedly found it. "Maybe."

I'd checked my bags after the first visit to the shrine. I hadn't seen anything like this. ". . . Did you plant this in my bag, Ana? To make me feel better after failing the tests?"

She blinked. "Uh, no?"

I felt my suspicion settle a little bit, but not completely. I'd been too specific with the question. "Did you plant it for another reason?"

"I didn't plant it at all, Lien. Honest. You found it."

"Did I find it because you put—"

"I didn't even know it was in the shrine, Lien." She folded her arms. "I can't tell you about details, because that would break the shrine's rules, but on your second trip into the shrine, you found a room I didn't even remember existed. It was one of the ones from before my time."

It was easy to forget that the shrine predated Ana's existence. I still didn't know what the shrine had been prior to her repurposing it into a home, but it was old. *Very* old.

I suspected it had something to do with the Ashen War, or something even earlier, like when the Buried had been first sealed. I'd once considered it likely that it had been a Destiny Shrine, housing a destiny crystal, but Ana had denied any obvious crystals . . . aside from her dungeon core, of course, which was crystalline.

I'd considered the obvious possibility that her dungeon core had once been a Destiny Shrine's crystal, but that seemed unlikely, unless something had transformed it. There were clear similarities to the legends of Destiny Shrines — with their ability to test people to see if they were worthy of a specific destiny mark — and modern dungeon cores. But the crystals in Destiny Shrines were massive — we're talking bigger than people — and had advanced intellectual and magical abilities. Anathema's dungeon core, as powerful as it was . . . wasn't that. It was the size of a child's fist — huge by gem standards, but nothing like a crystal shrine's core. And, so far as anything I'd read was concerned, dungeon cores didn't have the same intelligence that crystals did as Destiny Shrines.

I'm sure someone would have asked the crystal at a Destiny Shrine if they were related to dungeon cores at some point, but it was hard — most of the known Destiny Shrines had vanished during the Ashen War, and those few that had survived intact were now jealously guarded by powerful families and secret orders. I didn't know of any within the forest, but if the Queen of Rust and Salt had access to any, she wasn't going to tell me about it.

Anyway, even with a massive book collection, I'd never found anything written about the shrine. That might have meant it was simply an obscure subject, because of the shrine's presence in a faerie forest . . . or maybe it was just that Gramps didn't want me to find those particular books.

". . . My second trip? Not my third?"

It would have been more meaningful if I'd found it on that last attempt, after all. It would have vindicated my efforts, meant that I'd earned something through all of my pain.

But not everything worked the way storybooks told me they should.

"You didn't find *anything* useful on your third trip, Lien. You were so badly injured . . . look, I shouldn't be saying this, but don't ever try that again.

If it weren't me running the trials . . . you could have died. You're very brave, but there are limits to what passion and determination can accomplish on their own."

I looked down, suddenly finding the swirling liquid in my teacup very interesting.

We were all silent for a time. Internally, I wrestled with renewed feelings of failure, but eventually, Ana was kind enough to prod my less injured arm. "No moping. *Mapping.*"

"Right." I glanced at the map again, then turned to Gramps. "The hugely suspicious map. Was it you that put it in there?"

"I didn't plant it, either. I . . . didn't even know it was there. It shouldn't have been. In truth . . . I'm not sure you should have it."

I raised a quizzical brow. "You know what the map signifies, then?"

"I have an idea, yes. I recognize the area."

I felt my excitement growing again. "What can you tell me about it?"

"It would be better not to shape your image of it with stories. If that symbol signifies what I believe it does . . . you would be best to avoid it entirely, at least for now."

"Because it's dangerous?"

"In part, yes."

"Care to elaborate?" I asked.

Gramps took a sip of his tea. "I know of someone who once spent many years in that place. A sword master. One might have called them a Skyseeker, perhaps."

"A powerful one?" My heart soared at the idea.

"Undoubtedly, but that was a long time ago. They're long dead."

I frowned at that. "Is there a reason you're strategically omitting their name?"

"Yes."

". . . It wasn't one of my parents, was it?"

Gramps gave me a long look, a hint of sadness dragging his eyes and lips downward. "No, child. It was not."

I sighed. I didn't think he would lie to me, but I knew that look. He was definitely hiding something. Pushing wouldn't help. "Very well, Grandfather. I'll let you maintain your air of mystery for now. What are the odds there are actually usable swords there?"

Gramps sighed. "You have such a . . . focused mind at times, child."

"Easier to stay sharp that way."

Gramps rolled his eyes at my terrible pun. "There *may* be intact swords there. And if you did find one, you would likely be able to bring it here without incident. But child, you should not . . ." He hesitated, his head turning downward. "Do not get your hopes up about this place. The mountains are not considered human territory, so I will not stop you from visiting them, but you must not take any paths you find that would lead into their lands. And be wary, child. This map . . . it shows a place that the world has tried to forget."

Well, that's not an ominous statement or anything.

Warnings aside, I couldn't restrain my interest. If anything, the thought of danger made it *more* appealing. I'd always had bad habits in that regard.

"Isn't that all the more reason I should go?" I took another sip of tea. "You always tell me to learn what I can from the past."

"True." Gramps turned down to gaze into his own teacup. ". . . But at times, when you look too deeply into the past, the past has a way of looking back at you."

CHAPTER VII

SEEKING SOLUTIONS

In spite of my enthusiasm, I didn't leave for the mountains that night. I was still badly injured, after all, and I'd burned through or lost the majority of my traveling supplies during my trips to the shrine.

I spent a bit of that evening repacking a smaller set of items to prepare for a shorter journey.

Why?

I desperately needed a bath.

A bath in the healing spring, that is.

I still wasn't in good shape to travel, but after eating, I felt a little bit of my strength renewed. Not enough for any serious trek, but the healing spring was much closer than Ana's shrine.

I still wouldn't have made the journey alone, not at night, but Ana was kind enough to serve as my escort for the evening. We relaxed in the spring together, then headed back to Gramps's place to rest.

I slept better that night, knowing a journey was on the horizon.

The following day was another day of recovery. Even with the waters from Hero's Rest, my wounds were far from fully healed.

I wished I still had a healing elixir, but those took significant time to prepare. The process required taking water from the spring and extracting the healing essence from it, bottling that, and then repeating the process dozens of times before mixing it back into a new liquid base with a variety of healing herbs. I got started on the next batch, but it would take months to extract enough healing essence from the spring to make another fully functional elixir.

I went through my chores as usual, daydreaming about my upcoming quest (which had been mentally upgraded from "journey" to "quest" overnight). At lunch, I sat down with Gramps, waited for him to take a sip of tea, and then hit him with a surprise. "I want you to lecture me on something."

Gramps *almost* spat out his tea.

Almost. I was so close!

Instead, he just kind of coughed a bit, swallowed it, then raised a bushy eyebrow. "What are you conspiring at, child?"

"There's no conspiring! Well, minimal conspiring. Conspiracies require more than one person, right? And Ana was barely involved in this idea, so—"

"Plotting, then."

"Oh, yeah. Definitely doing that. I'm plotting how to grow stronger. Like, absurdly stronger."

Gramps rolled his eyes. "Of course you are, child. And what is your latest plot? This isn't another 'almost kill myself so I get an immediate boost of power' idea, is it?"

". . . No, but now that you mention it, I could start gathering the right type of essence to optimize near-death essence surges—"

Gramps set his cup down on the table gently, but somehow, the ringing of porcelain against wood seemed to shake my soul. For a moment, my words faltered, exactly as he'd undoubtedly planned. "I know a few people who trained with a style like that. You can visit them sometime, when you're older."

"Oh? Where is it?" I asked, suddenly excited.

"It's a lovely graveyard. I hope someone is still tending to it, after all these years."

"Oh." I sighed. "Okay, point taken, letting myself deliberately get near death for rapid advancement isn't always wise. Other risks, however . . ." I gave him the kind of mischievous smile only a thirteen-year-old could manage. ". . . I can handle."

"Within certain limits, perhaps. You are a fledgling. Creatures of higher levels of essence development could still crush you with the flick of a finger."

"Right, right, sure. Which is why I need to get stronger faster. I'm a *target* now. Everything saw me as a non-threat when I was pre-Candle. Now that I have my Heart Point formed, I'm fair game."

He frowned at that. "The strongest creatures will not risk harming you, so long as you stay within the forest. They are bound by alliances and traditions."

"Sure, but there are plenty of other creatures that still would look at me like a delicious snack. And . . . the creatures of the mountains aren't going to follow faerie rules of hospitality."

"All the more reason you should delay your visit. Or forget it entirely."

"Not happening."

"Then . . . should you encounter anything beyond you, remember this: run, hide, lie, or die. Those are your options, in order of preference."

I stared at him. One thing had stood out among the others. "Lie?"

Encouraging that to someone who had grown up among the fae was antithetical to everything that I had been raised to believe, but Gramps nodded seriously. "As a last resort, of course. Most powerful entities would see right through your lies."

"That's not why I'm objecting."

"I am well aware. Nevertheless, remember my words. You may need them."

I frowned. "I'll remember them. I won't promise anything else."

"Then you are not ready to leave," he insisted.

I groaned. "I'm already way, way behind where I should be, Grandfather. I need to catch up somehow."

"You need to stop comparing yourself to Ana. You're not a faerie. And by human standards, having a single completed Dianis Point at your age isn't bad."

". . . I'm not human, either, though. Am I?"

"No." He shook his head. "You're not. But you should expect your advancement rate to be more similar to a human's. And by that standard . . ."

"That's like saying 'you're rich compared to these people from a foreign country you've never visited.' I can understand it intellectually, Grandfather, but it's not applicable to my daily life. Especially when my weakness relative to the creatures here could get me killed."

Grandfather sighed, closing his eyes. "A better argument than your previous one, I'll give you that. But you can't hold yourself to an unreasonable standard."

"I'm not. I'm just trying to ask for help to feel capable on my own. I don't want to have to rely on you, or Uncle Eiji, or Ana, or anyone else to protect me. I want to be able to walk at night without fear . . . and not just here. I want to *explore*, Grandfather. I want to see the world outside these woods. I want to see human lands, and tengu, and des'vahi, and—"

"You are not ready for that. I will not permit it." His tone was absolute.

"That's exactly my point. That's what you always say. Help me *get* ready."

"What do you think I've been doing all this time, child?"

I shook my head. "I appreciate your lessons, Grandfather, and all of your help and guidance. But you're always focusing on my safety and telling me to slow down. I can try that, but I want you to help me."

"With one of your plots?" He asked.

"Yes. You see, I've been studying *Hartigan's Guide to Internal Essence Structures* . . ."

Gramps let out a "tsk" of disapproval, like he always did when Hartigan's books were mentioned. "And?"

"Well, I know you don't want me to try to unseal my bloodline ability on my right hand . . . but what if I could benefit from it without that? I've been reading about how star veins connect with the spirit, and it's possible that rather than breaking the seal open, I could bypass it and use it as an essence source—"

"It wouldn't work. The particular nature of that seal would not allow it — any essence that you allowed through would end up breaking it open from the opposite side. No." Gramps's tone brooked no argument. "There will be no *tinkering* with your seal."

"Why? It's my birthright, isn't it?" I stood up, feeling a rare surge of anger. "Why won't you even tell me who I am?"

"You . . . wouldn't understand, child. It's—"

"I have a *name*, you know." My hand flexed, not quite balling into a fist.

Gramps tensed. For a moment, I thought he was going to snap back at me. Instead, he simply raised his cup of tea again, closed his eyes, and sipped.

I barely restrained myself from slamming my fist down on the table. Instead, I simply trembled as I watched his insufferable silence.

He set his cup down. "You have several names. I know many more of them than you. But I know your meaning. You are still a child to me, but that is not meant as an insult. If it is acknowledgment of your identity you need, I cannot give it in the way you seek. For me to name you would be a mistake."

In spite of my growing frustration, I recognized that sage-like statement as revealing something beyond the words themselves. "You're saying you *can't* call me by my name?"

"I'm saying I *should* avoid it. Now, please. Sit. I understand I have angered you, and for that, I must express my regret. I know that this must be . . . difficult for you. To know so little of yourself, of where you came from."

I didn't sit. "I appreciate you saying that, but sympathy isn't enough. You have to tell me something eventually. *This isn't fair.*"

"Eventually," he agreed. "Yes, I suppose I will. For now . . . perhaps we could move back to your earlier topic?"

". . . I don't see how. You never approve of my ideas."

Grandfather closed his eyes briefly, looking pained. "I . . . will endeavor to be more supportive. Perhaps we could discuss something at a higher level, and I could assist in that way? Tell me more of what you have been thinking. And please, sit."

I took a deep breath, remembering at the same time that using such a method for clearing my mind was in itself something that Gramps had taught me. ". . . Fine." I sat, grudgingly.

"Now, tell me what brought this to your mind."

"It's . . . simple enough. I failed, Grandfather. And if I don't find some sort of advantage . . . Ana is going to keep getting stronger, too. And she'll keep making harder challenges for the shrine. I know you don't want me to compare myself to her, but . . . if I ever want to succeed, I need to be able to at least match her pace."

"Ah. A reasonable concern." Grandfather nodded. "Continue."

I was half-surprised he even acknowledged that point. I decided to take the opening while I could. "I'm going to be gone for a while to look for the sword, and I was thinking this might be the right time for me to work on some kind of way to increase my advancement speed. It doesn't have to be self-destructive. Just . . . anything to help me catch up. You're much stronger than I am. You must know a trick or two."

"Indeed. I know many. *Everyone* looks for ways to advance faster. People dedicate entire lifetimes to studying new techniques for improving efficiency in essence growth. In some cases, they even share that knowledge." He shook his head. "Rare ones, sadly. People often keep those secrets to themselves. The fundamental problems of advancement speed are simple enough. The first is resource scarcity — simply finding enough essence to absorb. The second is acclimation. Your body can only adapt to essence so quickly. Even with theoretically infinite resources, your speed to advance is limited by what you can handle. Flooding it with extra essence is a waste."

I could see where this was going. "Sure, I know all that. Most of it would usually go to secondary essence, rather than primary essence that I use to build my Dianis Point. And my body would have to acclimate to all of it, even if I wasn't using it."

"Precisely. And even more than that, the body processes essence faster if it's of a type the body is already used to. The more your star veins and Dianis Points are used to that specific essence type, the more quickly you can make use of it."

I nodded in understanding. "Sure. I've heard about the 'pure path' stuff, where someone only consumes one type of essence, and thus advances super rapidly. Seems like an absurd hypothetical, though, unless you're some sort of royal with infinite resources. But . . . I was thinking about this a while ago, when I was picking bladeberries."

"I don't know why you're bothering with those. I told you that you'd have to eat hundreds to make any useful contribution to a Dianis Point."

I shrugged. "Right, I heard you. So I ate thousands. Anyway, where was I? Right. I know where you're going with this. I know there are ways of stripping out unwanted essence to save acclimation time. I take it that's what you were going to mention?"

Gramps shook a single finger at me. "Precisely. There are ways of gathering essence and using alchemy to distill it into base components before absorbing the ones you want. There are also techniques for stripping unwanted essence out of the body. If this is done before the acclimation process begins, you can avoid stressing yourself . . . and thus, advance more quickly, since your body is only having to absorb one type of essence instead of trace amounts of any number of extraneous types."

"That seems like a huge advantage. Why doesn't everyone do it?"

Gramps laughed. "Rich people often do. It's time and resource intensive to go the alchemical route for separating essence into component parts. Your average person can't afford the cost, and for Skyseekers, the time spent on learning and performing the alchemical process is time that could be spent on other forms of training, which could be considered a disadvantage."

"What about just stripping it out of yourself with a technique, then, or other forms of separating the essence?"

"Removing it from your own body risks causing harm to your Dianis Points and star veins, and thus, it's generally not considered worthwhile. There are several ways to do it, but they're advanced. There are also non-alchemical techniques for splitting essence *before* absorbing it, but then you have to spend the time to learn those techniques, and they risk damaging the essence itself. Thus, there's a risk of resource loss, and Skyseekers without significant resources don't generally like the idea of losing advancement components."

I nodded in understanding. I knew I had the major advantage of living in an essence-rich area . . . but that came with a number of downsides, like the distinct lack of other people to train with in the area. In addition, the essence types weren't necessarily ones that suited me, and a plethora of unwanted essence could actually be disadvantageous if I absorbed them by accident. "Do you know of any techniques for separating or removing unwanted essence?"

"Yes. But none of them would be compatible with sword essence."

"Oh." I frowned, but I wouldn't let that disappointment stop me. "What about adapting a technique from a similar essence type?"

"That's . . . hypothetically possible, but very advanced work. People usually do not create their own techniques until Hearth-level or higher."

"There are exceptions, though, aren't there? The King of Mirrors created his Blackened Reflection technique when he was just a Candle, right? And the Smiling Sword Saint—"

"Apocryphal references at best. Firsthand accounts of that point in history are unreliable."

I frowned. "But it is possible. I've practically already re-created the legendary Sword Hand technique."

"You've created an elementary copy of the Sword Hand technique, yes. That's very advanced for your age, but . . ."

"I'm not claiming it's a finished technique, but I understand the basics. Adapting something that already works should be easier than making a new technique from scratch, right?

"Not necessarily. That depends on how similar they are. You may end up being better off trying to make something new."

I grumbled a little at that, but acknowledged the point. "Understood. I'd like to give this an effort, though, at least. Do we have any books specifically focusing on technique adaptation? And these essence-separating techniques?"

"Not specifically, but there's a large section on it in one of the books, yes. *Works of the Body and Soul, Second Edition.* Misleading name, I know. It's from an older tradition when 'soul' referred to the essence structure as well as the spirit. A bit abstruse, but useful for your purposes. Third shelf, top row, third from the right. As for essence separation, there's even less on that, but we do have technique scrolls for a few types that may be relevant. I'll retrieve them from the cellar later."

I blinked. Grandfather *never* let me see the scrolls from the cellar. "I don't suppose there are any sword technique scrolls down there that you could get, you know, while you're down there?"

"There are not. I have never had a reason to collect sword techniques. You may ask your uncle Eiji if he has any when he returns."

I grunted. Mildly disappointing. "What about other swordlike techniques that I could adapt?"

"One step at a time, ch—" He managed to stop himself from calling me "child" again, if only barely. "Grandson."

That was . . . better, at least. I felt another bit of my anger subside, just slightly. "O . . . kay. That might take me a while, if it works out at all. What about other methods? Anything I can do right away?"

"There are a few options, but they have their own downsides. Most of them impede long-term growth potential in some way."

I nodded. That seemed a little more reasonable. "What about things like pills and elixirs?"

"Those generally just contain essence, rather than changing your body's acclimation rate. There are some that could help, but they can be dangerous."

"I don't mind dangerous."

Gramps rolled his eyes. "Yes, I'm well aware. I'll consider teaching you about them, but not until you've at least worked on your basic foundation."

I considered pressing further, but I'd already gotten more than I'd expected out of the conversation, and I didn't want to risk the possibility that he'd take away the scrolls he'd offered from the cellar if I kept pushing too hard. "Any other tricks?"

"Plenty. In fact . . ." He smiled softly. ". . . I believe that brings us to your name day gift."

He slid the book across the table. I picked it up immediately and read the text on the cover.

"*An Analysis of Destiny Mark Acquisition and Bloodline Power Inheritance* . . . by Erik Tarren." I raised an eyebrow at him. He smiled innocently.

I'd long suspected Gramps had some kind of personal connection with the famous scholar, given the frankly suspicious number of Tarren-authored books in our household. At times, I'd suspected he was Tarren himself, but that seemed too simple. And Tarren was a renowned traveler — I'd never seen Gramps leave the forest. Uncle Eiji was the one who went out into the human world for supplies.

"Thank you, Grandfather." I bowed my head respectfully. "I'll read it soon. Based on the topic . . . I assume you're giving this to me to influence my essence selection?"

"Me? Ulterior motives? Perish the thought, child." He waved a hand dismissively. "But you *will* note that Tarren himself has a preference for branching paths over pure ones."

"Uh-huh." I lifted the book and shook it in the air. "It's clearly *Tarren* that wants me to take a branching route. I'm tempted to go with pure swords just to be contrary."

"That would be your right. You'll find the details of the destiny that leads to in the book, as well as a number of other sword-related destiny options. Chapter Twelve, I believe? I think you'll find some quite appealing. Perhaps Uncle Eiji's path will interest you?"

"His destiny is in there?" I blinked in surprise. "Isn't it supposed to be extremely rare?"

"It is, but you know, the famous scholar has his sources of information . . ."

"Right, of course." I rolled my eyes. I'd get to the bottom of Gramps's relationship to Tarren someday, but for the moment, I was more excited about the book . . . and maybe reading about Uncle Eiji's destiny mark, too. He could *fly*, after all, and that was pretty appealing . . . especially for a kid who had long wanted to fly far away from home.

I momentarily dismissed that thought. There would be plenty of time to daydream about exploring faraway lands later. For the moment, I wanted to check on something more immediate. "I can always start out just absorbing lots of sword essence and then change my path later if necessary, right?"

"That is true. It would not be unwise to begin that way for a time, while you learn more about your options . . . just make sure you don't overdo it. Once you have your Destiny Dream, you'll likely be living the rest of your life with that destiny. Once, people could earn more destinies by visiting Destiny Shrines, but . . ."

"Aren't there still Shrineseekers looking for the lost shrines?"

Gramps blinked. "I don't recall giving you any books talking about Shrineseekers."

I gave a wry smile. "I may have other information sources. It's true, then, isn't it? There are still people searching for them?"

He shrugged. "Perhaps in the outside world. But if there are any more shrines to be unearthed, they would be far from here. In the lands of fiends, Buried, and . . . humans."

"What about advanced destinies?"

He shook his head. "The chances of that are even more remote. I'm afraid those are almost impossible to earn in our environment." He sounded oddly hesitant. I'd clearly made a decision he didn't approve of, but he didn't seem to want to push it, at least for the moment.

"*Almost* impossible?" I asked.

"Very few things are impossible, child. But one should not build their life around the hope for one-in-a-million events."

That was wise advice and I intended to follow it.

I wouldn't *hope* for any one-in-a-million successes.

I'd carve my destiny by breaking as many rules as necessary.

CHAPTER VIII

SECLUDED SECRETS

The next morning brought the promise of adventure. A treasure map — okay, I wasn't sure if it was *literally* a treasure map, but it felt like one — hinting at the location of a long-lost sword . . . it was exactly the sort of thing that got my imagination running wild.

Which, of course, meant that Ana was even more excited.

"Swordswordswordswordsword—" she intoned as she fluttered in the air next to me. "What type of sword do you think it is? It could be a jian, since Skyseekers like them so much, or maybe a dao, but do you think they'd use different iconography for that on the map? Or maybe it wasn't a local Skyseeker and it's just using their symbology because a Skyseeker made the map or maybe a local—"

"Sentences need to end, Ana. And breathing is important, too. Please." I was happy that she was excited, but the running commentary could get a little too much from time to time.

"Sorry, sorry, sorry. I'll, uh, tone it down just a little. I'm just so . . . do you think you're going find a *magic* sword? There has to be one, right? A Skyseeker wouldn't use some ordinary thing."

"There may not be any swords, Ana. If the Skyseeker is dead — and, given what Grandfather said, they probably are — they may not have left any weapons. In fact, I see no reason why they would leave anything particularly important behind, unless they had to leave in a hurry."

"But . . . but . . ." Ana's expression sank. "If there is a sword, you'll let me try it, right?"

"Of c—" I had to stop myself before finishing that reply and adjust rapidly. "—concern to me is whether or not there is anything there at all. If there is, I would be pleased to show it to you if I can do so without any complications, such as, but not limited to, threats to the local area, myself, or yourself."

"Hmph. You are *zero* fun today." She folded her arms and huffed in perhaps the world's most stereotypical depiction of displeasure.

My rapid and awkward sentence adjustment had been a loathsome necessity. Ana was my best friend without the slightest bit of competition, but as much as I loved and trusted her, she was still very much a faerie. And saying "Of course I will" to a faerie, as I had so nearly done, was not something I did lightly. Making a promise to a faerie, even in a casual way, was effectively a binding contract. If I made such a promise and failed to deliver on it, I would — at a very minimum — lose a significant amount of trust with both Ana and the faerie community as a whole.

If she took it more seriously, I could face significant consequences. Breaking a promise to a faerie was one of those things that got people weird and often debilitating curses. I didn't think Ana would curse me personally for failing to show her a sword — in fact, I didn't think she *could* curse me, personally, since she didn't know that type of magic — but it was absolutely possible that some higher-powered faerie would hear her complain about it and decide to give me some kind of appropriate punishment. I'd imagine that would be along the lines of a curse that prevented me from seeing swords, for example, since it would be a poetic form of justice for failing to show one to Ana.

Or worse, they might change the mark on my cheek. That would be less funny and more heartbreaking.

So, yeah. Nonbinding language. It was a huge pain, both for me and for Ana, but it was a necessity. I'd considered workarounds in the past, but they weren't easily achievable. For example, it was theoretically possible that I could create a binding contract with the local fae authority — in this case, the Queen of Rust and Salt — that permitted me a certain degree of leverage to make statements of intent without them being considered binding promises. This was the type of thing high-level diplomats sometimes had done in the past because both the faerie and other species understood that different cultures have different cultural and linguistic proclivities, and thus, it was sometimes necessary to take precautions to prevent cultural disconnects from spiraling out of control.

Unfortunately, I wasn't a high-level diplomat, and I probably wasn't ever going to be one. I could have theoretically made a similar contract with Ana herself, but while that might have protected me from direct reprisals from her if I made a mistake, it wouldn't have helped if other faeries took offense, thus rendering it nearly pointless.

There were other ways around it — people invested with specific positions of high respect with local cultures, like faerie doctors (which is a person who works with faeries, not a faerie who is a doctor), generally had enough clout to say something like "that wasn't what I meant" and get away with it. I wasn't one of those, either, and didn't plan to go through the years of training to be one. I'd considered getting invested as a knight of the local court when I was younger, which would offer similar latitudes, but that would have placed me in the service of the faerie indefinitely. That wasn't desirable. My mark and title already gave me enough to worry about.

In order to placate my pouting faerie, I made a slightly more open-ended statement than my last one, while giving myself room to maneuver. "I'd love to show you a sword if I get one, but let's not forget that there may be rules that prevent it. What if the sword is soul-binding and can't be shown for a year and a day, for example? Or what if it's cursed, and I need to use it in two hundred and fifty-five battles before lifting the curse, and in the meantime, I will go berserk any time it is drawn?"

Ana's eyes widened. I'd successfully gotten her back into daydreaming mode, which was pretty much the ideal state to have her in when she'd been upset. "You think there might be a *cursed sword*?! Oh! Oh! I would absolutely love to fight you while you're berserk! Can you imagine? I'd be like, 'No, Lien! Fight it! You're stronger than this, I know it!' and then you'd give this like evil possessed laugh and tell me, 'There is no Lien, only the Sword of Infinite Chaos Death Darkness!'"

I rolled my eyes. "I think that name might need a little workshopping."

"Oh, don't look down on yourself. Lien is a perfectly fine name, even if no one else uses it."

I sighed. That had been an obvious trap, and one not dissimilar to the one I'd already avoided. Little things like linguistic ambiguity and wordplay were mostly harmless among humans — or so I'd heard — but among faeries . . . simple banter could easily turn into lifelong consequences.

Names were one of those areas where a degree of caution was always warranted, even when they were raised in jest. For example, if I responded to Ana with any indication that I didn't like my name, it was possible that the conversation would lead toward her (or more likely a faerie that was eavesdropping, which was about ninety percent likely at any given time in this forest) *taking* it. That would have been very, very bad. "I like my names — both my birth names and my nicknames. I was *referring* to the name you gave the sword. Does it really need chaos, death, *and* darkness?"

"I guess not, if you want your cursed sword to be *boring* and one-dimensional." She rolled her eyes. "Nothing worse than a sword with boring powers."

"I'd rather have any sword than none, but yeah, fair. Do you remember hearing anything about Skyseekers in this area that could give us a clue about who it might have been or any equipment that might have been left behind?"

She shook her head. "I don't tend to hear much about things outside the forest boundaries, unless it's relevant to our own history. I suppose there is one thing, though. Maybe we can look for more clues at Hero's Rest?"

"Briefly, since it's on the way, but I can't stop for long. The map isn't clear on scale, and I'd like to try to get to wherever this Skyseeker is supposed to be before sundown."

Ana pouted a little at that, but she understood. *Things* that came out after sundown were not to be trifled with as a mere Candle-level child. Moreover, it would be much harder to discern environmental threats, like ankle-eater grass and creeper moss, after dark. This would be doubly true in areas that were less familiar like the mountains.

It took a couple hours to reach Hero's Rest at a steady walk.

The area was breathtaking, even after seeing it a hundred times.

A waterfall at the base of the mountainside flowed and collected into a circular pool that sparkled with diamond clarity. The pool itself was only a few hundred meters in circumference, but it was too deep to see the bottom. It was also the origin point for the river that trailed onward to the south, which served as my primary point of reference for making my way back home when I'd first started wandering around with Ana as a younger child.

The whole area was surrounded by a ring of tall trees, stoic guardians that kept their distance from the tranquil waters. They were almost perfectly equidistant from the waterline, implying that they'd been planted deliberately in that defensive formation, or perhaps that they'd simply chosen to grow there. I gave the trees a quick glance, searching for any signs of kodama or other forest spirits, but didn't see any.

After that, we went to the side of the pool — after scanning for naiads, just in case — and, in the absence of threats, lowered our foreheads to rest them against the cool water's surface. It was a sign of respect for the local spirits, seeking to show that we were humble and courteous visitors. There was no visible response, but I thought I could just barely make out the sound of a distant chime in the breeze.

I smiled, and then, after a traditional count of three seconds, lifted my head.

The waters of this pool had healing properties. It was where I typically gathered water to make my elixirs. But I'd already done so within the last three weeks, and doing it again without waiting a traditional period had risks. Small ones, given that I generally left sacrifices any time I took the water, making it an exchange rather than an imposition . . . but I didn't want to gamble on it. I was much happier about risking physical harm to myself than offending spirits I'd spent years befriending.

What were the odds I was going to get critically injured during a simple investigation of some long-dead Skyseeker's home?

Not high, I assumed.

Hahahaha.

Oh, childhood me. To be that innocent.

Anyway, I didn't take the healing water. Instead, I turned to Ana to honor what I'd agreed to. "Okay. Let's search for a bit. I can stay for around an hour."

That last line was a deliberate clarification of something I realized I'd been too ambiguous about previously — I'd told her, "I can't stop for long," but that wasn't a definitive time range. Technically, she could have claimed that I was obligated to stay until just before sundown, since that was the only time marker in my original statement. An even greater stretch might have allowed her to claim that I didn't specify *which* sundown, but even most faeries didn't tend to push ambiguous language to that degree.

"Only an hour? Ugh. Fine. If you're so eager to get rid of me . . ." Ana fluttered off before I could get another word in, beginning her aerial search of the area. She was being playfully huffy, her teasing holding a degree of actual displeasure.

She's envious. She pointed me to the map in my pouch, and it was in her shrine, but she can't leave faerie territory to investigate it with me. I'll need to make sure I bring something back for her, if I can. At least a good story.

My own search began at the base of the large tree where we'd once found the remains of a glass bottle. Such a bottle implied that someone had once camped out there, or perhaps just traveled through the area. If I was lucky, it was possible that was the same Skyseeker we were interested in, and maybe they'd left some other clues behind.

First, I retrieved my shovel from the tree's base. It was a crude thing, made from solid stone that I'd spent months shaping into a useful form. I hadn't minded the work — it was necessary to be safe and respectful. Using a metal-bladed shovel and accidentally striking a tree root would have been considered a terrible act of violence, much like striking a tree with an axe would have been. And striking a tree with a wooden shovel would have been a grave insult, if not necessarily an assault.

Beyond that, I'd enjoyed working on it. I took a great deal of pleasure in making simple things in general, either out of wood or stone. I'd always wanted to do some metalworking, too, but I wasn't allowed to make anything in the Ghost Forge on my own, and there were no other forges I had access to.

Most of the things I made were . . . uh, let's just say they weren't of professional quality. I didn't have the patience or skill for detail work. So, when I started on a project that was more elaborate, Ana would usually help me with it. And by "help," I mean that she'd pretty much end up taking over as soon as the first steps were done. I'd smash a rock into small pieces, grind and carve the bits into basic figurines, and then she'd do the detail work and paint them for our war games. That sort of thing.

The shovel had been all me, though. And for that reason it was, uh, kind of terrible. Usable, but terrible.

Even with a stone tool, I had to proceed slowly to avoid hitting the roots — a simple nudge with such a tool would be tolerated, but any serious gouges in the wood could be considered an affront.

I dug deeper for about a half hour, searching for anything that might have been buried along with the bottle. Bits of clothing, perhaps, or any other articles that might have been kept in the same pouch as the bottle had been.

I found nothing, just as I'd expected. My best guess was that the bottle had been used to drink a healing draught from the waters nearby, then dropped in battle, or by accident. Sadly, the bottle pieces were so old that any trace of essence in it had been too diluted to track, even if I had the right skills for it.

Abandoning my shovel, I went and washed my hands in the water — an action I already knew the local spirits would consider innocuous, as simple cleaning was within the purpose of such a clear pool — then went and found Ana flapping next to the waterfall.

I gave her a soft smile. "We've checked back there a dozen times, Ana. There's nothing beyond the waterfall."

"There's *always* something behind a waterfall, Lien. You should know that. We just haven't looked hard enough!"

I tried not to roll my eyes at her faerie story tropes. Admittedly, this *was* a faerie forest, so following traditional narrative rules was more likely than in the outside world . . . but sometimes a waterfall was just a waterfall. Especially when it served as a boundary marker to other territory.

Still, I couldn't discount what she was saying entirely. There was always the possibility that we'd missed a hidden switch, a lever, or a false wall. Or an invisible treasure box — those were always possible.

So, at Ana's urging, I crept along the tiny rock ledge at the base of the waterfall, as I'd done time and time again. Twice, I almost fell into the water. It barely would have made a difference — I was thoroughly soaked by the time I reached the base of the waterfall either way.

Then, with only a moment of trepidation, I braced myself and pushed into the waterfall.

The force of the water slammed into me, but I was braced for it, and I didn't get carried by the current. I held tight against the stone wall, my fingers grasping the uneven edges of rocks on the mountainside as I fumbled my way toward the center of the fall.

As I moved, I prodded the seemingly solid mountainside, searching for secrets. Hidden switches, illusionary walls, tiny alcoves. Anything that was out of place.

I managed to make it about ten paces before I finally slipped. That was better than usual — the slick rocks beneath me weren't exactly a stable place to stand, and every step involved being battered by more and more of the onrushing water from above.

I hit the water hard, but that was nothing new. I swam to the surface, finding Ana floating in front of my face the moment I emerged.

"Again!" She grinned brightly.

I sighed.

I made one more effort, making it two steps farther along the mountainside, before being swept back into the water. Once again, there were no secrets to be found.

. . . Occasionally, I still wonder what might have happened if I'd made a third effort that day.

But I was soaked, I had places to be, and I had very different secrets to unravel. So, I emerged from the water, wrung out my shirt before slipping it back on, and then picked up my backpack and returned to the road.

Well, path, really. The way into the mountains was clear enough — a sharp gap on the northern side of the ring of trees around Hero's Rest — but calling it a road might be a bit disingenuous. It was a dirt trail that might have been well-traveled once, but in the many years since humans had been chased from these lands, it had fallen into disuse. The path wasn't completely overgrown — the local faeries had too strong an aesthetic sense to allow for that — but my boots were the first that had walked it in many years. I left soggy footprints as I headed to the mountain's edge. As the trees gave way to rocks and brambles, the trail turned upward and Ana stopped so suddenly it looked like she'd run face-first into a wall.

"I . . . can't keep going." Her shoulders sank and she drifted downward as her wings beat more slowly, a clear sign of her mood sinking along with her altitude. "I didn't think . . . I didn't know it would be this soon. Stupid mountains and their stupid boundaries."

I raised an eyebrow. "Is there a literal barrier here I'm not seeing?"

Ana shook her tiny head. "No, it's . . . I can *feel* where our territory ends. It's more like how you can sense sword essence. Beyond here . . . it's like the world feels like a different color. I can tell it's different and I'm not allowed to be there."

I couldn't quite feel what she could, but there was something ephemerally different about the air ahead. I wouldn't have sensed it if she hadn't said something, but . . . when I closed my eyes and concentrated, it felt like there was a subtle demarcation in the world. Like walking from one room into another, but on a massive scale.

It was strange, foreign feeling . . . but an exciting one nonetheless. In many respects, I was leaving home for the first time in my life.

"I'm sorry you can't come with me." I reached out my arms. She flew into them, hugging me tight with her tiny form. "I'll plan to tell you about what I find, okay?"

"You'd better! And you have to share the swords, okay?"

"We'll see." Again, careful language. I kissed the top of her head, then let her flutter backward to watch.

I hesitated for just a moment. Then, with a deep breath, I stepped into the unknown.

CHAPTER IX

SCYTHE

The mountain path was a long one, but I eagerly drank in the scenery as my still-wet boots clomped along the road. Every bright purple flower, every thorn-protruding cactus, every gray-barked tree, was a new and amazing sight. I had to force myself to remain on the trail, otherwise I could have spent days just smelling the flowers, testing cacti for poison, and climbing trees.

Fortunately, a life among faeries had helped me internalize the message "Always stay on the trail," especially in unfamiliar territory. The temptations of new experiences were strong, but my lessons were — for the moment — dominant.

The mountains were brimming with unfamiliar creatures, too. Without the presence of faerie dominance, and with humans long absent, beasts had claimed the territory for themselves. This was also a rare region where those beasts were, so far as I knew, entirely untainted by the Ashen Scouring — a transformative miasma that had swept through human lands and transformed many ordinary animals into monsters hundreds of years before.

As far as I knew, traditional animals still existed in human lands, but they were interspersed with numerous dangerous monsters. There were likely other territories that had never been touched by the blight, but they were comparatively rare. There were also Havens — cities and towns marked by the protection of the Saint, one of the members of the Hero's Party in the Ashen War — that could not be touched by the blight . . . but only humans had the Saint. And she had only sheltered her own.

Faeries and Skyseekers alike had guarded these mountains during the Ashen War, but most areas were not so fortunate as to avoid the scouring.

I knew that this place was special, but I didn't yet have the exposure to the demi-fiend monsters of the outside world to truly appreciate it. My education had been purely on words and paper — it wasn't until I saw the strange creatures of the human world many years later that I would truly understand the beauty of the natural creatures of those wild mountains.

That, unfortunately, led to some misunderstandings from time to time, like when I first noticed the massive beasts that were stalking me as I cautiously weaved my way up the mountain road.

One . . . two . . . three . . . four . . . that's at least five of them among the trees. Maybe more of them farther back.

I hadn't seen the exact species before, but I recognized the creatures as being some sort of very large feline. I'd seen cats before — I knew a family of witches, after all — but never of this size.

Hm . . . mountain cats, light-haired, very large . . . can't tell what kind of essence they have. Could be split tigers, maybe, or titan lions, or maybe those panthers that shoot bees, or . . .

That's six now.

Oh, why are they . . . oh, I've been remiss. This is their land and I haven't offered them a proper greeting.

I paused my consideration and walked straight toward the largest one. That was probably the leader.

"Greetings, great and wise mountain ruler. I am Lien, also known as the Edge of the Woods, and—"

The gigantic beast took two steps back, growling, while others moved into a half circle, flanking me.

That made me nervous, but I wasn't going to abandon my greeting quite so quickly. "I mean you no harm. I offer a humble trade for safe passage through your lands."

I knelt down and reached into one of my gift pouches, beginning to search through for a suitable offering, when the first beast lunged at me from behind.

I heard it, rather than saw it, and swung around to catch the lunging creature midleap. A flail of claws missed my face by inches and I grunted under the weight, then *hurled* the beast straight toward the next nearest one, purely on instinct.

The two cats fell in a pile, snarling as they found their feet. The others ceased their advance.

I scanned from side to side, evaluating angles of attack.

Then, as I heard them growling in unison, I did the same.

My right hand shot out to my side, essence flashing into the form of a blade extending from my right hand.

"*Stop.* I mean *no harm.*"

The beasts circled me. I shifted my stance to a more aggressive one, preparing to rush the leader. My eyes met their own.

Several moments passed while our eyes offered words that my voice had failed to communicate. Then, without warning, the beast turned away, as if they'd simply lost interest.

I watched cautiously as the other mountain cats retreated into the trees, just out of view. I waited for several seconds, then lowered my head.

"Thank you for the lesson."

I shook my head. That had been close to turning into a bloodbath. I clearly hadn't done enough to study the local creatures and their behavior.

Maybe my words had been taken as an insult, or my gift not presented quickly enough, or . . .

I shook my head and headed back to the road. I had time to worry about that later.

For the moment, I could still hear the creatures shifting just off the path. They were out of sight, but they were still watching me. Stalking me.

Perhaps they were just waiting to see if I left their territory, but . . . maybe they were waiting for a better chance to strike, too.

And if they did attack, I didn't know what my odds were. I hadn't seen them use any essence, and at the time, I assumed that meant they were hiding their power to use it at a more tactical point in the battle. Each individual cat could have had different essence types, too . . . or so I imagined.

I hadn't even considered the possibility that they were *ordinary mountain cats*. As a child of secret magic and faerie paths, to me mundanity was the strangest thing of all.

Even if I *had* considered it, however, picking a fight might not have been a good idea.

"Ordinary" beasts weren't necessarily powerless. Much like humans, animals could absorb essence. Some people distinguished between beasts with and without active essence powers by referring to the former by special names, most commonly the Artinian name "spirit beasts," but it wasn't always a clear line. In an essence-saturated area, even animals that didn't have obvious essence abilities like flight or fire-breathing would often have absorbed bits of essence simply through exposure, increasing their physical strength, speed, durability, and so on.

If the cats didn't have any essence abilities, I had a significant advantage against one. Even at Candle-level, I was considerably stronger and faster than an average human without any essence development. The shadow-hide boar I'd killed was both stronger and faster than any animal that didn't use essence.

There were two critical problems. The first was that while I might have had an advantage against one of them, that didn't necessarily hold true against a sufficiently large group. The second was that I had no way of identifying at a glance if they had essence abilities of their own — or even just essence-based improvements to their physical abilities. Once I'd completed a Viewing Point — one of the other Dianis Points in the body — I'd probably be able to determine the essence levels of things at a glance if I developed the right techniques.

Anyway, even if I could have beaten them soundly, I didn't really want to. I didn't mind hunting for food, but killing the local creatures without a good reason didn't sit well with me. This area was their home, not mine. I was just a visitor, and I had no reason to come in and start a fight, even if they were being inhospitable.

I continued on the path, eventually seeking shelter from the mountain cats in a dark cave surrounded by a pile of varied animal bones, which in retrospect probably wasn't the world's best place to explore, but I was short on options. And I did *love* exploring.

So, I glanced around near the opening of the cave until I thought they'd lost interest.

Such a variety of bones here! And such interesting damage. Looks like these bits were cut with some kind of scythe-like blade, and these were crushed with extreme force, and these . . . are those acid burns? Ooh, haven't run into anything with bone-dissolving acid in a while. Neat!

Fortunately, my clothes had mostly dried off during the pursuit, so I was only a little bit shivery in the cold of the cave's entrance.

Less fortunately, I quickly determined that I wasn't alone within the cave's walls. My first clue? The gigantic glowing eyes.

The many, *many* gigantic glowing eyes.

There are many different responses to fear. Running, freezing up . . . and my own first instinct, which was to attack.

I pushed that down. It wasn't useful, and worse, it would be painfully rude. Instead, I stared back at the eyes for a moment, then lowered my head to the cavern floor.

"Forgive me for invading your home without an invitation." I spoke in Morval, the primary language of local spirit beasts, rather than speaking the faerie tongue as I had attempted with the cats. There were a variety of other languages the creature — or creatures — might have spoken, but based on the eight eyes, the yellow gleam, and their size . . .

<Why come you here, morsel?>

Yes, that was "morsel," not "mortal." Honestly, being referred to as either was a bad sign, but the one that implied I looked like a small snack was probably worse.

The voice spoke directly into my mind, giving the impression of the same language I had spoken in, but telepathic communication was often . . . looser than speech. Especially when used to communicate with creatures that didn't default to verbal communication.

"I sought a brief respite here while seeking an ancient sword in the mountains nearby. I meant no offense with my intrusion."

I heard a chittering sound and the shuffling of movement as the eyes suddenly shot closer and gave me the first look at the huge creature's form.

Gigantic mandibles and antennae reached out from the eight-eyed head of the *akostrak*, better known as a "scythe spider" because of the creature's eight curved bladelike appendages. There was some debate about whether they were actually spiders larger than horses or if they were some other species that simply resembled conventional arachnids on a larger scale. That debate was currently irrelevant, given that there was, in fact, a consensus that *akostraks* ate people, and that was a much higher priority in my mind.

Fortunately, a few other facts came to mind, too.

<Seeking to rest? May rest for much time, sleep, after I bite . . .>

The chittering that followed sounded almost like laughter. Maybe it was.

Well, at least they're being straightforward about their intentions. That's refreshing. A faerie spider probably would have tried to trick me.

"Oh, but great and beautiful one," I began as jaws moved closer, knowing that some scythe spiders responded well to flattery, "may I instead offer you a gift?"

<Gift?>

The possibly-technically-a-spider paused and reeled up, lifting two legs in a gesture that I interpreted as curiosity. <What gift is gift?>

The repetition indicated a small telepathic communication error, but I didn't worry about that. Instead, I dug through my bags, debating what might be a suitable offering. I'd brought my traditional offering pouches and warding pouches on the journey, but spider gifts weren't on my list.

Eventually, I settled on something — a simple hand mirror. Presuming the creature could see in the dark, I offered it. "This will allow you to gaze upon the beauty of your own reflection at any time, great one. I can see nothing more worthy of a creature of such obvious power and influence as yourself."

<Know what a mirror is, morsel.> The creature reeled up and chittered again, giving the impression of a cackling old woman. <You may leave the gift and go, before too hungry and change mind.>

"Many thanks, great one." I left the mirror and hesitated. "I don't suppose you know how to find the sword I'm looking for?"

<Run now, little thing.>

In spite of the threat implied in that message, I didn't run. I stood and bowed my head once more, then retreated slowly.

Never turn your back to an *akostrak*.

. . . Not until you get a serious distance away, at least.

It was only when I was outside the cave that I ran. Not in fear, but with joyous laughter.

I'd only just started climbing the mountain and I'd already met such an interesting new person! Maybe, if I was lucky, I could even make a new friend.

CHAPTER X

SWORD SCHOOL

Retreating from the scythe spider wasn't exactly my idea of the best possible start to my career as a swordsman, but it did help to further incentivize me to grow stronger.

Next time, they won't think of me as a small snack. No, if I reach Torch-level . . . I should at least qualify as . . . a large snack!

And beyond Torch? Well, there'll be no snacking at all. Not if I get powerful enough to register as a threat. Then we can talk on more even terms, and maybe we can learn more about each other.

I wonder what kind of tea a scythe spider would like? I don't remember reading about that in any of my books. That seems like an obvious omission. I wonder why?

Oh, I'm being silly. They must have a broad variety of different tastes, just like fae and humans do.

Anyway, strength first, then we can talk again sometime.

Just . . . need to find the sword. Then I can get to reading those books and figuring out some more tricks to advance faster.

Staying on the path hadn't worked as well as it did in fae lands, so I changed tactics. I kept to the trees. Not literally hopping from tree to tree, mind you — I wasn't some kind of ninja. Not yet, at least. But rather than remaining on the obvious trail, I advanced through the brush within sight of it. This would cost me time, but presumably the lowered visibility among the trees would make it somewhat less likely that more local predators would notice me.

I couldn't do much to obstruct my scent. Sadly, I hadn't prepared for that, which was an obvious oversight. I comforted myself with the knowledge that the most dangerous creatures in the mountains would probably be following me through essence-based senses, meaning that disrupting my scent would be useless against them. This, of course, also meant that I couldn't really do anything else to hide from them, which was bad.

It was possible I wasn't old enough to be out on my own outside faerie territory yet. There was probably a good lesson to be found there, one that a wise child could have internalized and used to cut their losses and turn back home.

I was, however, much more of a stubborn child than a wise one. I'd like to say "brave," but calling myself brave right after I'd fled a threat feels like a bit of a stretch.

I pressed on, periodically checking my map and finding landmarks. A very large, triangular stone that looked like it warranted study by someone with more archaeological knowledge than I possessed. A moss-covered formation of upraised rocks that I almost missed — the top of a long-abandoned water well. The bucket and rope were long destroyed, but a rusted mechanism for raising and lowering said rope was lying half-buried in the grass nearby. Potentially salvageable, but of dubious use.

And finally, I saw it — a battered and illegible wooden sign.

I was almost there.

It took until the better part of the day's sunlight had faded to reach my destination: a flat section on the mountain with three small structures that had been ravaged by time and neglect.

The structures weren't on the map, but as far as I could tell, I'd found the location of the sword. It was possible it was a little farther on — the scale on the map was far from clear — but I was, at the minimum, near the right place.

My hands flexed open and closed in anticipation. I was *so close.*

The largest building looked to have been three or four rooms once, but with the roof collapsed, it was difficult to tell. The second building was a large single room, which at a glance I suspected might be a storage shed of some kind. The third was the smallest, and I took it to be some kind of ancient restroom.

I wasn't looking forward to investigating that one.

Behind the third building was something I *was* more interested in — a huge stone cylinder with some kind of metal bits on the exterior and deep etchings on one of the sides.

An obelisk of some kind? And are those etchings . . . wards, maybe? Might be a good place to keep a magic sword, if it isn't in one of the other buildings.

A soft smile spread across my face.

And if those are wards, and they're still active, then this could be a safe area even if it's abandoned. Even if they're not active, maybe I could get them working . . .

The buildings weren't the only signs that this place had once been inhabited. The rocky field right in front of the main building had still-visible lines etched into the ground to mark a square area . . . and within that square were six rough wooden figures in remarkable condition.

I took them for scarecrows at first, but my mind corrected when I came closer and saw their accoutrements — rough wooden swords in their hands and shoddy wooden helms on their heads.

I got even more excited.

Training dummies. *Intact* training dummies. Clearly, some kind of essence technique or enchantment must have kept them in better condition than the rest of the area, presumably the same kind of technique that prevented a Skyseeker from obliterating them in a single strike. It was possible that they had something to do with the obelisk, or perhaps the dummies themselves were warded.

It was a shame the same care hadn't been taken for the buildings, but this was a fantastic find regardless.

I'd found a Skyseeker's practice area. But more than that, the number of dummies implied that there had been more than one person training there at some point, unless a single Skyseeker was testing wide-area techniques or had the dummies set up with different abilities.

Would the dummies fight back if I attacked them?

I was about to step forward and find out when I realized I didn't need to—

The door to the largest building swung open.

I wasn't alone.

⊱ ⊰

A tall man yawned soundlessly and stretched as he stepped out of the doorway as if he'd just woken up from a long slumber. He wore long green robes and a rope for a belt, which gave me the image of some kind of mountain-dwelling hermit . . . which wouldn't have necessarily been implausible, all things considered.

He wore no obvious weaponry, but I still tensed when I saw him. Encountering any other person had risks, especially in a dangerous locale like that one. People who trained at swordplay tended to, you know, use swords. And while I could hope he was the kind of fighter that trained out of interest in self-perfection, or for athleticism, most sword fighters trained for the much more obvious application — getting better at killing people.

So, when he took a few steps out the door, and thus closer to me, I braced for possibilities.

Fight, my instincts told me. This was a useless urge, so I resisted it.

Run, my mind told me next, but I suppressed that as well.

Watch, I told myself, with years of practice. *There's much to gain from talking if he is friendly.*

Besides, if he's even one level above me — and he almost certainly is — fighting would just get me killed . . . and running wouldn't be much more likely to help me survive.

The swordsman took a few steps closer . . . and then he was ambushed.

A black-clad teen, maybe a few years the swordsman's junior, hurled herself at his back. I braced as the swordsman turned, caught her, and swung her around.

I could almost hear her say *Whee!* . . . but the *almost* was key there.

When they interacted, I didn't hear the slightest sound at all.

I frowned. *A sound suppression array?*

When he lifted her up, she bonked her head against his, and then he set her down. He said something, but again, I couldn't hear any words. I tried to read his lips, but I didn't understand what he was saying.

Oh-high-something? High because of the height, or a prayer, maybe . . . oh, no. He's giving an Artinian "Good morning," isn't he? I think those are Artinian-style robes. But . . . what are Artinians doing here?

I continued to watch awkwardly from a safe distance. I wasn't hiding, exactly. I actually gave a friendly little wave when they turned back in my direction, but . . . they didn't seem to notice me in the slightest. That was doubly strange. Was I too powerless to be worth their notice? Or was there something suppressing their senses, maybe, similar to how I couldn't hear them?

I continued watching as the black-clad girl maneuvered herself onto the man's back, and then he carried her just briefly before throwing her with surprising force at the next largest building. I winced on instinct before she impacted with it, but she simply flipped around in midair, kicked off the side of the building, and somehow *landed on the roof*. She looked down at the swordsman and bowed in a self-congratulatory fashion. He just sighed, shook his head, and walked over to her.

This was fascinating.

People *lived* up here. Teenagers, it seemed, not much older than me. Well, the green-clad man might have been in his twenties, maybe. Either way, they were being playful with each other. Siblings, maybe, or more likely just close friends. At a glance, they didn't look obviously related. The girl looked about average height and skinny, with short greenish hair that darkened to black near the roots. It looked like she'd dyed it and gotten bored with the color, then cut it herself with a lazy slash. The man was built like a brick wall, over six feet tall and probably twice her weight. Also, his hair was green, like his robes, but unlike the black-clad girl, it was *pure* green. Either he'd dyed it more recently or it was natural.

The green-clad man swung open the door to the smaller building, then went inside and retrieved what my eyes saw as priceless treasure—

A wooden training sword.

Not a rough-cut piece of wood like the type I'd made for myself time and time again (and occasionally painted silver, because, you know, it felt more like a sword that way).

I'd loved my own self-made swords, but I knew in an instant that this was different.

No, this was a *real* training sword, used by *real* sword fighters. One that was honed from the right kind of wood, built to the same length as a real sword of the right type, properly balanced . . . it was beautiful.

I say "wooden" loosely, of course. As I looked more closely, I could tell the sword wasn't entirely solid — it was some kind of phantasmal construct, perhaps as a result of an essence manifestation or technique. If it was, I wanted to figure out how to make one myself.

The black-clad girl hopped off the roof, doing a completely unnecessary flip before she reached the ground, and then retrieved one of her own.

I watched in eager anticipation.

I expected them to go to the wide-open dirt to square off against each other, but instead, they simply walked to the worn training dummies. Then, taking an identical stance — one that struck me as resembling a fencer, their bodies turned to the side and their sword-arm forward with their free hand off to the side — they began to train.

I watched.

I could have approached at any time, of course. I waved a few more times, and even called out "Hello?" once or twice . . . but they never replied to me. And honestly, that seemed like it was for the best. Interrupting sword fighters at practice was a good way to end up as a new training dummy.

Still, as I watched, my worries diminished. They didn't look overtly hostile, at least. That didn't mean I could lower my guard, but . . . this looked like a normal daily form of practice for a couple ordinary-seeming teenagers. Unless I did something to alarm them, I didn't think they'd have any good reason to kill me outright.

The language barrier was a problem, though. I knew a smattering of Artinian, but it was limited to necessities like "Where is the toilet?" and "I did not kill your relative," the latter of which had been reinforced by my books as being surprisingly necessary for foreigners to know.

I did not, however, know how to say things like "Please teach me your sword fighting techniques," which seemed like a significant oversight in my education process.

So instead, I contented myself to observing their movements.

I'd quote-unquote trained with Ana quite a bit as a child, but neither of us truly had any idea what we were doing. We'd both read books about sword fighting — both of the fictional and nonfictional varieties — and understood certain basics about forms and footwork for a couple different styles, but there was no substitute for seeing people who presumably knew what they were doing.

Uncle Eiji had taught me a bit more during his rare visits, but his fighting style was . . . unusual. His typical form was far from humanoid, and even when he tried to look like a human, his movements were lower, bent and crooked, with springing motions from extraordinarily powerful legs that were hard for me to copy effectively. His swordwork was a thing of raw and vicious beauty. He'd taught me a few strikes of his particular style, as well as a few basics about falling safely, but I couldn't properly adapt everything he did. Not at my childhood skill level, at least.

At first, I assumed that the green-haired man was the master of the location. His form seemed tighter, as he struck the training dummy over and over in what would have been vulnerable points on an ordinary human — head, neck, and heart. Conversely, the black-haired girl struck quickly, but with a lower degree of precision, and with her stance being just slightly different each time she reset.

After a while, I started to feel a little creepy about just watching them from a distance, so I decided to step closer and greet them again—

Only to stop immediately as the larger building door reopened and someone else stepped outside.

A child. The black-haired girl put her training sword down on the ground — something that seemed surprisingly disrespectful, from what I'd learned about sword culture — and then rushed over to ruffle the kid's hair. He looked even younger than I was, maybe seven or eight, but his hair was stark gray. He pulled away from the older girl's affections, blushing furiously, then ran over and scooped up her discarded training sword. She swore something, then raced off to the storage building to get another one.

I was about to focus on the kid, curious to see what his training level would look like, when the final figure came out the door.

She looked to be the oldest of the bunch, with curly shoulder-length red hair and an athletic build. She wasn't quite the height of the green-haired man and wasn't as wide, but she moved with a casual elegance that even the black-haired girl couldn't match. She carried a cup of some kind of steaming liquid in her right hand — tea, maybe? — and watched the others with what might have been an expression of fondness, if I could have seen her face.

Or any face at all, really.

Her facial features, like the rest of her body, were a blur, like my vision couldn't focus on her properly. As I squinted in automatic response, I realized it wasn't just a simple obscurement spell—

I could see right through her to the building behind her, too.

She wasn't completely transparent, just . . . mildly translucent.

It was only at that point that I took a closer look at the others and, upon squinting, I realized the truth—

I could see through them, too. Just barely.

They're . . . not really here, are they?

With that revelation in mind, I felt a mixture of relief and disappointment.

Something finally clicked with me that had been seemingly obvious — it was late afternoon, but they were clearly doing some kind of morning routine. This wasn't all that unusual to me, since I was often a late sleeper, but for a sword training school with at least four members, it might have been odd for them all to be treating near-sundown like the start of the day.

And beyond that . . . I didn't sense any significant amount of sword essence from them. There was a bunch of sword essence *somewhere* in the area, but if these were all sword fighters, they should have had a lot of it. True, they could have found ways to voluntarily suppress it . . . but given all the other factors, it was more likely that they simply were operating with a completely different essence type.

That part wasn't entirely disappointing. As much as I wanted to find the sword essence in the area, if they had some other type of power . . . that could be useful to figure out, too.

Still several things that could be going on here . . . let's experiment.

I finally stepped closer, approaching them directly and calling out. "Hello? I'm a traveler from the nearby forest. I mean you no harm."

As I expected, there were no replies from anyone in the group. Not the slightest acknowledgment of my presence.

I inched closer. And closer. No response.

Hm.

I listened. No matter how close I approached, I couldn't hear what they were saying. That was a clue in itself — perhaps they simply weren't generating sound at all, or maybe their forms were more closely tied to another plane of existence, which might have meant that any sound they generated was only audible elsewhere . . . or to people with enhanced senses in tune with whatever plane they were overlapping with.

Maybe if I build my Viewing Point, I could hear them . . . but that still wouldn't necessarily let me communicate.

I could try to touch one of them, or interject myself in their training process . . . but let's gather some more information first.

They continued their training. The sun fell below the horizon as I watched, noting the interactions between them. The green-haired man stopped several times to walk over and correct the style of the black-haired girl and the gray-haired child . . . and, in turn, the red-haired woman would occasionally pause and give the green-haired man advice.

After an hour or so, they paused working with the training dummies and moved to sparring practice. This I watched even more eagerly. The youngest paired off against each other at first, allowing the older pair to watch and instruct.

The black-haired girl weaved deftly around the attempted swings of the smaller boy, only occasionally deigning to even block his sword. Once, she hopped over his swing entirely, flipping over in midair and throwing her sword at him. This drew an inaudible "tsk" of disapproval from the older redhead, but as the child blocked it, the black-haired girl landed, charged, and tackled him to the ground. What followed was seemingly some kind of merciless tickling of the smaller child, which was very strange to watch without being able to hear any laughter.

The older pair sighed, ordering a reset. The younger pair cleared the field.

Cautiously, I walked closer to watch the older pair, eager to see the masters at work. As I grew closer, the translucence of the fighters grew more obvious, and I allowed myself to be less and less concerned about being obliterated by collateral damage from their fight.

But, just in case, I stood behind the black-haired girl to let her body-block for me. She didn't seem to notice.

The older pair raised their swords in an unfamiliar salute. I braced in anticipation.

I didn't even have time to blink. There was a loud *crack* and the green-haired swordsman's blade went flying, embedding itself into the ground nearby.

My eyes widened.

That had generated sound. What had been different? The simple power of the attack? Or had something about the technique allowed it to manifest more clearly in this world?

If that was a sword essence technique, maybe I could learn it by watching them. My first actual attack technique . . . that'd be a huge win if I could manage it.

There was just one problem — I hadn't seen *either* fighter even move.

That was . . . both an incredible display and simultaneously disappointing. How was I supposed to learn if I couldn't even see them?

The answer was obvious—

I'd have to start from the bottom and work my way up.

With a combination of nervousness and giddiness, I headed to the storage shed. The inside of the building was filled with crates, pots, and a wide variety of supplies.

There was also a very obvious bloodstain on the back wall and floor. It was long dried, but the blood must have stained the wood. I wasn't enough of an expert to be able to test what type of blood it was, and certainly not with the equipment I had on hand, but I was curious. Maybe I'd try to sort it out eventually, but for the moment, I had higher priorities.

Namely, swords.

I found what I was looking for easily enough — a series of weapon racks carrying a broad variety of training swords. All swords, specifically, but in a staggering variety — arming swords, longswords, sabers, rapiers, and even more exotic ones like falcatas and estocs.

I took a few minutes just to bask, inspecting each and every one. They weren't metal blades, true, but . . . to me, that room was the closest thing I'd ever found to a vault of priceless treasures. I wanted them all.

After careful deliberation, I picked up the largest sword I could find — a type of impractically huge greatsword called a zanbatou — and tested it in the air, narrowly avoiding hitting a support beam. That didn't dissuade me in the slightest. I'd have more room to swing it outside. I walked out the door, a bright smile on my face.

It was finally time for my sword training to begin.

INTERLUDE III

SPIRITS

"Wait, wait." Scribe raised a hand. Edge slowed his walking, which wasn't quite what Scribe had been asking for, but he admitted it was helpful.

He took a moment to catch his breath. They'd been walking for hours now, with Edge telling his story as they traversed a heavily wooded region just off the main trail. Thus far, they hadn't encountered any monsters — or any game animals, even — which was strange, but fortunate, as far as Scribe was concerned.

From his reading and minimal personal experience, Scribe knew that traveling off-road anywhere on the continent of Dania was a danger. As Edge briefly mentioned in his story, the continent had been affected by a strange miasma that twisted ordinary animals into beasts that were colloquially referred to as "demi-fiends," a broad category of monsters that encompassed everything from fire-breathing bears to lightning-maned deer. Beyond that, there were the less-ubiquitous but even more dangerous core-born — legions of monsters with less resemblance to conventional animals that had been created for the purpose of war.

If the stories were true, there were Buried on this continent, too, but he hadn't seen any of those yet.

The sheer quantity of monsters per mile on Dania was said to be the highest in the known world, largely due to the catastrophic war that had raged hundreds of years ago and left the natives of the continent scrambling to secure small patches of territory in the aftermath. These last refuges of surviving ancient civilizations were protected by powerful walls, wards, and Skyseekers.

Everywhere else was deadly . . . which was why he'd been traveling with a large caravan on a relatively well-traveled and supposedly warded road. Anything else was a horrific risk for a non-Skyseeker.

Of course, while Scribe wasn't a Skyseeker, he *was* a sorcerer — albeit a relative novice. In a pinch, he thought he'd be able to hide from most conventional monsters, but he wasn't sure how his concealment magic would work against those with enhanced senses. He hoped that his seemingly confident companion would render that unnecessary, since Edge seemed to travel the woods with a degree of casualness one might have normally ascribed to someone browsing a marketplace.

Thus far, it had proved moot, since no monsters or animals had approached them. Scribe had considered a number of possible reasons — luck, the areas nearest the roads simply being empty like the road itself, or Edge knowing the safe parts of the area to explore — but when he caught his first sight of a beast, he understood.

The creature, a black-furred mountain lion the size of a horse, took one look at Edge — then bolted in the opposite direction.

Even the deadliest beasts knew not to take their chances with things that were obviously more dangerous than they were. Dania, it seemed, was no exception.

This might have been comforting if Scribe didn't have the sinking feeling that he, too, could easily end up being the quiet swordsman's prey.

As Edge slowed to allow them to rest, Scribe dismissed that thought to clarify his earlier request. "You said you retrieved a sword. How did you know you could interact with the weapons? Were they more solid than the people? And . . . did you figure out what those people were? Ghosts?"

Edge blinked, seeming to refocus. "Oh. That's . . . I really should have explained that, shouldn't I?" He bowed his head in a gesture that seemed out of place for someone so obviously Scribe's physical superior. "Forgive me, I'm used to telling these types of stories to people I grew up with, who have similar magical traditions."

"It's no trouble. Your story has mostly been clear enough, and entertaining, but that particular element didn't make sense to me."

"Sorry," Edge repeated, "it's easy to forget that not everyone was raised with the same background as my own. So, to answer your question, no, they weren't ghosts. I actually did wonder about that at first, too — it is not an unreasonable assessment. Ghosts can exist in places like that, and repeating the activities of life is not an implausible behavior for them. A ghost, however, would have been much more likely to respond to my attempted greetings. While they have variable levels of sophistication, ghosts are generally aware of their surroundings and cognizant of changes. Their motivation tends to be to resolve the causes of their own death in some way, and thus, they are often eager to interact with outsiders . . . though not necessarily in ways that will actually help themselves. They are often confused, especially older ones. Malevolent ones exist, but usually those turn into wraiths or specters. In any case, if they were ghosts, I probably would have heard them speaking. Ghosts generally manifest with similar levels of physicality to each of the senses — meaning that if I could see them, I would probably be able to hear them with a similar level of ease. Thus, I concluded they were probably not ghosts."

"What were they, then?"

"That's the question, isn't it? Spirits mimicking the activities of people who used to live in the area were possible, but they seemed too genuine in their humanlike behaviors for that. Their affections for one another and distinct personalities didn't strike me as spirits playing at humanity — I'd seen that before and knew to look for the signs. And, moreover, such spirits would have been likely to approach me immediately. They tend to be eager for contact with outsiders. I also considered if they might be other types of phantasmal undead, rather than ghosts. Specters, wights, that sort of thing. None of them fit quite right. Sunlight made most spectral undead unlikely, and again, they would have probably tried to interact with me . . . and by that, I mean I probably would have been dead within moments of drawing their attention. I wasn't strong enough to handle anything close to a specter or a wight."

Scribe nodded in understanding. "So, not spirits, not undead . . . elementals, then?"

"Mm. Not precisely, and I didn't say they *weren't* spirits. They simply weren't spirits mimicking humans . . . or, rather, from a semantics standpoint, they only sort of could be classified as spirits at all. My conclusion was that they were a sort of bridge category between spirit and elemental — echoes. Are you familiar with the concept?

Scribe frowned, thinking. "I think I've heard bits and pieces, but not enough to be confident. What are they?"

"So, spirits tend to manifest in areas where there's a thinning between our world and the plane of spirits. Spirits — whole or parts of them — mix with essence from our world, giving rise to new forms of life. A spirit might bond to a tree, for example, giving life to a kodama. Echoes are essentially the same concept, but rather than being born from a breach between our world and the spirit plane, they correspond to the plane of *memory*. The semantics of whether they count as spirits get complex, since the essence they bond to in our world generally is spirit essence that was left behind on our world by a person or creature. Thus, they are composed in part of spirits, but not in the fashion that a typical entity classified as a spirit would be. They're almost the reverse of a classic spirit, in that sense."

"Semantics aside, they're born from spirits and memories, then?"

Edge nodded. "Primarily. But not necessarily the memories of those individuals, precisely. They're born of . . . it might be called the memories of the land itself, I suppose. An amalgamation of the memories of those that lived there, burned into the world and the fragments of spirit that linger there. For this reason, they are humanlike in behavior, but they tend to simply repeat the same activities over and over — whichever activities were tied to the bits of spirit that linger in the region. These may not even correspond exactly to real events from the past . . . rather, they tend to be amalgamations of events that serve as sort of an average of the activities that gave rise birth to the spirits."

"Huh. That's . . . wow. Okay. And these are common here?"

Edge shook his head. "No, not common. I'd heard of them, and even had supplies for defending against them, but the level of spiritual essence necessary to give rise to echoes is significant. In this case, there were probably a few factors that contributed to their existence. Artinians learn techniques called 'spirit arts' and use them in combat, harnessing the power of their spirits in training. Given that combat style, they probably left behind more spiritual power in training than the average Skyseeker. Next, repetition — some of those people probably lived together in that location and trained for years. Also, isolation. The location was obscure enough that no one was going there to harvest the spiritual essence that saturated the region. Gathering that essence before they had time to manifest would have prevented the echoes from forming. Finally, one more factor I'll get to later in the story."

"How long do you think the echoes were there before you found them?" Scribe asked.

"I've wondered the same thing many times. Could have been just a few years, but I expect it was probably decades, if not centuries. I did find some clues . . . but I'll get to that later."

"Understood. Sorry for all the questions."

"It's no trouble." Edge waved a hand dismissively. "In fact, I like questions. Please feel free to ask more if you have them."

"Will do. Now, you went to train with the echoes?"

"Right. Or, at least, I went to give it a try . . ."

CHAPTER XI

SPARRING

My fingers wrapped around the phantasmal greatsword. Gingerly, I lifted it from the display.

It's light, I realized in surprise. *Could be because it isn't fully solid, or maybe the original was just made of a lightweight wood.*

Swords aren't quite as heavy as many people think in general. A typical arming sword might be two pounds. A longsword — I use the term in the original sense, meaning a hand-and-a-half-sized weapon used by knights, rather than meaning a single-handed arming sword — might be three. A truly massive weapon like a zweihander might be six or so.

Based on the sheer (and largely impractical) size of this weapon, I expected it to be on the higher end of that, or maybe even higher. It was six feet long, putting it at about the same length as some zweihanders, but much broader — the blade was more than six inches wide.

An ordinary swordsman had virtually no reason to use that type of weapon, at least when fighting other people. You didn't need that broad a cutting surface to hurt another human in a duel. The extra mass would give it more force for hitting an armored target, sure, but you'd lose so much maneuverability and speed when swinging it that it wouldn't be worth the trade-off.

The advantages of such a large weapon came into play when your own abilities were beyond those of an ordinary human. With enhanced strength, someone could handle the added weight without difficulty, inflicting blows with tremendous force behind them. With both hands and enough strength, two-handed swords can be swung with deceptive speed, too — don't under-estimate how much of an advantage you get out of using both hands to move a weapon. Moreover, the wider surface area had a critical advantage that most people wouldn't intuit — the weapon could hold more essence. That meant that larger enchanted weapons could be more powerful, and in addition, larger weapons could handle the usage of more powerful techniques.

Finally, they had one critical advantage — they were extremely effective against large monsters.

Our continent is home to a wide variety of hostile creatures that cannot easily be reasoned with. Demi-fiends, core-born, even the Buried. Against the largest of such beasts, an ordinary sword is little more than a needle. The solution? *Giant sword.* In cases when you need to fight a monster that's the size of a building, there's no substitute.

Even for powerful Skyseekers, though, such weapons weren't perfect in all scenarios. Such a large weapon had limited angles of attack, restricting the wielder's flexibility. In addition, gigantic weapons didn't work well inside areas with limited room to swing them — cramped caves, hallways, doorways, that sort of thing. For that reason, most Skyseekers who trained with gigantic swords kept a secondary weapon for situations where it couldn't be used properly.

You might be wondering which of the practical reasons was why I chose to pick up the largest sword available. The answer is simple. All of those factors were carefully weighed into it, and one other very important thing.

I was thirteen years old.

I wanted the biggest sword because it was *awesome*.

With the sword in hand, I headed outside. In spite of my excitement, my chest was tight with nervousness.

What if the echoes saw me as a thief or hostile outsider?

I knew the answer. Best case, they'd realize I was a child and just hurt me a little to chase me off. More likely? They'd obliterate me. Echoes wouldn't have the full strength they held in life, but I estimated that they were at least two or three full essence levels above me — more than I could realistically overcome with tactics, especially against a group.

But I couldn't let a little thing like potential obliteration deter me from playing with swords.

I bashed the gigantic sword against the doorframe on the way out of the storage shed — oops — but that didn't seem to attract anyone's attention. Cautiously, I advanced to the practice field, picked an unused target dummy, and tried to mimic the stance Red was using.

Oh, right. That's what I called the redhead. A little reductive, I know. Without context, I named them all after their most identifiable colors. The big guy was Green. The mischievous shorter girl was Fade, because her green hair gradually faded to black. And the kid was Gray.

Anyway, I hesitated, watching the others for a few more moments, then...

Moment of truth.

I swung the sword at the training dummy.

Crack.

The sound, the first after an absolute absence of voices from the echoes, startled me—

And not just me.

The echoes spun in my direction simultaneously, focusing eerie half-solid eyes on my frozen form.

"Uh . . ." I stammered. "Hi?"

The echoes continued to stare blankly in my direction. Belatedly, I lowered my sword in an effort to ensure that they didn't see me as hostile or a threat.

Moments passed as I stood and stared right back at Red's strangely blurred face. She tilted her head to the side in apparent confusion, and then, after a moment of consideration, lowered her own sword and approached.

I stayed perfectly still, not sure what kind of movements would cause her to take hostile action. If Red chose to hurt me, I stood no chance of defending myself. My best hope would be that she wasn't sufficiently corporeal to deal real harm, but that seemed unlikely, given that I was able to hold one of the training swords without difficulty.

So, I tensed as Red got into swinging range, then closer, into my personal space — and, with an inaudible "tsk," lifted a hand and put it on my right arm.

I could feel the force behind her grip. It was solid, but without the warmth of a real hand. For a panicked moment, I wondered if she was going to break my arm with that terrifying grip strength . . . but she simply pulled my arm upward, then shifted and said something I couldn't hear.

After that, she pushed backward on my left arm, then pointed at my legs and shifted her own.

I blinked . . . then, as realization dawned, mimicked her motion.

She wasn't trying to hurt me.

She was *correcting my stance.*

She smiled, said something inaudible that I thought might have been the Artinian word for "good," and went back to her own training.

I stared for a moment . . .

Then wore a smile of my own.

I couldn't believe my luck.

I wasn't going to have to train alone.

The echoes continued training for another hour or so, then seemed to respond to something I couldn't hear. Red made a broad gesture, then headed back into the storage shed, dropped off her sword, and headed to the main building. The others swiftly followed her.

Curious and incrementally less concerned about echo-murder, I followed shortly behind them.

Gray left the door to the main building open as he passed inside. I couldn't tell if that was just one of his normal behaviors or if, maybe, he'd left it open for me.

Echoes had varying levels of awareness about their environments. I'd been extraordinarily fortunate that Red's level of reactivity was high enough that she was able to process my presence at all — and more so that she had seemingly incorporated me into her training scenario, rather than seeing me as a disruption. The situation easily could have gone much worse. Most echoes simply would have ignored me, but many others were known for attacking anyone that disrupted their standard routine.

Unfortunately, my luck didn't quite hold when I went inside the building.

The wooden floor creaked alarmingly as I stepped inside the derelict building. I froze, briefly startled, withdrawing before I could put too much weight on the floor, and glanced around to ensure that the rest of the room looked structurally stable.

It wasn't. As I'd noted before entering, one room was entirely collapsed, and the others looked shaky at best. The wooden support beams were cracked and worn. They looked like it wouldn't take much more than a swift breeze to cause them to collapse entirely.

. . . And the echoes were gone.

I glanced from side to side, scanning the room, but found no signs of their presence.

I did, however, find their likely objective — the long-collapsed remains of a wooden table with six splintered chairs around it. Only a single leg of the table was still intact. The chairs were in even worse shape, for the most part, but one still looked like it had three functional legs on it.

Not that it would do a lot of good if I couldn't stand inside safely.

I frowned, then took a quick circuit around the building, inspecting it further. Of the side rooms, the one that looked *mostly* intact was a bedchamber with the worn remains of three long beds and what looked to be a still-functional dresser. That was exciting enough — if I was lucky, that meant the dresser had wards that prevented the contents from degrading, and I could potentially find possessions that belonged to these ancient people inside.

But it wasn't the only preserved item in the room—

There was a bookcase. A *bookcase with books.* I could see the runes etched into the side of the bookcase glowing faintly, and I knew them well — Grandfather had similar enchantments on his own bookshelves.

There could be sword techniques in there.

I almost ran straight in the building when I saw that, but I managed to restrain my instincts. Further inspection told me that the ceiling was *riddled* with cracks. I'd say it was a miracle that it hadn't caved in already, but it wasn't miraculous at all — it was much more likely to be held in place by the same kind of memory essence that was maintaining the echoes themselves. That essence wouldn't hold it in place forever, however . . . and any disruption to the location had a high chance of making it fail outright.

Could I get in there and grab some books before it falls?

. . . Maybe. But that's a terrible strategy.

If the only thing I was risking was harm to myself from a roof collapse, I probably would have charged right in, or maybe even started working my way through the back wall behind the bookshelf to excavate it without disturbing the rest of the room.

. . . But if the building was linked to the echoes, anything I did to destabilize it further had a chance of destroying them. I wouldn't take that risk.

That put me in a difficult position. Could I remove some books from a distance somehow without disrupting the echoes? I didn't think just taking a few books off a shelf would harm anything, but I didn't have any techniques for manipulating things at range.

Maybe I could work on some kind of long-reaching blade technique that's solid enough to lift an object? Something deflection-aspected might work?

Swords weren't really designed to lift and move objects, but I wasn't a big believer in limiting myself to the original design intent of . . . well, anything, really. If I could find a way to make a sword dance, I'd do it.

Not that a dancing sword had any relevance or utility at that time, but you get the general idea.

I spent a little longer investigating the building from the outside, still hoping that I'd catch sight of a metal sword. Maybe the sword school itself was what the map had been leading to, but even if it was, they probably had metal swords there at some point. I had no immediate success, but I didn't let that discourage me.

The books were my best find, but they were out of reach, at least for a moment.

How can I reach them?

I dug through proto-technique scrolls, evaluating options for constructing methods of securing the building, but "make additional support beams out of swords" was probably my best option, and currently well beyond my abilities. I still wasn't confident I could even manifest a single functional sword, although simply having a phantasmal practice sword helped give me a much better template to work with for ideas. It still wasn't as good as a metal sword, but the practice swords resembled the balance and style of metal weapons more than anything I'd managed to find or construct on my own, and that similarity helped.

The sun fell as I tinkered with technique ideas, but I wasn't particularly worried. I'd packed my bag with the plan of staying at the site of the sword on the map for a couple days if necessary. The presence of these buildings just made things easier.

The main building might have been too unstable to make camp in, but the shed had seemed stable . . . and that gave me an idea.

I went back into the storage shed and took a better look around.

As I expected, it wasn't just for storing weapons. There were crates that might have once contained all sorts of emergency supplies, but I didn't bother with them — phantasmal food and water wouldn't do me any good.

Instead, I inventoried the tools.

The shed contained all sorts of them — everything from gardening supplies to mountain climbing gear. And, most importantly, there were basic crafting tools. Hammers, saws, axes, rope . . . everything I needed, really.

They weren't fully present in my world, but they would serve my purposes. There were even planks to use as building materials . . . but those were phantasmal, much like the tools themselves, and I didn't think using those would be a good idea. I'd stick with just the tools and get building materials the hard way.

It was getting late, but I wasn't anything close to tired.

If I didn't have a technique to repair the house . . . well, I could always do it the old-fashioned way, couldn't I?

I hefted a phantasmal wood-cutting axe. In spite of being only half-corporeal, the edge felt like it would cut just fine. I got to work.

⁂

With a bit of sword essence in my Dianis Point, I was significantly stronger, faster, and more durable than any human child my age without one. In truth, I'd probably been stronger than an ordinary human from birth, either as a consequence of the essence type from my sealed power or . . . whatever I actually was.

That didn't mean chopping down trees was going to be easy, nor something I could expect to do casually. In terms of difficulty, I knew that trees in an area that supported a sword school for powerful essence wielders were probably going to be extremely durable and essence resistant — otherwise, they'd likely get obliterated the moment someone slipped with a technique. Moreover, I'd grown up in a faerie forest, and I'd been taught not to cut down trees lightly. Dryads didn't take that well.

I didn't think I was going to run into any dryads — or kodama, or other tree-related spirits — up on the mountain, but I wasn't going to risk it. Instead, I searched the area until I found a tree that had already fallen on its own. That would reduce both my work and the risks involved. I tried not to stray too far from the buildings — I suspected that the area near them was at least somewhat safe because of lingering wards and the presence of the echoes, but anywhere far beyond it could be deadly.

That left me with a relatively small search region, but eventually I found what I was looking for. I checked to ensure that the tree was actually dead, testing the brittleness of the branches, searching for buds, and inspecting the roots.

May your next life be a better one.

I briefly lowered my head in respect, then lifted my axe and focused my essence.

I didn't have a true technique for my intended purpose yet, but I could feel the power in my body and intuit how to move it. Cautiously, I reproduced the same proto-technique I'd used when I'd first manifested my power, extending sword essence across the axe I was holding. I concentrated further, manipulating that essence to focus along the axe's blade, rather than spreading equally across the entire surface. Next, I concentrated on the composition of the essence, shifting it toward the slashing aspect, which would help make cutting easier. Using that aspect came naturally to me, but I noticed it immediately beginning to wear at the sides of the axe.

. . . Oops.

I shifted back to unaspected sword essence, which fortunately was easier to control without breaking the tool.

I can tinker with that more in the future. I need to build this into a fully functional technique like my Sword Hand soon.

For the moment, I had more pressing work to do.

I measured out the approximate length I needed to duplicate one of the phantasmal planks I'd seen in the storage shed, and then I lifted my axe and swung.

Thunk.

The axe carved through the wood with ease. I'd swung harder than I'd needed to, cleaving through the log and continuing in an arc, nearly swinging into my own right leg.

Eep!

I dropped the axe, startled.

My own sword essence wouldn't have cut me, but the phantasmal axe blade might have.

I took a deep breath, restrained my panic, and refocused.

Note to self: do not sever leg.

More cautiously, I looked around, then reached down for the axe . . .

Which, predictably, was gone.

I hadn't walked far from the buildings, but apparently, the force maintaining the echo had lost its cohesion as soon as the tool wasn't being held. That raised all sorts of questions in my mind — like how long it would have stayed if I had held on to it properly — but for the moment, I didn't have enough data to answer them.

With a sigh, I headed back to the shed and retrieved the very same axe, which had reappeared exactly where I'd found it. I could have chopped wood with my Sword Hand technique, but I was going for cutting wood in bulk, and I couldn't maintain it for very long. Not yet, at least.

As I exited the shed, I blinked as the door to the main building reopened.

Green walked outside, yawned, and stretched.

Moments later, Fade threw herself at his back, and Green lifted her and swirled her again.

. . . Their morning routine had started over.

I paused, debating for a moment, then set the axe back down.

House repairs could wait. Sword training was much more fun.

CHAPTER XII

STABILITY

Integrating myself into the training routine of the echoes of an ancient sword school was simple enough once I'd established the basic rules.

If I interacted with the training dummies, they'd briefly pause, then start to incorporate me into the scenario. As with my first test, Red seemed to react the most organically, but the others quickly followed suit.

Strange that Red is the most reactive, but the least . . . solid. She was probably the most powerful of the bunch, but something is making her manifest less clearly here. Maybe she wasn't here as frequently, or . . . something is making the world forget about her presence?

That was a mystery that I wanted to sort through eventually, but for the moment, I was happy to just get a work out.

Trying to get them to spar with me was equally simple, but also more dangerous. All I had to do was head to the practice field and take a position near where one of the fighters was going to line up, edging out whoever was supposed to be their original sparring partner.

I wasn't insane — I tried it with Gray first. He was a smaller child, after all. How dangerous could he be?

I got my answer quickly enough.

Crack.

The massive sword fell from my limp fingers, a smaller wooden one flashing to my throat.

I coughed, then took a step back and raised both hands in a gesture of surrender.

Gray laughed in silent glee, then made a simple one-handed gesture that I'd quickly picked up as meaning "reset."

I nodded, picked up my sword, and returned to my approximation of the neutral stance that Red had shown me. Notably, it was different from the stance that they were using — presumably because I'd chosen to use a massive two-handed sword rather than one of the same training weapons they were.

In retrospect, that had been an oversight. I'd added another variable without thinking about it. It would have been lower risk to add myself into the scenario if I'd chosen the exact same type of weapon they were using.

. . . But it had worked out, and I liked the bigger sword, so I stuck with it. At least for the moment.

Gray nodded to me, then waited for me to make the first move.

My eyes narrowed. I shook out the numbness in my hand. Then, cautiously, I advanced and took my first swing.

Gray flicked his sword upward with an expression more contemptuous than I'd expected an eight-odd-year-old to be able to manage. Apparently, he'd been taking bluster lessons along with ones in swordplay. His slight movement was enough to drive my larger blade upward, and then he shot forward with great speed, trying to close the distance between us.

I danced backward this time, not entirely caught off guard by his skill now that he'd punished my arrogance once. I'd never had any formal training, unless you counted a few haphazard lessons from Uncle Eiji, but I'd been practicing with Ana for years and that was worth . . . well, more than nothing. I knew that I had a reach advantage and had to use it.

As he closed, I swept my wide blade down at his legs.

If I could clip him, the rules of engagement seemed to indicate that he'd have to treat whichever part of his body I hit as being "wounded" and inactive. A hit to the torso would seemingly "kill" an opponent. Thus far, the trainees appeared to be deliberately avoiding hits to the head.

With an extra couple feet of reach, I hoped that disabling one of his legs would let me maneuver freely around him. It was a good plan, in theory.

In practice, Gray responded instantly, leaping upward, *landing on the flat of my sword*, and then jabbing me in the ribs as I stumbled under his sudden weight.

I dropped my sword, raised my hands in a gesture of surrender . . . then looked at my opponent with new respect.

Younger or not, Gray was *good*. Far better at this than I was and probably better than Ana, too. Ana might have had an advantage in raw power, but he'd clearly been training for some time. While he might not have been a match for the older fighters, I wasn't going to overwhelm him as easily as I expected.

He was a perfect training partner.

I continued sparring with him, losing again and again . . . but learning. Each time he outmaneuvered me, I noted bits of how he reacted, picking up elements of his personal style. His strengths. His limitations.

I lost every exchange anyway.

. . . At least for that night.

It was wonderful. Every loss taught a lesson, if I was wise enough to listen.

The next day, I'd try again.

As the students retreated to the large building for the third time, I finally let exhaustion overtake me. Their routine meant that they were always fresh when they started their "morning," which seemed to be about every three hours.

By the end of the third cycle, my arms and legs were burning and my stomach was growling loudly. I'd been hydrating periodically, but I hadn't eaten since morning.

I took some time to eat, then, exhausted, started to make my plans for the night.

I had a few options. I could try to head back home . . . but given how dangerous that had been during daylight, I didn't like the risk. It was possible I'd be able to handle it better now that I knew the path, but no, it was a terrible idea. I wasn't unfamiliar with night travel, but I was still new to this area and didn't know the threats well enough to take the proper precautions.

That left two other main options.

I could head off to make camp somewhere in the woods . . . or I could camp at the sword school. It was a simple matter of measuring the risks for each.

The answer might have seemed obvious, in that the sword school had thus far incorporated me into their scenarios without any hostility. There was no guarantee that they'd treat me the same way if they found me sleeping, though, and from what I'd seen of the echoes . . . they could be much, much deadlier than the local animals and monsters were likely to be. I also couldn't hear them, aside from the occasional crack of swords against one another. If they chose to attack me while I was asleep, I'd just die.

I picked that option anyway. As dangerous as they were, I preferred known risks over unknowns, and I thought I could take measures to mitigate the dangers of them just killing me in my sleep. The main one was simple — I'd just stay out of their way.

It was tempting to make camp inside the storage shed, since it seemed structurally stable and had a functional roof. I deemed that too much of a risk until I gathered more information. The larger building was likely to collapse . . . and I definitely wasn't camping in the outhouse, if it was stable or not.

I also considered camping up against the obelisk, but after investigating, I found that I couldn't read the glyphs on it. I was familiar with a couple different runic languages, and I suspected this was Artinian in style, but I couldn't parse it.

Eventually, I'll have to grab a book from home and translate these, but in the meantime . . . I can't be sure it's what is repelling the monsters, and I can't know if it's even safe to be close to it.

I did recognize that some of the deeper grooves in the back of the obelisk probably weren't runes at all, but rather indentations used for climbing it. That was interesting — perhaps it had simply been meant as a climbing challenge for the students, and the various glyphs would add challenges if activated?

It was too dark to risk climbing or tinkering with it, so I abandoned the obelisk for the moment.

Instead, I made a simple shelter right up against a tree right near the main building. I used the wood I'd cut from the fallen trees to form an initial structure. It wasn't much, but it would help keep the wind off me while I was lying down and serve as a structure that I could cover to provide myself with marginal concealment. From there, I watched the echoes do their next entire cycle. They never reacted to my presence.

That didn't mean that I was absolutely safe, of course, but I thought it was highly likely they'd stick with their routine unless disrupted. Still, I thought it would be wise to take a few extra precautions. I formed a circle of rocks around my shelter, then dusted the rocks lightly with salt.

After that, I made two additional circles. One, I filled with water. The final circle was charcoal. I had to be careful with that last part, since the charcoal bag still had vorinlief mixed into it, but charcoal was the best defense for echoes.

With that done, I had a basic threefold warding circle. I felt better once I had my shelter finished . . . but that didn't mean I could sleep.

My mind was still whirling with ideas.

Is there a metal sword in there, somewhere? If so, which room would be most likely to have it?

What techniques can I learn here? How can I improve my own Sword Hand technique? Can I figure out a way to move the phantasmal objects further? Would a phantasmal training sword be a sufficient focus for me to try out some of my other sword technique ideas, or should I need to get a real sword first?

As my mind jumped from idea to idea, I realized I was just keeping myself awake with that level of mental activity — a problem I ran into regularly — so I decided to try to settle myself down with a bit of reading.

I sifted through my backpack, first retrieving one of my filled essence vials to use as a light source. Then, I found the book I was looking for.

Works of the Body and Soul, Second Edition was probably the type of book that most people considered dry, but I found everything related to technique creation and adaptation fascinating.

As a child, I wasn't able to use magic — but that didn't prevent me from studying it. Gramps was a scholar of many things, magic theory being among them, and he had a number of books on how magic worked.

I *devoured* them.

(No, not literally. Eating books is an entirely different branch of magic, and one that, ironically, I haven't actually studied much about. But I digress.)

While Ana was figuring out how to use her own inherent abilities and absorbing additional power from Anathema, I absorbed knowledge and theory instead. If I wanted to compete with her in the long run, I knew I'd need significant advantages. And while many of my ideas for advantages were of the "crazy plan to make myself powerful fast" variety, I also had more methodical approaches. Athletic training was a part of that, as was my constant consumption of sword essence to ensure that I completed the Dianis Point I'd planned for . . . but my studies of technique creation were just as important to my long-term planning.

To understand what I'm talking about, let me back up a little and give you some context.

The deliberate uses of essence can be categorized in a few different ways.

First, there are manifestations. Manifestations are uses of power without any specific training behind them — it's basically the most fundamental thing you can do with essence of any type. For example, a fire manifestation would be just pulling fire out of your fire Dianis Point and pushing it out into the world, creating a burst of flame. You can think of this as analogous to calling in dominion sorcery, but rather than utilizing power from another plane of existence, you're pulling it from your own body. Combining manifesting with shaping, a term you'd probably be familiar with from dominion sorcery that has essentially the same meaning here, can still allow some variety in abilities . . . but for the most part, manifesting is just shooting out energy and then maybe shaping it a bit. This is what most essence users learn to do first, and often it's the only thing that people without formal training can ever do with their abilities at all.

That thing where I cut through Ana's sword? That was a classic manifestation of sword essence. Reproducing it to cut wood with an axe was another manifestation combined with rudimentary shaping. Manifestations were useful, but very limited unless you had extreme talent with them, like Ana did.

Next, there are augmentations. Augmentations are essentially the same thing as manifestations, but internal to the body, rather than external. There's some debate as to whether they're even different categories, but I think the distinction is worthwhile. For example, one could use an earth augmentation to shift earth essence to their arm, allowing them to hit harder on a punch.

There's nothing wrong with these rudimentary uses of essence. Everyone, even veterans, makes use of them to some degree. But to be competitive, powerful essence wielders utilize more-focused abilities called techniques.

Techniques are designed to use essence for highly specific ends. To do this, a technique creator determines their goal, then begins to assemble a technique by determining how best to use their available essence types to achieve that goal.

This might sound like something you can do on the spot — and, in the case of true experts, it may be possible to create a basic technique spontaneously. But technique creation is an entire field of research. Making the most powerful — and most efficient — techniques for any given purpose can involve weeks, months, or even years of research and iteration.

Let me give you a basic example.

From the moment I had sword essence, I could have projected it into the rough approximation of a sword shape and tried to cut things with it. This would be a basic manifestation and would have, to some degree, served the intended function.

But prior to completing my first Dianis Point, I'd read many times about the Sword Hand technique — a popular technique in literature about sword essence users. Unfortunately, I didn't actually have any descriptions for how the technique was performed . . . just what it looked like and how it functioned. So, I reverse engineered it to the best of my ability, reading through numerous descriptions of how it functioned and cross-referencing that with different aspects (sometimes called "subtypes") of sword essence.

Every individual essence type has aspects. Each aspect refers to something more specific than the main aspect — typically either a form, feature, or function of the essence.

Take metal, for example — gold, silver, and copper are all form aspects. Form aspects are the simplest; they're basically just more specific versions of the same basic concept.

Feature aspects are based on properties that the essence holds. These can be things that are properties of all essence of that type or a specific form. For example, metal feature aspects are things like luster and hardness.

Function aspects are things that the essence does that interacts with other things. Some scholars consider this the same thing as a feature aspect, but a level of distinction is useful for some specific essence types. In the case of metal, a function aspect might be something like magnetism, since it can attract or repel other things. You could argue that luster could be seen as a function, too, because it involves interactions with light, but that's getting into scholarly esoterica. The main line people use for distinguishing feature and function aspects is "internal versus external," but it's more of a spectrum than a line.

Typically, you see more form and feature aspects for essence types that correspond to materials, and more function aspects for essence types that correspond to things that aren't as tangible, like fire, water, or lightning.

I usually refer to specific aspects as "iron-aspected metal essence" and so on, although for simplicity, someone might just call the result "iron essence." The latter classification style can get a little confusing, because multiple different essence types can have identically named aspects — for example, you might see both "cutting-aspected sword essence" and "cutting-aspected knife essence." These would be similar, but different from each other, and thus, just using "cutting essence" would be a little misleading if we're talking about aspects. There can also be general essence types with similar names, which can be even more of a headache. Scholars try to name those subtly differently, like "sharpness essence" for the more general one, but with so many different essence types and aspects out there . . . you run into overlapping terms on occasion. To minimize confusion, I prefer highly specific aspect terms.

In order to form aspects from your own essence, you have to have a strong concept of that essence to build from, which usually means a sample of that essence aspect within your own essence structure — or just a really great grasp of the theory behind a specific aspect. In my case, my sword essence Dianis Point wasn't purely composed of unaspected sword essence — such a thing would be almost unheard of. I was able to identify at least a half-dozen different aspects of sword essence within it, which I'd undoubtedly collected throughout my life purely through exposure to them. I wasn't sure what all of them were, but I'd identified a few and figured out how to work with them to build techniques.

I could have just taken them all and mixed them into a sword shape and accomplished a rudimentary example of my concept, but that wasn't efficient — the sword essence types would dilute each other when mixed, reducing their individual functionality.

Thus, to create the effect I wanted, I designed my Sword Hand technique in layers — an inner "blade" formed from deflection-aspected sword essence, giving it solidity and the ability to deflect objects and other forms of essence, wrapped by an outer "edge" of cutting-aspected sword essence. To this, I added a third layer of piercing-aspected sword essence over the point, specifically to assist with thrusting attacks.

At this point, I had to determine the ratios of each type of essence to use for the creation of the blade, which involved a lot of math and would require trial and error to perfect.

Notably, at this stage, I did not have a finished technique. What I had was a hypothetical technique, one that was completely untested and may not have worked the way I hoped. I still continued to iterate on the theory behind it, simply by researching sword essence further to determine things like other valid aspects that might be more useful, but the improvement process couldn't occur until I could actually test it.

This is an extremely basic example of technique creation — and one of my favorite hobbies. But there was a huge gap between making hypothetical techniques and functional ones. For that reason, even with a solid knowledge of theory, I'd often have to do significant work to get something functional. More esoteric techniques required more research and practice.

There were stories of all sorts of amazing things that sword essence wielders could do — shooting waves of essence to cut things at a distance, cutting several times with a single swing, or even flying on swords . . .

But I couldn't even begin to work on those types of things without more practical understanding of how sword essence worked. I'd dug through dozens of books and scrolls trying to find ways to construct the kinds of sword aspects that might make a flying sword possible, but I hadn't found anything that sounded even close. Deflection-aspected essence could get a sword to repel away from something, but it wasn't a reasonable means of propulsion. I tried playing with several other ideas, but ultimately I had to settle for the fact that I had absolutely no idea how something like that worked.

I wasn't discouraged by that. I knew that my early efforts to create techniques would, for the most part, end in failure.

But now . . . with a new book to read through and some scrolls for functional techniques of other essence types to try to parse through . . .

I felt like I was on the right path.

I read through the book for hours and hours, refreshing my memory on certain basics and eagerly consuming every bit of new information I came across. Things like the math for how quickly specific types of essence dispersed when exposed to essence-free air (which likely didn't exist in nature, but still a baseline used for technique construction arithmetic), some additional interactions between antithetical essence types that could be used deliberately for creating unusual essence types, and that sort of thing.

Finally, I reached the section I was looking for.

To convert a technique, one must first convert each and every individual component part of the technique, then make sure those component parts are converted in ways that generate the same interactions as the original. Next, you must adjust essence values based on how effective the new essence type is compared to the old, their comparative rates of dispersal in air, and the planar constants for your region. (See Chart XI, Analogous Essence Types, and Chart XII, Planar Constants.)

In cases where there are no analogous subtypes for every function you want, you must find a similar combination of effects to approximate the same result or adjust your technique goal to account for this discrepancy. In many cases, you can offset any difference in technique functionality through sufficient shaping skill, but this will likely both slow the technique's use and decrease its efficiency.

For recommended technique-shaping exercises, see Chapter XII . . .

I kept reading, learning more of the details. In summary, the more distinct the original essence type and the one you were trying to use, the more difficult the adjustment process. Just doing the basics for adjusting any given technique could hypothetically be done in hours for something as simple as the Sword Hand technique, but actually getting it to function properly was a whole different story.

So, as someone with a pretty good background in theory and very little practical knowledge, I had a lot of work ahead of me if I wanted to adapt any techniques.

I didn't mind that in the slightest. Finally, after years of theory crafting, I had the freedom for my mind and body to run wild together.

As hours passed, I finally exhausted myself enough to make my mind slow down. Eventually, I cradled the book in my arms, pulled up my blanket, and slowly . . . very slowly . . . managed to make my way to sleep.

⁂

The next morning came without incident. No nightmares, which was a rare and pleasant surprise. I wasn't sure if the new environment had helped or if I'd simply exhausted myself so much that my mind couldn't form the dark dreams that often haunted me.

Either way, I was feeling pretty positive, aside from being absolutely freezing. I'd brought a blanket and cloak in my travel bag, and I'd used those, but the mountain air had been even colder than I'd expected — and wetter. The air was moist, and the wind chill after I sat up made that worse.

I shivered my way out of the shelter, changed into my one set of dry clothes in my bag, then watched the echoes again.

They were midroutine when I woke, and I wasn't sure if disturbing them after the practice started was a good idea.

Instead, I ate a small snack from my trail rations, then watched to try to glean what I could from their sword practice.

They're still just using basic swordplay. No actual manifestations or techniques, at least as far as I can see. Is that because they're echoes, or is this just a more basic routine that they're repeating?

I frowned, considering. If I wanted to learn sword techniques from them, I'd have to get them to use some. I wasn't sure if I could communicate that with them directly — they hadn't responded to speech. Maybe sign language would work?

I knew some Hunter's Hand, one of the local signing forms, but I didn't have a lot of recent practice.

They're probably speaking Artinian. Their sign language is different. I'd probably end up signing something like "please eat my face, great champion of waffles."

More research is warranted.

I kept observing for the moment, trying to mentally map basic actions. When Green thrusted, Red would perform a specific parry based on the angle, the spacing between them, and their timing. When Gray dodged an attack, Fade would follow it up with a flurry of others, keeping him on the retreat.

They had patterns. I wasn't fast enough to keep up with them — or even see everything they did — but if they had set actions they took under specific conditions, I could learn to use them to my advantage.

. . . In theory. I didn't know how much of their predictability came down to being echoes that repeated a certain set of things and how much of it was just, well, training. Drilling a specific move-and-response was a concept I was familiar with, but I wasn't skilled enough to identify if Red was just demonstrating a specific parrying technique repeatedly, or if she was actually working in a mechanized fashion.

A problem for later. For now, I can learn either way.

When they finished, I knew there would be some time before they returned to restart their practice loop. I used that time to go hunt for more wood, then added that to the pile.

It should have been a simple trip, but something in the distance had caught my eye — something that looked like a gleam of metal. It was brief, and investigating it hadn't led to anything close by, but after dropping off the wood and doing one more round of practice, I went back.

A hint of light could have meant anything, or simply been an optical illusion . . . but to me, it was a hint of a metal, the glimmer of a distant sword blade, and my imagination carried me forward.

I took deeper breaths as I climbed higher, following the winding mountain road until I reached a flatter area with a mist-shrouded forest. The fog was thick enough that I couldn't see more than a couple feet ahead of me, but just once upon approaching, I thought I heard something like the sound of metal clashing against metal.

I frowned, thinking back on stories Gramps had told me about mist-filled forests. There were lots of different varieties of life-stealing vampire mist, soul-eating mist . . . most commonly, though, there was the kind of mist that misdirected you into losing your path.

I considered briefly, then stuck a finger into the mist.

Well, it doesn't feel like it's eating my soul. Probably? And I'm not bleeding out.

So . . .

I grabbed a random stick from the path, marked an X on the still-muddy dirt, began to drag it forward, then stepped into the fog.

I managed to walk for about thirty seconds before I found myself walking back out of the mist. I was absolutely confident I hadn't turned around.

Oh, I see your game, mystery mist.

I walked back in, this time closely following the path my stick had made on the ground to see if it turned around at some point.

It didn't. At least, not as far as I could see. In fact, after a few feet, the path I'd carved simply vanished.

That's . . . huh. Okay. Illusions, then. Or . . . if it's a memory essence thing, it might actually be physically resetting the condition of the area. And messing with my memories, too. Tricky, tricky. Okay, let's play.

I spent hours experimenting — throwing things ahead of me to see if they vanished, searching for specific stones that might contain teleportation glyphs or illusion markers, even sitting down and waiting to watch what happened to my marks.

They never vanished right in front of me. No, it was the moment that I turned away that they'd be gone.

"Spirits of the wood, spirits of the mist, spirits of illusion, I mean no harm. I am merely here to follow a map, seeking a sword." I removed the map, showing it to the empty air.

If anything heard me, there was no reply at all.

I still left a small offering at the base of one of the trees — an empty essence vial. When I came back on my next loop of entering and exiting the mist, it was gone, but that didn't mean anything. I might not have even been looking at the same tree.

Ultimately, I found the mist extremely exciting, but I couldn't solve it right away. Instead, I headed back to the sword school.

My plan was simple enough. Train with the echoes when I could, learning their style to the best of my ability. If sword essence manifested — as I knew it was likely to when people were training with swords — I could gather that to strengthen my own essence. During downtime between training, I'd gather more wood and explore the area, keeping my eyes out for any clues about the mist. I'd test other ideas with the mist as they came, or perhaps if I had another form of essence to use to counter any tricks it held.

When it was too dark to explore, I'd read my books and work on theory crafting for technique construction and modification.

As soon as I had enough, I'd start using the wood to see if I could make some repairs to the structure. I wanted to get in there right away, since I was still hopeful there would be metal swords stored inside, but the more I examined the place, the worse the damage looked. I'd need other supplies to fix it — most notably nails, or maybe some kind of adhesive — but hopefully I'd either be able to find some in the storage shed or get some back at home.

I guessed it would take a week or so to get the half-collapsed building repaired to the point where I felt it was more or less structurally stable enough to explore it thoroughly. I could probably get to the bookshelf and dresser sooner if I was careful, but I didn't want to be impatient. This place was a long-term investment, and if I caused the structure to collapse further, I could bury any remaining swords in the rubble. Moreover, I didn't know if the echoes would fade away entirely.

So, I had a plan . . . but one with a critical flaw.

Food.

I'd brought enough for a couple days, since I knew I was likely to make camp at the site of the sword on the map, but I knew that wasn't enough time to repair the building enough to search it thoroughly. And, more importantly, I wasn't going to be done with this place as soon as I investigated the building.

This school had the potential to provide me with months, if not years, of training . . . if I was able to make proper use of it.

So, how was I going to eat?

Hunting local beasts was an option, but a dangerous one. Every encounter I'd had so far had been too dangerous for me to handle on my own. Granted, I hadn't focused on trying to find game animals, but . . . I didn't like my odds of handling anything big I ran into.

I considered the possibility that I could do it in the small area around the school — it was likely that the presence of the echoes was a deterrent to any local predators and there also still seemed to be some functional wards in the region. I wasn't seeing a lot of other wildlife nearby, either, though. If I kept to the areas just outside the wards, maybe I'd manage something . . . but I wasn't sure if it'd be enough to keep me going.

Another option was local plants. There was some plant life right near the school, which made that lower risk . . . but I hadn't identified anything edible yet. Granted, I hadn't been looking closely. I decided to look into that soon.

Finally, I could always go home . . . but I didn't want to do that more than necessary. If I had to do it every few days to gather supplies, it would significantly reduce my time for training. That wasn't necessarily terrible — taking breaks from training to do other things was generally considered a good idea — but I was excited and wanted to focus on learning swordsmanship, at least for a little while.

. . . And, of course, I could always get eaten by something on the way home or back. Traveling was a risk.

So, I started with the safest local approach and searched the surrounding area for edible plants.

It didn't go well.

I found a lot of plants I could identify. Grasping root, itchthorn, deaddrops, falsefang . . . all threats or irritants, rather than food supplies. None edible.

I found a bunch of plants I *couldn't* identify, too. Only one of those looked like it might be a lead, but the bright red berries were just as likely to be poisonous as promising. I'd look those up when I got back home, but in the meantime, plants weren't a good option.

At least, not the ones that were already nearby.

I mentally kicked myself for not carrying any seeds. If I'd planned ahead, maybe I could have started a garden . . .

Which led me to another question.

How had the people at this school fed themselves?

The school was in a remote location. Admittedly, I didn't know if there had been towns nearer to the locale when it had been built . . . that might have been hundreds of years before, back when humans had settlements in the region. Maybe they'd just gone to the market every once in a while.

But if not . . .

I searched the area again, this time focusing on the ground. In the decades or centuries that had passed, the signs might have vanished, but . . .

There.

I found it just behind the main building — a few pieces of thin wood that I'd previously ignored as just being abandoned lumber. Some pieces were missing — likely moved by the wind or buried — but the essence in the region had preserved the remaining wood to a limited degree, much like the buildings themselves, and I recognized the layout as a simple structure: a fence.

Upon inspecting the layout of the region within the formerly fenced area, I inspected the soil. There was nothing growing there except weeds now, but based on the texture . . . I was pretty sure the fenced area had been used as a garden. Or possibly an animal pen, but I couldn't find any animal remains in the dirt, so I found that somewhat less likely.

The empty garden wasn't a huge find, but it was potentially useful for a couple reasons. First, it implied that the soil there had, at least at some point, been nutrient-rich enough for growing something. Whether that was still the case wasn't certain . . . and if it had ever been successful as a garden was also unknown . . . but it was better than just trying to plant something near a random tree and hoping it would grow.

Probably.

Second, it meant that using that locale to grow things *probably* wouldn't disrupt the echoes, since they had likely used it for that purpose during their own lives.

I was no expert at growing crops, but we had a garden back at home and I understood some basics. I'd never particularly enjoyed growing food, but if I could make it work, I could hypothetically make the area self-sustaining and train for longer periods of time.

. . . But not immediately. I didn't have seeds, nor did I have the expertise to know exactly what was viable to grow in the region. And even if I did have seeds, getting food to grow took time.

So, I had a plan . . . but one I couldn't act on immediately.

I spent the next two days in the area. I trained with the echoes when I could, gradually acclimating to the basics of their style. I gathered more wood to use as repair supplies, temporarily using the lumber as the foundation for a better shelter.

I hunted game nearby to supplement my meager food sources, but succeeded only a couple times. Not enough to live off for an extended period of time.

I searched a little more broadly for local plants that might serve as food but found nothing certain.

When it was too late at night to continue my searching for food, and during downtime, I had a wide variety of things to keep me busy.

Since I hadn't found any significant source of sword essence to absorb yet, I was reliant on food I'd brought for most of my essence. That wasn't enough for my advancement to go as rapidly as I wanted, so a few times per day, I performed a simple conversion technique.

First, I'd draw some of the usable essence out of my Heart Point, just like I was going to use any sort of sword essence technique. Rather than using it directly, however, my next step was to convert the essence into the same composition as the Heart Point itself. This involved compressing the essence from an energy state into a more metaphysically solid state, similar to the Dianis Point itself. Once converted, I then gently shifted the essence back to the Heart Point, where it naturally merged together.

Some older-fashioned folks called this "cultivating" essence, but I preferred the more technical term of "primary essence compression." This was probably because I was a pretentious teenager.

Primary essence compression was something virtually all essence wielders performed while they were in areas where they didn't have a source of their necessary essence types available. It was a great way to prevent starving your essence growth completely, but it wasn't enough to keep someone advancing at anything close to maximum speed. It could also only be performed a few times per day safely, and even then, it would bite into the number of times you could use your essence for other things safely during the day. Thus, it wasn't something you could generally do if you were also practicing essence techniques at the same time.

All in all, it prevented my progress from coming to a complete halt while I was in an area without sword essence, but it wasn't a good long-term solution by itself.

Aside from practicing essence compression, I continued reading through the books Grandfather had given me and made significant progress, but I wasn't leaving myself a lot of time to read each night, so I didn't finish the books right away.

I read through the technique scrolls he'd given me as well. He'd picked out three essence separation techniques, and I'd studied enough to understand the basics of how to attempt to adapt them.

One was designed for water essence, which was about as far from sword essence as one could get, but the concepts were still important. The idea was to create a water essence "bubble" within your essence structure to surround whatever the "new" essence was, then wait as the component essence parts naturally separated within the water based on their properties. After that, you would "split" the bubble, keeping the parts you wanted, and using the water to "erode" the remaining parts you didn't want to keep. This was the most complex of the bunch, but also sounded the safest. Unfortunately, there wasn't any application of sword essence I was aware of that seemed even remotely similar.

The most overtly similar to sword essence was a scroll that involved using fire essence to burn away other essence types in the body, which seemed like the type of thing I could theoretically adapt, but with a high degree of danger involved. Burning essence inside your own body — or otherwise destroying it with another type of obviously attack-focused essence — had the risk of damaging your star veins or Dianis Points. Beyond that, it was very easy to accidentally damage the essence you wanted to keep, losing some or all of it.

The third scroll contained a method for using stone essence to "wedge" apart different essence types. This had a lower risk of accidentally damaging a star vein or Dianis Point, but an even higher risk of damaging the material you wanted to keep. Simply prying essence apart wasn't likely to keep it fully intact. Of the three approaches, this one seemed like the one I would be most easily able to emulate, but I also found the idea dissatisfying. If there was a good chance of breaking the essence I wanted to keep, it might have been even less efficient than just leaving the essence alone.

I briefly experimented with adapting that technique using deflection-aspected sword essence, but after I destroyed two batches of bladeberry essence entirely — the last dried bladeberries I'd been carrying — I ran out of things to test with.

By the end of the next two days, I was half-starved but still pleased with my overall progress. I might not have made any new techniques, but the discovery of the sword school itself was priceless. Cautiously, I made my way back home. The wolves that followed me barely bothered me at all.

CHAPTER XIII

STORM

Ana appeared next to me the moment I stepped back into faerie lands. I would have called it uncanny, but I understood her trick well enough. Her dungeon was linked to the entire region, and thus she had some degree of sensory awareness over the entire area. She'd probably felt something as soon as I'd stepped across the boundary.

"You're back! Where's my new sword?"

I laughed. "No luck on that yet, unfortunately. But I did find *something*. Let me tell you a story . . ."

I explained to her during the journey home, enjoying her extreme emotions as I slightly embellished some of the story here and there. Not lying, mind you, just . . . a few of the kind of colorful touches that make a story grand.

"And what did you do after you defeated the Dragon God King?" Ana asked, eyes wide.

I might have veered into creative storytelling a bit from time to time. Fortunately, that wasn't "lying," either, as long as I made it clear that I was *telling a story* and not a purely accurate depiction of what had happened.

"Well, after I returned the handsome prince to his homeland, I came straight back here to tell you about it."

Ana nodded sagely. "As well you should. Now, tell me the historically accurate version?"

I nodded and told the story again, but you know, with fewer Dragon God Kings. She enjoyed that *almost* as much, and it helped us discuss my actionable options for the future.

"Hm . . . echoes . . . do you think you could find the breaches that are causing them?"

I pondered that. "Maybe. I don't have the right essence types to sense breaches between the planes. And it might not be a breach, could just be a natural thinning."

"On that scale? Doesn't seem likely." She shook her head. "I mean, there are ley lines leading up there, but . . . no, I think you're looking for a breach."

"That's going to be tricky. I could probably find a bunch of essence if I actually locate the breach itself, but without any detection-focused essence types, I don't really have a good way to track it."

"I mean, it's probably at the school somewhere," Ana offered.

I shook my head. "Maybe, maybe not. It's possible there's some other site nearby that's powerful enough to be generating echoes throughout a significant part of the region."

"Sure, sure, but have you seen echoes anywhere else?"

"Not that I'm aware of, but I haven't searched too broadly yet."

"Any other clues?"

I pondered that. "There's a suspicious lack of sword essence for all the sword fighting they're doing. It's almost like it's being pulled somewhere."

"Ooh. Maybe there's a dungeon near the school? Or *under* it? All the best schools have dungeons."

I blinked. "That's . . . possible, I suppose. That would constitute a type of breach, just not the type I was considering. I'll give it a look next time I visit."

With that in mind, I made my way back to Gramps's cottage. Home. It had only been a few days, but somehow, it felt even more comfortable than I remembered.

The next day, I sat across from Gramps, sipping tea and nibbling at a scone. "I don't suppose you have any magical items to lend me for detecting a breach?"

"I wouldn't want to make things *too* easy for you." When I opened my mouth to object, he raised a hand to stop me, then continued. "Even if I did, however, I don't have anything like that on hand."

"And you couldn't make one? I know you have at least one detection-focused essence." Gramps still wouldn't tell me his exact essence types. I knew many of his general capabilities — long-distance sensory abilities, teleportation, speed, and something that seemingly let him be in multiple places at once — but he was surprisingly cagey about what powers he held. He clearly had some motive for keeping that to himself, maybe something to do with his past or identity, but he wouldn't budge on it.

"I do have sensory abilities, but nothing geared toward object creation of that variety."

"Okay. Then I'll need to do it the hard way. I can search the area for signs of dungeon entrances . . . and maybe see if I can pick up where the sword essence is flowing, too. It's too subtle for me to sense the flow right now, but maybe if I build up enough, I'll be able to sense it better."

"A prudent course of action. You should also work on building up additional essence types. You could expedite this process significantly with a Viewing Point."

I shook my head. "Still not sure what I want to do about that. I've been reading the books you gave me, but I haven't made any choices."

"You have time, child."

It didn't feel that way.

Every day I debated was another day of being weaker than everyone I knew. Still, I wasn't willing to ruin my future by rushing things, either. I'd make my choices when I was ready.

With that in mind, I finished eating, packed more food, supplies, and seeds, and once again left my home.

The return journey to the sword school was easier. Not because I'd grown stronger from a couple days of training — any combat skill I'd made in such a short time was both negligible in scale and inapplicable without a blade in my hand. My essence might have grown fractionally stronger from the food I'd been eating and primary essence compression, but not enough to make any difference.

No, the return journey was easier because I was better prepared.

One trip back and forth wasn't enough to have any sort of exhaustive idea of the threats in the area, but I could prepare for the ones I'd seen and extrapolate a bit for there.

Wolfsbane for wolves.

Splitpaw for cats.

And absolutely nothing for giant spiders, I just won't go into that cave.

The scent of the herbs I carried would repel most animals of the appropriate varieties. Such a thing was never certain, especially if I ran into demifiends or spirit beast variants, but those would be problems of an entirely different scale and would have to be tackled through different means (mostly fleeing rapidly).

Let me amend my earlier statement — my preparations *might* have been why I had an easier time. I didn't actually see any mountain cats or wolves on that particular trip. Maybe that was because of the repellent scents of the herbs, but maybe I just was luckier. I planned to make sure I was properly equipped for each future trip either way.

Beyond those herbs, I took a variety of other supplies with me on the return. A jar of adhesive. A solid hammer. Nails.

We didn't have any nails that contained iron, since the local fae wouldn't approve, so that meant I was working with bronze. It wasn't ideal, but they were good enough to get the job done. Even getting bronze items was difficult. Auntie Temper didn't generally work bronze, so we only had a limited supply that Uncle Eiji had brought in from foreign lands. I had, of course, asked him to bring me a bronze sword when I was young, only to be refused for the same reasons Gramps had articulated to me on my threefold name day.

I also managed to convince Gramps to trade me three empty essence collection vials in exchange for a few new Crowns figures I'd carved. He probably would have just given them to me, but exchange culture was a major part of faerie society, and I liked to be able to give things back when I asked for something, even with family.

Besides, I loved carving figures. I expected I'd make some more during my downtime at the sword school. I was planning to make a House Dianis set soon, focusing on the historical figures that Dianis Points were named after.

Anyway, I didn't know if my figures actually had any real value, but the essence collection vials did. They were a mainstay of essence wielders, consisting of two basic functions.

First, the vial itself had a glyph carved into the side that could be activated with the word "collect" or sending a tiny bit of essence into it after the cap was removed. This would cause the vial to draw in essence from the environment, pulling in whatever was present and compressing it within the vial.

Next, the cap itself. All you had to do was screw the cap back on and it would seal the essence inside with a stability effect, keeping it preserved for later use.

Essence vials like these were fundamentals of trade between essence wielders everywhere. Essence manifested in such phenomenal varieties and many types were extraordinarily difficult to find — you'd never find volcano essence manifesting in the middle of a city. Not unless someone had constructed that city in a very poorly thought-out location, at least.

As such, vials like these could be used to grab essence from remote places, then trade it for other essence types the owner needed or other valuable resources.

They also had a second useful function for people like me.

Essence is everywhere, but it's generally too diffuse for a low-level essence wielder to do anything with. You can think of those small amounts of essence as being like moisture in the air. The way an essence collection vial collects essence is analogous to drawing in air moisture into a usable supply of drinking water.

Without essence collection vials, I was limited to only absorbing essence from areas where it pooled in very large, obvious amounts, like from nodes or certain specific foods. With vials, however, I could go virtually anywhere and get some kind of essence, even if it was too small in quantity for me to even detect.

That didn't mean the essence would always be useful, though. I had to be careful — using an essence collection vial in an area without a single dominant essence type would just draw in a mixture of whatever random ambient essence was in the air, which was generally close to useless. And each essence collection vial could only be used once.

I knew the theory of how to create more essence collection vials, but that process itself required the use of essence types I didn't have. Thus, either I had to rely on Gramps to make me more, or I'd have to pick up other essence types to be able to make them myself.

I didn't plan to do the latter. While the essence types that could be used to make vials were extremely useful, I didn't think they synergized well with sword essence. Instead, my plan was to try to build a Breathing Point relatively soon, which would let my body do virtually the same thing — draw in small amounts of ambient essence from the environment — albeit only of types related to the essence in my Breathing Point. A Breathing Point wouldn't offer me the utility of being able to collect and trade more essence, but it would help me be able to support my own essence growth without having to worry about carrying more items.

Aside from all that, I'd also made sure to prioritize bringing essence-rich food and drinks with me. Dried bladeberries, jerky, dried fruit, lots of tea. I needed to make sure I was constantly taking in essence and processing it, and the area near the sword school simply didn't have the resources available to support my essence growth. Not yet, at least.

Food supplies weren't the last of my preparations for the journey back, nor even the most important. Even overstuffing my huge backpack, I simply couldn't bring enough essence-rich food to last more than a week or two. So, I picked up seeds, plant cuttings, and fertilizer.

Plants from a faerie forest tended to be extremely potent and could grow much faster than ordinary ones . . . but they carried extraordinary risks.

Ordinary apples were delicious. Faerie apples were even better — both in taste and in that they contained useful essence — but you had a tendency to forget that you'd eaten one after eating it, unless you took special precautions. This could lead to overeating, but the real risk was that if a faerie offered to let you eat *an* apple, and you ate more than one without realizing it, you could end up in debt to said faerie.

That's just one example, of course, and one of the more mundane ones. I don't even want to get into how dangerous faerie carrots are. I didn't bring any of those — the chances of attracting vorpal bunnies alone wasn't worth the risk.

No, I'd stick with the easy ones. I'd been both growing and eating fae fruits and vegetables my entire life, and thus I knew the necessary methods for handling the common varieties that we kept around our home. Surviving each meal wouldn't be a particular challenge.

The trickier parts were twofold. One, I'd have to make sure I could make them survive outside faerie territory, which could be a problem for certain plant species. The established garden area had probably grown things before, but I didn't know if my plants would be compatible. That's where my specialized fertilizer came in — contents are a bit of a trade secret, sorry — and I hoped it would be enough to let the plants grow.

The second major issue was that planting faerie plants elsewhere could, in theory, be the type of thing that convinced faeries that the garden was their territory. To ensure that didn't become a problem, I had to put up a boundary marker around the garden — essentially claiming the garden as belonging to me. The local faeries wouldn't be likely to resist that claim, since I was taking things from my own home garden (well, Gramps's garden) to plant, and he had already established that particular region as his own territory.

The boundary markers were simple enough — I repaired the fence around the sword school's original garden, wrote a series of glyphs on the wood indicating my claim, and then signed it with a glyph that represented my personal identity. Then I spat on it. No, really. People talk a lot about using blood to mark deals with faeries and other entities, but really, any bodily fluid will generally serve the same function. (Some are considered more respectful than others, of course, but spittle isn't actually thought of in a negative connotation in most faerie courts — it's essentially the same thing you're transmitting when you're sealing a deal with a kiss.)

Bleeding on the fence would have marked it more clearly, but it also would have risked attracting predators that were sniffing around for blood, which wasn't ideal. Blood might have alarmed the echoes, too, which could have created a problem. Also, I'd learned early on in life that when you have the option to avoid cutting yourself, it's generally best to do that.

So, with the garden marked, I got to planting things, making sure to go through the appropriate processes for each. I watered the faerie apple tree sapling I'd brought and spread a thin layer of honey along the area where it met the soil to encourage healing and growth. I planted the mirrorwheat upside-down, knowing it would flip over as it grew. I sang soft melodies to the silvervine grapes to encourage them to grow healthy and strong. I planned to play my flute for them, too, but it was better to do that at night.

Even with the accelerated growth of faerie plants, it would take a few days before anything had grown to a point of being edible, but I'd brought more ordinary foodstuffs along for this trip to keep me functional in the meantime.

With that, I'd dealt with one of the greatest threats to my long-term survival in the area . . . but I'd neglected something even higher in importance.

Water.

I'd found a nearby river with clear water to use, but it was outside the protective region around the building, and I didn't want to risk walking there several times a day like I had during my first stay. It was even more important now that I was planting things in a garden — I needed more water than just what I'd require to drink and bathe with.

No, if I wanted a sustainable area, I needed a stable water supply.

Time to get to work.

I considered digging a well. I had a shovel and I'd seen an abandoned well not too far away, which implied the possibility of underground water somewhere in the region. But while I might have been physically capable of excavating a pit eventually, it would have probably taken days to get something usable, assuming I found water at all.

No, that wasn't efficient, especially when someone must have already done the work. The fighters at this school would have needed water. Granted, it was possible they just ferried water from the river in buckets — it wasn't all that far — but they probably had a well of their own or something analogous to it.

I spent a solid hour searching the general area. There was so much overgrown brush on the outskirts of the school that a well could have easily been hidden among the bushes, but I didn't have the luck of finding one.

When the students came out to train, I joined them again, taking a few hours to think while I exhausted myself.

. . . Then, as I returned from putting my phantasmal wooden sword back in the shed, the skies began to darken.

I glanced overhead. Dark clouds were gathering.

Might rain soon. Hm. I should probably find some shelter. Wish I'd brought some barrels . . . if it rains frequently up here, I could just gather rainwater and—

I stared at the obelisk and something clicked.

If it rained up here often enough, I wouldn't have been the only person with the idea to collect the water.

It can't be that simple, can it?

I walked to the side of the obelisk, carefully reaching out one hand to touch the surface, ready to pull back if angry glyphs sprung to life to eradicate me.

Nothing happened.

Emboldened, I moved to the back side, putting a hand in one of the deep indentations, and as moisture gathered in the air, I began to climb.

The obelisk wasn't massively tall — only twenty feet or so — but if I'd waited until the rain fell in earnest it would have been a dangerous climb.

When I reached the top, I found that it was completely flat and almost entirely solid stone. I frowned at first, but felt around with my fingers.

There. A crack. And . . . something metal?

I'd seen some metallic parts on the outside, too, but I hadn't touched them. They looked like switches of some kind, and I'd worried initially that they had something do with making the obelisk more dangerous to climb.

But now, with more context . . .

On a hunch, I pushed on the metal bit.

Click.

The stone rooftop of the obelisk loosened, exposing a larger crack.

A wide grin spread across my face.

It's a release for a locking mechanism. And . . .

Click.

I relocked it.

Excellent. It still works.

I unlocked it again, then shoved the solid stone circle on the top. It slid outward so quickly I nearly lost my balance and fell, but I managed to grab the rim of the obelisk with my other hand and secure myself.

Thunder cracked in the air.

Need to hurry. But . . .

With the stone circle pushed out of the way, I leaned over and saw what I was looking for—

The interior of the obelisk was empty. Hollow. I could see more glyphs etched into the sides and bottom of the obelisk, their light still holding strong in spite of the many years the structure must have been unused.

Whoever had made this place had set up a gigantic water drum with a latch to seal it shut. It was wide and tall enough to store enough water for far more than just me — more than even a few students could have used for drinking. I couldn't get a good look at all the glyphs, but surprisingly, some of them were familiar — they were simple but effective designs for cleaning and resilience. The school had probably used it for their gardening, and perhaps other purposes aside.

I could figure out that part later.

For now, it was perfect for my purposes. Climbing up and down to gather water would be a pain, but . . .

As I glanced at the hollow interior, I examined the other metal bits I'd seen from the inside and realized I'd missed something obvious. They weren't parts of some kind of complex magical defense system or climbing configuration — they were faucets at varying heights, most likely for people outside the structure to drain the water for different purposes.

It was a small stroke of luck, but an incredibly important one.

As the rain began to fall, I hurriedly climbed down the side.

Water wasn't going to be a problem after all.

. . . I may have phrased that last part poorly.

As it turned out, water was going to be a problem, albeit not of the kind I'd expected—

I was going to get soaked. And, given the chill in the air, that could be a problem.

My meager shelter of stacked wooden boards wasn't going to keep the rain off. I briefly considered trying to cover it somehow, but there wasn't time.

After a moment of deliberation, I took the obvious route and ran inside the storage shed. It was still largely intact and the roof would protect me.

Oh, why'd I hesitate?

That's simple — there was a slim chance that I'd be murdered in there.

I was no expert on echoes, but I knew that they principally repeated behaviors that the world remembered. Thus far, the echoes had simply performed the same routine over and over, but a significant change in environment could result in echoes behaving differently.

Most likely, if they changed their pattern at all, they'd simply do something like take shelter from the rain themselves. Maybe they'd play in the rain, if they were feeling adventurous, or perform some kind of rain kata. I'd be excited to see that.

But as I sat awkwardly on the floor of the shed, I couldn't help but focus on the long-dried bloodstain on the wall and floor.

Someone — or something — had fought here, or nearby, and bled a great deal. If they hadn't died, they'd probably at least been very seriously injured.

. . . I didn't know anything about the conditions under which that had occurred. If there had, say, been a sword fight in the shed during a rainstorm . . .

Well, that would go badly for me, wouldn't it?

I watched the door carefully and sat as far from the bloodstain as possible. I hoped that even if a fight had occurred here during the rain, staying far from the area with the blood would avoid marking me as a participant. Still, fights tended to travel, and if I'd picked a spot where the fight had started, rather than the injury point . . .

I shook my head. I didn't have enough information. Maybe one of those books in the house had records?

It was worth exploring at some point, but I was still worried the place would collapse as soon as I walked inside. And beyond that, something else was on my mind.

The soft tones of the falling rain and the contrasting cracks of thunder brought fond memories to my mind. Days of dancing with Ana among the raindrops under the watchful eye of Uncle Eiji.

I remembered the first time I saw lightning flash from the sky — and Eiji catching it in his hand, holding the bolt like a javelin, then compressing it between his hands.

Ana and I watched in awe as he rolled the bolt into a ball, smiled that distant smile of his, and then tossed the bolt into his mouth and bit down with a thunderous *crunch*.

I'd known that Uncle Eiji was no one to be trifled with even before that — he was a Skyseeker and a shapeshifter. The humanoid form he'd worn that day wasn't his original body, but he wore it while watching me when I was very young to avoid scaring me. (I don't know if it was necessary, but I was very little, and Uncle Eiji was extremely cautious.)

As a slightly older child, I'd realized that even Uncle Eiji probably wasn't fast enough to catch lightning midflight — rather, he'd probably used a technique to deliberately attract it to his grasp. Still, such an action was a tremendous demonstration of his own Heart Point essence:

Storm.

Much like sword essence, storm essence was a confluence of a wide variety of types. Lightning, rain, and thunder were all components of storm essence, and each of those was a compound essence as well. That level of complexity meant that storm essence was extremely rare, generally only manifesting within storm clouds themselves. It was also unstable, generally dissipating rapidly back into the world when it wasn't claimed.

I'd often wondered how Uncle Eiji had obtained his first storm essence. Had he been born with it, perhaps as a bloodline power? Had he traveled through a great and terrible storm to find a lightning-struck monument atop a high mountain? Had it been a gift from a beneficent spirit?

I hoped to one day hear that tale, but much like Gramps, Uncle Eiji was often secretive about his past.

And so, as I often did, I thought of Uncle Eiji during the storm . . . and flipped open a book to read. My name day gift.

An Analysis of Destiny Mark Acquisition and Bloodline Power Inheritance, by Erik Tarren.

Gramps had told me that Uncle Eiji's destiny mark was mentioned in there. With the rain pounding around me, I wondered if perhaps I could learn more about his power . . . and, with luck, perhaps even enough information to seek out a way to harvest some storm essence of my own.

Be patient, I remembered Uncle Eiji's voice telling me. *The forward paw tests before the others strike.* It was one of his favorite sayings, and so, I listened.

I flipped the book open, then skimmed the introduction to get to the relevant section.

Upon reaching Torch-level, a person will go through a "Destiny Dream" — a type of dream where a person undergoes a series of choices that results in earning their destiny mark. Despite the name, Destiny Dreams do not require sleep. They are near-instantaneous visions that occur at the time the appropriate essence threshold is reached.

Destiny marks offer a second, parallel form of progression to standard essence development. While your traditional essence development deals with the "reflective" layers of self — the spirit, shade, and so on — destiny marks interact with what are commonly called the "extrapolated" layers of the self.

These interactions are complex, and addressed in more detail in the sections dealing with each layer of the self. In summary, however, the most relevant thing to understand is that once you have a destiny mark, that destiny mark connects your core self to a specific subset of your Destined Selves — possible future versions of yourself that are extrapolated based on your current abilities. It is this element of a destiny mark that allows them to enhance nebulous elements that are typically difficult to improve with sorcery, such as your proficiency and precision with specific types of spells, tasks, and weapons. While a traditional enhancement spell might increase speed or strength, it is difficult for most spells to emulate certain other benefits of training, such as giving the ability to play a musical instrument. Destiny marks can do this by granting you a fragment of your own potential ability.

Destiny marks also provide other advantages beyond extrapolated skills. Most destiny marks have a "signature ability," which is essentially a technique that is built into the mark itself. This technique generally provides a function that offers vast benefits to someone fulfilling that particular destiny, and improves as the destiny mark itself does.

Much like essence wielders themselves, destiny marks grow stronger over time — but through a much simpler framework than essence advancement. To improve your destiny mark, all you have to do is "fulfill your destiny." Basically, do whatever the role is that is connected to the mark. The more specialized the mark, the more specialized the requirements, though sometimes basic tasks still work in a less efficient fashion. A Fighter mark improves through any combat. A Swordsman mark might improve a little bit through general combat, but improves much more significantly through fighting with a sword.

The available options in a Destiny Dream are based on the types of essence in the body at the time the Destiny Dream occurs. Destiny Dream options appear to be largely driven by primary essence in completed Dianis Points, but there are accounts of options in dreams that appear to be driven by incomplete Dianis Points or secondary essence — these are simply rarer, and occur more often in cases where the dreamer only has one or two completed Dianis Points at the time the dream occurs. Destiny choices are rarely clear: instead, they appear to be metaphorical for the paths that each potential destiny mark takes.

Note that while having more essence types in the body at the time of a Destiny Dream generally means more options for destinies, it is also possible for the presence of specific essence types to disqualify someone from a destiny. There are several "pure" destinies that require having an overwhelming amount of a single essence type, typically meaning that is the only essence type where they have a completed Dianis Point. The Pyromancer destiny mark is only available to people who exclusively have fire essence Dianis Points, for example. While there are apocryphal cases of Pyromancers with other Dianis Points, these exceptions are rare and poorly understood. This can be contrasted with the Fire Wizard destiny, a hybrid destiny of Wizard and Pyromancer that may sound similar, but involves meeting the requirements for the Wizard destiny and also having access to fire essence.

I skimmed over a bit more of the introduction to get to more pertinent information. Eventually, I reached the part that excited me most — descriptions of specific destiny types.

First, I read over some of the most common ones — things like Worker, Farmer, Potter, Weaver, Blacksmith, and that sort of thing. While some of them were surprisingly useful — the enhanced endurance that Workers could gain had quite a bit of utility — they didn't interest me.

I picked out a few that weren't combat focused but still had some elements that interested me. Explorer and Tracker, for example, both could be useful if I ended up wanting to be a Shrineseeker or a monster hunter — both professions I had considered.

But, if I'm being honest, there was never much of a chance I'd focus on anything that didn't involve fighting. It was my primary passion — and it was what my Heart Point was all about. I couldn't ignore that.

I could scarcely contain my excitement when I found the section on combat destinies. Fighter, Rogue, Wizard, Healer — all the classics. From there, more specialized ones. Bruiser, Ranger, Knight, Berserker, Martial Artist, Bard . . .

Why was Bard in the combat section? I still don't know.

Those more general ones didn't really work for me, either, although I did briefly consider Ranger. Having grown up in a faerie realm, I knew that Rangers — along with Druids — were among the few destinies that the local faeries respected, even among humans. I'd even heard tales of a wandering human Ranger or Druid being allowed to visit the court every few years, but I hadn't encountered any myself, as far as I was aware.

That kind of respect could be useful, but I still didn't think they suited me perfectly.

Eventually, I found what I was looking for — rare and heavily specialized combat destinies.

This section includes some of the most sought-after forms of combat-focused destinies. Many have extreme or improbable requirements, often including either combat essence and a more esoteric type. Others specifically require sword essence, which is disproportionately common as a requirement compared to the other weapon essences, such as bow, spear, and dagger essence. There may be just as many destinies for those other weapon types, but the popularity of swords as a weapon has led to more information on their destinies, which creates a cyclic effect as others learn about these destinies and actively work toward acquiring them.

Another factor is that stories of legendary swords are common compared to other weapon types. Swords like the Song of Harmony, the Tenebrous Thorn, the Alabaster Moon, the True Blade, and the Dominion Breaker are often seen as goals for these sword-wielders.

Some silly folks even think about earning Luck's Touch, but that's absurd. No one takes anything from Aayara, the Lady of Thieves.

Spellsword

Essence Requirements: Any weapon essence and at least one prime dominion essence type.

Rarity Level: C+

Signature Ability: Spellstrike — Allows the Spellsword to infuse a weapon with essence and deliver it through a melee attack. While other destinies can accomplish this through training or specialized techniques, this destiny mark's ability both automates the infusing process and enhances the effect. Higher levels of Spellswords allow for complex weapon bindings, which can store multiple spells simultaneously, alter a stored spell into a persistent effect, or even permanently imbue a weapon with additional power.

Description: A powerful offensive destiny for those who wish to blend combat and magical abilities, with the downside of coming with generally low defensive abilities. Note that contrary to the name of the destiny, this can be obtained and used with any weapon essence, not just bladed weapons.

Breaker

Essence Requirements: Any combat-focused essence type, as well as striking essence, breaking essence, piercing essence, or a similar essence type.

Rarity Level: B

Signature Ability: Breaking Touch — While active, this ability continuously channels essence through the hands, discharging it destructively on contact. This is extremely effective against most forms of physical and magical defense.

Description: An offense-focused variant of the Martial Artist, frequently used by Skyseeker schools that have attack-focused unarmed combat styles. While this is popular for striking-focused hand-to-hand combat, it is limited in utility for any other combat style until higher levels, when it can be used to channel essence through weapons and other objects.

Blademaster

Essence Requirements: Sword essence, no other essence types.

Rarity Level: A

Signature Ability: Sword Instinct — Temporarily improves the wielder's instinctive ability at wielding swords and using sword techniques, allowing even an untrained Blademaster to fight with seemingly preternatural reflexes and skill.

Description: This is a "pure" destiny that requires that the wielder focus exclusively on sword essence. It's a specialized form of the Weapon Master destiny that can only be used with swords but has greater effectiveness when using them. The rarity level does not reflect difficulty in obtaining the destiny but rather a lack of popularity due to the flexibility loss by staying with only a single essence type until reaching Torch-level. The destiny has grown in frequency after the popularization of stories of the Smiling Sword Saint, a legendary Skyseeker who is commonly believed to have used the Blademaster destiny to the point of reaching the Sky level of essence development. In spite of the stories of the Smiling Sword Saint's prowess, modern scholars advise against taking such a focused destiny, as the disadvantages of specialization generally outweigh the benefits of the destiny.

Sword Lord

Essence Requirements: Sword essence and one of the rulership essence types (e.g., rulership, nobility, conquest, or royal essence).

Rarity Level: S

Signature Ability: Conquering Blade — Allows the essence wielder to manipulate the inherent abilities of nearby swords, enhancing the powers of their own weapon or diminishing the properties of enemy blades. At higher levels, this is said to be able to manipulate sword essence on the battlefield as well.

Description: One of the extraordinarily powerful "lord" series of destinies, this is a highly popular target for sword wielders of noble descent. Lord destinies provide both tremendous personal power and, at higher levels, extreme broad-area utility. This is especially true after the establishment of a personal aura at higher essence levels — see the section on essence levels for more on this subject. Due to the well-known potency of this destiny and related destinies (e.g., other lord destinies), all of the rulership essence types are generally hoarded by the highest-ranking nobility, making it extremely difficult for outsiders to obtain this destiny.

Storm Fang

Essence Requirements: Sword essence, storm essence.

Rarity Level: S

Signature Ability: Sword Storm — Allows the user to generate bolts of cutting lightning from the essence wielder's body and weapon, which lash out at enemies. This is especially effective when fighting opponents who are carrying metal, which the cutting lightning will lash out to in order to cut and electrocute whoever is carrying it.

Description: One of the few cases where rarity does translate into combat power, the Storm Fang is considered one of the strongest possible weapon-based destinies. They excel at both offensive combat and area denial, with their Sword Storm making them deadly to even approach for equal-level fighters with metal weapons and armor . . .

Paladin

Essence Requirements: Any weapon essence, any divine essence. Certain essence types also disqualify this destiny — notably darkness, fear, death, and nightmare. People with the criteria for Paladin that have one of these essence types are instead qualified for the Dark Knight destiny.

Rarity Level: S

Signature Ability: Divine Power — The Paladin gains abilities determined by the deity that grants them essence. According to legend, this often involved manifesting divine powers in their weapon, being able to conjure a weapon infused with divine power from nothing, or being able to manifest a divine companion.

Description: The Paladin is a "lost" destiny, one we only have myths and legends to draw from to discuss. It is believed that they were anointed as personal weapons of the gods, gaining vast and strange powers based on the deity they served. There is sufficient historical documentation to indicate that such a destiny once existed, but both the destiny itself and the supposed "divine essence" often attributed to it no longer appear to be found within the world. Most scholars believe that this destiny was lost during the fall of the Empyrean Empire. It is listed here for the sake of completeness, but it is not advised for anyone to attempt to seek out this destiny.

Hero

Essence Requirements: Unknown

Rarity Level: S+

Signature Ability: Unknown

Description: Much like the Paladin, the Hero is a lost destiny. Unlike the Paladin, there is some doubt as to whether the Hero destiny ever actually existed, or if it is simply a destiny ascribed retroactively to the leader of the legendary group that defeated and sealed the Ashen Lord. Stories of the requirements and powers of this destiny vary so heavily that attempting to list them all would require an entire separate book (which I, for one, have no intention of writing).

A few characteristics remain common in stories of the Hero destiny. Typically, the Hero is said to be a champion of the helpless, to oppose tyranny, and above all other things, to be brave, even in the face of overwhelming danger. It is this author's opinion that these characteristics share a single key element — they're the types of behaviors that are likely to lead any would-be Hero to an early grave.

For obvious reasons, I do not advise anyone to attempt to seek out the Hero destiny.

I considered each of these destinies in turn.

Spellsword is much more potentially flexible for offensive combat — I could pick up multiple essence types that work with it and learn to switch between them for different types of fights. Ice for slowing things down, lightning for fighting people with metal weapons . . . yeah, that suits me pretty well.

As appealing as that was, Breaker spoke to me on a more personal level. Not only was it an offense-focused destiny, which I preferred, it was also closely related to the destiny of one particular ancient dragon. I wasn't sure if Verthrimax's Iron Breaker destiny was a hybrid between Breaker and something else, or if it was an advanced destiny that required starting out as a Breaker and advancing later.

Verthrimax had been powerful in his youth. Legendary. If I could unlock his destiny, I was confident he would teach me how to use it. There was an appeal to the idea of being the successor of a legend, but . . . I didn't think his legacy was my own. He was, first and foremost, a fighter of flame and claw — I didn't know if his destiny could even be used with swords. And while the more basic Breaker destiny could be used with weapons at higher levels, I'd be stuck with only using it for unarmed combat at first. That wasn't ideal.

I was, of course, immediately tempted to seek out the seemingly impossible Paladin destiny. Who didn't dream of legendary powers?

. . . Upon further thought, I abandoned the idea rapidly. Not only would I be chasing an improbable goal, there was a greater problem:

I wasn't interested in pledging my life to the service of anyone. Not a human, not a faerie queen, and *certainly* not one of the gods. The gods had done enough damage to our world without more swords to wield.

Obviously, I wanted the legendary Hero destiny. It had the same mystique for being a "lost" destiny as the Paladin did, but without the downside of having to pledge my service to a deity . . . at least, as far as I knew. With so many conflicting stories about the destiny, it was possible the Hero did require service to someone or something, but I didn't know.

As amazing as the Hero sounded, I discounted it as an option almost immediately. If I happened to stumble on a means to obtain it, I'd try my best, but I didn't want to plan my whole life around something that might not even exist. I'd put some effort into research and ask Gramps about it further, but I wasn't going to let my heart get broken by pursuing it and finding nothing.

That left the Sword Lord, Blademaster, and Storm Fang destinies. They were tempting on a similar level to the Spellsword and Breaker, if not more so.

Sword Lord was extremely tempting. I'd grown up with stories of powerful lords and their absolute dominance on the battlefield. If anything, the description in the book seemed to be underselling their potency. S-ranked destinies weren't always the strongest available, but there was absolutely no doubt in my mind that Sword Lord was as powerful as the rarity implied.

If even half the stories about Lord Valissar Talis are true, this is one of the strongest destinies possible. He's only a couple years older than I am and they say he's matching people two levels above him. At this rate, he might end up being the youngest Talisian of all time.

Unfortunately, the scarcity problem was just as real as the power of the destiny. I didn't have access to any sort of rulership essence. There was undoubtedly some within the Court of Rust and Salt, but it was likely being held by the rulers themselves — the queen and her various children.

The queen has a daughter around my own age, so she's probably first in line for any rulership essence they have on hand. Still, they might generate more of it than the royal family actually needs.

Maybe I could trade something of similar value for some rulership essence if I find it up here. The fae can't enter this region, so if there's something truly rare, that might be an option . . . and, I suppose, there is that favor I'm owed . . .

I put that in the back of my mind as a potential option, but it seemed unlikely to work out. What was I going to find that had similar value to rulership essence? Even most of the environment-specific essences simply couldn't compare to the value of rulership essence of any variety. I'd have to find something truly outstanding to have any hope of a trade, and I couldn't count on that.

The Blademaster had a couple critical advantages. First off, obtaining it would be comparatively easy. I already had sword essence and I could get more gradually just by visiting locations I was already familiar with to collect nodes, bladeberries, and similar resources. If I was lucky, I'd eventually find some manifesting at the training ground or nearby, too. The singular focus sounded like it suited my mentality, too.

And who didn't want to emulate the path of the legendary Smiling Sword Saint? She was one of the most famous fighters in history, up there with the King of Thorns, the Blackstone Assassin, the Lady of Thieves, the Impervious Forest Goddess, and the Seven-Branched Sword Deity. They said that once, she fought a thousand potential challengers for the title of the greatest warrior on Dania . . . at the same time. And she won.

The only person to ever defeat her was her lifelong rival . . . and given that he eventually ended up as a god that ruled much of the outside world, that was a pretty big deal.

I'd grown up with stories about her . . . but I'd grown up *with* Uncle Eiji.

And Uncle Eiji was a Storm Fang.

I'd seen him fight monsters that stood taller than the greatest trees of the forest. In his youth, he'd fought off entire armies, crushed Fiend Lords in their domains, and outfought dragons in the sky.

He was, perhaps even more than those legendary figures I'd so often read about, my role model as a sword fighter.

. . . But was his path my own?

I didn't know.

I thought about that for many hours as the rain fell upon the old shed's roof. The echoes of the place never disturbed me, and eventually, I decided that they would be unlikely to come to me during the rain.

Eventually, I wrapped myself in my cloak and curled up to sleep, dreaming deeply of futures near and far.

CHAPTER XIV

SCABBARD AND SWORD

Weeks passed. My garden grew more slowly than I would have liked, forcing me to hunt a bit in the surrounding area. I had to be cautious to avoid the hunting grounds of the larger local beasts, but I eventually managed to find a few paths where I could hunt small game without competing with the native predators. I started recognizing the tracks and territory markers for some of the stronger beasts in the area, too, and that helped to avoid getting in their way.

The echoes reappeared as soon as the rain ended, resuming their own training routine. I trained with them, slowly honing my abilities through both exercise and the growing amount of sword essence in my Heart Mark.

Meanwhile, I also continued repairs on the largest building in the clearing using the wood and supplies I'd gathered. I reinforced it from outside at first, then very cautiously stepped within and worked on the damaged support beams. With more supplies, I didn't feel the need to rush my pace, so I didn't work as much on it each day as I'd initially planned to. I was continuously prepared to rush outside if something started to collapse, but it never did.

I eventually fixed the table that the echoes seemed to be focused on, then began the process of rebuilding the chairs. That was going to take a while — I basically needed to remake most of the chairs entirely, and carpentry had never been my strength. I managed to get the one mostly intact chair functional in those first few weeks, but I expected it to take months before I rebuilt the other five. I simply had too many other things to do, and as curious as I was about whether it would change the behavior of the echoes, it wasn't my immediate priority.

Between the repairs and the training, I was getting stronger, but not fast enough. I was building up my secondary essence with food and tea I'd taken from home, and practicing each day to increase the strength of my star veins and Dianis Points, but that wasn't enough. My only way of increasing my primary essence was through essence compression and another rapidly diminishing set of bladeberries I'd brought with me. As such, my primary essence improvement was actually slower than it had been back at home, where I'd long ago mapped out the local sources of sword essence — including my own house.

I needed to find a local external source of sword essence to harvest if I ever wanted to catch up to the standards of my home.

I could start bringing my sword collection up here, or build others . . . but no, there are already practice swords here.

Why isn't sword essence manifesting here?

I asked myself that question many times as I trained. Even if the phantasmal swords didn't "count" as swords for manifesting essence for some reason, we were specifically practicing swordplay — that was a textbook method of forcing sword essence to manifest.

Are the echoes absorbing the essence before it reaches a density I can perceive?

That seemed plausible. Echoes didn't have the same kind of essence that humans or fae did, but they did use essence themselves. It was possible that they had Breathing Points, or some equivalent of them. If even one of them had a Breathing Point built for sword essence, that could allow for them to draw in sword essence from the local area with each breath they took.

Breathing Points allowed for essence of the appropriate type to be absorbed passively, even when only small amounts of the essence type were available in the area, making them one of the most important Dianis Points for any essence wielders to develop. Since this was such an obvious advantage, anyone who didn't already have a reliable source of their primary essence type typically built a Breathing Point as their second Dianis Point. If they built a Breathing Point that was similar enough to their existing Dianis Points, they could use the essence absorbed through their Breathing Point to fuel their other Dianis Points' development, albeit very slowly. Someone couldn't advance at maximum speed simply training on their own through a Breathing Point, but it was much better than not having any essence source at all.

Maybe I should look into building one . . . but if the echoes are absorbing the essence, and they're stronger than I am, it wouldn't actually solve my problem at this location. They'd still absorb the essence faster than I could. Maybe I could get scraps in the time periods when they're not manifested, but it wouldn't be efficient.

. . . But wait. If the echoes are absorbing the essence, wouldn't I be able to sense it from them?

I frowned. My own essence sense wasn't very well-honed, but I'd been sparring with the echoes at close range. Unless they had some kind of additional essence type that concealed their essence, I should have sensed sword essence if one or all of them had an active Dianis Point of that type.

A concealment-focused Dianis Point isn't impossible, but . . . what if the sword essence is simply manifesting somewhere else?

The latter possibility intrigued me. If the school was tied to something else — like another location, or a specific object — it was possible the sword essence generated there was manifesting elsewhere or being drawn there so rapidly that I couldn't sense it. If I had divination-focused essence, or even just a Viewing Point established, I could have searched for it with relative ease. As it was, I was only barely able to sense the presence of sword essence in any given area. I didn't have any other kind of detection abilities yet.

I continued searching the area, heading farther up the mountain road and trying more approaches to the mist-shrouded forest. I'd enter it from other angles, walk in backward, try spinning around every few steps, charge in different directions at full speed . . . nothing quite worked. I thought I'd made it deeper a few times, hearing something distant that sounded like the scrape of steel against stone, but I could never be certain it was more than my imagination.

Fortunately, that failure didn't dampen my excitement about a very different type of progress.

After two weeks of repairs, I deemed the largest building secure enough to enter. One room was still completely collapsed and would take longer, but I'd shored up the damage in the other rooms enough that I felt that I could step inside without risking bringing the entire roof down on my head.

Finally. Let's see what we've got in here.

I stepped inside.

⁂

There were no legendary swords to be found, at least at a first glance. No weapons at all, really. That was mildly disappointing, but it was roughly what I'd expected.

The real treasure was one I'd already been aware of — the bookshelf.

As I'd expected, the books within had somehow been preserved by wards on the shelf. As I lifted the first tome, I didn't even find dust on the surface. Whoever had enchanted the shelf had been serious about preserving the knowledge within.

I flipped the book open in excitement . . . and promptly let out an exasperated sigh.

It was, of course, written in Artinian.

I knew a smattering of the language, but nowhere near enough to read a book in it.

A quick search of the shelf showed me that most of the other books were in the same tongue. I found a few in other languages, but none of them were ones I could read.

It was still a great find. Undoubtedly, Gramps could read some and tell me about the contents . . . if the books could survive being taken out of the proximity of the shelf. I wasn't sure about that.

I closed my eyes and sighed.

Why had I expected any different?

Disappointed, I sat down heavily on the floor.

Creak.

I immediately shuffled back up in alarm, worried I'd started a collapse—

But the creak had come from below me, not above.

My eyes widened as I processed that, and then I cautiously bent down and inspected the floor more carefully.

It was extremely subtle . . . but there was a thin line in the floor in the exact shape of a square.

This is . . . either an incredible structural flaw, or more likely . . .

A trapdoor.

I tapped the floor around it, then the square itself.

Hollow.

Very definitely hollow.

My mind flew to fantasies while I searched for a latch. Was this where they hid the powerful ancient swords that they very definitely had somewhere in the house?

Was this the secret passage to their deadlier training ground for more advanced students, filled with traps and monsters?

Was this a hole that led directly into the land of the Buried, sealed for ten millennia with the power of ancient long-forgotten gods?

Nah.

Turned out that it wasn't even much of a trapdoor. Just a hollow square without a latch that, upon being carefully extracted, revealed a small hole in the ground.

There was no ancient sword in the floor, no buried hero, no deadly trap or monster.

. . . But there was something. A slender object wrapped in dark blue cloth with a note fastened carefully to the top.

With trembling hands, I reached out to lift the note free from the wrap and . . .

Velthryn.

I recognized the language in an instant. The language of the center of the continent of Mythralis. The land my own parents had come from.

And as I read the note, my heart both sang and sank. It read:

Dear E,

No, it's not knives this year! You already have more than you need. But I did still want to get you something practical, and something that suited you. With your box, I figured you wouldn't need much in the way of storage, but sometimes it's useful to be able to wear something without having to reach in there, so . . . I hope this helps.

If you find this ahead of time, just go ahead and put it back and pretend to be surprised for me later, okay?

Happy name day,

—Siy

The note was pristine. My joy at finding such a treasure was tarnished by the sad knowledge that it had never been read before.

I closed my eyes hard.

I hope you lived and died well. May you have a safe journey to your next life and meet each other again.

I lowered my head respectfully to those who must have fallen many centuries ago.

That left me with a choice.

Did I dare to take an unopened name day gift for an ancient stranger?

You bet I did.

I unwrapped it immediately. A smile slid across my face.

And I fastened the gleaming black-lined scabbard to my left side.

I left an empty essence collection vial in place of the empty scabbard I'd taken. It was the closest thing I could offer to something of comparable value, and in spite of the fact that I wasn't in faerie territory, the tradition was a part of me.

Days passed as I continued to train. Those days quickly turned into weeks, then months.

My routine was split between practicing basic sword work with the echoes and attempting to work on creating sword techniques.

Within a few weeks, I'd worked out a viable formula for sandwiching various sword essence aspects into an improved Sword Hand technique. I could slice things apart with the edges, thrust with the tip, and use the main body of the blade to lift or otherwise manipulate objects. The critical improvement had come from figuring out how to adapt a hardness aspect to sword essence. I had three examples in my books of different hardness aspects — stone, metal, and density — and from studying those three, I was able to construct a rudimentary hardness aspect that was usable for my own essence type. I used that as an additional layer inside the deflection layer, making the essence blade more structurally stable.

When I lifted a training sword with my other hand and bashed it against the essence blade, the essence blade was sturdy enough to remain intact. The downside was that the more complex essence structure was trickier for me to maintain, in terms of both concentration and the essence toll on my body. That was good for exercising my star veins, but it would be a limitation in actual combat. If I had to deal with fighting a large group, running out of essence could be a problem . . . but hopefully, I'd be able to build my available essence pool before that became too much of an issue.

After getting that improved variation on my Sword Hand technique to a point that satisfied me, I began working on a few other experiments.

The first step was applying what I'd learned to try to improve my ability to project essence around an existing weapon. While the Sword Hand technique was useful for situations where I was completely unarmed, ultimately, I wanted to wield weapons and benefit from their own unique abilities. I'd daydreamed since childhood about unleashing the power of swords like Anathema — and to do that effectively, I needed techniques that supported blades, rather than replacing them.

Simply projecting my Sword Hand technique while I was already holding a weapon would, predictably, blast the weapon itself to bits. So, to avoid that little problem, I needed to work on a variation that projected the essence field around the weapon, rather than through it.

This wasn't too difficult — but even with that step, I found that the structure of the blade didn't work quite right. The deflection-aspected essence that I used toward the core of the Sword Hand technique's structure for solidity repelled whatever I was hitting before my actual sword reached it, which was the opposite of what I wanted — it basically rendered the sword itself useless. So, I restructured the essence "sandwich" to remove the deflection-aspected layer, instead using unaspected sword essence in that section, but retaining the slashing-aspected essence around the edges, a thin layer of hardness essence at the very center, and piercing-aspected essence at the tip. I was a little worried that the hardness-aspected sword essence would prevent contact in the same way, but in practice, it seemed to wrap against the weapon to reinforce the item rather than preventing contact.

Perfect.

When it was finished, I needed to give it a proper test. Naturally, that meant I needed a worthy opponent.

"Hmph. Insolent mortal. You dare challenge me, the ruler of all fiends?"

Ana sneered and tossed a goblet filled with red fluid to the ground. It shattered immediately, drenching the forest floor in what was probably some kind of berry juice.

I forced myself not to smile in approval. Shattering a goblet was a classic villain move, but smiling wasn't appropriate for my role. "You've conquered your last kingdom, vile villain."

"Oh? And who, exactly, is going to stop me? You've lost your powers, hero. You've lost your sword. And your dearest love lies helpless in my clutches!"

Darryl, never ceasing to be amused by Ana's theatrics, waved lazily from within his conjured prison. He couldn't be bothered to put any enthusiasm into his performance, though. "That's me, captured love interest that's twice as powerful as either of you. Seems reasonable."

"Quiet in the prison, prisoner!" Ana threw another goblet at Darryl. I hadn't even seen her conjure it — she was definitely getting faster at conjuring things. Or maybe just sleight of hand. Possibly both.

Darryl deftly caught the goblet, flipped it before the liquid within could spill, then sat down and took a sip. "Cragberry? Not bad."

"Oh, yeah, I got it in — hey, I said quiet!"

I took that moment to strike.

Don't judge me. I knew Ana was still much stronger than I was, and everyone knows that it's very heroic to attack an opponent with their guard down if they're extremely strong.

My wooden sword flared as I charged, my mind focusing on the pattern of essence types that I'd practiced a hundred times. As my blade flashed downward, it flared with power.

Sword Sharpening Shroud.

My sword flashed downward with greater speed than I'd ever managed—

So fast, in fact, that I didn't have a chance to stop it before my sword landed against her arm.

. . . And bounced harmlessly off a golden bracer, manifested in a fraction of an instant.

The Golden Raiment technique, I realized. *She's been working on making it a little more literal — and she used it almost instantly this time.*

I'd managed to cut a gouge in the bracer, but it hadn't broken through to the body beneath. As my blade bounced backward, Ana swung her gaze back toward me, then flicked her empty fingers in my direction. I jumped back just in time to dodge a wave of force that manifested in the area where I'd been standing.

I raised my sword in a defensive stance, eyeing Ana warily.

I'd never seen that technique before.

"What's this, hero?" Ana floated upward, golden armor forming over her entire body. "It seems you have some fight left in you after all. A new technique, is it?" She raised a hand to her chin, then gave a classic evil noblewoman laugh. "You'll find that I have a few tricks of my own!"

As a half-dozen phantasmal knives appeared in the air around Ana, I couldn't help but smile.

And thus, the battle began in earnest.

⊹⊹ ⊹⊹

In the end, the hero lay defeated — but the berry juice was pretty good, at least.

And so was the view of the stars. Ana, Darryl, and I lay gazing upward in exhaustion in the aftermath of our three-way battle.

Darryl won the battle after exploiting our exhaustion to break out of the prison. He defeated both of us with a cleverly laid paralysis ward he'd created by subtly shifting the wine on the forest floor with some kind of liquid-manipulation technique. He was the least exhausted of us, but still more than happy to recline and stare upward at the constellations.

"They say the skies look different in other lands," I said after many minutes of silence.

"Of course. Different stars, different magic," Darryl answered, turning his head toward me. "Don't know why you find that so fascinating. They're beautiful, sure, but stars are stars."

I shook my head. "That's like saying 'faeries are faeries.' It may be technically true, but it's willfully ignoring the differences to focus on the similarities. There's beauty in the differences between things, however small. You're with me on that, right, Ana?"

Ana snored loudly in answer.

"I'm going to take that as a 'yes.'"

⊹⊹ ⊹⊹

After that, I bundled Ana up, and Darryl escorted us back to Gramps's house. Given how late it was, I convinced him to stay at our home for a change. It was pleasant enough to have company that I convinced both him and Ana to stay for three days, after which I made my journey back to the sword school.

I loved my friends and family, but I had work to do.

With the Sword Hand and Sword Sharpening Shroud techniques more or less usable, I was ready to move on to working on newer and more exciting techniques.

There were a few general concepts for techniques that every essence wielder wanted to develop eventually — offensive, defensive, mobility, and so on. I hoped to be able to eventually build sword essence techniques to cover each category, but for obvious reasons, that was easier with some things than others.

I started with trying to build an offensive technique, given that it was the style that synergized with the essence type the most clearly. Even that wasn't as simple as it sounded.

I considered several options, most of which were based on stories of famous techniques or the abilities imparted by specific destiny marks.

I wrote down notes on each.

First, something to increase my striking power for individual attacks. My Sword Sharpening Shroud is a good start, but as Ana proved, it's too diffuse to cut through a serious opponent's defenses. For things stronger than I am, I'm going to need something more focused.

The Spellsword destiny has a function for delivering techniques through melee attacks. Can I simulate that and simply release blasts of sword essence on contact?

There are also famous stories of swordsmen projecting waves of sword essence at a distance. If I could learn how to do that, perhaps I could do the same thing at point-blank range as well, providing myself with both a ranged attack option and increased melee attack power.

Consider multi-sword conjuration and control, similar to what that Artinian Sword God was supposed to be able to do. Might feel too similar to where Ana is going with her skillset, but she can't complain if I pull it off first.

Iteration option: if I can figure out ranged sword attacks, experiment with alternate delivery methods. Can I do this without swinging? Project essence through my aura, maybe? The stories say the Smiling Sword Saint could cut people at great distances without even moving. Some sort of inverted Breathing Point technique to saturate the area with essence and control it, maybe?

Consider "charged" attacks as well. There are lots of stories of techniques that involve accumulating or converting essence for a few seconds or longer, then releasing it in a tremendous attack. Given how quickly opponents can move around, this seems impractical for things like duels, but maybe for fighting a single huge and slow monster? Figure out how charging up attacks works.

Oh, and spin attacks for hitting everyone around me. Try that, too.

I was tremendously excited to get started. This was the type of thing I had dreamed about since childhood — constructing powerful techniques that would serve me throughout my long and illustrious career as a swordsman. There were lots of options to test out, and I hoped to be able to rapidly develop each of them so I could move on toward creating other varieties of techniques.

I, of course, began by failing at step one.

I stepped up to a training dummy during one of the "off" periods when the sword school's echoes were not present, hoping that they would not find my experimentation disruptive to their cyclic routine. I'd considered experimenting elsewhere, but the risks of aggravating predators by throwing dangerous techniques around were too great. Besides, if I managed a working attack, I didn't want to obliterate too much of the environment. The dummies were reinforced with power that I judged too significant for me to cause them serious harm . . .

For now.

I lifted a phantasmal sword, focused sword essence into my right hand, and slammed the blade into the dummy, releasing the essence on impact.

The dummy was unimpressed.

. . . My phantasmal sword, however, was shredded to bits.

Huh.

I lifted the remaining bits of the hilt of the training sword, looked from side to side to see if anyone had noticed, then tiptoed to the storage shed to lean it up against the wall.

. . . They won't know it was me. Probably.

I coughed, glanced around again, then grabbed a different sword from the wall.

Hopefully the broken one will re-form later.

Anyway . . . developing a striking technique, take two.

I'll get it next time.

Three days and five hundred and twelve attempts later, with a newly regenerated copy of the first practice sword I'd taken from the shed, I took a deep breath and began my next attempt.

Okay, back to basics, and working from there . . .

⁂

Step one: form my Sword Sharpening Shroud.

I concentrated, projecting a wavering field of sword essence around my phantasmal sword. I'd continued to iterate on it throughout the process of creating my new technique, and currently, I'd removed the hardness essence at the core, since it was interfering with the next step in my current process.

Through repeated attempts, I'd managed to figure out that I could project more sword essence through the Sword Sharpening Shroud itself in a burst — but the results weren't particularly impressive. It hit somewhat harder than just a single attack with sword essence wrapped around the sword, but it also tended to make me lose my concentration on maintaining the original technique, so it didn't feel particularly worthwhile as an attack.

Practicing that same idea helped me maintain the Sword Sharpening Shroud better, but the results of the attack continued to be underwhelming, at least by my standards. So I tried a variety of different experiments, before settling on something a little more imaginative.

Ana would have approved.

⁂

Step two: cut my own sword essence aura in half.

This was the first tricky part, at least in terms of figuring out a good methodology, if not in execution. Simply shaping my Sword Sharpening Shroud into two different "blades" was possible, but for my particular technique to work, I needed to be able to do it more or less simultaneously with the next step, and concentrating on complex shaping while doing another manifestation was tricky. Even just keeping my Sword Sharpening Shroud technique stable while manifesting any other sword essence type was hard enough at my skill level.

I'd considered practicing a technique that simultaneously created two different Sword Sharpening Shrouds and maintaining that, but early tests proved that it was simply too challenging to make it work without having them interfere with each other or the practice sword. It was certainly doable, but harder than the shaping approach.

Instead, I'd come up with a way to cut that step and simplify the process.

There was an aspect of sword essence that came very easily to me — something that I'd used instinctively when I'd first fought against Ana. So far as I could tell at that point, it was something related to cutting-aspected sword essence, but somehow more specialized. I hadn't properly classified it, but the name didn't matter. I could use it as easily as blinking.

I sent a burst of that then-unnamed essence through the center of my own projected blade, cleaving my own Sword Sharpening Shroud technique into halves.

Doing it was easy. Intuitive. And something that, under ordinary circumstances, would be considered completely useless. There was a high chance of destabilizing my technique every time I did it, and I'd had to practice repeatedly to be able to retain the structure after splitting it. Even then, if I simply hit something with my sword right afterward, it was even weaker than a simple burst of unaspected sword essence would have been, since I'd removed a portion of the essence blade. I'd tried that anyway, of course, and the results were predictably underwhelming.

More importantly, I'd ended up "trying" it by accident on dozens of occasions simply because my timing was off for the next part.

Step three: shatter the blade.

I swung downward toward the dummy, executing the last part of my technique. This was both the most important part of the technique and the least intuitive.

Deflection-aspected sword essence was primarily used for defensive techniques. It was the foundation of many techniques designed to enhance parrying, enabling specific sword techniques to knock a weapon far off course, or to deflect magical projectiles that couldn't normally be affected by a sword swing. Both were well-explored applications — driving an opponent's sword off course was a tried-and-true way to create an opening, and deflecting spells was integral for a melee-focused Skyseeker to survive fighting opponents who hurled offensive techniques from range.

But through attempt after attempt at working with my very limited supply of aspects for technique creation, I realized that the second approach had potential—

If I could deflect an opponent's energy-based attacks, what would happen if I used it on one of my own?

The instant before my sword met the dummy, I sent the surge of deflection-aspected essence through my hand, just as I'd done dozens of times before.

. . . And stumbled as my sword passed straight through the dummy.

I blinked in confusion, lifting the still-intact phantasmal sword in my hand.

What happened? Did I make a mistake?

I frowned, raising my free hand toward the training dummy—

And watched as it slowly fell into four separate pieces.

Oh.

I glanced around from side to side, and, seeing no one around . . .

I cheered straight into the distant skies.

After a brief celebration, I glanced awkwardly from side to side to make sure that none of the echoes had noticed me murdering the poor training dummy, then went to my supply bag and retrieved some adhesive.

I wasn't sure if it would work, but I managed to glue the four slices of the dummy back together and get it into some semblance of resembling the original state.

That must have been enough, because when the echoes returned, they didn't seem to notice that anything had changed. I wiped my forehead in relief.

I'll . . . be a little more careful next time.

I wrote down notes on the exact final composition of my technique. I didn't expect to need the notes — I'd drilled each piece of the technique into myself through so much practice and iteration that I could scarcely conceive of how I'd ever be able to forget it — but it would be helpful to have my technique's first working form handy if I decided to continue to iterate.

I'd written down dozens of different less-than-functional versions, too, taking notes on where each failed.

Timing was critical — sending the burst too soon would destabilize the technique before impact, and sending it too late obviously didn't accomplish anything.

The angle and origin point of the burst were also important. To accomplish the effect I needed, I needed the two essence blade halves to separate at roughly ninety-degree angles from each other. Picture a V shape extending outward from the crossguard of the sword. Too shallow an angle wouldn't make a significant enough difference in the attack's output, but too much of an angle or a poor origin point could potentially make parts of the attack miss entirely.

The intensity of the burst was also important. Too little deflection-aspected sword essence wouldn't nudge the blades much or at all. Too much would destabilize the technique.

Many of the previous attempts had failed because of slight variations on any of the above, or combinations of them. I also knew that even with a "working" version of the technique, I still had a lot of potential work to do to improve it further.

I took some notes on some basic areas of potential improvement.

Improve power. This is likely straightforward; increase essence expenditure in each portion of the technique while maintaining the same ratios.

Improve range. Adjust baseline essence expenditure during initial blade formation. Marginal increase to essence for splitting the blade to compensate for needing to split a larger area. Adjust origin point of burst and angle of deflection to retain same angle of impact. Slight adjustment to deflection-aspected essence as well because of larger surface area.

Improve margin of error for impact timing. Consider methods that may allow for the deflection-aspected essence to be released automatically simultaneous with contact. Speculation: stability-spectrum essence may allow for this. While sword essence itself is technically on the stability spectrum, no currently known aspects allow for this function. Examine possible usable aspects for this purpose.

Improve splitting function. Splitting sword essence into more than two pieces would hypothetically allow for more "cuts" on impact. Adjustments required to sword-splitting stage to split into more than two pieces, increasing essence cost and technique complexity. Significant increases in complexity for deflection step; requires additional essence, simultaneous application of deflection-aspected essence to multiple areas, new calculations for angle and origin points for deflection, and new calculations for amount of essence to cause successful deflection without disrupting technique stability.

The last of these was by far the most significant change — one that would, in time, potentially help develop the technique into something much more impressive. It was, however, vastly greater in challenge than the other types of adjustments, save perhaps for improving margin of error, which I suspected would require research into entirely different aspects than the ones I had at my disposal.

Obviously the last two were the most interesting as well, but after a few failed experiments on those, I realized I'd built something functional enough that I should practice what I had rather than continuing endless complex iteration. I still played with tweaking the range and power in marginal ways, but for the most part, I just used the same baseline technique over and over. It was an impractical technique for the moment — the requirement of near-perfect timing made it challenging to use against a moving target — but that level of cutting power . . .

That felt *good.*

And with enough practice, I'd be able to use it with less conscious thought, maybe even quickly and intuitively enough to make it usable in real combat. If not, I could still take the lessons learned from constructing it and utilize them in other technique ideas.

Of course, I hadn't forgotten the most important part of technique creation:

It needed a name.

After a few days of practice, I settled on something surprisingly simple.

I called it the Shattering Sword.

⊱ ⊰

Over the weeks that followed, I experimented with a few other technique concepts, but I found most of my other ideas to be considerably more challenging.

Projecting sword essence at a distance simply . . . didn't seem to work. I could create a longer blade of essence and sweep it forward to hit somewhat more distant opponents, but I didn't have any early luck with trying to "throw" sword essence outward — it just dissipated if I released it from my body. That didn't strictly make a wave of sword essence impossible, but with as little essence as I had to work with, I couldn't manage anything significant.

I got a little closer by forming a Sword Hand technique and then using deflection-aspected essence to deliberately deflect my own technique away from my body on a predictable trajectory. Aiming that took some practice, but it was technically possible. I still ran into the problem of the essence dissipating rapidly in the air, though, and I couldn't make any significant impact on a target with my minimal essence available.

I tried to make a spin-attack variant, but it didn't really work out, either. The Shattering Sword was designed for an instantaneous power release, not a prolonged one. I tried to practice splitting the blade through shaping, then sending bursts of deflection-aspected sword essence into the split blade to send fragments of sword essence outward while I spun around, but . . . it was a mess. It didn't really accomplish anything other than some mild collateral damage. I simply didn't have enough control or power to make it a worthwhile area to pursue at my current skill level.

Conjuring and controlling swords was a completely different area of technique research, and while I did test out a few more ideas for improving my Ultimate Blade Creation technique, I didn't accomplish anything significant. I was getting better at approximating a copy of one of the phantasmal practice swords, but it was still vastly more practical to just . . . use a sword.

Charging up a more powerful version didn't make a lot of sense, since I was already continuously focusing sword essence around my weapon to make the technique work. Trying to build up another supply of sword essence simultaneously was theoretically possible, but it would have worked better with another Dianis Point to work with, or possibly somewhere external to "store" the essence I was charging.

Maybe I can figure out a way to work on that later, but I don't have enough essence to work with yet, and charging up an attack remains impractical in most circumstances. Better to keep this idea in the sheath for now.

I had enough to work on, and it was generally considered better to practice and improve one technique for a while before branching out into a ton of others, anyway.

Even with only one mostly functional new technique, I felt like those were months well spent. My curiosity eventually got the better of me, though, as well as my impatience.

Throughout my time practicing techniques, I'd continued to search the area for sources of sword essence to absorb, but I had no luck.

I wondered for a time if the scabbard had been what was absorbing the sword essence in the area, then converting it into something else. I wasn't particularly sensitive to essence at my level, but over weeks of practice, I decided that was unlikely — I didn't feel any changes within the essence of the scabbard even when I was wearing it, nor did it seem to interfere with my sword techniques.

Over time, I grew convinced there was still something else nearby that had sword essence within it.

There's still a sword around here, I just have to be patient and keep searching. I'll find it eventually.

I wasn't good at patience, but I tried my best. And it helped that the training itself was fun.

The sword essence within my body continued to grow stronger through my daily primary essence compression, but without an external source of essence to absorb, my Dianis Points' growth would be limited. In order to grow stronger at a reasonable rate, I needed to both continuously exercise myself and have an external source of essence for my body to process.

To make sure I was still absorbing enough sword essence to keep my body processing it constantly, I made periodic trips back home. I'd long ago mapped the local areas where sword essence could be found — the Ghost Forge, the Rust River, and that sort of thing — and I took the time to visit each of them periodically to gather enough to push my body to saturation before returning to the sword school.

I hated the inefficiency of it. Losing days of training to travel wasn't fantastic, and even with that method, I wasn't getting enough sword essence to keep pace with people like Ana. My sources simply weren't dense enough with sword essence for that, even if I cleared them out at every opportunity.

Still, the trips weren't entirely wasted. I used each return home as a chance to visit my friends, as well as an opportunity to brew more of the healing elixir for Verthrimax and bring it to him. As usual, he showed no signs of improvement, but I always hoped that the next dose would prove more successful than the last.

After a couple months, I began to attempt to grow plants that would generate sword essence in the sword school garden. This was an absolute failure, likely due to whatever was preventing sword essence from manifesting in the region as a whole.

Need to solve that mystery first.

So, I kept exploring. I continued training. Occasionally, I thought that Red gave me . . . or perhaps the scabbard . . . a look of recognition.

Was she the one who had given the gift? Or perhaps the intended recipient?

Or was it all just in my mind?

I wished I knew.

I continued repairing the house and studied books on Artinian I'd picked up during my periodic trips home. At night, I'd study letters to see if I could eventually learn how to translate the books on the bookshelf.

I finished replacing the chairs around the table. This had a subtle effect on the echoes — one of the first tangible impacts I'd managed — in that they sat down at the table for a few moments before they vanished. That was it, though, at least for the moment. I tried to sit down with them and engage them in various ways, but nothing worked. Not right away.

Maybe once I get the whole place fixed, they'll adapt further, but that might take a while.

Eventually, I finished digging out the remains of the last collapsed room. I searched it with great fervor, hoping to find another relic as valuable as the scabbard.

. . . But in that place, the past had been torn to shreds.

Once the destroyed roof had been cleared, I could tell that what I'd found was an ancient bedroom. The bed itself had been slashed in half with a single strike. The dresser had been blasted through the center with some kind of obliterating force that left nothing remaining of the section that it tore through. The remaining clothes within had fallen to tatters.

The most important place was undoubtedly the mantelpiece that was designed to hold a single long sword—

But the mantel, too, had been cut to shreds. And in that case, the effort was much more complete, more obviously deliberate. It had been shredded into so many pieces that it took me days to find and reassemble all the pieces necessary to even realize what I was looking at.

I searched the rest of the room, but it was all mundane.

Everything of value had been stolen from that place long ago.

It was more than halfway to my fourteenth name day when something unexpected happened.

Gray's sword flicked from side to side, a clear distraction. He was a fast little guy and loved to keep moving his blade to try to fake me out on when and where he was going to strike.

With his shorter reach, he always had to close in to tag me, but his superior speed made that simpler than it should have been against an equally powerful opponent.

I didn't know *how* he was as fast as he was at what looked like eight or nine years of age, but it didn't matter. Maybe I'd crack the secrets to his powers eventually, but at the moment, I needed to focus on the fight.

I'd been getting better at anticipating his thrusts and deflecting them, but he was still so much quicker than I was that he'd usually just follow up with a secondary attack, taking my knee out or flicking upward to graze my cheek.

. . . And the others were much, much stronger.

He'd beaten me into the ground more times than I could count . . .

But not that day.

No, when he came in for his thrust, I batted it to the side, then hopped back instantly to avoid his attempt to close the distance between us while my sword was out of position. He adjusted easily, ducking under my clumsy attempt to swing at his shoulder, then swept up toward my right elbow.

I'd anticipated that, too.

I released my left hand from my sword's grip, then grabbed his sword by the blade. His eyes widened—

And I poked him in the chest with my sword.

Gray froze for an instant . . . then released his grip on his sword, grasped his chest, fell backward, and played out the world's most dramatic death scene.

I burst into laughter. I couldn't hear him, but I could see him laughing, too.

I reached a hand and . . . for the first time, I was the one helping him back to his feet.

It was just a simple sparring match, but . . .

I'd won.

I'd finally won.

INTERLUDE IV

SEARCHING FOR SIGNS

Scribe followed in the swordsman's trail, splitting his attention between listening to the story and observing his environment. He'd grown up in a forested area himself, and thus the densely packed trees and foliage weren't entirely foreign, but the sheer variety of plants — and, from what he could glean from the distant noises, animals — was a heavy reminder that he was not at home.

Noting yet another unfamiliar bush, Scribe frowned, hastily scribbling a few lines and a sketch in the margins of his current journal.

Vivid blue berries with a hint of what looks like frost on the exterior, in spite of the weather being well above the freezing point. White flowers, green vine.

He was scarcely done with that sketch when he reached the next unfamiliar flower, a bright purple bulb with dark gray petals that seemed to be rotating around it.

Scribe paused at the strange sight, taking a step to look closer, but Edge stepped into his path.

"Don't touch it, you won't like the results."

"But I wasn't—" Scribe blinked at his own outstretched hand. When had he . . .

With a hiss, he pulled his hand back and turned to Edge. "Hypnosis? From a *plant*?"

"Hah, you'll see a lot stranger before we finish our trek. Anyway, hands to yourself."

Scribe hastily nodded and stepped away from the plant, making a deliberate effort to look away from those rotating petals. "What would have happened if I'd touched it?"

"Oh, spinwire isn't as bad as some, at least by itself. It'd keep you fascinated while it wraps you up. Some predator would eventually come by if you didn't break yourself free. The beast eats, the plant feeds on leavings. In this area, you'd probably have a reasonable amount of time to get free. The hypnosis isn't particularly strong against humans, but at that point, you'd have to contend with the vines themselves and the paralytic on their surface, which can get tricky."

"Spoken from experience?" Scribe asked.

"Never been caught by one, but I've seen animals get trapped. By the way, if you do see any animals caught like that, don't be the one that kills and eats them. That paralytic from the vines can get into the animal, and while it won't kill you, it's not great. No, I haven't made that mistake, either."

"Of course. You seem like the type that frees the hapless folks you come across in the vines?"

The swordsman gave Scribe a curious look. "Hm. Do I? Would I cut a plant apart, depriving it of its means of feeding, in order to save someone? Would that not be against the cycle of nature?"

Scribe gave Edge a dubious look. "If there's a cycle of nature, people are a part of it, and so is their agency to rescue others. Sure, maybe a plant needs to eat, and so do the animals of the forest, but I wouldn't prioritize that over a human life."

"You value humans over other life, then." It was a conclusion on Edge's part, a statement, not a question.

Scribe shrugged. "Sure. I mean . . ." He hastily accounted for a slim apparent mistake. ". . . humans and humanlike entities. I'd consider your fae friends the same. I would absolutely value a pixie above a plant. Wouldn't you?"

"Perhaps. But what if that plant is the bond of another fae? What if the animal that preys upon a trapped person is a spirit beast, as intelligent as a human? Is it right, then, to deprive it of its prey?"

"I'd rather act on what I know than speculation on the hypothetical possible intelligence. I'd like to think you would, too."

"Perhaps. But I've found that hasty decisions can often lead to critical mistakes." Edge seemed to consider that, then kept walking.

Scribe considered prying further but decided to keep his focus on the path — and anything further he needed to avoid. If he saw another of those hypnotic plants, he could blind himself immediately, or potentially break the effect through an attempt at deception shaping. It wasn't his area of expertise, but deception was a prime dominion tied to sight, and he did have some minimalist training. He couldn't counter any trained sorcerer, but a hypnotic plant? That might be doable. Assuming it was using deception, of course. This continent and its obscure hybrid essence types made a lot of his typical techniques less viable than usual.

That was, of course, likely a part of the point of sending him there. His master did enjoy making him grow through absurd challenges. And while he felt his usual bitterness at considering her, he admitted that access to essence sorcery was legitimately exciting. The advantages of being able to combine two sorcery styles were manifold, even if Edge himself had downplayed them somewhat.

He doesn't need the advantage as much, Scribe realized. *He's used to handling all these threats on a daily basis. For someone in my position, something like a single completed Dianis Point could easily mean the difference between life and death.*

For a few minutes of silent travel, Scribe's mind wandered, until it settled back into something more closely related to the topic they'd just discussed.

"Yes," Scribe said finally. "I think you would."

"Hm?" Edge turned his head back but kept walking. "Would what?"

"Ah, resuming the previous talk. I think you'd save someone from the plant."

"What makes you say that?" Edge's tone was curious, testing.

Scribe jerked a thumb vaguely toward the town they'd come from. "Back in Winch, there was a missing child. You went out in the woods and found him, saving him from some kind of giant wolf. If you really were so fixated on the cycle of nature, you'd have let the wolf eat the kid."

Edge's lips turned upward in mirth. "Ah, you've stumbled into another trap."

Scribe immediately panicked, jumping back and looking down.

Edge burst into laughter. "Not like that. I mean, in terms of assumptions in the conversation. You're safe." A few moments later, he added, "The closest pit is three whole paces to your left."

Scribe glanced to the left, seeing nothing. "Oh, now you're just messing with me."

"Maybe." Edge walked over, then picked up a rock, then tossed it at the nearby ground—

And a gap opened up in the world, nearly swallowing where Scribe was standing. He scampered forward to avoid the spreading hole, while Edge laughed again.

"Maybe not."

Scribe hissed. "This place is a death trap."

"Yeah . . ." Edge sounded wistful. "It's wonderful, isn't it?"

Can't tell if he's teasing me or if he's genuinely nostalgic for murderous plants and animal life. Is it better that I think that it's the latter? No, it's probably worse.

"For some people, I'm sure," Scribe offered neutrally.

"Right." Edge smiled. "Anyway, the trap. I did go out to the woods to find the lost kid, of course. I followed the tracks. Wasn't actually that bad — the kid had wandered off in the morning after the rain, rather than during it, and that meant muddy footsteps that hadn't been washed away. Got more interesting when I found other tracks that intersected them. Several sets. Monster tracks."

"Monsters? How far from town was this?"

"Not far." Edge furrowed his brow, shifting his hands as if measuring in the air. "Half a mile, maybe. Havens generally have a longer repulsion range for monsters than that, but Winch wasn't a full Haven. Their wards barely reached outside the gates themselves, and the kid wasn't on the trail."

Scribe, of course, processed the fact that monsters being that close to a town meant that it was equally possible that monsters were around at their current distance from the road. That wasn't a surprise, but it wasn't fun to think about. "What then?"

"The child's tracks shifted — longer, heavier. He'd started running. The monsters had, too. I followed them for a while. Then I hit the wolf tracks, and the kid's tracks disappeared. From there, I followed the wolf's tracks — and the blood."

"B-blood?" Scribe knew the kid had survived, but he hadn't seen if he was injured.

"Yeah. Wasn't time to test the type, but I had a pretty good picture of what had happened at that point — or, at least, a couple options. I knew I was limited on time. I ran until I found the wolf with the child in his jaws."

And fought the wolf to — no.

With how Edge reacted earlier, that doesn't make any sense. He'd led in with the fact that I'd made a false assumption.

"How badly was the wolf hurt rescuing the child?"

Edge stopped walking, looking Scribe up and down, seeming to reassess something. After a moment, he touched his forehead with three fingers in something that Scribe took as an unfamiliar gesture of acknowledgment. Respect, maybe.

"Good. You caught it." His tone shifted slightly, showing a hint of excitement, perhaps because he was pleased his audience was following his implications. "It was bad. Not fatal, but if I hadn't arrived when I did, he might have lost a leg. He was intelligent, but not capable of speech. When he saw me, he was going to run at first, but his leg buckled. I had to pull down my hood to show my face. That made the already panicked child scream, but fortunately the wolf recognized the mark and knelt down when I showed open hands."

Edge sighed. "I couldn't talk to the kid, but as much as he clearly didn't want to go anywhere with a faerie-touched, being in a wolf's jaws wasn't much better. I convinced the wolf to set the child down, then treated the wolf's injuries as best I could. We drew signs on the ground to exchange information — I identified myself as being with Eiji's pack, and the wolf understood. The wolf was a loner, and once he'd shuffled off the responsibility for the child, he left to heal, and I took the child home."

"And the monsters?"

Edge shook his head. "They scattered after the wolf put up a fight. I considered going back out to hunt them after dropping off the child, but hunting a couple monsters in the wild would be like taking a handful of sand out of a beach. Sure, it technically would make an impact, but acting on that scale is pretty much a waste of time."

"Even if those monsters are actively hunting people?" Scribe gave him a dubious look.

"'Actively' is a strong word. The kid stumbled into their territory — I saw their markers all around it. I never actually saw what they were, but if they were smart themselves — which they very well might have been — they were probably just guarding their own home. I don't even know if they would have hurt the kid. They never got the chance."

Scribe could see the reasoning, but he couldn't quite agree. "Doesn't that mean someone else could just wander into that specific territory later?"

"Sure. And I'm not going to say that monster hunting is inherently wrong, or anything. I've considered monster hunting as a career, in fact, but I'd focus on monsters that are aggressive toward civilization, rather than those that are just defending their own territory. I didn't have enough information to know if hunting those particular creatures would be right or wrong. I imagine the town, upon hearing about what happened, will be more careful about watching their youngsters for a while and prevent any immediate repeats. If they really want to, they can hire monster hunters to go out and investigate that area, but it's equally likely the next kid who goes wandering will walk in another direction and stumble upon something entirely different. Anything more than a little bit outside civilization is just . . . like that."

"And that's . . . just . . . accepted here? That the wilds are just overflowing with deadly creatures?"

Edge shrugged. "It's the way things have been for ages. Even before the devastation of the Ashen Lord's coming, monsters were common on the continent. There have been efforts to clear out certain regions, but that's usually the work of entire national militaries, and it often goes badly. Most successes have been limited to expanding the effective safe zones around existing havens."

"What about those monster hunters you mentioned?"

"There are several organizations dedicated to that sort of thing. Guilds, mercenaries, and branches of other larger groups. Most of those groups tend to be reactive, meaning they send people to go out after something goes wrong, or a major threat is identified. There have been more proactive groups, but they tend to be focused on the reclamation of ruined prewar cities, hoping to reclaim lost shrines and build new Havens."

Scribe could hear his tone shift a little bit when he talked about reclaiming shrines and cities — there was something wistful in that. "Is that what you're planning to do?"

"I've been thinking about it. Being a Shrineseeker was one of my childhood dreams. It's still something I intend to do at some point, but . . ."

"But?"

"I have other responsibilities." Edge absently reached up and touched his faerie-marked cheek.

". . . Something for your faerie court? Are you working for them?"

"In a sense, perhaps. I owe a debt," he said somberly. "One that is not easily repaid."

"Isn't that mark a sign that they owe *you* a debt?"

Edge raised an eyebrow. "That's more than I told you."

"I did a fair bit of reading before I came here. It's not always accurate, but . . ."

"You're not wrong. The mark is complicated. It's a mark of the court's favor, but it's not exactly a debt. It's a sign of both respect and responsibility."

"And that mark is court-specific?"

"It is, but most courts will take it positively, as will many beasts in lands adjacent to the court. Even in courts on the far side of the continent and beyond, I'd likely be treated better than an ordinary unmarked person — but with added risks and expectations. And outside fae lands . . ."

"You're seen as an enemy." Scribe gave Edge a sympathetic look. "Thus, the hood. But . . . I have to ask. Even from the hints you've told me in your story, I know you have some knowledge of herbs. Why not just make some sort of cosmetic to cover it while you're in human lands?"

Edge recoiled as if struck. ". . . I couldn't do that. It wouldn't be right."

"How is that different from wearing a hood?"

The swordsman frowned, searching for words. "The hood . . . it's a guise, something that is intended to be removed at any time, and for the wise or perceptive to be able to see past. If I wore something more concealing — like a mask, or cosmetics — that would be hiding the mark, rather than disguising it. That would dishonor the mark and my bond to the court."

That felt like a completely artificial distinction to Scribe, but cultural norms were just like that sometimes, so while he found it foolish, he couldn't say it was all that dissimilar from any number of traditions in his own homeland. "How'd you earn it?"

Edge smiled at that. "Which part?"

"Ah. The leaves are separate, aren't they?" Scribe nodded. "The first one, then."

The swordsman laughed. "You have funny timing, asking that now."

"Oh?"

"Well, as it happens, it was for rescuing a child who had wandered off into the woods."

"I imagine it wasn't a human child, in that case."

"No." Edge's expression lost a bit of humor. "They were not the lost children. They were, unfortunately, the monsters."

CHAPTER NEGATIVE I

STEALTH SOVEREIGN

I was knee-deep in the Death of Iron, reaching for a sword I knew I shouldn't touch, when it began.

It was a razor-thin margin before my twelfth name day, and I was behaving badly. Frustrated at my lack of tangible progress toward completing a Dianis Point, I was trying to directly siphon off essence from one of the sealed swords in the river. As I mentioned earlier, I didn't succeed at that until I was thirteen, so . . . you can guess at how well it was going at eleven.

Anyway, it was a bad idea, but that rarely stopped me. I knew that if Gramps found out, he would not approve — both because of the possibility for tension with the fae and because I could hurt myself by playing with sword essence beyond my level. But Gramps, on that rarest of occasions, wasn't around to stop me. No one was. Or so I thought.

Gramps was traveling with Uncle Eiji as a part of an escort for the Queen of Rust and Salt herself. They were on their way to another fae court, which was a rare event in modern times. Historically, the fae courts used to gather frequently for seasonal events in whichever court's power was at their peak — but that had ended hundreds of years before, when many of the courts had been sealed during the war. For centuries, our court had been completely alone, but about a decade and change earlier, the situation had changed somewhat. A second war between humans and fiends had ended disastrously for the latter, allowing humans to push back into a large swath of territory that had been fiend-controlled for centuries. This territory included multiple fae courts, and in the aftermath, our own court reestablished a tenuous connection with them.

Now, every three years, those newly freed courts met with our own in a neutral gathering place — bringing much of their power, including allies, to prevent any betrayal. I didn't know where this gathering place was, but I knew that Gramps was providing transportation. Teleportation was one of his main talents, and from what I understood, not one that the local queen shared. Historically, the fae courts had traveled through some sort of underground caverns or portals connected to ley lines, but that had been blocked during the war. I didn't know much about it — that was secret stuff, even to me.

Anyway, I was a child lacking any significant supervision, and that was rare. So, naturally, I was playing with deadly weapons.

My hand gripped the hilt of a fallen sword tightly, my eyes closed. I spoke aloud, trying one of the techniques I'd read about. "Sword, please lend me your strength. Sword, please lend me your strength. Sword, please lend me your—"

"Lieeennnn!" I startled, spinning around with a humbly honed stick held in my off hand to find Ana floating behind me. She deftly dodged out of the way, more than used to my "hit whatever surprised me" response. I started to apologize as usual, but her demeanor startled me so much that I fumbled over my words.

There was something on her face that I didn't think I'd ever seen before — not on her, at any rate.

Ana was afraid.

"I . . . uh, Ana? Are you okay!"

"It'snotmethat'stheproblem!" she half rambled, half shouted. "You need . . . come quick!"

I blinked, then lowered my stick to my side, as if sheathing it. I didn't have a sheath at that point, but that sort of movement had always come naturally when lowering a weapon.

Ana flitted off to the southeast, faster than I could hope to trudge through the water, and I felt my own sense of alarm growing as I shouted, "Slow down!"

"No, you hurry! It's . . . it's bad, Lien!"

I did hurry, but there wasn't a lot that I could do to run against water resistance. When I hit the ground on the other side of the Rust River, then I finally did run. I'd always been a fast runner, even before I'd started absorbing sword essence to increase my body's physical capabilities, but even with speed being one of my stronger traits, I couldn't keep up with Ana's flight speed. I wasn't even Candle-level at that point, and she was already getting close to Torch-level. Beyond that, flying was, well, flying.

I struggled to keep pace, my own alarm growing as we passed deeper through the southern woods.

This was a forbidden place for fae. I'd walked these woods before, because I wasn't actually considered one of them, but even I had to be extremely cautious.

The Rust River was the physical barrier that marked a clear delineation between fae territory and human territory. Traveling across the river was death for humans — the swords within proved that. But like I mentioned earlier, the area just to the south was more of a buffer zone between humans and fae. Neither humans nor fae traveled that zone without good reason, at least in theory.

If we'd been running to the southwest, rather than the southeast, we'd be heading toward an ornery dragon's tower. That, at least, would have made some sense . . . we'd been there many times before, even at that age. But the southeast . . .

We were running straight toward a human village. That was strictly forbidden.

I hoped for a few moments that we'd turn northeast, toward the Willowbark Witch — but no such shift happened.

"Ana, we need to . . ." I panted. "Where are we . . ."

"The border! Lien . . . someone *crossed it*!"

I stumbled, nearly falling. Someone had crossed? Was it an invasion? Had the humans come to push into our lands while our most powerful people were away?

If so . . .

How in the world were *we* going to stop it?

"How large is the human army?" I yelled. A sane person would have stopped running toward the threat with my assumption, but I felt my heart beating faster, and not just because of the sprint. No, I was excited to face whatever humanity had to offer.

I didn't have the presence of mind to be as worried about that as I should have been.

"It's not an army . . . it's . . ." She spun around, flying back toward me. "Stop! Stealth!"

I rushed to a tall tree, then crouched down. Ana floated down toward me. I wasn't fantastic at hiding by fae standards, but hopefully, whatever the threat was wouldn't know to be looking for me.

My heart continued to hammer as Ana landed on my knee, looking up at me. "It's . . . there are only three of them, but . . ."

"Three what, Ana? What's happening?"

"It was just a stupid game!" Tears welled up in her eyes. "I . . . Lindt and I were practicing our guises, and someone new came to play, and she had an idea, and it sounded really fun, and—"

My eyes narrowed, a picture beginning to form in my mind.

One traditional part of fae culture that had not faded even in the absence of contact with other cultures was the playing of different roles. The ability to slip in and out of different guises — essentially, characters or personas — was both a form of entertainment and considered a critical survival skill. Ana took to it much more easily than most, given that her specific essence types allowed for her to conjure costuming and props at a whim. She also genuinely enjoyed it more than virtually anyone I knew, aside from myself. It was one of our many shared loves.

We played with others fairly regularly, but usually close friends. Lindt, the witch's children, Eiji's pups, that sort of thing. Newcomers were rare, which made them both exciting . . . and dangerous, since they would not always have the same boundaries we did.

And at a time of the meeting of the courts . . . well, boundaries were naturally going to be pushed. I had, after all, been doing it myself.

"You tried to play with humans," I concluded. "Ana, you know that's—"

"I know, I know! And I didn't, okay! I tried to stop them, but she . . ." Ana gave me a hurt expression. "Okay, I didn't try very hard, but I told them it was a bad idea, and they wouldn't listen, and I . . . I know I should have insisted, but . . ."

I understood the problem immediately. "And you can't follow them. Okay. I'll go in and try to extract them. I can pass for human, I think, even without any glamor. This newcomer happen to be a glamor specialist?"

Glamor was a local term for illusion and shapeshifting techniques — basically, anything that could facilitate a guise. Ana's object creation techniques were on the borderline of what might be considered a glamor by some, but not by others.

"No, I wouldn't have worried as much if she was. And Lindt . . ."

"Lindt is a five-inch-tall pixie. Yeah, not exactly subtle. How'd they think—"

"He's hiding in her pocket. Or he was, but — Lien, you have to hurry. They *already caught him*."

"Oh, resh—" I stood up suddenly, throwing Ana off my knee, then catching her and steadying her with my free hand. "How far?"

"They tried to run and almost made it back." Ana pointed. "Be careful, Lien, they . . . they might kill you if they figure out you're not human. But . . . I can't go, I tried, but the moment I get outside the woods, my wings fail. Until I hit Torch, I can't go too far from—"

"I get it. Go get more help, okay? The witch, the dragon—"

"The witch went to the meeting, and the dragon is blind, Lien, he . . ."

"I get it. Find someone stronger than me. I'll buy what time I can." I reached out, pulling her close for a brief hug with the sudden realization that I might not be coming back.

I saw tears in her eyes as I pulled away. "Be careful, Lien."

"Aren't I always?"

I turned and ran, but not before I heard her whisper "Never" into the empty air.

⊱ ⊰

I found them almost immediately. That part, at least, went about as well as I could have hoped. They couldn't have been too far from the border, of course — Ana's sorcerous senses didn't extend beyond fae territory. At first, I assumed she'd watched them from the sky, but that made less sense as I approached and saw how dense the tree cover was.

I didn't get a clear explanation of how she'd known what had happened until much later, but the more important part was right in front of me.

Just as Ana had said, there were three of them — adult human men, the first I'd seen. From their garb and general appearance, I judged that they were just . . . people. Ordinary humans, townfolk from nearby. A farmer with broad shoulders and a heavy beard. The next was likely a hunter, from the thick leathers he wore and the axe and dagger on his hips. Maybe a woodsman? And the third, with arms thicker than my thighs . . . I guessed a blacksmith, probably, or maybe a miner.

I felt a brash bit of confidence then.

They weren't fighters, unless one counted the woodsman. No weapons of war. These weren't Skyseekers or veteran knights, just ordinary, fearful people.

I'd grown quickly for my age, already having reached nearly six feet tall. That gave me a reach advantage over most of them, especially with my stick, if it came to a fight. I was skinny, to put it kindly — others might have called me "scrawny" — but I didn't realize how much of a downside that was, having never been in a serious fight. The fact that most of those men weighed twice what I did made me think they'd be slow.

That was . . . a miscalculation, to say the least.

I didn't approach with the intent to fight, of course. I'd hoped to talk them down, maybe offer some sort of trade, or explain that the pixie was just a child playing—

That lasted precisely to the point that I saw that one of them, the farmer, was holding Lindt in one hand and using his other to pull on the pixie's wings.

"Stop! Stop it, you're *hurting him*!"

The voice came from an unfamiliar figure — presumably the newcomer that Ana had described.

She was, at present, being held back by the blacksmith, though she was making an enviable attempt to break free. I saw her jam her foot into one of his feet, and he winced, but didn't let her go — he just pulled her tighter and lifted her off the ground. She tried to kick backward, but the angle was poor enough that her leg bounced off him with virtually no impact.

As they looked at her, so did I — and recognition hit me.

The girl was about my age, but more than a head shorter and dressed like what I can charitably describe as a "peasant girl," if peasant girls wore immaculately tailored and perfectly clean clothes and an excess of "simple" jewelry.

As far as guises went, it . . . wasn't an expert effort. But if she was new to the idea, that wasn't exactly surprising. Honestly, I would have known it was off from the moment I'd seen that her dress had pockets. Everyone knew human dresses weren't like that — they were known for being deliberately inconvenient, largely as a part of human rituals to inconvenience women as much as possible.

That amateur effort at disguise probably would have given away the game in itself, but there was a clearer problem.

Her long, perfectly braided hair was much the same coppery color as the river water that still soaked my legs.

Oh, vek.

This wasn't just some random "newcomer." There was a reason this girl hadn't been playing with us before—

We were far too low in status for that, after all.

And at once, Ana's panic became clearer.

This wasn't just about Lindt, as much as we both loved him. When I saw her hair, I understood her identity in a moment, in spite of never having met her—

And I knew that if humans harmed her, it wouldn't be a matter for boys with sticks to solve.

It would mean *war.*

I ducked behind a tree before being noticed, cursing. I didn't have much time, but I took a few moments to circle around the humans. Not completely, just enough to look like I was approaching from the south, rather than the north — meaning that it would look like my origin point was the human town.

"Hey, what are y'all doing?" I yelled as I approached, trying to sound like a human peasant boy myself. "Let the girl go!"

The humans turned to look at me, just as I'd hoped.

"Beat it, kid!" the hunter yelled. "You *know* you're not supposed to wander this far from the village. Go home."

"Pa told me to never let men lay hands on a girl like that! You let her go, right now!"

I took a few steps forward, raising my stick menacingly. The hunter looked appalled at the accusation, though the others just looked *angry*.

"Look, kid, it's not like that. We found her hiding a *faerie*, see?"

I played at frowning as I continued to move closer, almost into swinging reach. "Is that what he's got there? But why you holding her, then—"

"Lien, help! Help!" Lindt yelled as one of the men loosened his grip on the pixie to stare at me—

Eyes narrowed from the men in understanding, and then the game was up.

I spun on a heel and smashed my stick straight into the blacksmith's face.

There was a loud *crack* as my stick impacted his jaw.

That would have been more satisfying if the sound had come from his body, rather than the breaking of the stick.

The man reeled back in surprise, letting go of the girl, his face bloodied by the blow — but barely.

The girl dropped to the ground and swung around immediately, slamming a fist into his throat, but that had even less impact than my stick had.

And then, as I held my broken stick in shock, the hunter was moving — far faster than I could. To my credit, I managed to get my stick into something like a guard position before he closed the distance between us. To my, uh, lack of credit, my attempted block did absolutely nothing as he stepped inside my guard and punched me in the chest so hard that I thought I felt my ribs beginning to buckle.

I coughed and fell to a knee, losing my grip on the stick instantly. The hunter grabbed my hair as I fell, painfully wrenching my head upward.

I tried to swing a fist, but he caught it with his other hand easily—

"When I hit you, *stay down*." He pulled his free fist back to strike me again. I raised my other hand to try to block, but I was neither strong or fast enough.

He would have downed me with that punch if a fist-sized rock hadn't hit him in the back of the head.

He blinked, dazed, his grip on my hair loosening, but he didn't go down.

In the moment while he was surprised, I pulled his dagger out of the sheath on his hip and pressed it to his neck.

"When I hit you," I told him, "stay down."

Then I slammed my forehead into his nose.

He fell backward, losing his grip on my hair—

And I stood just fast enough to be grazed, rather than floored, by a punch from the blacksmith.

The swing clipped my chin, and I stumbled backward, falling onto my rear but keeping my grip on the dagger. I tasted blood and my jaw felt off, but adrenaline kept me moving as the blacksmith rushed me. Distantly, I saw the girl rushing to Lindt's aid, only to get immediately clobbered with a slap across the face hard enough to knock her to the ground.

As the blacksmith reached for me, he stumbled, and my eyes widened as I saw the source—

Roots had reached up from the ground to grab his ankle.

Wood magic was something I was more than familiar with. It was common among kodama, dryads, and many other kinds of fae—

But it wasn't one of Lindt's essences, and I didn't think it was the girl's work, either. The style didn't fit what I knew of her, and she was down on the ground, not looking at me. I doubted her skill was sufficient to help from that angle.

As the blacksmith tripped, he fell right toward me—

And I still had a dagger in hand.

I could have ended him there, in spite of his greater strength. I saw it in a flash — areas of vulnerability.

Throat, eye, heart.

I could have struck for any of them, though my instincts pushed me toward slashing the neck. The latter options were less certain.

In a moment, I'd raised the dagger—

No.

Then flipped it in my hand, slamming the heavy pommel into the blacksmith's forehead.

His eyes fluttered as his mouth opened, apparently trying to say something before he hit the ground and went silent.

I didn't have time to wonder if I'd accidentally killed him. That was always a risk with trauma to the head, and if I'd managed to knock him out for more than a few moments, he might suffer lasting damage regardless. Knocking someone out was neither easy nor risk-free, but I couldn't afford to hold back more than I had.

I mumbled a "sorry" and pushed myself up, knife still in hand. If I had knocked the man out, rather than killing him, there was a high chance he'd wake in less than a minute, unless I'd hit him way too hard. The hunter was already rising in spite of my advice, but vines had begun to shoot from the ground to wrap around him, holding him in place.

That just left the farmer. Lindt was still struggling in his grip, and the girl was still on the ground.

I took a few steps closer, knife in hand, and looked him straight in the eyes.

"Let. My. Friend. Go." My grip on the dagger tightened, which wasn't actually a good fighting instinct, but it probably added to how intimidating I must have looked, especially given that my pants were soaked in water that, in retrospect, probably looked like I'd been wading through the blood of my enemies.

The farmer stared at me for a few moments, trembling, then opened his hands wide.

"We . . . meant no harm, but we won't be toleratin' no faeries on our land—"

"Shut up." I stepped forward, watching his eyes widen as he stepped back, away from my upraised dagger. "I'm taking the faerie and the girl and going to faerie lands. You will take your friends and go home. You will not follow us, nor will you make further trouble for the fae. Do you understand me?"

"Y-yes, sir, I understand."

I heard a groan from the blacksmith, but when I turned to glance in his direction — a bad instinct — more vines were rising to envelop him.

Fortunately, the farmer wasn't a trained fighter. He didn't punish my glance away by closing the distance to strike, as the hunter might have.

No, he took the chance to run, leaving the other villagers behind.

I stared after him for a moment, perplexed.

I had never seen cowardice like that before. Not in an adult.

The important part, though, was that Lindt was free. He'd fallen to the ground as soon as he'd been released from the farmer's grip . . . which was a bad sign, because he should have been flying.

I knelt at his side immediately, tucking the dagger in my belt, and my hands clenched into fists at the sight.

One of his wings was visibly broken. I'll spare you the description.

"Hurts . . . Lien. It hurts." His tiny eyes looked at me, filled with tears.

"I'm going to get you home." I picked him up gingerly, tucking him into my arms.

Then, belatedly, I turned to look at the lesser priority — the fallen girl who was stumbling to her feet.

"Can you walk?" I asked her, standing and stepping closer to meet her.

"I . . . I . . ." She stammered, her eyes wild, her body shivering.

Shock. Not good.

I did something you probably shouldn't do with someone of her status: grabbed her hand and pulled it to my chest. "You'll be safe with me. Stay with me, okay?"

Her eyes met mine, seeming to focus. "I . . . am grateful for your aid."

"Let's go."

I shifted my hand and began to tug her behind me, keeping the injured Lindt tucked under my other arm. And together, hand in hand, we fled the horrors of the human woods.

The moment we breached the border of fae territory, I didn't find Ana as I'd expected — but I did find someone else.

Cascade, one of the eldest of the witch's children, stood waiting with a dark frown on her features. She snapped her fingers at me, then gestured toward the bundle in my left arm, and I understood immediately.

Lindt had lost consciousness during the walk. Instinctively, I tried to reach for him with my other hand to hand him over, but the girl gripping it wouldn't let my fingers go. She was holding onto me with a knuckle-whitening grip.

Rather than force my hand free, I shifted Lindt awkwardly with my other arm and hand. Cascade stepped in with a frown to take him before I could drop him.

"This is bad." Cascade winced as she inspected his tiny body. "I can stabilize him here, but I can't heal him completely. I'll need to set his wing first, or it won't heal properly. Are you two . . . ?"

"I'm uninj—" I coughed midword, feeling the pain burning in my ribs again for the first time in several minutes. "I'm stable. Get to him first. You can help me later."

Cascade glanced at the fae girl clutching my hand — and the latter stepped back silently, half hiding behind me.

It took me a moment to realize she wasn't just being shy.

Cascade wasn't a part of the court. And after what she'd just been through . . .

"It's okay." I squeezed the girl's hand. "She's a friend. One of the witch's daughters."

The girl trembled, but that seemed to help a bit. "The witch. Yes, of course. She is . . . we, are, as always, grateful for her assistance in these trying times."

It sounded like a rehearsed line, but that was still improvement.

"Will you two be okay on your own for a bit?" Cascade asked, directing the question toward me.

"Yes. And thank you for the help. The vines . . . were those you?"

"Vines?" She frowned. "No idea what you mean. Need to go and see to this as soon as I can."

"Go."

A simple nod and Cascade disappeared in a blur. I wondered at Ana's absence, but before I could call out to her to see if she'd appear, the girl grabbed my arm with her other hand.

I turned to find her silently crying.

I . . . didn't really know what to do with that, exactly. Sure, I'd made my friends cry a few times, usually by hitting them too hard by accident or saying the wrong thing, but this was . . . an experience beyond the scope of what I understood.

So, I stuck with basics.

"It's going to be okay. You're safe now."

She trembled. I brushed tears out of her eyes with my free hand, which was, in retrospect, incredibly forward for someone of my status.

She responded by burying her head in my chest and bawling. This, I suppose, made some sense.

I'd cried over less than almost losing a friend, both before and after that day.

I held her there for a bit, knowing she needed the outlet, and trying not to feel too awkward about it. Occasionally, I glanced around to find Ana, but had no luck.

More importantly, I looked for whoever had made the vines.

That was . . . odd.

Other fae wouldn't generally leave the woods. They wouldn't necessarily have as much difficulty crossing as Ana did — she was a special case, because of her tie to the sword, and the forest itself — but going into human lands was an extreme transgression. One that would generally be punished severely.

That was likely why Ana had come to me first — that, and because I was already standing at the border to the human lands. Most fae wouldn't have even come that close under ordinary circumstances.

Had she found someone else that had been willing to risk crossing? Given who I was currently holding awkwardly in my arms, that was a possibility — saving her was potentially important enough to risk censure by the court. *Not* saving her would have had far worse repercussions.

But I saw no one.

Was . . . a human ally possible? A druid, perhaps, or a ranger? I'd heard of humans with both professions, but they were extraordinarily rare in modern times. But . . . if a human druid or ranger was present, that didn't explain why they didn't intervene more directly. They should have had a number of tools to resolve the situation with less risk.

As I continued to ponder, finally the girl pulled her head away, wiping at her own eyes. I reached into a bag at my side, fumbling for a piece of cloth for her to use as a tissue, and offered it to her. "To wipe your face. This is unimportant to me and I require nothing in return."

She seemed to understand the ritual words I'd used, accepting the cloth, wiping her eyes, and blowing her nose loudly. "I . . . am grateful for your assistance."

Apparently, she was coherent enough to remember to watch her own words, which was a good sign. "Are you feeling well enough to return home? I could . . . escort you."

It was a genuine offer, though I admit that I was conflicted. Escorting someone of her status ordinarily was something that would have appealed to me immensely—

But there was still a mystery to be solved, and that was at least equally compelling.

"I . . ." She folded the cloth I'd given her, then tucked it into one of her pockets. "That will not be necessary."

She straightened her posture, and with it, her *presence* seemed to change. I felt a chill run down my spine as her essence washed over me, stronger because we were still in direct contact.

With no further hesitation, she freed her remaining hand from mine, taking a breath, then slipped a nondescript ring off her hand.

And with that, she changed.

Her features sharpened, showing paler skin and freckled cheeks. Her ears showed their points, and her facial features shifted just slightly, making her cheekbones sharper and more pronounced.

The greater change was in her outfit. Her simple dress shifted to one that was luminous and resplendent, a mixture of the rust red, salt white, and purples that were worn among the highest nobles of the court.

As someone who grew up among the fae, I don't say this lightly—

She was breathtakingly beautiful both with and without her chosen guise. I'd noticed it before, but I'd had higher priorities. With the threat of death no longer looming over us . . .

I was *still* more interested in the mystery.

It's not that a beautiful girl didn't appeal to my younger self. But a genuine mystery to solve? A possible human ally to the fae, or perhaps a fae with unknown motives?

I had to actively focus my efforts on the lovely girl, rather than the forest we'd come from.

Fortunately, I didn't have to wait much longer.

She took three steps back, still watching me, then spoke into the air.

"Talisian, I require your assistance."

Instantly, I heard the sound of something like a wind chime in the air—

And he was there. A knight in wooden armor, just as the legends told.

The man was tall and slender, his pointed ears showing clearly through his own bright red hair. He wore a lustrous mask that matched the glitter of the silver blade at his side.

It was one of the few metal weapons allowed in the kingdom of the fae, for silver was their element, not that of the hated enemy. And the sword was not the true weapon—

That, of course, was the Talisian himself.

The Talisian Order may be known to you, even in your own lands, but I will summarize briefly, for I suspect the tales you've been told have been twisted.

Talisian is the name of a royal guardian — the one who is many. To be a Talisian is to leave your own name behind and, instead, become Talisian.

To leave one's name aside is not a small thing for anyone, and it is thrice so for the fae. I knew that this Talisian must have been one of great renown once — all Talisians were such — but he had set that aside, along with all his individuality, to become a knight in service of the royal family.

There were other knights of the fae courts, but to be Talisian was to be *more.* A Talisian was spirit-bonded for life to someone of great import to the court, generally one of the royal family. In these times, there were very few Talisians remaining — meaning that not even every member of the court had such a protector.

They were, without exception, people of incredible power, talent, and, above all, absolute loyalty.

As a child, I had often dreamed of being a member of the Talisian myself—

But even at eleven, I had begun to balk at the idea of sacrificing my own name . . .

Especially when I had yet to discover what my true name even *was.*

"My lady." The knight lowered his head. "You have called and I am at your service."

I felt something brush against me, then — Talisian's essence was extending over the area, creating a region under his control. This was, I felt, a prudent move, even if it set me . . . well, on edge.

The girl looked at him with an expression of something bordering on sadness, for reasons I could not understand. "You may rise, my knight. And be not concerned — there is no threat to me here."

"That," Talisian said as he raised his head toward me, his wooden armor gleaming in spite of the lack of metal, "remains to be seen, my lady."

The young girl stepped right between the two of us. "Cease this at once, Talisian. This . . . brave one . . . saved me from humans. At great personal risk, no less."

"From—" Talisian staggered back as if physically struck, his hand going to the sword at his side. "Where are the humans? I will see an end to this invasion in your name, my lady."

"Calm yourself, my dear knight." She stepped forward, putting a hand on his cheek. His eyes closed immediately, and he seemed to sway for a moment before they reopened.

That . . . that was an interesting power, I processed, feeling only a hint of her essence as it brushed over me and sensing another mystery. The Talisian was at least a layer above us, if not more. The young girl couldn't have possibly been strong enough to compel him with any sort of technique, not under ordinary circumstances.

But if he's bonded to her, that may render him susceptible to certain types of essence abilities she has. Especially if they have a subordinate bond.

". . . Of course, my lady. Forgive me. Your safety is, of course, my first priority. I should escort you home immediately." He glanced to me briefly. "And this one helped you, you say?"

"Selflessly, and with no request for recompense." She turned to me. "I owe you a debt, brave one. *We* owe you a debt — my court, my family, and myself. And it is a debt of life that we owe."

The scale of what she had just said was staggering enough that I understood the alarm in Talisian's eyes.

She had not only outright stated that she owed me something — rare among the fae in general — she had said it three times, with greater emphasis each time.

A threefold debt . . . with a threefold scope to it, identified in the central step, marking the parties that owed the debt as her as a person, her royal family, and, of course, the entire court.

And she'd called it a *life debt.*

"My lady, that is . . ." Talisian gave her a pained look. "I cannot gainsay you on this matter, but what you have offered . . ."

"I offer it truly and without hesitation. If he had not arrived when he did, one of my court, little Lindt, almost certainly would have perished. And I might have as well."

"If those are your words, then it is so," Talisian conceded. "But as I am both in your service and charged as your . . . guide . . . I must implore you to set reasonable limits on such a statement, my lady."

The girl, seeming to have regained some of her spirit, offered a fraction of a smile. "You would not abuse this gift, would you, brave one?"

I felt something change as she said those words a third time — a chill on my skin, a burning in my veins, and a warmth in my heart.

I couldn't discern it then, but I felt that something had begun.

"No, my lady." I bowed my head in respect. I was not of her court, but politeness cost me nothing.

"Before we offer gifts," Talisian noted, "it would be traditional for the boy to offer his name."

Realizing that somehow I'd never actually introduced myself to either of them, I felt a bit of embarrassment at my foolishness. "I will tell you my name, but not as an offering. I am a guest in your lands, and my name is incomplete, so it is not mine to give."

"Understood, and I did not intend to take it," Talisian said, waving a hand. "I alone cannot."

I understood my mistake then — it would be safe to "offer" my name to a Talisian, as he could carry none but his own. Still, he did not appear offended by my effort to remain safe. "I am called Lien by my family and close companions. To others, I am frequently called Edge, a translation of my name, and also a sign of respect to the great Eiji, whom I call uncle."

"You are the grandson of the traveler," Talisian realized. The girl looked at him in confusion. "Forgive me for my earlier behavior, then. Your grandfather is known well as a friend of the court, and you should have likewise been extended trust."

"I understand, and I am not offended. I bear no mark of the court, and given what just occurred, I can see why you might be concerned for your lady's safety . . ."

I trailed off straight into an idea.

Keen eyes watched me from both faces, but the girl was the one who spoke.

"You have a gift to ask for, then?"

"It may be presumptuous, my lady, but something does come to mind. You have offered me a threefold gift, correct?"

"With some degree of flexibility, given the circumstances." She glanced to Talisian, and he nodded. "You need not ask for it all now."

"That is good, though I must note that you have already given me the first part of a gift."

She gave me a quizzical look. "How so?"

"Intentionally or otherwise, you have named me three times."

Talisian gave her another brief expression of alarm, and then, without hesitation, put a hand over his face. ". . . You did, didn't you? And *deliberately*. And with *that name*? What have I told you about—"

"That's enough, Talisian. I knew what I was doing, yes. But since he did not ask for it, I do not consider it a part of the gift he was owed. And he has already repaid it, by telling us his own name, and asking for nothing in return."

"That is . . ." Talisian breathed heavily. "A bit of a stretch, my lady, for what you—"

"Very well, then. I shall give him a lesser name to use for now, if you feel that *saving my life* was not enough to earn it."

I'll admit I was a little confused — I didn't quite see the significance of the name she'd given me. Not at the time. I hadn't studied the right languages enough just yet.

"If he had *definitively* saved your life, then I would offer no objection, but as you said, he saved one of your subjects and *may* have saved your life, and thus—"

"Very well. Lien, will you accept a lesser title than the one you were offered, with the understanding that the greater title may still yet be earned?"

Sensing something political in play that I was not aware of, I discerned that it would be impolite to refuse. "I don't suppose I could ask to carry the greater title immediately, if I used it as a part of my gift?"

"I would ask that you do not," Talisian said, "for you do not yet understand what you ask for, and if I am not mistaken, you are not ready for the burden of it."

While I could sense that his primary goal was protecting the girl, I took his words to be honest, as fae ones generally were. "Very well. I will do what I can to earn the greater title at a later time, then, and accept the lesser one now."

"In that case, I will determine which title is appropriate based on what you ask for with your gifts."

I nodded in understanding.

A threefold gift from someone of her stature . . . I could have asked for almost anything. But I also knew that asking for something absurd would potentially earn me enmity, rather than respect, especially from Talisian. That was the last thing I needed.

And so, I began simply.

"I fear that I am not aware of the lady's name."

She let out a giggle. "That is what you would ask for? That is hardly worth even a fraction of a gift."

"*Take the win*, my lady," Talisian urged in an overly loud whisper.

"Let's call this a bonus for being willing to accept a lesser title."

Talisian groaned audibly.

The girl leaned in close, then whispered something in my ear. Something I'd already guessed at, but that her words confirmed.

I felt a prickle along my skin as she pulled away from once again being very, very close to my body.

. . . Which gave me, as a follow-up, something that was admittedly an eleven-year-old's idea of a reasonable idea.

"Is there anything else you wish of me?" she asked, still standing very near.

"There's . . . something, actually. I have long been a guest in these woods, but if you would consider it appropriate, I would rather be known as a friend."

"Such would be a traditional reward, true," she mused aloud, as if she hadn't been suggesting it herself, "and I can think of a few ways in which such a mark could be given. Can you think of one you would like?"

I could see the mischief, then. The playfulness that had gotten her into trouble in the first place, wandering into places she had no business being.

That was the first thing I truly liked about her.

"Well . . ." I glanced at Talisian, who was trying to stifle a laugh, and then said to her, "I wouldn't want to presume, but . . . how about a kiss, princess?"

She blushed bright scarlet—

Stepped closer, ignoring a knight's objection—

Stood up on her toes—

And with surprising swiftness, pressed her lips against my cheek.

My eyes closed as I felt the warmth of her against me. She must have done the same; our eyes opened again together.

Then she smiled, blushed again, and said, with all of the regality that she had remaining, "WellI'dbetterbegoingnowbye!"

And then she turned and bolted into the woods like a deer.

I stared after her, blinking rapidly.

Talisian watched her go for a moment, then leaned in close to me. "Nice going, kid. I think she likes you. You're in for some *real* trouble now."

Then he clapped me on the shoulder once, laughed, and vanished in a flare of rainbow-colored lights.

I patted my cheek in disbelief.

That . . . that was my first kiss.

It wasn't, technically. I'd been kissed by people who were family before, and *possibly* by Ana while playing, but neither of us thought that counted, so it didn't.

I wasn't entirely sure that being kissed on the cheek counted, either, but in my estimation, if it had managed to embarrass a princess, that was probably good enough.

That was significant enough that it managed to distract me for at least at least three seconds before I did the most absurd thing imaginable and ran straight back in the direction of the human town.

I still had a mystery to solve, and the trail was growing colder with every passing moment.

⊱ ⊰

I retraced my own steps, first at a run, then at a jog to conserve speed and to lower the risk of stabbing myself in the leg with the knife I was still wearing in my belt.

It was only at that point that I realized the very likely *iron* knife was probably why Talisian had been so cautious when he'd first arrived. Honestly, I was incredibly lucky he hadn't punished me for bringing it into faerie lands.

Either he was very nice, or he'd prioritized the happiness of the princess. Possibly both.

I'll abandon it at the border of faerie lands later. For now, I might need it.

I was a little reticent to leave it behind — it was the closest thing to a metal sword I'd managed to find up to that point, and technically, I'd earned it in battle. I could have argued that to the fae, and they might have let me keep it, given that I'd taken it from humans in the defense of a faerie. That was a pretty good argument — but one that would cost me more than I'd gain out of it.

I might be able to ask for a sword as a part of my reward, I considered. But that would come with obligations. *Asking for a sword directly from the princess would, symbolically, be like offering myself into her service.*

I groaned at that layer of complexity. I'd consider workarounds at some point . . . but I had a more immediate thing to think about.

Where would the vine-maker go?

I returned to the site of the fight first, using extreme caution. It was nearly nightfall, which made hiding easier, but it also made the next part harder—

Searching for tracks.

I swept the area, searching vantage points that might have been used for someone watching the fight from a distance.

I knew that my efforts might have been futile. If whoever helped us was powerful enough, concealing tracks was possible with many types of magic. And if they were a fae helper, well, they very well could have just been flying.

Fortunately, and confusingly, the tracks weren't hidden at all.

I found them easily — a pair of footsteps that were easily discerned from both my own and those of the human men. Both because they were slightly smaller than my own footsteps, and because they were steps taken by bare feet.

Humanoid, so they could be a human child around my age, or a fae with a humanlike body. Which narrows things, but only slightly.

Teenaged human druid or ranger? Fae willing to break the rules?

Either was possible, or numerous other options. I didn't need to narrow it further right away, though — I needed to follow the tracks.

They were, fortunately, easy to follow. The muddy ground left an easy trail, and there was no obvious effort to conceal the steps. They were moving at speed, both to the location and away from it, rather than attempting concealment.

That's . . . odd. If they were moving swiftly, why did no one see them? Misdirection, maybe? A false trail? Or . . .

I got my answer soon enough, when a vine snagged my ankle and I nearly face-planted into the mud.

I say "nearly" because, in this instance, I was actually ready for that exact move.

As the vine gripped my ankle, I controlled my fall. A proper forward roll wouldn't work with my ankle grappled, so instead, I simply caught myself on both hands, pushed up, and flipped myself over, kicking a second vine as it rose. My hand went to my knife, and I nearly pulled it to cut the first vine, but instead, I refused further violence.

"Stop! I'm a friend. You helped us earlier."

The first vine tightened around my ankle painfully, but the second paused in midair.

"F-friend?" came a quiet distant voice, uncertain.

"Yes, friend. You helped me save my friends, and therefore, you're a friend."

Simple logic, really, but it was sometimes easiest to communicate simple concepts, especially with someone who was unknown.

After a few moments, the vine let go of my ankle. I rubbed at it painfully, looking around with a frown, seeing no one.

"Why follow if . . . friend?" came the voice.

"I wanted to tell you that I appreciated the help. And, if I'm being honest, I wanted to see who helped us."

Another pause, and then I heard footsteps approaching. "No iron. Bad."

"Right. I'll throw it away. I'm going to take it off my belt slowly." Cautiously, I removed the dagger and tossed it into the mud. "I took it off one of the people we were fighting."

"Bad people. I saw. You helped glowy-friend."

I raised an eyebrow at the stilted language. I pushed myself to a seated position — and found myself nearly nose-to-nose with someone new. A girl who was covered in vines, leaves, and mud. She smelled like pine needles and the sky after a storm. She must have used some sort of concealment essence to sneak up on me so easily.

"See me, now." She smiled softly. "Hello, friend."

"Hello." I smiled in return. "I'm Lien." I extended a hand toward her.

She looked at my hand curiously, then leaned to sniff at it. "Nice hand." She poked at it with a finger. "Oh! Very soft skin. I like." She beamed at me. "You're hurt."

I blinked, feeling the pain in my ribs again that I'd been ignoring. "You can tell?"

She nodded hastily. "Touched skin. Oh! Hurt when bad man hit you. I heal."

She pressed a hand against my chest. A warm light enveloped me and I gasped as the pain flared, then vanished.

I'd been magically healed before, but rarely so directly. I typically relied on potions and healing water. There were plenty of healers among the fae, but Gramps didn't like me to rely on them — he felt magical healing made it less likely for me to learn lessons — so I'd only been healed like that for serious injuries.

"Th-thank you. I appreciate that. Do I owe you anything?"

She blinked at me. "Why?"

I looked at her more closely. Her ears were pointed, like I'd expect from fae, not from a human. Less pronounced than usual, maybe, but definitely pointed. But she didn't know about fae gift culture, and her language skills were . . .

"Among the fae — that is, the people nearby with the pointed ears like yours, and the people we saved — when you do something nice for someone, they are supposed to do something for you in return."

"Oh!" She brightened. "That's . . . nice! I, uh, like flowers, and sometimes meat, and sweet things, and . . ." She frowned. "Pretty rocks?"

I laughed. "Let me see . . ."

I went through my bag, finding something easily — an acorn filled with honey, half-splattered with mud during my fall. I wiped it off. "There's something in here called honey. It's a sweet thing. Do you know it?"

She shook her head. "Hon . . . ey?"

I opened the acorn so she didn't try to eat the shell, handed it to her, then grabbed a second one from my bag and opened it, licking the honey to demonstrate.

She frowned, then mirrored the gesture. Her eyes widened. "Sweet thing!"

I couldn't help but smile at her reaction. She glanced at me again, then feverishly consumed the honey.

". . . More?"

I smiled, then handed her a handful of acorns — all I had left. I owed her a lot more than that, after all.

She accepted them, clutching the acorns to her chest like treasure.

"What are you doing out here by yourself?"

Her expression sank.

"Not allowed." She pointed into the distance, toward the human town. "Bad people."

I frowned, thinking again of her ears, and her garb, and the brown of her hair. She looked like a dryad, if perhaps a strangely . . . fleshy one. With fewer obvious signs of her wooden nature than most. I gestured toward the faerie court. "What about that way?"

"Not allowed." She frowned. "Not . . . my people."

I blinked at that.

Is . . . she a fae from another court?

And if that's the case . . . how in the queen's name did she end up here?

She was far too young to be out on her own.

"Your parents?" I asked.

She only seemed to half understand me. "Tree far away. No one there."

I felt my heart ache at her statement. "And there's no one to look after you?"

She frowned. "Wolf-friends. They not here now."

Oh. Eiji's people have been looking after her? That makes a degree of sense, and I know he is gone right now, but . . .

No, she helped as much as I did with that incident.

I made a choice then, standing up slowly. She stood with me, her eyes full of panic as she dropped an acorn, but I caught it. "Here, I'll help carry those and give them back to you la — no, never mind. This is better."

I took off my belt, took off a pouch, and opened it for her. "You can put the acorns in here, then just carry the bag."

She accepted it without question, putting the acorns inside. "Leaving, friend Lien?" I could sense a hint of sadness in her tone.

"Not alone." I told her. "Not if you'll come with me." I extended a hand to her. When she still didn't understand, I took her hand in mine.

". . . Warm." She looked at me in confusion. "Where going?"

I gestured to the fae court. "This way."

"Not . . . my people," she insisted. "They . . . not let me in."

"Oh, they will now," I told her. "After all, a princess still owes me two more favors."

"Two more flavors?" she asked. "Like . . . more sweet things?"

I laughed, thinking of the kiss on my cheek. "You know, there might be."

"I go with you, then!"

I laughed. She was misunderstanding a bit, but I would make sure she had new sweets to try — she'd earned them.

We walked through the woods together, while she awkwardly began to pluck acorns out of the bag and pop them in her mouth with a single free hand.

"Before I introduce you to the court, I'm going to need something."

"My sweets?" She looked at me, briefly concerned.

"No, those are yours. What is your name?"

"Oh!" She brightened. "Silly me. Near my tree, there is stone. It says, 'For the . . . Falynne,' I think?"

For the fallen? Her tree . . . it's near a gravestone?

"I . . . don't think that's your name."

She scrunched her nose. "It's not? Oh. Other name wolfies gave me, then. I like that one, too."

She spun to look at me, with a big grin on her face and honey on her lips.

"They call me Eliree."

INTERLUDE V

SUBTEXT

As the swordsman finished that part of his tale, he gestured toward the base of a tree. Scribe, understanding the gesture, sat down to rest his aching legs.

It had been a long walk.

The swordsman sat down across from him, immediately pulling out a flask of water to drink. Scribe didn't blame him — it had been a long walk, and a lot of talking.

Scribe took a smaller drink of his own. Then, half-consciously, he reached up and fiddled with the earring on his left ear. "So, you got a kiss from a princess. On the cheek — meaning that's the source of the mark?"

Edge nodded. "The first leaf of it, at least. I earned the other leaves later."

"Ah, a changing mark, then, like an attunement. And that's how you earned the name Edge of the Woods as well, I take it? That's the lesser title you were promised?"

"Right. When I walked back into the forest, Talisian showed up immediately, questioning why I'd left and returned with a stranger. I explained, and he agreed to help Eliree in exchange for one of the favors I was owed."

"Fascinating. And that was the first encounter with Eliree? You said she was your first love, yes?"

"She was." The swordsman let out a deep breath. "In a way, at least."

"I find it amusing that you discount the *princess who kissed you* in that assessment."

Edge laughed. "That was more of a ritual than a romantic gesture. And it was on the cheek."

"You did emphasize the fact that she was blushing. Twice."

"Okay, so yes, there was clearly a romantic subtext, sure. But I didn't see her again for years, and Eliree . . . when I introduced her to the court, she was thrilled to be able to meet new people, but she was still very shy to most. The court gave her a 'guest tree' in the Brightwood — a tree that had lost its own dryad years earlier, which she was able to form a weaker binding to. That made her a sort of honorary Brightwood fae, a middle ground between being a guest and a local. A status not unlike my own, as one newly marked by the court. She was well-liked, and even loved by some — Auntie Temper basically adopted her the moment that I introduced them. But she'd been lonely for a long time, and she didn't feel quite like she was one of them. Not exactly."

Edge sighed. "I knew the feeling. It's . . . not the same, being an outsider, even if you're treated well. And as we got to know each other, we understood that we had something in common, that no one else our age shared."

"Ah. The commonalities of outsiders. That seems a good reason for an early bond." Scribe nodded. "Still, you could have pursued a *princess*."

Edge laughed. "Who says I didn't? But we'll get to that later. To answer your earlier question more clearly, yes, that's how I earned my title. After Talisian agreed to help Eliree, he told me something else, though. 'You did well today, young Lien. It's a lonely thing, living on the boundaries, never quite belonging — but you made it your strength today, and more than once. For that, I offer my gratitude, and fulfill a princess's promise on her behalf. By my will, by my word, and by my wish, I name you Edge of the Woods.'"

The swordsman exhaled deeply. "When I went home that night, I was glowing with pride. I'd earned a faerie's kiss and a title. I'd made a friend in Eliree. And . . . more than that, I'd done something good. Something *brave*. At the time . . . I couldn't have imagined the consequences."

Scribe saw the swordsman's shoulders slump, more than they had since he'd first seen the man turned aside by the villagers in the aftermath of the fire.

"Consequences?" Scribe frowned, searching. "That was . . . what, maybe seven or eight years ago?" Something clicked. "Wait. The inquisition? That began a few years later, though, wasn't it?"

"It didn't start that day." He closed his eyes for a moment. "Not exactly. But that was the spark. Perhaps if we'd seen it more clearly, it could have been stopped before it spread."

Scribe looked at the swordsman a little more closely, seeing, perhaps for the first time, the burden the young man was trying to carry. "You can't possibly blame yourself for what happened that day. Those children were out playing before you arrived — and while you helped to rescue them, I doubt 'child with stick' was the image that helped drive the people into a fervor."

"No." Edge gave a bitter laugh. "That part wasn't my fault, of course. It was, however, when I first got *involved*. My failures in that conflict . . . they would come later."

CHAPTER XV

SKY

As my training continued, I landed more and more hits on Gray. After a few more weeks, I was beating him nearly a quarter of the time. I still couldn't match his speed, but my reach advantage helped significantly, and beyond that . . .

I knew his tricks. I acclimated to every motion he made, burning it into my body and memory. I learned to counter every thrust, how to dodge every riposte.

. . . But there were some gaps that couldn't be so easily overcome.

When I tried the same thing against the older students, I faced different results.

Fade dodged my swing with contemptuous ease, then danced in to trip me with a sweep of her leg. I tried to dodge, but she was far too fast. I fell.

I tried again.

This time, I braced for the sweep, hoping I could remain stable if I lowered my stance just slightly and . . .

I fell.

I tried again.

The next time, I jumped over the sweep. That almost worked, except that she kicked me right in the knee when I landed. A sharp pain shot through my leg as I fell yet again.

I tried again.

The pattern continued for days and days. Fade remained well beyond my reach . . . and Green and Red were still so fast that I could barely perceive their movements.

Barely. But I could see them, now. Not every individual movement, but hints here and there.

I started to pick up some differences in their styles, too. Red focused on economy of movement, generally turning aside my attacks with graceful parries that barely involved shifting her weapon at all. Fade was all about speed, less likely to parry and more likely to simply shift out of the way of an incoming attack entirely. Green favored using beats, rather than standard parries — meaning that he'd counter an attack by smashing my sword out of the way to create a larger opening than an ordinary parry would. Of the three, I found myself emulating Green's style the most closely, both because I found it intuitive and because I still favored using a needlessly gigantic weapon.

Between sparring sessions, I continued to search the area for the sword I still believed might exist, but I didn't find one. I didn't go far, but I tried to range out a little farther from the school each week.

As time passed, I focused more on trying to actively learn to utilize my sword essence. Practicing swordplay would utilize it to a limited degree, but if I wanted to pursue swordsmanship seriously, I needed to learn specific techniques. Unfortunately, without a technique teacher, I was limited in what I could manage.

Most of my technique training time was spent simply practicing my homemade techniques in different configurations. I'd try wrapping essence around various different types of objects to make them usable as bladed weapons — the more obscure the object, the better. I'd throw leaves like darts, weave rope into a cutting whip, and slap invisible opponents with sword-essence-imbued gloves.

As I practiced, I confirmed that it worked best when I was carrying something that approximated a sword. Swordlike objects, even wooden ones, made it easier to focus sword essence intuitively in a way that didn't damage the weapon. I didn't limit my training to just swordlike stuff, but it certainly reinforced the idea that getting a real sword would improve my combat ability and training efficiency.

Beyond that, I kept tinkering with technique creation and modification, allocating a bit of my essence each day toward expanding my repertoire. I didn't succeed at making any new techniques during that time. As I reached the third quarter of the year, I felt like I'd at least made some progress at improving how quickly I could compress, convert, and release essence, which made techniques easier to execute.

Through those months, my secondary essence had increased significantly, generally improving my physical capabilities, but I'd barely managed to increase my primary essence at all.

I didn't have a spell or ability for exact measurement available, but I knew that there was a system for measuring the essence necessary to advance. Completing a Dianis Point required six "units" of essence. Don't overthink this number if you're more familiar with Mythralian domini measurements or Kaldwynian mana measurements — none of them are on the same scale.

It required a total of eighteen units in the body — enough to make three completed Dianis Points — to reach Torch-level, the second level of essence development. As soon as I had that much essence, I'd have my Destiny Dream and get enough power that even Gramps would have to admit that I was ready to see the world . . . at least in theory.

After several months of work, I'd gone from having roughly six units of essence in my Dianis Point to having . . . maybe seven, if that.

That wasn't anywhere close to acceptable. If I assumed that I was earning roughly two essence units per year, that would be about five more years until I hit Torch. That wasn't actually bad by ordinary human standards, but it wasn't exceptional, either. Dedicated Skyseekers often hit Torch-level at around fifteen . . . and even that was behind the curve compared to people like Ana.

It probably wasn't fair to compare myself to someone who was born with a Dianis Point already completed, but virtually everyone I knew was like that, so I *felt* like I was behind.

And, of course, I still needed to make a firm decision on my path.

It was six days before my name day when the sky came crashing down once again. It wasn't truly the second rainstorm that I'd experienced, but the thunder and lightning felt the fiercest since that first time I'd taken shelter in the shed.

I felt something different in the storm that time. Maybe it was the tingling feeling on my skin, or the scent of something burning with power in the air.

Or maybe it was something inside my own body and mind — the certainty that it was time to make a choice.

I wouldn't hide again. Not this time.

I sheathed a phantasmal practice sword on my hip, raised a handmade umbrella, drank a freshly brewed Threatseer Tonic, and went out to face the wrath of the storm.

⁂

The rain battered heavily against my crude umbrella, every beat reverberating with the tonic's enhancements to my senses, but I made steady progress up the mountain road. I wasn't quite as worried about being ambushed on the road while the sky was raging — most ordinary animals would be finding shelter, and the more dangerous creatures would see me whether I was on the road or not.

I took some extra precautions regardless — my belt pouches were stuffed with various monster-repelling supplies, like my aforementioned wolfsbane. I doubted they'd be sufficient for anything truly dangerous, but I'd scouted this road a few times before and determined a few likely escape routes if anything attacked me early on.

And if not . . .

Well, I wasn't completely defenseless.

The phantasmal wooden sword in my scabbard wasn't going to be much use in a fight by itself, but wrapping something in sword essence was the first trick I'd learned, and I'd gotten much better at using the Sword Sharpening Shroud while practicing my Shattering Sword technique. The sword wasn't the huge zanbatou type that I'd been practicing with the most — that wouldn't have fit in the scabbard — but I'd tinkered with all of the swords enough to feel safer with one on hand.

Assuming, of course, that it still existed after I drew it.

I still wasn't sure how far I could take the phantasmal sword from the shed without it vanishing into nothing. My best guess was that the scabbard, which was tied to the location the echoes came from, was helping to maintain the echo's integrity. The scabbard's essence might have helped, too. The scabbard was effectively what you'd probably call a "magic" or "dominion-bonded" item, but I had no idea what the functions were. Maintaining a sword placed inside it seemed pretty logical, though.

So, all in all, I had a weapon I could use this time, but not one I could rely heavily on. I still needed a real sword. I could have cobbled together a wooden spear or bow, but they wouldn't have interacted with my essence nearly as well, and making a wooden sword would have taken far too long.

I traveled up the road for what felt like hours, nearly slipping and falling in the mud on more than one occasion. The wind howled around me, but I didn't mind that — I'd always loved the feeling of the wind on my skin. The raindrops coming down at an angle were a bigger problem. I kept having to change the angle of my umbrella to make it functional at all, often limiting my own visibility, which was bad. Even then, my lower body quickly ended up getting soaked, with only my head and shoulders staying anything approximating dry.

I pressed on, higher than I'd climbed before. Eyes watched me from the sides of the road as I passed. First a single pair, then another, then . . . dozens.

But there was no assault. Either my precautions had helped, the rain stopped them, or whatever creatures lurked in the brush were simply uninterested.

Breathing came with more and more difficulty as I ascended.

The Last Breath, indeed. Definitely leaning toward the "low air" explanation over a hero dying up here. I suppose it could be both.

Even if nothing came out to eat me, climbing too high was a risk — the combination of low air, cold, and wet was as likely to mark my end as any monster's jaws. Inwardly, I cursed myself for failing to brew a potion to augment my breathing. I knew a few options for that — they were designed for breathing underwater, but I suspected they'd work just fine for high-altitude climbing. If I had the materials on me, I might have stopped to make one, but I didn't.

I trudged on.

I didn't need to make it to the summit. Not that day. I just needed to make it to the rise where the land met the sky.

I grinned as I saw a mist falling over the path up ahead.

Almost high enough.

It was a simple enough plan. As I mentioned, storm essence mostly manifested inside storm clouds. Under ordinary circumstances, that meant you had to have powerful abilities like flight or teleportation to retrieve it.

In the highest mountains, you didn't have to fly to reach the clouds—

All you had to do was climb.

I felt something tingling on my skin as I continued moving. Electricity flowing in the air.

If lightning decided to jump straight to me . . . well, that would be bad. I wasn't carrying any exposed metal, fortunately, and I was deliberately carrying items to ground me in case a burst of electricity did come by way — but I still didn't like my odds if a bolt hit me, or even close by. My body was more durable than it had been before I hit Candle-level, but my essence type wasn't great for resisting electricity. A lightning strike *probably* wouldn't kill me instantly, but it could easily leave me with bad enough burns to prevent me from making it safely back down the hill.

The danger made my heart pound faster, but I didn't stop.

Climb. Keep climbing, I told myself. It was easy to convince myself — right up until the point where I reached the mist.

And, for the first time, I felt something new.

It was subtle, almost imperceptible. If I hadn't consumed the tonic as a safety measure, I don't think I would have noticed it.

The sheath on my hip was shifting on its own.

Not out of any sense of awareness, mind you, nor was it blatantly flipping over or anything. It was, however, experiencing a very slight *pull* in the direction of the mist, like the world's weakest magnet was acting on it.

I took a deep breath. In fact, I took several.

I closed my eyes and formed my Sword Hand.

And, just like with the scabbard, I could feel it. Attraction. Something was attracting my sword essence toward the mist. Something distant, but strong enough that I could feel it calling like a siren's song.

This was it. This was what I'd been looking for — a potent source of power related to my own Heart Point. A possible answer to the mystery I'd been pursuing for months.

But if I followed the road . . . I could still feel the power of the storm in the air, still raging all around me.

If I pressed on, I was confident I'd be able to find a source of essence related to Uncle Eiji's path. Storm essence was a rare and powerful find, far more so than sword essence, which I could already generate on my own (albeit slowly).

And so, I was faced with a choice—

Did I press on, seeking to follow Eiji's path?

Or did I turn aside from the road, into the unknown?

If I absorbed storm essence into myself in a sufficient quantity, the path of the Blademaster destiny would be closed to me. But if I didn't do it then, I had no idea when another storm might come by with the intensity necessary to generate essence.

What if I made the wrong choice?

. . . This is a ridiculous false dichotomy. The mist has been here for months. It's not going away.

I gave the mist one final look.

I'm on to you, mystery mist. I'll be back.

Then I headed up the path, walking another solid mile before my footsteps breached the borders of the clouds.

I reached into my bag, pulled out a bottle, and spoke a single word. "Collect."

Then I hurled it and ran away. Not in fear, mind you, but out of rational self-interest.

I ducked behind a rock just outside the cloud. I didn't have to wait long — the effect was nearly immediate.

My vision went momentarily white as lightning flashed within the cloud. The thunder struck me next, so close that it rattled my ears and sent me stumbling back toward a cliffside that suddenly seemed much closer than I'd remembered.

Nopenopenope.

I teetered at the edge of falling but barely managed to steady myself by slamming my umbrella into the ground. The shaft of the umbrella wobbled dangerously close to snapping, but I managed to lever myself back into a standing position.

I didn't realize until after I'd pushed myself back up that I'd lodged the umbrella into solid stone. I'd instinctively managed to wrap it in sword essence without even thinking about it.

Huh. Neat.

Less "neat" was the condition of the umbrella itself — I'd jammed the stick portion into the ground to prevent myself from falling, but that meant that the "dish" portion designed to keep water off me was entirely ruined in the process.

Oops.

I was going to get absolutely soaked. I mean, even more soaked than I already was.

Still, as the rain pounded down on me . . . I laughed.

I'd done something only experts were supposed to do — I'd wielded my umbrella like a sword without even considering it.

There was potential there. But for the moment, I needed to worry less about my lofty sword future and more about the still-flashing lightning ahead of me.

I exhaled a deep breath. I could barely see where I'd hurled the vial in the cloud ahead, but it was still in there . . . along with the cap, which I'd dropped when I'd stumbled backward.

Cap first. It can't be far.

The rain continued to pound on my shoulders. I shivered as I dug through the dirt until I found the cap, and then, without any further hesitation, I rushed into the cloud.

There probably was a safer method for my madness. If I'd prepared a little better, I might have wrapped a length of string around the vial before hurling it into the cloud, then simply pulled the vial back on the string.

There's a good argument that I should have simply considered that vial a loss and gone home, but I'd never been good at giving up, even when I absolutely should have.

I rushed the cloud with what is probably best described as "manic abandon" . . . but not entirely without preparation.

Without any way to truly defend myself, I resorted to what came naturally to me — I extended my sword essence from my hand, then tried to wrap it around my entire body.

Aura-style techniques are extremely common. Many are defensive in nature, whereas others are intended to threaten opponents or aid allies.

In my case, I wasn't doing any of these things — not exactly.

If lightning was going to try to hit me, I hoped to cut it in half.

This wasn't actually a realistic expectation, and I knew that even at the time. I simply didn't have the essence level necessary to cleave through a bolt of lightning. Not yet. But I hoped that if a bolt did decide to fly my way, the haphazard aura of sword essence would at least deflect the lightning and help mitigate any damage I suffered.

It was a meager effort, but better than nothing.

With that in place, I rushed for where I'd last seen the vial . . .

And found absolutely nothing.

I had a moment of heart-stopping panic as blinding light flashed . . . but when my body wasn't burning in the aftermath and my vision cleared, I saw it.

A glow on the ground nearby, where the raging winds had pushed the vial. It was still open, still collecting essence. The lightning had been absorbed.

. . . And I wasn't going to push my luck any further.

I rushed the now-visible vial, suppressed the sword aura around my hand, and grabbed it. Then, with my other hand, I slammed the cap on top of the vial and rushed full speed out of the cloud.

I laughed again as I stumbled out back into the mountain air, but I didn't stop running. Not for quite a while. Even just being near the cloud was a risk, and while the essence vial wasn't going to be attracting more lightning now that it was capped, I was still in danger.

I rushed downhill until I was exhausted, and then slowly but inexorably, I made my way back to the relative safety of the long-abandoned sword school.

There. That's one more option available to me now.

I didn't have to make an immediate choice about my path. I'd trapped the lightning, and I could absorb it — or trade it, or sell it, or gift it — at my whim.

The mysterious mist could wait another day.

I nearly collapsed when I made it back to the storage shed. I was bitterly cold, wet, and exhausted . . . but I had it.

A single source of essence, flickering wildly within a glass bottle.

And it *was* essence — it wasn't just that lightning had happened to strike the vial. I could still see the crackling energy flashing within the glass, as if trying to escape.

I couldn't know if it was actually *storm* essence, however. It had come from within a storm cloud, true, but it was possible that I'd simply managed to leash a bit of lightning essence. An expert would have known enough to distinguish them, but the electrical power of the essence was bright enough that I couldn't tell if there was anything beyond that inside the glass along with it.

I set the bottle carefully aside. Rolling over on top of it and cracking the bottle while I slept would have ended badly. Then I stripped off my wet clothes and switched into the backup pair that I'd stored in the shed.

It was still cold. Dry clothes helped, but not enough. I had left my blanket behind in the shed, too, and it was still dry . . . but it was a thin thing and didn't feel like anywhere near enough to keep me warm for the night.

Should I start a fire?

I have flint and dry wood in here . . . but if I don't control it, the whole place could go up in flames.

I briefly debated my options. The only structure nearby that seemed likely to withstand a fire was the stone obelisk that stored the water. I'd opened that to fill up with the rain, so I certainly wasn't going to go try to start a fire inside it. It was still raining outside, so starting a fire out there wouldn't have worked.

I debated trying to set up a controlled fire pit inside the shed, but it was just too much of a risk to try it without proper preparation.

I might need to make some improvements around here . . . like a chimney. Otherwise . . . winter is going to bite me hard. It's colder this year.

I settled for wringing out my hair, then curled up in my meager blanket and shivered my way into sleep.

⁂

I woke up still cold and miserable, but the rainfall had ended.

Training resumed with a glorious dawn. I flexed frigid limbs and returned to fighting, but performed poorly.

After the first session, I ate a meager meal, then started a fire in a stone ring near where I'd built my original shelter. That helped me both warm my blood and make myself some hot tea, which helped get me functioning again.

When I finished my tea, I didn't return to training. Instead, I evaluated the clear sky . . . then prepared for another journey.

It wasn't polite to keep a magic sword waiting longer than necessary.

Sure, the map might have just been talking about the sword school, but I still had my heart set on the possibility that there was a treasure hidden and waiting to be found. Finding a source of sword essence had sent my imagination exploring the myriad of possibilities of what I might find.

Retracing my steps back to the mist was easy. In the daylight and drier weather, I made faster progress, too.

But the clearer weather brought greater risks, too. I had three close calls with mountain beasts.

I didn't retreat from any of them this time.

Instead, each time I encountered a threat, I raised the stick that remained of my battered umbrella, took a ready stance, and projected a Sword Sharpening Shroud. Then I stared at the bear, or the wolf, or the mountain cat . . . until *they* fled from my demonstration of power.

. . . Which was good, because while I was better prepared for a fight with seemingly ordinary predators now, I wasn't sure I had good odds at a straight fight with the large groups that tended to hunt together on the mountainside.

I could have run, of course, but that simply wasn't my style.

I still didn't know if it was my bravado that chased the beasts off or the strongly scented materials I was carrying, but it was nice to feel like I had combat techniques I could use if I needed them. That, at least, felt like some tangible progress. Whether my sparring with echoes had translated into any actual combat ability . . . that remained to be seen.

I'll find out soon enough.

There was no doubt in my mind that a magic sword — if it was a magic sword I was sensing, and not some other kind of sword essence — would be guarded.

I imagined a series of trials to determine if I was worthy, or perhaps some kind of ancient graveyard filled with ghosts of long-dead heroes. Or maybe it was just the kind of sword that was stuck in a rock, or a tree, and I'd need to meet some kind of arbitrary requirements to draw it.

Those last ones always seemed a little silly to me, but I'd brought a hammer and a stone hatchet in case stubborn sword-sealing materials were an issue.

Eventually, I reached the boundaries of the forest where I'd sensed the essence.

Hey, mystery mist. Mind if I come in? Probably not, since you're basically a magic cloud, so . . . I'll just step inside.

I took a drink of the meager remains of my Threatseer Tonic — I hadn't prepared more than one dose, so I was down to drops — and stepped into the fog.

It wasn't as easy to sense the pull on my scabbard without a full dose of the tonic . . . but now that I knew a bit more of what I was dealing with, I had a better idea of how to solve that.

Sword Hand.

Once the blade of essence formed around my hand, I focused on it — and immediately I could feel something tugging at the essence. It wasn't strong enough to disrupt the technique, and I don't even know if I would have sensed it at all if I hadn't been deliberately checking for it, but my connection with my own essence was stronger than my sense for the scabbard.

And so I held up my hand cautiously, and I followed the pull. As minutes passed, I knew I'd walked farther into the mist than ever before, and I let my Sword Hand fade.

After a certain point, I no longer needed it. The pull grew stronger and stronger as I walked — and as it did, the senses grew along with it. The feeling of blades pressed against my skin. The smell of freshly oiled iron drawn free from leather. The taste of copper on my lips. The scabbard was visibly shifting as I moved, like the needle on a compass.

As I approached an area where the fog was so thick that I couldn't see beyond it, I could hear a ringing melody, familiar and soothing in spite of never hearing the like before. It was the rhythmic sound of blades striking against other blades . . . not one, not two, but dozens. A harmony of steel. I walked closer, feeling a compulsion to join their song.

I walked through the wall of mist . . . and all at once, it parted.

I stared at the ruins of an ancient arena all around me — stone seats and splintered statues of warriors of the ancient past.

On the opposite side of the arena stood a lone figure. I use "figure" because "person" is too frail a word to describe a legend.

Her rough-cut black hair whipped in the wind, and a jagged scar traced from below her right eye down to her chin. Her white robes shimmered like metal, and she wore no less than six swords sheathed at her hips. The last of them was the most distinctive to my eyes. The pommel was a brilliant white gemstone, which was strange enough on its own, but the handle itself was also forged from white rock rather than metal.

She watched me with eyes the color of steel.

I could feel my heart skip a beat when the corner of her lips turned up just a fraction.

I knew who stood across the arena. I'd have known her from even one of her features; from the scar, from the swords, from the eyes.

And most of all, from the threat of a smile.

Oh, no.

No, no, no.

That's . . .

The Smiling Sword Saint.

They said she could divide a nation in twain with a single grin.

No, not because she was a one-in-a-million beauty. She wasn't the heroine of a two-copper romance.

When they said she could divide a nation with a smile, they meant she could literally *cut a nation in half* by making a facial expression.

When I looked at her, I didn't see beauty. I saw *violence*.

And while you might argue that that had a beauty all its own, at that moment, I was more worried about being the recipient of said nation-murdering violence.

My eyes widened. My heart slammed in my chest . . . then calmed.

Then, slowly, I lifted the muddy stick in my hands and fell into a combat stance.

. . . Somehow, I didn't think it would help.

CHAPTER XVI

SWORD SAINT

"Well, well." The Smiling Sword Saint stepped forward casually, not seeming to notice that the stone ground beneath her was cut to shreds with each step. "Looks like I've found myself a distraction."

I saw something flicker in her eyes. A hint of mirth, maybe. Or madness.

I was *really* hoping it wasn't madness.

It took every bit of my will to restrain the urge to do something foolish.

She wasn't deliberately outputting any sword essence. Not a hint of it. She didn't need to.

Even the shadow of her restrained strength was more than enough to crush my body and soul into powder, if she wished it. Or even if she didn't, and she merely slipped.

It's just an illusion. A projection. She isn't really here.

This is a memory, a—

She lifted her hands in front of her, then lowered them. "Hm. Seems like I'm a fake."

I blinked. How'd she picked up on that so quickly? *If she's like the other people I've seen, she shouldn't be able to . . .*

"Could have made it more convincing, but I can't say I mind the change of pace. Pleasant. Did I ask for this? No, don't answer that. Better if I don't know that little detail." She stretched her arms slowly, one after the other, as if feeling them for the first time. "So, this . . ." She jerked a thumb around. ". . . is what, a memory crystal? A shade stone? Did I finally drink and gamble away so much that I'm making memory crystals for . . ." She sniffed at the air. ". . . *a first-stage essence wielder*? No, you're *veking* with me."

I might have responded to her use of antiquated Artinian-style language for essence mastery if I had the chance, but no such moment was given. She snapped her fingers.

The stands around us vanished.

The sky darkened.

And I stood in a new arena — one constructed from countless whirling blades. Thousands, perhaps tens of thousands of them. They were everywhere — even the ground beneath me had been replaced by a shifting sea of steel. Paradoxically, they moved so quickly that the ground felt almost stable, but I didn't try my odds at moving.

Instead, I focused on the airborne blades around me, watching their rapid movements for predictable patterns. It was a futile task.

Too many. I can't read them.

As the blades spun dangerously close to my skin, I tried to adjust into a defensive stance to prepare myself for any that chose to strike, but my stick shattered in my grip. I didn't even see what struck it.

I dropped the fragmented stick and reached for the phantasmal sword on my hip on instinct, only to find it missing.

It would seem that even my resolve to die with a sword in my hand had been a miscalculation.

"Honored Saint of the—" I began.

She waved a hand. There was a flash of steel as something moved too quickly for my eyes to trace.

I felt a single drop of blood trickle down my face.

"Cut this nonsense, kid. You have *one word* to tell me why you're here."

I didn't hesitate. "Training."

She lifted a finger.

A half-dozen swords descended from the sky and cracked into the stone around me.

"Training? *You?* You're practically a child, and not a very talented one, from what I can see." Her eyes narrowed. "Why the *vek* should I train you?"

There was a sword hovering at my throat, then. I didn't see it move.

My eyes narrowed to meet her own. "The legends about you must have been an exaggeration."

The blade cut closer. I felt blood flow from my neck. "Wanna die that badly, eh?"

I shrugged. "I didn't think the Smiling Sword Saint was the type to threaten *talentless children*."

Her finger twitched. I felt the sword cut deeper.

I glared at her.

"Hmph." The blade pulled away, floating to her lazily. "Seems you've got a bit of steel in your spine after all."

She wiped a finger along my blood on the surface, raised the finger to her lips and licked. “Sword-type essence. Bit of a slashing flavor to it. Interesting. You hiding your strength from me, kid?”

I shook my head. “No.”

“You’ve got a sword heart, but you’re powerless. Useless.” Her lips twitched again. Distantly, I heard metal *crack* as hundreds of the flying swords surrounding us fell to pieces. “Interesting. Interesting!”

Then she laughed. Lightly, at first. Then louder, deeper, until she bent over at the waist.

“How hilarious! Such a dichotomy. An opportunity!”

Her quarter-forged smile and mirth vanished in the next instant. Her lips flattened, her eyes going dark. “I am, very likely, going to kill you.”

My hand shot out to grab the hilt of one of the swords flying next to me. I may not have been able to read the tide, but a single blade . . . “Then . . . I suppose I’ll have to cut the odds.”

My fingers clutched the hilt, seeking to wrest it out of the air. If I was going to face the Smiling Sword Saint, I’d do it with a sword in my hands, defying her to the end.

. . . But the sword didn’t budge an inch when I pulled. It turns out flying swords controlled by the will of legendary Skyseekers aren’t particularly easy for mere Candle-level essence wielders to move. I barely managed to release my grip before the flying blade pulled my shoulder out of its socket.

“You are *adorable*,” the Smiling Sword Saint offered. “I’ll cut you slowly, to savor it.”

Unfortunately for me, her idea of “slow” was fast enough that I heard a deafening crack like thunder the instant that she moved.

Then she was right in front of me, and I felt blood flowing from my left arm.

It was no ordinary cut. My arm *burned*, the sword essence that she’d used cutting through both body and spirit.

I should have screamed. Perhaps that would have given me an outlet for the agony.

Run, hide, lie, or die. Gramps’s instructions for how to handle an overwhelming enemy echoed in my mind, but over the cacophony of blades and the sound of my heart slamming in my chest, I could barely hear them.

My hand shot out again. This time, I flared my sword essence, shifting it to encompass a sword at the same moment I grabbed it.

The sword stilled in the air. Then, with great effort, I *pulled*. The blade resisted . . . but only for a moment.

In the next, I was in a defensive stance, a greatsword of lucent silver in my hands.

The memory of that first sword still burns within me. The first blade of metal that I ever held.

I raised it in front of me in a defensive stance, bracing for her next strike.

It was only at that moment that I realized she didn't even have a sword in her hands.

Had she drawn one of them and sheathed it faster than I could see, or . . . ?

I didn't have long to contemplate. I focused my essence, preparing to fight.

Sword Sharpening—

"No." Her hand was a blur.

The blade of the sword in my hand fell to a thousand pieces.

"I'm not teaching you to parry, kid."

She raised a finger.

Pain blossomed in my right shoulder, and as I glanced down, I could see a spreading blossom of blood.

And with that spreading blood, I felt it. That same burning energy as before. Sword essence, flowing freely within my body, tearing with every inch.

This time, I screamed.

And, with that scream, I did something foolish, purely on instinct.

I stepped forward and swung my broken blade at the Smiling Sword Saint. A burst of power surged through the shattered sword, forging a blade of essence stronger than I'd ever wielded before.

I didn't connect, of course.

"Better." The sword saint's voice slammed into me like the flat of a blade, blasting the wind from my lungs. Then there was a flash of movement in front of me.

Then my body was pouring blood from a dozen burning wounds.

I would have screamed again, but at least one of them had torn across my throat.

Another slit the area just above my right eye, bathing my vision in red.

I felt my knees hit the ground.

Sharp.

That was the feeling inside my body, inside my blood. Inside my soul.

My breaths came in ragged rasps as blood flowed freely down my body.

She appeared in front of me again, bending down. Her nose was very nearly touching mine. "Had enough, kid? I figured this little dream thing out. Could cut you free now, before you bleed out all over my imagination. How 'bout it?"

I could barely see her in my bloodstained vision, even as she pressed closer. Her lips were pursed, waiting for my reply.

I closed my eyes, focusing the frail fragments of my remaining energy. Sword essence.

I had my answer. I knew what my instincts guided me to do, and I wouldn't deny them. Not this time.

That was when I slammed my *veking* forehead into the face of the Smiling Sword Saint.

I accomplished very little. It was like slamming my head into a steel wall, if said wall was covered in razor blades. The razor blades themselves were little more than offended by the sudden presence of my head.

But it was a pretty good signal about who I was.

And, as my head pulled back from the blow, in the brief instant before her hand caught my hair and pulled my neck back, I saw something different in her expression.

Her lips were turned upward not in violence, but with something subtler.

Is she . . . happy with me?

That was my last thought before she cut me a thousand times.

After that, there was only blackness tinged with silver.

⁂

Waking up was a surprise.

Not just because I'd woken up in the storage shed of the sword school with no idea about how I'd gotten there. No, I was more surprised that I'd woken up at all.

The injuries I'd sustained from the sword saint . . . they were real. Very real, and without treatment, very likely fatal. I still wasn't sure exactly what species I was, but most things tended to die if they bled enough. And I'd been bleeding . . . well, a lot.

That part hadn't stopped. Not *entirely*. There was enough fresh blood on my arms, my hands, and the floor of the shed to show that I hadn't been magically fixed.

Not entirely, at least. With a trembling hand, I reached to my throat. I found scarring there, but no open wound.

Someone must have treated it with an essence technique, I realized blearily. *Or perhaps a very direct application of a healing potion or poultice.*

My hands were a different story. Some of the injuries had closed, but there were other tiny cuts that continued to bleed freely onto . . . well, everything.

I tried to move again, tried to push myself to my feet . . . but no. My body failed. I succeeded only in trembling.

Agony.

There is no way to describe the kind of agony that comes with your essence being cut a thousand times. There's something deeper inside you than any bone, any tissue, deeper even than the scattered fragments of your consciousness. Something of the *self,* a mess of essence, spirit, shade, memory, and layers beyond that composes the core of any individual.

. . . But within that same agony was something else I felt within that distant sense of self, burning beyond the pain.

It was there in my heart and in my veins, shining brightly in the wounds that she had carved.

Sword essence. That power had already flowed deep within me, deeper than I'd known, but the sword saint's cuts had unleashed it like a torrent that flooded through every part of me. When I closed my eyes and focused, I felt it in every cut that still bled freely in spite of treatment, in every half-healed scar.

And I had many, many new scars. Fortunately, those were only on the surface of my body. Essence scars could slow the process of gathering and using essence. Enough of them could prevent advancement completely.

She'd injured my essence structure, but not in a way that had caused scarring. No . . . if I understood what I was sensing . . .

She'd done quite the opposite.

There are channels within the body that cause essence to flow from one Dianis Point to the next. There are many names for them in different cultures, but I'll use the simplest — star veins.

I probably should have explained this before I mentioned them earlier, shouldn't I? I can get ahead of myself at times.

Anyway, these star veins are used to process essence within the body, moving it in and out of Dianis Points. They're basically the bloodstream, but for essence.

I suppose it's worth mentioning that there are other types of star veins, too. Technically, the star veins I've been talking about are a specific type called either essence veins or core veins, depending on who you ask. The other star veins were beyond my ability to do anything with at that point. They connected to higher layers of self — things like spirit veins, shade veins, and memory veins, each of which connected the core self to other parts of the self. Those other star veins were typically sealed and inaccessible until higher levels of advancement, but I'm digressing, so back to the main point.

Typically, essence within star veins ends up doing one of two things. It either settles in a Dianis Point to become primary essence, or gradually flows out of the star veins to disperse in the physical body as secondary essence. In ordinary circumstances, if you absorb essence and already have a completed Dianis Point of the same type, most of the new essence would go straight to the Dianis Point.

Focusing inward, I could sense that this was anything but an ordinary situation.

The Smiling Sword Saint's cut had shredded everything within my star veins, while preserving the veins themselves. I'd been flooded with so much raw sword essence that it had absolutely shredded everything else that my body had been currently processing — save, perhaps, for a thin line of strange essence I could sense flowing out of the seal on my right hand.

Some of the sword essence was already flowing around the Heart Point in my chest, attracted to it and beginning to settle as essence of the same type normally would. But as I focused on my mental image, I realized there was *far* too much — my single completed Dianis Point couldn't process the sheer flood of essence within my body.

And, if I allowed the essence to simply continue ravaging through my star veins, they might begin to bleed.

Or worse, my very Heart might break.

I grit my teeth as I concentrated on the persistent flow of essence, bending it to my will.

You are my sword, and I will wield you as I choose.

The flood of essence was many times what I'd managed to shape before, but I drew it easily, feeling it shift at my command.

It would have been easy to burn that essence in a technique, and perhaps the safest approach. Attempting to wrestle with so much sword essence in my body was asking to be cut. Even masters could harm themselves with a careless draw.

But I'd been given a gift by a master, and I wasn't going to forsake it. I could already sense the new strength that came with binding a fraction of that essence to my Heart Point — and I wanted *more.*

There's enough essence here to make the foundation for a whole new Dianis Point. Probably a whole unit of essence, maybe more. If I grab hold of enough of it, and hammer it into place, like folding it into steel . . . could I solidify it manually?

If I could do it, I'd have the foundation for two Dianis Points of the same type — and once I completed the second one they'd compound each other. If I made it a Breathing Point, I could absorb sword essence more easily, too . . .

It was a tempting prospect, one that would give me nearly enough power to catch up to Ana in a single decision.

No.

A hastily forged sword is brittle and likely to break.

A Dianis Point was ordinarily completed over the course of years, through layer after layer of careful work. Trying to build a foundation for a completed point in a single action was theoretically possible, but it was like trying to forge a sword in a single night — the results would be inferior to one built with proper attention and care. Perhaps someone more skilled could have done it without risk, but I was barely starting to learn how to wield my essence.

I wouldn't sacrifice my future for an immediate benefit.

Instead, I hissed, focused on the flood of essence further — and, with great effort, I began to funnel it directly into my body.

Manually converting the essence flowing through star veins into secondary essence wasn't an uncommon practice. People who prioritized secondary essence could be deceptively powerful for their level of essence advancement, which had advantages in terms of being underestimated. And having at least some secondary essence of the same type of Dianis Point was good for making your body inherently resistant to your own type of essence. Not as good as having a dedicated Shield Point of that type, but the effects were potentially cumulative with a Shield Point, and many people chose to use a Shield Point for a different essence type than their Heart Point for added flexibility.

So, I knew that converting primary essence in star veins into secondary essence could be done. I'd read about how to do it. I understood the theory.

But I wasn't converting a sliver of essence. I was trying to convert nearly as much new sword essence as I'd accumulated over the last entire year.

Well, if this kills me, at least it'll be a spectacular end.

I pictured the essence in my mind, focused on the places where it flowed, and formed a nascent technique.

Draw Sword.

I gripped the essence and *pulled.*

The pain was incredible. I should have fainted, but my mind's grip on my essence was tight, and I wrenched harder and harder until the essence slowed . . . then ripped outward into my body.

I think I did faint, then, if only briefly.

I remember my head hitting the ground, a burst of stars, and then my muscles spasming. I gripped my arms with my hands, trying to steady them, my jaw tightening.

I should have put something in my mouth to bite down on before trying that. Fortunately, I didn't quite dislocate my own jaw.

I don't know how much time passed while I lay there, wrestling with myself in agony. When the pain finally reduced to a more manageable degree, I was absolutely drenched with sweat, and still covered in the blood from my earlier wounds.

Fortunately, converting the essence from my body hadn't shredded me from the inside out. I'd *felt* like I was shredding myself to bits because I'd pulled out too much essence in a single moment, but my own sword essence must have offered me some protection. Any damage I'd suffered had been superficial.

Even so, there had been the risk of causing myself serious harm, both in terms of the possibility of my body rejecting the massive essence push and, you know, just knocking myself out or worse from the agony.

As my hands continued to tremble, I pushed myself upward into a sitting position, then raised my fingers in front of my face—

And laughed through bloodstained teeth.

Not a bad day, all things considered.

. . . But I think I'll skip practice tomorrow.

⁂

After washing my wounds and drinking some water, I collapsed again, and slept for nearly an entire day.

The next few days were absolutely miserable. I could barely move. My wounds, aside from the one that had been healed by some mysterious savior, needed better treatment — but I didn't have the strength to handle them properly. I didn't have any of my healing elixir left, nor did I have the supplies to make a proper poultice.

In the end, I had to settle for simply cleaning them periodically and wrapping them. I simply didn't have the supplies to do anything else, and I didn't have enough strength to make the journey home.

My situation was bad enough that I considered calling for help. It was possible that Gramps was monitoring me from a distance. I considered the possibility that he was the one who had dragged me to the shed and dropped me there — it was likely within his capabilities. Outside the forest, I wasn't sure who else might be able to get to me. Ana couldn't wander outside of the forest's boundaries, nor could most full-blooded fae. The witches could, but they probably weren't watching.

Ultimately, my pride was too strong to literally call for help, so I simply settled for a slow and painful recovery. I focused for the next few days on just resting, drinking water, and eating. Fortunately, my injuries always seemed to heal cleanly.

It was nearly a week before I was back to anything resembling normal, and even then, I had to be cautious to avoid reopening my wounds.

While my body was still barely functional during that time, my mind was spinning. I read through more and more of the books I'd borrowed, studied the technique scrolls further, and theory-crafted new ideas.

But more than the books or scrolls, I had something new to focus on—

The power that had nearly torn my body asunder.

The Smiling Sword Saint had nearly killed me, but she'd given me three gifts.

First, a massive supply of sword essence. Even after a week, my body was still processing both the essence that had gone to my Dianis Point and the portion I'd shoved into my body as secondary essence. I'd absorbed more sword essence from that attack than I had in the last several months combined.

Second, by overloading me with so much power, she'd given me the insight to begin developing a technique for sword essence conversion into secondary essence. My hastily assembled Draw Sword concept wasn't a real technique yet, but it had still mostly functioned. The sheer amount of pain the process caused meant that I absolutely needed to figure out a way to improve on it — I could handle it, but I didn't enjoy it or thrive on it like some. The obvious answer was that I simply needed to find a way to do it more gradually rather than rushing the process, but upon more consideration, I figured out a couple of alternatives.

I could convert the sword essence to a different aspect — one that wasn't designed to cause as much damage. The Smiling Sword Saint's technique had used something similar to slashing essence, which was inherently focused on attacking. If I re-aspected the essence into something more like deflection-aspected essence, it probably wouldn't have hurt my body nearly at all — but the impact of deflection-aspected essence on my body's development would have also been more defensively focused, and that didn't feel quite right to me. I was an attacker — that felt like a part of me.

Maybe I could convert it into unaspected essence, for a more balanced benefit . . . or, perhaps, I could change it into a mix.

That led to my next idea — converting the essence in "layers," similar to how I formed my Sword Hand, but in reverse. Slashing essence on the inside, surrounded by a layer of less-damaging essence, like deflection. That felt . . . unintuitive, but perhaps it was something I could iterate on more, especially if I could find another essence type that worked better for the concept.

Next time I'm hit with this much essence, I'll be ready.

The third gift from the Smiling Sword Saint came to me when my mind was clearer and I was less focused on the very obvious benefits.

Her technique had, intentionally or incidentally, served a function I'd been wrestling with for months—

She'd wiped out all of the non-sword essence in my star veins. By doing so, she'd removed everything else my body had to process, allowing it to focus on sword essence exclusively.

If I could emulate that, I could form a new technique.

I still could barely walk, but my mind could function, and I had small sources of other types of essence. There were trace amounts in my dried meat and fruit.

I popped a piece of jerky in my mouth, closed my eyes, and concentrated.

Let's get to work.

Three days later, on a cold night with a clear sky and brilliant stars shining above, I made my way home.

CHAPTER XVII

SMITH

Ana manifested in front of me the moment I crossed the invisible line marking the boundary of faerie territory. "Woah! You look like you got into a fistfight with an iron maiden!"

I grunted, leaning harder on my new walking stick, which had replaced the one that had been tragically taken from me by the sword saint. "That's . . . shockingly close to what happened, in a sense."

Ana fluttered closer. "That sounds amazing! I mean, terrible, but also amazing! What was it? A golem? A girl golem? A . . . *girl-em*?"

"We're not making that word happen. I refuse." I sighed.

"You're no fun." She folded her arms and then sat down on my shoulder. Fortunately, she was presently only the size of my hand and the weight of . . . I don't know, an apple, maybe? Even then, I grunted at the sudden shift. "Oh! Sorry, sorry! You're horribly injured and I forgot instantly again."

"It's fine. I'm mending. Most of the remaining damage is internal."

"That is . . . not fine, Lien. That's worse. That's so much worse. You do *get* how that's worse, right?" She leaned closer, jabbing a tiny finger into my cheek.

I shrugged, then winced again at the movement. "I think the Smiling Sword Saint knew what she was doing."

"The S . . . Smiling . . . Sword Saint?" She froze, comically falling backward off my shoulder in exaggerated shock. I reached out with a single hand and caught her before she hit the ground, which she clearly wouldn't have, but the effort to play along was important to us both.

"Yep. Don't faint, now. That'll make it much harder to explain . . . and I've got quite a story to tell."

Ana accompanied me back home, listening intently with stars in her eyes. No, not literally. She's not a fragment of . . . never mind. That's someone else.

"You seem so much stronger now." She sounded almost wistful. "I mean, not that your Heart Point is that much stronger, but . . . you're faster and stronger. Was it really that much secondary essence?"

I nodded. I was still healing, but I'd been feeling the difference, too.

I'd absorbed a lot of secondary essence in my life — so much I couldn't even hope to calculate it accurately. There was some small amount of essence in every meal I'd eaten for my entire life. That was true for many people in essence-rich areas, although I expected that it was more pronounced in my case than in most average cases. Gramps favored essence-rich meals, and few people had the advantage that I did of a knowledgeable essence wielder to guide their meal intake since childhood. Nobles and royals, certainly, or perhaps children raised in Skyseeker sects — but I certainly had an advantage over the average person in that regard.

Of course, my body could only process so much essence at once — anything else was wasted. So, it wasn't like I was worlds ahead of anyone who grew up in a more ordinary area. They were still probably getting close to their maximum essence acclimation speed even with more ordinary food, or so I assumed. There was probably a fair bit of variation.

Anyway, I'd probably consumed many times more essence of various types than the amount of sword essence in my Heart Point during my lifetime as a whole — it was just converted into secondary essence with a broad variety of applications, most of which were subtler than what sword essence gave me. Sword essence would primarily increase my physical strength, especially my striking strength, and have smaller benefits for my durability and speed.

The majority of the essence I'd absorbed would have virtually no impact on my strength — it would be things that were super common like life essence, water essence, and air essence. Of the common essence types, stone essence was the one that was used most directly for building strength, and that wasn't commonly found in food and drinks. Gramps did make tea with stability essence, and that definitely had helped — over hundreds of drinks — to strengthen me . . . but it was one factor among many, many others.

I had, of course, already built up a fair bit of secondary sword essence throughout my life as well. Even with a completed Dianis Point of that type, not all of the sword essence I absorbed went to primary essence, and while I could have pushed more of the essence I consumed in that direction, I hadn't focused on that. And my ability to even try that was a recent thing — up until my Heart Point was completed, my body had simply been splitting the essence between primary and secondary automatically, with no control over it on my part.

So, I'd built up a considerable amount of secondary sword essence in my body even prior to meeting the Smiling Sword Saint — but not an overwhelming amount. And while it had strengthened me with each bit I'd absorbed, across my lifetime, the newly gained essence provided a noticeable benefit to my physical abilities because it was so specialized and I'd pulled in so much at once.

It was hard to estimate, since I was still injured and didn't have any actual equipment or spells for measuring my physical characteristics, but I had to guess that my strength had gone up by about ten percent through the absorption of the Smiling Sword Saint's essence. My durability and speed had also improved, but maybe only by about half as much.

Moreover, my secondary essence wasn't the only improvement. I hadn't been able to guide the essence as much as I'd wanted, and I was still processing some of it, but . . . if I had to guess, I'd probably gained nearly a full unit of primary sword essence.

That may not sound like a lot, but it had happened in such a short time frame that it was an absolutely absurd level of improvement for the amount of time it had taken.

Of course, it had also come with horrible injuries and a long recovery period. During that recovery period, my physical conditioning would suffer, and that was nearly as important as essence development. And, uh, there was the risk of death. Someone had saved me, but I didn't know if it was the sword saint herself or someone else. Since I didn't know, I didn't have any idea if they'd intervene again if I was wounded a second time . . . and I had no idea if I would have survived the throat injury without help.

I wasn't going to risk that kind of thing repeatedly. The extra strength felt amazing, and I wanted more, but I wasn't going to go charging in without a plan.

Not in that specific instance, at least.

Just as important as the risk was that it wouldn't benefit me to go through that process repeatedly. My body was saturated with sword essence for weeks after my encounter with the sword saint. During that time, trying to absorb more essence from any source was largely pointless. It was like trying to eat when I was already full — I wouldn't get anything out of it.

So, I wasn't exactly going to work "get hit with absurd power by the Smiling Sword Saint" into my standard workout routine. It sounded like the kind of absurd training regimen someone at a Skyseeker sect might go through, but it didn't actually make any practical sense, at least for me. But if I could find a way to get her to give me sword essence in a more controlled fashion . . . well, that would be a different story.

Eight essence out of eighteen. That's solid progress. Finally.

Ana and I said our goodbyes outside Gramps's house . . . or . . . my house, if it still counted. I wasn't clear on that. I'd been living away for months, and . . . had I moved out? Was I an errant teenager living on my own now?

The answer was obviously "No," but I was a kid with an overactive imagination.

"Come." The door swung open wide as I approached. Gramps was already sitting at the table, pouring two cups of tea. "I've been expecting you."

I'd almost missed his weird ancient wizard theatrics. Okay . . . maybe I had missed them a little.

I rested my stick by the door, slipped off my muddy boots, and came inside to sit in a real chair for the first time in months.

"Don't slouch."

I hadn't missed everything about Gramps, though.

With a sigh, I made an effort to demonstrate sitting up straighter, then accepted my cup of tea. "So . . . I'm back."

"Ancient and wizened as I am, my eyes haven't failed just yet."

"What about your memory? Did you know I was gone?"

"Hush, you. Drink your tea."

I did. It was great. I'd missed his tea.

"There are things I need to tell you."

A bushy eyebrow went up. "Are there, now?" He poured more tea.

"I met the Smiling Sword Saint."

Gramps, an essence wielder so advanced that he could step across a country in less than the beat of a hummingbird's wings, nearly dropped his teapot.

Nearly.

I saw his hand tremble, I promise.

". . . No, you didn't."

I grinned. "I did. I mean, obviously, she's long dead. But I saw her anyway. An echo. And a powerful—"

There was a brief flash of blue centered on Gramps's eyes. A sensory technique, drawn from the essence in his Viewing Point, one of the Dianis Points I had not yet completed. His eyes flashed across me, scanning. "You . . . gods around us, what has she done to you?"

"It's fine, Grandfather. She just—"

"It's not fine!" I froze as he raised his voice. Gramps never raised his voice. He never panicked. He never . . . didn't know what to do. "The *seal*. It's . . ."

His voice lost cohesion. His eyes shut.

And I, very deliberately, closed my own eyes to concentrate on my right hand.

I could sense it there — a concentration of power that was bound in place by what felt like near-unbreakable chains.

"Near," however, was the operative word in that statement. There was a trickle of essence flowing from that hand throughout my body. I'd sensed it even when I'd first been cut by the sword saint, but I'd been so focused on dealing with the immediate problem that I'd ignored it—

Perhaps a part of me had known even then that it meant the seal was damaged.

Maybe that was a part of why I'd smiled so brightly that night.

It was foolish, I knew that. But that power . . . however terrible . . . it was a part of me. I knew that as intrinsically as I knew my own hand.

I still didn't know how I'd gotten the seal or why. I doubted I'd been born with it, but it had to have been applied very, very quickly — I had a strong memory of my childhood years. Stronger, perhaps, than an ordinary human should have, but not necessarily enough to be suspicious in itself.

Anyway, I'd had it a long time, and Gramps had always been cagey about it. And, you know, a bunch of other things.

Ancient wizard motif. I got it. I wasn't surprised when he kept secrets — it was all part of the aesthetic. I was deeply annoyed from time to time, but it was normal.

. . . Or so I thought. I was a kid, and I was used to that type of thing being ordinary. In retrospect, it was kind of an awful way to treat a child.

But I digress.

Gramps was quietly panicking, so I just . . . kind of mentally reached toward the seal and . . .

And I felt the crack.

It was a tiny, hairline thing.

My lips trembled, but not in terror. I hoped that Gramps didn't notice. And once I sensed the weakness, instinctively, I . . .

"Do *not* tinker with the seal." Gramps's hand was on my own. My eyes flickered open.

"Sorry, Grandfather. But don't you think it's about time you tell me what it is?"

He paused, breathing deeply. Then, in what amounted to one of my greatest surprises, he actually gave me something of an answer.

"It is . . . a legacy. One that I hoped you would never have to face. And one that you are, in absolute certainty, not ready for."

That was better than I'd ever gotten out of him in the past, so I felt a little emboldened. "What *kind* of legacy? It's a bloodline power, right?"

"Not precisely, but you may think of it as being similar. The seal blocks your connection to something that . . . you don't want to be involved with."

"Shouldn't that be my decision?"

Gramps stared at me. Hard. I didn't flinch.

Shockingly, he did. "When you are an adult, perhaps. And educated enough to make a reasonable decision. But for now . . . what kind of child turns down an offer for immediate power, even if there are consequences?"

"Uh, me. This guy, right here, actually." I waved my other hand. "See, when the Smiling Sword Saint pushed sword essence and cleared out the rest of the essence types in my body, I realized that I could use it to build a foundation for another sword essence Dianis Point—"

"Absolutely not! You'd risk making a weak foundation, one that could shatter at the slightest hint of damage!"

"Easy, easy." I squeezed his hand. "I already *made* that choice. I realized it on my own. You don't see the foundation for a second Dianis Point in my body, do you?"

"Then . . . I am proud of you. You show more wisdom than I have given you credit for. Forgive me, but the seal is different. I do not wish to underestimate you, but . . . if you knew the nature of the seal, the temptation to use the power within it would be great, and the consequences harder to foresee than damage to your essence."

"Why?"

"It is . . . a complicated story. One that I am not yet ready to tell. Forgive me, child."

". . . I get it. I don't like it, but I understand that. But . . . respectfully, Grandfather . . . if it's already damaged . . ."

He nodded slowly. "Yes. You'll need to know about it eventually. And I will tell you at the appropriate time. For now . . ."

He squeezed my hand and . . . there was no special visual effect, no sound, no clear signifier . . . but the crack in the seal vanished in my mind's eye.

"You resealed it?"

"I patched it. I cannot repair the seal properly. It is beyond my abilities."

Now it was time for my own eyebrow to shoot up. "Beyond your . . . how? Do you mean it's a different type of magic, like from another continent? Or simply too powerful?"

"A mixture of both problems, I'm afraid."

"Then how did a mere echo of the Smiling Sword Saint damage it?"

Grandfather shook his head. "It is a tragic facet of our universe that things tend to be easier to break than they are to repair. And . . . beyond that . . . even a memory of the sword saint is not to be underestimated."

He sighed, pulling his hand back and raising his cup of tea with a steadier hand. "Tell me what you saw, child. And we will discuss what must be done."

⊱ ⊰

"So," Gramps concluded, drumming his fingers on the table as I finished my tale. "You've been busy."

"What gave you that impression?" I offered him a slight smile.

"I'm proud of you for avoiding some of the obvious failures you could have made."

That was about as close to a direct compliment as I could have expected from Gramps, so I took it as positively as he'd intended it. "Thank you, Grandfather. I would ask for your insight on the Smiling Sword Saint. What was her nature? She seemed much more self-aware than the echoes, and spoke of herself as being an 'illusion' or a 'dream.'"

"In spite of being a reflection of the actual sword saint, she will not have anything close to a full scope of the original's abilities, and thus her ability to accurately assess her own nature would be limited. She probably believed she was conjured by something like a dream crystal or a shade stone. Those are both variations on memory crystals that allow for interaction. They were more popular as training tools in her time, and they're still in use in places like Skyseeker sects. It is probable that she believed herself to be a construct within one of these devices."

"Meaning . . . she didn't know she was actually hurting me?"

"Potentially. It's plausible that she was striking you with the intent of showing you how sword essence can be used to filter out other essence, as you speculated, then allowing you to practice that concept and use the shade stone again for other instruction. If this was her presumption, it was obviously erroneous . . . but we should not assume that was the case. It is also possible she was aware you would be harmed and simply didn't care."

I frowned. "That doesn't sound very heroic. Wasn't she supposed to be a hero?"

Gramps snorted. "Heroes. I've taught you about those before. Tell me, what is it that decides who gets to be a hero?"

"Let me remember the Tarren quote. 'The nature of a hero is to be one who stands above all others . . . according to the values of their own culture. To the Xixian Empire, Vyrek Sul was a hero above all others, for there was a government-mandated book upon every shelf to tell them so.' Is that about right?"

"Your recollection of the phrasing is passable, and you have accurately distilled the core concept."

I resisted the urge to roll my eyes. "But even if I take Tarren's cynicism at face value, he's talking about a very specific type of hero there. Vyrek Sul was an emperor. The Smiling Sword Saint was a peasant—"

Gramps actually snorted. "You've already proven my point. No, she wasn't. That farmer-to-hero story? An absolute myth. She had elixirs poured into her from an early age, much like half the so-called prodigies out there."

"Then . . ." I frowned. "Even so, her deeds . . ."

"I won't deny that she accomplished things we would have considered heroic from *our* perspective. This was less in her role as a duelist, however, and more in her role as a battlefield commander in the war against Xixis. And I'm certain that the people of Xixis had names that were far less kind than 'hero' for her."

"Okay, okay." I raised my hands in surrender. "Fine, I can accept that a war hero isn't a war hero to the other side. But what motivation would she have to be that aggressive toward a teenager? If she knew that we weren't in a dream, that is . . . she could have killed me, couldn't she?"

"Absolutely. It's possible she tended to your wounds when she realized that you'd lost consciousness and she was still there. It would explain why you found yourself partially treated at the sword school."

"But that would imply that she'd transported me there herself, yes? Would an echo have the level of cognizance necessary to do that, or any concept of where I might be safe?"

"Unlikely, but not impossible. She sounds too self-aware to be a typical echo, at any rate. There are other possibilities. She wasn't a ghost — her behavior and appearance would have been fundamentally different. Not likely a shade, either. They generally don't retain that much of their personality. Did you remember what I taught you about breaches?"

"Sure. They're tears in the boundaries between planes. Echoes manifest when there's a breach between our world and the plane of memory. If there's a breach from the plane of spirits, it'd be a spirit manifesting, rather than an echo."

"Good. There are also combinations. These can occur when there's a multilayer breach."

I frowned. "That can't be common. Breaches themselves are pretty rare."

"Yes. But a locale where the Smiling Sword Saint once practiced? She very well may have opened up one or more breaches on her own, or through fighting against a similarly skilled opponent."

"Or training her sword school?"

"Possible." Gramps stroked his beard. "But I recall nothing of her having a sword school. And she had two apprentices, not four."

"You knew her?" I blinked. I shouldn't have been surprised by that, but I still was. Gramps was powerful, but the Smiling Sword Saint was a *legend.*

"In a manner of speaking. Let's not dwell on that for now. Suffice to say that I doubt that place was her school, precisely. It is a curiosity to me. Perhaps it is from an earlier point in history, and a younger version of her is one of the students you saw. Perhaps it is an echo from later in time, and the master of that school was one of her students."

"Do the physical descriptions of the students offer us any insight?" I asked.

"Sadly, no. I will think on it. For now, I believe the school itself is safe enough for you to continue to train, but if the sword saint behaves like the other echoes you've encountered, she won't remember you on your next visit. Every time that you visit her, there's a chance that your first words will be a fatal mistake."

"I could try to repeat the same thing I did last time."

"Certainly. But how *perfectly* can you repeat the introduction to your first encounter?"

I shook my head. "Not closely enough to ensure her behavior doesn't diverge, especially if she's more self-aware than the echoes. She was reading my body language — that in itself could be different enough that it would influence her behavior. And even if I could match what I did precisely . . . just repeating that exact same experience wouldn't make much sense. If she'd cut me just a little deeper, she might have permanently damaged my star veins or Heart Point. I'm not sure repeating that would be a good thing."

"True. And she would sense you differently in any subsequent visit — your increased amount of sword essence would make you feel different."

I nodded. "That could be a good thing. She might not . . . look down on me to the same degree."

"Valuable, if she sees you as a student. But if you cannot ensure that expediently, she may eliminate you as a potential threat."

"Could I really be a threat to someone like her?"

"Now? Obviously not. But she may see you as being a potential future threat, which may be enough."

". . . Right." That was disappointing, but it was consistent with what I'd expected. "I understand. I'm not foolish enough to go back there without a plan, but I can't give up on it, either. I was hoping, perhaps, you could help me find a means of interacting with her more safely?"

"We can discuss it. Based on her aggression, it's possible that she is being influenced by the sheer quantity of sword essence in the area. If she is a spirit or echo, and you've identified that locale as being a place where the sword essence in the area is being funneled . . . she may be something like a 'sword spirit,' in which case her behavior would be at least partially dictated by that essence type."

"Meaning that she's more dangerous than the real sword saint because she's more a construct of sword essence than a person?"

Gramps made a tsking sound. "Now, child. You know better than this. A construct of spirit and sword essence that can hold a conversation with you and make decisions very likely *is* a person. There are many, many types of people in this vast universe that take different forms."

"I'm sorry, Grandfather. I didn't mean to dismiss her as a person. Forgive my rudeness. Still, the question itself remains."

"Is she more *dangerous* than the Smiling Sword Saint? Not on the absolute scale, given that she's much weaker. Weaker is relative, of course — at her peak, the Smiling Sword Saint was at a level of essence development that would have been taken for godhood by many cultures."

"You mean Sky-level?" I asked, momentarily awestruck. That was the mythological level that Skyseekers sought — and so far beyond anything I'd experienced that it was hard for me to properly evaluate.

"Perhaps. I cannot say for certain if she reached that level. But even if she was a step lower, that would be strong enough to rival many of the strongest beings left living alive — the faerie queens, the human emperor, and our ancient dragon friend among them. To your question, however . . . this copy would be far weaker. She would be a copy from an earlier period in the sword saint's life, and lack the full strength the saint held in that time period. Without knowing the exact date of this copy's creation, it would be impossible for me to accurately evaluate her strength . . . but even if she is vastly weaker, as I suspect, the direct answer to your question is 'Yes.' She may not be as powerful as the original sword saint, but is she more *dangerous* to you, specifically? Certainly. A sword spirit will, as a general rule, think of little more than combat and may possess fewer instincts toward limiting the damage they cause. Her core motivation will be to do what a sword does — cut, pierce, and so on."

"What about to protect others?"

Gramps gave me a sad look. "That may be something a sword *can* be applied to, child, but it is not, as a rule, what a sword is for. Not for the overwhelming majority of people, at least. And sword essence takes after how people as a whole have defined the sword . . . at least so far as we understand it. The nature of sword essence and other tool essences is a subject of constant debate, but the fact remains that entities born from it tend to be . . ."

"Living weapons."

"... That is one way to put it, yes."

I wanted to argue that, to fight it. Something about that assessment cut me on a deeper level than I could put into words.

I wanted to tell him that a sword could be different, or that sword essence could be different, or that I could change the nature of a blade I wielded...

But the words turned to rust in my mouth.

What did I know about it, truly? Very little.

I had only the sharp feeling that something was wrong with his assessment. It was strong, but not clear enough to articulate into words.

"More tea?" Gramps asked.

"Yes, please." I offered my cup and he poured for me. I swirled it around in my cup, watching and imagining the pool as something deeper, like a lake of tea. Were there lakes of tea in the world? It seemed unlikely, but if I never got away from home, I'd never have the chance to try to find one.

"If you're going to stir your tea, there's a proper way to do it."

I stopped, abashed. "Sorry, Grandfather. I..."

I blinked. The liquid kept moving for a moment, swirling on its own, without any further action on my part. It was almost like the water remembered what I'd been doing, even after I stopped. That was absurd, of course — the water wasn't remembering anything exactly, it was just a matter of inertia causing the water to continue to move — and it was the type of thing I'd observed on numerous occasions before.

But sometimes the simplest of observations can lead to life-changing conclusions.

"This is a solvable problem, isn't it? I just need to get her to remember me."

Gramps frowned. "You say that as if it is a simple thing, but echoes and their ilk are bound to a cycle of behaviors, as you've observed yourself with the sword school."

"I think they've started to recognize me at the school. Gray, at least, shows some signs of it. And if the sword saint is more self-aware, it might go faster for her."

"I'm not certain I agree with your core observation — could it be that your own behaviors have adapted in a way that facilitates Gray's appearance of recognition, since you fit better in with the training now?"

That was difficult to dispute. "I don't know. But even if it isn't working with Gray, the sword saint being self-aware offers an opportunity, doesn't it?"

"Perhaps. She's still bound by her own nature. As are we all."

That was a bit of a weird end to the statement, but I ignored it. "... Then all we have to do is cut the chains of her nature."

Gramps rolled his eyes. "Oh, is that all? I don't know why I didn't suggest fundamentally altering the nature of a godlike being. It's very obvious, now that you mention it."

I took a sip of my tea, then continued musing aloud. "It might be. Hyperbole about her power aside, if we assume her problem is being a static entity that is defined by omnipresent sword essence and whatever limited memories define her, both of those factors can be potentially changed."

Gramps seemed to give that more consideration. "Perhaps. If there's a source of the sword essence aside from her, perhaps it could be removed, changing the amount she has access to and reducing her hostility. But it's most likely within her area of influence, if such an external source exists, so finding and changing or moving it would be quite a feat. And if you change or remove it, she may simply cease to exist."

That did pose a problem, but it left another option. "What about her memories? Ana's shrine has the ability to suppress memories, so that clearly can be done. What about reinforcing memories, or giving new ones. There's . . ." I snapped my fingers. "Memory crystals. Memories from crystals cut themselves into your mind with greater clarity than ordinary memories do. What impact would they have on an echo?"

There was hesitation in Gramps's movements. The way he lifted his cup was just a hint too slow, the way his eyes refused to focus on me as he considered. "I don't know."

"But . . . it's worth trying, isn't it? If there's any chance that they could help her learn and grow . . ."

"An interesting experiment, to be certain. But one that risks your life on the possibility of success — and moreover, one that does not solve your secondary problem. Even if she should retain a degree of memory from each encounter, there is no guarantee that she would accept you as a student."

Gramps was right, of course, but that couldn't stop my enthusiasm.

That, too, was running on inertia now.

"That sounds like a problem for future Edge." I smiled. "Now, if you'll excuse me, I think I have a few memories to make."

Memory crystals were relatively common in human lands but scarcer in my homeland. It wasn't that memory essence itself was uncommon. It was simply that the residents of my homeland rarely bothered to complete Dianis Points using it — at least in modern times.

There had been a more cerebral bent to the local fae before the days of war. Before my home had been the Court of Rust and Salt.

Now the local fae had little need for essence of art, dreams, and memories. Perhaps that was a part of why Ana and I had such an affinity for one another — her mastery of imagination essence was a form of skill that was truly rare among her people, at least in the modern day. Imagination essence was something of a throwback to the faeries of old — the ancient beings from before the days when humans, fiends, and faeries warred. I'd heard that there were other courts where imagination essence was more common, but anything of that type was rare in our local court.

Sadly, imagination essence itself wasn't quite the same as memory, and creating memory crystals was not among Ana's abilities. It was possible that one of the witches had memory essence, but if they did, they hadn't told me about it.

I knew of only one person who had memory essence — and fortunately, she was one of my favorite people in the world.

It took the better part of a day to make the trek to the far western border of the court, beyond the Dead Reaches and south of the Widow's Walk.

It was there that one fae made her home, alone and not alone, banished and blessed.

It was there that the Ghost Forge burned.

Though the night was rapidly encroaching as I approached, the forge's white light burned bright, even from a distance. The stone building was the solitary intact structure among hundreds of crumpled corpses of ancient stone.

Here, at the borders of the Old Gate, faeries and humans had once made a home together. And here, the betrayal of humanity echoed with every footstep in the dust, every heartbeat in my chest, every drop of rain that eroded the foundations of what had once stood before.

. . . But none of that bothered me. Not that day, at least. I was far too excited to get maudlin about ancient human backstabbing.

I approached the colossal stone doors of the forge, smiling as I heard the melodic ringing of a hammer, and knocked three times.

The clanging of a massive hammer *paused*, bringing with it a deafening silence. The forge's light flickered for an instant.

Then, after a pause, I heard an all-too-familiar voice. *"In."*

My smile widened as I pushed open the forge's massive doors and saw, once again, the wonders within.

Metal glimmered brightly in the lights of the white fires of the perpetual forge, though many of the implements within needed no such external illumination.

The colossal room contained thousands of metal objects — from forks to horseshoes and bracers to blades. Bronze, copper, and silver lined the walls, but the colors of metal were often lost in the incandescence of potent power. Blades burned with inner fire and frost, while other tools simply glittered with regal radiance.

. . . Among these many metals were the forbidden iron and steel. A source of great power and pride for their owner, but also the cause of her exile.

The walls themselves did not hold every weapon or item, of course. The smith was hard at work as always. Nothing but perfection could be tolerated in her work, be it forging items anew or maintaining the old.

And so, I took my place in line behind a colossal two-handed axe, which hopped a step to the right to give me more space to come inside and close the door. "Appreciate it, Choppy."

The axe tilted downward in acknowledgment but didn't talk. He was the quiet type, unlike Slashy, the curved sword that bounced excitedly in front of him. I mean, Slashy didn't talk either, but he was much less quiet in his silence. He spun in place, flipped over, and then bounced on his tip in way of greeting.

"Oi! Yer gonna ruin the floor 'gain if you keep at that, Slashy! 'N your blade besides!"

Slashy flipped back onto his hilt, then lowered his curved blade in dejection.

I leaned forward and whispered in a conspiratorial tone. "Don't let her get to you, she's going to redo the whole floor again in a month either way."

"I *'eard* that!" A massive hammer swung in my direction — not close enough to hit me, but merely in a gesture that carried enough force to incidentally push me back. "Quit bein' a bad influence! My work is piled up enough as it is."

"Can I help?"

I heard a snort. "You can certainly try."

Auntie Temper lowered her massive hammer and waved with her free hand toward a much smaller anvil on the other side of the forge, where a variety of much smaller tools were lined up. "You can take care of the kids."

I nodded, backing out of the line. "See you later, Choppy, Slashy."

I headed to the back of the Ghost Forge, keeping a distance from the actual forge itself to avoid blinding myself or being burned simply through close proximity to the ever-burning flames.

Then I pulled up a stone stool and took a seat at the smaller anvil, where a small (meaning human-sized) phantasmal hammer was already hard at work tapping brightly burning metal of a small dagger.

I was out of practice, but I knew what to do. I reached over to the nearby table, then slipped on the heavy apron, face guard, and gloves that were still located there.

Freshly washed, of course, in spite of my recent absence. I felt a little bad about that, but Auntie Temper wouldn't have tolerated anything else.

Then I picked up my tongs and hammer, both of the physical variety. "I'll swap in, Sir Smashington," I told the phantasmal hammer. The glimmering hammer wobbled a little in the air, as if exhausted, and then went to rest on one of the shelves nearby. The dagger currently on the anvil flipped upward, as if curious. "Hey, Stabby. It's just me, Edge."

Stabby was a young one and I was worried at first that she might not remember me, but she did a little happy bounce on the anvil before lying back down, so I felt a little better. "Looks like Sir Smashington already handled most of the work on you, but let's get finished, shall we?"

Auntie Temper let out a whistle.

Dozens of other small weapons hopped off the walls, adding to the existing line.

"Since yer here, we can make up for some lost time."

Hacky, Bashy, Quillon, Quarter, Cutter, Clanker . . .

This is going to be a long night.

I didn't mind.

I never could be upset about an evening spent with friends.

⊹

Ah. I suppose the Ghost Forge might require a bit more of an explanation, doesn't it?

In the war between humans and fae, there had been many losses on both sides. In most cases, these were of the kind you'd expect — soldiers on the battlefield.

But there was another type of loss that few understood, and fewer still paid any heed.

Children left without a home.

Of these, some were of the obvious variety — those of flesh and blood.

But there was another kind of orphan, one often neglected or forgotten even by those few who understood them.

They were the orphans of bonds.

Trees that suffered the loss of the dryad to which they were bound, or the dryad without a tree. In these tragic cases, one would often simply die without the connection, though at times a new bond could be forged — one lost and lonely soul bound to another. The court did everything in their power to save who they could by forging these new bonds . . . at least in most cases.

In the aftermath of the war, as our queen rose reforged with terrible wrath, there were those surviving few that remained too close to the image of our enemies.

Weapons of war once bound by blood and spirit to the invading army.

In a war between entities of terrible power, there were numerous spirit-bound weapons, armor pieces, and other objects that were left to litter the battlefield. And though only a comparatively small portion of these items were self-aware at the time that their owners fell, spirit-binding items can, on occasion, grow into something greater — especially during events where great power is put at work.

And so, in the aftermath of the war, there were dozens of spirit-bound items without a home. Many with only the faintest of awareness, some with none at all, but in other cases . . .

Some were as much a person as you or me.

This, of course, put the Queen of Rust and Salt into a difficult position. Were the items once bound to the spirits of our enemies to be treated as enemies as well? Or were they simply to be thought of as tools, as our enemies themselves had often treated them, reduced to objects without responsibilities for their allegiance?

And what place was there for metal weapons in the Reign of Rust?

When it seemed that the queen's vengeful wrath would sunder all that remained, Auntie Temper had extended her hand. She was a young woman then, but a veteran of the war. She had lost much, including her own bonded blade.

Perhaps that was why she chose to save them all.

She gathered the lost and brought them to a bloodstained ruin that had once had been a symbol of unity between two peoples. A place no other fae would willingly take shelter.

And with them, she forged a home in exile. Away from the rest of her people, not truly hated, but neither could she be said to be accepted.

But she had all the love she needed — for she had made a new family of her own.

It was deep in the night when the forge's fires dimmed — they were never truly exhausted — and Auntie Temper set her colossal hammer aside.

I mirrored her gesture with my own much smaller one, removing my visor to wipe the sweat that matted my hair to my forehead. It was a problem Auntie Temper never seemed to have.

As the last of the weapons we'd worked scuttled back to their shelves to sleep, I stretched my aching arm, removed my work gear, and then turned to Auntie Temper as she did the same.

Then, with a slowness that matched the smile spreading across her lips, she stretched out her huge arms.

Auntie Temper gave the best hugs.

She pulled me in tightly with strength that, if the stories were true, came at least in part from the blood of titans flowing in her veins. Given her stature and power, I could have believed the tales of her descent, as farfetched as they might have been.

But her strength was not a crushing force. Not to me. It was the strength and warmth of unconditional protection. The strength of love without reservation.

I hugged her right back with all my might.

The eight-foot-tall woman released me after several long moments, then turned her big head down to look at me. "You've gotten taller."

I had to laugh at that. "Still a long way from matching you, Auntie."

"That's a good thing. You still get to use regular doors." She let out a much grander laugh than my own, then hastily put a hand over her mouth as she noticed the sleeping swords stirring on a nearby shelf. "Oh, I'm . . . pardon. I'm sorry, kids. Go back to sleep."

Sheepishly, she waved me to come outside. I followed her.

We moved to a nearby ruin, climbing atop the stones that might have once been a building wall to gaze upward toward the distant stars.

We were quiet for a time. Auntie Temper tended to shift between bouts of silence and boisterousness in general.

We weren't so different, in that. In many ways, among my family of the forest, she was the one I found myself in the most.

"What brings you here, Edge? My congratulations on finally wakin' your sword essence, but I doubt you hope to sharpen yourself here. And Ana isn't with you, so . . ."

I nodded. Just as I saw myself in her, I knew she understood me. She knew I wouldn't be visiting without a reason. She wouldn't be offended by that — her own life was defined by her work, by her progress. She could never fault me for being very much the same. "In your work, you use memory essence to repair damaged tools and weapons, right?"

She nodded. "Wounds of flesh may repair on their own, given time. But for my children, other tools are needed. Not just for the nicks and cuts, but for older wounds, cuts that run deep throughout their minds and souls."

". . . Would such a power be able to help an echo to remember different things?"

"An echo? A strange question. What is this about?"

So I told her. It took some time to catch her up, but she never minded listening. I was glad for that. In some ways, someone in the family that would listen was the most important thing I could have asked for.

"It is a clever idea, Edge. I cannot say if it would work — you know too little of this being's nature. Tell me . . . is it truly worth trying to take this in such a hurry? Could you not train for a few decades, then return when you could defend yourself properly if she assaults you again?"

Though she understood me in many ways, we did have one critical difference — Auntie Temper was patient.

Perhaps that could be attributed to her long life span. She was already hundreds of years old, and if the spirits were kind, she would likely live for hundreds more. Thousands, maybe. I . . .

I didn't know what my life span was.

I didn't know what I was at all.

She must have seen my expression then. "Perhaps not such a long wait, then. Surely, there must be safer training alternatives?"

"There could be . . . in the world outside. But Grandfather will not allow me to leave to seek them. Not until I meet his standards for being 'ready.'"

"And thus, you must find a way to train here and now." She nodded, putting a huge hand on my back. "I understand."

I sighed. "Do you think this is a foolish idea?"

"Yes, without reservation. But if it is important to you . . ." She nodded. "I could use some help around here. Perhaps a full apprenticeship would be too much of a commitment, but for a year or two of help, I could offer you the help you need with forging new memories."

It was a generous offer. An extremely generous one, in fact.

I took some time to quietly consider it. "I don't think I can wait that long, either. I . . . I'm worried about Ana. She's been behaving strangely. And beyond that . . . I need to do this. To find a way to strengthen myself, to move on with my life."

She lowered her head. Perhaps in thought, perhaps in disappointment.

"Very well, then." Auntie Temper restrained the pain in her words as she asked the next question. "What do you have to trade?"

It was a necessity with fae. She could not simply give me what I asked for, not without setting a dangerous precedent. I was her extended family — she had acknowledged me as such when I was young, and allowed me to call her "Auntie" — so she could have made an exception. But faeries, even those in exile, were often creatures of tradition. And given all she had already sacrificed of her culture, I couldn't ask her to sacrifice anything more. Nor would she volunteer to.

She was treating me as an adult, not a child. One capable of making my own decisions, paying my own prices, and dealing with my own consequences.

It was a choice that must have been difficult for her.

. . . My own choice was a hard one, too, but in a different sense.

What did I have to trade that was of enough value?

I had precious few possessions of my own. I'd hand-carved many wooden figures over the years and given her some in the past, but wood tended to burn. It was a poor fit for her environment, as well as her . . . well, temperament. I'd made some stone figures with Ana, which would work better, but I didn't have any extras at the moment — I'd already given them all away. And making some with Ana's help meant they wouldn't be as appropriate for this type of trade, since they wouldn't be my work alone.

Most traditional small gifts, like those in my pouches, were not sufficient for this sort of trade. No acorn with honey could pay for the creation of even a single memory crystal — not with their scarcity in this region.

And I needed more than just one crystal for what I was hoping. I needed many, many crystals for my plans. Enough that she would need to take time away from her work to help me create them, which was a significant imposition for someone with her lifestyle.

"Three weeks," I responded after a time. I took a breath, then reached into a pouch on my side with great hesitation.

If she wished for me to pay a price, I needed to pay one that had sufficient significance.

". . . And this."

I pressed the vial of storm essence into her hand.

And so, as Auntie Temper's power opened the Smiling Sword Saint's path before me, I saw Uncle Eiji's path fade away.

CHAPTER XVIII

SWEET SURPRISE

I had agreed to three weeks of service easily, having done such labor a number of times in the past. Certain numbers — one, three, seven, one thousand and one, and various iterations thereof — were traditional numbers in fae culture and often used for deals, contracts, and promises.

Three weeks was a very reasonable time period, but one that I had unwittingly contrived to overlap with a special three days.

And so, when I awoke on the final day of my service, it was to a particularly perky faerie floating above me and cheering, "Happy threefold name day!"

I sat up steel straight at the sudden sound, my hand flying to my side and essence flaring within. Sleep had never come easily to me, nor did it flee readily in the moments that came after waking . . . except, of course, when I was startled.

Ana just giggled and flapped up to the ceiling of the ruined building where I'd made camp near the smithy. "None of that, mister! You wouldn't want to offend someone as powerful as I am, would you? I'm nearly Hearth-level now!"

I groaned, blearily processing her proclamation. "How close are we talking?"

She grinned brightly. "Oh, close enough. I bet it'll only be another year or two! Had a second dream, too. Not a full-on Destiny Dream, mind you — still only have one mark — but I think it might have still had a hint of destiny in it. And it was a good one, filled with trials and travails and treasures and torrents of tigers—"

I quirked an eyebrow at that last part, which was about as far as you could get with questioning a faerie's authenticity without causing offense.

"Maybe just a couple tigers," she amended, "but they were huge! And made of titanium!"

That was . . . more plausible, maybe? It was a dream, after all. "Well, I suppose congratulations are in order, then. Unless you've become the first faerie in existence to abandon their destiny, that is."

She snorted. "Not likely, mister! I gave those titanic titanium tigers a good thrashing and earned my new power! I could show you, but . . . oh, what a shame! Is that the forge I hear in the distance? The one where you have to work on your name day?"

I sighed, my shoulders slumping slightly. ". . . Please tell me there's tea, at least."

"Obviously." She reached into seemingly nothing, her eyes flashing brighter gold as she withdrew a cup of steaming liquid. I blinked. That wasn't an application of her imagination essence, as far as I could tell. Had she been working on generating more dungeon essence in her own body, perhaps, and mastered storing items in an extradimensional space? Or was this an element of something new — perhaps a new essence type she'd been working on in secret? "What sort of tyrant do you take me for?"

A cup of tea helped rouse me to some semblance of functionality, after which I had a small breakfast with Ana and marched off to my day of work at the forge. Auntie Temper behaved no differently from the preceding days, though I knew that a faerie with memory essence like herself was absolutely certain to have remembered my threefold name day.

I let myself wonder briefly if she would let it go unremarked — I had promised service, after all, without any expectation of special treatment, and that was my own failing — but I should have known better.

It was some three hours past nightfall, my muscles strained to exhaustion and my eyes burning through a day of near-unceasing work, that we finally removed our smithing gear and sat down in her humble dining room for a much-deserved meal. And it was at that point that she made her preparations clear to me.

Fae were remarkable in their variety, as with any intelligent species, and there are few truisms that apply to every member. In my many years living among the fae, however, I met only a scattered few that did not share a love of sweets in their myriad varieties.

Auntie Temper was no exception to this inclination — but because of the circumstances of her near-banishment, rarely was there an opportunity to find such indulgences at her table. As a barely tolerated outsider, she had few faeries who would even acknowledge her in conversation, and fewer still that would make trade. And, as far as she was from fae culture, she refused to deal with the humans that bordered her land at all. Some lines would not be crossed, even by one such as she.

Only those others that lived on the borders of fae society — those outsiders that were a loose family of their own — would deal with her, and even those scarcely with any regularity.

And so it was a great surprise and mystery to me when Auntie Temper, who suffered so long in her isolation and had so little of her own, contrived to arrange for me to have a name day cake.

It was the most wonderous of sights — a table-length pastry in the shape and dimensions of a winged-hilted sword that struck me with a strange sense of familiarity and awe. Even the frosting was silver.

I gaped at the sight of the tremendous silver-frosted cake as she set it down, expertly sliding a plate and silverware across it to me.

"Don't make yourself sick. 'Appy threefold name day, young Edge."

She lifted a cup of cider to her lips, giving me a curt nod, and then gestured to the silver knife set by the cake.

I couldn't help myself from standing up to hug her, refusing to maintain proper fae etiquette in one small way.

I'd never been much for cake, but like many of life's rules, it had exceptions.

"Thank you, Auntie."

She sighed, leaning heavily into my hug, then gave a laugh choked with more emotion than I'd expected. ". . . No debt is owed," she assured me automatically, as any good fae might when responding to unneeded thanks. But knowing my intent, she uttered a rarely heard phrase in those winding woods where I lived: "And you're welcome."

⋄⋄⋄

We spent the few meager remaining hours of the evening in quiet celebration. Loud and raucous games may have been Ana's style, but even when Ana arrived, she managed to keep her enthusiasm restrained in acknowledgment of Auntie Temper's silent preferences.

And so, we sipped at cups of cider, ate delicious sword cake, shared stories, and played quiet games.

When midnight approached, Auntie Temper delved into her storeroom briefly, then returned with a box that was obviously intended to be a gift. A part of me was very briefly disappointed when she had not come back with a sword—

But as my imagination wandered, I realized that she already had given me one earlier in the day — the only kind she could without amending the seven-year term of service needed to earn a blade from the forge.

. . . It was a greater boon than I had initially realized. From batter to frosting, the cake had been infused with sword essence. I'd sensed some immediately, but with the distractions of the day and my exhaustion, I hadn't immediately processed just how much power had been contained within. She'd likely spent multiple entire essence vials on the cake, which was as grandiose a gift as I'd ever received.

Her warning not to overindulge in the cake made a little more sense, then. It was not merely an adult warning a child not to overeat their sweets, but a master of essence warning a novice not to immerse their body in too much essence to process all at once.

Fortunately, such a potent pastry would not be wasted, even if I'd only managed to dent it in my first meal. Ana's new mastery of extradimensional spaces was applied immediately, and she was more than willing to store the cake in stasis in exchange for a meager slice. I ended up giving her more than one slice, of course, both because cake was better with friends to share it with and because she had almost certainly helped Auntie Temper conspire to bake it in the first place.

As my body processed the cake, my mind processed my second gift.

Auntie Temper flicked open the latches on the box, showing a row of glittering crystals inside. I gawked at the number of them — three rows of seven — more than I'd ever seen in one place at any given time.

"Your memory crystals, as agreed upon for three weeks of work and the vial you offered in trade. A promise made, a promise kept."

I accepted the bond solemnly in agreement. "A promise made, a promise kept." I began to remove the crystals from the box, knowing intuitively that the crystals were what had been agreed upon — not the container they came in. Auntie wouldn't have trapped me in such a way, but it was rote habit to respond in such a fashion.

She shook her head. "That is not needed. As it is your threefold name day, I offer you the box as a second gift."

It was a thing of strange black metal, one that was not familiar to me, but from the etchings within, I suspected it to hold some kind of minor enchantment — perhaps something related to preserving the contents. Such was common, and a simple thing for one such as Auntie Temper. I knew her well enough not to question if it contained iron — she would not have given it to me if there was any risk of it drawing ire from other fae upon my reentry to the woods proper.

"I accept this generous gift, Auntie." I turned over one of the crystals. "I must confess that I do not understand how you already made my crystals, however, without drawing from my memories actively."

I'd worked with memory crystals before, and seen a few varieties, but usually the person with memory essence had to create them while someone was actively thinking about a subject. The memory-worker could then draw from those memories to create a coherent crystal that could be viewed by anyone who knew how to activate it.

"These are a bit of my own design," Auntie Temper explained. "With some inspiration from this wee one and her creative mind." She gestured at Ana.

Ana beamed. "Can I explain? Can I, can I?"

Auntie gave a patient laugh. "You've earned that much, little star. Go ahead."

"Okay, so, these aren't just memory crystals — they're a compound of memory essence and forge essence. They start out 'unforged,' until you tell it to 'begin forging' and think about something. Then it'll let you record those memories, and you can tell it to 'stop forging.'"

"That's . . . impressive. But what happens if my mind wanders?"

"Oh, that's fine. You can say 'reforge' and start it over if you have to."

I frowned in consideration. "Actively remembering something isn't usually as coherent as experiencing it. I know that when I've used your memory crystals before, my recollections were clearer than anything I've been able to remember on demand. Do these work the same way?"

"Not quite," Auntie admitted. "When I'm forging a crystal for you, I have some direct control over the content, which I use to make sure the memories are what you want to store. With these, the crystal will work to make a memory more complete, but it can't filter anything out. When you think of a core subject for the memory, the crystal will draw from associated memories on the topic. Basically, you want to think about something like 'the first time I met Ana,' and it will do the rest automatically, but if there's a particular part of that you'd rather not include . . . well, you're best not showing that scene at all."

I nodded in understanding. "This is a wonderful—" I almost said "gift," then remembered that it wasn't one. It was a trade, albeit one that she'd over-delivered on. "Innovation. It should serve my purposes well."

"I'd hoped it might." Auntie gave me a genuine smile. "You've made me proud, young Edge. Your arms have grown near as strong as your heart, though with the way the latter grows, I know they may never catch up."

"I . . ." I was a little abashed, but I managed an embarrassed smile. "I appreciate that, Auntie. You've taught me much, and offered me a great deal."

She gave a quiet grunt of acceptance, then took a breath and went to the wall to lift something else, hefting a deceptively heavy object in her hand and setting it in front of me. "Let it not be said that I would leave you on your threefold celebration with only two gifts in hand."

I stared at the object in front of me — one of the simplest in the building, and one with deceptive utility.

To an untrained eye, it was an evenly cut rock. And I wasn't great with rocks, truth be told. Fortunately, this was far more resilient than most, and with a utility that could not be denied.

A spiritsharp stone.

One of the iconic tools of the Ghost Forge, a spiritsharp stone was a whetstone — a tool used for honing the edges of blades — of simple use and vast application. While an ordinary whetstone could be used to keep the edges of a weapon or tool sharp, a spiritsharp stone would hone the essence and spirit of a blade, maintaining — and sometimes even improving — the powers of a weapon over time. Even mundane weapons honed with a spiritsharp stone would, according to stories, gradually develop abilities according to those of the wielder.

And so, in giving this gift, Auntie Temper had given me one piece of a path to crafting a blade of my own . . . or sharpening any I came to wield.

I pressed the stone against my chest, feeling the essence within, which seemed to pulse in accordance to the beating of my own heart.

"I'll cherish this gift," I said with the utmost honesty.

"Good." Auntie gave me a curt nod, but I could tell her own heart was warmed by my acceptance. "That's that, then. It's late now, and *I'd* cherish some sleep." She stood from her chair. "Thank you for visiting, young Edge and Ana. Know that you are always welcome . . . and if you ever should lose your path, your family will be here to help you forge one anew."

CHAPTER XIX

SHARPER

It was too late to travel, so Ana and I slept in my shelter near the forge that night. I cradled the spiritsharp stone to my chest throughout the night like many children would hold an animal, for it was a precious gift and reminder of my family's love.

In the morning, I felt stronger. Truly, the power of cake cannot be denied. In truth, as significant as the gift of the cake had been, I could not have gleaned such an immediate benefit from it even a year before. Not only was my body's acclimation rate naturally improving as I aged, but the work of the Smiling Sword Saint had a profound impact. My Heart Point had greedily consumed the cake-given essence as I slept, and by the morning, I felt ready for a few bites more.

I would still be cautious not to push my body too hard — I was still healing from the minor injuries to my star veins, and oversaturation could have caused significant damage — but as I healed, I knew I would be able to tolerate more and more.

I was still far behind Ana, her Torch-level capabilities still too much for me to match . . . but, for the first time, I felt like I had a competitive edge that might help me catch up.

. . . Even if I still didn't have a sword.

I was a little disappointed that I hadn't managed to earn a true blade — or, possibly *the* True Blade, one of the legendary weapons I'd long daydreamed about wielding — during the year since my first awakening. But with my power redoubled in my body, my confidence had returned twofold as well—

And so it was that I, Edge of the Woods, student of the Smiling Sword Saint, did endeavor again to attempt Anathema's challenges.

The journey took nearly a day and a night, with visits to the same friends of yore that I had celebrated with the year before, though this time

I slept at the base of the shrine itself to confront the shrine at dawn's first light.

Upon the final day of my threefold name day, I strode into the shrine's doors, a sword forged from my own essence in my right hand—

And found myself flat on my back in the next moment I could remember.

"Well," I groaned, "that was predictable. Time for round two."

When I headed home that evening with my left arm held in an imagination-wrought sling, I didn't cry.

I smiled.

At least I can walk this time. And . . .

My mind latched on to a half-faded memory of a blade that burned black and silver.

I'm getting closer.

CHAPTER XX

SAINTLY STEEL

When I headed back up the mountainside to the sword school, I was better prepared this time. Not just in terms of supplies, although I certainly tried to pack better every time I took a new trip.

No, I was stronger. It wasn't easy to evaluate progress within a stage of essence wielder advancement — not unless you had a specialized skillset for that purpose — but I could tell that the essence within my body was sharpening. I'd grown incrementally stronger, faster, and more resilient throughout the year, as befitting anyone who increased their sword essence, but the days since the sword saint had cut me had been a marked improvement. Now that I had a food source infused with sword essence, I was likely to continue to improve rapidly.

At least as long as the cake lasted.

I couldn't count on the food itself to be my only source of supplemental sword essence for long. If I wanted to continue to make rapid progress, I'd still need to find a way to gather sword essence regularly within the mountains. That was simple enough on the surface — I'd figured out that it was pooling near the Smiling Sword Saint — but in practice, that meant I was going to be risking my life any time I wanted to gather it. Unless, of course, we could come to an arrangement.

One of the most obvious issues was that I simply didn't appear to be powerful or skilled enough to warrant the sword saint's interest. There was no quick and easy fix to that problem, but her final attack — or, rather, the lingering aftermath of it on my body — had given me more than one idea on how to experiment.

As Gramps had explained, one of my problems with advancement speed was that my body had to acclimate to any essence I absorbed — not just sword essence. I'd already tinkered with trying to make techniques for getting rid of the wrong essence types that my body was in the midst of processing, but I hadn't had any success—

But the sword saint had. Whether it was deliberate or not, she'd wiped out everything other than sword essence that had been inside my star veins when she'd hit me, and that meant that obliterating other essence types through using sword essence was possible.

This wasn't exactly surprising — I'd seen similar techniques in the scrolls Gramps had shown me. Simply passing sword essence through my star veins might cut the other essence out, but I'd likely lose some sword essence in the process, and I could hurt myself, too.

When I returned to the sword school, I sat and considered this problem, then focused on what I'd already been able to do with sword essence and how I could properly apply it.

The answer that I came up with was simple in concept, but much more challenging in practice.

Gramps had told me about two different ways people cut out the essence types they wanted — using alchemy to separate the component parts before absorbing the essence, or destroying the unwanted essence after it went into the body.

Without the tools, knowledge, or resources, I couldn't use the alchemical approach—

But I *could* do the same type of thing in my own body, couldn't I?

I'd seen something similar in the technique scrolls regarding earth essence, but at the time, I hadn't been able to figure out a way to make it work with my knowledge of sword essence aspects. The idea hadn't really appealed to me at the time, either . . . but if I could combine the earth essence method with something more like the fire essence method of obliterating the other essence . . .

That had potential.

Instead, days after I'd gotten all of the benefits of the cake that I could and my star veins were feeling unfortunately empty, I ate a handful of bladeberries and watched the essence flow through my body.

Then I focused on the strange essence that I'd used to split my own sword apart for the Shattering Sword technique.

My essence sense wasn't exactly exceptional, nor was my ability to manipulate it — but that particular aspect of sword essence, the power to cleave things apart—

It came to me with a strange sort of ease. The kind of ease that should have worried me, if I'd considered it a little bit more closely.

Instead, I closed my eyes, focused, and cut.

I felt it pass through me, like a hint of a razor, and the essence of one of the bladeberries split apart into constituent parts.

I paused, momentarily stymied by the simplicity of it.

I'd made techniques before, but this . . . I'd succeeded instinctively, on my first try.

I didn't celebrate immediately. I repeated it, again and again, splitting the essence of the other bladeberries I swallowed and reproducing the results. Only when I could sense each independent component of each berry was I satisfied that I'd done it—

And that was a great accomplishment in itself, but I wasn't done.

Splitting the essence apart had the advantage that I could then take the sharpness-aspected essence and convert it into sword essence for my Heart Point, just as I might have with a sword mote. That allowed me to use it all directly for primary essence, rather than allowing some of it to dissipate into secondary essence. That would help give me an important tool for improving my advancement speed.

This isn't to say that I planned to neglect my secondary essence growth, either, of course — but it would give me more control over how I chose to distribute the essence in my body.

The next step, however, was even more critical—

I converted the sharpness essence immediately, using it to reinforce my Heart Point.

Then I focused again, remembering the surge of power that had obliterated all of the non-sword essence in my star veins—

And I hacked the remaining essence of the bladeberries to pieces.

With the part of the essence I'd desired already absorbed into my Heart Point, there was no risk of hitting the wrong essence and damaging it. I still had to avoid cutting my star veins themselves, or hitting a Dianis Point, but that was easy—

I remembered the pattern for the sword saint's essence flowing through my body, and I mirrored it.

This process, unlike the first stage, wasn't completely perfect on my first effort. I didn't hurt myself, but when I was slashing the essence apart, the minimal amount of sword essence I was able to pass through my star veins directly wasn't enough to completely obliterate the other essence types I'd absorbed. I eliminated some of it, but copper wasn't easy to carve into nothingness, even with a sword—

So, ultimately, my efforts weren't wasted, but they weren't absolutely exhaustive. Some bits of copper essence would remain, absorbed into secondary essence. That would slow me down marginally, but I couldn't help but be gratified by how well the process had gone.

I raised my quill and began to write. It was good to document my progress, both for my own reference and for future sword essence practitioners, assuming I could ever find someone to pass my own techniques on to.

Writing the instructions was easy, but I struggled for some time with what was often the hardest part of technique construction.

In the end, I wrote the final line at the top of my technique scroll. The name.

I called it my Star Sharpening technique.

Days passed. I continued to improve it.

With practice, I'd cut harder and faster, until I'd left nothing remaining of the essence I wished to destroy.

⁂

Weeks passed as I continued to train at the sword school, absorbing every bit of essence that I could from the power the sword saint had infused into me, the cake, and the massive bag of bladeberries that I'd taken with me on this particular trip.

The year had only started, but I was feeling great. By carving virtually every other type of essence out of my diet, I was building up sword essence in my body near-exclusively. I split that roughly fifty-fifty between primary and secondary essence, with the knowledge that I could have been advancing faster if I focused more on primary essence, but that it would weaken me compared to the power I could have at the same level.

There were different schools of thought in terms of primary and secondary essence allocation. The majority of a person's overall power came from their primary essence, but much of that power came in bursts of improvement as one increased in essence wielder level.

Going from Candle-level to Torch-level, for example, was expected to provide an immediate improvement of about a quarter to whatever attributes were related to the essence types the person used — so, for a sword essence wielder, things like strength, speed, and durability.

Certain specific "landmark" levels — those that involved the transition into another layer of the self — provided larger benefits. Usually, these were quoted at being around a fifty to seventy-five percent improvement . . . and instantaneous. It was a tremendous boost, comparable to the benefit I'd felt when I'd first hit Candle. But those huge gains could be years — or even decades — apart . . . if someone ever achieved them at all. The average person would only see that improvement when they first hit Candle and maybe one other point in their lifetime, if that.

Secondary essence, however, improved a person's power incrementally while they continued to advance through each stage. With a fifty-fifty split of primary and secondary essence, a person would see about another twenty-five percent improvement going from Candle to Torch from their secondary essence — so, about the same as the jump between Candle and Torch, but gradual, rather than all at once.

This meant that overall, the benefits of advancing secondary essence were somewhat lower, since the jumps between layers provided a greater benefit than secondary essence did on a per-unit basis. For that reason, Skyseekers often focused very heavily on their primary essence, allocating as much as seventy-five or eighty percent of their essence toward their Dianis Points and advancing vastly more quickly as a result. This resulted in people hitting extremely powerful stages at younger ages, but with lower relative power compared to people of the same level who took a slower and more balanced approach. When someone wasn't constantly facing imminent danger, this was a pretty good idea. Skyseekers and others who followed this route would have greater overall power for their point in life than anyone else, as long as they survived and went up to higher layers.

Conversely, relic hunters, Shrineseekers, and other adventurers tended to focus more heavily on secondary essence, eschewing rapid advancement for incremental improvements that could be lifesaving in a dangerous situation. These skews were typically less extreme, more like a sixty-forty split in favor of secondary essence. This was generally considered a wise strategy for helping to survive in the dangerous environments that Shrineseekers traversed, but they'd end up being weaker for their age than pure Skyseekers, at least once those Skyseekers hit higher layers.

There were other factors that made things more complex, too. Skyseekers who remained at their sects often had the ability to control their essence intake much more closely, only absorbing essence that they wanted, which would allow them to focus on strengthening the aspects of themselves they wanted to improve. Adventuring types could rarely be as picky, and thus, while they might end up with more secondary essence in total for any given level, they'd end up with a wide variety of essence types that didn't necessarily synergize.

My hope was that by sticking with absorbing sword essence near-exclusively, but going for a fifty-fifty essence split, I'd end up with some of the advantages of both approaches. In theory, this would make me stronger than average for my essence level in the specific areas I specialized in, but I wouldn't advance as quickly as a dedicated Skyseeker would.

Now that I finally had a place where I could get sword essence, I was eager to pursue it. After a few weeks of recovery time and improving my body, I was ready to take the risk.

Idly, I fiddled with one of the memory crystals as I walked. I experimented with forging and reforging memories within, then viewing them to see the results. There were a few possible things I considered recording for the Smiling Sword Saint, but ultimately, I settled on something simple.

I left my backpack and most of my possessions behind at the sword school as I approached the Smiling Sword Saint's arena. I carried only a handful of items, knowing that virtually anything in my possession could be easily destroyed if the sword saint chose to cut it.

And so, with a memory crystal in my pouch and a phantasmal sword at my hip, I stepped into the mist and braced myself for blades.

I found myself inside an arena of stone, ringed by an empty stadium. It was much the same as when I'd first visited the place, the thousands of floating swords absent in favor of a complete reset to the conditions before the sword saint had noticed me. This was not unexpected, but I didn't quite understand the mechanisms by which those swords had first been summoned, so I hadn't been sure what the place would look like when I arrived.

A black-haired woman stared at me from across the arena.

I took a step closer to her, keeping my hand away from my sword. I didn't want her to break it immediately, after all.

"Well, well." She stepped toward me, tilting her head to the side with curiosity. "Looks like I've found myself a distraction."

I took another step forward.

"That's close enough, kid. You're . . . what, midway to your second stage? And barely that. Pathetic. What brings a child like you here? This is clearly some sort of illusion, but . . . what could you hope to gain from visiting it?"

I raised my right hand, extending it to my side. A blade-shaped projection of force cut the air. "I'm here to train."

She tilted her head downward, her lips twitching. "What makes you think I'd train a talentless weakling like you?"

I lifted my left arm, allowing the sleeve to fall down and reveal a trail of still healing cuts and scarcely-fading scars from where she'd first struck me there. "You already have, once."

She raised her eyebrow. I braced myself for the possibility that this would be some kind of fatal eyebrow-related killing technique, but if it was, it still hasn't hit me yet. "Think I'd remember something like that. Don't take many students. Don't take *any*, in fact."

Her hand moved toward her hip. It was a warning gesture, since she could have easily drawn one of her many swords and killed me with it faster than I could have processed the movement. Or, you know, just manifested a reality-altering sword field, or cleaved me in twain with a blink, or . . . you get the idea.

Still, even knowing that, I admit to a degree of nervousness at this part of the exchange.

"Ah, wait, hold on. You're an echo, or something like it. I've visited you in the past, you just don't remember. Here, wait." I reached into a pouch at my side, then tossed a glittering green gemstone toward her.

Her wrist moved. The gemstone fell to the ground in pieces.

Well . . . that's a miss. Sorry, Auntie.

"Stay your hand, boy. Make no further movements." She held a glittering blade in her hand, her eyes narrowed. "Explain."

"Ah — ah." I froze, as she'd instructed. "Memory crystal. It was a memory crystal."

A piece of crystal floated upward toward her other hand. She snatched it out of the air. "Hm."

I continued waiting.

"It seems it was. A mix of essence, though. Not a bad taste to it. Metallic. Familiar. And what did you wish to show me?"

I took a breath. "Five minutes of my memories. It showed the last time I visited you, and, uh, your training."

"I gave you five minutes of my time?" She frowned, tossing down the fragment. It splintered further.

"Ah, no. Actually, the crystal always records five minutes, but I wasn't in here that long. We talked for a minute or two, and then you, uh, trained me a little."

"Define 'trained.'"

I considered how best to phrase that. "You hit me with a sword essence technique that I suspect was intended to make me stronger."

She gave me a disdainful headshake. "So, you were even more pathetic back then."

"No." I shook my head. "I was just as determined as I am right now."

She snorted. "At least you have a bit of steel in your bones. Fine. That must have injured you badly. And you think I'd teach you something else this time?"

"In fairness, you haven't actually taught me anything yet, unless we're counting 'how many places can someone bleed from at once' as a lesson."

"Oh, that is a good lesson. But not what I would have been teaching you, little blade." The Smiling Sword Saint's lips quivered for a moment. "The Trial of a Thousand Scars. You must be snapped to come back here after that. Why'd you return, kid? You feel like bleeding a second time?"

I shifted into a ready stance, hand floating near the hilt of my phantasmal sword. "Isn't it enough just to want to see my master smile?"

CHAPTER XXI

SEQUENCE OF SCARS

The Smiling Sword Saint frowned at me.

I gave her a sheepish look. ". . . I thought it was a pretty good line."

"It was a presumptuous line." She tilted her head to the side, examining me. "Why would I bother teaching a mere child, and one without any power?"

"I'd imagine you'd want to finish what you started. You probably had some objective when you carved these into me." I gestured at my skin. "I can tell that your technique both infused my body with sword essence and cut out extraneous essence types to facilitate rapid absorption. My best guess is that you felt that I was behind where you wanted me to be for my age, so you did something to accelerate my growth. You might have wanted me to make it into a technique, too."

"I didn't tell you that, though, did I?"

It was more of a statement than a question, but I responded regardless. "No. I just parsed that from the state of my body in the aftermath."

"Well, I've got me a *thinker*, have I?" She gave a brief snort. "Got a clever edge to you, won't deny that, but you've missed a critical weak point, boy."

I frowned. "Which is?"

"If you were too weak for me then, you're still useless to me now."

"In terms of raw power, perhaps. But I've read about you, and—"

She laughed. "You've read about me? Go on, please, tell me all about myself."

I sensed a trap in her words, but I had few options. "You were a master of a broad variety of techniques — and the path toward mastering them could begin even at my stage."

She scoffed. "Technically true, but why would I waste the time?"

I glanced around from left to right, moving nothing other than my eyes, just to be safe. She'd been clear she'd respond badly to any sudden movements.

"Well, far be it from me to keep you from all the *other* exciting things going on in the limited space where you sort of exist."

The sword saint snorted. "You think you can get me to teach you a technique because that beats the sheer boredom I'd be facing otherwise?"

"Uh, yeah, honestly, that was pretty much the plan. I was also considering various bribes."

She slapped her legs. "So honest! It'll get you killed, definitely. But it's refreshing! Okay, kid. You want me to teach you a technique?"

My heart brightened. I . . . was this really happening? Could it be that my plan was . . . actually going to work?

Was that allowed?

"I'd be thrilled by that. And . . . if it isn't too much to ask, I don't have a teacher for swordsmanship in general. I was hoping you'd be willing to give me a more formal lesson."

"Don't push it, kid. You're . . . what, twelve?"

"I just turned fourteen."

She shook her head. "And still so weak. I was pushing close to Regalia-level at your age."

I gave her a shrug. "Don't know what to tell you. I'm not you. I wasn't born a prodigy. But I'll work hard, and I think I could make you proud in time, if you'd let me."

"There's a wide gulf between those with talent and those without, kid. Very few could bridge the gap between where you are now and where you should be, if you want to follow my path. I don't know anyone who started that far behind and managed to catch up."

"The Emperor of the Conquered Suns." I folded my arms.

She raised a brow again. "Never heard of him. Did he do anything impressive?"

"Well, for starters, he killed you."

In an instant, she was right in front of me, peering into my eyes. I felt an intense surge of pressure in the air and the instantaneous feeling of metal pressed against a thousand places on my skin at once. "What did you say?"

I stared right back. Her threatening aura probably should have terrified me, but in that moment, it only spurred me forward faster. "He's the one who killed the *real* you. Years and years ago now. And he started with practically no power at all. Didn't even get into a sect at first, from what I hear. They looked down on him because he was a foreigner, and because of his eyes. He trained slowly, over the course of a long life, until he surpassed you."

She continued to stare at me, then spun around and took another couple steps away in utter silence.

For a moment, I wondered if she'd whirl around and cut me in half for my insolence.

But instead, her next words were quiet. Contemplative.

The sword essence in the air quivered . . . then stilled.

"How was the fight?"

"It was before I was born," I explained, my tone even. I sensed that coming across as apologetic would have been a mistake with her, even then.

"But you heard he killed me. You must know something about what happened."

I nodded. "Sure." I paused, considering my next words. "I don't know what age exactly you're copied from. Are you familiar with the ruined world of Talvas yet?"

A slight inclination of her head. "Sure. Tried to fight off the Sun Eater, ended up ruining their own planet so badly he didn't even want the remains. Probably a lesson to be had there, too. Why?"

"That's where you fought him. Needed a place to do it without the collateral damage spreading too far, I suspect. If you've heard of it, do you remember how many suns it had?"

"That's a foolish question." She turned, then glanced upward toward the sky, then back to me. "Thirteen. Not a common planetary setup, but not that strange, either."

"There *were* thirteen." I smirked. "There were eleven after your battle."

She froze.

Then, after a moment, she bent over double, bursting into laughter. "Emperor . . . of the Conquered Suns. We . . . destroyed them?"

"Technically, he did, from the way the story is told. As you fought in the void above the world, he managed to knock you into one of the suns. Then he crashed a second sun into it. Both were destroyed, and you were annihilated along with them."

The slightest edge of a grin formed on her face, and with it, the world below her splintered.

"Mag . . . magnificent." She drew in a deep breath, then sighed. "Such an incredible way to die. But is it certain I did not survive?"

I gazed at the woman who was asking me, in utter seriousness, if she could have survived two suns exploding on top of her.

You'd think that would have been a good time to wonder if I'd made a terrible mistake, but no.

Seeing her own doubt, somehow, I had to wonder, too. ". . . Well, they never found a body. Which is, uh, probably because of what happens when suns explode. But I suppose . . ."

"You suppose?"

"Anything is possible." I shook my head. "But it seems unlikely, given that you have not shown yourself in the years since. And the two of you were longtime rivals. If you lived, well, you likely would have challenged him again by now."

"Rivals . . ." she murmured, in a tone akin to prayer. "I had a rival, did I? And he destroyed two suns to defeat me." She raised a hand, covering her face. "How beautiful. If only I could remember . . ."

She turned toward me. Were those . . . tears? Her expression shifted back to stern in a moment, however. And then she said, "I have an important question."

"Okay?"

She nodded, more to herself than to me. "This . . . Emperor of Conquered Suns . . ." She paused, frowning. "Is he currently seeing anyone?"

I blinked. My jaw dropped just a little. "Like . . . you mean a wife? Or a lover or something?"

"No, obviously." She waved a hand dismissively. Her gesture left a stone pillar next to me shredded into dust, seemingly without any intent on her part. "Why would I be concerned about something as unimportant as that? I was asking if he has a new *rival*, foolish boy."

"I . . . don't think so? I don't believe I've heard of one. He's probably even stronger now, not a lot of people could possibly challenge him."

She tilted her head down. "Good. Very good." She clapped her hands together.

Another two pillars cracked, falling to pieces. I side-eyed the destruction, then looked back to her.

She spun toward me. "I will train you today. You will not return again until you have three memory crystals, all of the same composition as the last. They are capable of recording whatever you wish, yes?"

"Yes. But . . ." I blinked. "But three? Why?"

"You will prepare two with memories in advance. One of our first meeting, and one of today. The last will be left empty."

I felt a subtle smile crossing my face. She'd come up with largely the same plan I'd been thinking of on her own. "You're going use the last one on yourself, since you don't normally maintain any memories between my visits. Perfect."

"You'll need to bring me another blank crystal every time. Can you do that?"

I nodded to her. "I agree to your terms."

"Good." She gave me a curt nod in return. I heard one of the pillars nearby splinter in response to her gesture. "Now show me what you've got, kid."

I took a deep breath. I'd known there would be a chance she'd ask to see what I could already do, but that didn't exactly make me *less* nervous.

After a moment of hesitation, I extended my hand to my right side. "First, the Sword Hand technique."

I gripped my essence and formed my blade—

And found the Smiling Sword Saint right next to me before I could process any movement, lifting my right arm and processing it.

"Is this what passes for a Sword Hand technique these days?"

I frowned defensively. "I mean . . . it's a rudimentary technique, but . . ."

"I can see why you wanted a new teacher. Who taught you this resh variant?"

". . . I, uh, kind of made it myself."

The sword saint was right in front of me. She tilted my head downward, staring at me eye to eye. "You made this technique."

"Yes?"

"Say it again. Clearly."

A little annoyed, in spite of the obvious danger, I narrowed my eyes straight at her. "I. Made. This. Technique."

She shook her head, releasing my jaw and stepping back. "No teacher, no scrolls? Nothing?"

"Neither. I did study stories of people using the Sword Hand technique, as well as general theory, in order to approximate what—"

She shifted an eyebrow. I felt something — deflection-aspected sword essence, maybe, or something very similar — push my jaw closed.

"Hmph. Well, it's terrible, but I suppose that's to be expected if you made it yourself from spare parts. If that's the best you've got, though, I'm not wasting my time.

I bristled, feeling a slight affront to my pride. "That was just the first thing I built."

She gave me the slightest hint of a frown. I felt a gash spread across my cheek, and in the distance, I heard the sound of a tree falling to the ground. "You're telling me you've already made more than one technique at Candle-level?"

"Well, I wouldn't consider any of them *completed* techniques, and in the case of the latter two—"

"Latter two? No, no. How many techniques do you plan to show me?"

". . . Five? Maybe six?"

Her lips twitched in irritation. I felt a brush of sword essence flow into me as it ripped across my ribs.

My eyes narrowed at the implied threat from her essence as I felt the hairs on the back of my neck rise, but I didn't let it bother me. This was what

I wanted. Her attention, deadly as it might have proven if I misspoke. "I'll just show you the best one I built myself. It's an attack technique—"

She snorted. "Hit me, then. And be quick about it."

I didn't hesitate. If the Smiling Sword Saint's echo was only a tenth as powerful as the original at this stage in her life, she'd still be a thousand times my own power. I had no chance of hurting her.

So I grabbed every hint of sword essence I could muster, then slammed my sword into her chest.

Shattering Sword.

She didn't move. My technique blasted into her, the sword essence fracturing and splintering harmlessly on impact. My phantasmal sword shattered into nothing in my hands.

The Smiling Sword Saint stared at me.

". . . What . . . the *vek* . . . was *that*?"

I looked back at her, now uncertain. Had I done something wrong? Should I have warned her before I struck, or was my technique so rudimentary that she'd been offended?

Before I could open my mouth to stammer an answer, she had her hands on my shoulders. "Show me that again. *Now.*"

I glanced down at the rapidly fading hilt of the phantasmal sword in my hand. "I'll need a sword."

She took a step backward, releasing me—

Then, wordlessly, I grabbed one of the swords from her belt and slashed her with it.

Shattering Sword.

My sword essence *flared* across the newly drawn blade, even the facsimile of one of her own blades carrying vast power, hundreds of times beyond my own.

I heard a loud crack as I slammed the sword into her—

And for an instant, I saw the slightest hint of surprise on her face.

My technique shattered harmlessly, just as before. But the sword remained intact.

In the moment where I recovered in the aftermath, I processed the fact that I had, without asking, drawn a sword off the belt of someone who was thousands of times my superior. This was the type of impetuous action that, if one somehow managed to actually succeed, could be considered an insult to such a degree that it would not have been unusual for her to cut me in half in an instant for my presumptuousness.

But she did no such thing. Instead, she stared downward and said, "You wielded my sword."

Gramps's teachings were to be humble, to apologize for my impudence, but . . . something about how she looked at me, how she'd behaved up to this point, told me that was wrong. "I needed one to show you my technique. You could have stopped me — you're probably dozens or hundreds of times my speed. But you didn't think I could use it."

"No." She continued to watch me. "I didn't. The technique. Again."

I shifted my stance, raised the sword, and brought it back down.

Shattering–

She caught the sword in her hand. No, not just the sword — the essence, too. She'd somehow frozen it in place, keeping it stable.

"This is . . . you truly made this technique yourself?"

"I did."

Her lips twisted, and somewhere in the distance, a pillar twisted in the center, collapsing to the ground. "How many years did it take you?"

"Years?" I blinked.

"It's a straightforward question."

". . . I made this technique in three days."

Her hand twitched on the blade of the sword. My technique collapsed. The sword's blade crumpled like paper. She stumbled back, bending at the waist . . .

I worried for a moment that I'd done something terribly wrong, until I realized that she was laughing. Laughing so hard that I couldn't even hear the sound.

"You . . . made that technique . . . at Candle-level . . . with only one essence type . . . in *three days*."

". . . Yes?" I glanced again at the twisted sword — her own sword — that was in my hand and frowned. Had I offended her somehow?

Her hand was under my chin again a moment later, a single finger pushing it up. "You wouldn't lie to me about something like that, would you?"

"No. Could have done it in two, if I had a metal sword. You want to fix this one and loan it to me?"

Her finger twitched and I felt blood blossoming across my neck. "You're impetuous, even for a child."

"I get that a lot." I flipped the hilt of her sword around, offering it back to her. "If you don't want to loan me the sword, I'd settle for just a technique."

"Of course you'd settle for that. Well." She shook her head, then stepped back. "It seems like there might be some raw steel for me to work with here after all."

She snatched the broken sword out of my hand, resheathing it in a blur. I felt a hint of disappointment, but it had been worth a try.

"What are you teaching me?" I asked.

"Nothing. You're still too weak for that."

I felt my heart sink. "But—"

"Remove your shirt. I don't need to ruin one every session. And what was it you said earlier? You already learned how many places can someone bleed from at once."

I processed that and realized what she was about to do.

Oh.

Yeah, okay, that makes sense.

At least, if I stay conscious longer this time, maybe I can show her what I've been working on for my third and fourth techniques.

I slipped off my shirt. At least this time, I wouldn't have to buy a replacement.

"When do we be—"

Then the pain came.

Oh.

⊹ ⊹

I barely remember the first time I woke up.

I remember the sharp pain, omnipresent throughout my body.

I remember the blurriness of my vision as my eyes feebly attempted to open.

I remember trying to raise my right arm and failing.

I remember, faintly, a feeling of warmth. Something immediate, yet distant. It brought less comfort than it should have, given how extensive my injuries were.

What I remember best, oddly, is the scent of pine, strange and yet familiar. Had I been more aware, I might have processed it and understood elements of my situation much earlier.

I don't remember speaking, exactly. I feel like I must have, because someone must have responded, bringing water to my mouth. I drank, liquid sloshing over my lips and face during my feeble effort. Then the blackness came again.

When I woke next, I was alone.

⊹ ⊹

I don't know how long I slept, but it must have been through at least that day, and perhaps others. It was nighttime when I managed to unlimber the shields from my eyes, and I was, once again, inside the storage shed at the sword school.

I closed my eyes immediately, remembering where I'd been and feeling the now-familiar welling of sword essence within me.

Ugh. I didn't manage to resist losing consciousness for even a moment. Wish I could have shown this to her.

. . . But even so, there's work to do.

I focused on the sword essence, preparing to draw it out — and hesitated.

I didn't have any lack of courage, but that didn't mean I enjoyed extreme, consciousness-shattering levels of pain. And given what had happened last time, I wasn't exactly in a hurry to repeat it.

So, instead of wrenching the essence straight out of my body this time, I focused on the intense flow of power that cycled through my body.

My mind was clearer this time. I wasn't as badly wounded, because of either my increased sword essence providing me with more resistance, the sword saint cutting me differently, or additional care from my mystery healer. In any case, as I extended my senses, I could feel the essence around me more easily than before — and the essence next to me, too.

The scabbard at my side felt *closer*, now. The essence within it was more tangible, almost like a part of me. I didn't know how that had happened, but it meant that I had a sample of the essence to work with. And with a sample, I could change other sword essence to the same composition.

When I'd last considered drawing essence out of my star veins into my body, I'd considered building a shell of deflection-aspected essence around more offense-focused essence within . . . but that didn't feel *right*. Deflection-aspected essence wasn't meant for an edge, nor was it built to be a container.

But now?

I grinned as I realized I'd had the solution on me all along.

There was nothing better than a scabbard to safely contain a sword.

With my eyes closed and my will focused, I began to convert the essence swirling in my star veins into layers. The outermost layer would be a protective wall of scabbard-aspected sword essence. And within, I would shift the essence into a shape of a proper blade — with slashing essence on the edges and unaspected sword essence within.

With the essence whirling within my veins shifted to the new aspects, I grasped it firmly.

Draw Sword.

And this time, the draw was smooth.

Sword essence flowed freely from my star veins and into my body. The technique itself was near-instant, but once the essence had been moved, it would still take weeks for my body to process it. Still, the hardest part was done, and painlessly this time.

With that process completed, I focused on the remaining essence still in my star veins and pressed it gently against my Heart Point, making sure I didn't overwhelm it with too much.

Good.

I sat up, still wobbly from my injuries, but feeling stronger than ever before.

I washed my wounds. I ate a light meal.

Then I closed my eyes, smiling as I felt the new power slowly building in my body.

If I kept using this technique . . . I was going to get very, very strong.

Thank you, Master.

I'll forge this body into something sharper than you'd ever imagine.

CHAPTER XXII

SHARPENING SKILLS

It took me just over two days of recovery before I could move enough to resume the most basic of physical training exercises . . . and I use that term loosely.

After Gray knocked the sword out of my hand for the third time, the small child looked at me with an expression that might have been pity.

After the fifth time, whereupon I dropped my sword entirely on impact and had to grab my right arm afterward to stop the muscles from spasming, Red stopped training with Green to walk over, put a hand on each of my shoulders to steady me, then shook her head and pointed toward the storage shed.

I got the message.

I picked up my sword and glumly put it away.

I spent the next couple of days continuing my gardening work and technique research.

The Smiling Sword Saint had seemingly been impressed by my signature Shattering Sword technique — yes, I thought of it as my signature technique at that age, since I didn't have any other "unique" ones I'd developed independently — but I wasn't anywhere near done with working on it.

So, I spent much of my time conceptualizing variants.

After the sixth day of recovery, I finally got to work.

Next time, even she's going to have to admit that I'm worthy.

Shattering Sword Variant #7, attempt four thousand ninety-six.

Step one, channel sword essence.

I felt a familiar surge from my Heart Point, essence flowing more easily through my star veins than it had even a few days before.

If nothing else, every time I'm visiting the sword saint is bringing tangible benefits for using my essence . . . and this practice is helping, too.

Still, I wasn't willing to settle for that. I was going to make a technique that would shatter the skies themselves — or, maybe with a little less hyperbole, impress someone that I deeply respected.

Step two: create inner scabbard.

Through weeks of study, I'd determined that the scabbard I'd found in the building contained at least three distinct essence types, but the most prominent was the sword aspect I'd been able to sense and use while working on my Draw Sword technique. The name I was calling it was straightforward enough — scabbard-aspected sword essence.

As I'd realized while trying to safely convert my essence, the function of a scabbard was to safely contain a sword. That was useful for the Draw Sword technique, but it wasn't by any means the only application I could think of. And one of those ideas tied back to one of my original concepts for how to build an attack technique.

As I converted my sword essence into the scabbard aspect, I spread it over the entire sword. This was one area where I'd failed repeatedly before, since intuitively, scabbard essence seemed like it should only be used to cover the blade of a sword — but to make the technique that I wanted work, I needed to protect the entire weapon.

I'd made my first several attempts at designing this technique without such protection, and let me just say that it's a good thing that the phantom blades reappeared periodically. I lost a lot of swords that way — and then, in later phases, many hilts when I initially just tried to protect the blade.

Now, with a scabbard protecting the blade, I could tinker with my original plan — and that led me to the next step.

Step three: create outer scabbard.

I created a second envelope of scabbard-aspected essence around the weapon, but this one also wrapped around my hand. This had required some further experimentation, since I had to find a slightly different composition of scabbard essence that had less physical resistance to prevent it from being so stiff that it limited the mobility of my wrist. The current composition still had a little bit of resistance to it, but not so much that it prevented me from moving my hand.

The important part was that I left a space between the two different "layers" of scabbard essence. Basically, I was creating a scabbard that held the entire sword, then a second scabbard that contained empty space around it.

Step four: sword into scabbard.

I breathed in and out, gradually channeling cutting-aspected sword essence through my Heart Point into my hand. Even if I couldn't create an instantaneous burst of devastating power, if I had a few seconds to fill a container with essence . . .

In theory, I could create a much stronger field of sword essence, which I could later "unsheathe" into an attack. This was my answer to a "charged" attack, like I'd considered when I'd first been experimenting with techniques months before.

In practice, my scabbard usually exploded.

This was the part where I'd done the most experimenting, and it was the easiest place for things to go wrong. Scabbard-aspected sword essence was excellent at containing sword essence, but it seemed that there were, unfortunately, some reasonable limitations on that power.

Time and time again, I tested those limits, figuring out the exact ratios of scabbard-to-slashing essence that could be contained.

I could have stopped there, just filling the scabbard with as much cutting-aspected essence as possible and dispersing the scabbard. This would have technically fulfilled my goal of a stronger attack, but the output wasn't orders of magnitude greater than my Shattering Sword technique like I'd hoped, and given the complexity, it simply wasn't a strong enough technique to be worth the effort to stop there.

So, I kept going.

My initial sword creation techniques had failed because I hadn't structured the blades correctly, and simply using cutting-aspected essence for an attack was an obvious failure. I'd already found that a proper sword needed to be created in layers.

Building my Sword Sharpening Shroud technique inside the scabbard was a little tricky, at first, but doable—

And completely underwhelming. With the edges composed of slashing essence, it broke through the scabbard nearly as quickly as pure slashing did, with even less impressive damage output.

I tinkered with just using unaspected sword essence inside the sheath, but while that was much easier to contain without breaking the sheath, the essence itself simply wasn't as potent for attacking.

I tried variant after variant, making minor changes until I realized that I'd made a fundamental error—

I'd been treating the "sword" component as having multiple aspects, but thinking of a "scabbard" as only needing a single one.

I couldn't identify the specific essence types in my actual scabbard, beyond the one I'd figured out, but the core idea was simple enough — scabbard-aspected sword essence was useful, but anything could be made stronger with additional support. And sword-aspected essence types could, as I'd already proven, synergize with each other and be used in atypical ways.

With this knowledge in mind, I'd created my scabbards differently during this particular test. Rather than purely forging them out of scabbard-aspected essence, I constructed them from layers of scabbard-aspected essence on the innermost layer, hardness-aspected sword essence around that, and deflection-aspected essence on the outermost layer. This three-aspect scabbard would, in theory, prevent the sword essence from bursting through the scabbard and destroying it, unless the amount of essence within it was truly overwhelming.

I, of course, was attempting to use a truly overwhelming amount of essence — at least by humble Candle-level standards. My intent was to burn through my entire pool of essence in this single attempt. It would be exhausting, but if it worked . . .

Well, I'd find out the results soon enough.

I continued pushing my sword essence into the scabbard, watching with grim determination as cracks began to form in both the interior and exterior scabbard layers. Even with the three-aspect setup, the scabbard wasn't impervious to harm. But I'd planned on that, too.

Step five . . . ready sword.

I raised my sword into a ready stance.

Wait for it . . . wait for it.

Step six . . .

Strike!

I brought my sword down toward the training dummy.

Step seven—

Shattering Sheath.

In the heartbeat before contact, I performed the last part of my technique—

I didn't unsheathe the sword, as I'd originally planned. That still would have likely resulted in a powerful attack, but . . . an ordinary one. And I liked my attacks to have a certain flair.

So, instead, I took the remaining, splintering fragments of the sheath—

And I changed them into cutting-aspected essence, just before impact.

I saw a flash of silver as I made the change, the air itself seeming to *crack*—

My sword passed through the dummy's barrier with ease, but I didn't slip and fall this time like when I'd first completed the Shattering Sword.

The dummy, however, did fall. Not in four pieces.

. . . No, I'd split it into more like four *hundred.*

I gawked at the sight.

It wasn't that I'd . . . exploded the dummy. Not exactly, since the pieces didn't fly outward, and there wasn't really a detonation.

"Minced" might be a good word for it, or "shredded." It was like I'd repeatedly passed the dummy through a gigantic omnidirectional cheese grater.

I stared at the obliterated remains for another moment, then knelt down.

. . . I don't think I can glue it back together this time.

I patted the shredded dummy's remains.

I'll remember you, even if the world forgets.

And as for the technique itself . . .

Oh, I'd definitely remember that, too.

CHAPTER XXIII

SWORD SKILLS

I spent another three weeks recovering from my injuries, as well as exploring my new Shattering Sheath technique.

During that time, I continued processing the essence I'd absorbed, into both primary essence for my Heart Point and secondary essence to improve my body.

I estimated that my sword essence had leapt up another full unit during that time frame. Between that, the sword cake, and other small bits of essence I'd absorbed, I estimated my total essence to be at around ten units.

Still not even close to Torch, but I'm advancing much more rapidly with her help. I've managed to gain roughly four units of sword essence in just over a year. At that rate, I'll hit Torch a little after I turn sixteen.

That was still too slow for my tastes, but . . . it was getting closer. There was an effective maximum to how much essence my body could process at any given time, even with things like the sword saint's bombardment and any tricks I managed. At my age, that effective maximum was somewhere around twelve units per year, and I'd probably managed to get very close to that — it's just that most of it was secondary essence, since I didn't have a reliable source of sword essence, and even my sword essence was being split between primary and secondary.

It was tempting to try to apply more of the sword essence toward primary essence, but if it kept coming in bursts like what the sword saint hit me with, that simply wasn't feasible — my Heart Point simply couldn't process that much at once. I still needed to find a reliable source of sword essence that could be absorbed incrementally at my own pace.

I tried to apply what I'd learned from creating the Shattering Sword technique to forming a ranged attack, but I didn't meet with any early success. Forming a scabbard of essence and trying to project that with deflection-aspected sword essence was possible, but getting it to "unsheathe" itself in midair proved too difficult — I couldn't effectively change the essence composition after it left my body at my current skill level. If I tried to "unsheathe" it at the same time I deflected it outward, it tended to veer wildly off course.

I figured that might have been possible to improve with timing, but given the amount of time it took to prepare, it was even less practical than the Shattering Sheath was — at least for the moment.

A spin-attack variant of the Shattering Sheath ran into a similar problem — I was releasing all the stored essence in a near-instant burst when I "unsheathed" it, meaning that I couldn't really hit more than one target before the essence dissipated. Just spinning around in a circle with a Sword Hand out was closer to what I'd been going for, but it didn't have enough power. I tried a few variations on combining the ideas, but ultimately, I didn't have any breakthroughs right away.

Ultimately, I resolved to do what I'd done with the Shattering Sword and focus primarily on improving the foundations of the technique before trying to make any more versions. My practice focused largely on executing the technique faster each day, since any sort of technique that required time to execute would leave me vulnerable while I prepared it.

After the three weeks had passed, I still wasn't confident that the technique would be useful in an ordinary fight. I was, however, pretty sure the sword saint was just going to let me hit her with it — and that she'd be surprised by the results.

With perhaps a little bit too much confidence, I made my way back to the now-familiar arena where my master trained forever in solitude.

"Well, well." The Smiling Sword Saint narrowed her eyes to examine me. "Looks like I've found myself a distraction."

"Greetings, Honored Saint—"

"Save it, kid. What are you doing here?"

"Training. I have memory crystals for you that should explain things further."

"Memory crystals?" Fortunately for both me and the environment, she maintained a neutral expression.

"They contain some of my previous memories of our meetings, as well as a blank crystal."

"Why would that be — ah. I'm an echo, or something, is it? Hm." She sniffed at the air. "Seems a little strange to offer memory crystals to a memory."

"It's a part of our preexisting agreement. I've visited you in the past and offered you—"

"I get it." Her lip twitched. I heard something crash in the distance. Was . . . that a mountaintop sliding off nearby?

I suddenly felt grateful that this mountain range was largely uninhabited. At that altitude, even animals would be sparse, and most of those in the area would be birds, so they'd survive. But . . .

I *really* needed to make sure I didn't irritate her.

"Don't overexplain. Got it. Can I get my crystals out of my bag?"

She gave a snort. I didn't sense anything destroyed by that, which was somehow even more concerning. "I don't know, can you?"

I hastily retrieved a crystal. "I'm going to toss this to you. Please don't cut it down in midair this time, I have a limited number."

"Heh. That does sound like me. Okay, kid, toss." She gestured with her right hand. I tossed her the first crystal, which included a recording of our first meeting.

Her eyes closed for a split second. "Boring. Next?"

She . . . saw it that quickly?

Memory crystals were generally watched in real time. Was she bluffing? Or . . . did she have accelerated cognition to the extent that a several-minute recording could be processed in an instant?

Perhaps it was a property of being connected to the plane of memory, but . . . maybe she could just think hundreds or thousands of times faster than I could. That was terrifying, if it was true, perhaps even more so than her combat abilities.

Destiny Dreams are near-instant, I remembered. *Maybe she just has a technique that allows her to view memory crystals in a similar way?*

I was curious, but I also knew better than to pester her with questions. I tossed her the second crystal.

Again, her eyes shut briefly.

". . . Huh."

When her eyes reopened, her expression was . . . contemplative.

"You didn't fake this, did you?"

"No." I shook my head immediately. "I don't even have the ability to do that. Memory isn't one of my—"

"Yeah, yeah. Sword essence and whatever you've got in that hand. *That's* curious, by the way." She frowned fractionally, causing a tremor in the ground beneath us. I casually stepped to the side to avoid a growing fissure. "But that's talk for later. But no, I didn't mean you faking it yourself. Whoever made these could have fabricated memories."

I shrugged. "Possible, I guess, but out of my area of expertise. If there's something in there you're skeptical about—"

She was face to face with me, then.

"Show me your best technique, kid."

I took a step back. Not out of fear, but because she'd stepped in too close to draw my sword from my belt properly, and I didn't want to open by grabbing her own sword a second time.

As my hand gripped the blade on my hip, I concentrated, then ran through the process I'd carefully practiced more than four thousand times.

I hadn't practiced drawing straight into the attack, but it wasn't particularly difficult — in fact, the scabbard itself served as an additional source of scabbard essence that I could have drawn from to build the technique, if I'd been willing to experiment with that. For the moment, I fueled the technique with my own essence alone, slashing upward across the Smiling Sword Saint's chest—

Or, rather, I tried to.

Shattering Sheath.

My technique exploded outward as expected, but a hair before my weapon and essence impacted the sword saint, she moved backward in a blur.

I found her standing ten feet back, well out of range of the attack. It might have been my imagination, but I thought her eyes had widened just fractionally, though they quickly normalized the moment after she reappeared.

For a moment, we simply stared at each other.

Finally, I lifted my sword to rest it against my shoulder and gave her a questioning look. "Shall I do it again?"

Her brow furrowed. I felt a slice across my cheek, but it wasn't deep. "That was a different technique from what you showed me in the crystal."

"Yep."

"Last time, you told me you were using your best technique. Today, I asked you to show me your best technique."

Ah. I understood her confusion now.

"My apologies. I intended no deception. That *was* my best technique, but that was a month ago."

"A month." Her tone was completely neutral.

"I mean, roughly, not in exact days—"

"Who else has been teaching you?" she asked.

I shook my head. "It's like I mentioned in the previous visits. I've been studying the swordplay of various echoes in the area, but I don't actually have a teacher. The other echoes aren't coherent like you are, they just drill the same things over and over — basic swordplay and footwork. My uncle knows a sword style, but he hasn't been here since my last visit. I developed this technique on my own. It's a variant of the one I showed you last time, so it wasn't too hard—"

"Stop." She waved a hand. "Demonstrate the previous technique you showed me."

I nodded, then simply swung my sword in the air and used the Shattering Sword.

She caught my arm on the way down, stopping my movement. "Hold it."

I froze, struggling to interrupt the technique midway and pause at the stage just before the impact, meaning the sword blade was currently split into two.

"Hm." She flicked a finger at the split blade. I heard a "ting" like metal impacting against metal. "What do you call this?"

I blinked. "That layer? I'd call it cutting-aspected sword essence. It's the outermost layer of my Sword Sharpening Shroud technique, which is constructed from—"

"Where'd you learn *that* technique?"

"I made it? I mean, obviously there's plenty of precedent, and I—"

She shook her head. "Stop. How many types of sword essence are you using here?"

". . . In the technique as a whole? Not a lot, just slashing, piercing, deflecting, and unaspected. Oh, and hardness, right. I added that last. That's for the Sword Sharpening Shroud, of course, whereas—"

"Stop." The Smiling Sword Saint put a hand to her forehead, then exhaled. *"Why?"*

I blinked, hesitating. I wasn't sure I understood the question. "Why . . . only use those aspects? I haven't been able to figure out many others yet. I've been having to find examples, which is hard — there aren't a lot of swords in the area I live in, and—"

Her jaw tightened. I felt my left leg twist suddenly, followed by a surge of agony. I fell backward with a yelp, barely managing to maintain my technique as I hit the ground. She hadn't told me I could dismiss it, after all.

Trembling in pain, I used my free hand to rub my leg. It wasn't broken — it was more like I'd suddenly pulled a muscle without warning.

The sword saint looked down on me, watching with narrowed eyes. "You have no idea what you're doing, do you?"

". . . Not really," I admitted. "If I've offended you somehow, I—"

"You've got your blade flipped."

I raised an eyebrow at that expression, then turned to my still-active sword technique. "It's . . . double-sided?"

"No. Ugh. That's . . . a sword training expression. It means you misread something. You're not using too few aspects, kid. You're using *far* too many." She sounded pained. "Not in that what you're doing is wrong. It's just too advanced for your level. Many stages too advanced."

"Ah. I suppose it's certainly harder to make techniques with several aspects, but when I was trying simpler ones, they seemed underwhelming by comparison. And with enough practice, I was able to get these pretty reliable—"

"Enough practice?" Her hands flexed in the air. Fortunately, it was two pillars that suffered this time, rather than me. "You made that last technique in a month. Your starting point technique used five essence aspects. Your next technique up used six, or maybe seven, depending on if you're counting the thing you used to split the blade apart as the same as the outer edges. A seven-aspect technique is something masters would take years to refine. At your level? It shouldn't even be *possible*."

I . . . had no idea what to say to that. "But . . . in the stories . . . people like you just make up techniques on the spot. In the middle of a fight."

The Smiling Sword Saint sighed . . .

Then flopped lazily to the ground, right in front of me.

"You can dismiss the technique, kid. I've seen what I need to see."

I frowned, dismissing the remains of my sword technique.

She seemed to take a moment to find the words that followed. "Don't believe everything you hear in stories. Not about me, certainly, but not in general."

"I . . . I'm sure some stories are exaggerated, of course. But making techniques in combat is something there are hundreds, even thousands of examples of."

"Yeah, sure." She looked at me. "Do you know what those usually entail? I'll give you an example of one of mine. Lycanthrope ambush. I use metal essence, so I added a silver aspect to one of my simplest attack techniques — one I'd practiced for years — to bypass their defenses. There you go, kid. That's what a mid-combat technique development sounds like. Adding one new aspect to something you've got a ton of practice with, which generally is a very simple technique in the first place. Anything beyond that has too many variables."

I nodded. I did run into thousands of failures while trying to experiment with my own techniques, and I knew that trying and failing something complicated mid-combat was likely to get me killed. ". . . Okay. That much I can understand. But even so, why would it take years and years to research something like my technique? I suppose I benefited from a lack of distractions, but that shouldn't make a difference in orders of magnitude."

"Most people your age can't even use more than one aspect at a time. Maybe two, and in those cases, they're generally drawing from different essence types, which is much easier."

Was . . . that true? I frowned. Then it was my turn to ask a question. "Why?"

"Come on, kid. How many things can you normally do at once? Sure, some actions are easier to pair up than others. You can talk while walking. You can clap your hands while walking. But try doing all three, and maintaining a specific pattern of clapping, and a specific walking cadence — and it gets harder and harder. Now, some of your steps are sequential, rather than simultaneous, but for something like that slashing technique you showed me last time, you have to maintain the basic five-aspect technique throughout the entire process, then complicate it further by splitting it, then blasting it outward."

"I . . . can understand what you're saying, I guess. But why would using sword essence exclusively be harder?"

"Using multiple aspects of any individual essence type is harder. Think of it this way — it's easier to conceptualize the difference between red and blue than it is to think about the difference between two shades of gray. Trying to make a technique out of several shades of gray, each of which has to be exactly the right shade of gray in the right configuration, is vastly more difficult than putting together something that is, say, red outside, green inside, and blue on the tip."

That made a degree of sense, at least, but it wasn't what my experience actually felt like. I said as much. "I . . . huh. I suppose after a certain point of practice, I don't really feel like I have to think about each step actively. Like, I conceptualize each essence type I'm doing when I'm building the technique, and figure out the essence ratios and all that, and modify them as needed — but once I've settled on a stage, it doesn't feel like doing several things at once. It's more like . . . when you're walking, you don't think actively about every step. Lift leg, shift weight, lower leg, shift foot—"

"You're saying you use sword techniques as intuitively as walking, once you've developed them." The sword saint's tone remained neutral, but there was an intensity there that she didn't — or couldn't — hide.

"Not every part," I admitted. "There are some stages I think about actively — generally, the beginning and end of the process."

"Sword Hand, now," she commanded.

I was manifesting the technique immediately, my hand sticking out to my side to avoid cutting either of us.

"Did you think about how you built that?"

". . . No. Not really?"

"Meaning that for simpler, or more familiar techniques, you may not even need to consider the initiation and completion stages." She looked at the blade. "And that's still a three-plus-layer technique. Okay."

She nodded to me. I didn't feel any change in the environment, but I did sense a change in her. She'd come to some kind of conclusion, but I wasn't sure what it was. "You need to be careful who you talk to about this."

I blinked. "Why?"

"Because, kid, that level of intuitive use of techniques is not *normal.* And yes, before you ask, I could do that sort of thing myself, though maybe not in quite the same way that you do. But I couldn't have done it when I was your level. I'm not going to say it's literally unprecedented, and I've heard of people with similar talents for other types of essence use. But usually, it's something like some kid with the blood of a fire elemental being really good at lighting things on fire. But even with a fire elemental . . . no, I don't think they'd be actively drawing from that many aspects. They generally intuit manifestations and shapes, not *techniques.* And swords . . . no. You . . . you might be something new."

"And . . . that's bad?"

"No, kid. Except maybe for your life expectancy." Her lips quirked upward, just a bit. I felt a slice spread across my shoulder. "You see, if I were the original Smiling Sword Saint, I would have just marked you down as a future threat."

I simultaneously was intensely flattered and actively had to resist the urge to panic. Panic, of course, in my case meaning "attack uselessly and die," since as we've established, my flight instinct was broken-to-nonexistent. Instead, I simply said, "So, teach me, then. Teach me to be a threat to you."

"Now that," she laughed, shaking the entire arena, "sounds like it could be fun."

She gestured upward. I stood, and she stood languidly along with me.

"But first, you're too weak."

I put my hands up. "Okay, but before we go through the whole thing where you nearly kill me with that Trial of a Thousand Scars again, can you actually teach me a technique or two?"

"Wasn't going to do that," she said. "Not right away," she muttered quietly. "But you pose a good question! And the answer is no."

I frowned. "But why? If I'm understanding you right, it sounds like . . . making and using techniques is what sets me apart. Learning one of your techniques should be possible, too, right?"

"Sure, you could learn the theory. But you couldn't use any of the useful ones."

"Why? I mean, I'm sure many of them are designed for so much essence that I couldn't possibly use them at my level, but you have to have lower-level ones that you used when you first started."

"Sure. But you can't use them, either. Because you *only have sword essence.*" She shook her head. "That's what you need to work on, kid. You might be some sort of *prodigy* at constructing sword essence techniques, but that doesn't mean you can do everything with that by itself."

I took a moment to consider, then gave what I felt was a reasonable answer. "But . . . being purely sword-aspected . . . there's almost no one that can make that claim. That has to be advantageous, right?"

She stared at me for a moment, her eyes narrowing again. Then she said, with a hint of skepticism, "You're serious."

I nodded. "I know getting sword essence first is rare, but it's true. I'm—"

"No, stop." She raised a hand. One of the arena pillars collapsed, shredded into pieces. I ignored the destruction, having grown more used to it by that point. "You're . . ." She sighed, and I saw the shimmering of blades in the air around her. "You actually believe that's a good thing?"

"I, uh, respectfully . . . yes?" I was a little confused and more than a little nervous.

She took a step forward, raising her hands. The air around her trembled, and for a moment, it seemed as if the very world might buckle at the pressure she exuded.

"Everything you just said is terribly, pitifully, wrong."

I forced myself not to take a step back. "What do you mean?"

Her right hand tightened. "First, tell me why you think there would be an advantage to only having sword essence."

"Well, I would be a rare case of someone who could dedicate myself fully to the sword. You've already seen what I can do with aspects — I could keep refining that further, rather than splitting my focus, and through doing that, I could reach greater heights than an ordinary sword fighter. And beyond that, when I get my Destiny Dream, I'll be eligible for the Blademaster class, like you."

She actually let out a small laugh at that. I heard a crack in the sky above, like distant thunder. "Like me? Do you think I only have one destiny?"

"I, uh, the legends say . . ."

"No, child. I don't only have one destiny. I have *many*. So does every excellent fighter I've ever known."

I held my hands up. "Okay, sure. But that was later in your career, right? Your Destiny Dream must have been—"

"What's a Destiny Dream?"

I blanched.

I had made a terrible, obvious error.

I took a breath. ". . . They didn't exist in your time, did they?" I shook my head. "Right. You were born hundreds of years ago. Okay, let me give you some context."

"I'm listening, but don't waste my time."

I nodded. "So, destinies. You used to get them from traveling to crystal shrines and taking their tests. That's not possible anymore — at least, not for the most part."

Her expression darkened. "What happened?"

"A few hundred years ago, there was a colossal invasion. Or, accident. I don't know what started it — a planar incursion from another species that people call 'fiends.' Huge war. During that time, the crystals became major targets for the invading army, given the power they provided. Many were hidden or destroyed. Others were protected by major sects, royal families, or that sort of thing. The war concluded with the invading species conquering nearly two-thirds of the continent before a cease-fire was reached. We live in the remaining one-third, and those crystals that weren't hidden away or destroyed are almost entirely controlled by powerful factions that took control of them during the war. What that means is that virtually every shrine is now nearly or completely inaccessible as a means for getting access to additional destinies."

"You let an enemy just take two-thirds of the continent?" She fumed. The air around her trembled, and she looked as if she was about to stomp off to fight a war on her own. Which . . . admittedly, seemed physically possible, if she was able to leave the area.

"Ah, no, I mean, certainly not me personally, this was hundreds of years before I was born—"

"But humanity! What are we *doing*?"

I raised a hand to calm her. "Getting there. There was a second war much more recently, pushing the fiends back further, creating a sort of neutral region between the human and fiend lands. This was just before I was born, and there are always those that want to push further — but there are also those who wish for long-term peace."

"*Peace?* With an invading species from another plane of existence?"

"It's more complicated than that. They claim we summoned them to be slaves."

"Yeah, I suppose that tracks. People are idiots. Okay. Fine, keep talking. Dreams?"

"Right. So, either during or after the war — mixed stories and all that — there was a group of somewhere between five and seven major figures that were the leaders of the allied nations against the fiends. One of these people that everyone agrees existed was called the Sage, based on having the Sage destiny, some kind of advanced destiny, or maybe a step beyond advanced, if that's a thing."

The sword saint nodded. "Plausible. Keep going."

I was surprised enough at that part sounding plausible that I almost stopped, but I managed to find my words and keep going. "So, with the loss of access to so many crystals, the stories say that the Sage found a way to commune with them. Some say he sought out an ancient god, or the Skylands, or something. Either way, he managed to set up some kind of massive ritual that made it so that everyone who reaches the second level of essence development — I don't know what you called it, we call it Torch now — has a dream. Some of them are straightforward, others involve adventures and trials. It's basically like going into a crystal shrine, but through a dream, rather than in the real world. Succeed, and you get a destiny."

"Genius. And the power it would take to connect every living person to the crystals . . ." She frowned. "Say, is this Sage still around? How good a fighter is he?"

I laughed. "Best guess is that he's long dead, along with all the other legends of that era."

"Shame. You run into his echo, you let me know, yeah?"

I couldn't help but feel a smile sliding across my face. "Provided I can make it back here alive, yeah, I'll do that."

"Good. Anyone else worth fighting from that era?"

"Well, I suppose there's the Ashen Lord, and the Hero, and . . ." I got a mischievous look. "And I'd be more than happy to tell you about them sometime, after you teach me a bit more about what I've been doing wrong."

"Oh, cheeky. Okay, kid. Let's talk about how terrible your strategy is."

I groaned. That wasn't the direction I was hoping things would go.

"So, your logic is that you're going to get Blademaster because you're limited in destiny availability. It's not a bad destiny, but why limit yourself to sword essence?"

"Ah, that's the thing with these dreams. They determine which trials you take based on your essence — and certain essence types can cause you to be excluded from trials. Blademaster requires only having sword essence."

"That's . . . an incredibly bad system. When I meet this Sage, I'm going to have to get him to fix it after I beat him. Assuming I leave enough of him." She groaned. "Even if that's a terrible system, though, your plan is awful. Sure, Blademaster is useful, but useful enough to give up every single other essence type? That's *terrible*. It's obviously not worth the effort."

"I mean, I could get other essence types later," I tried. I hadn't really been planning on that, but I wasn't sure. "But even if I didn't, what's so wrong with only having one essence type? Being purely focused should be an advantage in specialization, right?"

She took a breath. "Did your elders teach you that?"

"I mean, uh, not exactly. Like I said, I don't have a sword teacher. And while my uncle and grandfather have taught me some things, they didn't really encourage me to follow a certain destiny. If anything, my grandfather dissuaded me from doing that kind of thing, but he wasn't this specific about the reason. I . . . got the idea from a book."

She nodded slightly. "That explains much. But this concept of specialization is something they are teaching in books?"

"It's seen as one possible path to greatness. They call it the 'pure path,' and it's seen as allowing someone to reach the greatest heights in any given style."

She lowered her head. "That is . . . some of the most absolute nonsense I've heard in my entire life."

"What?"

She snapped her fingers. A flood of swords appeared in the air around her, hundreds at once.

I froze for a moment, then awkwardly raised my hands into a guarding position. I couldn't possibly stop that many swords if she attacked, but . . .

The swords flowed upward, toward the sky. "Sword essence. Air essence. Aura essence. Area essence. These are the essence types I used to create this particular effect. Without any one of them, the technique would not be possible." She snapped her fingers. The swords vanished. "Virtually every technique I have requires multiple essence types. The same is true for any advanced sword fighter."

"But . . . surely some of your techniques only use sword essence, or could be adapted to it."

"Not a lot of them." She seemed to consider that. "Certainly nothing usable at your level. There's a version of my Rejoinder technique that only uses sword essence aspects, but it wouldn't be worthwhile to even bother with as a Candle."

"What about the Sword Saint's Smile?"

She laughed. "Come on, kid. Think about it. You've probably played with sword essence quite a bit by now — how well does sword essence by itself work for long ranged attacks? And beyond that, the Sword Saint's Smile is an advanced technique. It's built on the foundation of others, and even those use more than sword essence. The Cutting Remark is my foundation technique, and it uses air essence to move sword essence when I talk."

"But . . . if I stay on the pure path, maybe I could adapt them . . ."

She stepped forward again, shaking her head. "This 'pure path' of yours is nonsense. You claim to have pure sword essence? You're wrong."

"I . . . am?" I frowned. "I mean . . . I know I have secondary essence of a bunch of types. Everyone does. But, as far as the Destiny Dreams go, I assume it's mostly talking about completed Dianis Points."

"Sure, maybe for your dream thing, that's what matters. Two problems, kid. First, you already have a different type of essence in a Dianis Point of a different type, or something like it — in your right hand."

It was strange to hear clear confirmation of what I'd suspected for so long. I already had another source of power, one that had been a part of me since before my earliest memories. I simply couldn't *use* it.

"The seal." I felt my hands tightening in frustration. "Whatever essence is under it is inaccessible to me. I . . . don't know if that counts. I still don't even know *what* it is. I think it's more like a spirit bond than something from my bloodline."

"Sure, probably is. But it's still connected to your Dianis Point and providing you with another type of essence. The seal is in essence form, too. Don't you think that whatever causes your dreams to be based on essence types is going to pick that up?"

"I . . . don't know," I stammered. "That's . . . but I can't even use it. That wouldn't be fair."

The Smiling Sword Saint laughed. "What in the world gave you the impression that any of this was *fair*?" She shook her head, the world trembling around us as she continued to laugh. "If there's a fair system for power distribution anywhere, I haven't seen it yet. I'll grant you that whoever this Sage was seems to have put some thought into it, at least. That's better than some places, and it's good that he was trying to help provide for people who can't walk to a shrine. But fair? No, it can't be. Not while humans — or, you know, any other intelligent species — are involved in the system."

"Okay. Fine. Let's say the seal, or the power within it, counts against me and I'm not eligible for Blademaster. I can still *focus* purely on sword essence and sword techniques."

"And therein lies your second problem, kid. You think that's a good thing? Think about it. You're drastically reducing your options that way."

"But I'll be stronger at it if I keep my essence as pure as possible, right?"

She made a disgusted face. "Ugh. That's such a narrow view. Sure, there are essence types that conflict with each other, but no one has pure essence. And I'm not just talking about secondary essence — even your primary essence isn't 'pure.' That's nonsense. Your particular sword essence, for example, isn't pure. It has an emphasis on sharpness, greatswords, and slashing attacks."

"But those are . . . more like specializations, aren't they?" I tried.

"What do you think those specializations are? They're differences in essence composition. Meaning, you're not dealing with unaspected essence."

I knew that, of course. But somehow, I still just thought about my Heart Point as being sword essence, and thus meeting the absurd requirements for Blademaster, without considering the details. "Okay, sure. There are subtle differences there, and my essence might be slightly aspected. But I could still focus on trying to train sword techniques exclusively and get better at them than others, right?"

"No!" she practically shouted. Distantly, I heard trees fall. "Spirits, you're awfully fixated on this idea. Okay, *listen*."

She sighed. "There's *nothing special about only having one type of essence*. Yeah, you can put more time into studying it, sure, but that's not going to amount to the same level of usefulness of training multiple things."

"Why not? I mean, I feel like I'm good at making sword techniques. Wouldn't focusing on that make sense?"

Her expression softened just slightly. "You *are* good at making sword techniques. Better than good. But how do you know if that only applies to sword techniques if you've never studied anything else?"

I opened my mouth, then closed it to consider. After a moment, I finally answered, "You have a point."

"Well, yeah. Of course I do."

"But . . . let's say I want to compete specifically in swordsmanship. Doesn't it make sense for that to be my focus for my essence, even if I practice other skills outside that?"

"No. Not to the extent you're thinking, at least. Let me ask you this — do you think someone is going to be a better fist fighter if they only exercise one arm?"

"I . . . no. Of course not."

"And a group of adventurers — is it best if they're all swordsmen?"

I shook my head. "No. You'd want a balance. Someone who can heal, someone with a shield, someone who can find traps . . ."

She nodded. "Good. You have some minimal sense, then. What makes a good sword?"

I pondered the question. "Proper balance, good construction, proper materials . . ."

"What type of material is better for a sword — iron or steel?"

"Steel," I answered immediately.

"Right. And what is steel?"

"It's . . . an alloy." I nodded, understanding her logic. "It's stronger than the component parts alone."

She reached out, strangely slowly. Her hand moved to my shoulder.

And though I had to push down the urge to defend myself, I wasn't cut by her touch.

"Listen, child. Purity is one of the oldest of lies. Nothing is truly pure, and purity itself has no inherent value. We are all alloys, and like a sword, strengthened by the blend of our component parts. This is true for both individuals and groups. One person, one group, or one culture that is fixated on purity is far weaker than one that embraces the advantages that differences provide. And if you truly wish to be a master at swordsmanship, you must understand this. You must learn to hone your different parts to work in tandem. Only then will you know true strength."

I . . . didn't know what to say to that.

I paused, looking at her, taking a breath, and thinking.

I knew she was right. That my path to this point, as much as it hurt to admit it, had been focused on an idea that was predicated on a glorification of the concept of purity. That in order to be good at something, I had to fixate on it entirely, to the exclusion of all else.

But that was demonstrably false, wasn't it? Even a sword was made of many parts — a blade, a hilt, a crossguard, the wrap around the hilt . . . If I simply focused on one aspect, wasn't that like being a blade without a hilt? Maybe I'd be sharp, but I'd still be useless.

And internally, I must have understood part of it from the start. I was already experimenting with several sword aspects, after all, rather than just unaspected sword essence.

It was so simple a concept, and yet it had eluded me until she'd spoken it.

I nodded to her. "So, if I want to be a great swordsman, what I need to do is figure out the best essence types to build the sword style I want. To make the strongest possible alloy."

"Now you're getting it." She released my shoulder, then turned and stepped away. "Our lesson today is done."

I frowned. "But you didn't . . ."

"Teach you swordplay? No. I taught you something more important. Go think about it. And when you return, you will tell me the next step for your own path."

I nodded. I was disappointed, but relieved that she was willing to see me again at all. "Thank you, Master. I will consider my answer for next time."

"I'm not your master." She stepped away, her voice growing quieter.

"Not yet."

That was the last I heard before I stood in an empty arena, alone with my thoughts.

CHAPTER XXIV

SYNERGY

It was strange being in the Smiling Sword Saint's arena without her being present. I didn't actually know how she'd vanished.

Had she actually left the area? Could she do that? Or had she just . . . sort of temporarily ceased to exist?

I still didn't know exactly how she worked. I hadn't been able to study the exact essence composition of the area, or the nature of the breach between planes at the location. Similarly, I wasn't sure how the sword essence was being drained to this spot.

Or, somewhere a little farther, actually. I frowned, feeling the shifting of sword essence in the air. It was thick around me, but drifting slowly straight ahead.

Had the sword saint moved a little farther into the region? Or was something else entirely bringing the sword essence to the area?

I considered investigating, but I didn't think the Smiling Sword Saint would be happy if I followed her. She'd effectively dismissed me, and if she had some other place of residence farther up the path, she hadn't invited me there.

While I wasn't willing to take the risk of offending her — not when I could simply ask her the question during a future visit — I was willing to take a more minor risk.

"I'm going to use an essence collection vial," I said out loud, just in case she was still listening. "I don't have a good source of sword essence anywhere nearby, and this will be a big help. If it doesn't end up collecting sword essence, I'll consider using whatever I get. If you can hear this and don't want me to use the vial, just let me know and I'll stop."

There was no response. So, carefully, I reached into my bag and uncapped an essence vial, then activated it.

I sensed two things immediately.

First, sword essence rushing toward the vial as it activated—

And second, something *resisting* that pull.

My expression narrowed as I tried to sense more about what was shifting the essence away, but I simply didn't have enough understanding of my essence sense to be able to determine the cause. Instead, I waited until the vial was as full as possible, then quickly capped it.

The capped vial *trembled* as the essence within it tried to escape.

Not good.

I rushed out of the arena and back toward the sword school. The essence vial's trembling lightened after I left the grove, implying that whatever force was draining the sword essence from the area was still present, but weaker at a distance.

The vials were built to be resilient beyond my level. Gramps had made them, but he hadn't built them to be the maximum strength he possibly could have — that would have been a waste of his time and talents for something as simple as a Candle-level essence vial. So, rather than shattering outright from the constant trembling, the essence vial simply gradually cracked as I kept moving.

I passed the sword school, then kept moving. If the vial had broken apart, I would have tried to absorb the essence before it escaped, but fortunately, it remained intact.

The vial's trembling only ceased completely when I crossed the barrier into fae territory at the mountain's edge. It was nightfall, then, and a poor place for me to spend the evening — especially alone.

Fortunately, I wasn't alone for long.

"Lien! You're back!" Ana appeared in front of me almost instantly, fluttering close. "And sooner than usual! Did you bring me a present?"

I blinked. It *was* almost Ana's name day, wasn't it?

I briefly considered the vial, then dismissed it. Ana had a constant source of sword essence available — she didn't need it. Not like I did, anyway. Finally, I shook my head. "Don't have one yet. I'm still thinking of ideas."

"Don't worry! Maybe just tell me a story about your adventures?"

I smiled. "Nothing would make me happier. Escort me home?"

She shifted forms, reappearing at my side at a height that nearly matched my own, now wearing a gold-trimmed three-piece suit. "Of course, good sir. It would be my pleasure." She extended an arm, and I slipped my arm into it to hook them together. Then we began the long walk home.

⁂

Late that night, I tucked Ana into bed. She'd managed to stay awake throughout the entire walk but had fallen asleep nearly the moment we sat down at the kitchen table.

I, however, was far from ready for bed. I poured myself some water to drink — since tea was the opposite of what I wanted for my next task — and then opened the barely intact essence vial.

I wouldn't have opened it immediately if I hadn't been confident that the essence inside was sword essence — I didn't want to absorb something else without studying it — but my senses recognized the contents. Sword essence must have been the densest thing in the area, although it had been rich in other essence types as well.

Without the disruptive effect from the mountain range, the essence in the vial had compressed, and all I had to do was take the essence out and absorb it directly, like an ordinary node I might find in the environment.

I trembled momentarily as the compact sphere of essence passed through my skin and into my star veins. It was far denser than I'd expected, providing nearly enough essence to saturate my star veins entirely. With effort, I began to compress as much essence as I safely could into my Heart Point, then took the remainder and forced it into my body with the Draw Sword technique.

The process didn't take more than a few minutes, but it left me exhausted. I took the time to leave a quick note for Gramps, briefly debated eating something, then decided against it. Then I went to bed, and as an unusual change of pace, I fell asleep in minutes.

When I slept, I dreamed of thousands of swords. Walls and walls of them, surrounding me — and, somehow, seeming a part of me as well.

I reached out toward one, feeling as if I was at the very edge of grasping something important—

And then awakened, alone. I mean, aside from the dozens of wooden swords that I still had in my room.

I lifted the one in my bed gently, frowning and examining it.

What was that?

Maybe it was just a dream, but it felt different than usual. More tangible, like a hint of something.

Something related to my Destiny Dream?

It was too soon to reach my destiny, but perhaps I was instinctively reaching toward it somehow.

I considered asking Gramps about it, but I decided against it. I had more important things to ask about, and something about that dream felt too personal to share.

I dragged myself out of bed, finding Gramps already sitting at the kitchen table.

"So, you've returned. Come, tell me what you've learned." Gramps gestured to the table, and I sat. I found food already prepared and helped myself, once again avoiding tea in favor of water, since my body would be processing the sword essence from the vial for several days. Any further essence I tried to absorb would be wasted.

While I was eating, I explained what I'd experienced. Gramps looked concerned at times, but contemplative.

"You walk a dangerous path with that teacher, Grandson."

I nodded, naïvely thinking that I understood. "I know. She could kill me at any time, either deliberately if she feels threatened, or even by accident. I'm not exactly thrilled with that, but any high-level sword technique teacher could kill me if they get angry."

"Perhaps, but she lacks motivation to control herself that a standard Skyseeker instructor would have."

"I don't exactly have those lining up to teach me, Grandfather. Now, if you want to take me to a sect and provide me with an introduction . . ."

He sipped at his tea. "We both know that would not be possible."

"Right. So, I appreciate your warning, but this is the best chance I have — and I'm taking it."

"Very well."

I blinked. I'd expected more of a protest. The conversation stopped abruptly for a moment, but after sipping more tea, he asked me another question.

"Have you given much thought to what the Smiling Sword Saint said?"

"Sure. She's encouraged me to diversify my essence types. And before you say that you've encouraged the same thing, I know. It's not that I wasn't listening to you, I just—"

"You needed to hear it from an expert in your own field of study, rather than someone from a completely unrelated discipline. That is not unwise, in itself. I also do not blame you for wanting a second opinion on anything I teach you. It is often wise to seek out alternate opinions on subjects, even when you have spoken to a single expert. I do not hold it against you to seek knowledge elsewhere."

"Thank you, Grandfather. I know not everyone would be as understanding."

He waved a hand dismissively. "Given how your mind works, I'm certain you already have a number of ideas on what you want to do next."

I nodded. "I debated a bunch of things on the way here. If I'm willing to be completely open to any option . . ." I paused, taking a breath as I considered how to phrase things in a way that Gramps would approve of. "It's staggering how many essence types there are. So, I've been trying to narrow them down by usefulness."

"Knowing you, most of them still probably involve swords."

I groaned. He really did know me too well. "Well, that *is* the most obvious way to get synergy, isn't it? And in terms of compounding essence between multiple Dianis Points, the more similar the essence type, the stronger the effect, right?"

"Yes, that's generally true, but there can be synergistic relationships that exist outside the direct relationship of having two near-identical mana types. The degree of abstraction is not the only factor. Take metal essence, for example. The sword saint gave you the example of alloys being stronger than single metals. You could create a stronger essence type from merging two metal sub-essence types, but the strongest alloys are not purely from metal."

I nodded in understanding. "Steel has both iron and carbon, which is non-metallic. And if I extend that to sword essence, there might be better options than, say, just making another Dianis Point with greatsword-aspected sword essence."

"Precisely." Gramps snapped his fingers. "A greatsword-aspected Dianis Point would be helpful for making stronger attacks when you're specifically using a greatsword, but other essence types might provide similar benefits, while also adding to your flexibility. Some sword aspects might be viable as Dianis Point options, but you want to look primarily at feature and function aspects, as they can be more broadly extended than form aspects."

"That makes sense. What if I went with hybrids of sword essence and other types? If I go that route, I could get some more flexibility out of each. Then, I could build a Breathing Point of a sword-related essence and use it to fuel all of my Dianis Points."

"It is a strong approach, and worthy of consideration. But it also is an approach that incentivizes remaining in one place once you find a good source of essence, since you would need a tremendous amount of that one essence type to fuel all of your Dianis Points. Is that something you really want?"

I paused, then shook my head. ". . . No. It isn't. I want to see the world. But . . . I don't think that going for a broad variety of essence types would be any better for a traveler, would it?"

"The general consensus is that it is, yes, as long as you choose some essence types that are broadly available. The idea is that you don't expect to have a source of essence for every Dianis Point everywhere you're going — instead, you have several diverse essence types that allow you to get some of at least one of them in every area. The classic traveler's approach is to take at least one of life, air, earth, or water — you can find sources of those in any location."

". . . But none of those pair well with sword essence, either as a hybrid or simply compounding with sword essence on their own." I frowned, contemplating. "There isn't really any common essence type that synergizes directly with sword essence, is there?"

Gramps seemed to hesitate for a moment, then answered. "Death essence technically synergizes with sword essence, but that path is frowned on for a number of reasons."

I could understand his concern, but he didn't have anything to worry about in terms of that influencing my choices. "Yeah. Not planning to go that route. I do like having an offensive focus, but I don't want to kill someone accidentally, nor do I want to eventually develop an aura that kills everything around me. What about something like metal essence?"

"That's relatively common and would be an option to consider, but you'd find it in the largest quantities in places like mines. Well, and shops, and armories. In all three of those cases, you can expect that the owners would be the ones collecting the essence. This might make it harder to obtain than some other relatively common types."

I pondered. "What about fire or stability? Those are both involved in some of the components of sword essence."

"Both are relatively common options for sword fighters and absolutely worth considering. Fire would give you ranged combat options, as well as defense against one of the most common forms of magical attack. Stability is more generally applicable for improving virtually any characteristic. Of course, there are some specific aspects of each that might also give you clearer benefits."

"Like the sharpness essence from bladeberries. That's a stability aspect, isn't it?"

"It is. And not a terrible option to consider, although you'd want to find a much better source than the berries themselves."

I drummed my fingers on the table. That was more promising than many other options thus far — it was something my body was already acclimated to, and sharpness had clear synergy with sword essence. It also had the advantage that it was only one step away from traditional stability essence, which meant that I could theoretically use it to learn stability essence abilities. That would take more work than using unaspected stability essence, but it was an advantage compared to something like cutting-aspected sword essence, which had a similar function to sharpness but was a much more complex composite and couldn't be easily converted into something like stability.

"I'll think on that one." I took another drink of water. "What about other general combat essence types? Like . . . combat essence itself, I guess. Or war."

"Both are functional options, although combat essence is closer to your sword essence than war is. I would also advise against war essence for political reasons. Being a walking siege engine invites a type of attention you may not wish for."

That made sense, and combat essence felt more appropriate for my general style, anyway. From what I understood, it was more focused on one-on-one fighting, whereas war essence was for large-scale effects, like throwing spells that obliterated entire fortresses. I was much more interested in focusing on things that would help me fight powerful individual opponents. "Okay. I'll think on those. Are there any other obscure essence types that might synergize with sword essence in ways I might not be considering?"

"There are many, child. Any essence type that interacts with a trait related to swordplay, for example, can have a synergistic effect on that specific aspect of using sword essence. Speed, strength, accuracy, focus, reflexes, senses — these are all aspects that can be found for certain essence types that you may wish to consider."

"But some of those would be aspects of things that might be opposites to components of sword essence. Like, speed is usually an aspect of motion. That could make me weaker overall, even if it makes me faster, right?"

Gramps sighed. "If you're truly worried about your absolute maximum possible efficiency, then yes, there would be some interference between using opposite types. If that's a concern, then you could get your speed out of something that provides a general physical benefit, like enhancement essence."

"What about transcendence essence? That could help with a lot of physical enhancements, right?"

Gramps snorted. "Oh, certainly. Good luck finding that. You'd be about as likely to find destiny essence."

". . . Wait, is that really a thing I could find? Destiny essence sounds pretty amazing."

Gramps groaned. "Forget I said anything. There are only a few known sources in the world, and they're incredibly carefully controlled by major governments. I won't say that it would be impossible to get some, but don't think of it in terms of your immediate plans."

I felt a twinge of disappointment at that, but I tried not to let it bother me. It wasn't a perfect fit for combining with sword essence, anyway. I wasn't strictly set on everything matching sword essence somehow, but it was my preference for at least most of my Dianis Points to feel like they had some kind of connected theme — it would make technique construction much easier.

"Maybe I'm thinking about this the wrong way. I already have two essence types, hypothetically, if there's something in my right hand."

Gramps's expression darkened. "You would be wiser to continue to think in terms of your other essence types."

"Why? You've always been so vague about this. I know, you'll tell me 'when I'm ready,' but I'm actively working on figuring out my essence types right now, and I need to plan for the future. If it's something as simple as 'do not break, the essence overflow will kill you,' that's something you can just tell me."

Gramps hesitated. ". . . No, child. That seal is not to protect you. The power you are bonded to would not destroy you."

I sat up a little straighter. "What's the risk, then?"

"It might not destroy you, Grandson. But it very well might destroy *everything else*."

I could sense it, barely. The essence behind the seal, thrumming hard, as if in anger — and seeking escape. "What *is* this seal, Grandfather?"

"One terrifying piece of an ancient mistake."

I turned toward him. "No riddles, Grandfather. What is the seal? Does it have something to do with why I've always felt close to Ana? To swords in general?"

"You are bound to a sword, as you have long suspected. Not in the same way as Anathema, but in a way that is equally important. I cannot tell you all the details. I say this not to be evasive, not this time. By that, I mean I literally cannot. I am bound even more surely than your hand." He raised his hands and mimed them being cuffed together. "But you are right, Grandson. You deserve the agency to influence your own destiny. The seal is damaged — it is only a matter of time before it breaks entirely. You must make a choice. If you wish to live a life of peace, you must find someone greater than I who can rebuild that seal — and never seek the truth behind it. Perhaps strengthen it further. But if the truth is something you must find . . . the key is within your hand."

I lifted my hand to look at it. ". . . How literal is that last part?"

"More than you realize."

"If I wanted to unlock the power within the seal, how would I do that safely?"

"There is no way to do it completely safely — such would be antithetical to the power within. But if that is your objective, you must find a way to unlock it one layer at a time."

"Layer? Does my seal have multiple layers?"

Gramps winced suddenly, as if struck, then reached up to put both hands on his head. ". . . I . . . you . . ."

I'd never seen him respond like that. I rushed closer, reaching out, until he vanished right in front of me—

Then reappeared a moment later, blinking rapidly, and then reached out to lift up his cup of tea to take a sip. His facial expression was completely neutral, unbothered.

"I'm sorry, child. What were we talking about?"

I stared at him. Then, slowly, I turned away from the wall, my heart hammering like a drum.

". . . Some essence theory ideas."

"Ah, yes, of course." He slipped the piece of paper that was still in front of him closer. "Synergy essence? An intriguing notion, isn't it?"

"Y-yeah."

I wasn't willing to risk a repeat of . . . whatever had just happened. I'd seen Gramps vanish on numerous occasions before, but . . . never like that. Never so violently, so . . .

I tried to calm my heart as I took a seat, resolving not to ask him anything further on the subject of the sword and the seal.

An image of him lifting his hands, miming shackles, played in my mind.

Sorry, Gramps. I . . . hope you're okay.

I poured myself another cup of water, unsuccessfully attempting to suppress my feeling of guilt.

I won't squander what knowledge you've given me.

I glanced back toward my grandfather's face, just for a moment, then turned away.

While Gramps hadn't given me the answers that I wanted that night, he'd given me something critical — a direction to follow. One that I hoped hadn't cost him too dearly.

Sometimes it takes a key to find another key. And with that thought in mind, I knew the next step of my plan.

CHAPTER XXV

SELF SHARPENED

It was late in the night when I realized that Ana had slipped out at some point, either while I was chatting with Gramps or before I'd woken up. I felt a little bad that I hadn't said goodbye to her, but a trip to her shrine would have been simple enough, or I could have just called out to her — she might have heard me and answered.

Instead, I plotted.

I finally had an idea on what I was planning to do for my next essence type. It was a considerably different concept from what I'd been originally planning on, but the more I thought about it, the more it felt *right.*

That wasn't the only thing I was considering, though. I needed a good gift for Ana's threefold name day, and possibly another for once she reached Hearth-level. She'd been gradually working her way toward reaching the peak of Torch-level, and I didn't expect it to be much longer before she made the jump to her third level of essence development.

That didn't bother me like it might have a year or two earlier. Even if she jumped ahead before I reached Torch-level, I finally felt like I was advancing, and if I figured out a couple good matches for my existing essence type, I could potentially catch up with her eventually — or even match her combat prowess without reaching her essence level.

Fighting at a level above your own was possible through several means.

Certain destinies were known to be exceptionally potent, allowing for deceptive levels of power. I hoped to get one of those, and destinies were another factor in why I didn't want to deviate too far from my existing sword focus right away — I didn't want to accidentally end up with a strange destiny if I, say, picked up fire essence before reaching my next level.

Specific secondary essence types — sword essence among them — were more combat focused than others. Focusing heavily on sword essence for my secondary essence type would give me a bit of an advantage against people who just absorbed whatever essence types they came in contact with. This strategy was common among Skyseekers, so it wasn't something I could count on as a major advantage against other people in the outside world, but it would help make me more competitive against people who had not chosen to do the same thing.

As far as I knew, Ana wasn't focusing her secondary essence to the same degree that I was — but she also continuously got secondary essence from her bond to Anathema, and much of that would be sword essence. So, while I might have had a bit of an advantage in terms of how much I was focusing on sword essence now, it wasn't going to be a tremendous advantage until I had a much longer period of time to exploit it.

Aside from that, people could challenge more powerful opponents through advantages like powerful equipment, individually potent essence types, personal skill, powerful techniques, tactics, strategy, and synergy between their essence types.

My hope, of course, was to take advantage of all those things — but so did everyone else that was hoping to be competitive.

For the immediate future, my clearest advantages were my apparent talent for technique construction and any power that I could get out of my upcoming essence choices. If I found a couple particularly powerful essence types that worked well with sword essence, then got a powerful destiny on top of that, I'd be in a much better place to challenge people like Ana that were a level above my own.

If Ana reached Hearth-level before I reached Torch, things would be much harder. Fighting up two levels was technically possible, but you needed to stack a large number of other factors to your advantage to make it plausible. Anything beyond two levels, or even a single level increase coincided with reaching into a different layer of essence development, was generally considered too much to overcome even with several other advantages. There were cases of it happening, but they tended to be very niche, involving things like ambushes, or truly legendary figures like the Hero herself, who was supposedly capable of fighting people a full layer higher due to the absolute absurdity of her destiny's powers.

I obviously wanted that power, but even as a child, I knew that fighting one level above my own was more than a worthy target to start with.

As I contemplated both Ana's impending name day and the possibility of her reaching Hearth-level, I knew that what she wanted most was what I'd wanted for myself for ages—

A proper sword to use.

Ana had access to Anathema itself, but the sword was affixed in place to power her shrine — she couldn't actually wield it. And she had had no better luck in finding a sword to train with than I had.

With that in mind, I spent a few more days near home to collect resources, researched a few more essence options for myself, then headed back to the sword school to make camp.

I had another visit to the sword saint in mind — and this time, I was hoping to walk away with more than just scars.

"Well, well." The Smiling Sword Saint took a step forward. "Looks like I've found myself a . . . distraction?"

The sword saint's lips shifted downward fractionally. I felt a momentary surge of pressure in the air around me, but I resisted the urge to fall to my feet.

A pillar near me crumpled. It was, of course, one of the same pillars she had destroyed during our last meeting — the entire place seemed to be fully reconstructed each time I visited.

The saint herself should have reset, too, much like the other echoes. But this behavior . . . there was a subtle difference there. One that might be dangerous.

Before she struck me down out of some kind of sense of caution, I spoke. "Honored Sword Saint, I have come for training and brought you a memory crystal of my previous visit."

"A previous visit? I don't—" Her frown deepened, but fortunately, she seemed to restrain her area-obliterating abilities that came along with her typical changes of expression. "Show me."

"I'm going to reach into my bag and retrieve the crystal, then toss it to you. You should also have a few other crystals already in this area from my previous visits. I didn't take them with me when I left."

Her eyes flicked to the side for a moment. "Fascinating. Go ahead."

I grabbed and tossed her the crystal. She restrained her cutting instinct and caught it.

"Probably would have been better to watch the others first." She waved a hand, and I saw several crystals rush toward her in a blur from somewhere in the area behind the arena.

They floated in midair in front of her briefly, and she snatched them out of the air one at a time, concentrating only briefly before releasing them.

Mentally, I noted the direction the set of crystals had come from and tried to extrapolate the distance based on their speed of travel. I wasn't planning to investigate wherever she was storing the memory crystals immediately, but I always tried to keep track of possible resources in case they'd be necessary for the future. If the sword saint actually moved around within this echo area, it also gave me another area where I might find her if she wasn't at the entrance.

At first, I'd thought she'd always manifested in exactly the same spot, much like the other echoes — but upon seeing the crystals moving, I wondered if she might be periodically active even in my absence, and not necessarily in the same locales. It was even possible that she was perpetually active, and simply moved to the arena and responded near-identically each time someone entered the area. I didn't have enough information on the subject to know for certain. Not yet.

After she examined each crystal for a second or so each, she fractionally nodded. I heard a distant tree bend along with her neck. "Show me that signature technique of yours again."

Immediately, I demonstrated the Shattering Sword technique. She hadn't approached this time, so I simply discharged the slash in midair.

"Not bad. Not much improvement this time, though. How long have you been gone?"

I felt a bit of shame at her possible disappointment. "It's only been a couple days, most of which was spent in travel."

I half expected her to chastise me for failing to innovate in that time, but she just waved a hand. "Makes sense. Where'd you go?"

"Home, to visit my grandfather."

"Literal grandfather, or someone like a sect leader?"

"More the former. Not biologically, I think, but he raised me."

"Ah. Needed to tell him all about your visit to the famous sword saint?"

I shook my head. "No, I'd told him about that previously. He's a scholarly sort, and I wanted to discuss essence options with him. Things that could define my future."

"And you let him choose your path for you?" An eyebrow went up. I felt a twisting pressure against my throat, but it was mild enough that I pushed through it.

"No, sword saint. I simply discussed ideas and theory with him. My path is my own."

The pressure lifted. "You've made a choice, then?"

"I've decided on a first step." I lifted my right hand. "I have power in here, something restrained. It might be a key to my development as a swordsman."

The sword saint shrugged. "Maybe. Might not be useful at all. People don't just seal Dianis Points on kids for no reason. It's either disadvantageous to you, or it's dangerous to someone else."

"According to my grandfather, at least, it's more of the latter."

"Lemme see."

She vanished, reappearing next to me, then grabbed my hand. For a moment, she seemed to inspect it purely physically, and then I felt a thin puncture in the center of my palm. It wasn't severe, and almost immediately, the wound sealed over.

"Hm." The Smiling Sword Saint released my hand, looking contemplative. "You've got some problems, kid."

"In what way?"

"Think your grandfather is right. No one makes a seal like this casually — it's complex enough that even I couldn't get a good look at all the parts without tearing it open. That's tempting, but you've got some things to think about first. If this thing gets completely ripped apart, the power within it is going to be released immediately. You'll have to learn to control that or deal with the consequences. And second, someone made this seal for a reason, and they might feel a bit put out if it's broken. And someone powerful enough to make a seal that I can't see straight through? Well, that's not someone you're ready to play with, kid. You still want to do this?"

I felt a bit of nervousness, but I nodded. "It's part of me. It's like I've spent my entire life fighting with an arm tied behind my back. Sometimes . . . I just want to be able to cut loose."

The Smiling Sword Saint's lips twitched upward. It was, up until that point, the closest thing I'd seen to a smile on her face.

It almost killed me.

The arena all around me vanished, cleaved into nothingness, but I remained unharmed, standing on a tiny patch of remaining stone.

The sword saint continued standing in midair as if the ground below her hadn't been obliterated.

"That," she said, "is what you will need to learn."

She gestured at the now-obliterated arena around me.

"Complete control over what you cut. Otherwise, you'll be constantly risking collateral damage to your allies — or, more mundanely, your environment and equipment. This will not be easy. Even I, on occasion, have difficulty with controlling the power at my disposal."

I didn't point out that "on occasion" seemed more like "constantly" in her case. The number of times I'd seen her restrain her power felt more like exceptions than the norm — unless, of course, she'd wanted to give me the impression that she was dangerously uncontrolled. That was certainly possible, but I didn't know her personality well enough to evaluate the odds of it.

"I think that whatever essence is in there is related to sword essence somehow. Would it truly be so different from having a standard Dianis Point of that type?"

"You feel that essence flowing through the little crack already in there? That's nothing, kid. You break that seal open, it's going to be a deluge. Whatever you've got sealed, it's a connection to an external power source — one that's orders of magnitude stronger than you are. With most spirit bonds and similar stuff, whoever is on the other side regulates the power they give you to an amount that you can handle. When you bond an item, usually you set up the bond yourself, and when doing that, you create a connection of a level you can handle. Whatever this thing is that you've got . . ." She shook her head. "The other side isn't limiting the flow properly. Lots of possible reasons for that. Maybe it's a person who is so strong they can't limit themselves to the extent you need. Maybe it's an item that someone else bonded you to without properly setting up limits on the item itself, either because they couldn't or didn't want to. Maybe it's something more esoteric, like a gateway crystal, a ley line, or another location. In any case, without the seal, you'd have been overflowing with power since whenever the bond was made. Maybe you would have survived that, if it's a power type that doesn't cause internal damage, but it would have prevented you from absorbing much other essence, and you'd have other side effects. You'd probably be emitting some of the essence all the time, like an aura, destroying your environment."

". . . Aren't auras like that usually only possessed by people who are much more powerful?"

"Sure. But the body will do it naturally to some extent, if you get truly flooded with essence you can't use. It's not easy to control, and it's not pretty."

I nodded. "So . . . I'd need to learn to control that power. But there's barely a hint of that power available to me right now — not enough to actually use for much. I can manipulate the thread of essence I have and mix it into techniques — it feels like some kind of extreme version of cutting-aspected essence — but I don't feel like that's enough for what you're talking about. How do I learn to control it properly without breaking the seal?"

"You're right." She gestured at my hand. "And you don't. You're going to have to break it open just a bit more, then learn to restrain it after that, if you can."

"And if I can't?"

"Well, then you'll be ruining your life at a very young age. Probably won't last much longer after that, unless you can exercise some modicum of control. Even if the essence doesn't shred you from the inside — which I can't say I'm as confident as your grandfather about — you'd risk cutting anything you interact with. You'd cut your food before you can eat it, cut your water before you can drink. Maybe even cut the air around you before you can breathe it."

I took a deep breath. "Okay."

Her eyebrow went up again. "You're not backing down from this?"

I closed my eyes, focusing on my right hand and feeling the power within. The tiny thread of strength that flowed out of it, and the distant power of something familiar. Something that, even while separated, was a part of me.

"For as long as I can remember, I'd been searching for my first real sword. But . . ." I took a breath. "I've had it with me all this time."

I spoke more confidently as I closed my eyes and raised my hand.

"This . . ." I closed my hand into a fist, feeling the thread of power within it briefly swirl. Then, with only the slightest of effort, I forged that strange essence into a gleaming blade of silver. ". . . will be my first sword."

When I opened my eyes, I saw the sword saint staring openly at the technique. "And what will you do with your sword, young man?"

"Wield it." I swept the essence in the air in front of me.

"For what purpose?"

I felt a hint of a smile cross my face. "That," I said confidently, "I'll figure out as I go."

The sword saint continued to look at the blade manifestation from my hand.

There was something subtly different about it that I hadn't even realized when I'd first formed it — the length and dimensions weren't those of a standard arming sword like when I usually formed it. Instead, I'd instinctively formed an essence blade that matched the dimensions of a sword I'd always seen in my dreams.

It . . . wasn't complete. The sword was hazy, ill-formed, indistinct, like a half-finished picture. Holding it, I could feel the familiarity — and the desire to find the missing pieces.

And the sword saint's eyes shone with something like recognition . . . and perhaps, for the first time, a hint of concern.

"You sure you want me to break this seal open for you, kid?"

I gave her a quizzical look. "Who said anything about having you break the seal?"

". . . Then what are you planning?"

"That's simple." With one final glance at the sword I'd formed, I allowed it to disperse. It was simple, intuitive. Easier even than working with normal sword essence . . . at least at that scale.

Working with a truly broken seal would, of course, be a different story.

"It's my sword. I'll unsheathe it myself."

It took some time to convince the Smiling Sword Saint to assist me with my plan. She called it things like "ambitious" and "creative," by which I could tell she meant "utterly insane."

But I wouldn't settle for anything less than breaking the seal through my own power.

It had taken me the time from leaving home to reaching the sword saint to settle on the plan.

I'd already tested seeing if I could damage the seal with sword essence or the essence from within the seal itself. The answer was a resounding "no," at least at the level of power I had available. I suspected that the seal was expressly designed with sword essence in mind and, more than likely, created by someone in at least the shade layer. That meant several levels of power beyond anything I could hope to affect — at least normally.

I'd considered trying to break the seal from the inside somehow, perhaps by altering the flow of power from whatever was on the other side, but that wasn't a reasonable option at my own level. I'd need to reach the spirit layer to be able to interact with spirit bonds with any degree of fidelity, and specifically, I'd want to reach Regalia-level — the middle level of the spirit layer — to be able to deal with spirit bonds to items, as I now recognized this to be.

That was likely decades off, and I wasn't going to wait that long.

I considered several approaches, including having the sword saint break it open for me. That, of course, would have been the simplest method. She'd already proven that she was able to damage it, even unintentionally. But I wouldn't be satisfied with someone else solving the problem — and more importantly, if she broke the seal herself, she'd do it in a way that I couldn't control. In all likelihood, if she decided to tear it open, she'd do it all at once. Perhaps she could limit her impact if I asked her to, but if I'm being honest, I didn't really trust her to follow my wishes.

The Smiling Sword Saint seemed friendlier now that she was interested in me, but that interest came along with dangers. She was a creature born from sword essence and memories, not the original sword saint — and her personality would be skewed by that, as Grandfather had already warned me. If she had an opportunity to release some vast amount of swordlike essence from within me all at once, she very well might do that, even if it went against my wishes. Perhaps she'd do it to see if she could learn a new aspect from the aura I ended up emitting, or perhaps she'd try to absorb the essence from it herself. With the seal completely broken, there was a chance she could even steal the spirit bond somehow for her own purposes.

She'd indicated that she couldn't sense the full extent of the seal — or the power within it. That was good, and I hoped to keep it that way. If the sword

I was bonded to was what I thought it might be, the risk of allowing her to interact with it could not be understated.

So, I'd formed a different plan. One that might allow me to learn to use the sword safely, and keep some part of the power of the weapon held back, both to prevent myself from being overwhelmed and to avoid tempting the saint.

The key was a word that Gramps had used — one that he had seemingly sacrificed something to say.

Layers.

The seal wasn't just a single barrier. If that was true, then perhaps I could interact with parts of the seal independently without breaking them all at once.

And once I had that idea in mind, a method for doing that was all around me. It was shockingly simple once I'd thought of it, but simple didn't mean easy — and I couldn't do it on my own.

I'd known for some time that the areas where I'd seen the echoes were breaches — tears in the layers between worlds. Layers like the spirit layer, shade layer, and memory layer, just like those found within the body.

And, if I wasn't mistaken, just like the layers I'd find within the component parts of the seal.

When I'd told this conclusion and my plan to the sword saint, she'd been a little surprised.

"Kid, I get that you're trying to figure out a clever way to access the power in your right hand more gradually and safely. That's creative. And completing a Dianis Point like you've described is . . . ambitious, at least. But . . ."

"Breach essence itself is dangerous." I nodded. "Unstable. Difficult to control. I know. I'll need to learn to use one dangerous essence type just to access another. I get it."

"I don't know if you do." She shook her head and the air around her trembled. "Breach essence is no joke, even at my level. There's a reason almost no one uses it — it's too impractical. Mess up with sword essence? Someone gets cut. Make a mistake with breach essence? Congratulations, you've ripped open an unstable portal to another plane of existence. Maybe you get pulled in, maybe something else comes out — and isn't friendly."

"There are safer ways to use it," I pointed out.

"Sure. Knew a guy who used it on his Advancing Point for real fancy movement techniques. Destructive teleportation. Very clever, until one day he used his technique and he was just . . . gone. Honestly, still have no idea what happened there. Probably better not to think about it."

"I . . . uh, yeah. That does sound pretty risky, I admit. Probably better essence types for movement."

"You think?" She scoffed. "There's better essence for almost everything. It's intensely dangerous, kid. *Chaos* essence is more reliable."

"That's why I plan to put it up here." I tapped my forehead.

"You . . . want the world's least stable essence . . . messing with your perception of reality."

I folded my arms. "It's still just essence. If I put it in my Viewing Point, I can use it to enhance my perception, but if it's causing trouble, I can just burn through the available essence or pull it out."

"Sure, assuming you're aware that it's causing you a problem in time. Things *happen* with breach essence, kid. Things you can't easily predict."

"Sounds exciting." I grinned. "Come on. You can't be that adverse to using deadly essence types. You're a sword specialist."

"There's dangerous and then there's crazy, kid. Breach essence isn't a sword without a crossguard. It's a sword without a handle."

I shrugged. "Then I'll make a handle for it."

"Ugh. Don't get clever with my metaphors, there is no way to make a handle — well, not easily."

"Already working on ideas for it. I could easily spirit bond something to that Dianis Point in a couple levels that adds a stability component to it — like, you know, literal stability essence. Or something that enhances my ability to control it. It's doable."

"Maybe," she conceded, "but why bother, when there are much more straightforward options that could get you similar results?"

"I'm not sure there are, actually. The things I have in mind . . ." I didn't want to reveal my hand too much, lest she object even more strenuously. "Breach essence is a good fit. It's a means to work on things across multiple layers at once, and not a lot of essence types allow for that. Sure, I could get something like spirit essence and be able to impact both the core plane and the spirit plane simultaneously, but that's just two layers. With breach essence, I could hypothetically see into any of them — or impact any of them — with just one essence type."

"There are other ways to do that, too," she pointed out.

"Yeah, I've looked into that. Constellations essence is the primary example. But unless you're going to fly up to the stars and pick some out for me on a regular basis, that's even less accessible."

"Definitely not doing that, yeah. But why do you even need to do that with a single essence type? It would be vastly simpler to just get the essence types for the specific layers you want to mess with — spirit, memory, that sort of thing — and take your seal apart that way."

"Maybe. But with the number of layers in the seal, I'd end up using every Dianis Point on that alone. More than all of them, actually."

The sword saint stared at me. "Wait. Just how complicated is this seal?"

We stared at each other for a moment.

"I thought you could see the whole thing," I admitted.

"I can see a corporeal layer, a spirit layer, and a memory layer. You're saying there are more than three?"

I got that look like a kid who'd gotten caught sneaking a snack after midnight. "Yes?"

Her expression turned more serious. "I'm reevaluating this. A seal of that complexity shouldn't be toyed with at all."

I folded my arms. "You made it clear that this was my choice."

"Oh, it is. I won't stop you. But let me be clear — any seal of that level of complexity needs to have a very good reason for it. People don't just casually make four-plus-layer seals. And if you said there are more layers than you have Dianis Points left . . ." She frowned. "It's a full seal, isn't it? Six layers?"

"Seven."

She gave me a skeptical look. "I . . . don't think I've ever seen a seven-layer seal. That would be for . . . I don't even know what that would be for, kid. People put raging gods behind seals less extensive than that."

I may have some ideas.

But I didn't say that. "I assume it's my birthright. Don't you want to find out what that might be?"

"Don't tempt me with treasure, kid. It's a bad idea. You might not like the results."

I didn't like the razor look in her eyes when she said that, so I took a step back and raised my hands defensively. "Fine, okay. I can take it slowly at first, feel it out. The important point is that I can't afford all those essence types to do it one essence at a time. If it proves too dangerous, I'm willing to go search for a source of seal essence to repair the seal in the future."

"Might be best to just get the seal essence first."

I shook my head. "I considered that, but there's no one here to teach me how to use it, and it's not in any of my books. I'd have to travel — and my grandfather won't let me travel until he thinks I'm strong enough. I need a sword for that, so . . ."

"So you're stuck. I see your problem. I still think there are better solutions."

"Such as . . . ?"

She folded her arms. "Just get normal essence types and ignore the seal until you're older."

That was . . . eminently reasonable, unfortunately. "I'll think about it. But for the moment, I'd like to start gathering breach essence. Even if I don't use it for breaking the seal, I still think the perception enhancements are worth having."

Her lips twisted in disapproval. "Maybe, just maybe, we can consider that a reasonable method of being able to see things across several layers with one essence type. That's clever, I'll admit, even if it's a niche approach with some clear downsides. But there's one major problem. I might not know you well, and even I know you won't be able to resist the urge to make a sword technique with breach essence in it. I give you a week."

. . . She had me there.

"I . . ." I took a breath, considering. "I can wait longer than that, until I have a better idea of what I'm doing. Focus on sensory stuff first. Seeing breaches would be useful for gathering more essence. And I bet I could make techniques for more clearly interacting with things like spirits and shades."

"And echoes?" She folded her arms. "Planning to use the breach essence against me?"

I blinked. ". . . No?"

Her eyes narrowed for a moment, and then she sighed. "Shame. Might have been fun to crush you."

She exhaled. The air in front of her shimmered with the exhalation, as if the air was being shredded. "Fine. Since it's obvious you won't listen to reason, I'll help with your little plan. What did you need me to do?"

I gestured at the area around us. "This place is either adjacent to or on top of a breach. It should have a bunch of breach essence . . . but, with your presence here, sword essence is still dominant. I don't suppose you could stop drawing in the sword essence in the area for a bit?"

She blinked, seemingly genuinely confused. "You think I'm the one drawing sword essence here?"

I stared at her.

". . . You aren't?"

"Nope." She shook her head. "If anything, my presence here might be a side effect of whatever is doing that."

That . . . was outside my expectations. When I'd found the echo of the saint, I'd assumed — obviously erroneously — that she was drawing a region's worth of sword essence toward herself continuously through using her Breathing Point. It was a simple explanation to the absence in the sword school — someone stronger was just drawing it all in. And she did have sword essence herself — she used it constantly. So, if something else was drawing in sword essence, she was either omitted from that somehow, or simply powerful enough to resist it.

I'd need to figure that out at some point, but for the moment, that was beyond my power to explore directly.

"Do you have any idea what is drawing in the essence, then?"

"I have a few ideas. I know the general area, and I've looked around a bit, but I can't remember exactly what I found. Tempted to investigate more, but I'd probably just lose my memory again. I'll probably take another look after you leave. Memories might set in properly with time, might not."

"I could go with you to look, and we could record my memory?"

She glanced behind herself, then turned back to me. "Tempting, but you're too interesting to get yourself killed with that right now. If something here is strong enough to make me manifest, you'd stand no chance if it doesn't like you, and I couldn't necessarily protect you. Maybe we can take a look someday, but you're too weak."

"For now." I stared determinedly in the direction she'd looked. A trail to follow, someday.

"For now," she agreed in a cautious tone. "So, giving up on the breach plan?"

"Not in the slightest. Even if you're not the source of the sword essence, can you simply clear it from a small area? Draw it into yourself, or nudge it toward where it's already going?"

"Hm. Yeah, I could, for a little while, but not long enough to form an essence node."

"Oh, right. I should have mentioned — I have empty essence collection vials. Just a couple left, and they're Candle-level, but . . ."

"I get it." She nodded along. "But even if I clear out the sword essence, breach essence might not be the dominant type."

"I was hoping you could clear out the spirit essence, memory essence, and shade essence from the same area. Just briefly. Hopefully that would ensure that breach essence would be the most concentrated thing remaining in that area."

She whistled. "Now *that* is ambitious. Do you know how hard it is to simultaneously shape four different completely dissimilar essence types?"

I gave her a little smile. "Well, if it's too hard for you—"

"Oh, you're on, kid. I won't just clear those four. You want breach essence? Fine. Toss me the first vial."

My smile broadened. She really couldn't back down from the challenge.

I tossed her the vial. She flipped it over in her hands. "Huh. New design. Be right back."

Then she was gone.

I blinked at her absence.

When she returned a full minute later, her hair was tousled and her robes had slight but noticeable tears. I tried not to stare in open wonder at that.

I didn't dare to ask what could have possibly harmed her.

Fortunately, she answered for me as she tossed me the vial.

"The breach essence was easier to collect from inside."

I blinked as I caught the glass container, now filled with a strange mixture of colorful translucent essence.

Inside? What did that even *mean*?

If a breach was like a thinning in layers between the planes of existence . . .

Did that mean she'd somehow traveled to an interstitial space between them? Was . . . that even something people could do?

"Quit staring. It's unnerving. If you've got what you need, you can leave."

I carefully slipped the vial into a pouch. "Actually, while I'm here, I do have a couple more favors to ask you about."

"You want more help? Not gonna carve your whole path out for you, kid."

"It's not for me. Do you have a sword I could use as a gift for a sword fairy?"

She looked at me like I was crazy. "You think I have swords that could stay intact outside of here? They're memories, kid. You'll need to find your blades elsewhere."

"Do you happen to know where I can find one?"

"Sure, if you want a sword that'll make you weaker, rather than stronger. They're in that place I mentioned exploring, the one where the sword essence is probably going. Lots of swords, but they're terrible."

She was being flippant, but I was genuinely excited by the idea of there being swords nearby. I'd been searching for so long — was I finally near to reaching my goal? "What do you mean by terrible? And where are they, exactly?"

The sword saint let out an exaggerated huff, briefly causing a burst of intense wind to push me back a few steps. I instinctively shielded my eyes, just in case the breath had a hint of sword essence in it. She ignored my defensive reaction, just shaking her head. "Forget it, kid. You don't want anything the Sepulcher of Sealed Swords has to offer."

I felt my heart beating faster as I processed the name. ". . . Sealed swords, you say? And where exactly might this sepulcher be located?"

"You're hopeless." She let out a sigh. "I'm not telling you."

"Please don't tell me it's some kind of ancient secret or forbidden knowledge. I can't stand that kind of thing."

"Pfft. No. Nothing like that, kid. I just can tell you're going to get yourself hurt if you go wandering over there."

"And you're . . . concerned? Isn't hurting me sort of the whole way that you've been training me so far?" I gestured at a still-visible scar on the back of my right hand.

"That . . ." The sword saint exhaled another breath, but no wind came along with it this time. "Look, kid. I owe you an apology. Not great at those, so it's gonna be brief. Shouldn't have done that."

I raised an eyebrow in confusion. "But . . . I learned so much from that technique you used. It hurt, but I've built more than one technique around—"

"I wasn't planning on that." She cut me off. "Speaking honestly, I was just hazing you. It was a tradition back in my sect. Trial of a Thousand Scars to see if someone is worthy of joining us. If you can't take a few cuts, you can't be a swordsman — that was the idea, at least. Honestly, it's *veking* stupid to start someone out that way. Could have killed you. But I was more instinct than person then. Still am, really, but . . . I'm getting more grounded. You keep feeding me those crystals, I might be . . ." She shook her head. "Never mind that. Doing it once might have been forgivable. Got something out of it, I guess. More than once, though? I was just being cruel, trying to scare you off. I'd like to say that's 'not me,' but no, it was. I do that to people sometimes. Not proud of it. But you didn't deserve that."

I pondered that for a moment, uncertain of what to say. I'd . . . been sure someone as skilled as the Smiling Sword Saint had been trying to teach me some kind of incredible lesson with the trial, or at least been trying to infuse me with enough sword essence to grow. If it had just been . . . well, a literal trial to see if I was good enough . . .

I had complicated feelings about that, ones I couldn't easily put into words. But the most important element of it was simple enough:

She'd given me an important test, and presumably, for the first time in my life, I'd succeeded without even realizing it. If I could do that with her . . . maybe I was closer to succeeding at Ana's trials than I'd realized, too.

As for her apology, well, I had complex thoughts about that, too. I tried to articulate the most important of them. "I accept your apology. And if you want to make it up to me . . . you could always tell me about this sepulcher where I can get my hands on a sword."

The sword saint stared at me for a moment, then burst out into laughter. "You really have a single-edged way of thinking, don't you? Fine, kid. The sepulcher is a storage space for swords that aren't wanted. Cursed swords, experiments that didn't work properly, ones tied to a *jashin* that the world couldn't survive another brush with. You aren't going to find much of use in there."

"Jashin?" I asked.

"Artinian word. Roughly translates to 'evil god.'"

"Oh." I suddenly felt just a hint more nervous. "Yeah, okay, that sounds bad."

"You think?" She sighed. "You'd be better off just having a blacksmith make you plain steel."

"Not exactly any of those around where I live." And I had to admit, my imagination was already running wild. There were so many stories I'd grown up with of legendary sword fighters wielding cursed blades — and even ones who'd learned how to redeem them into holy ones. "Can you tell me about the specific swords there?"

"Nope. Don't want to tempt you, and I didn't even confirm that the swords were still in their rooms. I wasn't interested in them."

"But there were rooms for swords?"

"Sure, but the place looked abandoned. Some fool looking for a sword might have looted them by now." She gave me a meaningful look.

"I take your meaning. You don't think it's possible any of the swords in there could be useful? I've heard stories of curses being removed, and experimental swords could still have useful functions."

"Sure, if you were a high-level Skyseeker and wanted to spend years trying to uncurse a blade, that's possible, but you're not, and it's usually a waste of time. As for the experiments, you're more likely to blow yourself up than get anything useful out of it, but I suppose there's a chance someone stowed something salvageable in there. But even if there is, you're not going to get them out. Not as you are now."

"Ah. Monsters that are too high-level for me? What sort of dungeon is it?"

She blinked. "Dungeon? I don't think there are any prisoners in there. I mean, unless you count a *jashin* or two sealed inside those weapons."

"Sorry, modernism. People call pretty much anything that contains a bunch of monsters and traps a 'dungeon' now. I guess in your day they probably would have called that sort of thing . . . a lair, maybe? What would you have called a place with tests and trials like the crystal shrines?"

The sword saint shrugged. "'Lair' sounds like there should be a big monster making its home in there, or maybe an evil wizard. I don't know if there's a more general term that encompasses both the sepulcher and things like the shrines, but . . . 'dungeon'? That's a strange one."

"Think it comes from the war with the fiends and their dungeon cores. As for why they're called dungeon cores . . . I don't know the etymology, actually. Might be because of the prisoners they used to take, early on, for political reasons. Or maybe . . ."

"Not interested in the history lesson right now, kid. But either way, this isn't what you'd probably call a dungeon, unless you use that term really loosely.

Used to be that people could just walk in and out, more like a museum. But like a museum, you can donate stuff, but you can't take it out. Not without the curator's permission . . . and he's probably long dead."

"Ah. So, the swords are sealed in a way that prevents them from being removed. Couldn't I just brute-force them out?"

"Not with just sword essence. If you had seal essence, or something weird like unlocking essence or theft essence, maybe you could finesse it. Probably would take a while, since you're so low level, but it might be doable. At that point, though — that's when it might turn into something more like what you're calling a dungeon."

"Ah. Traps to prevent someone from stealing one of the swords?"

She nodded. "Traps, guardian spirits, whatever they could do to prevent the swords from getting out. Some of those defenses have probably been worn down by time, or already discharged by others, so it won't be as bad as it would have been during the time the place was actively in use — but you're still going to be in a load of trouble if you try to unseal some kind of evil-sealing blade. They'd have built the defenses to prevent cultists from getting in and waking up whatever thing they worshipped, and you're not anything like on the level they'd be preparing for."

"Hm." I pondered for a moment. "You could help me with that, couldn't you? I pick out a sealed sword, you brute-force the seal and handle the defenses?"

"That wouldn't be properly earning yourself a sword, now would it? And let me reiterate — I think this is a terrible idea. Why would I help?"

"Fair." I shrugged. "Guess it's up to me to figure a way to handle it, then. Unless you know of any other areas nearby with swords?"

"Not a one, unless you're thinking of raiding the faerie queen's vault."

"Let's put that idea on the 'even worse ideas than breaking the seal on a cursed weapon' list."

The sword saint snorted. "At least you have some minimal sense, then. Can we consider this matter closed?"

"For now." I nodded. "I'll bring it up again when I have a better plan, though. One last question, then. If I can't get a sword right now . . . could I bring my friend for a lesson instead? She would genuinely love to meet you."

"You're asking for a lot of favors, kid. You're not even my student yet."

"True, but it's her name day coming up, and . . ."

"Oh, say no more." Her look shifted to one of serious consideration. I was a little startled that she'd given in so easily. There was a story there, one I wanted to hear, but I didn't feel quite ready to pry into that, especially if it might disperse my good fortune. After a moment, the sword saint said, "She's a sword faerie, right? Can she fight?"

I briefly wondered if I'd made a terrible mistake.

"Better than I can, but not in a way that would be capable of giving you a worthy fight. She's only Torch-level, and I don't think the fae would respond well if—"

"Please, kid. I know some teenaged faerie wouldn't be any match for me. I'm not going to pluck her wings. Bring her anyway. I want to see her fight *you*."

CHAPTER XXVI

SPARRING

The Smiling Sword Saint didn't smile as I asked her to sign a bunch of paperwork.

I was no scribe, but I knew my way around a few specific fae traditions where written contracts were an absolute necessity, even if I'd never previously had a chance to make use of most of them.

In this case, I was drawing upon a rare and unusual opportunity for Ana's gift to do something that would have, under ordinary circumstances, broken rules in ways that would have gotten us both into very serious trouble.

With the sword saint's signatures, I traveled back home. Given the value of what I was now carrying, I was, of course, ambushed as soon as I reached faerie territory.

"Drop your weapon and the backpack. Then raise your hands, real slow-like."

I half rolled my eyes, releasing my stick and allowing it to clatter to the floor. Then I grabbed my backpack, mentally checking to make sure that my most valuable breakable goods were in my belt pouches — they were — and began to slip it off my shoulders to comply with the demand.

I could sense the power behind me, and the danger along with it. Without a Viewing Point established, my essence senses were extremely limited, and my clear sense of that power could mean only one thing — I was up against someone with sword essence.

It seemed I'd be getting a duel even earlier than expected.

With my attacker behind me and taking advantage of the element of surprise, they'd assumed that dropping my phantasmal blade meant that I'd be unarmed. As a sword essence practitioner, at an overall higher level than my own, they probably could have sensed if I had other hidden weapons, after all.

But training with various aspects of sword essence, trying thousands of essence compositions and mixtures with different objects in my effort to develop additional techniques and find new functional aspect types, had gradually begun to change my approach to fighting. I couldn't quite put it into words yet, but I didn't need to. I acted on a mixture of instinct and training, unstrapping my backpack as if to drop it.

A backpack was a poor medium for unaspected sword essence. It was, however, a container.

No time for anything complicated.

I spun, simultaneously executing a minimalist manifestation, then hurled the backpack straight at the bandit behind me.

The cutpurse's eyes widened at the incoming projectile, but they reacted with admirable speed, bringing a gleaming cutlass down on the backpack—

Just as I'd hoped.

The bandit's sword-aspected essence met my scabbard-aspected essence and bounced right off, throwing their swing wide.

I charged in during the opening, swinging a fist straight at the bandit's chin—

But they were fast. Too fast.

By the time I'd closed the distance, the bandit's sword was sweeping back down, and I had to sidestep to avoid the swing, then duck under another immediately thereafter. After that, I took a couple steps back, resetting into a combat stance with my arms raised.

"So." The bandit's eyes gleamed gold. "You wanna do this the hard way, do ya?"

Sword Hand.

A blade of essence flicked to life, extending from my fingers. "Wouldn't have it any other way. But watch your step. You wouldn't want to land on that backpack."

The bandit's eyebrows went up. "Oh? Got another trap for me in there, do you?"

"Not exactly." I danced forward with an aggressive swing, deliberately pushing the bandit backward toward the now-fallen backpack.

The bandit parried easily with superior speed, but as I'd hoped, I'd thrown them off balance, just slightly. They were more than a full essence level above me, and even my unusual amount of secondary sword essence wasn't enough to completely cover that speed gap. Not yet, anyway. But while I was at a physical disadvantage, I'd been practicing swordplay at the school for over a year — and while my lessons had been anything but formal, there was a lot to be said for drilling the basics.

When their sword flashed at my face, I didn't try to smash it out of the way with maximum force as my earliest instincts urged me. Instead, I drew from watching thousands of repetitions of Red and Green's matches, and made a minimalist move — a simple tilt of my head to the side, allowing the sword swing to pass right by me while I stepped inside the sword's reach.

My opponent's weapon was longer and stronger than my own hastily conjured blade, but my own weapon had an advantage — flexibility.

As I stepped in close, I concentrated on the manifestation and reshaped it into a knife-length blade, drawing it upward toward the bandit's chin—

Only to stumble as one of my boots hit the caltrops on the forest floor.

The points didn't quite pierce my leather boot, but they sent me into a forward stumble. My swing went wide and my opponent was away in a flash, a parting slash cutting a gouge in my left sleeve.

"Got a few traps of my own," the bandit laughed. "More than you can handle, I'll wager. That's what you get for trying to fight on prepared ground."

I had to admit, a terrain advantage was something I hadn't properly accounted for. I kicked, trying to hurl the caltrop from half poking through my boot directly at my opponent, but it remained stuck in place. While my opponent watched in amusement, I groaned and hopped back on one foot, then slashed through the spike of the caltrop with my essence blade. That did the job, but I'd brushed against a second one of the bristly bits while I'd hopped backward. The forest floor was *covered* with them.

And my opponent, I realized for the first time, was subtly floating.

"Oh, that's . . ." I hesitated before calling it unfair, smiling instead. "A new wrinkle."

A floating opponent wouldn't have to deal with the caltrops, but they'd be easier to shift around with force without the benefit of traction — if I had a way of pushing solidly enough.

I can't outmuscle this, but . . .

An idea formed as the bandit began to stalk forward, dragging their cutlass across the ground menacingly. That was terrible sword discipline, but I supposed this wasn't the right time for a lesson.

Not one of that kind, anyway.

My eyes scanned the forest floor, finding the most open spot I could.

Now or never.

I shot forward three steps, then leapt, my blade extending as I swung downward in a massive cleaving motion.

A jumping attack was, against a faster and stronger opponent, generally one of the worst possible ideas. I was massively exposed while airborne, and superior speed could be used to reposition and take advantage of my opening. But I'd seen my opponent's combat style before, and I knew that if I made a massive and incredibly obvious attack, they'd feel the obligation to block it blade to blade. With a reach advantage from reshaping my weapon, I'd also limit their ability to take a second immediate swing and cut me apart after the impact, since our blades would meet at an angle that would leave me out of their immediate reach.

Not that I was planning to let them get another swing in.

An instant before our blades met, I tried something new. It wasn't a major shift, and it only incorporated ideas I'd already used — but it was, in the technical sense, a distinct technique.

I felt the cutting-aspected sword essence on the edges of my blade and flipped them into their near-opposite function:

Deflection.

When our swords met, rather than trying to cut straight through theirs, the impact blasted our weapons away from each other. The force of the impact destabilized my nascent technique, immediately causing my sword to vanish, but the attack served its function—

My opponent, still levitating, stumbled wildly backward in midair.

"Careful," I called out as I landed, "backpack!"

Their eyes flicked downward as they nearly stumbled right on top of the fallen bag. That gave me a moment to charge again, re-forming my Sword Hand technique and bringing it upward rapidly as I dodged a wild and panicked swing from their sword—

Then we were face to face, panting, my technique under their chin—

And a hidden dagger pressed right against my heart.

"So." The bandit's eyes focused on mine as they spoke from close enough that I could feel their breath. "What's in the bag?"

I could feel the dagger pushing through my shirt. In response, I brushed my own technique closer against their neck, each of us drawing the faintest hint of blood.

"Your name day gift."

The bandit's eyes narrowed for just a moment — and then, with a gleeful laugh, the pressure at my chest vanished.

"Well, why didn't you just say so?"

Ana tossed her conjured cutlass, which vanished just as the knife had, then bonked her forehead against mine affectionately. I let my own Sword Hand technique disperse. "And miss the fun? Besides, a little warm-up like this was a perfect introduction for your gift."

"Ooh. Now I need to know!"

Ana pulled back, and I had to dodge to avoid being smacked with her wings.

As she lifted my bag, I pulled the remaining bit of the conjured caltrop out of my boot and discarded it. Creating caltrops was a new trick but a variation on her familiar imagination essence conjurations.

Her use of sword essence, however . . . that was new. She'd told me she'd considered completing a Dianis Point for sword essence, but I hadn't imagined it would go so quickly. It had been just over a year, and forming a fully functional Dianis Point often took several, unless someone had a truly powerful source to draw from all the time—

Which, of course, Ana did.

I smiled at Ana's glee as she searched through my backpack, finding the letter written by the sword saint, but I couldn't focus entirely on that.

Seeing how she'd fought, I knew that even with all I'd learned, I was still at a disadvantage.

I still have a lot of work to do.

⊱ ⊰

We sat down together while Ana read through the first paper, her expressions shifting from glee at the gift, to shock at the signature, to . . . something sadder as she processed it.

She turned toward me with an expression of loss. "An invitation from the sword saint . . . that . . . that's incredible, but . . . Lien . . . you know I can't leave the forest."

I raised a finger. "I thought of that, of course. If you're thinking about your physical ability to leave, that should be possible for short periods now that you've hit Torch, right? And if you're talking more about the political side . . . if you keep reading the stack, there are two more things for you to see."

The first letter was addressed to Ana, in the form of an invitation from the Smiling Sword Saint to participate in an exhibition match against "Edge of the Woods," after which she would offer us both basic pointers if she was entertained with our performance.

It was the type of thing any young sword wielder would dream of — and Ana was no exception. But she was right, of course. Faeries of the Court of Rust and Salt were not permitted to go into human territory under normal circumstances, and certainly not to interact with humans. In Ana's case, she also had a greater responsibility than many others, since she was responsible for ensuring that her sword was cared for. She couldn't do that properly while she was absent, so she couldn't leave until the sword was claimed, even for nonhuman territory.

I had plans for both problems.

The first letter was a petition to the Court of Rust and Salt, which meant to the queen herself or whoever she designated to handle requests from outsiders.

The petition was to allow Ana, as a sword faerie, to visit the Smiling Sword Saint in a diplomatic capacity.

While faeries were rarely allowed to leave their lands, a direct request from an extremely powerful essence wielder for a diplomatic endeavor was a potential exception. I explained as much to Ana as she read it over.

"Maybe . . . but I don't know if the queen would even entertain diplomatic relations with a human. Not after the war."

I nodded at that. "Right, I thought of that. I think it'll go through, though, for three reasons."

I raised a finger. "One. The Smiling Sword Saint might have been human at first, but she reached a level of essence wielding where she could have been considered to transcend the limits of humanity."

"Flimsy. High-level essence wielders might be considered immortals, in theory, but they're still human at the core."

"Arguable, but that's also my weakest reason. Second . . ." I raised another finger. "I've read the text of the queen's ban against entering human lands. As with many courtly affairs, it begins with, 'On this date, I set forth this decree,' and goes forth to prohibit interaction with 'any human alive.' The Smiling Sword Saint lived and died before the date of the decree. She is, thus, outside the scope of the ban on interacting with humans. Given that she is very likely the most powerful entity in that part of the mountain range and has a clear territory marker, we can consider that area her own, by extension, that is not banned territory, either."

Ana seemed to consider that one. "There's an argument for that, but it has some prerequisite arguments that have to be made first."

"The next few pages lay those arguments out. I'm no expert at rhetoric, but I think it's pretty good. But that isn't the closing argument. This manifestation of the sword saint was born from spirit and memory — she isn't human at all. She's an echo, and thus has a distinct species type."

Ana set the papers down. "I . . . that might be right, Lien, but . . . even if it is, I don't think they'll let me leave. The shrine . . ."

"The third set of documents is designed to deal with that. That's actually for you to sign — it's a request to allow someone else to watch over your shrine in your absence, while it's temporarily closed. You close up the shrine for solstice and equinox festivals, so the idea of closing the shrine isn't without precedent."

"I don't know . . . it'd be a lot to ask someone else to watch the shrine . . ."

"I'll ask Gramps to do it, and to sign paperwork indicating he'd be willing to. No one is going to doubt that he has the capability to keep the shrine safe, especially while it's closed. He could also deliver the paperwork himself — I think that would lend it weight, since he's already considered a guest in good standing with the court."

She lifted the papers and clutched them close to her chest. "You really think this might work?"

"I do. And I'm willing to work to make it happen. Even if the queen won't let you slip away now, maybe when I earn your sword—"

Ana stood up suddenly, hugging me tightly.

"Thank you."

Faeries, as a rule, didn't thank anyone. The implication of a debt owed was a dangerous one. But Ana and I—

We were beyond debts owed.

I kissed the top of her head gently. "Think nothing of it. Happy name day."

She laughed and buried her head in my chest and I pretended not to notice her tears.

⊱ ⊰

We visited Gramps next, letting him in my plan. He reviewed my paperwork with far greater caution than Ana, tsked at places, but could make no alterations to the two sections that had already been signed. He did suggest some edits for the final part, which we made before Ana signed her segment.

Then, finally, he agreed to his part in the plan.

"I will see these documents delivered. You should not, however, expect an immediate response. The court moves at the speed of seasons, after all."

Ana and I both understood that, though I groaned internally. I should have accounted for that in my planning.

The result was simple enough — we would not be able to expect an answer until seasons passed, and more likely years. Based on the contents and the court, I expected a winter reply, and not necessarily the *next* winter.

That . . . wasn't entirely bad, though. We wouldn't be able to take advantage of Ana's gift right away, which made her pout a little, but internally, I felt a bit of relief.

A few more months to practice meant that maybe, when the time came to face Ana in front of the sword saint, I might stand a chance.

⊱ ⊰

Even without confirmation of my gift's success, Ana and I celebrated. For three days, we spent nearly every waking moment together, traveling and training, playing and partying. We met with others several times, visiting the Willowbark Witch and even the great dragon, who deigned to give Ana a gift of his own — a shed scale of such size and density that it took both of us to carry it.

It was a true treasure, one that could be forged into something potent by one of sufficient skill and power. We had no such thing, but that led to an idea—

And Auntie Temper was more than up to the task.

On the final day of our celebrations, Ana and I both still lacked true swords, but she had something of equal value—

A shield.

And though my chances of matching her in a fight shot drastically downward if she acclimated to the new tool, I couldn't help but share her excitement.

With Ana's name day celebrations completed, I returned home only briefly.

I pressed the vial into Gramps's hands. He frowned at the bottle, flipping it over and examining it carefully, then whispering something into the air that I couldn't quite hear. I took it to be a spell incantation — an old habit that was utterly unnecessary both on Mythralis and here, but one that had been drilled into him through years of practice.

"It is, as you hoped, breach essence." He looked much older then, his shoulders slumping as his hand curled more tightly around the vial. "You are certain you wish to follow this path?"

"If there's something terrible about this plan that you're not telling me, I obviously would rather hear it now than find out in ten years that there was a clear downside that I'd somehow missed. *I'm* not the stubborn one."

Gramps snorted at that. "You can be plenty stubborn. If you weren't, you would have taken my advice about the bladeberries."

I shrugged. "Maybe a little stubborn, sure. And I'm not going to abandon this if you just give me some vaguely worded omen, Grandfather. But if you want to tell me something like 'You will accidentally kill everyone you love with this essence,' yeah, sure, I'll listen to that. Is that the type of thing I need to worry about?"

"No." He seemed to decide something then, and with a hiss, he closed his eyes and pushed the vial toward me.

Hesitantly, I accepted it back, flipping it over to examine it, then hastily putting it in a bag on my hip. For one reason or another, he clearly didn't like seeing it. "What is it, then? Can you talk about it?"

"It is merely one step on a road that may lead you into ruin." There was a particular emphasis on that last word that I didn't miss.

"What sort of ruin? Are we talking 'damage my own essence structure' kind of ruin, or 'ruins of an ancient civilization' kind of ruin, or . . ."

"There is a potential for either." Grandfather sat back down. "Breach essence is among the least predictable essence types in the world. While sword essence is inherently dangerous, a sword has a guard and a grip. Breach essence has no safe place to grasp. The moment you introduce it into your essence structure, there is the possibility that it will break what is not meant to be broken."

"Like my seal, yeah. That's part of my intent, if that wasn't clear."

Grandfather shook his head. "As much as I may disapprove of that action, I will not stop you from pursuing freedom from the seal. The risks I speak of are both smaller and grander in scope. When people speak of areas where the boundaries between worlds are thin, they often think of terrain — places like your sword school or the mountains where the sword saint makes her home. It is easy to forget that is not the most common place where this occurs."

"The body." I paused, thinking. I knew, of course, that star veins connected between layers of the self. The physical body, the essence structure, the spirit, the shade, the memory, and so on. Those connections were how higher-level essence wielders built much of their power — they'd generate new sources of strength through higher layers of themselves. Spirit bindings, like what I suspected I already had on my right hand. Shade weaves, connections that allowed restructuring of the physical body. I knew power could be gleaned through the memory layer as well, but that was the work of such high-level essence wielders that I understood less about it.

Accessing elements of higher layers early was possible — in fact, some entire forms of magical practice were dedicated to it. Artinian Spirit Artists, for example, learned how to work with the spirit immediately, entirely skipping the essence layer of self. That specific method required some external conditions to work — their "Spirit Dedications" were not possible on the continent of Dania, as far as I knew — but there were essence wielders who had learned other means to tap into the spirit layer early. The most common method was simply completing a Dianis Point with spirit essence, then using that to open the connections between the essence self and spirit self completely, earlier than it happened automatically.

It was possible to access the other layers of self earlier than intended, too, but any form of alteration from the standard sequence of essence advancement had significant risks. The incremental process of unlocking new layers and abilities allowed the self to acclimate properly to each step, reducing the chances of catastrophic events. Star veins bursting from the extreme stress, spirits and shades mixing together in unpredictable ways, Dianis Points becoming untethered from their proper positions in the spirit structure . . . many, many things could go wrong.

Breaks in the essence layer were the most straightforward — they would generally leave parts of the essence structure unusable, or make them physically dangerous to use.

A broken spirit layer could lead to the loss of spirit bonds, or unstable flows of essence from those bonds. Worse, it could also lead to being extremely susceptible to compulsion through your bonds, often in ways that couldn't be easily detected. Oh, also, there was the chance of being taken over by ghosts.

A broken shade layer could lead toward the inability to recover from injuries, since the shade served as the template for bodily recovery. It also was a large governing factor in aging, and damage to the shade could cause irregularities, like parts of the body aging at different rates.

A broken memory layer was, on the surface, the most straightforward, likely causing literal memory loss. The effects could be more sophisticated, however, such as altering memories, or preventing the recovery of essence.

Obviously, these were all terrible results—

But when I thought about the idea of breach essence interacting with other layers of the self, I also saw *potential.*

If I could mitigate or eliminate the risks involved . . .

"I can see that you understand, but from your expression, you're thinking something unwise." Gramps poured us both some tea. "Tinkering with your essence structure is not something to be taken lightly, ch . . . Grandson."

"I don't intend to take anything lightly. But if I can control what I'm doing . . ."

"There are advantages and disadvantages." He waved a hand, and in an uncommon display of more overt magic, a stack of books appeared on the table in front of us. "You will read these before you finish completing your Dianis Point or make any attempts at using breach essence directly. You will also focus on your perceptions — layer by layer — before you attempt any direct changes to your essence structure, to the seal or otherwise."

"That's . . ." I looked at the stack of books. I didn't mind reading a bunch of additional theory — I loved books — but being forced to do it did remove a bit of the fun. Still, I understood his reasoning, and I wasn't such a fool that I thought I could handle experimenting with extremely unstable essence without studying. "Fair. But in exchange, I want you to prepare some more essence collection vials for me."

"In exchange?" Gramps scoffed. "I am doing you a favor, not the other way around."

"Fine, fine. What do you want in trade? I'm going to need a *lot* more vials before this is done."

⊱ ⊰

I spent the next couple weeks grudgingly working at home, doing chores for Gramps in exchange for more essence vials.

As much as I disliked being away from my sword training, it wasn't a waste of time.

On the first day, I absorbed the first vial of breach essence — or, at least, I tried to. In spite of planning for it and creating a layer of scabbard-aspected sword essence inside my star veins with the express purpose of trying to keep the breach essence from escaping, more than half of it dissipated before I could manage to get the remainder to "stick" into place and form a piece of the foundation for a Dianis Point.

That wasn't enough essence to meet my body's acclimation capacity, but being back at home meant I had more opportunities to do some catching up on collecting local essence, so I was able to return to my routine of collecting sword essence nodes from the Rust River, sharpness nodes from nearby, and bladeberries from everywhere I could find them. So, while I wasn't able to work on building my breach essence quite as quickly as I wanted, it helped to be able to catch up on my sword essence development a bit as well.

I still trained at swordplay at night, going through both my bladework routines I'd learned from the school and practicing the usage of my various techniques. I sparred with Ana, which gave me some practical practice, and even paid a few rare visits to Darryl and Eliree. The latter was a little standoffish, and understandably — I'd been away too much, and often without warning — but she seemed to appreciate the flowers I brought her in apology.

I had to walk back and forth from the sword school around once a week even while staying mostly at home, just to manage my little garden, so that meant there was still a chance to do a little bit of practice with the echoes on each trip.

Even with just a hint of breach essence in my structure, they seemed a little bit more solid to me. A little more real. And on occasion, when they spoke, I almost thought I could hear the sound of whispers upon the wind.

When I'd finished processing the first batch of breach essence and my required chores for Gramps, I took a couple extra vials with me, leaving the others at home, then returned to the Smiling Sword Saint—

And I was in for a surprise.

⊱ ⊰

"Well, well." The Smiling Sword Saint took a step forward, scrutinizing me. "It looks like you found your way back here after all."

CHAPTER XXVII

SIMULACRA

I stared at the Smiling Sword Saint.

"Lost your speech and spine, sword boy?"

I blinked, then shook my head. "No, just surprised. I didn't think you'd remember me. You . . . never previously have."

"That's quite an assumption." The Smiling Sword Saint didn't smile, fortunately, but I sensed a hint of mirth in her tone. "The crystals?"

"I have them. I'll reach into my bag—"

"Yeah, yeah." She waved a hand. I braced myself, but nothing in the environment was ruined by the gesture. "No need for the preamble. Toss."

I retrieved a couple memory crystals — my own memories of our last encounter and another blank one — and tossed them to her one at a time. She caught them easily, and I watched them vanish.

It would have been easy to assume she was just moving them too quickly for me to see, or perhaps storing them in an extradimensional space. But there was another option — one I hadn't expected.

"Are you . . . permanently absorbing the memory crystals?"

"Not all of them. Don't like the idea of mixing your memories in with mine too much. Wouldn't want to lose even more of who I am."

"But when you record your own . . ."

She nodded. "You get it. Not quite fully myself yet, but I can feel it." The Smiling Sword Saint flexed her hands in the air. "Every bit of memory I save, I get a little more *real*."

My heart beat a little faster when I saw the greedy look in her eyes that came with that statement.

Sure, I was happy that my would-be mentor remembered me, and in theory, things would only get easier for me the more she remembered. But seeing that expression, and knowing just how dangerous she was—

I couldn't help but worry that I'd been making a terrible mistake.

I pushed that worry aside, at least for the moment. There was no use in leaving a sword half-drawn, after all.

"Well, if you remember me, that certainly simplifies things. I've brought more vials for breach essence, if you're still willing to help me acquire more."

"Sure, kid. You keep the memory crystals flowing, and I'll be happy to help you break your soul to pieces. Who knows? You survive it, you might even end up being a little more interesting. But first, I think you're forgetting something."

Was I? I hastily considered whether I'd offered her anything else, but I came up with nothing. "Honored Sword Saint, if I owe you some service—"

"Not like that, kid."

She blurred, appearing right in front of me. "What did you first come here for, Child of the Sword?"

My heart beat even faster as I realized what she was implying. I couldn't help but grin in spite of my nervousness. In fact, I probably grinned broader because of it.

"Training." I looked at her, then bowed my head slightly.

"Well . . ." Her lips curled upward. ". . . then what are you waiting for? Get in a proper stance, kid. And let's begin."

I was shocked that the Smiling Sword Saint didn't correct my stance. If I'm being honest, I wasn't confident I knew what a "proper" stance meant, given that there were a huge variety of different "ready" stances based on circumstances and individual sword schools. My instinct was to take a stance similar to what I'd been practicing most frequently at the sword school, with my right foot extended, my knees slightly bent for stability, and my sword held near my waist at a slight upward angle.

It was a "middle" stance in many forms of swordsmanship, according to the books I'd read. I had no idea what the sword school I'd been training with called it. I still didn't even know what the school's name was, or what martial arts forms they used.

"Before I give you any instruction, I need to see what you can do." She waved a hand. Instinctively, I stepped to the side, but it wasn't an attack — instead, a dozen arming swords appeared in midair. "Take one, then return to your stance."

I blinked, then inspected the swords. They outwardly appeared identical, and my limited sense of sword essence told me nothing unusual about either, so I simply grabbed the one that was farthest away from me. Then I returned to my stance.

It was a little awkward — my chosen stance was primarily used for a larger weapon, like a Velthryn-style longsword or an Artinian nodachi or zanbatou. Arming swords weren't unfamiliar to me — they were basically the Velthryn-standard sword, and the type of weapon that most of the people at the sword school used — but while I'd practiced with them, the sword never felt quite perfect.

Huh. Now that I think about it, it's interesting that they're practicing primarily with arming swords at a school where everyone seems to speak Artinian. This scabbard is designed for an arming sword, too. I suppose if they're here on Dania, it isn't that strange that they'd be familiar with weapons from other continents, but . . . there's something to that, isn't there? Another small mystery, a piece of the greater one.

I didn't let myself get distracted by that for long. Instead, I watched the Smiling Sword Saint closely, waiting for her next move.

It wasn't one I anticipated. Not a swing of a sword, not a demand for a demonstration — not of the type I'd expected, anyway.

Instead, she watched for a moment, then said, "This one should do."

She snapped her fingers . . . and we were no longer alone in the arena.

A boy with short black hair appeared next to her. He looked to be about my age, but his features were much more like the sword saint's — in fact, as my eyes widened in shock, I realized he even shared her signature scar.

The boy blinked as he appeared, then immediately jumped back from the Smiling Sword Saint, letting out a low growl. His left hand shot out, and two of the hovering swords shot into his hands in a blur. "So, the master is right. There *is* someone abducting young talents."

The Smiling Sword Saint looked at the boy with narrowing eyes for a moment . . . then burst into laughter. "Oh, goodness. Look at you. So precious. So precocious. So *pretentious*. Was I ever really . . ."

She moved in a blur, appearing right in front of the boy. His swords flashed outward simultaneously in an X-shaped cut.

The sword saint moved so quickly I barely processed it — even then, I knew she'd slowed herself down so we could see what she was doing. She raised a single finger and swung it to the left and right, deflecting both sword swings with enough force to send the boy reeling backward. With each impact, there was a sound like metal striking metal.

Then, as the boy fell backward, she stepped in with a hand raised in a knifelike form — and brought it down.

To pat him on the top of the head.

"Silly boy. Or, girl, really. But you don't know that yet, do you? I'll give you time."

The boy — well, the person who *currently* considered himself a boy, whom I'll refer to as a "boy" to avoid overly complicating this explanation — froze at the touch, pulled away, and tried to raise his swords again, only to meet her gaze . . . and froze.

"You . . . you're . . ."

"Yeah, I'm you, idiot. Ancestors, you're slow. What a disappointment."

"A dream, then? Or a tribulation?" The boy stepped back, never lowering his swords.

"Nah. You're a copy of a memory of a memory. I brought you here to train this one." The sword saint jerked a thumb in my direction. Again, I braced for environmental disasters, but she seemed to be getting better at preventing those — in fact, I hadn't noticed any incidental cutting during that particular visit. Another thing to question later. "He's too weak for me to train directly. I've already nearly broken him a few times without even trying. You're still way above his pitiful state, even at your age, but he can't even hope to learn anything from training against me directly. So, he gets to be your pincushion instead."

I tried not to be *too* insulted by her assessment. Instead, I looked at the boy, sizing him up. He was a head shorter than I was, with features that looked like a mixture of Mythralian and Artinian. He wore traditional Artinian-style robes in white and blue, but they were ill-fitting, likely secondhand. Even so, they were layered in protective runes that would likely slow or stop a sword swing from someone of my proficiency level. His shoes were also Artinian-style, with an open top, and only a thin layer of cloth covering the upper foot.

A possible weak point, I considered. *No clear runes on the shoes or stockings.*

I also considered the neck — which had a small gap exposed — and the face, but given that I was hopefully supposed to be having a nonlethal spar, they were likely considered out of bounds.

The boy looked at me as well, seeming to pay attention to my presence for the first time. "Not much to work with, is there?"

"Try me. You'll find out soon enough."

He smiled at that. No city-cutting, just a genuine smile. Apparently, he wasn't at the age where his expressions could depopulate nations yet. "Well, I can't say I dislike that answer. What happens when I win?"

The sword saint responded immediately. "Same thing that usually happens when you win a fight. You get to live another day."

"Well, that's a bit of extra incentive, ain't it?" The boy shifted to face me completely, resting both swords against his shoulders. "Suppose I'll get to live to old age after all, then."

"You already did, once." I took a couple steps forward. "No one expected you to lose your final duel."

"Oh, yeah?" He rubbed his nose with a sleeve. "How'd their dance go?"

"Allow me to demonstrate the first steps." I took a deep breath.

Sword Sharpening Shroud.

A familiar cutting aura surrounded my sword. I'd need the extra power to be able to even hope to harm my opponent, whereas he'd need nothing special to cut me.

"Oh, terrifying. You have a sword technique that literally everyone has some version of. I'm shaking." He took a few casual steps closer, crossing most of the arena without care. "You got a name I should etch onto something when I bury you?"

"Since you're a version of my master, I suppose you can call me by my family name. It's Lien."

"Oh, classic. A sword-related name. Getting a picture now. Rich, arrogant young master gets a dream crystal to train, gets in over his head . . . then loses it."

I snorted, turning to the sword saint briefly. "Did your younger self really misread situations this badly?"

The boy appeared at my right side the moment I'd turned my head. In an instant, both swords were cleaving downward in a vertical cut.

I barely — just barely — managed to swing around and adjust, deflecting both swords with a single horizontal slash. That sent us sliding apart.

"He's not the one misreading," the sword saint said seriously, but I didn't have time to watch her.

Resh, I cursed as I fell backward, deflecting a hail of furious sword strikes from the boy. *He's fast. Too fast.*

In spite of looking like he was my age, his cuts were much faster than I could manage, and his form was impeccable . . . at least, as far as I could tell. As one of his swords swept up and left a gash along my face, I hissed in pain and displeasure. I wasn't able to predict the movement. I'd tried wielding two swords myself on a handful of occasions, but none of my books covered the forms, and the sword school didn't train in that style — at least, not during the particular exercise that they repeated over and over.

As blood flowed over my cheek, I ducked a follow-up swing, swung upward, let my sword get deflected, then stepped in to throw a punch. I was out of range, but it didn't matter.

Sword Hand.

A blade flashed out of my left hand as I punched, plunging straight for my opponent's chest—

And stopped dead as it hit him in the torso, fracturing harmlessly as the runes flashed on his robe.

He growled, leaving me with a slash along my left arm in reprisal, then stepped back with an appraising look.

"Another extremely basic technique, but . . ." He wrinkled his nose in distaste. "You shouldn't have been able to form that while holding a cutting technique on your sword. Not at your level."

"Not going to remark on the fact that I hit you with something that would have killed you without your robe?" I asked.

"No, because it wouldn't have. You're far too weak for that. But . . ." He gave me a toothy grin. "I hate that you managed a hit at all. You shouldn't have."

"Get used to disappointment."

His smile widened into something wilder — something almost manic. "Oh, I'm not disappointed in the slightest, *Lien*. In fact, this meeting might turn out to be the best thing that's happened to both of us in a while." He laughed. "Finally . . . it looks like I've found myself a distraction."

We danced for hours. Not continuously, of course. I didn't have the endurance for that. At first, each exchange left a shallow cut across my skin — a warning, a punishment, and a boast.

And he had every right to make those cuts. He was better than I was, without the slightest hint of doubt. I'd startled him with my rapid manifestation of a second simultaneous technique, since that was apparently rare at my level, but I couldn't repeat that success. He was ready for that specific trick now, and every effort I made to do something similar was easily rebuffed.

After the first hour, I'd begun to pick up on a pattern in his movements, with each assault followed by an exactly three-step retreat.

I counted it off — six swings from his sword, split into three sets of strikes with each sword — then . . . step, step, step.

Now.

I charged in reckless pursuit. He wasn't surprised, exactly — pursuing someone on the retreat was very standard — but I'd noted that he was just slightly off-balance when he took his third step back, and I took advantage of that to the best of my ability. I sidestepped a hasty swing to arrest my charge, deflected the swing from his off hand with my own sword, then—

I kept charging, straight into him.

I couldn't hope to beat him in speed, but I seemed to be able to match him in raw strength. With my focus on processing so much secondary sword essence, my strength and durability were outstripping standards for my own level. I'd also always been strong for my age, which might have been because of whatever my species was, or it might have just been a consequence of the heavy labor in my lifestyle. Probably both.

When I was inside his guard, I slammed a booted heel on top of his foot and crashed right into him. As our bodies slammed together, I sent out a burst of deflection-aspected sword essence. The sudden burst of power on the impact blasted us apart.

I slid backward across the arena, straight into a ready stance.

He was in a far worse position — I'd caught him off guard and sent him falling backward toward the ground.

Then, in one of the least plausible maneuvers I'd ever witnessed, he flipped both of his swords downward as he fell, jammed the points into the ground, and somehow used his momentum to flip himself over entirely—

Then, while flipping in midair, he swung both swords at me, sending two crescents of cutting force in my direction.

Vek!

I barely managed to swipe my sword through the projectiles as they closed in, smashing them to the side one at a time, and the raw force of the impacts as I deflected them was enough to send jolts of pain through my arm.

The boy landed on his feet, eyes once again appraising me. "That . . . was completely unfair. Underhanded." He jammed both of his swords into the floor in front of him. "It was *beautiful*."

"Thanks. If you ask nicely, maybe I'll show you again sometime." I gave him a wink.

"Quit flirting with my younger self. It's disconcerting." The sword saint turned to him. "And you. You let a Candle-level hit you three times. You're done for the day."

"But . . . I'm having fun!"

"Shut it. You were useful, and I'm counting this a win for you regardless, so you can keep living."

The boy frowned, folding his arms. "You sure grew into a tyrant."

"No," I mumbled, "I'm pretty sure that's someone else."

"What was that?" the sword saint asked.

"Nothing, just commentary on specific titles. Anyway, can you stop threatening to murder your past self? It's mean."

The Smiling Sword Saint stared at me. "Do you have a death wish, kid? Do you have any idea how much danger you're in if you talk like that to me?"

I blinked. "Of course I do. You could kill me for any number of actions I might take, whether they seem to be obvious provocations or completely arbitrary. I'm not going to deliberately antagonize you — I'm not suicidal

— but I'm not going to be cowed by the possibility that you might dislike what I have to say. You're my teacher, but that doesn't mean I'm going to stand for it if you're doing something unjust toward someone else. Even if that someone is . . . well, you."

The sword saint sighed. "Someday, you're going to mouth off to someone who isn't as kind and gentle as I am, and it's going to end very badly. For you, for people you care about, or both."

"Well." I rested my sword against my shoulder. "Then I'd appreciate your help in getting stronger to help prevent that."

"Think I can do that." The boy looked at the sword saint, and then at a nod he tossed his pair of swords into the air. They floated back into position alongside the remaining nine in the air, as if drawn there by magnetic force. Then he walked closer to me and extended a hand.

I passed my sword to my off hand, then took his in my own.

He slammed his forehead into mine immediately. I fell backward, hissing, and prepared to swing—

Only to stop when I saw the boy doubled over in laughter. "You should have seen your face!"

"I suppose I deserved that." I sighed, tossing my own sword aside.

It fell on the ground, rather than rejoining the others. The sword saint raised an eyebrow.

Awkwardly, I turned back to the laughing boy. "Was that a lesson? Never let your guard down, even when the match is over?"

"Nah." He smiled, brushing a stray lock out of his hair. "I just owed you a trick. Think we're even, now."

"Not quite," I told him.

"Oh?"

"You still owe me a name."

He stood up straighter, furrowing a brow. "Don't you already know, if you know the older me? It's the—"

"Not that one," the sword saint cut in. "That name perished along with our body and a pair of suns."

The boy gave her an incredulous look. "Say that last part again?"

"Later. For now, you have a choice — more of a choice than we ever had. Think hard."

The boy looked at Edge for a moment, contemplative. "Never did like being put on the spot. I'll take a bit on the forever name. For now . . ." He offered a hand again. I took it, bracing, but there was no trick this time. Just a steel-handed grip, one that threatened to hold me without escape. "You can call me Thane."

CHAPTER XXVIII

SIGHT AND SOUND

The months that followed were full of brutal bliss.

Each day, I'd wake, study the books that Gramps had given me on layers of the self while I ate, then begin basic drilling at the sword school.

I'd work on my garden for a bit, have lunch, read some more, then head to meet the sword saint and Thane for my *real* training.

The Smiling Sword Saint was not a gentle teacher. Neither, for that matter, was Thane. I left the arena each night with bleeding wounds, but each failure, each mistake, left harsh lessons carved into my memory.

As I learned, so too did Thane. I didn't know how that was happening, exactly. He didn't seem to function exactly the same way the Smiling Sword Saint herself did — if anything, he felt more real. My initial assumption that he'd been conjured purely through the sword saint using a newly completed memory essence Dianis Point fit less and less as time went on, but I couldn't get a clear answer out of the saint from where he'd come from.

"Don't ask me to talk about how babies are made, kid. Ask your grandfather or something."

I didn't press the issue. I'd figure it out on my own eventually.

As I practiced with Thane, my surprise attacks and tricks became too easy to anticipate and counter — so I developed new ones while I polished my skills and techniques.

I still lost every fight. Thane never revealed his exact level, but based on his demonstrated abilities, I expected he was likely at Hearth-level, two full levels above me. It was plausible he was already at Signet-level, three levels beyond my own, and simply hiding some of his capabilities.

If I was uncertain about his abilities, he seemed equally uncertain about himself. One day, he glanced at the sword saint awkwardly when she was training and, after a bit of hesitation, asked her a question that had clearly been cutting at him for a while. "Do I really look like you when I'm older?"

"Hm? Oh, no." The sword saint shook her head. "I never looked like this. Not physically, at least. Not unless I did something after where my memories end. This is a representation of what we *should* have looked like. It's also how I knew I was some sort of illusion or construct. Feels nice, to have my proper form." She stretched her arms. "You want to try it out? I could try to adjust you, but when I first made you, you were based on my memories, and—"

"It's too much." He let out a hiss. "I'm . . . going."

He stalked off somewhere. I didn't know how far he could go and continue existing, but I supposed that was his problem to deal with.

I couldn't understand exactly what he was going through. I'd worked with friends through exploring their identity before, but . . . there were elements to this that were beyond my experience. Beyond anyone's experience that I knew of, really. I could sympathize in that I didn't know my own parentage, nor my species — but that was a different issue, even if it was analogous in some respects.

"I could bring a friend up here to talk to him," I offered to the sword saint. "Darryl went through something similar, figuring out he was a boy. And one of his older sisters—"

"Eh. He's tough. He'll figure it out on his own eventually. For now, focus on your training."

I wasn't sure I agreed with that, but the sword saint was both Thane's creator and his future self, so I supposed I wasn't in any position to argue.

We resumed our training a few days later, when Thane stopped sulking. When he returned, he didn't behave much differently, but I noticed he'd started to wear his hair down, and he'd awkwardly applied some kind of cosmetics to his face. I asked if he wanted me to refer to him as a woman, but he told me not to bother. I wasn't fantastic at reading people, but from the glare he gave me when I tried to ask for more clarity, it was clear he didn't want any further questions.

That was fine. I understood.

Experimenting. Little steps. Whatever works best for him. I'll help if I can.

I had many steps of my own to make, as every loss to Thane quickly reminded me. And as my memories of mistakes began to lead to improved instincts, his own memories and coherence improved.

The sword saint was true to her word, gathering more breach essence for me each time I'd acclimated to a batch. From time to time, I visited home for more empty vials and to resupply, but it wasn't necessary often. As I grew in experience with the breach essence, I learned to control it more carefully in my star veins, losing less and less of it with each attempt. Within three months, I was absorbing nearly an entire vial's worth without wasting any — but it still took nearly a month for my body to acclimate to that vial full of essence. And during that time, my body couldn't handle absorbing almost anything else.

I had plans for fixing *that* problem, and I was more than excited to try them in spite of the risks.

During that time, I grew more comfortable training with the sword saint, and simply asked her if she'd be willing to make me vials of sword essence as well. She refused, largely for practical reasons. There simply wasn't enough ambient sword essence to collect in a vial — it was still being drawn elsewhere — and pouring her own essence into a vial wasn't something she wanted to do. She said that it would . . . diminish her. I didn't like the sound of that.

Beyond that, she reiterated that it was better to focus on working on my new essence type, rather than fixating on building more sword essence. So, for the moment, I listened.

As three months passed into six, something *snapped* into place inside me late one night as I treated my wounds, and I felt it—

New power, flowing deep within me. The kind of power that viciously resisted any form of outside control.

I closed my eyes and smiled, feeling the crystalline structure that I'd forged.

My Viewing Point was finally fully formed.

I could sense it already filling with power, usable breach essence ready to be wielded at my command. I pushed myself to my feet immediately, ignoring the pain burning in my arms and legs.

Let's see what this can do, shall we?

I'd read everything I could on the subject of breach essence, both in the new stack of books that Gramps had shoved at me and my older tomes and in a handful I'd borrowed and bartered from the Willowbark Witch.

To say that I had "ideas" on what I could do with it was an understatement—

I had pages and pages of notes. Dozens, if not hundreds, of compiled ideas for possible techniques. Many of them were completely useless, having been invalidated by subsequent findings in later books, but I had a half-dozen pages set aside with the best technique concepts I'd managed to craft. Things that might require work, but had foundations that I thought were at least within the realm of viability.

As much as my instincts pushed me toward immediately testing a new attack technique, on this one subject, I deferred to Gramps. This was a Viewing Point, which was strongly disposed toward sensory techniques.

With such a dangerous new essence type, even I wasn't going to tinker with using it for attack techniques until I had some kind of basic foundation in other uses.

And beyond that, a sensory technique would, in theory, give me access to something I had long awaited.

I walked from my shelter toward where I knew that the sword school would soon be gathering for their lessons, took a breath, closed my eyes, and formed my first attempt at a technique. It was little more than a basic augmentation, in truth, given that it only involved unaspected breach essence and a small portion dedicated specifically to memory-aspected breach essence. I focused that power inward, rather than outward, allowing it to coalesce around my Viewing Point and radiate into my body in a basic perception-altering technique.

It was only minutes later that the sword school began their loop—

And I heard the footsteps approaching from inside the building before I saw the students emerge.

Fade strode outward first, a bright grin on her face, waving to me in greeting.

When I waved in return, she yawned, and then, with beautiful clarity, I heard her voice.

"What are you waiting for? Grab your practice sword."

"Of . . . of course."

I rushed to the storage shed. Not just to comply, but to hide the tears forming in my eyes.

Finally, after nearly two years of practice, I could hear them.

⁂

When I returned, I found Fade staring straight at me. I lowered the practice sword I'd retrieved to make certain I didn't look hostile. She didn't look angry or afraid, though. Just . . . doubtful?

"Is something wrong?" I asked after a beat.

"There it is again," she said. "I . . . didn't imagine it."

"Imagine what?"

"You, ghost boy." She took one step closer, then another. "You can *talk*."

I blinked. There was a lot to process there. "Yes? I . . . always could talk. What's this about being a ghost?"

"'S'obvious. You're half see-through, you couldn't talk, you weren't solid most of the time. Hate to be the one to tell you, kid, but you're . . . super dead."

Wait, what? She thinks I'm . . . no, hold on.

"No, no, no." I put a hand up. "You've got it all wrong, I'm not—"

I hesitated. Was it a good idea to tell these people that they weren't actually, well, people? I mean, they *were* people — I couldn't doubt that, not if she was capable of making assertions like "this guy I can't perceive properly is probably a ghost" — but they weren't living humans, as they likely believed themselves to be.

Was sharing that the right thing to do?

Fade walked right up to me, then poked me in the arm with a finger.

"I'm — hey, stop it, ow — not a ghost." I sighed, grabbing at her finger as she kept prodding, but she deftly pulled it back.

"Huh. Seem solid enough. Less squishy than I expected a ghost to be. You must be getting stronger, ghost boy. Might be that I need to fetch . . . what's the word? Exor . . . priest?"

"Exorcist," I corrected, "and wait, hold on. You're speaking Velthryn."

"Uh, yeah. Obviously. You clearly don't speak Artinian."

I folded my arms, offended. "I've been studying, okay!"

"Uh-huh. Say something in Artinian."

"Uh . . . watashi wa . . . E . . . ji . . . desu?" I tried.

"You're . . . gonna need to work on your pronunciation, unless you just tried to confess to me that you're a pervert."

"I . . . uh . . . what . . . no!" I took a step back, barely. "I . . . how could you possibly get that out of—"

She let out a sigh. "Look, you said something that *sounds* like a word for . . . never mind. Just, uh, maybe stick with Velthryn until you've studied a bit more, yeah?"

I might have blushed a bit. "I couldn't actually hear any of you until now, so I've just been reading books. It's, uh, kind of hard to sound things out without examples, so . . ."

She snorted. "What were you trying to say?"

"'My name is Eiji.' Which is, uh, not exactly right, but that's the Artinian form of the name I've been given."

Fade raised an eyebrow. "I *guess* Eiji could be a portion of an Artinian name, but without a house, it sounds a little weird. What's your name in your language?"

I considered for a moment, but I saw no reason to lie. "I don't know my full birth name, but the portion I've been given is Lien."

"Huh. Isn't that Tyrenian? And . . . not to be weird, but a girl's name?"

I laughed. "I've heard that they use it for girls there, but where my family comes from, it's just a word for 'sword,' or 'blade,' or . . ."

"Ah, edge. I get it. I haven't heard that word in Velthryn before."

I shook my head. "It isn't Velthryn. It's Liadran."

"Oh. That's on the same continent, though, yeah? That's where—" She shut up abruptly. "You've got me sayin' too much."

I looked at her curiously. "Is that a problem?"

"Well, that 'pends on what sort of ghost you are." She wrinkled her nose.

"Still not a ghost." I sighed.

"Uh-huh. Seems like the kind of thing a ghost would say." She leaned closer — close enough that I could *smell* her, which was weird, because it was new — and brushed a stray lock of hair out of my face. "Oh, you're a *faerie ghost*. Sneaky, sneaky."

I rolled my eyes. "I am neither a faerie nor a ghost." After a moment, I amended the first part. "At least, I'm like ninety-nine percent sure I'm not a faerie. Admittedly, there are some uncertainties about my heritage, but . . ."

"Right. What's with the obvious faerie marks, then, Ghost Edge?"

I frowned. "Definitely not my name, and still not a ghost, but to answer your question . . ." I raised a hand and pointed at the petals. "Marks of favor from the local fae court. I helped them out, I got marked." I folded my arms. "I can't help but notice this is turning into a one-sided interrogation. Don't you have some sort of guest rights? I told you my name."

"Oh, clever. But you're not going to steal my name, Faerie Ghost!" Fade tapped at her forehead.

"Once again, most likely not a faerie, definitely not a ghost."

"Seems like the sort of thing a faerie ghost would say."

I groaned. "If you think I'm a faerie, don't you know that faeries don't lie?"

She squinted at me. "Likely the sort of story that faeries would tell people to get them to lower their guard. Then you're walking along one day, chatting all innocent-like, and suddenly, wham, your name is gone. You check your pants—"

"Why would you check your pants?"

Fade looked at me like I was being completely oblivious. "Where else are you going to write your name? Gotta tell your pants apart from the others in the laundry some—" She looked briefly alarmed, then hopped back into a guard position. "You'll never get my pants, Faerie Ghost Edge!"

I took a moment to stare at her, briefly reviewing the questionable choices that had led me to this point in my life.

I raised a finger, planning to say something, but my mouth closed again.

What did you even *say* to that?

Fortunately, I was saved from needing to respond by the sound — the lovely, clearly audible sound — of a yawn from inside the building, then the door swinging open.

Green stepped out.

"Who are you talking to, R—"

"No names!" Fade yelled in alarm. "Faerie Ghost Edge the Pants Thief will take them!"

. . . This was going to take some getting used to, but as Green gawked, I felt a smile crossing my face.

The title was a little excessive, but if that was the price I had to pay to make friends, it was one I would gladly pay.

⊹ ⊹

A few minutes later, the four residents of the sword school faced me in a half circle. I could see them all clearly now, save for Red's face, which remained a blur. That was a bit of a mystery — apparently, whatever concealed it must have been distinct from my inability to hear their speech. Perhaps the world had forgotten it, as I'd speculated before, but it was also possible that she simply had some kind of concealment technique perpetually active. I didn't know why she'd have something like that on while at her own sword school, but I'd heard of disguising techniques that doubled as anti-scrying measures, like the famous Mask of Kishor — it was possible she had something like that active to prevent her from being found by enemies.

"So," Red concluded, "you're not a ghost, but rather a resident of the local faerie forest that came here for sword training. And we couldn't hear you before because of some sort of barrier between planes?"

"That's about right." It was a true explanation, but not a complete one. They would assume that I was the one who was stuck between planes, rather than them, but I knew that the risks of telling them the truth about their own nature were significant — and, in this case, I opted toward what seemed safer. I could ask Gramps and the Smiling Sword Saint for advice before making any potentially devastating decisions.

Red and Green looked at each other briefly.

"Well, this, unfortunately, changes our dynamic a bit," Red explained. Now that I could hear her, her voice was much like I'd imagined. Warm, caring, effortlessly patient. "Up to this point, we thought you were a harmless ghost of someone who had died up here. Thought maybe you'd move on if we practiced with you a bit, gave you some attention. Was a little weird that you trained as much as you did, and seemed to learn, but . . ." She shook her head. "I've seen plenty of strange things before. If you're alive, like you claim . . . we can't treat you quite the same."

"I don't really need any special treatment. I just want to train with you on occasion, if that's okay. And, I suppose, basic guest rights, of course, so we both know the other isn't hostile."

"That first part is more of the issue," Red explained. "We . . . can't actually take on other students without permission."

"You're not the master of the school, then?" I'd known that was a possibility, based on the number of beds and the layout, but Red was so far above my abilities . . . she easily could have been a master herself.

She smiled softly. "Not quite. The master of this school and I have . . . well, a complicated dynamic. He's out right now, and my friend and I . . ." She nudged Green. ". . . look after the kids he keeps spontaneously adopting."

"More like we have to look after you geriatrics," Fade huffed. "Shall I fetch your walker, or are you feeling spry enough for the cane today?"

In spite of the blurred face, I was pretty sure Red wasn't much more than twenty. I stifled a chuckle, but Gray made no such effort. He laughed, then mimed walking with a bent back.

I frowned as I realized he hadn't said anything. "You're quiet," I noticed. "Something wrong?"

He frowned at me, then said something I thought I half understood in Artinian.

Green must have noted the confusion on my features. "Doesn't speak Velthryn. Don't speak much, either." He gestured to Fade. "Much better than I. And her . . ." He glanced at Red. "Native speaker."

I raised an eyebrow at Red. "You're Mythralian?"

"Yeah, guys, please, spread that around. Not like I'm, you know, being hunted by malevolent demigods or anything." She sighed, touching her forehead in apparent frustration. Turning back to me, she added, "Yes, I'm from Mythralis. And you?"

"Not sure, actually. Parents kind of, uh, abandoned me. Think probably the Selyr region?"

She nodded. "Been there. You've got the hair, but you're paler than most people from around those parts. Got a skin tone more like mine. I'm from way east."

"Whereabouts?"

She grimaced. "I shouldn't say, sorry. Not specifically, anyway. You know Valeria? Somewhere in that area."

I nodded. I'd seen maps of the continent. That put her home in the far northeast somewhere, whereas my presumed origins were more of the far northwest.

She was right about my complexion being pale, more like someone from Valeria myself. I suspected at least one of my parents originally descended from someone in that area, but I simply didn't know. It was possible my pale skin was more of a consequence of the essence types I'd been exposed to, or the differences in climate in this region from where my parents had grown up, or any number of other factors.

But that wasn't what mattered.

"So . . . you can't accept me as a student, because your master isn't here."

"Not my master," Red corrected in a tone that suggested she'd explained that fact many times before.

Fade nudged her. "Oh, come on. You're the first apprentice, you can call him master."

"Definitely not." Red folded her arms. "He's just teaching me a bit for a thing, that's all. He'd enjoy it way too much if I used a word like that."

"Shisho, then? Sensei?" Fade prodded.

"No. Not happening," Red insisted, then turned back to me. "The point stands that the master of the school isn't here, and thus we cannot offer you a position as a student. I'm sorry."

"That's fine. What about just . . . training with a visiting martial artist from another school?"

An exchange of glances.

"Look, I'm deferring to you." Green put his hands up. "You've known him for the longest, *first apprentice*."

"There are security risks . . . but I suppose you've been coming and going for quite a while already." Red frowned. "And you've already practiced with us a bit before." She seemed to come to a conclusion, nodding to herself. "No spirit arts. He'd be put out if we actually taught you one of his signatures. Basic swordplay is fine."

"That's more than fair. There's . . . just one more thing I need. I mean, aside from guest rights."

"Oh?" Red asked, "What's that?"

"Names. What should I call you?"

"No names for the Spectral Pants Thief!" Fade insisted.

"What have you been calling us up to now?" Red asked, with a brief glance toward Fade that indicated *she* was not going to ask what Fade was talking about.

"You're going to laugh," I warned.

Through the blur of her missing face, I thought I could see the hint of a smile. "It's about my hair, isn't it?"

"Maybe?"

"Ugh. Go get to the training field. I'll give you a reason to make me a better name."

CHAPTER XXIX

SHATTERED STAR

Days passed as I began a new training routine at the training school — one where Red gave me *actual instructions,* in spite of her insistence that I was "not a student." It was a novel experience, considering how long I'd been training in silence before, as well as the sword saint's methods of what I could only generously call "training."

"If you're going to use a sword like that, you need to loosen your grip with your off hand. Gripping it that tightly isn't helping you — it's slowing you down. When you're using two hands, your second hand just needs to subtly shift the sword. Don't use a full grip, you only really need a couple fingers with your off hand. Here." Red gestured at the sword, and I handed it to her.

When she gripped it, I watched her hands closely. I'd rarely seen her bother with a giant sword like this one during training — she preferred standard arming swords and longswords — but she clearly knew what she was doing when she held it. Watching her grip, I saw what she meant — her hands were both looser than when I practiced, and her off hand was barely gripping the sword at all. Rather than swinging it with full force as I did, when she moved the sword through the air, it was more like she was just using her hands to guide the sword subtly into the direction it needed to go.

It was, without a doubt, a superior method in terms of using the minimal amount of energy to accomplish a result. When she urged me to pick up her sword and swing at her, she demonstrated blocking by simply nudging my sword out of the way, barely moving her hands in the slightest. It was fast, not just on account of her actual speed vastly outstripping my own — her movements were efficient. She wasted no extra effort with any superfluous movement.

"See? Loose hands or you'll lose your hands. That's how I remember it."

It was a good phrase. Memorable.

. . . But her style still felt strange to me. Unintuitive. "Wouldn't your attacks be weaker that way?"

"Of course, but it's a sword, not a club. And yes, a sword this big might do some crushing damage, if you insist on using one *for some reason.*" Her tone was pointed, not at me, but at Green and his own large-sword habit. "But that's only going to be useful in certain niche circumstances. For the most part, you want to use a weapon like this with finesse. Let its momentum work for you, rather than trying to force it. You should just be using your off hand to shift the weapon like a lever. And if you really want to bludgeon someone, you can always flip to half-sword . . ." She demonstrated shifting the sword around for a technique that involved bashing the opponent with the hilt from a grip with one hand on the blade. ". . . and smash their helmet or whatnot that way, more like you're using a mace. Or, do what I used to do . . ." She handed the sword back to me. ". . . and carry a staff while you're traveling. They're useful for armored targets, skeletons, nonlethal bandit deterrents, and are *quite* comfortable for leaning on."

Her style still didn't feel quite natural to me, but I couldn't exactly refute her argument. And once I began to practice, I adapted quickly, finding myself able to shift my blade more quickly into both parries and strikes with my hands no longer clinging to my blade in a death grip.

I applied that same strategy to other two-handed weapons, not just the gigantic zanbatou-style ones that she disapproved of. It was equally useful when I used a traditional longsword in both hands, a style Red tried to encourage me to practice, rather than falling into the habit of "using swords of useless proportions," as she liked to put it.

Green reassured me that where he came from, gigantic swords were great — they were just favored by monster hunters who fought things the size of buildings. Red was more of a duelist, and her training was designed for human-sized opponents. I learned a great deal from both, but if I'm being honest, Red was the better teacher.

After a few days, I started calling her Red Sensei, which seemed to amuse Fade to no end. She, of course, continued to append new things to my name, until I'd eventually ended up as "Not-Apprentice Faerie Ghost Edge, the Extradimensional Phantom Thief of Named Pants."

Fortunately for conversation, she truncated that name in different ways each time she used it, occasionally swapping in other words like "Spectral" and "Spirit," seemingly trying them out to see how they fit.

After I'd finished completely processing all the essence in my star veins, I returned to the Smiling Sword Saint. There, I resumed our own lessons, and traded her another set of memory crystals for a vial of breach essence.

I absorbed the breach essence with ease. Now that I had a completed Dianis Point of breach essence, the essence was naturally attracted to that Dianis Point. With the Dianis Point completed, I no longer needed to force all of it into primary essence, and I allowed most of it to dissipate into secondary essence. I'd been focusing near-exclusively on primary essence since I'd first started absorbing breach essence, and I needed to let my secondary essence catch up.

The effects of developing secondary breach essence were subtle at first. It didn't impact my physical strength or durability as much as secondary sword essence did, if at all. Instead, I found that when I visited the sword school, I was able to hear the people there more and more clearly without requiring any breach essence augmentations or techniques. After two months, I stopped bothering with using manifestations to chat.

That didn't stop me from working on breach essence manipulation, of course. I primarily focused on training with the basic manifestation that enhanced my senses at the sword school, but I also began to work on attempting to narrow down various breach essence aspects for the eventual development of techniques.

This was trickier than it sounded. Breach essence was obscure, and even the rare books that Gramps had pushed at me had very little information on breach aspects. Through several sources, I eventually put together enough information to figure out some basics, and wrote down some notes for my own reference.

> *Most known breach essence types seem to be form aspects corresponding to the specific planes of the breach. For example, the location of the sword school has breach essence that leans heavily toward the memory aspect. The breach essence I've been absorbing from the Smiling Sword Saint's arena appears to be aspected toward both memory and spirit, which implies that there is, in fact, a multilayer breach. I suspect there may actually be more layers to the breach, which is somewhat alarming, but the Smiling Sword Saint will not allow me to travel past the area of the arena itself. I am, it seems, still "not ready."*
>
> *So, if we have spirit and memory aspects to breach essence, it can be inferred that aspects exist to each other layer of the self — and, perhaps, other planes of existence as well. At a minimum, this means layers likely exist for shade, dreams, destiny, and transcendence. Beyond that, I strongly suspect that I'll be able to figure out travel and constellations aspects, given their significant interactions with the core plane.*
>
> *Given that I have notes on the composition of travel essence in my books, I could likely reverse engineer breach essence of that type, but it's*

probably a bad idea. Unlike most breaches, travel breaches don't generally lead to directly analogous locations on other planes; they're much more erratic because of the spatial compression on the plane of travel. The same factor that enables teleportation also makes breaches of that type less useful, since they can lead great distances without easily calculated destination results. Still worth researching further in the future.

Aside from form aspects related to the planes, I've narrowed down a few other aspect types. Feature aspects include things like "visibility," "corporeality," "audibility," and broader features like "permeability."

Function aspects are largely related to the above, but with some notably more specialized elements, such as "passing through," "breaking through," and "tearing apart," all of which have very obvious combat applications. Once I have sufficient control, it may be worth experimenting with adding some of these aspects to one of my existing attack techniques.

I believe I have narrowed down several useful aspects for my essence acclimation rate improvement plans. Greater precision for technique handling is needed before I begin experimentation. This will likely need to wait until after I work on the seal.

After a period of focusing on breach essence, I went home for a bit, spending time working for Auntie Temper to trade for another set of memory crystals to replenish my dwindling supply. During that time, I also absorbed more sword essence in the region, splitting that evenly between primary and secondary essence.

With that done, I returned to the sword school and resumed my training there. To my delight, the students of the school remembered me in spite of days of absence, and picked up right where we left off.

While Red focused on teaching me basic swordwork and footwork — the only things she felt she was "allowed" to teach me and, I could tell from conversation, what she felt I needed most at my skill level — the Smiling Sword Saint continued to share more insights with me about the creation and usage of sword techniques.

I rotated between training at those two locations, usually doing a day or two of each and then resting and studying to allow my body time to recover.

Three months after achieving my Viewing Point, I was only a season away from my fifteenth threefold name day, and I was ready to test my first two breach essence techniques.

I'd designed the two techniques to be used in conjunction with one another, which made the process trickier. Working with breach essence wasn't quite as intuitive for me as sword essence, but I'd finished reading each of the books Gramps had given me more than once, taken copious notes, and practiced the manifestation of several different aspects individually before utilizing them in techniques. All that was left was to try them out.

For a proper test, I needed a different kind of target—

A person. One that I didn't mind horribly maiming, possibly forever, if things went terribly wrong.

No, I didn't go hit Ana with them. While she did have some unnatural recuperative abilities, I wasn't sure even she could handle recovering from what I was planning on, especially if I made a mistake.

Instead, I stepped into a now-familiar arena.

"Thane." I nodded to the swordsman across from me. "I'm going to try something new today."

"Oh? You thinking you might hit me, for example? That'd be a novel experience." He cracked his knuckles, reaching out in a practiced motion to call a jian — a straight sword of Tyrenian style with a minimalist crossguard — to his hand. He'd started favoring the sword recently, whereas I'd leaned into practicing with a broad variety of different weapons, rather than sticking with my preferred greatsword.

That day, though, I went with what I thought would be optimal for my test. A greatsword for reach, but something lighter than the absurdly thick zanbatou-style ones I'd started with. Specifically, I picked a five-and-a-half-foot-long spadone, a common style in the Terisgard region on the southern side of Mythralis.

I was planning to hit Thane, but I needed more than a modest scrape — something I had managed a few times — if I wanted to test my techniques. Well, the second one, anyway.

"Ready?" I asked, lifting the sword and testing the weight.

"You don't really need to ask, you're so slow that—"

I charged. I wasn't close enough for any real surprise attack — Thane was standing fifty feet away, and it still took me a couple seconds to close that distance at that age — but I did see his expression turn more serious as he shifted into a traditional defensive pose.

I sidestepped as he reached a hand behind himself, anticipating the thrown dagger that followed. As the dagger flew past me, Thane swung his sword with his other hand, casually sending a cutting wave of force in my direction.

Sword Sharpening Shroud. My sword gleamed with essence, and I slashed the shock wave in half, never slowing my charge.

Thane didn't step back — he simply waited as I closed in, moving one hand behind his back.

I swung as soon as I got in reach, a downward cut aimed at his right shoulder. He dodged, as I expected. He dodged the next several swings as well, tsking each time I missed.

"Going for a record on how many times you can miss me in rapid succession? That'd be new, I guess."

I didn't bother bantering back, not at close range. Banter was one of the most fun parts of sparring, but attempting it when I was in Thane's reach was just asking to be cut. I was simply too far behind him in both power and skill, so I saved my breath and focused.

Thane was practicing absence of blade, meaning that he was avoiding allowing his sword to come into contact with mine. This was a counter he'd developed for my style after the first couple times I'd surprised him with my Shattering Sword technique, which was very effective at hitting an opponent during a parry, since the different angles of the blades created by the technique often resulted in a successful cut to the opponent's arm.

With Thane's speed advantage, this wasn't much of a challenge. Not only was he faster than me by default, he'd recently started practicing a body-enhancement technique — something I still didn't have — which boosted his physical strength and speed even further. With his technique active, I was probably less than half his speed. That didn't make hitting him strictly impossible, but it required superior skill — which I didn't have — or some combination of luck, tactics, or mistakes on his part.

I couldn't rely on the first or last of those things, so if I wanted to land a hit, I needed a new approach that could still catch him off guard. It was with that in mind that I took a swing — not at him, but at the pillar next to him.

My sword's essence cut through the pillar easily — I'd missed and hit one accidentally enough times to know that. I'd gotten intimately familiar with the pillars, as well as the rest of the arena, over the last several months. It was easy to note small things, since the arena always reset to the exact same configuration shortly after I left.

So, in a preview of what I was planning, I aimed for a weak point. Not to topple the pillar, of course — I couldn't manage to cut that deep. I simply targeted a particular chunk of stone that already bore several gouges, angling my blade for my slice to completely sever it. Simultaneously, I sent a burst of deflection-aspected essence through my blade.

A massive chunk of the pillar blasted straight in Thane's direction. Thane dodged to the side in a blur — just as I'd anticipated. I briefly released my off hand, reached, and threw.

Throwing something with my off hand wasn't my greatest skill, especially while wielding a greatsword. There was something I could throw with just as much skill as Thane, however, or perhaps even the sword saint herself—

Absolutely nothing.

Thane dodged in anticipation of a dagger, knowing I had one on the back of my belt. When Thane saw nothing, he — with his more defensive style — was more cautious, rather than less, and avoided the entire area that the dagger could have conceivably traveled. And, just as I'd hoped, his rapid change in directions left him very briefly off-balance.

Star Shattering Sight.

My eyes flared as I invoked my first technique. Breach essence flowed through my Viewing Point in a mixture of three aspects. Core. Visibility. And perhaps the most important — layer-aspected essence, a rarely used feature aspect dealing with the overlap between the layers of self.

As the power flooded through me, my vision changed. I saw overlapping silhouettes in the arena — flickering shadows of people, motion, and hovering blades. I ignored those figments and focused on the target in front of me. And ahead, I saw the breaches I'd been looking for.

Breach essence was largely thought of as only being applicable to environments — places like the arena itself where the layers between worlds overlapped. This was an understandable mistake to make, given that those places were where you'd find breach essence in any notable quantity . . . but there were other places that qualified as breaches, at least to a specialist. Places that were so common that an ordinary person wouldn't even think to consider them—

That is to say, the layers within the body itself.

When I closed in on Thane as my vision changed, I saw those layers clearly, and the power contained within. I saw crystalline focal points of power inside Thane's chest, throat, hands, and right leg — the Dianis Points he'd already forged at this point in his life. I saw the thin lines that connected them with the central point, as well as others that were more difficult to perceive — more advanced star veins reaching into the spirit, shade, and memory layers, connecting with other forms of power. If I'd focused on those, perhaps I could have identified more, but I didn't have time.

I only had an instant of vulnerability to exploit. And with it, I aimed for the heart.

Off-balance, Thane still reacted quickly to a sword thrust straight at his chest — but his instincts pushed him into the wrong counter. His sword flicked to the side, as his training dictated, to push mine out of the way with the least force necessary.

Just before our swords met, I unleashed the Shattering Sword.

Thane's speed eclipsed mine enough that he almost managed to correct his error. As my additional blades manifested, he knew to counter two additional cuts, and he used his own aura essence and sword essence to manifest two flickering blades of his own in midair to intercept them.

His error was a simple one—

My technique no longer made two additional blades. I'd been practicing for months, after all, and I hadn't dropped my sword essence training to focus exclusively on breach essence.

It made *four*.

There was a resounding clang as Thane's floating sword intercepted half of my technique. One of my other cuts missed entirely, purely from being at a poor angle, but the other clipped Thane's shoulder, drawing blood. As Thane recoiled, I stepped in to try to close the gap between us, prepared to finish my rush with my new technique—

And predictably, that was when things went wrong.

I felt something sharp slash across the back of my right leg, then stumbled, half falling as I attempted to continue my charge.

Then Thane's fist met my face, and I hurtled backward far enough to slam into the pillar I'd cut earlier. I slammed into it hard, falling forward, barely catching the blur of Thane's rush to close the distance between us as I toppled.

I tried to catch myself on my sword as I fell forward, but that was the wrong move — my blade still had the Sword Sharpening Shroud active, and the point sank into the stone rather than bracing my fall properly. Before I fully hit the ground, Thane was there, smashing his sword into mine and wrenching it from my grip, then hitting me with the flat with a burst of force, sending me right back into the pillar.

As pain shot through me and my vision blurred, I saw Thane's sword sweeping up toward my neck. Purely on instinct, I grabbed the blade with my left hand. This was exactly the wrong thing to do, ordinarily, especially without gauntlets — but without consciously processing it, I wrapped scabbard-aspected essence around my hand as I grabbed it, preventing the blade from tearing my fingers apart.

Thane's sword froze in place as my essence held it tight. For a moment, we stared at each other in equal surprise—

Then, with a razor grin, I yanked Thane close, focused my essence, and slashed my right hand across his throat.

Star Shattering Sword.

Layer-aspected, corporeality-aspected, and breaking-aspected breach essence mixed with sword essence in my hand as I activated my technique—

And just as I hoped, the Dianis Point in Thane's throat *cracked* as my essence tore into it.

Thane staggered backward, releasing his grip from his sword to clutch at his neck. I flipped his own sword over, taking it in my right hand and renewing my Sword Sharpening Shroud technique, prepared to strike again, but paused as Thane fell, coughing, to both knees.

Thane's neck was bleeding, but only barely — there was a physical component to my attack, but most of the essence of the strike had been located on the layer that corresponded to the essence within the body. I'd designed the technique to damage Dianis Points and star veins, hoping it would diminish my opponent's essence wielding ability slightly with each successful use.

It had worked a little too well.

"Sorry, Thane. I didn't mean to—"

The Smiling Sword Saint moved in a blur to stand between us. "This round is over. Thane, it's your loss. Center yourself."

Thane coughed again, trying to speak and failing. The sword saint sighed in response. "Pitiful. He barely scratched you. Fix it."

"Honored Sword Saint, if you can't tell, it's not just a surface wound, I—"

"Hit the Dianis Point directly. Obviously. It's a clever technique. I've seen similar ones before, but not with breach essence. That's good thinking, very dangerous. Could have killed Thane with that. I like it."

I did not like that. "I . . . didn't think it would be . . ."

"Potentially fatal to cut someone's Breathing Point?" The sword saint snorted. "Might not want to practice the sword if you're that squeamish. But if you're that worried . . . Thane should be able to fix the damage simply by compressing more essence into the gouge you made."

"Not . . . enough . . . free . . . essence . . ." Thane managed, then burst into another cough.

"Ugh. Then cannibalize some compressed essence from another Dianis Point if you need to. It's your fault for lowering your guard like that."

I shuddered at the idea. Tearing out compressed essence from a completed Dianis Point and converting it was possible, but it was painful, and it would lower that Dianis Point's capacity until it was restored. That would slow down Thane's progression for a while. I hadn't meant to cause such a serious wound.

"And you." The sword saint turned to me, examining me. Then, after a beat, she reached forward . . . and put a hand on my head to tousle my hair. "Good work, kid. Keep trying to kill this version of me in the future. If you succeed, it'll make you that much more interesting."

⊱ ⊰

In spite of the Smiling Sword Saint's support of my use of a near-fatal technique, I felt more than a little conflicted as I headed back to the sword school.

I'd expected that the sword saint would fix any serious damage to Thane using memory essence. It was likely that she had the capability to do so — reverting something to a previous state was a well-known function of memory essence. That didn't make it easy, of course. Fixing damage to a completed Dianis Point with that method was very advanced, in fact . . . but not as advanced an application as forming an entire duplicate of your past self. If the sword saint could make Thane, I was confident she could heal Thane, too.

But I hadn't properly accounted for the sword saint's personality.

In the end, I'd offered Thane an essence vial to use rather than cannibalizing a completed Dianis Point's essence. The sword saint had smashed the essence vial and told me that Thane would heal on his own or not at all.

Resh. I need to find another place to practice with this. I can't keep doing that to Thane.

. . . But I'm not going to abandon this technique, either.

I considered trying it on the people at the sword school, but given that they were primarily memory constructs, I was concerned it might hurt them even more severely.

That left me with a few options to experiment with. I could use the technique while hunting for food — there was no real downside there. I did practice that for a few days, in fact, but prey animals were weak enough that I didn't really get much benefit out of the practice.

If I wanted to get everything I could out of the technique, I needed powerful, dangerous opponents . . . and ones that I wasn't concerned about hurting.

There were a few monsters that that applied to back home. Undead were an option, but their Dianis Point structures were somewhat different from the living.

The ideal targets were core-born — creatures conjured by dungeon cores, like the one in Ana's shrine. But I'd benefit little if I couldn't remember my experiences, and Ana's shrine could only be visited a few times per year.

And so, after a few more weeks of practice and a bit of preparation, I paid the Smiling Sword Saint a visit.

"I think I'm ready," I told her.

"Well, that's a statement that's ambiguous enough to be useless. Ready for what, exactly?"

"To earn a sword." I cracked my knuckles. "I think it's time I make a visit to the Sepulcher of Sealed Swords."

CHAPTER XXX

SUPPLIES

The Smiling Sword Saint stared at me. "You're serious?"

"Absolutely serious. Not only will it be a place where I can potentially earn a sword to wield, it's also a place where I can cut loose with my techniques without restraint."

"You may be imagining something different from reality, as usual. What exactly do you think you're going to be dealing with at the sepulcher?"

"Well, you said it's like a museum, basically, so I'm imagining swords on walls, or in cases. Presuming you were right, and the curator is dead, I'd have to find ways to defeat any security they still have to prevent them from being taken out. If I can shut that stuff down — or blind it — before I take a sword, I should be able to leave without an issue."

She shrugged. "In theory, sure. If you were Symphony, maybe you could treat this as a heist and manage to get in there and out without triggering the defenses. But, while times have changed, I somehow doubt you're the Lady of Thieves."

I looked at her in surprise. "You know about Aayara? I thought she was from after your time."

"Don't recall that name, but I've heard of Symphony, sure. Little surprised you have. She's still around, I take it?"

". . . Maybe," I said hesitantly. "Someone using that name is. But with you being your apparent age, I don't think Aayara would have been born yet, so—"

"Generational title, then. I know the type."

That was plausible, at least. Talisian was a similar example — several people had used the name throughout history, often multiple at once. Perhaps Aayara Haven was just one incarnation of the Symphony name . . . but one who had managed to hold it for hundreds of years by my own lifetime.

She was clever enough to have stolen virtually everything imaginable. Legendary artifacts. The names of cities. The heart of her rival, the Blackstone

Assassin. The Perfect Stranger, a chain of famous inns and public houses on multiple continents, including Dania. And, if one believed it, the entire concept of the letter *S*. People didn't name children — or other things, like techniques — with that letter lightly, at least not where I came from, because anything with an *S* name was something she'd notice and potentially claim as her own.

Bringing Symphony into the equation did give me some ideas on how best to deal with the problem. I'd read about her several times in books, and I knew a few tricks that they'd claimed she'd used. I had, of course, also read about the tactics used by her rival, the Blackstone Assassin. Both could be useful in a museum heist if I had the right resources. "So, I don't have her skills, but if she wanted to take something from in there, how do you think Symphony would do it?"

"Kid, there's nothing in that place that Symphony would want."

"Even the swords that are sealing ancient calamities from before time? She seems like the type that might put one on her mantel."

The sword saint sighed. "From . . . before time? That doesn't even make sense, kid." She sighed. "You won't find anything like that in there."

I tried not to let my disappointment show in my expression, but my shoulders might have slumped a little. Who *didn't* want a sword containing an ancient evil beyond imagination that they could gradually make friends with against everyone else's expectations, only for the being to ultimately sacrifice itself to save the wielder in their final battle?

"You're daydreaming about impossible things like those absurd stories with your faerie friend, aren't you?" the sword saint asked, sounding vaguely exhausted.

"Maybe a little," I admitted.

"Look, I wasn't just being flippant about there being 'one or two *jashin*' in there. Playing with power like that is dangerous, and not just for you. I don't care how good a thief you are — you'd have to be truly crazy to try to unseal one once it's been put down. I don't know anyone who could handle one in a fight alone, myself included. The effort to seal something like that doesn't take a few heroes — it takes the combined work of a civilization. And sometimes, the civilization *doesn't win*."

I shivered. ". . . Okay, no unsealing evil gods. I'll keep my hands off those, understood. But . . . uh, let's say there's just a . . . mildly cursed sword? Maybe something that, I don't know, gradually turns the wielder into stone or gold or something?"

"That sounds more like a badly designed sword than a cursed one, but sure. Might be that you'd get lucky and find that such a thing has lighter security, but more likely, all the swords are linked to the same defenses."

"Meaning defenses designed to keep people from stealing civilization-destroying god swords."

"Yep."

". . . This is actually a bad idea, isn't it?"

She chuckled. "Finally got it, did you? I'm amazed. Now, does that mean you're ready to give up?"

"Oh, no, obviously not." I waved a hand dismissively. "What it does mean, though, is that I can't handle the security in a direct confrontation — and that, if it's all interlinked, I have a responsibility to make sure I don't break it. I wouldn't want someone else getting a *jashin* sword because I was careless."

"How uncharacteristically thoughtful of you."

I ignored the jab. "That means . . . finding a way to disable the security, or making myself invisible to it. I have some ideas for that, but what would you advise?"

"Heists aren't really my thing, kid. Your guess is as good as mine."

I nodded slowly, plans coming to me. "Okay. Can I run some ideas by you, at least?"

"Not like I have anything better to do."

"Okay. You've been in there, right?"

"Sure, briefly." She shrugged.

"Can you draw me a map?"

She laughed. "No point. It's not very big. You'll see why when you get there."

I frowned. "Okay. What can you tell me about the defenses?"

"Didn't test them. Saw some inert golems, runes on the floors and walls, barriers. Typical stuff. I didn't pay a lot of attention; none of it looked like it would be a threat to me if I didn't, you know, try to steal the swords."

I coughed. "I get your point. Let's move on from the layout questions, then. I think I'm nearly ready to hit Torch. I don't have an exact measure of my essence, but with around six units of breach essence, and somewhere over ten sword essence—"

"You're close," she confirmed. "Don't know about your 'units,' but I can see it. You just need another slight nudge."

I took a deep breath. "Yeah, that's what I figured. And I have a few ideas on how to do it. The simplest would be my original plan. Break open my seal."

"Sure, kid. You could do that. You've got power under there, to be certain. Might be a completed Dianis Point, might not, but it'd push you over the edge. But could you control it?"

I frowned. "No. Not effectively, at least. I've tried tinkering with it, but . . . I can barely pull a thread of essence out of it in the seal's current state, and each time I do that, it feels like a risk without any real reward. I'd need full access to the Dianis Point to get enough essence out of it to learn proper control. I've considered just widening the existing damage a bit, to try to siphon out a bit of essence to practice with, but I don't think I have the precision to do that without breaking the seal entirely."

"Then it's simple — don't do it. Work on improving your general power first. The more you increase your overall essence level, the easier it'll be to manipulate essence in general. And if it's similar to sword essence, your control over sword essence will help, too."

I frowned. I didn't like waiting to open the seal, but intellectually, I'd already come to the same conclusion. "I don't suppose you know anywhere else that has a source of the essence type behind my seal?"

Something flashed across her features. "Not definitively. But . . . I think, if you keep searching, you'll find something. Or it'll find you."

That's more ominous than helpful. Do old people just take lessons in that kind of dialogue?

I shook my head.

I wasn't going to be happy about it, but waiting on breaking the seal seemed like the right answer, at least for now "I won't discount opening the seal in an emergency, but I'll hold off for the moment."

She grunted in response. "I take it you didn't come here with that as your only plan?"

"No. The most obvious alternative, of course, would be to ask you to gather another vial of breach essence. But I stopped at pretty much exactly enough essence to complete my Dianis Point, and it would feel more organic to expand my sword essence instead to double what I started with. I'd end up with around twelve units of sword essence and six of breach."

"Having an even number of essence units doesn't actually change your performance," the sword saint pointed out. "That's almost as silly as your purity fixation was."

I groaned. "I know, but from a practical standpoint, the ratio might influence my Destiny Dream."

"Still hoping to sneak a Blademaster destiny out of it?"

I shrugged. "I know that specific one is unlikely, but it's possible that having twelve units of sword essence is a prerequisite for something, and it's easy enough to reach."

"Except, of course, that you don't have a reliable source of sword essence."

"Right." I considered that problem for the thousandth time. "I don't suppose there's enough sword essence in the air to gather a vial yet?"

"Still no."

"I figured as much." I took a deep breath, my hand subtly trembling. "Which is why I was thinking about asking you to hit me with the Trial of a Thousand Scars again."

"Brave of you. But the answer is no."

I blinked. "Why? I know you felt bad about doing it, and you explained it's not really a training technique, but I've figured out how to—"

"No." She cut me off with a wave of the hand. "You're thinking of the problem the wrong way. I'm not saying you shouldn't ever undergo the trial again for sword essence. I'm saying you shouldn't advance to Torch right now at all."

I blinked at that. ". . . Why?"

"I'm not interested in taking the swords out of there, but I obviously took a look at the place. The sepulcher may not be a crystal shrine — not exactly — but it follows similar philosophical rules. Some of the defenses in there only activate, or activate differently, based on the level of the person who triggers them."

"Meaning that if I walk in right now, I deal with Candle-level defenses as a peak Candle, but if I hit Torch, I'll be dealing with Torch-level defenses as a pitifully weak Torch."

"Precisely."

"But you said *some* of the defenses. That means that some of them are level-independent. Wouldn't it be important to hit Torch-level for those?"

"It would be an advantage, yes. But given the dangers within . . . I think your greatest challenge is going to be one that is highly dependent on what you walk in with."

"I'd love it if you'd tell me more about that," I told her.

"I'm sure you would."

I groaned. "Fine. Be like that. One more unrelated question, then."

"Oh?"

"If I do break the security, what are the chances you could get it working again?"

"Don't push your luck."

⊹ ⊹

After we discussed my possible plans, the Smiling Sword Saint didn't seem much more confident in my success than before, but she agreed to at least escort me to the path to the sepulcher.

I didn't go straight there. No, first, I went home to gather supplies.

It took me three months to prepare. Realistically, I should have waited more like three years, given the risks, but I wasn't anywhere near that patient.

I restocked my warding and gift pouches first, did some work around the house that I'd been lax about, and practiced my newest techniques. I gathered more sword essence from the Rust River, drawing nearly all of it toward secondary essence for the immediate boost in strength and durability that it provided.

I'd need every ounce of combat ability I could get if something went wrong. And, knowing how my plans worked, I was erring on the side of preparing for *when* something went wrong.

After that, I went to Auntie Temper to trade. I spent three weeks working there in exchange for a custom commission. She wouldn't make me something as significant as a sword in exchange for that small bit of labor, but she was a blacksmith, not just a weaponsmith.

I left with a small set of enchanted tools — a key, a glass-cutting knife, and a grappling hook.

Auntie didn't have the traditional essence types used for stealth, and she told me as much, but I'd come up with a few ideas over the trip there and the weeks of work.

Memory essence was extremely flexible, even on its own. Combined with blacksmith essence and forge essence, they could work wonders.

The key was the most complex item of the bunch. It had three functions.

When pressed against a lock, it would use memory essence to recall the shape of the keys that had opened it before, then reshape itself using blacksmithing and forge essence into the proper shape.

When the blue gem on the top was tapped against a surface three times, it would send a pulse of its essence outward to try to force the surface to "remember" a time when it wasn't trapped. If there was a physical trap, forge essence would reforge that into a "disabled" position. If it was a magical trap, memory essence would try to remove it.

When the red gem on the bottom of the key was tapped against a surface three times, it would reset any traps to a functional state. In theory, this would work both on traps the key had disabled and on other traps that it could detect and manipulate.

The methodology for using the key was simple — tap to turn off traps, open lock, tap to reenable traps on the way out of the sepulcher. In theory, this would be a significant help. There were, of course, limitations.

Disabling traps with the key had a limited range — about three feet from where I was tapping, with the effect diminishing more at longer distances. It wasn't like I could just use the key once and disable every trap in the sepulcher — I'd have to either find the traps first and tap, or just tap somewhere that seemed likely, such as on the surface of a door or treasure chest.

Essence was another major limitation. The key would recharge itself gradually, but it would take days to fully recharge after being drained. The amount of essence used would depend on the power of the trap it was disabling. At best, I expected to get about seven uses out of it before it needed to recharge.

Finally, power was relevant. Auntie was an ancient and powerful fae. I didn't know her exact level, but I estimated her to be somewhere in the shade layer, maybe even brushing against the memory layer. That put her in the same range as many heroes and kings . . . but even she wasn't at the same level as people who would seal a *jashin* in a weapon. If that story wasn't just designed to scare me, it was likely that any defenses designed for that kind of power would be beyond the key to disable.

In spite of that being an issue, it was also comforting — I didn't want the key to accidentally break the defenses on a sword like that. My ideal scenario was to get in there, carefully retrieve a more innocuous weapon, reset the traps, and get out.

My other two items were designed to help with that.

Glasscutter was inspired by the comparison to a museum. It was a curved, silver-bladed knife with tiny runes written in Nyn all along the edge. The name was clear enough to imply the basic purpose, but it wasn't just enchanted to cut through glass — it was designed to cut through most materials slowly, while infusing memory essence into the subject to convince it that the damage was preexisting. It would function against both mundane materials and things like magical barriers, at least up to a certain level. In theory, if I worked slowly enough and the defenses didn't trigger the same instant that I touched the knife to whatever I was working on, Glasscutter would be able to gradually carve through something like a museum case without triggering anything that might respond to the damage.

This might sound redundant with the key to disable traps, but it was necessary if there was a trap that I couldn't — or didn't want to — disable. It was also a precaution for things like golems, which might be linked to something like a case in a way that wouldn't trigger like a conventional trap. I wasn't actually sure if Glasscutter would prevent a golem from waking up, but I certainly hoped it would.

The grappling hook was the simplest. When thrown, it would attempt to reshape itself to grip whatever it touched. This just made it easier to use than a traditional grappling hook, which I didn't have a ton of experience with. It also had some durability enchantments.

Auntie didn't work with rope, so I got help with that from a different source—

The scythe spider that had first chased me out of their cave.

I was strong enough to count as a "large morsel" now, which meant I was strong enough to negotiate. I traded a large bag of food for scythe spider silk, which I used to gradually weave the rope to go with my grappling hook between training sessions.

I considered brewing another Threatseer Tonic, but we were out of the necessary supplies, and it wasn't the right season to grow some of them. I wasn't willing to wait on that, but I did take the few days necessary to prepare another healing elixir. During that time, I began to hone Glasscutter's blade with my spiritsharp stone. It was designed to be a tool, not a weapon, but that didn't mean I couldn't use it as both if the situation called for it.

It was nearly my fifteenth name day when I finished my preparations, and with the Smiling Sword Saint at my side, I headed to the path to the sepulcher.

I didn't even make it to the front door before my plans began to fray at the seams.

The mists swirled around me as I stepped out of the arena onto a cobblestone path. The pathway itself led farther upward, toward the summit of a different peak than the one I'd explored during the rainstorm so long before. This place was perpetually obscured by the same fog that I always saw upon approaching the arena, but rather than parting, it remained heavy in the air, limiting my visibility.

It was less of a problem than it once was, at least in terms of being able to properly sense the path. The mist was a representation of the tearing between worlds, and with my breach essence, the obscuring effect was lessened . . . even if the result was more disorienting rather than less.

With each step, I saw flickers of the past around me. To my left, a hooded figure stumbled down the path, his right arm missing from the elbow down. He clutched a bundle to his chest with all of his remaining strength. An elaborate white scabbard hung at his side, lined with metal, but it was empty.

Is . . . he carrying a child?

My instinct, of course, was to rush to offer aid — but this had happened in the past, if it had indeed happened at all. And in a place like this, the flashes that I encountered were fleeting, not lingering echoes like the sword saint with the strong potential for nurturing into consciousness.

Perhaps I could have done something, even still — intervening briefly, offering the healing potion at my side and a memory crystal. Asking why, of all things, the scabbard at his hip looked and felt so familiar.

But I turned away.

To my right, a group of six figures approached the entrance to a castle wrought from pitch-black stone. They were focused, facing their goal with grim determination that came from the knowledge that their coming battle was a necessity, but one that many of them would not walk away from.

As the vision faded, one of them — a woman dressed in pitch-black with a rapier at her hip — turned toward me and offered an exaggerated wink before she vanished along with the others.

Did she just . . .

"Keep walking, kid." The sword saint flicked my right arm. "Nothing but phantoms beyond the road. Nothing to do with them."

I . . . couldn't quite agree, not after what I'd just seen. But she was right that I needed to focus on what I was doing, at least.

More distantly, I saw other fragments ahead.

A woman kneeling on a branch of a tree, wearing armor of leaves, drawing back a bow to fire at a distant target. She, too, felt familiar to me — something in the metallic glint of her eyes, the strangely sharp smile that mirrored one I'd made a thousand times — but I walked on.

A blacksmith's forge near a massive pit that was unnaturally smooth, as if the ground had simply been removed from existence. Within that pit, a tremendous pile of dull and shattered blades. Beneath them, distantly, I sensed one that wasn't so broken as the others — though the smith, I sensed, suspected, was too deeply absorbed in his continuing work to know or care.

I felt the temptation to go to that abandoned sword, knowing it was a diamond forged from coal, but I knew it was a fool's endeavor.

They're just memories, like the ones at the sword school. Keep walking.

More and more images flickered around me. I ignored them as best I could, until finally, one made me freeze.

A woman with curly red hair strode through a forest filled with razor-edged leaves and trees that reached beyond the clouds. She wore dark brown pants that had been recently cut, with fresh bandages wrapped around them. Her white shirt was unmarked, but the thicker leather vest over it had several tiny gouges that teased the stories of narrowly avoided cuts. She walked with purpose and confidence. Her face was striking, with dark eyes that seemed intensely focused on something in the distance. She wore an arming sword on her left hip that, even when sheathed, glowed softly with morning's first light.

She was familiar, yes, but not in the way of the others. This one was not a complete mystery, though I'd still had little luck at understanding the exact details of her nature and identity.

Red . . . ?

She was older, perhaps, but not by a large margin. A few years, maybe, though age could be deceptive with many species, and I couldn't presume that she had been human.

And, unlike any previous time I'd seen Red . . . I could see this woman's face.

Is this memory linked to the others? If I stepped closer, or called to her, would this version of Red remember me? Would she finally tell me who she was?

I took a step toward her without thinking.

Never leave the path. The old fae adage was as true here as it was in their lands — stepping off, I knew, meant stepping deeper through the liminal space. One step too far and I could find myself in another plane of existence. And, in spite of my growing strength, I was still barely beyond childhood. I did not have the tools to survive in the planes of spirit, shade, or memory.

But if I shouted to her from a distance, maybe . . .

"No." The sword saint's hand covered my mouth. She had just grabbed me when a rapier soundlessly pierced through a duelist's heart.

I couldn't even see an attacker — just a sword, jabbed through her from behind. From the incredulous look that crossed Red's face, she hadn't seen the attack coming, either.

Red's hands came up to the blade that had pierced through her, and with silence equal to her attacker's, she gripped the blade that had killed her and snapped it.

Then, wobbling as she stood, she turned around and jabbed the broken fragment at the empty air.

There was a warbling as someone appeared — a white-haired man dressed in traditional dueling garb, just as Red had been. He deflected the blade with an empty hand, giving her a look of surprise. "That should have killed you outright. You certainly shouldn't be standing."

"Get used to disappointment." Red's dark eyes narrowed as she processed her opponent, raising one hand to press against the bleeding hole in her shirt. Crimson stained her hand and her jaw was tight, but she still managed to raise the broken sword and make a universal "come at me" gesture with it.

"Alas, I think you're out of surprises. But I'd love to be wrong." The dance that followed was too fast for me to properly follow, broken steel tracing through the air, interrupting the assassin's charge a dozen times before his hand finally landed on the hilt. Then, with his other hand, he reached down and, almost gingerly, pried her fingers off the grip, one at a time. He flipped the broken blade around, pointing it toward her already bleeding torso.

"You really could have been something special," he said in a pitying tone. "He was right about your potential. For what it's worth, I never held anything against either of you, but blood begets—"

Red's hand moved in a blur to the light-forged sword at her side.

. . . And strained futilely against an invisible force.

"Ah, no." The assassin twirled a finger in the air. "Locked that in place before I stabbed you. I didn't *expect* you to survive being stabbed, but I knew not to take any chances."

Red whipped a hidden knife off the back of her belt with her other hand, but the assassin swept it out of the air with his sword and stepped in closer. "It's been an honest pleasure."

Then, with a cheerful smile, the white-haired man sliced his broken blade across Red's neck.

As Red fell to her knees, the white-haired man nodded once, then tossed his broken blade into the dirt.

He turned to walk away—

And Red, choking and coughing as she clutched at her throat, began to stand back up on wobbling legs.

"You're joking."

The assassin turned back around just in time for Red to lunge. Her blood-stained fist collided with his face, sending him staggering back a step.

He raised a hand incredulously, then vanished and reappeared behind her to viciously return the blow, a pitch-black aura around his right hand.

I heard a snap as his hand connected with Red's spine. When she fell that time, she did not rise again.

The white-haired man stared down at the unmoving woman in front of him, raising a hand to wipe at the bloody mark she'd left on his cheek. "Well," he mumbled, "I suppose you had one more surprise left in you after all."

And then, seeming to internally debate something, he took something out of a pouch at his side.

A single stone, so dark that it seemed to draw in the light around it. "I don't usually do this unless I've marked someone ahead of time, but you've earned it."

I tried to bite the sword saint's hand. I'm not proud of it, but I knew what he was doing, I knew who he was, and even if this was an echo . . .

I wouldn't let him take her spirit and put it in that stone.

"No." The sword saint's voice was firm.

I stilled, wobbling on my own feet as pressure knocked the air out of me.

"She's dead, kid. You can't stop what already happened. No one—"

A knife arced out of the trees.

The white-haired man spun in an instant, another sword appearing in his hand out of nowhere, as he deflected the hurled blade.

There was a loud sound as sword and knife met. The knife exploded, shrapnel pelting the swordsman. He wasn't hurt — the shards of metal that hit his skin bounced off without cutting him — but as he opened his off hand, the black stone within it crumbled into dust.

The white-haired man stood slowly, a bemused look on his face. "You're not supposed to be here."

Fade stepped out of the trees, though that name no longer applied. Her hair was pitch black, now, matching her eyes — eyes that no longer showed even the slightest hint of sclera. Strange tattoos covered much of the exposed skin on her face and arms.

Her expression was one of grief barely restrained by absolute fury.

"Blackstone. You *veking* coward," she spat, "you . . . you couldn't have beaten her fairly, so you . . ."

"Oh, don't be a fool, dear. Even at her best, she was no match for me. I'm simply not the type to take unnecessary risks." He waved his sword in the air, as if stretching his arm. The simple and effortless motion tore the space around where his sword passed, leaving wide gouges in the air. "And you? You're not half the apprentice she was, even when unburdened. And carrying what you are . . ."

"No, I was never her equal. I was always more like you," Fade whispered. "You'll see that soon enough."

A brace of knives appeared between her fingers.

The white-haired man's expression turned serious . . . and then, after a beat, he turned directly toward me. "Do you mind? This is a private show."

He snapped his fingers. The entire vision faded.

I'd stopped my pointless struggling, but it was a few moments before the Smiling Sword Saint released me from her grip.

"Someone you know?" she asked, finally.

"The other sword school. The woman who died—"

"Her stance. I only saw it for a second, when she went to draw her sword, but . . ." The sword saint lowered her voice to a whisper.

"It was perfect. The best I'd ever seen."

I stared at the emptiness for a moment, but the sword saint gently tousled my hair. "Come on. The past is the past. Learn from it, but keep moving."

I took her lesson seriously. I kept walking, studying the remaining images, but they no longer gave me pause.

But if there was one thing I'd learned, people rarely listen to their own advice. And for the briefest moment, the sword saint herself stopped at the sight of the last fragment of the past.

It was her. Her in her original body, kneeling bloody and broken. Her white stone sword that had given her a title and surname was shattered, only the top half held in her hands. She looked up at her opponent, if he could be called that. The creature that loomed above her was distorted, a tenebrous phantasm that stood like a man, but one that had no clear boundary from the encroaching blackness that stood behind him. I could sense his weapon only because of the flashing golden runes on the massive blade he held above his head.

I couldn't look at the sword too closely — I could feel the weight of it pressing down on my chest and something horrible within. As each rune glimmered, I could *hear* them, hear their eagerness for another to join their number.

My teacher stared at the sight. "Is that . . ."

"Nothing but phantoms, teacher." I gently took her arm. "Nothing to do with them. The past is the past."

With that, I dragged her forward. Powerful as she was, she let me guide her.

I was glad that she hadn't taken the same path I had. She hadn't absorbed breach essence. Her sensory abilities in general were much stronger than my own, but I'd experienced that path differently than she had, I was certain of it.

If she'd sensed what I did, she wouldn't have turned away. She couldn't refuse a challenge.

And without breach essence, the Smiling Sword Saint hadn't heard the laughter that echoed as she brushed past her killer's shadow.

CHAPTER XXXI

SEPULCHER

The mist parted at last, leaving images and memories behind. We were some distance away before the sword saint turned her gaze backward, perhaps seeking another glimpse at her final enemy.

I worried that she would turn back the moment I entered the sepulcher, seeking to confront him — not to save her former self but to test her current abilities against the one who had killed her.

I would have squeezed her hand to offer her comfort if such a thing was needed, but she was not hurt as I had been upon seeing Red's untimely end. No, the vision had not sparked doubt or melancholy within her, but interest.

"It's not really him. Even if you were to intervene—"

"I know," she replied. "But he's still alive out there, isn't he?"

"Most likely." I regretted saying anything about him before, but I wouldn't be dishonest. Not with her. "If he is who I believe him to be, he still reigns in another land. But you . . ."

"I don't even know if I can leave. I'm not quite real. And even if I could walk out of here, I'm not his match. I know." Her hands opened and closed in the air, and for a moment, the air itself tightened along with her grip. I stumbled a step, but she caught me. "Sorry, kid. Trying to be better about that."

"Were . . . you like that in life? Causing things like that with simple gestures?"

"Not exactly. Not at the point I remember, at least. My techniques were driven by such motions, but they were deliberate, easy to control. Now . . . I'm both less than my former self and more. My essence composition is different. I'm out of balance."

I nodded in understanding. "Maybe my grandfather could help? He seemed to know who you are, and he's powerful. Maybe he . . ."

"Don't want help from powerful strangers, kid. They've always got their own agenda. You'd be wise to remember that lesson."

I frowned. "If I followed that advice, I'd have never been taught by you."

"Yeah. That would have been wise."

⊹⊹ ⊹⊹

We walked on. The path beyond was an ordinary one, once well-used, but now eroded by time. I saw buildings by the sides of the path, or the fractured remains of them. A town, perhaps, or just a monastery or sect. I had to keep myself from wandering off to explore them — perhaps they'd hold treasures and secrets of their own, but I had a quest, and my teacher would not appreciate further distractions.

Eventually, the cobblestone road gave way to stone steps carved into the mountainside. Hundreds of them, chipped and worn, but still functional. I wondered how many others had passed this way, and how long it had been since the last visitor had come to the sepulcher.

When we reached the top of the mountain, I got an answer to the latter half of that question.

The sepulcher was there, though to my eyes, it looked more like a legendary palace. Six white stone pillars lined the entrance, each holding a single gleaming crystal. I suppressed the urge to climb the pillars and investigate the crystals, which were clearly enchanted.

I had a higher priority, which was immediately evident when I saw the entrance to the regal structure — two massive doors wrought of silvery metal, each etched with hundreds of runes.

The runes were hard to see. Part of that was because of the distance.

A larger part was because the doors had been ripped off their hinges and were lying nearly flat on the ground.

"Huh." The Smiling Sword Saint looked at the open doors with rare surprise in her expression. "Now, that's strange."

"Then . . . I suppose you didn't leave the doors open during your last visit?"

"Nope. And I didn't feel anyone else pass through my territory, either."

"Meaning someone with stealth skills like . . . like the assassin who . . ."

"Killed your friend? Nah." She shook her head. "Nothing like that. There's another path up the mountain that way." She pointed behind the structure. "It's a dirt road, barely more than an animal path. Didn't think anyone still used it."

"Do you think whoever did that is still inside?" I asked her.

"Oh, I'd say so, given that he's already headed in our direction."

I bristled in alarm, hand going to the scabbard at my side. It had a better blade this time — a copy of an arming sword taken from the sword saint's arena — but I knew that if I drew it, the weapon would rapidly fade from existence outside her area of influence.

"Are you going to handle this, or . . ."

"Nah. Have fun!"

When I turned toward where the sword saint had been to give her a groan of annoyance, she was already gone. I was alone — alone with whatever was inside the sepulcher, at least.

He emerged from the sepulcher a moment later. He was, without a doubt, one of the tallest people I'd ever seen. Not Auntie's height, sure, but *tall.* I'd have guessed him at six and a half feet, perhaps with a few extra inches if one accounted for the length of his spiked purple hair.

He wore mismatched armor, mostly leather, but with a steel pauldron on his right shoulder, scratched copper bracers and greaves, and a single demi-gauntlet of some kind of white metal on his left hand.

Beyond that, most of what he wore looked like someone had dumped out the entire contents of an armory.

A colossal axe was strapped across his back, with a dubious harness that seemed to be made from several interlocking belts keeping the blade from moving too far from side to side. On his hips he wore no less than six weapons — a longsword, two long knives, a mace, a warhammer, and a hand axe. In his right hand he carried a colossal polearm with a curved blade.

A naginata, maybe? No, more like a guando, I realized. He strode forward with confident steps. It was only when he came closer, the gems in the pillars around him gleaming silently, that I realized he looked no older than I was in spite of his prodigious height and absurd array of weaponry.

"So, you've come at last," the purple-haired man declared, jamming the plain bottom of his guando downward with enough force to crack the stone. "The one who would be my rival."

What?

I stared at him.

He stared back at me, eyes narrowing. Waiting.

Then, finally, the tension in his shoulders vanished, and he broke into laughter. "Come, come! You look exhausted. If we are to battle in the future, you must rest and eat properly first, yes? Sit, I will cook us a meal worthy of our battle that is yet to come!"

I blinked in stunned silence.

He ignored this, leaving his guando jammed into the ground, then unslinging the massive axe from his back . . . or trying to, anyway. When he tried to unhook it from the harness, one of the axe's blades got caught, and he stumbled and teetered backward, nearly falling over.

He continued shuffling with it for several seconds, only managing to get caught up in the half-dozen belts that were designed to keep it in place.

". . . Little help?"

I found myself moving in spite of my general caution, then helping him with his struggle, which reminded me of a deadly beast caught in a net. Eventually, I simply unclasped half the belts and he let the axe tumble to the ground.

"Phew. Thank you. That was probably the most dangerous situation I've faced all day, and let me tell you . . . that's saying something. Oh, and by the by, don't touch the blades of that axe. It's, uh, not good for your health."

I gazed down at the axe, noting that both blades were glowing an eerie green. "Cursed?" I asked.

"Or something." He plopped down unceremoniously on the ground next to the axe, very nearly cutting himself on it in the process, then grunted because he had landed on the mace. ". . . Oh, that's going to bruise. Again."

He sighed.

Still uncertain what sort of strange creature I was dealing with, I cautiously sat down in front of him. "I appreciate your offer of hospitality, but it is not needed. I simply seek the sepulcher."

"Nonsense! If we are fated to fight, we must first bond, yes? And what better way to bond than over food?" He shuffled, unfastening his sword belt and casting the whole thing aside, weapons and all, as if he was completely unconcerned about being next to someone he had already talked about engaging in battle with.

Is he truly that confident that he could defeat me, or . . . is it just a display of trust?

Uncertain, I unfastened my own sword belt — sitting with it on was admittedly difficult — and set it to my side. Still within reach.

"You have a good point about rivals, but I have to confess that I have no idea what you're talking about."

"Oh?" He went quiet then. "You didn't see me on the way up?"

He sounded almost hurt.

I blinked, processing.

If he had seen a vision of me, much like the fragments I'd seen before, that explained his behavior to some degree, but . . .

Those visions were of the past, not the future. Weren't they?

Then something clicked.

"You are a quiet one, friend."

"Thinking, sorry." I put my hands up. "The route I took up the mountain was over there." I gestured to my path. "I saw visions, but they're from breaches to the planes of memory, shade, and spirit. They don't show the future. But if you came up that way . . ." I gestured to behind the sepulcher.

"Ah! I see, I see!" He grinned brightly. "But, in spite of me seeing, please explain it, anyway!"

"Your path may be one that showed the future, while mine showed the past."

"Ahhh! Yes, of course. I was clearly thinking the same."

He definitely wasn't. Or, at least, he wanted to give me the *impression* that he wasn't.

Was he truly just . . . gregarious, and a bit clumsy? Or was that a form of obfuscation? I'd seen a few fae playing similar roles — often the brightest minds hid behind a dense guise.

"Perhaps while we eat, you can tell me what you've seen."

"Eating! Yes, of course, I'd nearly forgotten!"

He rose to his feet, then waved his hand. I pulled back a bit, wary, but there was no immediate threat — instead, a ring on his right hand flashed, and something massive appeared in midair and clunked to the ground.

Is . . . that some sort of . . . grill?

"How do you like your meat, friend?"

My stomach grumbled.

Rival or not, obfuscating demeanor or not, I liked him immediately.

* * *

An hour or two later, we finished eating. After recovering from the massive and frankly delicious meal he'd prepared, we reclined against opposite pillars.

I'd contributed, but only mildly, in the form of some spices from my gift pouches. He assured me that he considered that an even trade, given the "rarity" of my spices, but I took that as him simply being polite. In retrospect, given that he was likely from a faraway land, it might have been truer than I realized at the time.

During the meal, we'd talked a bit, mostly about our visions on the way up. He told me many things, but most importantly, he told me of our battle to come — one in which he admitted he had not seen a victor.

"But," he assured me, "that is not to be held here, nor today. We will be older then, and it will be held in a grand arena, before the adulations of a kingly crowd!"

". . . I think I would like that," I admitted aloud, more to myself than to him. "Did you recognize this arena?"

"I fear I did not, friend. But that makes it all the more exciting, does it not?"

I nodded along with him. "Then, if we are to fight later, does that mean that you will allow me to pass freely into the sepulcher now?"

"Indeed, if that is what you wish. My business there is already concluded."

"The axe? Is it from in there?" I asked, gesturing toward the weapon where it still rested.

"Nay, that is an old family thing. My visit to the shrine was one of study — a pilgrimage of sorts. I took nothing and left nothing."

I raised an eyebrow. "Not many pilgrimages I'm aware of involve tearing off the doors."

He blinked and, comically slowly, turned toward the entrance of the shrine.

"Egads! Who did that? When? *How*?"

I genuinely could not tell if he had just noticed the state of the doors for the first time.

"Not you, then?"

"Gods around us, no. I would never . . ." He shuddered. "This is a sacred place! One day, I shall find whoever was responsible and right this injustice!"

I was *deeply* skeptical about that last part. "Right. If that wasn't you, then did you see anyone else inside?"

"Not at all! Well, unless you're the type of fellow that sees golems as *people*." He chuckled.

I stared straight back at him. "What sort of golems?"

He frowned, presumably at my unexpected response. "Nothing to worry you, friend. Just standard security golems, for those unscrupulous folk who might seek to steal from this sacred place. You wouldn't do anything like that, would you?"

"Steal? No." I shook my head, speaking in absolute honesty. "But there may be something in there that belongs with me."

His eyes narrowed in sudden intensity. For a moment, his irises shifted, showing some kind of symbol I couldn't make out — and then it faded.

"Is that so?" he asked. "Well, so long as you stay away from the things that do not belong to you, we will not have a problem."

We stared at each other for a tense moment, and then I offered him a sharp smile. "I have no intention of freeing any ancient evils, if that's what you're worried about."

A moment of silence, and then he slapped his knee. "Ancient evils. Goodness! What have people been telling you? There's obviously nothing like that in there." He gave a nervous chuckle that sounded very fake.

"Well, if there isn't, I suppose I needn't be worried about making any mistakes."

"That—" He drew in a breath, then sighed. "Don't go poking where you don't belong, friend. If you really think something in there belongs to you — and I believe that you do believe that — stick to your target. Take nothing else. *Touch* nothing else. Understood?"

I nodded seriously, as appeared to be appropriate for the tone of the conversation. "I will do my best."

"That's all one can ever ask for, isn't it?" he mused aloud. There was probably a story there, but to my regret, I did not have the time to ask about it.

"Well, then. I suppose if you've completed your journey already, and we are not to battle today, then . . . I believe it is time for us to part ways for now. The night comes soon, and I must begin my own entry into the shrine."

"Ah, of course. If you came up the other path, you must . . . have a long journey home."

His eyes were more focused on me, then. Questioning. Knowing.

Then he gave me one of his very bright smiles and effortlessly pushed himself to his feet, so quickly that he could have easily grabbed a weapon before I stood.

But he did no such thing. Instead, he moved in a blur and offered me a hand.

I accepted it and allowed the huge man to haul me to my feet.

"Best of luck in there," he said, tilting his head down. "Don't get killed before we meet again."

"The same to you," I told him. "And before you go . . . who are you, exactly?"

He laughed deeply, folding his arms. "I go by many names, friend. But for you . . . You can call me Lance." A dramatic pause. *"Lance Rival."*

With that, he swept up his weapons in a blur — at least until he got to the guando, which was stuck in the ground and took a few seconds of awkward straining to remove — then dramatically ran and *leapt* off the side of the cliff.

I heard his laughter trailing as he vanished into the clouds below.

. . . Well, that's definitely a thing that just happened.

I picked up my sword belt and put it back on, feeling refreshed. The food was good . . . and moreover, it had some sort of essence in it that helped me feel stronger than before. Normally, I might have gotten rid of the extra essence, since it was an unfamiliar type, but something about it felt like it suited me just fine.

I'll see if Gramps can analyze it later. For now, though . . .

I walked to the torn-open doors of the shrine.

No more distractions. I have a sword to earn.

I cautiously stepped over the fallen doors, not wanting to trigger some sort of magical trap simply by brushing against the runes.

In spite of the damage to the doors, the interior of the shrine appeared to be pristine, at least at the entrance. The floors were the same pristine white as the pillars outside, but divided into large blocks. It gave the whole room an appearance that reminded me of a Crowns board, but with all white squares.

The entrance chamber was hundreds of feet across, with a slanted rooftop that, at its peak, was at least fifty feet above me. The architectural style reminded me of what I'd heard described about ancient temples, though the chill in the air felt nothing like the warmth I might have expected in a divine domain.

Even the torches that glowed with a soft blue hue along the walls didn't seem to emit any heat.

Fascinating. These are genuine magical items, just used to keep the place lit. Unless they're powered by something else in here, which is possible, but less likely. Hm. No visible runes on the outside, but maybe . . .

I immediately considered cutting one of the torches off and taking it to examine further, but I remembered Lance's warning, and I wasn't going to violate his trust instantly. He clearly had some kind of important agenda in this place, more than he'd been willing to say.

From context, I guessed he was related to either the long-dead curator or perhaps someone who had deposited one of the swords sealed within the place. Possibly both.

If there's actually a sword sealing some kind of ancient evil god in there, that would warrant someone checking in from time to time, if not someone permanently stationed here.

I wondered at that last part. If there was something that important, I'd expect contingents of knights to keep people out. Perhaps secrecy was the greatest concern? Or maybe keeping people close by continuously was another type of risk? Mind control from one of the swords, perhaps?

I didn't have enough information. So, naturally, I began to explore.

The center of the chamber held some kind of massive runic symbol, which I did my best to stay away from. It wasn't in any language I could read, but it was clearly glowing, and mysterious glowing things of dubious origin were pretty close to the top of my "dangerous" list.

They also had a tendency to attract my curiosity, but I'd get back to it.

The golems were less obvious than I expected. They were along the walls of the room, looking less like classic gigantic stone statues and more like empty suits of armor. I'd have considered them decorative suits if not for the obvious warnings I'd been given about the place, and, if I'm being fair, the glowing runes on each of them were probably a hint.

"Hello!" I approached the first security golem. "Any chance you're willing to tell me a bit about this place? History, contents, things to avoid?"

There was no answer. I tried again with each of the golems — there were a dozen of them — and tested a variety of different languages. There were no responses. Either they couldn't talk, or they weren't feeling chatty. That was a shame.

The purpose of the golems was clear enough — two of them flanked each of six doors along the sides of the room. The doors were similar to the titanic ones at the entrance, but these were fully intact, their runes glowing with inner light. Each door had an indentation at the center that was roughly diamond shaped.

Empty slots. Looks like they're designed for crystals like the ones embedded in the pillars outside, but these are missing. Either they don't need to be inserted all the time, or . . . maybe another looter got here before I did.

Er, not another looter. A single looter. I am not a looter. I'm . . . an adventurer. Completely different.

Adventuring further, I checked the floors.

At the edges of each door was a near-solid line of tiny runes that led toward the massive central rune formation I'd noticed earlier, then connected to it.

This whole place is interconnected. There must be a central power source somewhere, or something along those lines . . . probably literally along lines, I suppose, in this case. A larger crystal that interconnects with the others, maybe? Something like a destiny shrine crystal, perhaps one that was repurposed deliberately, or decided to cooperate? If so, it'd likely be associated with an essence type like stability, or maybe a specialized application like stasis. Alternatively, something like protection, or an aspect of that, like safety.

Briefly, I allowed my inner scholar to play a role in my visit, and I took a moment to copy down some of the glowing glyphs. Maybe I'd ask Gramps about them later, or look them up, but I hadn't brought my books with me. They would have weighed me down too much.

I didn't bother writing down the runes on the floor — there were simply too many of them. Thousands and thousands. It would have taken me all day.

Next, I inspected the doors and the areas around them further. Each door was made of the same silvery metal, and along each door was a series of metal plates attached to the wall, each of which was inscribed with helpful information. Well, I *presumed* they were all helpful. I couldn't actually read most of them.

The plate closest to each door was always in one specific language, one I couldn't read a single letter of. I did recognize it, though.

That's Scrawl, an archaic language that was used by magical scholars hundreds of years ago. I think Gramps could probably read this, but I've never studied it. It was obscure even in the time this place was built — it's probably meant for the people who worked here. It seems like these have more detail than the other plates.

Next were plates in Caed — the most common human language on the continent. I could only understand a fraction of those, but that was more than what I could get out of the Scrawl ones. Sadly, my comprehension was limited to basic concepts like "sword" and "imminent death."

Only three doors had plates that I could read completely, and even those weren't all in the same tongue. There were also a few more in obscure languages that I couldn't read, like Er'vhan.

Strange. Maybe the swords were placed at different times, and different curators did whatever translations they could at the time?

Two were in Nyn, which was the local fae tongue that I'd spoken throughout my entire life. That made sense, if I understood the timeline when the facility was primarily used — it had been used by local humans in the area at that point, too. The most unusual one was in Velthryn, which got me curious, but I decided to look at that last.

I took a look at the closest one in Nyn.

Here rests a storied sword of old,
Borne once by those of manner bold,
Wrought with magic fierce and true,
Enchanted thrice to cut and hew.
With its every battle fought,
As sword was raised and terror wrought,
Each deadly stroke of golden blade,
The sword did grow with orphans made.
Until one day, at witches' scorn,
The losses made the blade would morn,
And strength once granted now would weigh,
More than any heart could hold at bay.

A second, perhaps more helpful inscription, was written just above the longer one. It read "Unbearable Burden."

I took a few moments to consider what I'd learned. This was, at first glance, a sword of the cursed variety. Once, it had been enchanted to grow with power every time it killed, or possibly just injured, someone in battle. At some point, it had been cursed, supposedly by a witch . . . and now, it carried the weight of the lives it had taken. This seemed like it could mean emotional or spiritual weight, rather than merely physical weight, since a heart was also mentioned.

Or weight on essence, I realized belatedly. *The heart could refer to the Heart Point. It's possible the weapon isn't cursed at all, but rather, it puts immense pressure on the wielder based on all the essence it contains. That's especially possible if it's designed to connect to the Heart Point.*

To be certain, I was tempted to go for it immediately. Any weapon that grew in power over time had incredible potential, and given that I knew more than a few witches . . . maybe the curse was something I could get removed, if it existed at all.

But while I've never been accused of excessive patience, I also knew it would be wiser to keep looking — at least at the other inscriptions I could read, at a minimum.

I went to the next one with Nyn writing first. This tablet was remarkably more straightforward, lacking the usual poetry of the Nyn tongue, and it was also the plate that had the largest number of duplicate languages that I'd seen. Someone wanted to make sure that whoever came by could read the warning.

Sealed Sword of Artinian origin, identified in documentation by previous curator as "Wicked Accord." Believed to be a self-binding weapon if touched, offering vast powers related to regeneration, bodily reconstruction, and accelerated power progression. Exerts immediate and potent mental influence. As the wielder gains power, the sword's influence expands further, until the wielder is subsumed. Previous records indicate that extended testing of questionable ethical value shows that standard anti-possession and anti-compulsion measures can inhibit the loss of control, but all established methods have ultimately failed to prevent takeover. Previous security failure resulted in loss of curator [—] and three allied sect leaders, within the memory layer.

Noted to move periodically of its own accord. Suppressed through the use of thousand-layer chains and sixfold binding technique, but constant maintenance required, as seals degrade even with Sky-level suppression in place. Frequently targeted by cultists. Believed to be one of the sixty-four seals of the worldmaker Aetor.

I stared at the inscription. There was a section scratched out that I couldn't quite read right after the word "curator." Their name, maybe? That was odd, but it wasn't the most concerning part, of course.

After all the talk of ancient evils sealed in swords, I hadn't actually expected to find one. Certainly nowhere near the *first room* of the sepulcher.

I knew the name Aetor from Gramps's stories. Once, he was one of the creators of the world, as the name "worldmaker" implied.

Specifically, he was known as the Maker of Monsters.

As one might guess, Aetor and his creations didn't get along with all of the other creators — and their creations. There was a massive war that nearly shattered the heart of the world, or so it was said, and in the aftermath, Aetor and the other worldmakers were all sealed away — indefinitely.

There were several different variations on the legend, some claiming that the other worldmakers had sealed themselves with Aetor to keep the Maker of Monsters from escaping. Others claimed the worldmakers had all been sealed together because they were equally at fault for the war. In any case, Aetor was, without a doubt, something that would qualify as the *jashin* that the Smiling Sword Saint had been talking about.

There was a fragment of an evil god sealed in the next room, and I admitted I had an itch to figure out just how strong he was. And the benefits? Regeneration? Manipulation of my own body? Increased essence growth speed? Those were hard to beat.

. . . But I wasn't completely daft. I walked the other way immediately after making sure the door looked like it was properly sealed closed.

Not playing with that any time soon. Nope. Not a chance.

Next, I inspected the one written in Velthryn.

> *Sword of unknown origin, once wielded by a member of the Hero's Party during the battle against the Ashen Lord. The term "sword" is used loosely, as it was described as a shapeshifting weapon, settling in the shape of a sword because, in the words of the anonymous individual who contributed it, "we expected it to be one."*
>
> *Capabilities variable; appears to shift due to external variables, as with the physical appearance of the weapon. Demonstrates powerful beneficial abilities, including what appears to be some sort of probability alteration, but disables or inverts these benefits at critical moments. Confounds standard detection abilities. Sealed due to suspicion of high-level chaos and lies essence. Tentative identifier: the Traitor's Whisper.*

I nearly gasped.

A weapon wielded by a member of the Hero's Party? That was impossibly rare, if it was true. Roughly as rare as, say, something used to seal a fragment of an ancient evil god.

Truly, I was spoiled by the number of truly terrifying options in front of me.

Thinking objectively — or as objectively as one might be able to while in a facility that contained at least one weapon known to influence the minds of people nearby — the Traitor's Whisper had a few appealing characteristics. It didn't sound like it was actually cursed, nor was it clear if it was actually malevolent . . . it was just unreliable.

That was, of course, dangerous . . . but not in the same way that trying to carry around a sealed god fragment would be. And as for the specific properties of the weapon? Well, there was potential there, too. Shapeshifting weapons weren't uncommon, exactly, but they were always useful. I could potentially alter the weapon to take whatever shape I needed for any given circumstance, if I could figure out the mechanism behind the shapeshifting.

The description didn't directly state that the weapon was intelligent, although there was some implication of that in the idea of it "betraying" the wielder in times of great need. Without examples, it was tough to know if that meant the sword had any agency, or if it simply had some sort of cost for overuse that might have backfired on a wielder. My inability to read the longer notes in other languages was a significant problem there, one that I knew would be wise to remedy if I was serious about taking that sword . . . or any of them, really.

I wasn't the most patient person in the world, but I could always leave and come back. First, I'd want to spend some more time thinking about each weapon and exploring the facility, though.

Probability manipulation . . . I wasn't even aware that was possible. That's one of those things that Gramps insists people should never try to play with, like time travel.

Maybe with proper study . . .

I considered that an option to be the "safest" so far, given that the Unbearable Burden might have properties that could damage my Heart Point, and obviously the Wicked Accord was hilariously dangerous. I could feel my temptation to grab it, but I kept moving.

Next, I investigated each of the other doors, trying to glean what I could in spite of not fully understanding the languages. One of them had an Artinian-language section I was able to partially translate to something like "crimson," which I took to be a flowery rendition of "blood," which was a pretty typical thing for a cursed sword to involve. And speaking of "flowery," I think I saw a letter like "flower" in there, too.

Maybe something related to a blood-absorbing weapon? Oh, or generally stealing life essence from people it cuts . . . or the wielder?

That seemed plausible; life-essence-draining weapons certainly existed, and they were known to be highly dangerous. For someone with a combat style as aggressive as my own, a weapon that could heal the wielder by causing damage was an excellent match . . . but I simply couldn't understand enough information to know if this particular sword worked that way, or what the downsides would be even if it did.

Mentally, I noted the sword as the Crimson Flower, then kept moving.

One of the two remaining rooms had writing in a language I couldn't even recognize. In spite of only appearing to be in one tongue, it went on almost as long as all of the many translations of the sealed sword that supposedly held a fragment of Aetor.

When I came near that door, I felt something in the air — something that felt like it was moving me closer to the door. Not mentally, like a compulsion . . . nor was it a physical pull like magnetism or gravity. Something was physically moving me closer, but through a mechanism I couldn't perceive. I'd look at the metal, then look away, and I'd find myself an inch or two nearer to the door than I'd been standing previously.

That was alarming, to say the least. Was I moving without consciously realizing it? Was something altering my memory?

My enhanced perception from my Viewing Point could sense something, which implied it was planar in nature, rather than mental.

I tested using a bit of breach essence with the layer aspect to try to see what was happening . . . and my vision went white, with numerous versions of the room overlapping, but . . . just slightly out of sync.

I staggered backward, disabling the manifestation immediately. My vision was still slightly blurred, out of focus.

I . . . didn't know what I'd just seen.

The various layers of existence — core, spirit, memory, and beyond — were supposed to sit directly on top of each other. But near to this room . . . they didn't sit quite right.

I had no idea what could cause that kind of effect, but it was, in many respects, the most profound thing I'd experienced so far. Anything that could impact planar alignments was not only profoundly powerful, it was also directly related to my own skill set.

I found myself tempted, perhaps more than by anything else so far, but I knew I simply didn't have enough information. And beyond that, I still had one more room to look at. I wasn't going to leave without at least glancing at it.

I walked away from the door. That was . . . slower than it should have been, since it seemed like the distance grew with every step. Eventually, though, I made my way to the final room.

. . . And found that it had no description at all. The final plate was completely blank. I won't claim that was more foreboding than something that could alter the nature of the planes, but it was pretty concerning.

Empty, maybe? Or did something happen to the writing?

I found myself reaching toward that last door, but stopped myself at the last moment.

I had never intended to lift my arm.

Okay, mental compulsion on this one. Walking away now.

I took a deep breath, closed my eyes, turned around, and walked away.

I found myself standing in front of the same door I'd just walked away from.

Creepy. Okay.

Consciously, while looking at the door, I walked backward until I was near the center of the room. Then, I considered each weapon carefully . . . and also considered leaving.

Getting a book to translate the text would be the right way to do this. I should probably do that.

I didn't leave, though. Not because of my impatience — not entirely, at least. I had another reason for staying.

I hadn't found what I was looking for yet.

After all, none of those felt like where the essence in my right hand was guiding me.

It took a while of standing in the chamber to feel it, but as I walked around, I could feel the pull shifting, like the point of a compass—

And it was pointing toward the center of the room.

Or, more accurately, somewhere below it.

A grin crossed my face as I understood.

There weren't six chambers sealing swords in this sepulcher. There were *seven*.

I didn't step on the central figure immediately, in spite of the temptation. I was cautious enough to kneel down, tapping the blue gem on my enchanted key three times at each corner of the massive glyph, hoping to cover the whole surface area that way. I felt the key activate, attempting to disarm any traps, but I didn't see or hear anything else happen. Either it wasn't trapped or my key simply didn't find anything it could interact with in a way that would give me obvious feedback.

During that process, I noticed a tiny slot in the center of the glyph. It was crystal shaped, rather than key shaped, but I thought I understood the intention. I'd seen similar diamond-shaped symbols in the center of each door, after all. This one was a bit harder to see than the others had been because of the excessive glowing on the floor, but I was pretty sure it was the same shape as the others.

I could go get one of the crystals out of the pillars, but . . . but without knowing what they do, prying out an existing crystal feels like an unnecessary risk. Especially when I have another option right here.

After glancing around cautiously and considering, I gave it a try. I stepped onto the circle, since I couldn't reach the center otherwise, and when nothing happened immediately, I bent down and pushed my enchanted key into the crystal indentation.

I heard a loud click.

All around me, in twelve suits of guardian armor, blue flames flickered to lifc.

Oh, resh.

Then the floor beneath me began to fall.

CHAPTER XXXII

SUBTERRANEAN SECRETS

As the floor shifted, I rapidly processed the fact that the entire room wasn't dropping — just the circular segment I was standing on. I rushed forward and jumped, barely clearing the segment before it finished descending. I preferred rushing toward the incoming golems over falling into a classic pit trap.

As I landed, I began to form a Sword Hand technique, but stopped myself. The golems, in spite of marching forward, were doing so in a set formation.

They were coming in my general direction, but I wasn't their target. Not at the moment, at least — and I didn't want to change that by being immediately hostile.

Instead, I lowered my arm and watched cautiously as the guardian golems approached the still-descending circle on the floor. The golems formed a circle around the open pit, linking hands, and began to glow brightly as essence collected in the air.

I didn't recognize the exact type, but from the feel of it, it was something that most closely resembled my sword's deflection aspect — and told me the intent.

They're not attacking. They're making some kind of barrier to seal off the pit, now that it's open, presumably to stop whoever fell into the trap from—

No, that's wrong.

I frowned down at the circular section of the room that had descended, seeing that it was still descending . . . but not absurdly quickly. And given that I, a mere Candle-level essence wielder, had been fast enough to escape the circle before it descended . . .

I groaned in realization.

I hadn't triggered a trap.

I'd turned on, and subsequently escaped, some sort of magical lift to carry people to other floors of the building.

. . . And now it was down below, descending too quickly for me to safely catch up.

Presumably, there was some sort of reset mechanism somewhere on this floor, but at a quick search, I couldn't find it. And given how quickly the golems were moving to seal the area between floors . . .

I took a breath and made a decision. The barrier spell was almost finished, but it wasn't quite solid yet. I was running out of time.

"You're not sentient, are you?" I asked one of the golems. There was no response. "No? Okay, good. Hold this for me, would you?"

I slipped my backpack off my back, setting it down, and retrieved my scythe spider silk rope and grappling hook, then attached it to the leg of the golem I'd spoken to. I couldn't find anything else the hook could latch onto nearby — the stone ground didn't have indentations thick enough for the hook's spikes to get purchase.

With the rope attached, I lowered myself into the unknown.

Conveniently, the shaft that the central platform had descended was lit. Less conveniently, it was more than fifty feet long, eclipsing the available length of my rope.

That mattered significantly less when the barrier spell finished and bifurcated my rope.

I'd known that was a possibility, but I'd hoped that the barrier would be vertical, similar to the shaft itself, rather than simply covering the opening. That was apparently too much to hope for. I had to admit, simply blocking the pit was a more efficient design, even if it did lead to my descent being a little more rapid than I'd hoped.

Sword Hand.

I slammed my essence blade into the wall, digging into the stone. Fortunately, the shaft itself wasn't enchanted, at least not thoroughly enough to prevent me from cutting into the rock. I felt an abrupt jerk as my embedded blade arrested my momentum, then sighed and dropped the remainder of my rope, counting the time before I heard it hit bottom.

Another hundred feet, give or take. I'd survive that fall, but it wouldn't be pleasant at my level.

Climbing it is.

I conjured a second Sword Hand technique with my other hand, then slammed it slightly lower in the stone. Then slowly, awkwardly, I cut my way down to the bottom of the shaft.

The only light was from the barrier that was now sealing me below the surface of the world.

A number of stories came to my mind when I thought of creatures that dwelled underground. The ancient faerie tunnels beneath the world were first on my list, of course, but they didn't feel immediately relevant. I was more focused on the stories of the labyrinthine home of the Buried, the servants of Aetor, the Maker of Monsters, who had been sealed beneath the world along with him. From time to time, some of the Buried broke free from the labyrinthine passages they'd been condemned to, causing havoc and strife in the world until heroes or gods intervened in some way. This was always a considerable doing. One of the more popular stories involved the God of Stone reburying some of them by knocking a mountain range over onto the hole. Another legend told of the Blackstone Assassin and the Lady of Thieves working in a rare collaboration, tracking down one of the escaped Origin Beasts and tricking it into a different sort of prison.

I had to hope I hadn't just stumbled into the latter sort of location.

Obviously, I had plans for if the location seemed like the type of place I didn't want to be. I suspected that reactivating the lift would signal the golems to remove the barrier when it neared the top, and that would be my first test if I needed to escape. Otherwise, there were a few options. Breach essence was great for barriers. I'd consider that route if I needed to, but whoever made this place was unquestionably above my level, and I expected that wearing down a barrier maintained by twelve golems would take me a while . . . at least with my own abilities.

I checked my side. Glasscutter was still there — and as I mentioned, it could cut a lot more than glass. Barriers were one of the expected things on my "items to cut through" list for Auntie Temper, and I suspected that an item with her level of power would be enough to get through the shield much faster than my own abilities could.

Still, I had to assume the barrier was there for a reason, and breaking it might have unforeseen consequences — both of the "golems go berserk and attack me" variety and the "ancient evil escapes from below" variety.

More likely, I could just cut a hole in the stone to make myself a passage, then rebury that gap when I got out. It wasn't going to be fun, but carving in the parts of the lift's shaft had shown that something like that was hypothetically possible.

Seems like a pretty clear security flaw, I considered, *unless whatever is down here has less physical power to cut stone than I do. Maybe it's a different type of threat . . . or maybe the top of the lift shaft is tougher to cut than the section I tested.*

I glanced upward, considering the effort it would take to climb all the way up and test that.

Nope. Exploring first.

I picked up the remains of my rope briefly. I didn't have any good place to put it. I pondered wrapping it around my chest a few times, but while that was possible, any added defense from having an extra layer of silk rope as makeshift armor around my chest simply wasn't worth the loss of mobility. I left it on the platform.

Need some light. Fortunately, I'd brought flint, oilweed, and a stick — all the fundamentals for an old-fashioned torch. I wrapped the top of the stick with the oilweed, then struck the flint with my knife to make a spark, and illumination came along with it.

I took a quick look around. This section of the building was much rougher, seemingly shaped directly out of the mountain, rather than formed from that strange white stone. I could see unlit torches on the walls of a similar design to the ones in the area above, but no clear mechanism to ignite them. Aside from fire, obviously, which I considered, but I suspected some magical trigger was the right answer.

The room I stood within was comparatively small, roughly a ten-foot cube. I saw three obvious passages, splitting off in different directions like the points of a triangle with the platform room at the center. Each passage led off into darkness beyond my sight, but they weren't what interested me most.

The circle that had lowered — really, a platform — was now flush against the ground . . . and I still sensed what I was looking for farther below me.

There's another level below me. Possibly more than one.

I knelt back down, investigating the platform. Now that I knew it functioned as a lift, and that the gem section I'd triggered with the key functioned to lower it, I wondered if activating that section a second time would lower it further, or if it would raise it again. If I could find another area to insert the key, that would imply different keyholes for raising and lowering, but I didn't have a chance to find any.

While the light allowed me to see, it offered the same benefit to someone else.

"My, my. It seems we have a visitor!"

I nearly jumped at the voice behind me, somehow startled in spite of obviously expecting something.

When I turned, I wasn't faced with a horrible monstrosity like I'd anticipated, but the face of a kindly old man with bifocal spectacles. He looked like the gentle, studious sort, wearing a fine suit that might have been black, but it was hard to tell, because it was just as translucent as the rest of him. The rest of him meaning the approximately top half of a person, since his bottom half was simply swirling mist.

Based on his incomplete form, his translucency, and his demeanor, I quickly came to a simple conclusion — this wasn't another echo. Not exactly.

"Hello, sir." I bowed my head. "I hope I'm not bothering you with the unexpected visit."

It was always my policy to be kind to ghosts.

"Oh, not at all!" He clapped his hands. "It's been so long . . . I simply can't remember the last time someone came down and . . ."

A disturbing frown crossed his face. I interjected immediately, not wanting the ghost to wander into the sort of thoughts that could cause him harm. "You're the curator, I assume?"

He tipped his head downward. "Vantonio Morningway. And you, good sir?"

"Most simply call me Edge, Sir Morningway. No surname yet. Still hoping to earn one."

"Ah, I see. A great pleasure to meet you, Edge. You're a young Skyseeker, I take it?"

I shook my head. "Not formally, although I'm training beneath one. You could call me more of an aspiring Shrineseeker, I suppose."

"An explorer! How wonderful. That would explain your interest in this place, I suppose. I wish I could show you everything — we used to have such lovely displays — but alas, the defenses of this place have deteriorated over the years, and you may have to be satisfied with a truncated tour."

I blinked. "I'd be delighted by whatever you could show me," I said honestly. I hadn't been expecting any guidance, after all. I'd have to broach the subject of taking something out of the collection later, if he stuck around. I didn't want to alarm him, and more information was always useful.

"I see they've let the lights off, forcing you to use that thing. Disgraceful." Vantonio snapped his fingers. Blue lights flickered to life, the newly lit wall torches illuminating the chamber around me far more brightly.

Uncertainly, I kept my own torch at hand. It wasn't the type of thing I could magically extinguish and relight, so I just sort of awkwardly held it to the side in case I needed it.

"Come. There isn't much to see on this level, but we can take a quick look while we're here." I followed Vantonio down the first tunnel cautiously, aware that even in the presence of a ghostly guide, there could still be traps in the floors and walls. He was floating and half-corporeal, so even if he was ahead of me, he wouldn't necessarily trigger the same things I would — and as a ghost, he might not be fully cognizant of the dangers to others.

I didn't find any traps. Instead, we reached a room at the end of the hall with a simple, unadorned wooden door. "I present to you the most mundane of all places — the administration room."

He opened the door, displaying a simple chamber carved out of the same white stone as the facility above. A plain wooden desk and chair took up much of the simple room, but the true treasure was on the back wall—

A bookshelf. One that was filled with books . . . and appeared, in spite of the years, to be perfectly intact.

He must have seen my awestruck expression. "You'll find no books of secret magic in here, my young friend. Just bits of history and documentation on the weapons and tools stored here."

"That's . . . more than fine. May I?"

"I see no reason why not. Books are for reading, after all." He gestured to the bookcase but remained outside the room. That was a little odd, and I noted it for later, but I had more immediate things to think about. I set down my torch, propping it up against a nearby wall. With careful reverence, I lifted one of the books. It didn't fall apart immediately as I'd feared it might. Whatever power was here had kept it perfectly preserved.

It was in a language I couldn't read. Caed, of course.

Frowning, I put it back, then checked through a few others. "You wouldn't happen to have any translation tomes, would you?"

"Not on hand, I fear, nor would I be able to permit you to stay long enough for such a task. While you are welcome here for a tour, your stay must be limited to seven hours to avoid . . . certain risks."

"That's vague. You mean possession by the worldmaker-sealing sword up there?"

The ghost blinked. "That's remarkably insightful of you. In truth, such a thing has never actually occurred for someone who is simply present in the facility, so far as I'm aware, but that's what these precautions are for. Aetor's fragments must be strictly controlled."

I nodded in understanding. "Perhaps I could make another visit when I'm older and more versed in languages?"

"One visit per year," the curator explained. "That seems to be enough time to ensure that no problems occur."

I wasn't planning to stay in the area for more than a year — not if I retrieved my sword and successfully completed Ana's challenges — but I could always come back someday. "That's good to know, thank you." Unable to resist, I asked an impertinent question. "What about you? I mean no offense, but if being here too long is a risk, how do you do it?"

He didn't seem to take offense. "Oh, it's a reasonable enough question. This level of the facility is isolated from the chamber above by extremely powerful safeguards — even stronger than the ones on the individual rooms above. The curators like myself live and work down here, going above only when we must, and briefly. We have a number of other precautions, but I'm afraid I can't speak about them, as someone malevolent might seek to subvert them. Most importantly, however . . . I'm simply not powerful enough to be a concern."

I blinked at that last part. "What do you mean?"

"When this place was first built, the sect intended to garrison it full time with powerful enough people to resist any curses or other burdens the facility held. In time, that proved untenable — powerful Skyseekers simply do not have the patience to sit around and guard swords for decades or centuries. Mid-level ones could be persuaded to for rewards but still proved susceptible to possession and occasional urges toward foolish things like theft. Eventually a new policy was instituted. Curators for this facility would be specifically chosen from the weakest physical combatants in our sect — and those with no hope of significant advancement. That way, if one of us was taken over by one of the swords, we'd be able to be subdued rapidly without causing massive damage in the process."

"Huh." I'd never previously considered the idea that being low-powered might be advantageous for certain career choices. "And that strategy worked?"

He gave me a strange smile. "You'll have to judge that for yourself, my young friend. Come."

With great hesitance, I put the books back on the shelf, then picked my torch back up and followed. The next chamber was equally simple, but similarly, a treasure trove for one such as myself. The room was similar in size to the administration room and carved out of the same white material.

When Vantonio told me he was opening the "storage room," I was picturing a closet with a broom. There was a broom in there, but more importantly, there were shelves carrying supplies in great variety. Some were familiar — alchemical components, many of them rare — but others were new and terrifyingly exciting. Strange metal widgets and tools, bags of unusual sand and glass, and perhaps most obvious in value, several gleaming gemstones.

"This place holds the supplies we use for repairing damage to the facility. In older times, we'd also keep things for expanding the place here, but alas, resupply efforts have failed over the last several years with the fall of . . ." He frowned, still standing outside. "The kingdom of . . ."

Worrying that a failure to remember something would alarm him, I interjected, "What are these gems for?"

"Oh, those? Nothing, at the moment, but they're the base crystals used for embedded facility control functions." He frowned, gesturing to one of the crystals. At a closer glance, several facets of the crystal were etched with unfamiliar glyphs, but others were blank. The tiny writing was beyond my ability to read. "Looks like this one was mostly set up, but someone left it here without finishing it. Clumsy."

"May I look at it?"

"Be my guest."

I picked up the crystal. "What's it do, exactly?"

"You see the writing, yes? Depending on which side is facing down when it is inserted into one of the slots, it has a different function."

"Like up or down for the lift?"

"Precisely. This is up . . ." He pointed to a certain facet. ". . . and this is down."

I nodded. I couldn't memorize the entire set of glyphs that quickly, but I quickly picked out a couple prominent symbols — something like a square and a circle — to identify which was which. "And these other facets?"

"One is to raise a barrier around the area. There should also be one to lower the barrier, but someone left that out."

"Huh. That's odd. The other facets?"

"Secret, I'm afraid." He bowed his head. "My apologies."

"That's fine, I understand. I'm surprised you'd even tell me this much, to be honest."

"No harm in it. You're very much like me." Vantonio laughed. "You aren't strong enough to be a threat."

That was . . . fair. A bit brutal, but fair. "Right." I pushed aside my embarrassment. "Can I look around a bit more?"

"Of course, be my guest. I'll be back shortly — I need to see to the preparations elsewhere."

Then he headed back down the hall the way we'd come from.

I glanced from side to side.

Then, shamelessly, I immediately stole the unfinished control crystal. I shifted another crystal into the position it had been in, then replaced that crystal with an empty memory crystal from my bag.

"I offer this in fair trade for what I take," I said aloud.

A bit of fae tradition, there. There was no response, of course.

I didn't feel great about taking the crystal, but having a way to control the lift was too important to leave the crystal behind. The key had worked to lower it, but given the way the crystal had been described, I wasn't sure I could get my key to do anything other than lower the lift further — and while I fully intended to do that at some point, I also needed a way to get out of the place, ideally without setting off any alarms.

And . . . maybe this could open the doors to the sword rooms, too.

I glanced around, considering the other supplies. There were things that were obviously extremely valuable, the other crystals among them, as well as what looked like magical etching tools for cutting them — but I didn't take anything else. Not only would that likely raise suspicion, but I didn't feel right taking anything I didn't actually need to help me survive and achieve my goals. And, of course, both the sword saint and Lance had warned me against taking things that weren't mine.

On a hunch, however, I ducked down and felt at the floor, then scratched at it with a fingernail. Nothing came free, but I felt a familiar grainy texture, and I recognized the scent. It was something I carried nearly all the time, after all, and one of the things most strongly associated with my home.

The floors weren't adamantine or some similar mystical material — they were ordinary stone that had somehow been covered with an inordinate amount of another mundane substance. Enchantments must have kept it from simply scraping off when people walked on it . . . or scratched at it with a nail.

And, given some of the things I'd seen, I began to understand why such a precaution might be in place. A chill ran down my spine as I began to consider the best way to resolve my situation. It wasn't necessarily dangerous — not yet. I could have returned to the lift with my crystal and tested it, but instead, I waited.

I reorganized some of my pouches, shifting two in particular to be at the ready.

After a few minutes, Vantonio returned. "Finished here? Good. Please, come this way."

I nodded, the stolen control crystal safely tucked away in one of my bags. If he noticed, he didn't say a word. If anything, he seemed like he was in a hurry now, or just generally excited. He led the way back to the central chamber, then down the final hallway.

As we walked down the final hall, I tilted one of my pouches upside down.

"This room, I think, you'll find the most interesting thus far. It's where, historically, we've run tests on the things contributed to the facility."

"You mean like trying to remove curses?" I asked.

"That would be included, yes, but only after cautiously testing the parameters of such curses — if any. The primary purpose of the testing room is for gathering information, though admittedly, it is also the room for attempting modifications like you described. Historically, the sect has managed to repurpose a number of objects into something useful. This is generally performed by visiting experts, of course, as someone of our own level has no hope of being able to alter an object of the potency as those contained above."

I nodded in understanding. "And that's how you make room for more things up above, I take it?"

"It is," he confirmed, "though there were, at one point, two other facilities owned by our sect for other items that couldn't be stored here — or didn't fit the theme." He chuckled. "As a sword sect, naturally our inclination leaned toward gathering swords, but occasionally, you'd find other items that needed testing or containment as well. One of those places was destroyed, however, and now, the last remnant of that is held here."

We reached the door, and he opened it, then gestured ahead as before. "Please, after you."

I nodded, inspecting the room briefly before stepping in. Unlike the others, this didn't have any torches lighting the wall, but it was lined with the same white substance as the other rooms. It was larger, too . . . and I could sense a familiar mist permeating the air.

A breach. And a powerful one.

With both the darkness and the mist, I could barely see a thing until I stepped in deeper. There was a pile of something I could barely make out in one of the corners of the floor, and something reflective embedded in the opposite wall.

"These days, the testing chamber only holds one item, so I call it the Reflectory. A bit of a pun name. You'll need to forgive me for the terrible naming sense, it comes with the boredom and isolation."

I chuckled. "Reflectory because . . . is that a mirror over there?" I asked, cautiously taking a step into the room.

Immediately, I could feel the breach essence surging around me. On the opposite side of the room, I could sense something beginning to coalesce.

"It is *the* mirror, in fact. The most famous of them."

I couldn't help but step closer at that. "You don't mean . . . the World's Memory?"

"Indeed."

I couldn't help but be awestruck.

I'd heard legends of that mirror since my childhood — an item that could be used to gaze into the distant past. Once carried by the legendary scholar Erik Tarren, it was stolen by Aayara, the Lady of Thieves, and then . . . lost, under unknown circumstances.

And now, if the ghost was to be believed, it was here.

Several things clicked together in my mind at once. The vast power of memory that saturated the entire region. The echoes.

"Why is it here? How?" I asked with growing concern.

"As I was explaining, it was the crowning jewel of one of our sect's other reliquaries. Once it was here, naturally, we began to test its abilities — and found that, when combined with other powers, it could be used to do some truly incredible things."

"Like do more than gaze into the past," I realized out loud. "You figured out how to use it to bring the past here."

Vantonio sounded startled. "You're quite astute, my friend. You must have encountered some of the echoes outside this place?"

I turned to him. "Several, in fact. I've even studied with one of them. I believe she must have made use of this mirror to make a younger copy of herself."

"You met the sword saint, then." He sounded . . . concerned. "Did she say anything about her experiences with the mirror?"

"No, I'd originally assumed she'd just used memory essence to copy herself, but I suppose that would be quite a feat, even at her level. But she wasn't exactly an expert at memory essence, so this makes more sense."

Vantonio let out a sigh of relief. "Ah, she didn't spoil the surprise, then."

"Surprise?" I asked.

"You're quite clever to have figured out everything you have about the uses of the mirror . . . but through experimentation, we managed to take it a step further." He smiled. "A mirror that reflects the past is an invaluable historical tool, and obviously the applications of something that can manifest physical copies of things from the past are innumerable. But there are limitations — copies of past items, people, and so forth are weaker than the originals, and the mirror only has so much essence to work with. With ample time to work, we began to make modifications to bring forth the mirror's true potential . . . which could only be realized in conjunction with this facility's other items."

The mist in the room continued to swirl up ahead. ". . . Wait. You used the mirror in conjunction with one of the swords? Is that wise?"

"More than one, actually. As for whether it was wise . . . well, that's subjective, is it not? We did have a breakthrough, as you'll soon see. Please, feel free to take a closer look."

In spite of my growing trepidation, I stepped deeper into the mist. I had to know. As I grew closer to the mirror, the reflection within it gradually grew clearer, as did the remainder of the room. I began to make out more details — cuts and gouges in the floor, burn marks, and . . .

Were those bones in the corner?

Cautiously, I leaned a little closer. Definitely bones.

"Vantonio? What exactly do people reflect on in the Reflectory?"

"Oh, that's simple. The mistakes that trapped them here."

I spun and rushed the door, but not quickly enough. It slammed shut, the telltale blue of a barrier flashing around the entire room as it closed.

I heard a *crack* in the air behind me, then slowly turned again, and with dread, I saw him in the mirror—

Myself, but drained of nearly all color, leaning a paper-white greatsword against his shoulder.

His golden eyes shone and his lips turned in a predatory curl as he pressed his hand against the mirror's surface from the inside and began to push.

CHAPTER XXXIII

SUNDERED SEAL

There comes a time in every young person's life when they have to fight their evil double. I don't make the rules, that's just how life works.

There was a critical problem in my case, though — one that I hadn't fully accounted for, in spite of having a pretty good idea that I was walking into a trap.

A mirror version of myself was one thing. A copy version of me, maybe flavored toward evil somehow. A particularly creative version might have opposite abilities, like . . . maybe shield-related powers, rather than sword-related powers.

In those cases, I was pretty confident I could handle the challenge. It would be difficult to fight, to be certain, but as Vantonio had mentioned, something that was a past copy was likely to be inherently weaker than the original — and, moreover, the copy probably wouldn't have the full scope of understanding and control of their abilities that I did.

The Smiling Sword Saint, for example, had noteworthy difficulty in controlling her essence — thus, the casual and repeated destruction of her arena. It wasn't just an intimidation tactic or flaw in the original saint's fighting style. This sword saint wasn't identical, and thus, essence worked differently. Much of her power was likely emulated by memory essence, rather than actually derived from the original essence types, and thus, she wouldn't have the training to use it perfectly. In retrospect, it was remarkable she could control it as well as she could, given the amount of essence conversion she needed to do in order to manage any sort of technique.

I'd been planning to fight someone like that.

. . . But what I was looking at was something much, much worse.

The figure stepping through the mirror wasn't a reflection of the past. Those golden eyes, the pale-as-paper skin, the pitch-blackness of the petals on his cheek, the strange greatsword . . . those weren't me. Or, more accurately, they weren't my past.

From that, I realized the truth—

This copy wasn't made from a reflective layer of myself.

Vantonio, or someone working with him, had altered the mirror to allow it to do something truly incredible. The World's Memory wasn't reflecting the past. It was forming a version of me from an extrapolated layer. A possible future.

And if that was the case . . .

There was no telling how powerful he would be.

I felt a chill run across my skin. Fear, pure and unbridled, mixed with adrenaline. I trembled . . . and began to laugh.

I couldn't have asked for a better gift.

My hand went to my side, but not to my sword. Glasscutter flashed from its sheath as I charged the mirror, immediately jamming the silvery blade into the reflective surface—

Or, at least, I tried to. The blade hit a barrier, forming cracks in the surface of the protective shield, but bounced off harmlessly.

A few more jabs proved unable to break the barrier. I saw my mirrored self tsk at me from the inside of the mirror, shaking his head, and then he began to push harder from his side. Ripples continued to spread across the mirror's surface as he threatened to emerge.

"You won't break the mirror, even if you get through the barrier. It's a legendary artifact, boy. Do you really think you could harm it?"

Vantonio's voice came from outside the room, seemingly from everywhere at once.

Oh, this room doesn't just have extra security features. It has magic built for gloating over your doomed enemies, too.

Ordinarily, I'd take that kind of claim as a challenge — I felt like I could cut through any defense, if I harnessed my abilities properly.

But I didn't actually want to destroy the mirror. Attacking had been my first instinct, as it usually was, but seeing the copy inside still working on getting out, I had other, better options.

"Question," I said aloud. "Are those your bones, right there? Presumably from after you touched the worldmaker-sealing sword upstairs and got possessed?"

"I wasn't *possessed*," Vantonio insisted, "I was merely persuaded of the truth. That my sect had deemed me useless and written me off as a weakling, one that would never amount to anything. They'd considered me *expendable*, but I knew I could show them—"

"Let me cut you off there. My sympathies, that sounds difficult, but I think I know the rest, and I'm in a hurry. You were influenced by Aetor, took the sword, and went down to the mirror to experiment. Presumably to do something absurd like, say, bring an alternate Aetor out of it. It didn't work as planned. You died right here, and in an awful enough way that you came back as a ghost. And now, you've been trapped down here ever since, on account of the layers of salt on the floor."

"You missed the part where I lured a young fool into a trap."

I nodded. "It was a pretty good trap, I admit, if a bit slow." I gestured at my mirror self. The mirror's surface seemed to be stretching now, which was alarming, and I knew it was only a matter of time before he broke free. "But *you* missed the part where I lined the hall behind you with salt. So, you have nowhere to flee, once I get the door back open. And . . . you might not be an ordinary ghost, but I'm pretty sure that burning your bones would lay you to rest, right?"

I walked over to the bones with my torch.

"That's . . . no, you didn't, there isn't . . ." I heard a pause, then a hiss. "You've made me *angry*, boy."

More mist began to swirl in the room, rushing toward the mirror.

I formed a Sword Sharpening Shroud technique over Glasscutter and imbued it with breach essence, slashing through some of the essence rushing toward the mirror. The makeshift attack worked, dispersing some of the essence, but not all of it . . . and the essence continued to flow from all around me. I couldn't hope to stop it all. The figure in the mirror seemed to glow brighter with every moment, pushing harder against the already distorted surface.

"Disable the mirror." I stepped to the bones, lowering my torch. "Now."

"An empty threat. If you had magical flame, you would not be using that makeshift thing, and a simple torch would not burn hot enough to—"

I sheathed my knife, then used my free hand to pull herbs out of my pouch. I'd already moved it close. "What about if your bones were covered in oilweed?"

"You . . . wouldn't."

I tossed the herbs on the bones. "You sure?"

"I . . . there is nothing I can do to stop it. Once the mirror begins to form an extrapolated self, it . . . I couldn't stop it. Not even when I knew it would kill me."

"Well." I set my torch down. "Then I guess we're doing this the hard way."

It would have been easy to just burn the bones, but . . . I still had questions. And in truth, I wasn't disappointed at all by the way things had gone.

I'd tried to do things the safe way, like Grandfather would have wanted—

But that had never really been my style.

My mirror-self had almost broken free . . . and I couldn't wait to see just how strong he was.

I stepped toward the middle of the room, finally drawing the sword I'd borrowed from the Smiling Sword Saint. As a copy, it wouldn't last long, but I hoped it would work for this fight.

Then, as the copy finally ripped free from the mirror, I ran my sword through my charcoal bag and tore it free.

My other self finally stepped through the mirror, golden eyes bright with amusement.

I threw the charcoal bag at him. He deflected it with his sword effortlessly, as I knew he would — but the bag was already slit in half, and the force of his impact blasted it apart, spilling the contents across his strange white garb and the floor.

"Really?" He raised an eyebrow at me. "Charcoal, for echoes? You must be truly desperate — you know I'm more than that."

It was always strange to hear your own voice from an outside source — it never sounded quite the same. It was, however, doubly strange to hear it when the voice was distorted by the inestimable distance between worlds being compressed through strange magic. The result was that my echo sounded like he was simultaneously distant and right beside me, with an unusual musical lilt to his speech.

I raised my sword into a guard position. "Well, if you'd be kind enough to tell me which layer you're from, I could greet you more properly."

"Counting on your own overconfidence? Do I always use such obvious bait?" He took a step closer, lifting his sword, and stared straight at me, gold eyes glimmering as the remaining mist in the room swirled, then rushed into him. "Fine, I'll bite."

He smiled, mist swirling against his skin and strange patterns of red forming all along it. The room trembled, bits of the floor and ceiling cracking, and the barrier around us flickering wildly.

The barrier failing should have comforted me, perhaps, since it might have offered a means of escape — but I felt the same pressure that was shattering the room around us. Just a casual fragment of his power, effortlessly enough to cause more damage than I'd been able to deal with direct strikes from a magic blade.

I knew that turning my back on him right then would have meant death. The only way forward was through him — and that was growing less viable by the moment.

The room blackened, leaving us with little light beyond my torch and the illumination of my opponent's unnatural markings.

"I've never been afraid of the dark," I told him with more confidence than I felt.

"No." He took one step forward. "That's just it, Lien. You have your answer." His gold eyes shone bright even in the dark. "You're afraid of *me*."

Nightmare, I realized, *from the darker end of the layer of dreams. And for that, I have—*

Absolutely nothing.

Nothing but the sword in my hand.

With that realization came a kind of calm focus — the kind that came when I knew the time for intricate planning was concluded and the song was about to begin. I felt my anticipation burning, and from my reflection, I knew he felt the same.

Simultaneously, we cracked our necks, then began to circle each other.

"As eager as I am to get this started, I have to ask a question," I began. "What's your motivation? Kill me and take my body, so you can exist in this world?"

He shifted his footing, and I shifted my sword in response, but he didn't attack. Not yet. "Oh, no. I don't need anything as feeble as your form to replace you. That's someone else's strategy. Right, Vantonio?" My opposite laughed. "That pitiful thing can't leave here without flesh and blood. Barriers, golems, salt — none of it would stop him if he borrowed your corpse. Fool. Doesn't realize you're immune to possession."

"I am?"

"Oh, you must have gotten here early. Candle-level? You took some shortcuts, didn't you?" My other self frowned at me. "You're barely going to be a workout."

"I wouldn't make too many assumptions." I continued to watch him as we circled, observing his style of holding his sword, his footwork. He was clearly doing the same with me.

He's using the sword one-handed for now, meaning he has his other hand free to grab things from his belt. His outfit is similar to mine, but there's no telling what's in his pouches. No Glasscutter or other weapons, he's just got the sword. And his scabbard isn't the same as mine.

A brief flash of Star Shattering Sight showed me four completed Dianis Points in his body — his heart, throat, forehead, and left hand.

He's much more powerful than I am. Either Torch-level or low Hearth, since he has four Dianis Points that all look individually stronger than mine. But . . . that last one . . . maybe it's because he's a mirror reflection, but . . . if it's not . . .

"I won't underestimate you," he responded simply, "but the result will be the same."

He shot forward, testing. I blocked his first strike, just barely, and the sheer force of the blow blasted my sword out of the way like my arm had been hit with a hammer.

His sword drew two bloody lines across my chest in the moments while I recovered. I winced at the cuts, but pushed forward, forming a Sword Hand technique around my off hand and trying to jab him with it.

He laughed and simply stepped aside, causing me to miss wildly, then drew a bloody line across my arm with a cut that was too fast for me to parry.

I hissed, swinging widely with both blades, and he parried the two strikes with his single sword. Then, with deliberate slowness, he flicked a finger forward — and I felt a cut form across my forehead.

I stumbled back, reaching upward to feel at the bloody wound, my expression falling for the first time.

He wasn't *just* a higher-level version of me. He wasn't just better armed.

He was using the Smiling Sword Saint's techniques.

"Get it, now?" He gave me a jovial look. "There's nothing you can do to win this one. It's just as hopeless as when we tried to beat Ana before we hit Candle. You aren't even strong enough to see the gap."

I wiped away a bit of the blood from my forehead, grimacing. It wasn't deep, but head wounds loved to bleed, and there was a good chance it would end up temporarily blinding me if I didn't do anything about it.

I reached down with my off hand to grab my healing elixir, but his sword smashed the bottle before I even managed to get it off my belt.

"Come now, you don't think I'd let you recover. You certainly wouldn't give an opponent that chance, and you're much weaker than I am."

Well, that was a mistake.

I grimaced. The wound on my face was going to be a real problem if the fight went on too long. The chest wounds and arm wound were less of a concern. They were shallow in a way that spoke to deliberate control.

He was toying with me.

. . . And I could work with that.

I dismissed my Sword Hand technique, forming a Sword Sharpening Shroud along my sword instead. Then I began to move more sword essence, with as much subtlety as I could manage.

I hadn't been able to sense sword essence in the techniques that he'd been hitting me with. And, because of that, I had a hunch. An advantage that I might be able to use, even if it was incredibly slight.

"Nice sword there. Which one is it? And what happened to the others?"

"I combined the ones I wanted," he explained. "A skill you'd learn if you lived long enough." His lips shifted back into that same predatory curl that I'd first seen in the reflection. I had to wonder if that expression was exclusive to the obviously evil version of me, or if I just . . . looked like that sometimes. "You're stalling to think of solutions. Signaling the sword saint, maybe. Breaking down the door and hoping I can't leave the room. Hoping the ghost outside will figure out a way to dismiss me. None of them will work. Well, that last one might have, but . . ."

He rushed forward. He wasn't the fastest person I'd ever fought, but his speed was still overwhelming — far too fast for me to fight effectively.

I didn't try to dodge. After all, he was right about me stalling. He just wasn't right about the strategy.

I'd been charging up my Shattering Sheath technique.

I stepped forward, rather than backward, trying to get inside his reach. I'd likely take a hit in the process, but if I connected . . . I didn't need a clean hit on him. I just needed to get my sword close enough to either hit him, or hit his sword, and then I'd unleash every bit of power at my disposal.

And if he was anything like me, his defenses were much weaker than his attacks. One powerful strike might be enough.

For a moment, I thought I saw surprise on his face as my blade flashed closer to his skin—

Then he vanished in a blur, and my sword met only air.

I barely managed to retain the sword essence I'd been holding, rather than releasing it incidentally on the miss. I spun around to find my mirror standing next to the pile of bones.

"Looks like you already did half my work for me."

"No, wait!" Vantonio's voice came from outside the room, but my mirror wasn't listening.

He kicked the torch over. It spilled onto the oilweed-coated bones, which immediately ignited.

The bones burned bright blue.

A horrifying scream echoed all around us. The room briefly rippled and distorted as essence shimmered in the air, and then, with a cracking sound, the bones collapsed into ashes.

"Huh. More effective than I'd expected. Oilweed shouldn't burn that hot, but . . . I suppose it doesn't matter." My mirror copy turned to me. "Back to our little duel. You were desperately hoping to hit me with all your essence at once, I believe? Thinking that since I'm born from extrapolated essences, rather than sword essence, I can't sense it? That's cute."

I readied my sword, filled with nearly every bit of my power.

"Nearly" being the operative word. My technique still wasn't ready.

I attacked again immediately, knowing that staying on the defensive simply wasn't my strength. He dodged my first few swings entirely, then parried the last.

I had to improvise at that point. My Shattering Sheath wasn't properly charged, wasn't designed for that kind of contact, so . . . I split what I had.

Shattering Sword.

It wasn't a proper execution of the technique — I was cleaving and converting a half-formed scabbard, rather than my usual Sword Sharpening Shroud — but the resulting detonation of sword essence was more than enough to prove that I could, in fact, improvise a complex variation on a technique in the middle of a fight.

It might have worked if I hadn't been fighting someone even better.

Sword essence flashed across my blade as it met his, splitting and tearing at his exposed arm—

But I recognized the gleam of essence across his sleeve too late.

Sword essence, I recognized. *Deflection aspect, and . . .*

I didn't recognize it from previous use, but I understood the power as my sword essence met his — and rebounded back, cleaving into my arm.

Bloody gashes cut into my skin as I stumbled back from the results of my own technique.

If he'd simply reflected my own attack, I might have been immune. But he'd done something just a little different—

He'd used the Smiling Sword Saint's Rejoinder technique. As my own sword essence blasted into him, he'd flipped it and taken it as his own, pushing a portion right back into my body with his own particular power infusing it. I was still resistant to sword essence as a whole, but that just kept it from cutting my arm into a thousand pieces.

Instead, the retributive strike left me with a dozen new bleeding wounds, enough that I could barely keep my grip on my sword.

My nightmare laughed, not giving me a moment to recover. As I stumbled at the sudden agony, he left me with yet another cut of his own as a parting gift, this one along my left leg.

With that, he danced backward, swiping his sword in the air to clean the blood from the surface. "Is that it?" he asked.

I deeply hoped that I wouldn't ever taunt and monologue like he did if I ended up in a similar situation.

The answer to his question, fortunately, was "No."

I'd discharged most of my sword essence in the cobbled-together Shattering Sword technique, but not all of it. And, even injured as I was, I was still gradually flooding my blade with more, re-forming the scabbard layers I'd just detonated.

Maybe I should have abandoned that strategy. It was founded on an idea that he'd already disproven. He had real sword essence, and in wider varieties than I did. If he could manage the Rejoinder technique, his mastery also exceeded my own.

Truthfully, I simply didn't have any better options. If I didn't end him with my next strike . . .

Star Shattering Sight.

I saw the power flaring within his body, so far beyond mine — but those sources of strength could also be his weakness.

We attacked at the same time.

He was going to hit me. There was no avoiding that. My plan was a simple one—

I'd hit him *harder.*

His sword cleaved downward, while mine flashed up toward his heart.

Star Shattering Sw—

His sword flicked down at the last second, right before I could make contact . . . and my sword shattered, but not in the way that I'd hoped.

His blade cleaved right through mine, and when the essence within it burst, he simply *controlled* it. His free hand pointed and the massive amount of sword essence flashed across the room, crashing into the back door, tearing straight through the weakened barrier and the door.

I had only a fraction of an instant before his sword hit me. In that moment, I stole one of the techniques he'd taken from our teacher.

Rejoinder.

My chest flashed as deflection-aspected sword essence mixed with riposting-aspected essence enveloped it. It wasn't enough to cause the sword to rebound, but it turned a lethal strike into one that merely sent me flying toward the now-shattered doorframe.

I crashed into the wall hard. My vision went red on impact.

I had only a heartbeat to recover while he frowned at his sword hand, a tiny cut on his finger from my barely manifested technique.

"Well, you managed something. That's better than I expected." He briefly passed his sword to his other hand, grimacing as he pressed his wounded hand against his charcoal-stained shirt, then adjusted. "No more games, then."

I could barely move from the wall. The door had been blasted open, and perhaps I could have tried to run, but with an injured leg and a far faster opponent, I wouldn't have made it far.

I was too badly hurt to fight effectively, and too outclassed to hope for a victory even if I was fresh. Most of my sword essence was gone, lost when I used my strongest technique without effect.

But I still had one more thing I'd been planning to do for a while, and if there was ever a time to take a risk, fighting an impossibly strong alternate version of myself was the time to do it.

I had two techniques that were meant to be used together, but I didn't need the first. Not when the target was myself.

I formed a Sword Hand with my left hand, then focused.

Star Shattering Sword.

Then, with a deep breath, I jammed my left hand into my right palm.

For an instant, the pain was overwhelming. I felt something in myself *crack—*

"You fool, you can't—" My opponent charged, his eyes wide in alarm, but he seemed to be moving in slow motion.

But while my technique had only lasted for a moment of contact, I'd struck true. I sensed it as the pinhole I'd seen in the seal on my hand seemed to warp—

And all at once, the first layer of my sword seal shattered. And with that, my vision went black.

CHAPTER XXXIV

SILKEN SLUMBER

I blinked upward at a brilliant blue sky. I was on my back, which was a terrible position from a defensive standpoint, especially given my complete lack of cover. Fortunately, there didn't seem to be any imminent threats. I felt like . . . there should have been, but I didn't see any, and I couldn't remember why I'd thought I'd been in danger.

There was precious little visible around me in general, save for the soft grass beneath where I'd been lying and a few sparse trees I could see in the distance.

Where . . .

I felt a surge of concern. There was an obvious question. No, not that one.

Where . . . where is my sword?

I felt a surge of panic, then shifted into a sitting position and looked to my side—

And there it was, of course. The same place it always was, waiting for me. It was safe, stored in my seven-layer scabbard. It was . . . hard to look at, as if somehow both immaterial and impossibly solid, and I couldn't make out even a single individual feature of the weapon. Not the length, width, metal, or style.

But that felt normal at that moment, and it didn't bother me.

No, as I wiped my head in relief that the sword was still present, my concern came from somewhere else—

It was an awfully bright day for a world without a sun.

I pushed myself into a standing position, trying to get my bearings. I didn't recognize the area in the slightest, but fortunately, there was a cobblestone road nearby, as well as a slowly flowing stream. I frowned briefly, not remembering seeing them earlier, but I'd been on the ground and distracted. Terrain features didn't just arbitrarily manifest themselves, so they had to have been there earlier. Obviously.

I took one look at the road, which somehow felt comfortable, even without standing on it. There was a sense of warmth from the stones, a sense of safety, like it would lead me home to a comfortable cabin with a blazing hearth.

Boring.

I headed toward the river, which was flowing dangerously fast. Stepping in meant one was likely to get swept away by the current, dashed against rocks, and drowned. Of course, following the river also felt like a good way to head to civilization. People needed water to live, after all, and I could feel that there would be towns or even cities in the distance if I followed the water's flow.

Better, but . . .

I glanced back at the trees behind me. They felt the most like home, but . . . that wasn't what I was looking for, either.

I wanted something new.

I took a breath, glanced at the river, and took a few steps back. Then I concentrated briefly, flooding my legs with undefined power—

And took a few sprinting steps before leaping across the river.

It was a powerful leap — one that should have carried me easily across to land safely on the other side. Would have worked beautifully if the water hadn't cheated.

The river seemed to stretch, widening, even as I flew across it. Simultaneously, tendrils of water lashed upward, seeking to grab my legs and pull me below.

I instinctively formed a burning blade from my right hand, swinging and severing the questing whips of water before they reached me. I severed each watery tendril with ease, but that didn't solve the other problem. With the waters widening, I couldn't quite reach the other side — not on my own.

I felt a flash of something both familiar and new. A vision of something I'd both done before and hadn't done just yet. I saw myself, older and younger, hands held on a sword that shifted and . . .

I reached upward — both toward the sky and toward my other self — and the phantasmal blade that extended from my right hand changed into a cutting chain. I whipped it downward rapidly, slamming the bladed chain into a mountainside barely visible on the other side of the river. Then I commanded the chain to retract, pulling me straight across to the mountainside.

I slammed hard into the rocky cliff, having escaped the water, but not its reach. As my right hand's blade — once again in the shape of my sword's blade — plunged into the wall, I felt something grab my ankle and *pull.* I felt rock crumble as my blade tore through stone and I was pulled inexorably toward the water below.

... *Wasn't there solid ground beneath the mountainside before?*

I felt a surge of pain at the incongruity, but it was quickly eclipsed by the panic of being dragged toward the waves. I must have missed a tendril somehow. I couldn't quite see it as I glanced down, and with my hand-blade stuck in the mountainside, I couldn't exactly reach down to swing even if I could see it.

I knew I could form a second blade from my other hand, but the angle to swing still wasn't right. Instead, I focused inward, finding my strength.

Burn.

Flames exploded from my body. I heard a hiss of steam as the tendril grappling me writhed, as if in pain, then released the grip on my ankle.

And then I was free, my right hand forming a shorter blade to jam into the mountainside.

With a blade on each hand, I began to climb.

When I pulled myself to the top of the mountainside, I gawked at the sight of what awaited me.

I'd reached a strangely flat plateau, one that seemed to have been sculpted by magic rather than the simple work of time and erosion. In the center of that plateau was a platform constructed entirely out of some kind of pitch-black substance. I'd say it was "stone," because that was the feeling I got from it, but in truth, it was so black that I couldn't even look at it properly — my eyes had trouble focusing on it. I'd never seen a material that dark, but I'd heard of a few, generally substances related closely to void essence.

The platform was constructed from blocks that started about knee-high and went upward in layers toward a flat top, giving it the appearance of a half-built pyramid. The base at the bottom of the structure was maybe a hundred feet across in each direction.

There was something about the structure that felt inherently unsettling, like some animal instinct was telling me "Now would be a good time to be elsewhere." That same instinct was overridden by a much stronger instinct that told me that I needed something there — something I'd been looking for.

So naturally, I ran straight at the half pyramid, jumping onto the first step and then bounding my way upward toward the top. It was good that I moved as quickly as I did, because as soon as my foot hit the first step, it began to *sink*. I didn't panic — stone trying to absorb me inside was no stranger than anything else I'd seen recently — and rapidly manifested a bit of deflection-aspected essence on my feet as I bounced to the next step. That seemed to be enough to block whatever effect was trying to absorb me, at least during the brief contact I made with each step.

When I reached the last step before the top, the floor felt more stable, but I felt a sudden wave of exhaustion hit me, as if I'd been climbing for hours and hours. The last step was a much taller one, too — the block was taller than I was, obscuring my view of the absolute top.

Looking briefly back down — which was always a mistake — I gawked.

Maybe I *had* been climbing for hours. The half pyramid seemed to stretch up thousands of feet now, consisting of hundreds of the strange black blocks, rather than the few I'd climbed. The bottom of the mountainside — and the lake — were both visible below, though they were partially obscured by clouds . . . which were below me now.

. . . This definitely doesn't make any sense, but there are too many options to narrow it down, so . . . up I go.

I braced, ducking down and hopping upward to grab the rim of the stone above with the intent to pull myself up. I felt something surge through my fingertips, like an electrical shock. I was surprised enough that I nearly dropped off the ledge immediately, which would have been unfortunate, as there was no longer a ledge beneath me.

Nopenopenope, not falling.

Gritting my teeth, I formed a layer of scabbard-aspected sword essence around my hands. It didn't block whatever the sensation was, not entirely, but it dulled the pain enough for me to wrench myself upward, landing on the more stable substance on the top of the half pyramid.

As I pulled myself upward, I saw it — the power that had been calling to me.

In the center of the darkness was a silver sword, hovering suspended in midair. It hovered in the midst of six hexagonal pillars, each of which was wrapped in thin golden chains. Those chains extended from the pillars to wrap around the sword, holding the weapon in place, point facing downward. I noted that the chains were wrapped completely around the hilt and crossguard, but none of them were wrapped around the blade directly — instead, the chains had flat metal panels covering the segments where they would contact the blade, preventing the edges of the sword from touching anything directly.

Even at a great distance, I could sense the essence from the sword — deeply familiar and incomplete.

But that wasn't all that I saw. The same moment I pulled myself into sight of the sword, there was a blur from the other side of the pillar as a figure hurtled over the opposite side of the platform. I caught a glimpse of metal flashing upward, and then she was descending to land gracefully in a crouch, directly opposite from my own position.

As she landed, I met her eyes — one silver, one gold — and I *knew* them.

A wave of vertigo washed over me. We both blinked at the same time, awkwardly, I finished pulling myself to the top of the platform and into a standing position.

She watched me the whole time. I didn't blame her — the moment I was stable on the top, I was looking her over, too.

The girl was my age, with shoulder-length blond hair that darkened toward the roots, implying that she'd dyed or otherwise altered it. The base color of her hair looked to be black, or perhaps a very dark red, but I couldn't tell precisely at the distance.

She was tall, maybe a few inches shorter than I was, and built wiry and athletic. She wore an elaborate suit of armor formed from dark green scales shaped like leaves — a distinctly fae style, but one I hadn't seen. Over the scale armor, she wore plate gorget, bracers, and greaves of some sort of white metal.

Heavily armored, but not wearing anything to cover her face. Vanity, perhaps, or just extreme confidence. That or her essence style requires high visibility. Helmets can get in the way of some Viewing Point techniques.

She wore a tabard over the scale shirt, but it appeared to be completely blank. In her right hand, she carried a long spear seemingly made entirely out of metal, and on her left hip, she wore a classic longsword as a side arm. The grip was heavily worn near to the top, indicating frequent use, likely in a one-handed style.

I saw her taking me in at the same time as I assessed her, her eyes seeming to pay particular attention to the scabbard at my side. Then she offered me a twisted smile, one that spoke of gleeful anticipation.

I hadn't realized it, but I was wearing a sharp-edged grin of my own.

We began to circle each other, making mirrored movements around the edges of the platform. Fortunately, at this height, the material itself seemed stable to stand on — I no longer needed to use deflection-aspected essence just to stand. That was good, because I was deeply exhausted, and I had the strong feeling I would need every bit of essence at my disposal to survive what was about to happen. We watched each other closely, hands at the ready for someone to make the first move.

"You look familiar," I found myself saying, "but I can't place you. You're obviously dangerous. Aside from the hilt of your sword, your equipment is pristine, but with that exception, and the way that you're walking, you clearly have some fighting experience — you must just put a lot of work into maintenance."

She gave me an amused look. "You're just meeting me and you're calling me dangerous and high-maintenance? If you're here to seduce me, Auntie needs to get a better handle on her agents. You're off to a *rough* start."

I would have rolled my eyes if I thought I could afford to safely take them off of her for a moment. "I don't know who 'Auntie' is, but I'm definitely not here to seduce anyone. I . . ." I spoke with a certainty born of instinct. ". . . am here for the sword. But I'm very much like my teacher, at least in some ways. I don't mind a little distraction now and then. And as I said, you look dangerous. You might be fun."

My hand settled on the hilt of the sword at my side in obvious meaning.

"Ah. You see a cute girl in some kind of ephemeral realm and you want to . . . challenge her to a fight?" In spite of the tease, her smile only broadened. "*Now* you're speaking my language. This place is obviously a trap, but . . ." She stopped circling.

I did the same, lowering myself into a draw position.

"I'll admit, I've been known to walk into traps on purpose before, especially if they're compelling enough. So, on that note . . ."

She jumped.

My eyes widened as she simply vanished upward, a blur of vertical movement so quick that I couldn't possibly follow it. I had, however, seen her do something like this before and I had a pretty good idea of what was coming next.

Rather than dodging to the side, like a sane person, I shifted my gaze upward and swung my hands.

I didn't draw my sword. Instinctively, I knew I couldn't pull it out of that layered scabbard — not exactly. Instead, as I pulled my hands away from my hilt, I formed a phantasmal copy of the weapon in my hands, a sword of translucent glass with a silvery sheen. It felt more solid than the conjured blades of essence I ordinarily formed, like it was more real, in spite of being a copy.

The strange girl descended from the sky, a burst of speed accelerating her descent, her spear angled straight for my chest. She wasn't playing — her weapon struck out as she approached with deadly force.

I probably shouldn't have been able to block it, not when her speed was so great that I could barely process her, but as she approached, I saw a flash — a sword and spear crossing, again and again, echoing in harmony — and my arm moved to mirror the image, knocking her spear to the side.

The deflection wasn't perfect. Her expression showed absolute surprise as I knocked her spear aside, but she self-corrected, and the point of her spear grazed the right side of my rib cage as she landed. I felt a strange numbness from the wound, rather than conventional pain, but I didn't let that distract me. As she landed with a *crack*, I stepped inward, trying to get inside the reach of her weapon.

I wasn't an expert at fighting against spear wielders, but in those moments, every step felt like one I'd taken a thousand times before. My weapon had two principal advantages over polearms, at least in theory. The first was that a greatsword would, traditionally, be able to cut through the shaft of a pole weapon if used properly — that wasn't going to work as easily in this scenario. Her strange spear was pure metal, and it didn't show even the slightest hint of damage from the initial impact.

I saw a brief flash of cutting into that spear in my memories, but that was with a different sword — one that was closer to whole. I couldn't do that here. Instead, I knew I had to do what Red always did when she faced a longer weapon — get in too close for the opponent to maneuver properly.

As I rushed forward to try to take advantage of her recovery period after landing, I quickly realized no period existed. The moment she landed, she was sweeping her spear at my legs. When I hopped forward, trying to preserve my forward movement, she grinned, releasing a hand from the spear and waving in my direction.

A burst of force slammed into me in midair, carrying me backward — and with enough force to hurl me straight off the platform.

I coughed at the impact, then swung my sword downward. The sword changed shape, the center of the blade shifting into a chain and jamming into the black substance we'd been standing on.

Something didn't like that.

As I retracted the chain to pull myself back to the platform, I felt the entire structure rumble. My blade dislodged from the stone, but fortunately, my momentum was already carrying me back toward the surface. The structure was still trembling as I landed, throwing off my opponent's balance as she jabbed at my face while I recovered. I deflected that off-balance swing with my left palm, then swung my chain at her legs, but rather than jumping as I had hoped, she simply kicked the chain and produced a burst of force.

That kick half wrenched the sword from my one-handed grip, but I instinctively formed another chain around the hilt, lashing the sword around my wrist. Then, as she angled for another spear strike, I got back to my feet, retracting my sword's blade and reforging it into the proper shape.

To my surprise, she took a step back, watching me more cautiously now. "You're right. This *is* familiar."

I took a moment to step back as well, using one hand to reach toward where she'd grazed my ribs.

First blood to her, I grimaced. I pulled my hand back from the wound. On the plus side, there wasn't that much blood. On the . . . strange side, my blood was silver.

"A dream," I told her, more and more certain. "My Destiny Dream, I think."

Her eyebrow went up. "Well, you certainly like to escalate your flirting quickly. Calling me your *destiny*, now? That's an awfully bold claim."

I frowned. She was clearly still teasing me, but . . . from the tone of her response . . .

". . . You don't actually know what I'm talking about, do you?" I rested my sword against my shoulder. "And you're not part of the dream, either."

"Wow, that's a quick reversal. I don't even count as part of your dream? You wound me deeply." She put a hand over her heart. "Oh, wait, no. *You're* the one who's wounded. My mistake."

She's being evasive, both literally and figuratively.

I watched her take a few more slow steps backward, her eyes scanning for further threats on the platform. She was planning something, but . . . she was uncertain. I could take advantage of that, I was sure, but . . . curiosity was briefly overwhelming even my aggressive instincts.

"If this is a dream, and you're not a normal part of it, then . . . something went wrong. Or, something else is going on that led us here at the same time. Ley lines, maybe?"

"Thus far, none of your lines have been good enough to get you laid, trust me."

I groaned. "Okay, now you're being *deliberately* obtuse. I'm trying to sort this out."

"Obviously. And why would you think I'd want to help you with that? You're bleeding out, and you're the only thing left in the way of my goal."

"I'm not—" I felt my side again, a sense of vertigo overwhelming me briefly. Then there was more blood on my hand. I hissed. She was right, I was bleeding more badly, and . . .

"No."

Flames burned along my fingertips, cauterizing the wound. There was a brief surge of pain, and then it was gone. The wound was closed.

The girl let out a low whistle. "Not bad. Wasn't expecting you to get the mechanics that quickly."

That quickly?

". . . You've done something like this before." I looked at her with renewed caution. "Fighting in dreams."

"Comes with the territory. Shame that I'm meeting you right now. If we had similar experience, you might have been a worthy opponent."

She tapped the floor with a heel.

Then the entire platform *tilted*, sending me falling backward toward the edge — and the void that now awaited beyond it.

As I stumbled, she began to run up the slant toward the sword—

And stubbornly, so did I.

I couldn't match her blurs of speed, but as I took each step on the slanting platform, I manifested spikes under my boots, jamming them downward. Not only did those spikes allow me to remain running, what I gained in stability, my opponent lost—

Every time I drove my power into the platform, the entire structure trembled like an earthquake, the intensity growing with every step I took. As her own feet landed, the shuddering caused my opponent to stumble, but she caught herself with a burst of power.

"Knock it off!" she yelled, hurling another burst of force at me. It looked like nothing more than a distortion in the air, like a layer of mobile heat, nearly imperceptible—

Without even thinking, I brought my sword upward and cleaved right through it. I felt the remains of the essence wash over me harmlessly.

She gawked at the sight. "That's . . . you can't cut *motion*."

"You sure?" I grinned at her. "Because right now, I feel like there isn't *anything* I can't cut."

I charged. Not at the sword now. At that moment, I had eyes only for my opponent.

She turned toward me, running backward on the still-sloping platform, her spear lashing outward to skewer me on my approach.

No.

Deflection-aspected sword essence burst out around me, accented with a flash of magnetic memory. My power blasted her spear aside, and then my sword cut upward, tearing straight through the less-armored weak spot under her armpit.

In that moment, I learned that while I bled silver . . . she bled gold.

She blasted herself backward with another surge of motion, startled at the cut.

"Not . . . bad." She clenched her jaw in what looked like genuine pain. "But it's going to take a lot more than that to—"

The sky above us darkened.

I glanced skyward . . . which I realized was now more to my side than up.

I could barely process what I was seeing. It wasn't the passage of time, of day turning into night—

The darkness was the mere shadow of a claw. One that, as I watched, slammed downward — and collided with the sky itself.

The entire world trembled at the impact. Visible cracks formed in the false twilight of the sky. My heart slammed in its chest at the mere sight of something that massive, something so colossal that I couldn't even hope to see the full size of it at once, even from a distance that had to be miles away—

The claw receded briefly, but I felt my breath catch as I realized it was only pulling back for a heavier strike. I turned to the girl and found her turning toward me at the same time.

"That . . . that's . . ." In spite of her uncertain tone, she didn't look afraid, exactly. More . . . disappointed, perhaps? "We're out of our depth. We . . . we should wake up."

"We should," I agreed. "But hear me out, dream girl. Want to fight the impossibly dangerous monster instead?"

I glanced at the monster, the sword, then back to her—

And released a hand from my sword to offer it toward her.

"That . . . that's insane. There's no way, even if we had the sword . . . and . . ." I'd never seen a brighter smile than the one she wore in those next moments. "It's the best pickup line you've given me all day."

I ran toward her. Her expression shifted, uncertainty leaving her.

"Consider our duel on hold, but only for now."

She blurred toward me again, but not to strike this time. Her fingers stretched out toward my own—

I could almost feel them.

Then the sky shattered and the world was engulfed in nothing.

* * *

When awareness returned, I found myself in an unfamiliar room — although I use the word "room" loosely. I was sitting on a translucent platform of some kind of crystalline structure — quartz, maybe, or some kind of unusual glass. Below, I could see only the same kind of pervasive darkness that had swallowed my perception moments before, but it wasn't the only thing in the area.

As I stood, I took in my surroundings. The air was cool, but not in the same sense as a conventional winter night. There was a pervasive feeling that everything around me was frozen, both in the sense of temperature and in that it felt like things were . . . paused. I licked my lips subconsciously.

Tastes like . . . stasis magic, maybe? Huh. Am I back in the sepulcher?

Distantly, I could see several obelisks carved out of the same strange crystal as the floor below me, but no other obvious landmarks. There was no roof above me, no walls within sight — just more blackness.

Doesn't look like the interior of a building like . . . wait, I can remember the sepulcher now. Am . . . I awake?

I blinked, then snapped my fingers experimentally . . . and produced a burst of sparks.

Nope. Unless I've suddenly acquired a fire-related destiny — which makes no sense — I'm still operating on dream logic. Speaking of which . . .

What was all that?

I could remember what I'd just experienced with a strange level of clarity, without the loss of memory that came from waking from a dream. That, I supposed, was probably because I hadn't woken up yet . . . I was still asleep, just in a different type of dream.

Whatever that titanic thing was must have shocked me into a higher degree of lucidity . . . and then I tumbled here, either because the stress of that monster breaking into my dream sent me here, or because someone or something else transported me out.

I was trying to get into my Destiny Dream when I breached my seal, but . . . I think something may have gone wrong.

It's possible that trying to start my destiny seal in the middle of a nightmare monster while on top of a breach to the plane of dreams was a poorly strategic move. Is that monster connected to my nightmare double somehow? Is it . . . him, but manifested here?

And the girl. What happened to her? And the sword? And why can I use these other abilities? Just dream logic, or something else?

I searched around but saw no sign of either. Disappointingly, the giant monster was absent, too.

I frowned, thinking back as I began to slowly walk toward the closest of the upraised pedestals. I didn't know what they were, but they were at least a few minutes of walking away from my current position, which looked to be at some kind of central point.

I used at least three abilities that I don't have on the core plane. Turning my sword into a chain seems . . . odd, but it might be physically possible with just sword essence shaping, at least with a sword made purely out of essence. Deflecting an attack with an effect similar to magnetism is also plausible with deflection-aspected sword essence, but the effect was too extreme. Both of those felt like they were something different — metal essence, I think?

And then there's the fire. Metal stuff is similar enough to swords that it makes a degree of sense, but . . . fire? I don't have any skills remotely close to that.

There are two likely possibilities — either I'm simply able to use completely arbitrary abilities here because I'm asleep . . . or I'm already reaching into extrapolated selves for abilities somehow. Hm. Maybe this dream is allowing me to test out different destiny abilities, in order for me to have an educated choice? Or simply to see what I default to doing organically?

I'd read a fair bit about Destiny Dreams, but much like dreams in general, they were wildly individualized. There were varying levels of lucidity, interaction, and feelings of risk. "Adventure"-style Destiny Dreams weren't uncommon, but there were a couple elements in mine that were unusual — the use of abilities I didn't have, as well as encountering another person that seemed like she might be real.

People can dream up extremely realistic figures, I told myself, *and Destiny Dreams have an outside factor that makes them more complex. It's possible she was just a part of my test, or my imagination, but . . .*

I still found myself scanning the open area for her while I walked, hoping to find her.

I had no luck with a purely mundane approach, so I decided to run two tests at once. I could still conjure fire here — could I also come up with other arbitrary abilities?

I spoke out loud, using speech as a medium for trying to attempt a technique that was completely dissimilar from my usual ones. "Detect Dream Girl."

Nothing happened.

I frowned, attempting several other forms of tracking and detection magic, but with no results.

Hm. Might be that I simply don't believe I can use tracking magic, since it's so dissimilar to my usual skill set. Doesn't invalidate the possibility that this place simply runs on dream logic, but it is one point in favor of my abilities being based on extrapolated selves, rather than being literally anything.

Need to run a few more tests first, though.

I kept walking, seeming to take longer than I would have expected to approach the first pedestal. Either I was farther away, or . . . maybe I was going slower than I felt like. Was it because I was distracted?

Either way, I wasn't going to miss the chance to run a few tests. I'd had some degree of awareness in dreams before, but I had almost complete lucidity in this one, and there were higher stakes.

If I was actually in a Destiny Dream, I was still at a point where I was potentially determining my destiny through my behavior and choices. If I had the ability to actively influence that, I wanted to do so with as much agency on my part as physically possible — and that meant experimentation.

As I walked, I tested.

Fire works, so . . .

I held out a hand to my side. *Create water.*

Nothing happened.

Gust of wind.

Nothing.

Stone spike.

I froze as a rock manifested above my hand and shot outward into the distance, vanishing out of view while I blinked at it.

Huh.

Not . . . just fire, then. And I didn't do anything like this in the previous segment of the dream, which means I'm not entirely limited by what I'd already done earlier.

And what's more . . . I felt something when I did that.

It was like I was brushing against the edge of a memory, but one I couldn't quite focus on. It wasn't quite as clear as the images I was getting when using new abilities earlier. I speculated that might be either because my earth abilities were weaker, or perhaps because the increased lucidity in my current state was interfering in some way.

I finally seemed to be approaching the first pedestal, which was good, but I wasn't done with my tests. Hastily, I began experimenting with the other prime essence types, with some successes and some failures in the process.

In all cases, my effects were underwhelming in terms of power. I tried conjuring a giant fireball, just to see if I could, and only managed a sphere the size of my fist. My power seemed to be limited to something analogous to my current essence level, even if I was using new abilities. I didn't know if that was something to do with how the dream worked or something I was influencing myself with the expectation that things would work that way.

Either way, it meant I felt a little better about my lack of experimentation in the previous phase of the dream — I wasn't exactly able to throw around continent-breaking spells just by imagining them.

Meaning trying to fight that monster probably would have ended badly.

In spite of that, I still felt disappointed that I hadn't gotten to try.

Maybe with the sword . . .

I glanced around, searching for the weapon as well, but it was still absent. I thought I could still feel it, but it felt extremely distant and remote. I wasn't confident I was still sensing the same sword at all, in truth. The sensation was too weak for me to feel confident, especially in my dreamlike surroundings.

Maybe . . . with magic?

Something brushed against an edge of my memory then, bringing a fragment of a technique.

Sense . . . Sword?

I felt a flash of agony in my right hand, intense enough that I fell to my knees. I found myself clutching at it, deliberately cutting off my own technique the moment I was coherent enough to do so.

What . . . was that?

I tightened my jaw, still feeling an echo of true pain — something far more intense than the numbing injuries I'd suffered earlier. And the effect hadn't helped me in the slightest. I'd *felt* something related to the sword, but it hadn't given me anything useful like a distance or direction.

. . . Okay, note to self, don't do that again until I have a better plan.

I immediately tried to come up with what might constitute a better plan, of course, but something else got in the way—

An unfamiliar voice, emerging from seemingly everywhere at once.

[Dream state deteriorating. Cascading barrier failures detected. Please make your selection.]

I blinked.

What?

I looked around, obviously. "Hello?"

There was no response.

"Are you . . . my subconscious? Or, uh, maybe one of the destiny crystals? All of the destiny crystals?"

Nothing.

Hello? Can you hear me?

I tried speaking with my thoughts but didn't get a reply from that, either.

Whatever had spoken, it sounded . . . urgent. I didn't like the sound of "cascading barrier failures" — not unless I was making them in an opponent's defenses. Which, admittedly, sounded like a great technique to work on soon.

I took one more moment to try casting a communication spell, but nothing happened, so I ran to the closest pedestal. I reached it seemingly immediately once I began to deliberately rush, implying there was more than physical distance involved.

The pedestal was simple — it was a waist-high crystal block with a flat top that extended out a little farther in each direction. Basically, a crystal table. There were three things that were notable.

First, there were crystals on the table. Three of them, in fact, each roughly fist-sized. They reminded me of memory crystals, but they weren't the right color.

Next, there was writing on the table next to each of the crystals, as well as one word that was right at the base of the table. I didn't recognize the language, but I could read it, implying some kind of communication magic at work.

The word at the base was "Fighter."

The three words next to each crystal were "Demonstrate," "Reject," and "Select."

I gawked as I processed that.

"Fighter" was clearly referring to that specific destiny. Was this . . . just letting me outright pick my own destiny from the options available? That wasn't unprecedented — I'd heard of someone who picked their destiny in a similarly coherent fashion by choosing a specific page in a book that described the destiny they wanted — but it was relatively rare.

I probably would have felt a little happier about the prospect if I hadn't heard the ambient voice a moment later.

[Destiny selection required. Dream state failure imminent. Barriers—]

The voice cracked and faded.

That can't be good.

I wished I could communicate. I had questions, and . . . hearing the voice sounding concerned, I also felt the urge to offer help.

Was what was happening my fault somehow? Did it have to do with how I'd gotten into the dream? Or . . . the monster, maybe? Was that real, and actually trying to reach me somehow?

With communication attempts accomplishing nothing, I knew I had to make a choice.

I considered picking up the "Demonstrate" crystal for the Fighter, but dismissed it. If I was limited on time, I couldn't check a demonstration for every available destiny — and I knew what a Fighter did.

When I glanced around, the other pedestals seemed closer now — much closer. That was a little disorienting, but convenient, at least.

I checked the next one, then the next.

Knight.

Ranger.

Spellsword.

I blinked. Of those . . . Spellsword was the only one where I likely met the requirements, and even that was a stretch. It was possible that I'd met the other requirements through secondary essence, but I couldn't be sure, and I felt a degree of skepticism that I'd properly earned something like Knight.

Had I . . . broken things somehow?

I certainly couldn't complain about having more options, but I had to wonder what would happen if I chose a destiny type that I didn't have the proper essence for.

I looked around, trying to see if there were more pedestals in the distance, but I only saw a few more nearby. There were a total of seven available, and only three I hadn't checked yet.

The world around me trembled as I approached the next. The crystalline floors beneath me began to crack.

I expected to hear that strange voice again, but there was nothing. That was somehow even more concerning.

I checked the next closest platform.

Blademaster.

My heart skipped a beat.

This was it — the destiny I'd first hoped for, then given up on when the Smiling Sword Saint had explained that I already had more than one essence type. If I could still claim it . . .

My hand reached for the crystal to select it, then froze in place.

Was this truly what I wanted? It was a rare destiny, to be certain, but . . . I'd learned more than just my ineligibility for the traditional requirements of the destiny when I'd spoken to the sword saint. It was still a useful destiny, but having experienced the abilities I'd demonstrated in the dream . . . I knew that I could do more if I focused on more than sword skill alone.

Not purity, I told myself, *synergy is my strength.*

I rushed to the next pillar.

Sword Lord.

An S-ranked rarity destiny, one of the lord subtype, known for being so powerful that they could — on occasion — fight two levels above themselves.

It was an impossibly lucky find, one I almost decided on in an instant, but I couldn't suppress my overwhelming curiosity at the final pillar. And so, as the bits of the floor began to fall away, I jumped across a gap to the final pedestal and gazed at the name.

Heartbreaker Sword.

I had . . . never heard of that destiny. I reached down for the Demonstrate crystal, only to find that it was gone — and there was a hole already spreading near the base of the platform. It must have fallen off during one of the tremors.

I glanced behind me. Other pillars were beginning to fall into the void as the world around me collapsed, but the Sword Lord pillar remained, as if my will and indecision were maintaining its stability — at least for now.

Instead, I looked down at the platform that was in front of me. Heartbreaker Sword.

I couldn't test it, but in spite of the unusual name, I could extrapolate the likely function. The heart was the center of the essence structure of the body, connecting to every other Dianis Point. With that taken into consideration, a Heartbreaker likely was a destiny with functions related to damaging or destroying someone else's Dianis Points, star veins, and other essence structures.

It was how I'd already started to fight.

The rest of it was somewhat easier to guess. It sounded like a hybrid or variation of the Breaker destiny, similar to Verthrimax's Iron Breaker destiny, but sword-focused. At a minimum, that would mean that swords would likely be valid tools for using the abilities of the destiny, and it might even specialize in enhancing swordplay.

It's like it was made for me, I realized. *It's probably a result of the combination of sword essence and breach essence. Maybe even whatever essence I have behind the seal. This is the destiny closest to what I've chosen for myself so far.*

But if I can choose whatever destiny I want . . .

The world around me fell, leaving only this last pillar and me. I felt the floor beneath me crack.

In that moment, I reached down, formed a sword, and cut the words that would define my future.

Three cuts. That was what I'd hoped would make my own destiny.

The floor beneath me collapsed. I reached out, grabbing the crystal to choose my path. I heard a final phrase as the world began to shatter—

[Warning: Requirements incomplete.]

And silver light shredded the darkness as I fell.

CHAPTER XXXV

SEALED SWORD

My eyes opened, and with my awakening came memory.

My mirror image was charging toward me, his sword plunging unerringly toward the center of my chest. Absently, I sensed the sword essence now flowing along his blade, recognizing the technique that he was using as a copy of my own Sword Sharpening Shroud.

His lunge was a quick one, but no longer too fast for me to process. New essence flowed within my body, untapped, and I drew on it instinctively as his blade neared my chest.

With the back of my right hand flaring with deflection essence, I struck the flat of his blade. His sword deviated from the intended path, jamming into the wall right next to me, rather than my chest. I was surprised by the force of my own movement, but I didn't have much time to consider it, as my opponent dragged his sword straight through the stone wall toward my arm.

I lunged forward and upward, trying to jam my fingers straight into his chest. He danced backward, aborting his own attack and moving halfway across the room before I managed to stumble back to my feet.

I understood several things as I watched his expression.

I'd been right that he'd been much stronger than me before, insurmountably so. But by breaching my seal, I'd hit Torch-level and closed much of the gap. I suspected he was still a bit stronger and faster than me, but he was wary now, and I understood why.

With even one layer of the seal breached, I could sense the power that originated from it much more clearly. It was somewhere beneath us, in a deeper floor of the facility. I could sense other sources of it as well, other pieces that were connected to me, though they were far more distant.

And most importantly . . . I knew where I couldn't sense this essence.

My copy didn't have it. Either he'd taken a different path, or . . .

"You don't have the seal or the Dianis Point beneath it," I realized. "The mirror . . . it couldn't copy this essence type."

"You don't know what you're dabbling with." I could see it in his body language, then. Nervousness. Agitation.

The power beyond my seal was one that even nightmares feared.

"You're right, I don't know much about it." I took a breath, then reached into the seal for more essence. It was easy — easier than using sword essence, in spite of my greater amount of practice with the latter type. This was, after all, an essence type that I'd had within me for my entire life. And now . . . even only partially unsealed, it was mine to wield. "But I'm figuring it out with every swing. For example . . ."

Sealed Sword Creation technique.

With a hint of effort, I forged a familiar sword out of a mixture of my faint remaining sword essence and my newly awakened Dianis Point's power. It was a mixture of my Sword Hand and my nascent Ultimate Blade Creation technique, the one I'd never properly been able to execute until I had the last piece of what I needed. Something resonated as a phantasmal greatsword formed in my hands, and I could feel the other essence nearby calling to me.

I decided to answer.

I began to cleave straight through the floor.

"I won't let you." My copy charged at me, swinging horizontally. I swung upward to meet his blade, and as I'd hoped, he pulled his swing backward at the last moment, unwilling to let the swords meet, then jumped back into a ready stance.

I understood why, just as he did — if our weapons met then, *his* would be the one to shatter.

With that knowledge came a problem, however.

I had a full Dianis Point of powerful new essence to work with . . . but it was still a limited supply. His sword was seemingly a copy of a magical weapon, meaning he didn't have to spend essence to maintain it.

If he continued to wear me down, my conjured sword would eventually vanish.

I couldn't win a battle of attrition. Not unless one of my earlier tricks panned out, and . . . it was going too slowly, if it was working at all. At this pace, I'd bleed out.

My instinct was to press my advantage and charge . . . but given that he was still largely uninjured and faster than I was, I couldn't necessarily win a battle of aggression, either.

So I did the one thing that no version of myself would ever expect—

I took one swing at the empty air, the feigned strike causing him to step back defensively . . . then turned and ran right out the door.

I heard him following me immediately, of course. As I rushed down the hall, adrenaline dulling my pain, I cleaved each of the blue glowing torches off their stands, leaving them as impediments in my copy's path.

They didn't slow him down much. Neither did the line of salt that I'd left for the curator — he wasn't a ghost or an echo. Nightmares were different, and I didn't have the right weapons to fight that type of monster.

But I knew where to get one.

I reached the central platform, pulled the control crystal out of my bag, and jammed it into the diamond in the floor. Immediately, the platform began to descend — but the moments that it had taken me to reach for the gem and find the right side had been enough for my copy to catch up.

He leapt onto the platform, swinging downward at me in midair.

I met his sword with my own. There was a crack as our weapons met, and the force of the impact drove me back, nearly off the platform.

And, much to my dismay, his sword remained whole.

As he swung again, I understood why. He didn't have my new essence type, nor could his weapon stand up to the cutting power my strange essence provided — but he still had access to every trick that I did and more.

He had, absurdly enough, formed another entirely new variant on the Sword Sharpening Shroud while in the middle of running after me. This one was coated with an outer layer of scabbard-aspected sword essence, and as one expected, a scabbard prevented a sword from cutting.

. . . At least for the most part. I could see a hairline crack along his blade where our weapons had met. Apparently, the potency of my new essence was great enough to overwhelm his technique.

If he saw the cracks in his weapon, they didn't stop him. He didn't pause as he landed, taking another great swing. There was no holding back now as he aimed at my waist, trying to cleave me in half.

I deflected his swing, just barely, feeling a sting in my arms from my existing wounds — and feeling another open as he manifested the Shattering Sword technique on impact. I managed to reshape some of it, but he was, it seemed, still better at that — one of the blades cut through my defense, leaving me with another bleeding gash.

I tightened my jaw and swung in response as the platform rapidly dropped, descending into the darkness below. He danced backward, but I focused on my new sword and pushed, the blade stretching impossibly as I swung.

He manifested the Rejoinder technique as my attack connected — but my attack cleaved right through it, tearing a gash across his shoulder.

For the first time, I'd dealt him a serious wound. And the riposting-aspected essence hadn't even triggered from the attack — I'd cleaved through that, too.

He grimaced, raising his sword into a more defensive stance, taking deep breaths to focus.

We continued to descend, the lighting around us changing rapidly as we fell deeper and the torches along the walls bathed us in flickering illumination.

As one, we stepped away from the walls of the shaft as the platform continued to move, trading blows in the dancing dark.

Another cut along my leg.

A glancing wound across his arm.

A slash that nearly took off my ear.

A brushstroke across his entire rib cage.

My cuts were barely grazes — he always managed to move at the last second, turning a telling blow into a graze. But with each scratch, he slowed — more than the injuries alone could account for. And when I next struck his sword, he very nearly dropped it.

I took the opening immediately, lunging desperately, but he flicked a finger in my direction and a burst of force hurled me backward into the opposite wall of the lift.

I was momentarily stunned, giving him time to lunge, but his movement was sluggish compared to before. I sidestepped and his sword buried itself in the lift wall. I kicked his knee, sending a burst of sword essence into the impact, and he stumbled back with a hiss, dragging his sword out of the wall in the process.

He lifted his sword in both hands, his main hand trembling. And, for the first time, he seemed to realize why.

"Poison." He cursed. "The charcoal, right at the start of the fight."

"Vorinlief. I had it mixed in that bag for years. I had to gamble that you wouldn't remember it. You are, as you said yourself, born from something other than memory. And when you wiped your hand on your shirt, you poisoned yourself."

His grip tightened on his sword.

I smiled, remembering what Red had taught me.

Loose hands or you'll lose your hands.

I let my left hand relax near the lower part of the grip and took a deep breath, readying myself as the lift's descent came to an end.

Then, as we reached the bottom, we struck. I aimed straight for his heart—

But he was *still* faster than I was.

His sword flicked upward at the last moment. His eyes flashed with a technique . . . and power flooded through his weapon as it brushed, just barely, against my hand.

I wasn't the only one who knew the Star Shattering Sword technique. And while I'd been ready to test what would happen if I broke open a layer of my seal, I absolutely was not ready for what would happen if I tried to damage a second.

I felt the breach essence slam into the next layer of my seal — felt the cracks form — and threw my power into trying to reshape the attack. The cracks ceased to spread, preventing me from being flooded with more power than I could have handled, but the distraction served its purpose—

My conjured sword vanished, my focus disrupted and my essence bleeding freely into the air.

My mirror raised his sword for a final strike against a now-unarmed opponent.

And I did what I did best. I attacked, stepping in and slamming a fist into his chest, sending him staggering off the platform — and into the room beyond.

A room formed entirely out of a single, hollowed-out blue crystal.

It was titanic, reaching upward hundreds of feet, presumably nearly into the facility above us. There was no doorway, just a ragged opening where someone had cleaved their way through the rough-hewn crystal.

The room itself was near-empty, with a smooth crystal floor, and a single other occupant—

The sword.

The weapon was colossal, standing nearly at my own height, with the base of the blade being as thick as my hand. It looked to be wrought from a single piece of silver, with a double-edged blade of impossible sharpness, a crossguard of jagged protrusions that looked nearly as deadly as the sword's edges. There was no wrap on the handle, nor a proper pommel — instead, the bottom of the sword ended in a series of spikes that looked like they should be gripping a crystal but held only empty air. The center of the crossguard had three empty slots, making it obvious that the weapon had been intended to hold several crystals, but either they'd been removed or the weapon had never been properly completed.

The sword hovered in midair, suspended by an unseen force. I felt it calling then, stronger than ever before—

But I had someone in my way.

My mirror had fallen back from my strike, but he was still armed and, in spite of his wounds, more functional than I was. He glanced at the sword briefly, and he must have made the same estimation that I had—

If I managed to reach the sword, it would be all over for him.

So, he blocked the doorway with his body, raising his sword.

I wasn't going to be able to get past him. Even if I charged by him somehow, or staggered him again, he'd just cleave me in the back before I crossed the room.

He must have thought I was out of options, because he was smiling again, just slightly, as he struck again—

But not with his sword.

"This is your end, my friend. Tear to pieces."

There was a fraction of an instant as the essence coalesced, and during that time, I could see it—

Sword essence manifesting in midair, right in front of my neck.

He'd used the Cutting Remark technique.

He was even farther ahead of me than I'd realized, far more skilled at sword essence manipulation.

I didn't have a sword to counter it. I couldn't muster enough essence of any kind.

But like me, my opponent had an unhealthy tendency to focus on swords over everything else.

My left arm blurred straight up, the essence tearing deep into it but preventing it from cutting my throat. At the same time, I lunged forward, drawing Glasscutter and jamming it straight into my opponent's chest.

He glanced down at the knife, his face looking briefly perplexed, then settling into resolve. "Oh. She . . . she's going to be so disappointed. Again."

And then he shattered into a thousand pieces.

I frowned at the mystery of his final remark. I'd never found out what his goal was.

That bothered me, but not quite as much as the massive amount of bleeding I was doing. I didn't bother to pause to try to stanch my wounds. I didn't have the supplies on me — they were in my backpack.

I stumbled forward, grimacing at the pain from every step, and then finally, after everything, I went to claim my sword.

I understood more as I approached, trailing blood with every step. There were more runes etched into the crystal below, lines and lines of them, trailing back toward the platform I'd come from . . . and forming a circle on the ground above the weapon.

I couldn't read them, and I didn't bother to try. I could feel something coming from those runes — and the circle — that felt familiar.

A seal.

A seal that was, I finally understood, connected to the whole of the sepulcher . . . and powered not just by the remains of this titanic crystal, but by every single sword that remained sealed above.

Someone had wanted to make very, very certain that this sword was never claimed again.

If they didn't want me to take it, they should have written clearer instructions.

With that, I jammed Glasscutter into the barrier. It flashed and sent another fresh surge of agony through my arm. I dropped the knife. It hadn't made a scratch on the barrier.

I took a breath then. I knew the answer. Gramps had given it to me, though I hadn't understood it at the time.

The key is within your hand.

My right hand still burned from where my copy had struck it, but I could already feel the Dianis Point drawing in more power. I felt it resonating with the sword that was just ahead of me. I drew on that connection, forming a faint blade around my right hand, and touched the barrier.

Sparks flashed from the barrier as it repelled my attempt to cleave through — but then the walls of the crystal around me flashed. I heard a strange tone reverberate through the air.

And without any further resistance, the shield vanished into nothingness.

My sword fell from the air. Effortlessly, I caught it.

And for the first time in my life, my grip on a weapon's hilt felt perfect.

CHAPTER XXXVI

STORIES

I staggered out of the sepulcher, barely capable of walking, but triumphant. I'd used the borrowed control crystal to raise the platform back to the ground floor. Using it had removed the barrier at the top of the shaft and reset the golems, allowing me to exit without difficulty.

I had my sword still in my hand, clutched with the kind of desperate need that I'd never known. Holding it was like I could feel another limb, a part of myself that had been always been present, but numb. But with every passing moment, my certainty increased.

I had found only a fraction of what I was missing.

Four gems missing . . . and it feels like other parts are incomplete, rough. There are seven layers to the seal. Was . . . whatever this sword once was . . . split into seven pieces as well?

That made the most sense to me, but there were other possibilities. Perhaps there were more pieces than layers, and not all of them bound to myself. It was also possible there were fewer pieces, with some pieces bound to more than one layer of self.

I had to wonder at their motivation.

Sealing a powerful, dangerous weapon made a degree of sense, of course — but if it was truly something that the previous wielder didn't want anyone to reach, it should have been harder to access.

As difficult as the sepulcher was for me, though . . . it wasn't particularly well guarded by the standards of higher-level Skyseekers. There's no doubt that the Smiling Sword Saint or someone of a similar level could have walked in there and taken anything they wanted. She'd clearly visited the mirror to make Thane, so . . . she could have gone further. Even that final barrier probably wouldn't have stopped her, but she wasn't interested in the sword.

The crystal seemed to open the barrier for me deliberately, perhaps sensing the connection from my essence . . . So was this some sort of test for me? Something set up deliberately to make sure I was ready for the first piece?

I frowned at that. What would the purpose of such a test be? It would only determine if I had reached a certain power threshold — there was no element to the test to determine worthiness, at least that I'd sensed.

Maybe worthiness isn't a factor. It's likely someone planned for me, specifically, to claim the sword at a specific time. Gramps knew about it, at least to some degree.

But if that's the case . . . why did that mirror version of me seem so afraid of it?

What did he know that I didn't?

I shook my head. There were too many things I didn't know. Speculation would only get me so far.

There was someone with answers, and though he'd never given them freely, now that I had the sword in hand . . . I had to try.

I stumbled forward. I'd bandaged and treated my injuries as best I could, but it was still going to be a long and difficult walk home. And before I could speak to Gramps, I had another conversation to hold.

As I stepped out of the sepulcher, I found her waiting. The Smiling Sword Saint didn't look particularly happy to see what I was holding.

"So." She leaned against a nearby tree in what I might have thought was a casual pose, if I hadn't seen the tension in her shoulders. "You found yourself a sword."

I nodded to her. "I did. My sword, I think, or a part of it. Thank you for taking me here."

Perhaps that was a part of why she's here. If I presume that this was all calculated by someone as a test, maybe they knew about the sword saint being nearby — or maybe even caused this version of her to manifest here deliberately, knowing she would teach me.

Or, perhaps, that she'd keep other people out.

That felt very plausible to me — most higher-level Skyseekers that could have blasted through the sepulcher easily wouldn't have interacted with the sword saint the way I did. And if she was deliberately set up as a guardian, and they intruded on her territory, well . . . that would have ended badly for anyone below the memory layer, at a minimum.

And yet, if she was a guardian, how had Lance gotten inside? Did he work for whoever was responsible for the saint's presence?

As I paused outside the entrance to talk, the sword saint watched me carefully, with a degree of scrutiny I'd never seen before. There was . . . concern there. I wouldn't call it fear, exactly, but a degree of caution that I didn't think I could have warranted. It was obvious the sword was the source, but I didn't understand why.

"You recognize it?" I asked.

"Not exactly." She shook her head. "Not completely. It looks . . . similar to depictions of a weapon I've heard of before, but the dimensions are slightly off, and . . . I'm sure you noticed, but it's not whole."

I unconsciously shifted the weapon, inspecting it further now that I was outdoors. The colossal sword was lighter than I would have expected for the size, likely due to the strange silvery material that had been used to construct it. The blade was straight and unusually thick, but that didn't keep it from thinning to absurdly sharp edges that I knew intuitively could cleave right through almost anything, if I wasn't careful enough with it. The hilt and pommel looked almost like weapons themselves, all threatening points that lacked ornamentation.

Overall, it looked . . . unfinished. Or, perhaps, like it had been taken apart and reassembled incorrectly.

"These gaps in the hilt and pommel look like they were built to hold crystals that are missing. I also get the sense that other alterations have been made, likely to the blade. It feels . . . off to me, somehow, but I can't tell exactly what was done with it."

"Makes sense. Wouldn't do to leave gaps in a sword like that, no matter how well enchanted. It's just impractical. As for the sword, though . . . I think you might want to put that back."

I blinked in surprise and felt a sudden stab of betrayal at the very idea. "Why . . . ? I mean, I know you advised me that the swords in there could be cursed, and some of the things in there definitely *were* dangerous, but I don't think . . ."

"It's not cursed, at least in the conventional 'do three tasks or this sword will do horrible things to you' sense. I don't sense that it is sealing away an ancient evil, either. Glad you left that one in there. But kid, if the sword you're carrying is anything close to what I think it is, you're going to get attention. Dangerous doesn't even come close to describing it. It's . . . the kind of sword that shouldn't exist. And since it does, it's going to draw looks. The kind of attention you can't handle at your level. I'm not sure even *I* would want to be carrying that thing. Not that I couldn't handle it, mind you," she said with a hint of what felt like false pride, "but I wouldn't want the annoyance. It's not worth it."

"Would it be that attention-grabbing even while it's incomplete?"

She shrugged. "That will make it harder to detect and identify, true. It might even be usable like that, with practice. But if someone truly powerful *does* figure out what you're carrying, there's no way you're going to be allowed to keep it. Best case, you get robbed. More likely, you get tied up, interrogated, then left in a ditch while someone goes and finds the other bits and puts together something *truly* terrifying."

"I'm not sure anyone else could use them. It's . . ."

"Bound to you, yeah. I can tell. Someone really set you up for failure, kid. But I wouldn't let that give you any false confidence. Bonds can be broken. You should know that better than most, given your skill set." She let out an exhausted breath. I felt the familiar prickle of metal against my skin, but she'd controlled herself enough to prevent me from being cut. "Can't say I get the motivation behind putting this here, close enough that you'd be sure to come for it in time. Feels like a cruel joke — or the act of someone truly desperate."

"Desperate how?"

"Can't say for sure. Feels like someone executing a plan halfway, maybe. Maybe you were meant to find the sword, but I doubt you were intended to find it like this. Not now, not while you're this weak."

I didn't take her assessment personally. If she was saying that this sword was significant enough that people at her level or higher were interested, she was right — I *was* too weak for it.

But I wasn't putting it back, either.

"An idea, then." I shifted the sword — and noticed that she moved subtly the moment I did so, as if on guard. That nearly startled me into freezing, but I continued my action — slipping the sword into the sheath at my hip.

. . . Or trying to, anyway. The sword was too big to fit into it entirely, but fortunately, the material had a bit of give, and I managed to slip most of the blade in there.

Immediately, I felt something change in the flow between my hand and the sword. It wasn't suppressed like it had been when the sword had been suspended in the crystal chamber, but . . . the power flowing from it was reduced somewhat, at least. That sensation wasn't comfortable for me, but it wasn't awful, either — like wearing a pair of gloves that were just a smidgen too tight. I could deal with it.

Especially once I saw the resulting change on the sword saint's face. She eased up noticeably when I'd finished the action. "That . . . looks ridiculous."

"I'll need to get it adjusted. Or get a bigger one. But . . . whatever aura was making you uncomfortable . . ."

"The scabbard suppresses it. More than I would have expected for a simple thing like that." She looked the scabbard over curiously. "Was that given to you?"

I shook my head. "I found it in the sword school nearby. I don't think it was meant for me, but . . . if it was made by the master of the school, or one of the students there . . ."

"It might have been designed for a similar style of weapon," the sword saint concluded, "or at least by someone with enough power to hold it. Plausible. It's not just that it's weakening the sword, though. It's drawing on another property of scabbard-aspected essence you don't see too often. Scabbards don't just protect a sword — they conceal it, and make people feel more comfortable around it. That aspect is in play here. It's making the sword less . . . obnoxiously noticeable."

"Meaning you think it'd be safer for me to keep it?"

"Safer, yeah. Not *safe*. But you're less likely to get mugged just walking down the street, at least. You'll want to find a more permanent solution eventually, but . . ." She seemed to make a decision, pushing herself away from the tree to stand up straight. "I can let you leave with it."

I stared at her for a moment. ". . . And if I hadn't had the scabbard?"

Her voice was as cold as steel as she replied.

"Well, then, my student. We'd be having a different kind of conversation."

⊹⊹ ⊹⊹

Having narrowly avoided an early retirement into a different kind of sepulcher — or possibly the same sepulcher, if I'm being honest — I kept the sword sheathed on the way home.

That didn't stop Ana from sensing me the moment I stepped out of the mountain range and into the forest.

"You're back!" She wore a finely tailored suit this time, all dark green. "Just in time for the festival! Come on, you can — waitwhatisthatohspiritsisthata—"

I hefted the sword, which was presently half-sheathed and leaning against my right shoulder, since it was too large to keep on my belt. I'd tried — it just had dragged on the ground. "Hello, Ana. This," I told her, "is my sword."

There was a brief pause as Ana stared directly at me. I stared back. Then, finally, she opened her arms wide.

"Congratulations!!!!!"

Ana half threw herself at me. I caught her carefully in a half hug, half dance that spun her around in a wide circle. "Thanks, Ana. For everything."

"No debt is owed, blah blah blah. Now give it here, like immediately. I need to try it out and see what it does! Is it magic? Silly question, I can feel the sword essence from here, like woah, that's a lot, and—"

"Breathe, Ana. You can . . . lift it while it's in the scabbard. No drawing it, though. Absolutely no drawing it. Like, possibly, ever."

"Is it cursed by a power beyond all imagining?"

"More like cursed *with* a power beyond all imagining."

I could practically see the glow in her eyes. "Tell me *everything*."

⊱ ⊰

I told stories to Ana all the way home, and most of them even were true.

I passed Grandfather several times in the forest on the way home. Many of him were watching me that night, silently, with an undertone of concern and . . . perhaps condemnation.

But I didn't feel like the latter was directed toward me.

"I'm home," I announced as I opened the front door. It wasn't needed, of course.

"You're early," a version of Gramps said as he looked at me from his seat at the kitchen table.

I got the sense that his words were referring to something other than the hour of the day, given both the tone and the fact that it was already past nightfall. Gramps waved toward the opposite chair, so I took it.

"You will have questions," he said.

"I do." I lifted the sword and set it down in front of me on the table.

"Tell me, Grandfather. What, precisely, is this sword? How is it connected to me? And . . . where can I find the rest of it?"

EPILOGUE

SILENCE

The swordsman went silent.

Scribe gave him a curious look. "And the sword? Did he tell you what it was, and where to find the other pieces?"

"More than he had previously, at least. But even he didn't know the full story."

". . . And the part he did know?"

"That's a long story. A story for another time, if at all."

Scribe blinked. "What do you mean?"

"We're about to hit the inn." Edge waved ahead of him. "Just a few minutes out, and I don't like the idea of telling my story around . . . perfect strangers. Especially this part. This is a subject I can't speak lightly about, even now."

"Even if they won't understand the language?" Scribe asked.

"Especially if they won't understand the language. These . . ." He gestured to the markings on his face. ". . . will arouse enough suspicion if they're seen. If we avoid speaking a foreign language, there's a chance we can make it through this without any unpleasant incidents. Assuming you're willing to do the talking?"

"Of course. That was the deal, after all." Scribe nodded. "But one thing . . . when you continue, would you mind telling me the historically accurate version?"

Edge's lips slid into a grin. "You remembered that line, did you?" He folded his arms as he walked. "What makes you think I'm not already telling you the historically accurate version?"

"Well, dropping that little line into the story could be seen as a hint in itself. But beyond that, there have been some small incongruities."

"Oh?" Edge's eyebrow went up, looking sincerely curious. "What sorts of incongruities?"

"Mostly minor things. Subtleties, some of which could just be coincidence. For example, you have a habit of saying something like 'I did this for exactly three reasons.' It's always three. Often, it feels like you came up with an extra item for whatever the list is just to make it three."

Edge laughed. "That's . . . less a fabrication and more of . . . a storytelling tradition. The number three is important where I come from — along with four, six, seven, and twelve. Even you should be aware of the last."

"Sure. Twelve prime dominions, and we often see systems of base twelve as a result. Twelve hours in a half day, that sort of thing. I'm sure some of the other things are just . . . let's call them stylistic elements. But there are a few things that really don't match up."

"Intriguing. What sorts of things?"

Scribe tried to get a read on Edge's reaction there, but the swordsman's expression had shifted back into being . . . neutral. Concealed. It was nothing unfamiliar to Scribe, but it was somewhat concerning, given some of the topics he'd considered raising. "Well, for one thing, your behavior in the story . . . if you'll forgive me for saying so, I don't think you're describing yourself entirely truthfully."

"I'd hardly be the first storyteller to portray myself in a slightly slanted light. Most people have complicated views of themselves but want to be seen in a positive way."

"Of course. But you're not just portraying yourself positively — you emphasize your failures and weaknesses significantly in certain areas, although perhaps not in others. I can sense some regrets, perhaps. But I'm not really speaking in terms of positives or negatives. Your personality, as far as I've seen it, doesn't quite match with that of the version of yourself in the story."

"How so?" Edge's tone was cautious, guarded.

"I'd say the point that stands out the most is your attitude in combat. In the story . . . you're playful and excited every time you encounter a risk. I've met people like that. Plenty of them, in fact. People addicted to battle. It seems plausible enough as a personality trait — especially if one considers that your behavior might be influenced by sword essence, or the mysterious essence you were born with. But I've seen you fight twice. In both cases, you were calm, collected. Perhaps when simply dealing with the fire creature in the rain, I wasn't able to see it, since you hopped up to the roof — but I saw you clearly with the bandits. There was no . . . playfulness. No banter."

"People change." He sounded a bit melancholy as he said that. "They get older, and . . . they learn."

Scribe frowned, sensing he was walking into dangerous territory. "I can believe that, too. Perhaps you're simply not as innocent as you were, then, and lost your joy for battle, but—"

"No." Edge's tone was firm. "I haven't. Not in the slightest." He shook his head. "But in those cases, there were innocent people at risk. And what I've learned is . . . there are times that I can't play. Not when I'm not the only one who can get hurt."

Oh. Perhaps that was a reasonable explanation. Maybe he'd . . . lost someone, or hurt someone by accident, or . . .

"Sorry," Scribe said. "I didn't mean to accuse you of anything, or bring back bad memories, I'm just . . ."

"No, this is enlightening. I rarely get to hear how I'm perceived from the outside, and certainly not from a human. Please, go on. Are those the only oddities you noticed?"

"No," Scribe admitted, though he was concerned to push further. He calculated briefly.

Best to raise these suspicions now, rather than letting him learn more about me before the talk. At this point, if he reacts badly . . . I still have a couple tricks he hasn't seen. I might escape.

"You claimed you don't speak the local human language. That's why you need me to talk." He was matter-of-fact.

"I understand a few words, here and there, but I'm not conversational. Why?"

"I almost missed it," Scribe admitted, "given the emotions of the scene, and the threats. But during the encounter where you saved Lindt from the humans, you spoke to them. They wouldn't back down, but you understood them, and they understood you. Thus, either that part of the story was false, or your claim to not be able to speak to humans is false."

Edge paused in his step, turning to face Scribe completely. ". . . Fascinating."

Scribe felt a shiver run down his spine, taking a step back out of instinct. Not that a bit of distance would save him from someone of Edge's speed — he'd need more drastic measures if he wanted to escape.

There was a breathless moment, and then Edge shrugged, looking away. "Might be that I've overplayed my lack of understanding a bit. I've been known to tailor my stories to my audience, both for entertainment and for other reasons. It's only natural. But there's another factor in play. Those humans spoke a local dialect — one born from communication between humans and fae in the region in the ancient past. There are multiple human languages here, many different dialects. It's not so easy to understand, by comparison."

Scribe straightened a bit. The explanation was . . . plausible, but dubious. Still, some of the tension had left, since the swordsman had chosen not to react with immediate violence. "I see. And Eliree? The reason why she spoke in a disjointed, animalistic fashion when you met her, but not — as I understand it — perhaps a single year later, when you encountered her by Ana's shrine?"

The swordsman turned back to him. "That's even simpler. She had plenty of time to talk to people once I introduced her to the local court. It wasn't that she didn't understand the language at all before — a year of conversation did wonders for her."

"Perhaps. But I can't help but feel that you decided at a certain point to avoid talking about her."

"Truly? What makes you say that?"

"You were injured and knocked out during your first couple visits to the sword saint. Someone treated your wounds. It wasn't the sword saint. Doesn't make sense with how you described her personality. That means it's someone who the sword saint either didn't detect or didn't see as a threat. Eliree is a tree spirit with a tree 'far away' — meaning, perhaps, up in the mountains, rather than in the forest where you grew up. 'For the Fallen' seems consistent with the type of thing that might be written at a grave for fallen warriors, which could easily be located near a place called the Last Breath. And Eliree's powers were related to shade, offering her both stealth and healing capabilities."

"And your conclusion?" the swordsman asked quietly.

"Even if she wasn't the one who helped you — and I think she was, if that part of the story was true at all — she would have, at a minimum, been a clear suspect in your mind. Unless there's something I was missing about her, like perhaps you knew that her tree was in a completely different spot. But you'd mentioned eyes following you from the forest, and her guest tree was on the way north through the Brightwood, which given how you've described the forest . . ."

"You've been paying close attention. That's good. I'm genuinely flattered." He tilted his head to the side. "But you're aware that in faerie culture, accusations of lying are quite serious. I've mentioned that before."

"And yet you've also emphasized repeatedly that you're not fae. Thus, you shouldn't be offended to the same degree, even if you're from that culture."

A slow nod in response. "I suppose that's true. Still, you're pushing me deliberately. Testing. Why?"

"Because I have suspicions. Ones related to another incongruity — one I've been debating asking about. But I do not wish to cause . . . undue levels of offense. I've genuinely enjoyed your story, and—"

"Ask your question, Scribe." The swordsman shifted his stance, opening both hands wide, presumably some sort of demonstration of harmlessness.

As if Scribe would believe that, after seeing — and hearing — what the swordsman was capable of.

Well, I've made a terrible mistake. But he's not going to back down now, and . . . I need to know.

"I want assurances that you won't kill me — or, you know, significantly maim me — for asking."

Edge frowned. "You think I'm the sort of person who would do that?"

"I think you're the sort of person who would respond to a request like that with a question, which is in itself a concern."

A smile spread across Edge's face. "I have no intention of killing or significantly maiming you."

"Swear it three times. And be specific. I'm not talking about your current intention. I want to know that you won't kill me if I say something you don't like."

"Ah. Someone *has* been paying attention. Very well. If, during this specific conversation, you ask a question that offends, alarms, or otherwise antagonizes me, I will not kill or otherwise seriously injure you in response to it. I swear this three times: by my will, by my word, and by my wish." He closed his eyes for a moment, as if sealing the ritual phrase. "Satisfied?"

"Not particularly, given that you could have fabricated the whole 'swearing three times' concept at an earlier point in the storytelling process, but suspicion is in my nature. That's *me* being honest."

"A shame that you don't think you can trust me. We'll have to see if we can do anything about that later. Now, ask your question."

Scribe took a deep breath, then nodded, half to the swordsman and half to himself.

"Early in the story, you had some very interesting technique names. Ultimate Blade Creation technique, for example. As the story progressed, however, the style began to take on a more consistent quality. After a few hours, your new techniques all started with the letter *S*." Scribe took a deep breath, trying to suppress his nervousness. "So, I'll postulate this. You began to rename your techniques later on in the story deliberately — and you wanted it to be noticed."

"You're very perceptive." Silver flashed in the swordsman's eyes. "That was subtle enough that I wasn't expecting you to pick up on it. I wasn't sure if either of you would."

"What do you mean?" Scribe asked.

"It's simple, really." The swordsman took a step forward. "As I said much earlier, I enjoy tailoring my story to my audience. And I began to make a few changes once I was reasonably confident about who my audience really was."

Scribe moved a hand behind his back, ready to make hand-signs if needed, but he knew he wouldn't be fast enough. "I'm not sure I understand."

"Oh, I think you do. Granted, I don't think you planned this from the start, but I do think you picked up on what was happening even faster than I did." He gestured to Scribe's bag. "That's probably why you took the pieces of the arrows. You suspected something — or you knew something, and you didn't want me to see the same thing you had. I still haven't managed a good look at the arrow bits, but I imagine that they'd be just as unsuited to the bandits as the rest of their equipment. I have a good eye for that, like I hinted."

"Your observation about the maintenance of equipment the girl had in your Destiny Dream. *That* was a hint that you knew about the bandits?"

"Some clues in a story can be clearer than others. Maybe that one was a bit of a stretch. Anyway, the bandits themselves were an oddity, but there were other possible explanations for that. It took a few other oddities to make the situation clear. It was a little bit too much of a coincidence that you happened on me at the same time as the bandits did — and that walking off the path when we did would put us directly in the path of a certain roadside inn. The Perfect Stranger."

"You didn't tell me that was the name of the inn we were traveling to."

"That was deliberate. I wanted to see if you'd slip and say it yourself, since I hadn't mentioned it. I did mention the Perfect Stranger during my story, though — just to see if you'd react to the name. You did, but to your credit, it wasn't extreme enough to make me feel any more suspicious. You might have just recognized the name." He took another stabilizing breath. "But I recognized more than that. I grew up hunting game in a dangerous place. I recognize what it looks like to herd prey. And between the bandits and the Perfect Stranger, I knew *I* was being herded. All I needed to know is if you were responsible."

Scribe shivered. "I didn't know about the bandits, nor did I arrange for them. Nor did I know about the inn until you told me about it."

"I believe you." The swordsman nodded. "You were, it seemed, just one piece on the board. And you played your part admirably."

Scribe made a quick hand-sign. It wouldn't make him invisible, but if things came to blood, it might offer him a slim chance to escape. "How do you know I was involved with . . . whoever or whatever was trying to herd you?"

"There are three things that gave you away." He smiled, as if amused by his reference to earlier in the conversation. "Your name was obviously a hint, but not confirmation on its own. Your particular skillset being related to sight magic was a larger one — it's rare even on Mythralis, and people with it tend to have certain connections. But either of those could have been excused with proper context. No, it was something more direct that gave you away. You have a habit of playing with your ear when I stop or start talking. Or, rather, the earring. And while I'm not a specialist in your type of sorcery, I do have a general idea of how dominion-marked items work — the types of items one might wear on an ear. I know who would employ people like you. And for what it's worth . . . I'm sorry."

Oh, vek—

Scribe stepped backward again, reaching upward in a familiar gesture, but he wasn't fast enough. Even being ready for it, the swordsman was too fast, silver forming around his hand as he struck.

The pain was sharp, but brief, and . . .

A moment later, the swordsman was back where he'd been standing.

Scribe's hand reached up, coming back stained in blood.

The swordsman shook his head with a sigh, then tossed the earring casually up in the air, then caught it again. "Not a bad toy. Subtle. You like that word, don't you? It's one of yours, isn't it?"

"Don't. You don't know what you're . . ." Scribe stammered weakly.

"Oh, I think I do. I've been waiting a long time for this, in fact."

The swordsman lifted the earring in front of his face, his lips spreading into a wide smile.

"My greetings to Aayara, Lady of Thieves. I believe you have something that belongs to me."

APPENDIX I

ESSENCE SORCERY

A Message from the Pen of a Scribe

As instructed, I've been collecting information on the local style of sorcery for quite some time, but it's only been in recent months that I've managed to find a reliable source. During my travels, I encountered a young swordsman who practices the art of essence sorcery. He is not what the locals call a Skyseeker, exactly, though he appears to pursue power in a similar fashion. The Skyseekers appear to be more of an organization (or perhaps several organizations) that have places of learning called "sects," whereas this swordsman grew up in the wilds, raised primarily by a variety of nonhuman species.

Including wolves, if he is to believed. Yes, literally raised by wolves. The humor of asking someone who is raised by wolves to teach me complicated sorcerous theory does not escape me, but I assure you, I have taken steps to verify the veracity of his tales. Or, at least, the pertinent portions for this report.

The swordsman refers to himself primarily as Edge — a nickname seemingly derived from the birth name Lien. Yes, Lien, the Liadran word. This Edge may be only a teenager, but his understanding of the functionality of essence is formidable. Much of this information seems to have come from the teachings of his so-called Grandfather. I can surmise from the context of the story that Grandfather is a scholar of some repute and one originally of Mythralian origin.

It couldn't be . . . no, I shouldn't make assumptions that grand in scale without more significant evidence. There are many other scholars, after all. It couldn't be *the* scholar, could it?

You would have told me if he was around here, wouldn't you? Never mind, of course not. Question withdrawn.

Continuing on, the local form of sorcery is what we refer to as essence sorcery back in the homeland. Edge uses this term as well, but I'm unclear on if that is actually the local term or if he simply uses it because of his own Mythralian education and heritage.

The basic foundation is that essence sorcerers gather ambient essence from nature and absorb it. Once they have absorbed enough essence of a particular variety, they can compress that essence themselves, creating a container of essence in a set location called a Dianis Point.

Yes, like House Dianis. Noteworthy.

A completed Dianis Point is a crystalline structure that automatically fills itself up over time with the same type of essence that was used to make it. This provides a steady, reusable source of essence, much like certain dominion-marked items work. A fascinating concept, but one that seems entirely too simple to me.

I can see why building up essence in the body might cause the body to build more of that essence, but these discrete containers seem . . . odd. Artificial. Arbitrary. And things only grow stranger from there.

There are, apparently, a set number of valid Dianis Points . . . and the location of each Dianis Point is relevant to how it functions. And as one completes more Dianis Points, both the points themselves and the person's overall essence can reach higher "levels," which grant new abilities.

These parallels to the crystal marks and attunements of the continent of Kaldwyn make me wonder . . . is this essence progression structure some kind of equivalent to how they work, but one that the residents are born with? If so, is this is an organic distinction in the species, or one that comes from the machinations of local gods or other powerful entities?

This bears more investigation, but my sources of reliable information on the deities of this land are minimal. Most seem to believe the gods have moved elsewhere or died. I will continue searching for more.

In the meantime, I have a few more specific notes that you might find useful.

First, the levels of essence development. There are many of them, but I have made some notes on the first few, which Edge seems most familiar with.

The first three levels are referred to as the Essence Layer or Core Layer, and the levels in this layer of development all have names related to fire. This is, according to my research, a combination of older traditions referring to essence as "inner fire" and because essence sorcerers see the auras of this layer as being either clear, orange, or red, depending on their intensity.

Candle (Clear to Light Red)

- *Reached by:* Completing a first Dianis Point. This appears to be largely an automatic process, as the body processes essence, but it can be guided through attempting to absorb as much essence as possible of a specific type, much as Edge himself did. Some species are born with already completed Dianis points, and thus, already at Candle-level from birth.
- *Power Gained:* Internal essence sense. Able to clearly conceptualize and interact with your internal essence structure. In addition, your ability to sense essence in the environment is enhanced.

Torch (Red)

- *Reached by:* Completing three Dianis Points or overloading a smaller number of Dianis Points with essence.
- *Power Gained:* Upon reaching this stage of essence development, the person will undergo a Destiny Dream. Upon waking from the dream, the person will have a destiny mark, which grants different abilities based on the specific mark. For example, destiny marks might be things like Warrior, Wizard, or even Farmer. Once someone has a destiny mark, that mark can also improve over time, but this is a separate and parallel form of progression. Destiny marks are an entire field of study in themselves, and I will write about them more in a separate report. Briefly, however, these destiny marks supposedly draw from alternate versions of the self for power. If true, this is absolutely absurd, and I feel cheated at being stuck with merely a single mediocre self to work with. Ugh.

Hearth (Orange)

- *Reached by:* Completing six Dianis Points or overloading a smaller number of Dianis Points with essence.
- *Power Gained:* People at Hearth-level gain the ability to form spirit bonds. These can be with other entities or between two of their own Dianis Points.
    - Forming a spirit bond with another entity has the advantage of allowing the person to get essence of another type, which they can use directly or intermix with the essence in the Dianis Point you linked it to. For example, you could link a Fire Dianis Point to an Air Dianis Point on another entity, allowing you to mix the two to create lightning essence.
    - In addition, spirit-bonded individuals gain a strong sense of each other. As the bond strength progresses, this can allow for remote

sensing of the other, telepathy, sensing the health of the other entity, et cetera.

- My studies have indicated that this is the most common method by a large margin. Among nobles, spirit bonds are formed between partners in marriage ceremonies. This is seen as a means of ensuring loyalty and forming a tangible connection between houses. Ordinary civilians may form spirit bonds with their spouses, parents, grandparents, siblings, or children.
- Powerful adventurers and Skyseekers often seek out spirit bonds with exotic entities — phoenixes, kitsune, wani, and other legendary beings.
- Binding two Dianis Points together allows for intermixing essence types between separate parts of your own body, rather than just being able to mix outlying parts with the Heart Point. Basically, this creates a secondary essence "route," which allows for direct interaction between two otherwise unrelated Dianis Points.
- This is mostly useful when someone needs to form an additional spirit bond while they're alone, if they are intentionally hiding their power, or if they have a specific Dianis Point they do not want to link to someone else.
- For example, if someone has an extremely dangerous Dianis Point or a rare essence type, they might choose this option.
- An essence wielder that is isolated (e.g., someone stuck in prison and planning a prison break) might also try to do this.
- Note that spirit bonds are initially fragile and require time to develop into something permanent. Much like star veins, the amount of essence that can be safely passed through spirit bonds also improves over time.
- Spirit bonds can be removed, but this can apparently be dangerous. I do not have sufficient information on this subject to explore it in detail at this time and will need to do further research.
- I am also currently unaware if spirit bonds persist beyond the death of one bonded individual.

The next layer is the Spirit Layer. These levels all refer to objects or concepts associated with nobility, which makes sense — in most time periods, only nobles could afford the resources necessary to reach these stages. In modern times, many merchants, Skyseekers, and adventurers also reach these stages of development, but the ancient names remain.

Signet (Orange to Yellow)

- *Reached By:* Completing your first spirit bond and "solidifying" it, similar to how a Dianis Point is completed. Also, continue to develop your essence in your Dianis Points to a certain level.
- *Power Gained:* Internal spirit sense. Able to clearly conceptualize and interact with your internal spirit structure. In addition, your ability to sense spiritual power in the environment is enhanced.

Regalia (Yellow)

- *Reached By:* Completing three spirit bonds or increasing the level of a smaller number of spirit bonds significantly. Also, as per usual, you must continue to accumulate more essence in your Dianis Point.
- *Power Gained:* Create spirit regalia. This allows you to fuse items into your spirit. This works similar to spirit bonding elsewhere, but it ties the item directly to a component of your spirit. You cannot have both a spirit bond with a creature and a spirit regalia piece tied to the same Dianis Point (under normal circumstances). Basically, this lets you equip an item on your spirit and incorporate/discorporate it at will, as well as mix essence with it.

Crown (Yellow to Green)

- *Reached By:* Completing six spirit bonds or increasing the level of a smaller number of spirit bonds significantly. (Also, more essence.)
    - At this stage, I've also heard rumors of something called a Shadow Trial, where one must confront their "inner self." This is not a subject I have studied in great detail, however, and this may be unreliable. It is noteworthy that this may not occur at this level, or another. If it is a parallel to the Destiny Dream, it should occur a level earlier. If it has to do with the shade, it logically should likely occur later, during the Shade Layer.
- *Power Gained:* Create Shade Weave. This allows you to bind things to your shade, allowing for physical transformations of the body. For example, one could bind their shade to a spirit beast — say, a cat — and gain catlike eyes as a benefit. I'm unclear on the limitations of this, but clearly, this offers significant potential benefits if one is able to find a powerful creature to bind to.
    - Upon completing this, a person may then begin to form Shade Weaves, which allow for physical transformation of the body.

After this, there's a Shade Layer, which is color-coded to green, and a Memory Layer at some point after. There may or may not be other layers between

Shade and Memory. I should also make it clear that my information on this subject is what I have gleaned from brief conversations and poorly translated texts; it is not to be taken as perfectly reliable.

I know virtually nothing of the names or powers of specific levels beyond the Spirit Layer at this point in time. I've heard that there is a Sky-level, which appears to be a theoretical maximum, and likely is at least a layer or two beyond the Spirit Layer if it exists. This appears to be one of the possible sources of the Skyseeker name. It may also refer to a physical land that Skyseekers are attempting to find — some kind of divine island in the sky.

Notably, these level titles primarily are used to refer to people, but individual Dianis Points also are sometimes referred to by these level names. In those cases, the level name indicates the expected amount of essence that someone should have in a Dianis Point at that level. A person could have Dianis Points at a lower or higher level than their overall personal power.

Next, the individual Dianis Points.

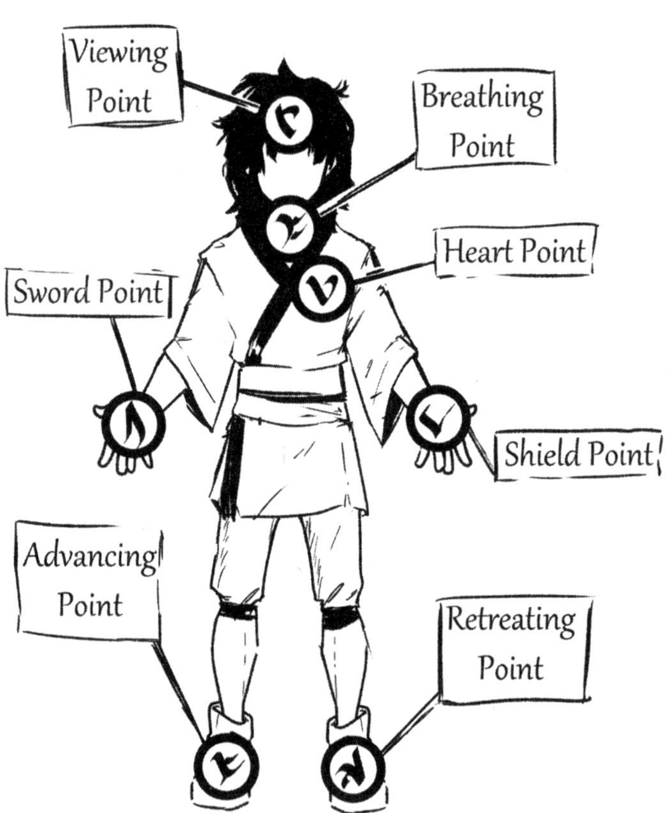

- The Heart Point in the chest is the center of the essence structure, influencing all other points to a limited degree by spreading some of the essence there to every other Dianis Point. In essence (hah!) it seems like the Heart Point can link to other Dianis Points to create the local equivalent of deep dominions from prime dominion essence types.
    - It may be more complicated than that . . . their essence types seem to exceed the variety of dominions. They have complex compound essence types that derive from more than one prime type. I'll write more on this later.
    - The Heart Point is the first Dianis Point humans seem to develop, and the essence chosen for the Heart Point is one of the most integral for long-term development.
- The Viewing Point is in the center of the head. Essence formed in the Viewing Point influences perception.
    - For example, someone who accumulates flame essence in their Viewing Point develops the ability to sense heat, allowing them to perceive people in the dark. Useful, at least for those people who don't have sight sorcery.
- The Breathing Point is in the neck. The Breathing Point determines how a person draws in essence, making it arguably the most important of the Dianis Points.
- The Sword Point in the dominant hand allows the essence within it to be used for direct offensive techniques.
    - For example, holding ice essence within the Sword Point allows someone to form icicle weapons or hurl shards of ice at their opponents.
- The Shield Point in the offhand is the defensive mirror to the Sword Point, allowing the essence within to be used for defensive purposes.
- The Advancing Point in the dominant foot is the principal point for movement techniques, such as increasing speed and agility.
- The Retreating Point in the other foot allows for the essence within to be used for stealth, concealment, and other forms of defensive motion.

Essence manifests in a truly staggering number of varieties in the natural environment here. I am still uncertain about the mechanisms behind this, although Edge has mentioned "breaches" — locations where there is a connection between our world and other dominions — and I believe these may play a critical role. Moreover, I have noted that although elementals exist on this continent, there is a distinct absence of Harvester and Gatherer classifications of elementals. It is possible that essence nodes would manifest naturally in areas of high essence concentration on other continents as well, but that these elemental subtypes prevent that from occurring. This may warrant some experimentation when I return home, or at a minimum, some further research during my stay here.

I intend to see if I'm capable of completing Dianis Points myself, but first . . . I need to make some hard choices.

And on that note, I will leave you in suspense, Auntie. If you want to know what else I find, well, you can send me reinforcements.

Otherwise, hope that I don't die.

Yours in service,
Scribe

APPENDIX II

TYPES OF ESSENCE

From Lien's Perspective

Essence can be found in innumerable varieties. Many of these correspond to the dominions found in the stars, but others are much more specialized, having been born from the convergence of numerous features of the core plane.

While most essence types are strongly associated with natural environments, essence motes can (and do) come into existence anywhere. Populated areas tend to be sources for variants on life essence, essence from building materials, and various mental and perception-focused essence types. The sheer number of people present in these areas means that there is more competition for this essence, however, and thus motes that manifest are generally found and collected before they can collect into powerful cores.

Most essence users choose to build their own essence based on types they personally have access to. For example, forest fae will generally gather life, wood, and similar essences from their own environment. A blacksmith might gather the forge essence that manifests from their own work, either to use it to increase their own abilities or to sell to someone wealthy. Nobles often spend tremendous sums purchasing cores for their chosen essence types.

Many types of essence correspond to what are found in the dominions referred to in Mythralian sorcery. There are many other types, however, which we refer to in a couple different ways.

Specialized versions of dominion essence types exist. These are called essence aspects. Aspects can be divided into three categories: form, feature, and function.

For example, iron, silver, and steel are all metal form aspects. Oak and teak would be valid wood form essence aspects.

Hardness and luster are metal feature aspects.

Magnetism is a metal function aspect.

More specialized essence types are harder to find but can be more powerful in some situations.

Skyseekers are taught not to bother with these unless those types would provide a clear advantage: for example, silver or diamond might be worth taking, but oak is generally too niche to bother with.

Specialties that have strong, broad concepts are better options. For example, rather than taking protection, armor or shield would both be strong alternative options for specializing.

There are also complex combinations of essence called hybrid essences. These involve combinations of two deep dominions, three prime dominions, or even broader mixtures.

For example, metal combined with ruin creates rust essence.

Combining spirit and communication creates bonding essence.

And so on.

Hybrid essences exist in thousands of varieties. Virtually any combination of essence types can form a hybrid, although some essence types have better compatibility with each other and merge more easily. Hybrid essences can also consist of other hybrid essences, or combinations of hybrid and nonhybrid essence types.

A clear example would be my own sword essence. Sword essence consists of weapon essence, which is in itself a hybrid essence, combined with sharpness essence (an aspect essence of enhancement), and purpose essence (an aspect of another hybrid essence type).

Weapon essence itself consists of battle essence (which Mythralians call retribution essence and Kaldwynians call dawn essence), tool essence (a combination of purpose essence, enhancement essence, and stone essence), and some more purpose essence.

And then if you go even further, battle essence is a combination of fire and enhancement.

So sword essence is complicated. Many hybrid essences are like that — Uncle Eiji's storm essence combines rain, air, thunder, and lightning, for example. As a general rule, the more hyperspecific an essence, the more component parts it has, and the more difficult it is to find organically occurring in nature.

As a result, someone who wants to use one of these unusual types has to find or make locations where very specific conditions are met. This is an entire field of study in itself, but the summary is "Find a place where there's a lot of that specific thing and very little competition."

This is obviously easier said than done, since rare essences are inherently valuable. Swords do not, in most locations of the world, grow on trees (although we've been earnestly working at that for a while, back at home).

Given that fully manifested nodes of these hybrid types are so hard to find, it's often easier to take alternative approaches to gathering them. The most common of these is the use of a Breathing Point, which can allow you to absorb and process ambient essence that is not in large enough quantities to manifest a node. This is absolutely integral to the development of essence for anyone serious about the prospect of advancement, and it's the reason why many people choose a Breathing Point that matches their Heart Point.

Another major method is to assemble the essence you're looking for from component parts. This is generally viable only after you have at least some of that essence type in the body to use as a blueprint, but after that, you can learn to gather the component essence types and merge them together within yourself to create a target hybrid essence. For example, I could gather weapon essence, sharpness essence, and purpose essence, and then mash them together into sword essence. This is the only viable route for advancement with some truly esoteric essence types, but fortunately, sword essence isn't so scarce that it is a strict requirement for me.

Finally, it's possible to take some of the usable essence out of a Dianis Point and compress it into the container itself. This is called primary essence conversion, and it's a very slow process, but it can be done as a means of continuing to improve your Dianis Points when no other essence is available for absorption.

APPENDIX III

LIEN'S SWORD TECHNIQUES

From Scribe's Perspective

Lien described a number of sword techniques throughout his story, as well as what he referred to as "proto-techniques," meaning ones that he had not finished developing to full functionality. I'm noting these for future reference. While I do not intend to attempt to reproduce these, it's always wise to be aware of the capabilities of one's traveling companions — even if I suspect that some of his tales may be a hint exaggerated.

- **Ultimate Blade Creation** — A proto-technique for conjuring a sword to use in combat.
- **Sword Hand** — Lien's elementary technique for forming a blade of essence. Rather than just being a raw manifestation of sword essence, he crafts it from a "sandwich" of different sword aspects, creating an approximation of a sword blade that can cut, thrust, and repel other blades.
    - **Sealed Sword Creation** — A combination of his Sword Hand technique, his Ultimate Blade Creation technique, and the essence from his sealed hand. Conjures a powerful two-handed sword that mirrors the form of a sword that is familiar to him.
- **Sword Sharpening Shroud** — A technique for wrapping a weapon in a field of cutting energy. Like his Sword Hand technique, this is more complex than it sounds, involving multiple layers, but it's designed not to repel weapons and instead allows both the sword essence and the blade within to deal damage.
    - My strong suspicion is that he has also developed a variation on this technique that heavily emphasizes the "hardness" aspect of

sword essence that he spoke of. This would help explain how I have seen him cut things with seemingly impossible objects, like a strand of wheat — the hardness aspect would theoretically allow the object within the field to remain stable while the cutting field tears through whatever is around it. This is purely speculative on my part based on the abilities he has already explained to me; it's possible that he has an entirely different technique for that purpose, or that his wheat-wielding was simply misdirection for some other type of attack that I was not capable of perceiving.

- **Shattering Sword** — Lien's supposed "signature" technique, at least for the week he made it. This involves taking a Sword Sharpening Shroud and splitting it into halves deliberately, then using deflection essence just before impact to blast the blades of essence outward. This theoretically creates three or more points of impact for the slash, rather than a single one. This sounds useful both for inflicting damage at multiple points in a single attack, which is obviously useful in itself, but also for the potential to strike an opponent's arm when they are parrying an attack, or otherwise damaging an opponent from unlikely angles. Given the split nature of the attack, the damage at any individual impact point is more limited than a focused attack would be, but likely still considerable.
    - **Shattering Sheath** — A variation on the Shattering Sword technique. This version of the technique involves Lien creating a layer of scabbard essence to "charge up" his attack inside, and then before impact he converts it into a slashing aspect. The result is an explosive release of sword essence in several directions simultaneously. If Lien weren't seemingly immune to his own essence, this probably would have killed him repeatedly. As it is, I'm glad I know he has this, because it means I know to stand very far away from him any time he gets into a fight.
    - **Star Shattering Sword** — A variation of the technique that incorporates forms of breach essence in order to damage a target's star veins and Dianis Points. The effects can range from temporarily reducing a target's ability to use essence in that location to being completely debilitating.
- **Draw Sword** — A technique used for converting sword essence flowing through star veins directly into secondary essence used by the body. To do this without causing himself absolutely absurd amounts of pain, he creates a protective barrier of scabbard-aspected sword essence around the rest of the essence, then "draws" it into himself. This is the

only technique that Lien has demonstrated that I believe I may be able to learn directly from — not that I intend to use sword essence, but if I begin to develop any analogous essence type, the core concept behind it might be applicable to any form of secondary essence development. Of course, that would require building up a Dianis Point or two first . . .

- **Star Sharpening** — Lien's technique for splitting essence in his star veins into component parts, then eliminating the unwanted essence types. While he claims to have recorded his methodology for doing this, I'm dubious as to how easily it could be replicated by a typical sword essence wielder. His process appeared to involve the unusual essence type from his strange sword bond, which may or may not be a typical aspect of sword essence. Hm. Perhaps if I had access to that technique scroll, as well as some scrolls demonstrating the composition of standard sword essence, I could compare them to reverse engineer the composition of his more unusual essence type . . . from there . . . yes, there's potential in this idea. But I'm digressing, and that's poor form for a scholar, even a humble scribe.
- **Star Shattering Sight** — A breach essence technique that allows Lien to visualize Dianis Points and star veins in the body. A companion technique to Star Shattering Sword, this is used first in order for Lien to see his targets, and then he uses the sword technique to strike them.

APPENDIX IV

CHARACTERS

From Lien's Perspective

A list of our intrepid heroes:

- **Lien**, our protagonist. That's me, although most of the locals call me Edge, or more formally Edge of the Woods. That latter part is a title that I earned for my service to the local faerie court. And speaking of faeries, up next we have . . .
- **Ana**, a xiphiad, better known as a sword faerie. "Ana" is short for "Anathema," the name of the sword she was born from. Technically, her name is also Anathema, but no one reasonable calls her that, except for . . .
- **Gramps**, the old man who raised me. He's some kind of weird ancient Skyseeker or something. I don't know his whole deal. I don't think he's my real grandfather, but he raised me after my parents were apparently killed in a suspiciously typical Dark Lord–style murder thing. I'd probably be more upset about it if I remembered them. As it is, well . . . Gramps is my only real family. I suspected he has a close connection of some kind with . . .
- **Erik Tarren**, legendary scholar and world traveler. I grew up with lots of books he wrote. I strongly suspected that he might be might be in my family, too, or my grandfather's actual identity. I didn't have any other immediate family, but I've was always close to . . .
- **Uncle Eiji**, an ancient shape-changing demi-beast, who basically serves as a second (and much nicer) paternal figure. He's still super old and crochety at times, but at least he brings me stuff from the outside world, like cool trinkets. And, more importantly, news. Oh, and I suppose that means that his kids are family, too, like . . .

- **Auntie Temper**, who isn't actually Eiji's mate — though I'm sure they'd both be hugely amused by *that* idea — but she's still my aunt and my family. She runs the Ghost Forge, a smithy that serves as home to many spirit-bonded weapons that were damaged or abandoned after a disastrous war between humans and faeries. She's an exile from faerie culture, and thus, she naturally gets along great with other strange people like Eiji and me. She occasionally gets visits from a few other faeries in spite of being banished, like one of my mischievous little friends . . .
- **Lindt**, a faerie with the appearance of a tiny ten-year-old boy, who loves to wander out of where he's supposed to be.
- **Eliree**, my first love. Half dryad, bound to a mysterious tree outside the normal faerie lands. She's also a potent healer.
- **Current**, a naiad, and Flow's twin. Doesn't appear in this story, but I thought about the twins next, so I'm writing them down anyway.
- **Flow**, a naiad, and Current's twin.
- **Verthrimax the Iron Breaker**, a great and powerful dragon who was blinded protecting the forest hundreds of years ago. If the faerie queen is the queen of the forest, he'd be the king. I mean, not in a "they're a married couple" sense. Probably? I don't ask questions about that sort of thing. Anyway, he's ancient. Maybe . . . too ancient. I worry about him.
- **The Willowbark Witch**, a powerful practitioner of foreign magic and alchemy who lives on the eastern side of the woods, along with her children:
- **Belladonna**, the oldest child at roughly twenty and a full witch.
- **Cascade**, a few years my elder and an ocean witch.
- **Darryl**, just a few weeks older than me and a shadow witch. The only male witch in the family.
- **Flare**, a few months younger than me and a fire witch.
- **Root**, eight years old and an earth and crystal witch.
- **Poppy**, a five-year-old with a talent for plant magic.
- **Blink**, the youngest child at three years of age, and possibly a ghost. An actual ghost, though — not an echo, like . . .
- **Gray**, the echo of a small child at an abandoned sword school. Extraordinary talent for his age.
- **Fade**, the echo of a teenaged girl with fading green hair at an abandoned sword school. Dexterity and trickery-based fighting style.
- **Green**, the echo of an adult swordsman at an abandoned sword school. Strength-based combat style, with skill at both swords and unarmed fighting.

- **Red**, the echo of an adult swordswoman at an abandoned sword school. Impossibly skilled, impeccable technique.
- **The Smiling Sword Saint**, a historical master of swordsmanship who died in a legendary duel with her rival hundreds of years ago. I discovered an echo of her at an ancient arena and sought her training, with mixed results. She eventually conjured another echo . . .
- **Thane**, a younger copy of the Smiling Sword Saint, forged from her memories. Manifests as male, since the sword saint presented as male when she was younger. Still prefers to be referred to as male at his current age.
- **Lance Rival**, a . . . probably(?) human Skyseeker who came to visit the Sepulcher of Sealed Swords for some kind of pilgrimage. Looks about my age, but he's colossally tall, even without his spiked purple hair. Tremendous strength and speed. Believes I'll one day be his rival, which sounds like it could be pretty exciting, even if it would make Ana jealous.
- **Vantonio**, the ghost of a curator of the Sepulcher of Sealed Swords.
- **Dream Girl**, a young woman who appeared during my Destiny Dream, wielding a strange all-metal spear and wearing armor of green leaves. She had one golden eye and one silver eye in the dream, as well as unnatural blond hair that revealed black or red near the roots. I . . . think I know her somehow, but I don't know how. She seemed to be after my sword. No, not like *that*. Okay, maybe like that, too — she was kind of a flirt. Anyway, I don't know what happened to her after the dream, but I have some ideas, now. And speaking of the present, I just met someone interesting . . .
- **Scribe**, a human from the continent of Mythralis that I met while traveling between human cities. Given that he uses an *S* name, has illusion magic, and is from Mythralis, it's incredibly obvious that he has some kind of connection to the legendary . . .
- **Aayara Haven**, the Lady of Thieves. Demigoddess and child of one of the gods of the continent of Mythralis. Also known as Symphony, she famously runs an organized crime syndicate known as the Orchestra with influence on several continents, likely including my own. The fact that cities that are safe from monsters are called Havens has not escaped my notice.

APPENDIX V

DESTINY MARKS

An excerpt from An Analysis of Destiny Mark Acquisition and Bloodline Power Inheritance, by Erik Tarren:

Destiny marks are the signature of the Torch-level of essence development. Numerically, Torch is the second level (after Candle), although many organizations consider it the first "true" level because of the significance of the mark itself and refer to Candle as "level zero." This artificial distinction helps to demonstrate the cultural impact of the destiny mark — without one, a person is not generally considered a real essence wielder.

In some cultures, the destiny mark is also seen as a symbol of adulthood. This can cause significant difficulties in areas where essence is not abundant, and therefore "adult" status can be difficult to reach — often requiring a coming-of-age ritual to seek out significant sources of essence in the wild to harness for power.

In modern times, such rituals are uncommon, given that the environmental dangers outside of Havens vastly outstrip the capabilities of low-level essence wielders. Instead, reaching Torch-level at a relatively young age is seen as a mark of status and ambition. This has led to some unusual opportunities for commoners and newly minted nobles to outshine more prominent noble families because of the interaction between essence development and bloodlines. This will be discussed in greater detail later in the book, but the simple summary is that having a bloodline power slows essence development at young ages, requiring extreme resources and unusual training methods to allow those with a bloodline power to keep pace with those who do not.

The most important determining factor in acquiring a destiny mark is essence. Completed Dianis Points in the body are the main determining factor in which destiny marks are available through a Destiny Dream, although other factors may also influence this (see Chapter XXXV, "Destiny Dreams," for more on this).

It is commonly believed that many of the rarer marks, such as the Paladin destiny mark, are not available to anyone who has several disqualifying essence types, such as darkness or fear essence. For this reason, essence selection for the purpose of working toward a specific destiny can be complex, and many essence wielders cautiously limit which essence types they build.

Destiny marks have levels, much as essence wielders do — three levels corresponding to the Core Self, three for the Destined Self . . . then things get more complex, as you deal with things like the Dream Self. This is far more advanced, and outside the scope of this introductory chapter. Most people never reach the level where they are interacting with their Dream Self through their marks, which is likely why the marks are still called destiny marks, rather than a more accurate name, like Extrapolated Self Marks. For more on the later layers, I recommend *Hartigan's Treatise on the Advanced Manipulation of Post-Destiny Selves*, ideally the second edition, as I find that his third edition introduces too much speculation.

After a destiny mark has been gained, additional essence types can be developed in Dianis Points without impacting the mark — at least at the earlier phases of essence development. It is possible for a destiny mark to change into a more advanced form of mark if certain prerequisites are reached, but this is complex, and almost always purely advantageous.

In the past, it was very possible to acquire more than one destiny mark, though you will only ever gain one through your Destiny Dream. Additional marks can be earned through trials in various crystal shrines, but these shrines have long been isolated, destroyed, or otherwise lost. In those rare cases where someone is still able to earn multiple marks, it is possible to switch which destiny you are currently primarily using. This is called "changing your destiny," and it involves switching which destiny is currently connected to your Heart Point. You can only have one destiny connected to your Heart Point at any time, and this is the only destiny you will fully benefit from. You may learn to connect other destinies to other Dianis Points as well, but you will only receive lesser benefits from each, which are related to the Dianis Point's specific properties. For example, connecting a destiny to your Breathing Point allows it to continue to improve over time, much like if it was your primary destiny, but you will not be able to actively use the full benefits of the mark.

Some organizations still actively pursue the acquisition of additional destiny marks. These people are collectively referred to as Shrineseekers, although Shrineseekers can belong to many different organizations — the Explorer's Guild being the most famous.

More on additional destiny mark acquisition as well as crystal shrines can be found in Dianis's *The Pursuit of Destiny*, Volumes 1–3.

Destinies exist in a wide variety of forms. While the most commonly discussed are those used for combat, such as Fighter and Wizard, these aren't the most frequently obtained. The vast majority of destiny marks are simple profession-based marks, such as Farmer, Cook, and Merchant. These are obtained by forming Dianis Point combinations related to the profession — for example, a farmer might have Dianis Points consisting of food essence, growth essence, and harvesting essence.

I say "might" because there are many ways to reach the same destiny. While there are generally estimated to be a few hundred destinies, there are at least tens of thousands of types of essence and millions of possible permutations of essence combinations. Thus, there are many different ways to end up with the same destiny.

In addition to essence types in Dianis Points, there are ways that a person's essence can be influenced by outside factors, such as spirit bonds and ancestral curses, but those are so rare that they are difficult to study and account for. Please see the chapters on these individual topics for more information.

Because of the differing scarcity of specific essence types, as well as the frequency in availability of some specific combinations of essence, different destiny marks can have hugely variable degrees of rarity. For this reason, major organizations use a letter-based rarity system for describing the rarity of any individual destiny. This ranking system begins at E, for the most common, and advances to D, C, B, A, and finally S, the rarest category of destiny mark. There's some discussion in the scholarly community of using even more obscure rankings for seemingly unique marks, but that has yet to be settled at the time of this writing.

Rarity does not always translate to power or usefulness. A hybrid destiny like Fire Wizard may be rarer than a standard Wizard, but their narrower focus in abilities comes at a cost of flexibility. Moreover, rarity does not even always imply specialization — some destinies are simply rare because it is unusual for any one individual to gather two or more completely divergent essence types, or because they are using an essence type that is considered suboptimal for their chosen profession. For example, it would be rare to find someone who uses both fruit essence and war essence. I can only speculate about what kind of strange destiny this would lead to, as I have never seen such a combination chosen.

The following section includes descriptions of many destiny types. This is not by any means exhaustive; it is merely a selection of some specific destiny marks that are common, useful, or noteworthy.

Worker

Essence Requirements: None.

Rarity Level: E

Signature Ability: Keep Working — When this ability is used, the Worker gains a resurgence of stamina and focus, allowing them to maintain exhausting tasks for a much longer period of time. Unlike many similar abilities, this does not appear to have major costs for repeated uses, though like any signature ability, it uses a portion of the connected essence pool, and thus, it can only be used a limited number of times in any given day. This ability makes Workers popular for exhausting tasks, as one might expect.

Description: The only destiny with no known requirements. This is effectively the "default" destiny and can be achieved by anyone, regardless of essence type. There are even a few amusing tales of noble children accidentally stumbling upon this destiny in their dreams — well, amusing as an outsider. I'm certain that the child and their family found the event somewhat less funny.

In spite of being extremely common — and directly associated with commoners, which attributes a certain stigma — it's generally agreed by scholars that the Worker destiny is actually extremely useful. Not only does a signature ability that improves stamina have myriad applications and broad utility, the other abilities granted by the Worker destiny are similarly focused on improving routine daily tasks, such as improved focus, improved sleep efficiency, and improved recovery speed. Not only do these benefits allow for better performance in the majority of professions, but the reduced toll on the body can help improve the destined's day-to-day life.

Farmer

Essence Requirements: Any essence type related to domesticated animals, herbs, vegetables, fruit, and so on. In addition, general essence types such as growth essence, harvesting essence, herbal essence, and similar types can meet these requirements.

Rarity Level: D

Signature Ability: Improve Growth — The Farmer has an embedded technique that can be used to imbue essence into a crop to improve the crop's rate of growth, health, and quality. As the Farmer grows stronger, this provides greater benefits to the crop.

Description: Among the most common destinies, the Farmer helps improve the production rate and quality of crops. Additional abilities can help improve the chances that crops will survive extreme weather conditions. Higher-level Farmers gain abilities that are tied to sensing the health of plants and animals, as well as detecting shifts in weather before they occur. Even higher-level Farmers have been known to obtain abilities related to improving the growth and health of domesticated animals as well, though these are more poorly documented.

Hunter

Essence Requirements: Tracking essence, bow essence, any predatory animal essence, trap essence, or any similar essence type.

Rarity Level: D

Signature Ability: Sense Path — An extremely useful sensory ability, Sense Path is an embedded technique that highlights all forms of tracks and trails in the Hunter's perception with varying degrees of brightness, depending on how much essence remains on each trail. This is a deceptively potent technique and notoriously difficult to emulate simply by using tracking essence itself, because of the extremely low essence cost compared to conventional techniques, the fidelity of the brightness differentiation, and certain additional features, such as the technique automatically shifting to enhance senses other than sight if needed by the user.

Description: While the Hunter's iconic ability has clear utility for finding prey in the wild, as one might expect, it also has other important uses in the modern era. First, it can be used to identify the tracks of threats in a region, such as local monsters, and how old the tracks are. This is extremely important for avoiding such threats during a simple hunt for food and equally useful for directly hunting monsters when needed.

Notably, this can also be used to track ordinary people — meaning Hunters are also extremely helpful for finding lost children, tracking thieves and escaped prisoners, and other similar tasks.

Finally, Sense Path can be used on occasion to find obscure pathways, such as secret doorways inside dungeons, or obscure entrances into ancient ruins.

Merchant

Essence Requirements: Any essence with a financial component, such as greed essence, trade essence, gold essence, and so on.

Rarity Level: D

Signature Ability: Appraise — A potent sensory technique, Appraise allows the Merchant to identify certain characteristics of an object at a glance, such as the condition and materials of an object. Higher levels of Merchants can also identify magical properties, detect forgeries, and even use this ability to see an estimated value. There are entire scholarly essays dedicated to guessing how that last function actually works, given that it appears to somewhat accurately account for market conditions and fluctuations.

Description: As one might expect, Merchants develop other skills related to the purchase, sale, and evaluation of goods. Nearly every profession benefits from a connection to one or more people with the Merchant destiny, especially at higher levels, when Merchants are capable of identifying essence types on sight.

Explorer

Essence Requirements: Motion essence, travel essence, walking essence, running essence, climbing essence, or a similar essence type.

Rarity Level: D

Signature Ability: Sure Step — While activated, this ability massively improves balance and coordination, as well as providing a smaller bonus to speed, strength, and perception speed. This allows for generally improved athletics while active but most clearly improves tasks related to movement, such as climbing up mountainsides, jumping across gaps, and avoiding traps.

Description: The abilities of Explorers, much like those of Workers, are deceptively useful for how easily they can be obtained. Not only does Sure Step provide benefits for nearly any physical task, but the other abilities gained by higher-level Explorers provide similar benefits to balance, coordination, and general physical ability. High-level Explorers may not have the flashy combat abilities of traditional combatants, but they are remarkably adept at handling the many physical challenges and puzzles found in ancient dungeons and crystal shrines.

Fighter

Essence Requirements: Any combat-focused essence type, such as combat essence itself, war essence, or any form of weapon-specific essence.

Rarity Level: D

Signature Ability: Walk It Off — A similar function to the Worker's Keep Working ability in many respects, Walk It Off allows for continuing an activity well beyond the point where it would normally be incapacitating — but rather than actually restoring stamina like Keep Working does, Walk It Off simply suppresses negative effects temporarily. This makes it less ideal for simply continuing tasks for a long period of time, but it is much more broadly applicable, as Walk It Off allows for the suppression of a much wider variety of issues — the pain from injuries, fear, paralysis, and other debilitating effects. At higher levels, this can make a Fighter truly terrifying, as they're capable of simply ignoring massive wounds for extended periods of time — but they often collapse as soon as the ability ends.

Description: The Fighter is the "default" combat destiny. If one does not plan their early essence development, it is easy to end up as a Fighter simply by not having one of the exact essence combination types for a rarer destiny.

The iconic ability of the Fighter is useful for responding to a variety of circumstances. Much like the Worker, a Fighter can perform tasks for an extended period of time because of their Walk It Off ability, though this requires active use on the Fighter's part. The main advantage to Walk It Off is that it can be used in response to necessity, allowing it to function as a counter to many problems, such as debilitating spells and techniques, unexpected injuries, or exhaustion.

Rogue

Essence Requirements: Stealth essence, lockpicking essence, deception essence, or similar types.

Rarity Level: D

Signature Ability: Stealth — One of the most well-known and feared destiny abilities, Stealth allows the Rogue to blend in with their surroundings, making them harder to notice. At higher levels, this goes beyond camouflage and can make the Rogue entirely invisible, as well as hide them from other senses.

Description: While often associated with thieves, spies, and assassins — and indeed, many of them do use this destiny — the Rogue is also extraordinarily useful for other tasks. Rogues often pair well with Hunters for tracking and ambushing game animals as well as avoiding monster threats. They also make incredible general scouts for both armies and exploration-focused groups, such as Shrineseekers.

Healer

Essence Requirements: Life essence, healing essence, curing essence, or similar essence types.

Rarity Level: C

Signature Ability: Diagnose — While certain forms of magical healing can deal with injuries directly, more obscure issues — especially things like disease and poison — cannot be accurately treated without proper identification. Diagnose is a simple but powerful tool for determining any maladies affecting an individual. At early levels, Diagnose primarily identifies injuries and simple diseases, but at higher levels, it can provide staggering levels of detailed information about conditions that the target is suffering from.

Description: The very existence of this destiny puts the quality of life in many cities on Dania well above that of other continents, especially for those who are afflicted by long-term maladies that would frequently go unidentified in other countries. Healers are not as common as many of the preceding destinies, but there are still generally several in every major city, and often one can be found even in smaller towns — frequently in positions of prominence, because of their utility. Healers are highly respected, and for good reason.

Martial Artist

Essence Requirements: Any combat focused essence type, as well as discipline essence, meditation essence, focus essence, or a similar essence type.

Rarity Level: C+

Signature Ability: Battle Meditation — Accelerates the Martial Artist's perception, seeming to slow the battlefield to allow the Martial Artist time to consider actions. At higher levels, Martial Artists gain enhanced predictive abilities, sometimes described as being able to see the next several moves in a battle before they occur.

Description: A fantastic option for potential combatants, with some limited usability for noncombat applications, such as sports. However, some higher-level Martial Artist abilities have an unarmed combat focus, limiting the utility of the destiny for other forms of combatants.

Wizard

Essence Requirements: Prime essence.

Rarity Level: C+

Signature Ability: Spellcasting — This lets you cast spells by saying specific preexisting incantations. Simple, no? Hah, obviously not. Such a function cannot possibly exist without significant complexity and major downsides.

This is perhaps the least understood function among the relatively common destinies, even among people with the destiny itself, and for good reason. The underlying functions of this destiny push the limits of what destiny marks are capable of, providing a simply staggering variety of abilities for someone who is willing to study.

First, the basic description of the function is true enough. If you know the words to speak, the Spellcasting function attempts to generate a specific effect. Typically, Wizards learn these specific verbal incantations from other Wizards, although many can also be found in books, scrolls, and a variety of other written formats. It's also common for Wizards to see a few incantations in their Destiny Dream when they select the Wizard destiny, which allows them to begin with a few spells, provided they remember the dream.

The Spellcasting ability functions by taking advantage of the requisite essence type for the destiny — prime essence. Prime essence — also known as "gray mana" or "primary essence" — is a combination of all twelve prime dominion essence types. The Wizard destiny takes advantage of the "rule of single step abstractions." This rule indicates that essence can generally be converted into any essence that is only one step removed from it. Spellcasting allows the Wizard to convert prime essence into any of the component parts, allowing for the generation of a massive variety of spells.

This may sound so flexible that it immediately outperforms all other destinies — and, indeed, there are many that find the Wizard destiny to be one of the most useful of all destinies, especially among those with access to spell books and scrolls. The fame of this destiny is why it is relatively common in spite of the comparative difficulty to find prime essence — wealthy people often buy prime essence for their children, and thus there is a massive market for wizards to make and sell it. Notably, this also means that people from less wealthy families may attempt to earn the Wizard destiny simply for the purpose of eventually making more prime essence to sell. Generating your own essence isn't easy for most destinies, but Wizards have a fairly common spell for it, which in itself is a massive incentive to take the destiny.

Much could be said about the overabundance of Wizards compared to natural essence scarcity, and it has been said in other places — but in spite of the popularity of this destiny, one must understand that it has real and significant limitations.

The conversion of essence from prime essence to any individual prime dominion type is extremely inefficient. When converting essence between types, there's always a loss based on how similar the base type is from the target essence type. Generally, a one-step conversion of an individual type to a similar type, such as fire to heat, results in about a twenty-five percent loss. Prime essence, however, contains twelve parts — one of which is identical to the target type, two of which are similar, six of which are distant, and three of which are impossible to convert. Without going into a tremendous amount of math, converting prime essence back into any individual essence type that it is composed of results in the loss of over half of the original essence.

This means that a Wizard's spells are more than twice as expensive, in terms of eventual essence cost, as simply creating a technique from the original essence type.

For many, this efficiency loss is worthwhile because of the flexibility offered by the destiny — but even this flexibility is not without limits. A Wizard is limited by the spells they are able to learn, and powerful spell incantations are often kept carefully hidden by specific guilds and organizations.

Moreover, a Wizard's spells are limited to being constructed from prime dominion essence types — at least at first. Higher-level Wizards can create deep dominion spells, but most Wizards never reach this stage.

Finally, Spellcasting has the natural limitation of requiring verbal components. This renders the destiny almost impossible to use for people without the ability to speak, as well as specific species that do not have the capability to easily form the specific sounds that are used for the words of spells. Moreover, since the destiny works from specific prewritten spells, it can be predictable in combat situations, especially for experienced combatants. There are workarounds for all these difficulties, but they can be complex and challenging.

Description: In spite of the limitations of the Spellcasting function, Wizards are an extremely potent destiny and strongly recommended for anyone looking for flexibility. Several basic spell examples are listed in the appendix to this book, and others can be found in the companion volumes *Exploring Your Destiny*, Volumes 1–3.

Vanguard

Essence Requirements: Any weapon essence and shield or armor essence.

Rarity Level: C

Signature Ability: Deflection — Forms a portion of the Vanguard's essence into a protective layer around their body, reducing the damage they suffer from attacks.

Description: The Vanguard is the quintessential defender for any group, often putting themself in the way of harm to shelter their allies from harm. At high levels, a Vanguard can wade through the assaults of weaker monsters or lower-level essence wielders without suffering any harm. At higher levels, the Vanguard develops a passive version of their Deflection ability, allowing them to be defended even while asleep — a function that has no doubt saved a variety of Vanguards from would-be assassins and other threats.

Duelist

Essence Requirements: Sword or dagger essence and at least one essence of the following: dexterity, reflex, agility, cunning.

Rarity Level: C

Signature Ability: Duelist's Dance — Vastly improves the Duelist's combat reflexes and speed, allowing them to dodge, deflect, and disarm with grace and ease.

Description: As one might expect, the Duelist is a popular option for single combat. While the benefits of the Duelist are similar to those of the

Explorer, they provide a larger benefit in a shorter burst, and the function is more heavily skewed toward speed and agility. Outside combat, Duelists are often professional athletes, although the reflexes of the Duelist also make them excellent as a replacement or supplement for Rogues at the role of disarming traps and picking locks.

Berserker

Essence Requirements: Any weapon essence and at least one essence of the following: anger, rage, conquest.

Rarity Level: C

Signature Ability: Rage — The Berserker is capable of burning massive amounts of essence in a burst, increasing their strength and endurance drastically for a short time, while also suppressing pain and providing resistance to certain debilitating effects.

Description: The Berserker is an excellent destiny choice for warriors who want to be able to fight powerful individual monsters — or groups of smaller ones — that would be beyond their ordinary capabilities. This is often necessary in extremely dangerous regions of the world where a young essence wielder may otherwise be helpless in the face of any enemies they encounter. In spite of the terrifying name, a Berserker does not always lose control when using their signature "Rage" ability — while this can happen, it is possible and common to train to retain control, at which point this ability is limited only by how quickly it drains the Berserker's essence.

Ranger

Essence Requirements: Any weapon essence and at least one essence of the following: plant, animal, tree, nature.

Rarity Level: B

Signature Ability: Nature Bond — A Ranger has a strong tie to the natural world. This allows them to form spirit bonds with plants and animals at an earlier-than-standard level of essence development. Perhaps more impressively, it also allows for the Ranger to bond more than one creature to a single Dianis Point, allowing for a larger-than-standard variety of spirit bonds, as well as complex relationships with these bonded entities.

Description: The Ranger serves as an excellent destiny for martially oriented essence wielders who are focused on hunting, exploration, or kinship with nature. A Ranger is frequently an integral part of any group that seeks out ancient ruins lost among the wilds, serving as both a guide through dangerous plants and a potential diplomat to intelligent beasts. At higher levels, Rangers are passively protected from certain natural threats, such as poison and venom, and have enhanced senses related to environmental dangers.

Knight

Essence Requirements: Any weapon essence and at least one essence of the following: valor, glory, honor, riding.

Rarity Level: B

Signature Ability: Challenge — The Knight's signature feature provides them with powerful temporary benefits when challenging a single target. This also incorporates an attracting effect on that target, drawing their attention toward the Knight, which is amusingly quite similar to the much less renowned Brawler destiny's Taunt ability. While Challenge is active, the Knight gains a variety of enhanced combat abilities, such as strength, speed, and resistance to magic. The principal downside is that this destiny burns through essence extremely quickly, leading to exhaustion in the aftermath of a challenge. In earlier days, this was frequently paired with destinies like Fighter or even Worker to compensate for this downside — but alas, such is no longer likely because of the loss of so many shrines.

Description: The Knight is a popular destiny for noble warriors, because of the prestige associated with the title and their potency in limited-duration combat situations, such as duels and tournaments. Knights are (unfortunately) also often employed to hunt down wild mages and witches, given their somewhat exaggerated reputation for a general resistance to magic.

Weapon Master

Essence Requirements: At least three weapon essence types (e.g. sword essence, spear essence, and axe essence).

Rarity Level: A

Signature Ability: Weapon Mastery — While active, the Weapon Master gains intuitive proficiency with any weapon they pick up, allowing them to wield even the most obscure weapons as if they had significant training.

Description: An unusual destiny, one that allows for an untrained fighter to potentially match the skill level of a trained veteran . . . at least on paper. While this can compensate to some degree for a lack of training, a veteran's instincts will be honed from years of actual training, allowing for better decision making. That said, a Weapon Master's abilities are still supplemented by training, and a Weapon Master with many years of practice is truly a formidable fighter no matter what they are carrying.

Spellsword

Essence Requirements: Any weapon essence and at least one prime dominion essence type.

Rarity Level: C+

Signature Ability: Spellstrike — Allows the Spellsword to infuse a weapon with essence and deliver it through a melee attack. While other destinies can accomplish this through training or specialized techniques, this destiny mark's ability both automates the infusing process and enhances the effect. Higher levels of Spellswords allow for complex weapon bindings, which can store multiple spells simultaneously, alter a stored spell into a persistent effect, or even permanently imbue a weapon with additional power.

Description: A powerful offensive destiny for those who wish to blend combat and magical abilities, with the downside of coming with generally low defensive abilities. Note that contrary to the name of the destiny, this can be obtained and used with any weapon essence, not just bladed weapons.

Breaker

Essence Requirements: Any combat-focused essence type, as well as striking essence, breaking essence, piercing essence, or a similar essence type.

Rarity Level: B

Signature Ability: Breaking Touch — While active, this ability continuously channels essence through the hands, discharging it destructively on contact. This is extremely effective against most forms of physical and magical defense.

Description: An offense-focused variant of the Martial Artist, frequently used by Skyseeker schools that have attack-focused unarmed combat styles. While this is popular for striking-focused hand-to-hand combat, it is limited in utility for any other combat style until higher levels, when it can be used to channel essence through weapons and other objects.

Blademaster

Essence Requirements: Sword essence, no other essence types.

Rarity Level: A

Signature Ability: Sword Instinct — Temporarily improves the wielder's instinctive ability at wielding swords and using sword techniques, allowing even an untrained Blademaster to fight with seemingly preternatural reflexes and skill.

Description: This is a "pure" destiny that requires that the wielder focus exclusively on sword essence. It's a specialized form of the Weapon Master destiny that can only be used with swords but has greater effectiveness when using them. The rarity level does not reflect difficulty in obtaining the destiny but rather a lack of popularity due to the flexibility loss by staying with only a single essence type until reaching Torch-level. The destiny has grown in frequency after the popularization of stories of the Smiling Sword Saint, a legendary Skyseeker who is commonly believed to have used the Blademaster destiny to the point of reaching the Sky level of essence development. In spite of the stories of the Smiling Sword Saint's prowess, modern scholars advise against taking such a focused destiny, as the disadvantages of specialization generally outweigh the benefits of the destiny.

Sword Lord

Essence Requirements: Sword essence and one of the rulership essence types (e.g., rulership, nobility, conquest, or royal essence).

Rarity Level: S

Signature Ability: Conquering Blade — Allows the essence wielder to manipulate the inherent abilities of nearby swords, enhancing the powers of their own weapon or diminishing the properties of enemy blades. At higher levels, this is said to be able to manipulate sword essence on the battlefield as well.

Description: One of the extraordinarily powerful "lord" series of destinies, this is a highly popular target for sword wielders of noble descent. Lord destinies provide both tremendous personal power and, at higher levels, extreme broad-area utility. This is especially true after the establishment of a personal aura at higher essence levels — see the section on essence levels for more on this subject. Because of the well-known potency of this destiny and related destinies (e.g., other lord destinies), all of the rulership essence types are generally hoarded by the highest-ranking nobility, making it extremely difficult for outsiders to obtain this destiny.

Storm Fang

Essence Requirements: Sword essence, storm essence.

Rarity Level: S

Signature Ability: Sword Storm — Allows the user to generate bolts of cutting lightning from the essence wielder's body and weapon, which lash out at enemies. This is especially effective when fighting opponents who are carrying metal, which the cutting lightning will lash out to in order to cut and electrocute whoever is carrying it.

Description: One of the few cases where rarity does translate into combat power, the Storm Fang is considered one of the strongest possible weapon-based destinies. They excel at both offensive combat and area denial, with their Sword Storm making them deadly to even approach for equal-level fighters with metal weapons and armor.

This power comes with two significant downsides. First, activating the Sword Storm has an extreme essence cost, and low-level Storm Fangs often burn through their essence pool so rapidly that they cannot engage in sustained battle.

Perhaps even more important is the scarcity of storm essence itself. Given that storm essence generally only occurs within storm clouds, it is almost unheard of in regions that do not have this type of weather. Even in rainy regions, storm essence is hard to obtain, manifesting only briefly within the clouds themselves. This makes it both difficult and dangerous to obtain. Some locations where lightning strikes can also briefly manifest storm essence, but the risk factors involved in staying in lightning-ravaged regions also make this an unpopular option to pursue.

Paladin

Essence Requirements: Any weapon essence, any divine essence. Certain essence types also disqualify this destiny — notably darkness, fear, death, and nightmares. People with the criteria for Paladin that have one of these essence types are instead qualified for the Dark Knight destiny.

Rarity Level: S

Signature Ability: Divine Power — The Paladin gains abilities determined by the deity that grants them essence. According to legend, this often involved manifesting divine powers in their weapon, being able to conjure a weapon infused with divine power from nothing, or being able to manifest a divine companion.

Description: The Paladin is a "lost" destiny, one we only have myths and legends to draw from to discuss. It is believed that they were anointed as personal weapons of the gods, gaining vast and strange powers based on the deity they served. There is sufficient historical documentation to indicate that such a destiny once existed, but both the destiny itself and the supposed "divine essence" often attributed to it no longer appear to be found within the world. Most scholars believe that this destiny was lost during the fall of the Empyrean Empire. It is listed here for the sake of completeness, but it is not advised for anyone to attempt to seek out this destiny.

Hero

Essence Requirements: Unknown

Rarity Level: S+

Signature Ability: Unknown

Description: Much like the Paladin, the Hero is a lost destiny. Unlike the Paladin, there is some doubt as to whether the Hero destiny ever actually existed, or if it is simply a destiny ascribed retroactively to the leader of the legendary group that defeated and sealed the Ashen Lord. Stories of the requirements and powers of this destiny vary so heavily that attempting to list them all would require an entire separate book (which I, for one, have no intention of writing).

A few characteristics remain common in stories of the Hero destiny. Typically, the Hero is said to be a champion of the helpless, to oppose tyranny, and above all other things, to be brave, even in the face of overwhelming danger. It is this author's opinion that these characteristics share a single key element — they're the types of behaviors that are likely to lead any would-be Hero to an early grave.

For obvious reasons, I do not advise anyone to attempt to seek out the Hero destiny.

ACKNOWLEDGMENTS

Thanks for reading, everyone! Let's get into some inspirations for this story.

This book is my tribute to what I call my "green tunic boys," a surprisingly consistent descriptor for many of my childhood heroes.

It all started with Peter Pan. He was the first story character I really identified with. I remember being thrilled when my mom made me a Peter Pan costume, which I used to participate in a Peter Pan contest at the mall where I grew up. I won the contest, of course. (Take that, four-year-old version of Mallory Reaves.)

(This was, in some respects, the start of my lifelong rivalry with another author, who also participated in that costume contest as an equally young child. But that's a story for another time.)

Anyway, I loved Peter Pan. I loved that costume my mom made me. My dad painted a portrait of me in that costume. I insisted on being depicted with a sword, however, rather than Peter Pan's dagger. Even at that age, I thought swords were cooler . . . probably because of the next couple guys on the list. Thank you to my parents for always encouraging my creativity, with both those things and numerous others.

Just a year or two before that contest, I'd been introduced to the wonders of the Nintendo Entertainment System. The first game we owned was the combo cartridge of *Mario* and *Duck Hunt*, but that didn't ever really interest me.

The game I fell in love with was *The Legend of Zelda*.

I didn't play it at all at first. I watched my older brother and his friends play, carefully paying attention to everything they were doing.

And one day, still around three or four, I picked up the controller and started playing a new game. I'd memorized the locations of everything I could — heart containers, hidden passages containing rupees, the White Sword and the Magic Sword.

I can say without exaggeration that it was a life-altering experience.

From that time onward, poor Peter Pan was eclipsed in importance. I never forgot him, exactly, but Link was my favorite.

And he'd remain my favorite even after I was introduced to the other people on my list. Link is still one of my favorite characters. I'm not ashamed to say that *The Legend of Zelda* is one of the inspirations for virtually everything I write.

But I wasn't done meeting heroes in green tunics.

The next was, perhaps, the most traditional: an archer you've probably heard of by the name of Robin of Locksley. Or, if you're not being a nerd like I am, Robin Hood.

Robin Hood was a large inspiration for my love of the forest, woodsmanship skills, and childhood archery practice. You can see all that in this story, but you also see a somewhat subtler influence: my love for characters with meaningful names. Robin Hood was probably the first character I was introduced to who used a pseudonym based on his own name, as opposed to something like Clark Kent having an unrelated superhero name.

Aside from that, a green-tunic-adjacent fellow named Aragorn was certainly another inspiration for my style. Like many others, I loved *The Lord of the Rings* as a kid, and Aragorn — especially in his Strider persona, as a ranger — was another fantastic model for me to draw from with a ranger-esque foresty protagonist. Moreover, Aragorn was a model for a protagonist who is an excellent swordsman, but still a kindhearted man who is defined less by his martial ability and more by his honor and healing. He is, in many respects, what I feel Edge aspires to be.

Finally, a more obscure one: *Lone Wolf*, from the series of gamebooks by Joe Dever. If you're not familiar, the *Lone Wolf* books are similar to *Choose Your Own Adventure* books, but with a persistent character, skills, items, and statistics. They're basically single-player role-playing games in book form. I found these as an elementary school kid and absolutely loved them.

(Notably, Landen of the Twin Edges in my other books is loosely named after Lone Wolf/Silent Wolf, who has the canonical birth name of Landar.)

Anyway, my green tunic boys have a lot of common elements: surviving in forests, struggling against forces that generally greatly outnumber them, fighting with edged weapons (usually swords, unless you're Peter), and that sort of thing. Peter and Link also have faerie companions, so you've got your source for Ana right there. And three of the five have some kind of magical power that interacts with their swordplay.

So, if you're looking for the main inspirations, look no further. I'd say Peter and Link are the main two, but they're all involved.

Ana is very clearly a Tinkerbell and Navi analogue, but with certain elements of her interactions with Lien heavily influenced by my own childhood games with my dear friend of eternity and occasional rival, Mallory Reaves. She's also the model for Red, but the story behind that is tied into deep elements of Red's backstory that you'll have to wait to learn more about.

Fade is based around a character by Carly Thomas. I'm going to stay vague on this to avoid giving too much about her away, but you'll learn more about that in the future, too.

The witches, Gramps, Auntie Temper, the unseen (for now) Uncle Eiji, and the faerie royalty all owe a great deal to the Noel family. Joshua Noel and Rowan Noel-Williams were two of my closest childhood friends and two of the earliest PCs in my D&D games for this setting. Their parents, Larry and Elys Noel, were also two of the earliest Dungeon Masters who ran games for us when we were kids. Larry and Elys always had an air of magic and mystery about them — in honesty, they still do. I still consider them family.

Also, Rowan and Elys baked me a sword cake. I don't usually take that clear of inspiration from real-life events for my fictional characters, but that one was too appropriate not to reference.

Aside from that, this series clearly owes a lot to other Japanese games and anime. Much of this draws from the same inspirations as many of my other works — classic games like *Final Fantasy*, *Dragon Quest*, *Ys*, and *Lufia*. In terms of manga and anime, I'm heavily inspired by Yuusha/Maou narratives, which include everything from watching *Slayers* on VHS in the 1990s to more recent titles like *Maoyuu* and *Frieren: Beyond Journey's End*.

There's also some minor influence from "boy who grows up with monster" stories, like *Dragon Quest: The Adventure of Dai* and *The Faraway Paladin*, although I began this story before watching either of those. I still love both series, and there's a lot of overlap.

I also drew some inspiration from shonen battle manga in general. In particular, my magic has some overlap with *Hunter x Hunter*'s Nen, and certain scenes — particularly with the Smiling Sword Saint and the mirror at the end — have some parallels with Ichigo's training in *Bleach*. Star Shattering Sight has some inspiration from the byakugan in *Naruto*, as well as the Mystic Eyes from various Type-Moon works. And speaking of Type-Moon, Edge definitely has some strong parallels with Emiya Shirou from the *Fate* franchise, as well as some inspiration from *Fate/Zero*'s Berserker, Gilgamesh in the same franchise, and so on.

There's also another layer of inspiration that comes from Chinese cultivation/xianxia novels, as well as Western stories inspired by them. Some of my favorite examples are Will Wight's *Cradle* series, Yrsillar's *Forge of Destiny*, and Sarah Lin's *The Brightest Shadow*. This inspiration can be seen most clearly in the style of different levels of essence development, which more clearly resembles a cultivation structure in this story than the more gamelike level systems used in my previous books. The layers in particular are very similar to what you'll often see as "realms" in cultivation books. The various dreams, as well as the echoes of previous people and events, also have some resemblance to elements of Yrsillar's work. The ultradangerous environment also has some parallels with Will Wight's *House of Blades*. Verthrimax's name was probably subconsciously influenced by the dragon from the movie *Dragonslayer*. That wasn't intentional, but it's super similar, so . . . hey, let's call it a reference!

Now, with that out of the way, I'd like to thank the people who helped make this story possible.

First and foremost, let me thank my literary agent, Paul Lucas, and his assistant, Eloy Bleifuss.

Next, I'd like to thank all of my beta readers: Tobias Begley, John Bierce, Eli Brandt, Nick "Ghost" Chevalier, Heather Crosthwaite, Yvonne Etzkorn, Justin Green, Krista K., Michael Kelly, Markus Kemppainen, Jonah L. L., Mallory Reaves, Rebecca Reeves, Jess Richards, Andrew Ritchie, Bruce Rowe, Christine Rowe, Lorne Ryburn, Izzy Trejo, Will Wight, Andy Winkle, James L. M. Wolter, and Brandon Yee. Finally, thanks to everyone for reading this book! I hope you enjoyed it.

ABOUT THE AUTHOR

Andrew Rowe was once a professional game designer for awesome companies like Blizzard Entertainment, Cryptic Studios, and Obsidian Entertainment. Nowadays, he's writing full time.

When he's not crunching numbers for game balance, he runs live-action role-playing games set in the same universe as his books. In addition, he writes for pen-and-paper role-playing games.

Aside from game design and writing, Andrew watches a lot of anime, reads a metric ton of fantasy books, and plays every role-playing game he can get his hands on.

Interested in following Andrew's books' releases or discussing them with other people? You can find more info, updates, and discussions in a few places online:

Andrew's Blog: https://andrewkrowe.wordpress.com/

Mailing List: https://andrewkrowe.wordpress.com/mailing-list/

Facebook: https://www.facebook.com/Arcane-Ascension-378362729189084/

Reddit: https://www.reddit.com/r/ClimbersCourt/

Podium